THE V

$$\Sigma T \Sigma X$$

SCHÄFFER & OJEDA VERLAG

Description:

The story of a young German couple and their three children during the years 1936 –
1946.

First published by Schäffer & Ojeda Verlag

First Edition

ISBN: 9798531384577

ASIN: B0978NTR6F

Cover photo & design: © Queñon 2021

http://stevenhugh.wordpress.com/

THE WAR

Steven Hugh Kenyon

Chapter 1

Inge screamed out in terror. The heavy dull thud of the initial impact was accompanied by a succession of splintering smashes, ending in the tinkling of small shards of glass finding their resting place. It was a moment of acute fear for the young woman, the homeliness of the sunny biergarten in Berlin pierced by a bursting sound close to her. Her heart raced; more than just the jumble of sharp noises beside her, there was the sense of something enormous and invisible about to attack.

Around Inge, heads turned, first to her and then to the source of the disruption: a young waitress was hurrying to clear up the mess, nimbly picking out the larger fragments from the gravel to place them into the jagged head of the smashed beer glass. A waiter came rushing out with a large metal brush and dustpan, while the customer at the table and his male companion were playing down the incident, responding to the rushed apologies of the hapless waitress by flirting with her. A few pairs of eyes still lingered over the scene of the smashed glass, as well as the embarrassed face of the now calm Inge nearby, before returning to their drinks and conversation partners.

She snickered into her right hand, her left hand over her thumping chest, looked down in a deep blush at the table. "I feel such an idiot," she then said quietly. "But it took me so by surprise." She made as if to continue speaking but stopped, did not want to reveal to him how she had just been distantly daydreaming while he was studying the drinks list; carried off yet again back to their wedding day barely a week ago. Hence the acute shock when that intense inner vision had been broken by a falling beer glass.

She felt it would come across as silly of her to let her husband know that, delighted as she was with every minute they were spending together in Berlin, she could not but help to let her mind drift back. Back just a couple of days previously to when she entered the church back home in Lüneburg in a long flowing gleaming white bridal gown that her mother and sister had spent weeks preparing and sewing together; with sequins, puff sleeves, a fine veil of Brussels lace, white silk gloves, and a short frilly train. She had seen herself in the mirror and found she looked both regal and stylish as she had never imagined possible for herself before that day.

At the altar her father Georg standing stiff but contented beside her; the nervous moments as the priest prepared himself; her dry throat before the vows; the warm family smiles. Her husband standing tall and erect in church with his short thick pitch-black hair, hazel eyes, winter-pale and summer-bronzed skin, broad shoulders and thick muscular arms, looking awkward but infinitely handsome in his best - and one and only - suit. So many flowers of so many shapes and colours; the later banquet *"ein königliches Mahl"* - fit for royalty, as everyone had said in wonder (whereby the waiters knew it was barely at the level of standard, let alone haute, bourgeoisie). Like a popular and much shown film, she could still sit through every last second of the wedding day in her mind and never tire of the scenes. In fact, those very scenes seemed to emanate more from the picture movies she had watched in cinemas rather than her own - up to that point very ordinary and dull - life.

Horst asked twice more if she was sure that she was alright, if she didn't feel faint or dizzy. Inge reassured him with a dismissive laugh. She said there was no reason to be concerned, repeatedly assured him that she was alright: *"Kein Problem, mir geht's gut* (No problem, I'm fine)," she said with a weak voice, her heart still knocking. She gulped down some water.

"Aber bist du dir sicher? (But are you sure?)" He frowned, was clearly concerned. Especially when appearing fragile, which Inge often did in his eyes, she was a sight of great beauty for him. In her bashful, insecure look there was a force that controlled him fully. Her long straight blond hair that hung down simply and unpretentiously over her narrow shoulders; her blue-grey eyes that shone with good humour; her pale and slightly freckled skin; her ungainly, self-conscious manner of carrying herself: he adored her physical presence. With the wedding freshly completed, he felt she was now a part of him, a deep intrinsic part of his own being. Nothing could have made him prouder than her acceptance of his role as protector and companion the day they married.

"Yes, Horst! Yes, of course," she insisted. It was just a silly little fright, she continued, not even worth discussing. She indicated for the waiter to bring them two more beers: this time she would join her husband in a stronger drink to calm her nerves. "I love it here," she said with a heartfelt sigh, enjoying the sensation of breeze and sunshine on her skin. "So peaceful, so relaxing, and so close to the city centre, too."

They had arrived in Berlin on the evening of Wednesday 29th July 1936 and checked in to the Hotel-Pension Funk in the Fasanenstraße. The entire trip – train tickets, hotel accommodation, spending and restaurant money – was a gift in the form of a fund that numerous friends and family members had contributed to. It was to be a grand honeymoon, the perfect finale to a perfect love story. Dreamily passing a week in the dazzling capital, in a fairy-tale fantasy on the arms of her newly wedded husband; a man who was handsome, caring and reliable. Berlin stretched around them as an endless garden of stone and grass, asphalt and traffic, glass and steel and trees. Proud and majestic, pompously Prussian, a king of cities that could not fail to impress at every turn.

They themselves were no great sport enthusiasts, took only a passing interest in sporting events. But that year's Winter Olympics, held in February in Garmisch-Partenkirchen in southern Bavaria, had fired up the imagination of many whose interest in the tournaments had been meagre up till then. Interest in the Summer Olympics of that year promised to eclipse that by far. In fact, coverage of the event in the media had grown to such feverish proportions that Berlin was widely considered *the* place to be that summer, both nationally and internationally. They themselves had contemplated various destinations, all of them rural, for their ideal honeymoon location. The idea of Berlin in August had arisen unexpectedly and with initial skepticism, but eventually thrilled them with the prospect of not only visiting – for the first time in their lives - their own nation's dynamic capital, a budding world city in itself, but moreover of taking part in this historic event, these much-publicized Games. As the cliché went, and it had been stated in their family circles on several occasions thus far, it would be 'the visit of a lifetime'.

For people of such modest financial means as theirs, such an extravagant holiday – which necessitated paying for hotel rooms and taxi fares and meals in restaurants - was a rare event that should be lived intensely and to the full; one that was only affordable due to generous donations in the form of pecuniary wedding gifts, and an occasion that was unlikely to be even approached in opulence again in the next decades.

Alone arriving at a hotel and being shown to a room, having a young man bring up the luggage behind them, that was an experience in itself. Horst had the presence of mind to tip, and with a banknote that otherwise back home would have fed them for an evening. The fresh bedlinen and immaculately kept room, the polite and discreet service; and most of all the wonderful view from the hotel window of the broad Lietzenburgerstraße ahead with its trams regularly gliding by and below them the Fasanenstraße with the bustle and chatter of its stream of excited pedestrians. At 8 *Reichsmark* a night, breakfast included and with their own bathroom, it was a small luxury for them; but when they inquired and found out that the Adlon would have been 18 RM, they felt a sense of relief that eased what otherwise might have led to a guilty conscience.

On their first day they went for a walk in the area around the hotel, in the Charlottenburg district just to the west of the central park area Tiergarten. They orientated themselves in the district which was elegant and, though busy, still relatively relaxed in comparison to the touristic madness of the city centre. They examined the local restaurants and cafés, located the shops and kiosks that they preferred. At a nearby bus-stop they waited with wide-eyed wonderment at the traffic density and caught one of the large white double-decker buses trundling with punctual regularity round the city, each with different slogans painted on the side; in this case *Ozonil*, a brand of washing powder. Inge thought this was a charming idea to brighten up the city transport and reminded herself to look out for the product once she got back home.

They enjoyed the idle fun of sitting cuddled up together in the bus and losing themselves in the elevated streets of the unceasing city. Upon getting off at the end of the route, they found out they were way over in the south-east part of the city, near Treptower Park. Initial disorientation turned to delight when they realized they could take a river boat trip down the Spree from a spot close by, returning back in a westerly direction. After a pleasant cruise, they alighted near the impressive baroque Charlottenburg Palace, not far from the hotel and high up on their list of places to visit. After an extensive viewing and strolling round its adjoining park area they continued on, enjoying the loud heady street atmosphere. They made their way with leisurely pace up to the famous 'Ku'damm' (Kurfürstendamm) shopping street where Inge wanted to see the elegant boutiques. There, as planned, they picked out a modest, not too costly store and bought her a dress – navy blue chiffon to wear to dinner - with an envelope of notes that her sister Gisela and brother-in-law Martin had given them at the wedding reception for that very purpose. They came out all smiles and walked on past droves of pedestrians, lines of leafy trees offering shade under the bright sunlight, stopped to admire the elegant Kaiser Wilhelm Memorial Church; it sprang up before them like a medieval fairy-tale castle. "This is such a beautiful city," Inge breathed as she held her husband's hand tight. "I hope it stays just like this forever."

Despite its austere charm and impressive dimensions, for someone from the province such as herself there was so much that reminded her of home as well. The proudly hanging flags – with the familiar black swastika in a circle of white, on a bold scarlet background – that she knew so well, that radiated vitality and homespun solidity. Here they were draped from every possible spot, billowing in the wind like walls of sheets in their sheer numbers. In some parts of the city, especially around official buildings of importance, they hung in huge sizes, forming waves of flowing fabric in red, black and white that tastefully adorned the streets and increased her sense of security.

Police officers were ubiquitous and extremely polite, always eager to help out. They had asked them on two occasions the way, once to the Savignyplatz S-Bahn station, another time to the nearest public toilet, and the responses had been gracious and well-explained. Everywhere and at all times they found the Berliners to be a friendly, witty and open-hearted folk; not at all the abrupt or coarse citizens that they knew from commonly held stereotypes. Rather they came across to the couple as fulfilling all the better ideals of Prussian constancy and correctness, and in that was confirmed their deep love of their country, their people. Furthermore, that seemingly effortless and natural hospitality was not just meted out to German tourists. She had seen and noted with satisfaction how foreign visitors were likewise accommodated with all due politeness. She had heard her fellow countrymen slowly and patiently explaining things not only in a clear simple German to foreigners having difficulty with the language, but sometimes in French, in English, even in Italian on a couple of occasions. They walked on in deep satisfaction and took in the fine, often intricate architecture of the long wide streets. By the early afternoon the wind had calmed, the sky was a dazzling blue with puffs of white serenely pushed along.

In the evening they located a modest restaurant near to Steinplatz and were so happy with the service, the food and, above all, the prices; so much so that they returned a few times. The interior décor was simple but charming, and for a very affordable 2.50 RM came belly of pork with carrots and potatoes for Horst, and bean stew with bacon and potatoes for Inge, both including a glass of beer.

On the Friday they decided on a long walking tour around the centre of the city, now loudly buzzing with the excitement of tomorrow's grand opening. Already before the wedding day they had compiled a comprehensive list for their sightseeing, augmented by tips and suggestions from friends and family. They hoped to take in as many of the famous sights as possible, to dutifully cross the items off the itinerary, to be able to talk with at least some basic knowledge about them, and relate it all once they got back home.

They walked a few blocks to the Hardenbergstraße, from there up to the Berliner Straße and turned right into that majestic broad avenue with its dense forest of trees on both sides, thick traffic humming incessantly by them. In three lanes in both directions, no less - Inge noted in amazement. Yet well-regulated too, all drivers turning off the street in an orderly fashion as copious numbers of vehicles intuitively coordinated the rules of traffic. Taking in the view of so many automobiles in such structured movement, both Inge and Horst sensed how here was the strong beating heart of a dynamic nation. It was attractive and compulsive, drawing in even the casual observer with fascination.

After a good twenty minutes of briskly invigorating walking they reached the Brandenburg Gate, lingered to catch their breath and admire the stone effigies and the thick pillars of the structure which stood as a solid and imposing entrance to the city, swastikas swaying between them. From there, the excursion turned left and headed up to the Königsplatz to see the *Reichstag*, the German parliament building. "The axis of the nation," Horst's supervisor at the fire station, Hans Lenz, had said back in Lüneburg with a vehement nod, after the wedding on the eve before they had set off for Berlin. His wife had added, "Whatever you do, you must definitely take a good look. Oh, I do so envy you!"

From here out emanated the dynamics and political power of the whole Reich, they grasped with the instinctive awe of young people in their capital for the first time. "The heart of the nation indeed!" said Inge, paraphrasing. Horst had the literal sensation of a swelling heart and sang a couple of lines of the national anthem: "*Von der Maas bis an die Memel, von der Etsch bis an den Belt*" ("From the Meuse to the Neman, from the Adige to the Fehmarn Belt"), in reference to distant waterways that marked the geographical boundaries of their land. They laughed after he finished his short serenade, kissed and hugged. A few passers-by heard him and looked over with smiles, in inner approval at the handsome image of both young married love and deep patriotic love.

The *Reichstag* was a splendid, imposing building: a colossus in layers of intricate stonework, a gleaming mass of columns, windows crowned with pediments, and sculptures; bordered by ornate avant-corps corner towers. It drew their eyes to its stepped and pillar-lined entrance bearing the engraving dedicated to *Dem Deutschen Volke* (The German People). In front of it was a small area with lawns, small trees, and a sputtering fountain. They gazed up at its idiosyncratic characteristic central dome, still bearing the scars of the infamous fire of three years earlier.

Inge shook her head and commented, "To think someone would want to burn down something so beautiful."

Horst shrugged, "Communists - what do you expect? At least they were caught, but the damage was already done."

After a pause, during which they looked around and all over the building, their hands shielding their eyes from the sun, he added, "You know, the parliament does not meet up here anymore. Since the fire they hold the sessions over there in the *Krolloper* (Kroll opera house) on the other side of the square," he indicated a group of stately buildings across the way from them.

Inge said, "So when they show the parliament meeting in the cinema in the *Tonwoche* news, and with the enormous eagle behind them on the wall, that is not actually happening in the Reichstag, but over there at the opera instead?"

"Exactly."

"Oh", she said, somewhat disappointed. "So why did Herr Lenz from the fire station say it was the heart of the political power if there is no-one there to make all the speeches and announcements?"

"The Reichstag is still important. More so than all those debates or discussions. It is symbolic, really. With the building, I mean, it is more than the building … it is the power that counts." He felt confused by the question which now cast doubt on the importance of the grand edifice before them, formerly so bloated in their admiration. "Either way, at least we can tell everyone back home that we have seen it now, that we were actually here on this spot." Inge agreed and felt that was surely the most important thing.

After a while staring at the Reichstag building, which had now altered in their minds from frighteningly impressive to somewhat forlorn, they walked on to see the nearby *Siegessäule* (Pillar of Victory). It was a column-shaped tower with the bronze statue of the Roman goddess Viktoria atop, with a laurel crown in one hand and in the other a standard bearing the iron cross. There was something in the strong majestic pose and the rich gleam of the feminine figure that filled Horst with emotion. They stepped into the red granite base through a circle of smaller pillars, Inge reaching out to glide her hand over the smooth surface. There they gazed at the vivid tones of murals depicting battle scenes and images of heroic statures, then made their way up the column shaft inside the tower, trudged up the winding staircase to the top. They stood out on the platform to survey in awe the surrounding area, the packed streets and squares, the massed traffic, the sprawling green of the Zoo gardens. From that vantage point the Reichstag improved considerably as it reclined palatial and sovereign under the warm summer sun, tranquil amid the urban bustle all around, and they could better appreciate it from the higher perspective.

They returned to their route passing by the Brandenburg Gate. "I had always wanted to see it and now I can see it twice!" exclaimed Inge with her childish gushing enthusiasm that Horst found so endearing. From there they continued on down the broad avenue Unter den Linden, with its central double bank of trees and dense traffic on both sides; passed an impressive array of buildings crammed with flags and bordered by hanging streetlamps. They saw the fine Victoria Hotel and the Opernplatz square, adjacent to the avenue where they caught a glimpse of the magnificent Opera House; went past the Prinz Heinrich palace and the German State Library with its statue of Friedrich the Great in equestrian pose; on through the slew of Prussian architectonic glory before final arriving at the classical *Neue Wache* (New Guardhouse). Here was to be a memorable highlight for Horst when they arrived, and as he had hoped, just in time to witness the ceremonial changing of the guard in front of the memorial. Smartly uniformed guards marched stiffly outward in formation, legs kicking high to a horizontal position, at which Inge nearly applauded, as the new set of guards moved sideways in the same militaristic fashion, preparing to take up their new positions and relieve their comrades. Horst watched with envy as a pair of well-dressed and clearly affluent Americans photographed the event, clicking numerous times on their hand-held camera.

It was also at this point that Horst noticed how few uniformed men they had seen during their brief stay so far in the city, despite the high number of young men he personally knew who had been called up for military service. The brown and khaki uniforms of the SA and the Hitler Youth seemed to be also conspicuously absent. He had subconsciously entertained a different, more martial image of the capital and felt a certain disappointment. The smart uniforms and visual displays of discipline that accompanied a strong military presence were, he felt, an integral part of this new – and undeniably successful and prosperous – land. It was only right therefore that the capital, of all cities, should proudly exhibit them.

Inge too had noticed discrepancies between her previous reflections and assumptions, and the reality she now perceived. This conception she assumed to be characteristic of Berlin in general and was unaware that most of it had been artificially created, and that solely for the duration of the Games. There were none of the omnipresent glass-fronted public stands and showcases on the street displaying and selling the popular *Der Stürmer* paper, when back home they would be all around in plain view. This came as a relief to her, for there was something she found very unpleasant about the publication, with its ugly caricatures of hirsute hook-nosed Jews and its permanent front-page slogan *"Die Juden sind unser Unglück"* ("The Jews are our misfortune"); it continually shouted out this same bold statement that she could not imagine being the case, and she found it ridiculous and indicative of paranoia. Nor was there the usual sight of groups of young SA officers, leering in sinister watchfulness on the pavements in their brown uniforms, standing outside Jewish businesses to aggressively enforce the boycott and or occasionally paint '*Jude*' ('Jew') in dripping white onto shop windows. Jews must be more tolerated and have an easier life here in Berlin, she therefore concluded. That in turn made the city yet more appealing to her, together with its international flair produced by so many languages, fashions and facial types that crisscrossed the streets around her. To be sure she had in the past few months often heard words such as "*friedfertig*" (peaceable) and "*völkerverbindend*" (connecting nations and peoples) used in connection with the upcoming event, to such an extent that she now associated this tone of vocabulary directly with the Games. Noteworthy for her was how many of these latter details, not to mention this interpretation, were completely ignored by her husband; but this was not a topic of discussion that she had any intention of entering into with him.

A feature that had greatly impressed Inge was the richly diverse linguistic texture of the Olympic city. She herself had had absolutely no aptitude for foreign language study at school but was fascinated by the ability in others, finding that even those foreigners simply speaking in their mother tongue must be in possession of a great talent. Everywhere she went she had been picking up snatches of other languages. She recognized English and French from her old school years, while there were others flowing in vowels that she guessed might be Italian or Spanish; also the hissing and consonant-laden Slavic tongues caught her attention. Japanese, obvious by the physiognomy of its speakers, possessed a hacking, aggressive sound for her, contrasting to the plethora of smiles and humble bowing of heads that these people radiated. On one occasion she heard what she perceived to be a wild and ugly version of German and, upon querying her husband, found out it was Dutch. "I could even understand some of the words," she laughed, finding the whole linguistic mêlée around her quite fascinating. Her curious gaze had often settled on the red armbands worn by some of the police and security officers that read in gold lettering "*On parle français*" and other versions in various languages; all this she found captivating.

Once the changing of the guard was over and Horst was satisfied with observing the stiff officers, they continued marching on; over the bridge that crossed one of the smaller sidearms of the Spree river, past the *Lustgarten* with its elegant court garden and fountain, across the neatly kept lawns until reaching their next port of call for the day, this time Inge's choice: the Berlin Cathedral. They stood before it and gazed upon the beautiful exterior with exquisitely adorned stone walls, bold columns topped with pediments, intricately hewn sculptures; its crown of four green copper domes with bell towers, the central one extending out in huge dimensions. Awestruck by its solemn magnificence they lingered for a while outside, as if intimidated by the luxury of detail; in devout silence despite the surrounding city din, before stepping almost gingerly inside to move quietly round the solemn interior. There in its belly a gentle hush reigned. It was a strange and enticing peace that they now encountered for the first time since their arrival in the metropolis.

They sat down at the end of a pew; Horst placed his arm around his wife's back and she cuddled up to him. From there they regarded the golden altar and the towering organ pipes behind, all around them a flowering of elaborate sculptures, paintings, chapels, staircase and pulpit. Though generally enchanted with the bluster of central Berlin, in this moment Inge had needed this deep harmonious peace. She experienced a sublime sense of consonance with everything and everyone around her. And her mind drifted off again to that most perfect of days in her short life so far, only three days ago: "I, Ingeborg Maria Hartmann, take you, Horst Grün, to be my husband. I will love you, respect you, and cherish you for all the days of the rest of my life…"

With spiritual batteries renewed, they returned to the noisy streets outside and headed off down this central artery to their final destination for the day, the famous Alexanderplatz. They reached the roundabout overlaid with grass and stopped to catch their breath; around it flowed an unrelenting traffic of bicycles, trams, motorized vehicles; on all sides a steady stream of pedestrians from the native dwellers firmly stepping forward on their business and to the tourists idly wandering and staring. The rapid modernization of towering steel and glass structures was surrounding and enveloping the more traditional features of Berlin's past, such as churches and statues. Strung on high were endless lines of swastika bunting; at night the square was lit up by a multitude of electric bulbs. Further on, a covered pedestrian bridge connected both sides of the street at second floor level and boasted an advertisement for '*Hertie*', Germany's first department store; few metres below the U-Bahn emblem gleamed and steps led down into Berlin's striking modern underground train system. The city was vibrant, interconnected, brashly self-confident.

Already in the short space of their visit they had walked down so many of the capitals wide open streets, all so broad and lined with towering buildings of six, seven storeys, sweeping up into the sky. They were draped with masses of bunting and small flags, displaying the national flag of the Reich in red and white with black swastika alternating with rows of the official Olympic flag of five coloured circles on a white background. The coats of arms of the various *Länder* of Germany could also be seen fluttering and helped to brighten up the dizzy though sometimes monotonous whirls of flapping fabrics.

The stark and idiosyncratic Nazi symbol, which in itself produced an emotional effect on all visitors of whatever origin, was furthermore featured in immense elongated flags that hung down from on high from a few of the more important official buildings, such as ministries. In comparison to all the merry bunting, these larger drapes swayed with grandeur and gravitas in the warm summer light.

Despite the enormous scale of the capital and the sheer overwhelming number of people and vehicles, the familiarity of the omnipresent swastika imbued the city with a homely, almost cosy, feel for many of the provincial German visitors, including Horst and

Inge. Moreover, the streets were clean and well-kept, the atmosphere was lively and festive, and even the homeless seemed to have miraculously disappeared (in fact they had been quickly removed well in advance, transported to housing in the city's periphery for the duration of the Games). The blocks of buildings were all neatly maintained and freshly painted, the shops packed full, offering a great selection of goods and doing roaring trade, the locals on their best behaviour and exceptionally (some cynics added: unusually) friendly. Prussian military march music was carried on the breeze, bright garlands decorated shops and other businesses.

Returning back down Unter den Linden, Inge paused once again to take in the thick traffic of cars, vans and little blue buses, still astonished at how coordinated the course of this traffic was, seeming so effortless on the one hand but at the same time so rigid and correct, as if controlled by omniscient precision. The yellow and brown trams rumbled by with the occasional toot of a horn to warn any unwary pedestrians caught inattentive in the middle of the street, as she had been on the first day already. There was so much information to absorb, she felt easily dazed by the enormity of it.

Eventually they drew away from the central *Prachtmeile* – the glamour mile – and headed back westwards towards their hotel. On the way there they entered the extensive grounds of the Zoo, strolled around the botanical gardens, watched in fascination the elephants and lions and other exotic beasts in their compounds. Here in a busy biergarten they decided to take a rest and have some refreshments. Inge was by now worn out by all the touristic tumult and Horst was itching for a beer. They located a table to their liking near to the edge of the outside seating area, with an impressive view of the gardens around and the milling crowds of locals and holidaymakers.

And it was here, some minutes later, that a large beer glass slipped from a waitress' tray and crashed to the ground, frightening the life out of Inge who had been daydreaming away on the table next to her.

Chapter 2

The following day, Saturday 1st August, Horst and Inge set out for the stadium in the late morning; caught the S-Bahn, in itself an exciting first-time experience, followed by a bus to the Olympic Stadium. Soon they were joining up with the streaming throngs of attendees, all eager and ebullient under the warm August sun. The sky shone in a beautiful azure with a few fuzzy dashes of clear white cloud over a gleaming and dynamic Olympic city. The atmosphere was one of joyful innocence and summer festivity, as almost all visitors, both domestic and foreign, would later recollect with fond nostalgia.

Horst and Inge had received tickets for the highly coveted opening ceremony, plus seats for a further series of sporting events during the following days, as a wedding gift from Horst's supervisor Hans Lenz and his colleagues Schönbeck and Hase from the fire station in Lüneburg. They in turn had managed to obtain said tickets through a friend of a friend who worked at the *Reichsministerium des Inneren* (German Ministry of the Interior); as Lenz himself had commented, a good contact in a ministry was the best way to achieve the impossible. This opportunity was taken by the wedded couple to be an immense stroke of both luck and generosity, and indeed it would have been the only way for a modest working-class couple like Horst and Inge Grün to gain entrance to such a historic event.

At the stadium they passed almost nervously between the imperious twin stone towers of the Eastern Gate: narrow and dizzily high cement structures with a clockface to the left and a swastika to the right, connected by the five Olympic rings. Jostled in the eddies and flows of over a hundred thousand attendees, Inge and Horst found and took their seats. As the stadium slowly filled, the crowd waited in electric expectation for the arrival of the Führer. Meanwhile the airship Hindenburg crossed overhead, grabbing all eyes to follow it floating across the blue skies of Berlin. Inge and Horst shielded their eyes from the sun and looked up in wonder at their first live glimpse of the strange craft, a beige bloated form bearing large swastikas on the vertical empennage. Around them eighty thousand spectators were gazing up in unison, gasps were heard.

Inge looked back down and around her at the crowd, had an awareness of unity with the immense mass around her. It was an electrifying moment, a strong emotional and physical sensation. Before, she had always shied away from larger gatherings in her hometown, particularly those organized in recent years by the National Socialists, in which fervent emotion would be unleashed in the joy of belonging to a greater group, of participating in a greater good. But this time she felt the sensation acutely, as well as the enchantment that the sight of the airship produced. This feeling would later be reinforced in the course of the ceremony by all the regular bouts of frenzied cheering and arm raising, wherein she would find herself drawn in irresistibly to the pride and excitement of belonging to such a much-loved Fatherland. A Fatherland that surrounded and embraced her; an entity as masterful as God and seeming as wide as the world itself; of which she as a German was an intrinsic part, and likewise her nation was an intrinsic part of her own being. It was a huge privilege, she felt in her budding awareness of this identity, and furthermore, like her recent marriage, a bond to be taken with the utmost sense of commitment.

Punctually at 15:00 came the long-awaited arrival of the Führer himself, heralded with a martial fanfare at the Marathon Gate. With dramatic pomp (carefully staged down to the last detail), flanked by a small entourage of Party ministers, Olympic officials and uniformed guards, he made his way across the arena to the delirious cheering of the crowd. The music, a march theme by Wagner, accompanied him in homage. On his way to the stand, he was met by a small blonde girl, dressed in a white pageant dress and with daisies in her hair. She was grasping a bouquet of flowers and raised her other arm in a typical Nazi salute, though over-enthusiastically pointing right up to the sky. She curtsied in awe as the Führer bent forward with a warm smile to receive the flowers.

He proceeded on up to stairs, humbly followed by his cluster of courtiers and attendants, to take his place at the *Führerloge* (the Führer's box in the balcony) from which prime spot he would observe - whenever work permitted it - some of the next fortnight's sporting events. He greeted the assembled spectators with a subtle movement of his hand and the wild howls of devotion went up again. Inge and

Horst too, like thousands around them, were carried off into a state of exaltation by the passion of the moment. The Führer's standard was hoisted and it was as if an emperor stood before them. The orchestra struck up the national anthem and all (Germans, at least) in the audience sang along with the first verse: *"Deutschland, Deutschland über alles, Über alles in der Welt..."* ("Germany, Germany above all, Above everything in the world..."). This was duly followed by the Horst-Wessel song, the anthem of the NSDAP, with arms stiffly raised: to be sure, an intimidating experience for some of the foreigners in the crowd.

After another blast of Olympic fanfare as trumpets, horns and trombones blasted their motif around the audience. The flags of the participating nations were hoisted around the *Führerloge* where Hitler stood. A circle of national flags from the participating nations was hoisted in regal solemnity; closing up the forming circle came a group of white Olympic five-circle flags, all fluttering in unison. As the brass instruments finished their call, another huge wave of Nazi salutes (known by the euphemism of the 'German greeting') swept through the audience. This time it seemed to engulf and cover everyone, even the foreign visitors. For the Germans present, including Horst and Inge, it was perceived as a deeply moving, if not magical moment: the participation of the whole world in their own deeply felt patriotism, an undeniable confirmation of the new-found strength of their nation. In less than twenty years, they had gone from humiliation to glory; the ecstasy was irresistible.

There was a highly dramatic as well as efficient and punctual feel to the proceedings, like watching a well-oiled theatrical work. It communicated all the stereotypes that the audience had come to expect of Germans: order, discipline, punctuality, diligence, coordinated obedience. The Führer presided from the balcony for the rest of the ceremony; an inscrutable figure emitting a quiet but burning energy, sending the odd nod of acknowledgement into the crowd, exchanging some words to the side with his companions. Eyes followed him continually with all the possible emotions in the world. One way or another, no-one remained untouched by the presence of the eccentric but commanding man from Braunau am Inn. This event was to be his show, as many had already come to realize on this first day; it had been meant to be that way from the very beginning.

Prussian marching music struck up and it was time for the participating national teams to do the rounds of introductory honour. The Führer watched down benignly. A ripple of excitement passed through the crowd as each team emerged, though in such politicized times some were naturally greeted with more enthusiasm than others. Led by a team member bearing a lowered flag, the teams marched around the track in tight formation, facing the audience with an impassive iron gaze. The men were in the great majority but the women team members marched along with equal vigour. They strode on round the track, passing by the *Führerloge* to receive the regulatory Nazi salute from Hitler as they came under his glare.

The audience raised their arms to the athletes in the 'German greeting' and some teams also gave that salute back: the Austrian and Italian athletes responded in kind, as did the Rumanians. Also the French, apparently, striding past in their black berets; and the Greeks as well, the originators of the modern games who had kicked off the parade of teams and showcased at the front a happily waving man in traditional fustanella. It should be noted that both French and Greek athletes seemed almost bewildered at finding their own arms raised in this manner, as if caught out in some strange unnatural act that was the result of a last-minute change in choreography. There were later rumours that they had simply not known, in terms of height, where the traditional Olympic salute ended, and the Nazi salute began.

Most teams though did not return the Nazi salute to the crowd. The Swiss marched by with modest calm steps and a nonchalant look, as if unimpressed, almost embarrassed, by the bombastic display of their Germanic cousins. The Americans removed their hats in a swift single movement and stared at the crowd with stolid indifference, earning some boos by refusing to acknowledge the Führer's presence with a lowering of their flag as they passed by him. The Swedish and Danish teams also removed their white hats with a flourish and held them at waist height while marching. For the British it seemed more of a leisurely though brisk stroll, than an actual march; likewise with the competitors from the (still British) India. The Japanese by contrast, dressed in solemn black, marched by in sharp jerks and glowered at the crowd.

The Americans had been the penultimate team to parade around the arena. This huge and potentially most powerful nation was by now slowly emerging onto the world stage and here at the four-yearly Olympic Games they had become the traditional champions so far. The order of teams was thus carefully planned, then in many quarters it was expected to be a battle of titans this time round, between the United States and Germany. Finally the German athletes came out into the arena to an intense explosion of acclaim. Cheers and clapping, whistles and shouts and shrieking, all combined to form a wild cacophony of jubilation to greet the home team. Germany thus completed this series of rounds, marching in strict formation and with clear Nazi salute; first the women dressed all in white – hats, blouses, long skirts; then the men, also all in white – trousers, blazers, hats. They were led by an athlete bearing an enormous swastika that was dutifully lowered before the grinning, quietly joyful gaze of the Führer. Afterwards there would be artillery fire, speeches, flag waving everywhere and the incessant cheers of the crowd. But what most struck Inge that afternoon were the gleaming white uniforms of her team, and especially those of the women. Gliding forward in their long flowing skirts with arms raised ahead, they were an image of femininity with a spectral unearthly touch, one that stayed with Inge for the rest of her life. Horst too found the image moving, though his feelings were less sublimated than his wife's, being closer to erotic arousal.

Now that the athletes had completed their rounds, there followed a heavy, almost fearful silence. Hitler's voice, with its characteristically clipped tones, resounded around the stadium: *"Ich verkünde die Spiele von Berlin zur Feier der IX.ten Olympiade neuer Zeitrechnung als eröffnet!"* (I declare the Berlin Olympic Games for the celebration of the IX. Olympiad of the modern era to be opened!")

The audience had half-expected a raucous speech to come afterwards, and some had dreaded that it might descend into yet another long-winded affair. As it happened, there came only a brief silence; today the Führer had deigned to leave things at that one simple sentence. The crowd however showed no sign of disappointment and responded immediately with thunderous cheering and cries of "Heil!"

The brass instruments smashed out again the regal motif and the Olympic flag was hoisted on high. Thereupon a large flock of pigeons was released. They rose up into the sky in a cloud of shimmering greys; confused and swaying one way, then the other. There came a deafening volley of artillery fire, leaving the now terrified birds in desperate search of a route up and away from this torture. (Rumour later had it that such was their terror that they defecated in mass over the area where the national teams stood below, covering mostly US athletes in a splatter of grey goo. But it would have been an act of petty schadenfreude to report it that day in the press, and accordingly no-one did.) The orchestra played an Olympic hymn that had been specially composed for the occasion by Richard Strauss, and this was the announcement of the imminent arrival of the mythical flame.

At the Eastern Gate the last in a long series of torch bearers entered, who had run through numerous cities during the previous weeks. He was a young lean man, blond and bronzed in white shorts and singlet, bearing the mythical flames from Olympia. It was a magnificent moment, particularly for those who had followed in the press or TV rooms how that same torch, originally lit in the ruins of Olympia, had travelled all across Europe through Athens, Delphi, Sofia, Belgrade, Budapest, Vienna, Prague and finally on to Berlin. (That the flame had been briefly extinguished during anti-Nazi protests in Prague was not shown or discussed). The torch bearer raised it up high and the crowd began to cheer in near frenzy at the sight of man and fire: the very first time this visual treat – destined to be repeated ad infinitum - was staged at the event. Flanked on both sides by masses of spectators, he ran down the broad steps and into the arena; ran clear across it in front of the assembled national teams looking on at this solitary man in his smart white kit. He ran up another flight of steps on the opposite side to reach the cement podium where the large metallic structure supporting the basin stood waiting. There, to an awed silence, he paused; and that pause was monumental. All around the stadium there was an awed hush, clapping hands stopped frozen in the air, only the sporadic click and flash of cameras.

The torch was raised high, electrifying the mood in anticipation, before being placed into the top of the basin with one bold sweep of his arm. A mass of fire erupted, tongues licking out in all directions until the fire became more concentrated and flamed upwards, belching up thick black smoke. The choir and full orchestra struck up the Olympic hymn with heraldic pomp. On a huge display board, that would later show all information concerning races and tournaments and the results thereof, was engraved a quotation from Pierre de Coubertin, founder of the modern Olympic Games, in German in large black capital letters: "*Möge die Olympische Flamme leuchten durch alle Geschlechter zum wohl einer immer höher strebenden, mutigeren und reineren Menschheit!*" ("May the Olympic flame shine through all generations for the good of an ever higher aspiring, braver and purer humanity!"). The fire, that had come all the way from southern Europe up to Berlin, would burn there for twelve days and eleven nights.

The renowned weightlifter Rudolf Ismayr, who had already won gold four years previous in Los Angeles, swore the Olympic Oath on behalf of the host team. However, he deviated somewhat from the usual recitation by seizing the German flag with its swastika and raising his right hand in a Hitler salute. After that, the orchestra and choir struck up Händel's '*Halleluja*' and the teams commenced their tightly organized march out of the arena. There followed an impressive series of choreographed performances by young German athletes under the title *Olympische Jugend* – Olympic Youth. No less than ten thousand young men and women performed synchronized running and dance routines around the entire area of the field, producing a myriad of patterns and shapes with their white kits gleaming against the background of the dark green lawn. There was a theatrical number featuring medieval knights which depicted, according to the prospect, the nation's warriors fighting and dying a hero's death. It seemed somewhat out of sync with the Olympic motif of peaceful international sport connecting nations, but the crowd thundered their praise nonetheless. The '*Ode to Joy*' from Beethoven's Ninth Symphony filled the stadium and the opening ceremony was brought to an end. An immense number of torches were lit to form a sea of flames at the side of the arena, while a dome of light was produced in the sky over the stadium by strategically placed flak searchlights, that illuminated the surrounding area throughout the night. (No-one at the time appreciated just how premonitory this image was.) Bells rang out from nearby towers; it was time for the spectators to depart. The show was over for that day.

Like those around them, Horst and Inge had clapped, cheered, shouted, raised their arms in salutes, all throughout the ceremony. Like the others, they had also felt the warm thrill of crowd excitement on a summer's day; the gushing pride of patriotism as their team strode by. They both enjoyed that sensation greatly and it gave them a sense of confidence, of a deeper meaning that was outside of their own little day-to-day dramas, with the typical banalities and struggles and gaffes. They experienced the strong desire to be part of something larger than this simple existence; something that extended beyond their humble frets and worries, that held ethical weight, that encompassed the vivid essentially of existence.

Inge and Horst held hands tightly, occasionally gave way to hugs of pure joy. They were so happy to feel such love, and to be away from home and from all domestic and professional duties; carefree on holiday and well entertained. They squinted, blinded by the afternoon sun as they attempted to make out the features of their cherished Führer more clearly. From their position in the stadium he was a distant but still easily recognizable figure, in his emblematic uniform and cap.

They had been thrilled by the ceremony and the stadium, but were also conscious of the sleek management behind it all; not only of that day's opening ceremony but of the look and feel of the whole Olympic event. Things were changing for the better, and it was a change that you could not only believe in but could actually perceive. It was top-notch professionalism in every way it touched them to the core. The music had been perfect: stirring and emotional, with such acoustic precision that it was carried to every corner and made them feel a part of the proceedings rather than mere spectators. They had sang along heartily with the Deutschland-Lied, the national anthem, where that simple but heartfelt repetition at the beginning - "*Deutschland, Deutschland*" - had such a soul-laden ring, like a child calling for a parent. Horst in particular had joined in with the Horst-

Wessel song with gusto and had felt through that communal singing how he was less a simple individual – just another worker, another married husband - but instead part of a wider group. Here in the stadium in harmony and union with thousands around them, he achieved a sense of spiritual nobility, of inner value. In the collective group, bound by common cause and common song, there was something indescribably sublime that had only existed in this form in this moment. Once the crowd dispersed, they were back on their own again. The coolness of bare existence returned – it was like waking from an excellent dream; while Horst acknowledged inside that he missed that fiery warmth of comradeship.

Inge had little interest in politics, neither the current raucous mood at national level nor the distant tugging and pushing of international relations. At family reunions she had listened in, generally with indifference, on long, heated discussions between men about German troops returning to patrol in the Rheinland or the masses jubilantly greeting German troops after the referendum in the Saar territory and what the French would now have to think of that. A lot more than she did apparently, she had mused.

Horst, however, was fascinated by the whole political thematic and would breathlessly relate to her item after item of fresh hot news, despite her showing only mild interest. Not that his zeal in any way irked her or led to a single moment of irritation. She always enjoyed his conversation, whatever the subject matter. She took great pleasure in hearing his speech, from the cadence and tone (he had a baritone voice which softly rose and fell and carried the humour of a gentle chuckle) to his manner of speaking (never overbearing or aggressive, usually striving to adapt to her mood in the moment). He could be opinionated, even strident, with others, but in her company he softened appropriately. That was one of the principal reasons that she loved him.

She had seen often husbands talk brusquely, even aggressively to their wives. There was even the memory of hers, when a local man and friend of the family had thumped his wife in the face following a hot row in a local *Bierstube*: the woman had crumpled, literally stunned by the knock-out blow, and afterwards had not been seen out for over a week. There had been other, more minor cases of domestic verbal abuse, too. But most relevantly she knew well the tone that her own father employed with her mother. He had never raised his hand and struck his wife. But he had often raised his voice and used vulgar disrespectful language on many occasions; to which her mother had invariably bowed her head and let out a long sigh, looked round for some little chore, usually sewing or darning, to occupy herself with, to try to assuage the angry moment and divert attention with activity. Inge had sensed, ever since she was a young girl, how her mother sat silently fuming but fundamentally submissive. She loved her father, and he adored and thought the world of her, but his voice could be strident and rough-edged with drink; unpleasant like the stench of his schnaps-filled breath. More importantly than those sharper vivid scenes, there had been the frequent small put-downs, inserted with such ease into his discourse when talking to her mother. "I told you not to talk about things you do not understand", he would sneer at her, if she wandered off what he considered the correct conversational route for women. "What a stupid thing to say! How ridiculous!" he would exclaim, even when the present company was large. "That's enough children's talk for one day, these are serious issues." Witnessing this with such frequency had firmly shaped Inge's notion of how she imagined marital life for herself, and what it should not be.

Horst was just that very different companion that she had hoped for. He never spoke loudly, never criticized harshly or unduly; he called her "*meine Prinzessin*" (my princess) and generally treated her with such respect and care that she could almost feel she was being elevated to that very level. It thrilled her to be special, to belong to that one special man who was so very unique and made her feel equally unique. After the honeymoon and upon their return to Lüneburg they would have their own home together, a modest little apartment that they were planning to move in to together in the Rotenbleicher Weg. She had said little to others about her thoughts and musings, at most a few confessions to her sister Gisela, and so devoted was she to the relationship that she could not imagine airing personal concerns or formulated views for all the public to observe. That would be an area of life reserved for the attention of Horst. And so her mind wondered back to the wedding; back to her husband and her ideas of, and sketchy plans for, their married life ahead.

The day after the ceremony, they returned to the stadium to attend athletic events in the afternoon. It was a cooler cloudy Sunday with fleeting drops of light rain and Inge felt comfortable in the now familiar surroundings and city. They watched the Men's High jump final and Men's Shot put final, the latter gold going to Germany and allowing them to cheer and stand for the anthem. The music was always the most emotional part of the experience for her. She and Horst hoped for more gold medals next time; to enjoy the moment when the entire arena listened in jubilation as the athletes stood together on the podium and the winner looked proudly onward with the right arm raised.

Later they went for a walk in the extensive Olympic grounds around the stadium, where the fields for further matches and tournaments outside of the main athletic attractions would be held. There was a small amphitheatre on the edge of a woodland area that was to be designated for theatrical performances and readings during the course of the Games, all connecting the ancient civilizations of Europe to the modern might of the Reich. There nearby, Inge located the *Langermarckhalle* (Langermarck Hall) that she had been searching for, with its war memorial to the fallen of the *Langermarckschlacht* (- Battle, English: First Battle of Ypres) in November 1914. Over it towered a thin austere grey-stone bell tower known as the *Führerturm* (Führer's tower). She told Horst that they would have to return here on the third and final visit in order to leave a little bouquet of flowers in remembrance. This had been a favour expressly requested of her by her father Georg, whose brother had been killed early in the war, in that battle at the tender age of eighteen along with tens of thousands of German soldiers. (It had been a tactical error, a military disaster of the highest proportions, and was – as with so many military defeats - accordingly revered as a near mythical event. It had become a symbol of modern German heroism and a useful tool for Nazi propaganda, though for Inge's father this tribute merely concerned the personal loss of a beloved brother.)

Inge and Horst stepped inside the area to read the inscriptions hung on the wall in hushed silence. Horst shuddered in sorrow to think of how many young men had tragically lost their lives in the past for the sake of his country. This experience, he pondered afterward and without commenting on it to his wife, also reminded him that it was the duty of his generation to ensure that their sacrifice should not go in vain. They had fought to make their nation great, and great it now clearly was. He thus considered it the responsibility of the people of this nation to ensure that it stayed that way.

Monday was spent visiting Potsdam, a Prussian jewel just a short train ride from Berlin; later sightseeing the palace *Sanssouci* there and walking round its magnificent park. On their last evening in the capital, Tuesday 4th August, they returned for a final visit to the Olympic stadium in the afternoon. This time on show were the heats of men's 200 metre sprint and women's Discus throw trials, finishing with the final of women's 100 metre sprint. An American won and their hopes for a German gold, pinned on Käthe Krauß, ended in bronze; and so it was the American *Star-Spangled Banner* (by now becoming pompous for them) that once again filled the stadium.

The day ended with the Men's Long jump final, with gold going once again to the USA, and namely to the black American star athlete Jesse Owens. It was his second gold already, having stormed to victory the day before in the Men's 100 metre sprint, and he was set to become the major star figure of these Games. The Germans had hoped for a victory from their own Luz Long, but he went away with silver. Like many spectators, Horst and Inge caught a glimpse of the two athletes Owens and Long engaging in a touching and genuine hug of fraternal respect at the end of the contest which, Inge felt, gave the contest a warm human touch. As chance would have it, this very same scene, that had so captivated Inge, was caught on film and a shot of it turned out to be the perfect picture for the NS-Party to project itself outward with visual positivity into the world; an image of brotherly respect, and even tenderness, between the different races of the planet. Naturally nothing could have been further from the truth; but the important thing – as was well understood among the administrators and designers and political agents who had been commissioned to produce these Games in this particular style - was how to construct a new and more meaningful truth in its place.

(Luz Long in turn had no idea how his spontaneous hug had been used for political purposes that day but he did remain in close friendly contact with Jesse Owens for the rest of his short life. He was called up to the *Wehrmacht* in 1941 and died in action in Italy in 1943.)

But it was the following event that Horst had *really* been looking forward to: the first round of the football tournament. It was the only sport, out of the many and very diverse ones on offer, that held any true interest for him, and he was very keen to watch Germany's first match. He was not to be disappointed. It was a "bloodbath", he later grinned and shook his head in merriment at the thought of the 9:0 victory against hapless Luxembourg. "We slaughtered them, those poor peasants."

"So many goals!" exclaimed Inge with glee, who had witnessed that day her first ever live football match. "I never imagined it could be that exciting."

(Horst would however laugh on the other side of his face later that week. Once back home in Lüneburg he followed the Games on the radio at the apartment of his brother-in-law Ernst and listened to how Germany was beaten 0:2 by Norway in the Quarter Finals that Friday and so kicked out of the tournament by the plucky little Scandinavian nation. Indeed, it is said that this surprise defeat caused a deep depression throughout the entire nation that day.)

In the evening they dined at a fine traditional restaurant called *Zur Letzten Instanz* which Inge had read about in a guidebook as being the oldest restaurant in Berlin, dating back to 1621. They had telephoned for a reservation and been in luck. It was located significantly further to the east, though not too far from Alexanderplatz, and involved a convoluted route with two bus rides and a walk through the central area. They arrived breathless and took their seats. It was simply adorned and horrendously expensive. Inge reacted with a start when she opened the menu and saw the prices; the waiter having overlooked her receiving the *Damenkarte* - the ladies' menu with merely the dishes listed and no prices indicated – and having mistakenly given her the men's full version instead.

"We can't possibly afford this!" she whispered in panic, aware that she had already given up her coat and drunk some of the water on the table. Alone the first item her eyes rested on, '*getrüffelte Gänseleber*' (truffled goose liver), cost an arm and a leg. Horst, though equally shocked, retained his composure and assured her that they most certainly could. He reminded himself internally that he had a steady and reasonably paid job; that there would be few, if any, holidays for many years afterwards; and after a brief calculation he ascertained that he did have just enough cash to get through to tomorrow afternoon if he ordered modesty himself. He began to skim through the prices to locate the cheapest options on offer.

Horst asked the waiter the way to the WC and was gone for some minutes, during which he was counting his banknotes again in order to double-check his calculations. The man from the couple at the next table was talking loudly, in fluent German with a strong French accent. Inge eavesdropped as she idly scanned the wall opposite. "I find the generous urban image impressive alright, that cannot be denied. Impressive, but terribly cold. There is something here that causes me discomfort, something that was missing, that you would normally expect from a German city. Here, I miss the solidly evolving building structures and architectural ensembles, the old granite churches with windows aspiring to heaven, the distinguished patinated monuments. Instead, you have all these staggered modern sandstone constructs in Hohenzoller-style and this...this giddily thrown-together mixture of Romantic, Gothic, Baroque and Renaissance styles. These glitzy department stores and all these endless uniform rows of houses. No, what I'm missing here is that quaint charm and inviting atmosphere of older places, that...that architectural flair that comes from cities that have formed gradually and harmoniously grown up. The little corners with no apparent function, the blank polished stones formed by centuries of walking, the dark little cafés with the old furniture and the musty smell of the glorious past, the narrow and secretive side streets that surreptitiously connect the principal municipal arteries."

He took a hearty gulp of white wine and continued instructing his partner, "No, Berlin can only impress but it can never seduce. Of course, that is exactly what you would expect from a Prussian project that needs to be strictly completed in a limited space of time. It can grow as huge as it wants, but when all is said and done it will never compete with other European cities. Even when compared with other German cities like Frankfurt or Cologne, it is far behind." He went on to ask his companion if she also wished for another glass of wine, which she declined, and he called over the waiter just as Horst was returning to the table.

Inge, happy to contradict the overheard opinion, said to her husband with a wide grin and a lowered intimate voice, "You know, I am loving every minute of our time here in Berlin. It is a wonderful city. I am so glad we came."

Horst, making himself comfortable in his seat, smiled, "Aha, and what do you love so much about it?"

"I don't know....so much! The long wide streets. The tall rows of houses, and all so neat. And it all being so big. You can just lose yourself in it. And the churches, and the marvellous shops and cafés. The...the huge department stores. It is like a whole new world."

"It is very impressive," said Horst, echoing the adjective used by the French man nearby, which Inge found uncanny. "That is for sure. You get a sense of the future here."

"That is exactly it!" said Inge. "It is in the future. Not in the past, but in the future: that is where it belongs. That is where the capital should be. You know, I bet that in a few years all the world will be talking about Berlin and the things that happen here."

"Happening here and in the whole of Germany!" said Horst and raised his glass. "Cheers!" they toasted with glazed eyes and smiles of young love.

"Everything has been so well organized for the Games, don't you think?" said Inge. "And Berlin is just perfect. It is so amazing. Everything functions like clockwork."

"I have to admit, I am pleasantly surprised. I thought Berlin would be different, somehow."

"How do you mean?"

"Well, rougher, more chaotic. Dirtier even. I have always heard that it can be a tough city. Dangerous at times, too. But the whole time we've been here, everything has worked out perfectly. Like you say, very well-organized. And pleasant too. Clean, orderly. Although I think that is something that we Germans do well."

"Now the whole world gets to see what we are capable of," said Inge. "I do hope they hold the Games here again some time. I would love to come back and live it all over again."

Horst smiled and wiped his long thick moustache. He said to Inge with lowered voice, looking briefly over his shoulder, "You know, someone back home, no names mentioned but you will know who I mean, he was saying there is a rumour that if the Führer gets his way, they are going to hold the Olympics in Germany all the time in the future. And that they are even planning a huge stadium that no-one else in the world could even compete with."

Inge gaped. "Can you imagine that? Each and every time, here in our own country. That would be just perfect for us. So, what has been your favourite part so far?"

"Difficult to say. I suppose the whole of the opening ceremony. That certainly kicked it off with style. And when they had all those birds fly up. And then the torch bearer came in and when he lit the flames. It was very well done. I would not be surprised if people were not talking about how they organized it all for years. Imitating it even! What about you?"

"I loved the story about the oldest contestant, the Austrian - did you see that?"

He frowned. "When did you see that?"

"We saw an interview with him in one of those television boxes they have put out on the street. Don't you remember? And I read about him in the *Berliner Illustrierte* too. He is a general from Austria, a horse rider, and he is competing in the "equestrian eventing", they said. He is seventy-six, Horst. Can you imagine that? Taking part in the Olympic Games at seventy-six. You have to admire the determination of that kind of person. They never give up."

Horst nodded glumly. "I can't even ride a horse. Did you see how they could all spring up during the High jump? Incredible, like gazelles. And the sprinting. I could never even dream of running that fast."

Inge admonished him with a smile. "Horst, don't be silly! These are just games. They are running for fun. When you run, it is for a serious reason."

Horst's mouth curled up in the largest of grins as he observed his wife. This person was the greatest gift life had given him: an attractive, fascinating, and above all consistently supportive companion. He reached over the table to squeeze her hand; she giggled as she squeezed it back. The waiter was suddenly standing over them, asking for the order with a tired look and monotonous tone. He had noted that they had finished off all the bread in the little basket and had already put them down to provincial folk splashing out exceptionally and well above their means. The couple glanced at the menu and ordered at the cheapest end of the selection: tomato soup, green salad, Wiener schnitzel with boiled potatoes.

They sat and felt almost conspicuous in these noble surroundings, but the food arrived promptly and was delicious. As was the bottle of white wine, still wet with condensation in the cooler bucket; a modest Côtes du Rhône Reserve that they, though not great drinkers, finished off with relish and could have gone on for more. Most importantly, they had come to realize that their mutual company delighted them, even after a whole intensive week together and, in combination with the excitement of Berlin and the soft charm of the restaurant, this made the moment eternal.

After they had finished and were preparing to leave, Horst had taken Inge's hand again. She said, "Imagine we could have taken a photograph of this moment. Of us sitting here together at the table, just that. So that we could remember it," and they laughed at the silly thought. Horst, though, made the internal note that one day – hopefully not too distant - he would buy his wife a camera.

Apart from the two further visits to the Stadium, they occasionally tried to push their way into one of the very popular and usually brimming full public *Fernsehstuben* (TV rooms), that Inge had mentioned during the meal and that were to be found all around Berlin, enabling as many people as possible to follow the latest development in the Games. Not only the athletics in Berlin but also the sailing events taking place in the Baltic Sea around Kiel. This was the first time that the Games had been transmitted lived on radio and television and was a big thumbs up for the advanced state of German technology. All across the country the audiences followed with great interest on cinema or television screens, or much more commonly next to the radio, the race to heap up as many medals as possible for the Fatherland. They followed the prestigious competitions in their millions, such as the 400 metre relay races, the Men's Shot put and Javelin (which featured the popular Gerhard Stöck), the pentathlon, the final slog of the marathon, the weightlifting exploits of Egyptian competitor Khadr El Touni, the High and Long jumps. It brought great excitement, not to mention bonding, each time Germany won gold and the stirring melody and chords of the national anthem vibrated through the radio. Often it was turned up higher in those victorious moments in order for listeners to both inwardly rejoice in, as well as outwardly demonstrate to those around them, their unswerving loyalty. It could be said that these Olympics were the first time that an event was felt with such fervour and such proximity by a whole nation, all in real time. People didn't just listen to the results emanating from the Games, they experienced them. Thus Berlin's superiority in the Games and its contiguity to the Reich, reinforcing its politically central position, became unquestionable.

Right at the beginning there was the major highlight: the Men's 100 metre sprint. The race was won by Jesse Owens, who was a hot favourite for gold. Perhaps surprisingly, considering the racist ideology reigning in the country at the time, he enjoyed much admiration and respect from the general public. Despite his popularity among many ordinary Germans, who recognized the virtue of a young man of humble background making history, the German media and press were expected to be hostile toward the dark-skinned American. They put down his spectacular run of wins as being akin to the stamina and cunning ingenuity of the big cats, like a panther sneaking out of the jungle.

(Following one of his four gold medal wins, which eventually made him a household and legendary name at these Games, he was personally approached by Adolf Hitler who, to the astonishment of many, greeted him and warmly shook his hand. Upon returning home to the United States, his welcoming committee was far less enthusiastic in a still segregated America. He received neither a congratulatory telegram nor an invitation to the White House. Indeed, Owens later recalled that Hitler was far more friendly towards him than his own president (Franklin D. Roosevelt), though propaganda measures were soon put into effect by the US media in order to reverse the nature of the story.)

Back home in Lüneburg, the show was closely followed by Inge and Horst's families. In particular Horst's cousin Carsten liked to annotate and absorb technical facts and numbers in large quantities, and regurgitate them whenever possible. He was convinced that he was doing his fellow Germans a great instructive service in that he always had the correct information at hand to provide clarity and detail to any conversation. So it was with the results of the Games and in terms of the medal count these were very satisfactory for him and for all Germany. The final tally achieved exactly the desired effect and helped to further lift the mood of the nation immensely that summer. Germany had won with a resounding 33 gold medals (37, if you counted Austria, which Cousin Carsten did not at the time; the mere suggestion of this interfered with his statistical approach and produced in him a near state of anxiety) against the 24 golds of the Americans; 89 medals for the Reich in total, against 56 for the US in total. Hungary and Italy were very distant third and fourth respectively.

It was the final day in Berlin for Horst and Inge; tomorrow they would catch the train back and return home to Lüneburg. While on their last wistful promenade through the city centre, Inge bought a souvenir for her sister Gisela to thank her for all the help and organisation that she had provided before the wedding. It was a small figurine on a stand, of an athlete running with the Olympic torch held ahigh, around 25cm in height, in white porcelain and bearing a black swastika engraved on his chest. She felt it was a very appropriate gift and would also communicate that which had been for her the most memorable moment of the whole visit; the electrifying lighting of the torch and the immensity of the hushed arena that first Saturday during the opening ceremony. It was a cherished memory, purchased to be shared with a loved one, and it left Inge feeling fulfilled.

For her parents she bought copies of the official souvenir magazine. The cover attracted her, with a white marble Greek goddess looking across a dark blue background as rays of light blue sunlight pierced down from above through the five hanging Olympic rings. As with the figurine, the visual aspect had attached an emotional bond that she found moving. She bought two copies, one in German for her father and one in French for her mother who, unlike her father, still spoke a little and had fond memories of the year spent there as a girl: she knew that that way her mother would feel a little special and appreciate being able to read something that her spouse could not.

Chapter 3

Returning buoyant from the excitement of the energetic metropolis, Horst and Inge encountered a warm and familial welcome home in sedate Lüneburg. All were eager to tell them of how the Olympic Games had been extensively covered not only by the press but also, for the first time ever, live on the radio and even with film excerpts in the cinema news. This had filled many with the rousing sensation of participating, through the latest technology, in the Games: watching from the domestic comfort of living rooms an event of such magnitude actually taking place in that very moment of time. So widespread and professional had been the coverage, that some related that it was almost like they had been there themselves. They also quickly admitted there was of course nothing like seeing the actual event live, not wishing to take the wind out of the young couple's sails when they were so enthusiastically chatting about their experiences in Berlin and their visits to the sporting events and festivities. Between the Winter Games in Garmisch earlier that year and the Summer Games just over, the general view was that Germany had staged two exceptionally well-organized spectacles. It had played the perfect and friendly host, had shown the world its society and culture from the best side, and furthermore gone on in the principal show in Berlin to prevail with a convincing win in all medal categories: the general satisfaction could not have been more complete.

Gisela was Inge's older sister and closest member of the family. She was a blunt-tongued wife and mother who with her sturdy frame and dark curly hair, her skeptical attitude towards all those around her, and her domineering manner, barely resembled Inge. The sisters had always got on well since childhood and during the period of wedding preparations Gisela had made particular fuss of the couple, delighted to see her sister joining her in marital stability. She was glad now to see them back safe and sound from Berlin and, though wild horses wouldn't have dragged Gisela herself to the capital, she was fascinated by the idea and very much looking forward to hearing about their experiences with all luxury of detail. Moreover, she was already hinting right upon their arrival in Lüneburg, as she accompanied them home on foot from the railway station, of an important and imminent announcement that was soon to be made by the parents of Gisela's husband, Martin Landeck.

The next day, following some whispered discussions between Gisela and Martin behind the scenes, the news was privately divulged in one breathless swoop when Gisela caught her sister leaving work from the bakery in the early afternoon. She took Inge straight to her own house, where she had prepared a relatively lavish meal, and even served chilled white wine in order to create the appropriate atmosphere in which to share her information.

Martin's parents, Anna and Volkmar Landeck, had announced the week before their intention to hand over the running of their *Gasthaus Sonnenschein* (literally: Guesthouse Sunshine) in Lüneburg to their eldest son Martin and daughter-in-law Gisela. Anna and Volkmar were both now in their sixties and had decided to retire back to a large rural cottage that belonged to Anna's elderly mother Brunhilde in nearby Adendorf. Brunhilde was an octogenarian widow of an iron will, with an unpredictably fiery temper and an innately sadistic disposition toward the male sex. Her hard character had not been tempered by the passing of time but her general cognitive grip was not what it once had been, so she now found herself in need of someone to take care of her and be close at hand. Anna was her only child so the task naturally fell to her.

Brunhilde herself was very pleased with the new living arrangements. She would have the certainty of ministering company on the one hand, while on the other she would have no qualms at all about making Anna's and more pointedly Volkmar's lives a misery wherever she had the chance. She was cunning too, knowing how to apply pressure quietly and inconspicuously; how to close conversations with simple off-the-cuff insults that burnt deeply for days. All in all it was a very satisfactory plan for the matriarch. Anna was somewhat apprehensive of this set-up, having always kept a friendly but distant relationship to her mother thus far, but was aware that her filial responsibility lay indisputably there. It was the only socially acceptable route. Volkmar positively detested the old woman and always had. He assumed though that her demise could not be far off; after that the cottage and grounds would be theirs. So long, he was sure, he could bear his mother-in-law's bad humours and sharp jibes.

Volkmar had not been well for some time, suffering from a persistent and throbbing backache, plus a painful right knee when walking. He felt mentally alert and loved to discuss current affairs, but was often physically weary. These days he enjoyed sitting for hours in people's living rooms, reading and chatting now and again to anyone who would spare the time to listen, and managed to get himself driven by car from one place to another whenever possible. The sudden increase in the production and private acquisition of motor cars in the country in the last few years had come as a godsend; and he knew only too well whom he had to thank for this new era of *'Motorisierung'* (motorization). "There is nothing that the Führer has not put right in this country. Everything has been a blessing," he would pronounce with clear contentment in his pale blue eyes. He loved the topic of automobiles and had become quite knowledgeable on it, mentioning the type of car a given neighbour might possess even while not being aware of that person's name.

His wife Anna also had health issues. She had been experiencing sporadic spells of dizziness and nausea, as well as a periodic loss of balance, and had consulted a well-known and expensive physician in Lüneburg, Dr. Lübbe, in his practice in the Lünertorstraße. She had undergone various tests there, all to no avail. There did not seem to be any clear physical ailment to which her ongoing condition could be ascribed. Dr. Lübbe proposed a visit to a specialist in Hamburg, a prominent expert in the field of cardiovascular disease, and this was to take place in early September and at considerable expense.

Given their age and general physical condition, the Landecks had decided that passing the management of their modest but beloved business over to Martin and Gisela would be the perfect solution to their situation, explained an exuberant Gisela to Inge over lunch. It turned out that they had already sounded out the young couple on the subject ten days before, during the honeymoon of Horst and Inge in Berlin. After all due consideration they were all now ready to formalize that decision. Gisela had been helping out, on and off, for a few years now, and knew her way round the business; while their son

Martin, they had opined, possessed the solid character that was perfect for management.

Martin's brother Dieter, the younger of the Landeck's two children, was involved in a promising career in the army that included a recent promotion to the position of *Unterfeldwebel* (Sergeant). He had also been consulted, so as to ensure complete familial concord, and as expected had expressed his complete agreement with the arrangement proposed and his own complete lack of interest in any participation therein. An appointment had been made at the notary from the law firm *Anwaltskanzlei Briegel* in October to finalize all legal aspects. In this way, Anna and Volkmar hoped then to see Martin and Gisela, together with their own three children, firmly established in the Gasthaus as soon as possible, hopefully before Christmas.

Inge was thrilled by the news and only had congratulations, embraces and the best future wishes for her sister. She knew how perfect the position would be, and internally thought that Gisela would bring the practical know-how and robust attention to duty that Martin might sometimes be lacking in. All in all, it would be the perfect plan, she was sure.

"Anna was saying just the other day how you never can tell how things might look a few years further down the road," Gisela expounded as they were finishing their food. "And she is quite right. You never do know. But there is so much security in property and in a family business. So naturally we accepted immediately. Well, Martin accepted for us, what with him being the actual heir, after we had had a discussion on the subject beforehand. He was not so sure at first about some of the minor details but fortunately I was able to set him right." She sighed with contentment as she sipped her wine. "Everything is looking so rosy now. And to think I will be running a hotel soon."

Gisela was clearly in the process of hatching big plans, Inge found, as her sudden and inapposite usage of the word 'hotel' suggested. The *Gasthaus Sonnenschein* had already been in the Landeck family for four generations. It was a modest but well-liked establishment, the exterior fashioned with deep red bricks which bordered the arched windows in their gleaming white frames. The ground floor consisted of an ample restaurant and adjoining kitchen, a spacious entrance hall and storage facilities, and with a back lounge that functioned as private quarters for the proprietors. Above this came three storeys and an attic, containing a total of eleven bedrooms all told: three small single rooms and a large double room on the first floor, three ample double rooms on the second and third floors, and at the top was a snug attic room under the triangular roof with a double bed and private bathroom which would be taken by Gisela and Martin. It was still unclear however where the children were to sleep. Gisela considering putting the two boys Sigfried ('Siggi') and Erich, eight and six respectively, in one of the single rooms; and have the girl Katrina, nine years old, sleep by her parents. Martin had in turn wondered whether it would not be wiser to have the youngest child Erich, heavily handicapped by a withered left leg due to a Polio infection in his youth, sleep with them instead, as he obviously required more care. Gisela saw his point and would like to have slept with the boy near, but argued: "In that case, he would have to climb up all those stair every day to go to bed." And with Katrina growing up fast, it also seemed more sensible to give the girl her own room at some point. But there was no really adequate solution, Martin concluded irritably, until each of the children had their own room; which meant they might as well go back to their old apartment over in Moorfeld as the Gasthaus would barely provide them with enough to pay the utility and staff costs. Gisela, like her mother, expressed her frustration with long extended sighs, and at this point exhaled profusely and desisted from discussing the issue further.

"There is the income from the restaurant as well," Inge reminded her. "To my knowledge it has always been popular in town. Whenever I have heard people mention the Gasthaus at the bakery, they usually speak very highly of the restaurant. It has a good reputation and is well located too."

The restaurant, situated at the front of the building, offered a pleasant view out into the street, with the ornately gabled buildings opposite. It had three old windows, in need of replacement and fronted with thick beige curtains, and the walls were covered with panels of rich dark-brown walnut wood. A few hanging lights hung sporadically round the walls in milk glass shades that emitted a soft glow which nonetheless left a heavy gloomy ambiance in the room. The few pictures that decked the walls were of mostly rural themes: cows grazing, wheat being harvested, ducks on ponds. The central artistic feature at the back of the restaurant, wedged in between two small windows, was the Landecks' pride and joy - a large engraved and painted woodland scene of hunters armed with rifles, standing to the left of a stag and deer couple. Dense thickets of thorns and tendrils of plants, sporting the occasional vivid red and blue flowers, entwined about the scene and up and around the window frames.

The menu offered mostly southern German and Austrian cuisine, though occasionally graced with a touch of Italian influence in the last couple of years. It was a well-liked and oft-visited establishment, thanks in no small measure to the talent and steady reliability of the cook, Walter Schönbrunner - originally from Austria and now well into his sixties, though as fit and energetic as any young man. Not only local residents frequented the restaurant but also tourists came eagerly in spring and summer. Hence its good reputation produced first-class publicity for the comparatively commonplace level of accommodation at the Gasthaus itself.

Gisela said how she too had picked up similar comments on her travels round town, which was a welcome datum to her ears. (She did not like to rely on her own judgement of the restaurant's offerings for the simple reason that she heartily ate almost everything placed before her and rarely came across anything not to her liking). She only hoped that both she and Martin were up to the mammoth task ahead and that they would be able to keep up the good reputation of the *Gasthaus Sonnenschein* and its restaurant, by offering a solid working attitude combined with a sensible business strategy. She had told Martin as much herself and he had been very impressed by the sound of it.

There were however some factors that made her nervous. Primary among them was that with the retirement of the Landecks had also come that of the previous manager, a cousin of Anna, and in turn that of his granddaughter who had worked there as a waitress and now planned to study for a secretarial post. That would leave only the chef Walter from the original staff once the change in ownership had been established. Gisela told her sister how she planned to take over the managerial role herself, in which capacity she would be assisted by her husband. Inge, knowing her sister's ambitious nature all too well, concealed a smile at the thought of the reserved and taciturn Martin and his future role.

What the Gasthaus lacked in space, it more than made up for in its prime location. With this, the lodgings had been built up through the years to a well-frequented, renowned and lucrative business. It was situated on the Rosenstraße, in a central compact area of commercial activity, just a couple of minutes walking down from the Marktplatz and its elegant town hall in one direction; an equally short stroll down to the Ilmenau river in the other. From the noble Am Sande street and its large open square and general hub, it was just a five-minute-walk to the Gasthaus. Most of the businesses they worked with were all to be found here along the tight and cobbled streets of the town centre.

Convinced of her ability to successfully carry on with this traditional family business, and seeing herself as treading in unambitious footsteps, Gisela also had no shortage of innovative plans for improvement. These included an extensive internal renovation to be carried out over the next few years, once she felt she had attained the necessary experience and feel for the profession. Her desire was also that in the course of this renovation she would be able to convert the eleven bedrooms into twelve, perhaps with luck even thirteen. Furthermore she talked enthusiastically of *Lüftlmalerei*, the art of mural paintings on the outer walls of buildings which she had once seen, depicted in a magazine, of a painting on a Gasthaus in a Bavarian village. The property featured had looked almost identical in size and form to their property, which naturally made the idea seem very appropriate for their own venture. She had already put a great deal of thought into the contents of the paintings, which would encompass the light of an entire day from morning to early night, including horses and carts moving through the mural as a constant motif, gas lamps in the twilights scenes, big piles of straw bales, and central would be a hot sunny midday scene displaying strong farmers working with pitchforks and hoes and clearly sweating. "A tribute to rural times gone by but not forgotten," she had told a puzzled Martin.

"The restaurant has a mural design on the wall inside, too," commented Inge, when she heard of Gisela's renovation ideas.

"Exactly, exactly, and so my plan would be to have a large painting on the front wall that would complement the internal mural. It might even come to be a talking point in town. That would be the most wonderful publicity you could hope for. People love paintings, especially happy ones. Of course, this would be quite a major investment and so will have to wait a couple of years until we have the financial means. Which is a shame as I already have most of it worked out in my mind," Gisela concluded, lightly tapping three fingers on the table. It was always regretful in business when the boundless imagination of the mind so quickly and nimbly outperformed the dull considerations of reality.

As a married couple, Inge and Horst moved into their new home together: a small and dark two-room 35 m² apartment in the Rotenbleicher Weg, but ideal for both of them in terms of distance to work. For Horst it was a short jaunt to the Feldstraße and the bus-stop that took him to the *Feuerwache* (fire station) in the Moorfeld district. For Inge, employed at the *Bäckerei & Konditorei* (bakery & confectionery) *Strauß* in the former Lindenstraße, recently re-named the Adolf-Hitler-Straße, it was a brisk ten-minute walk to work. The apartment had a bedroom, a tiny bathroom with toilet and a small room for cooking and eating. The light was dim as its position meant it received little direct sunlight, and it could get quite damp in winter and smell musky, but they viewed it as a good start in life and were very happy to live there. The apartment had been unfurnished, containing only a rough basic stove, but their families had helped enormously to organize the basics for them to move in: a double bed and an old chestnut wardrobe for clothes, a dressing table and chair in the bedroom for Inge, a cheap but sturdy table in the kitchen to eat off with four different wooden chairs, and an armchair; none of which matched.

Inge's parents were Georg and Corinna Hartmann, who lived modestly in a small apartment to the south of the town. Corinna was an amiable woman, much liked in town, who worked part-time in a nearby dry-cleaning and laundry business. Georg, who had been injured in the Great War and suffered from ongoing headaches and dizziness, lived from his pension. He was a prickly and cantankerous man, old before his time, who had few friends and enjoyed his life that way. He was often rude and patronizing to his wife, who endured in grim silence the verbal hostilities that her husband dished out on a regular daily basis.

They had had three children: Gisela, Ernst, and Inge. None had liked the family atmosphere and all had been keen to leave. The girls had married young (Gisela at barely eighteen and Inge at twenty), which common wisdom considered the preferential route for women to a new home and life; while their brother Ernst had gone into the banking profession and, working his way with diligence up the career ladder, had a good position for his age at the local branch of the *Vereinsbank,* which in turn afforded himself an attractive apartment near the centre. He was somewhat of a loner and stayed out of the family affairs on the whole, although his various medical ailments meant that Gisela kept a protective eye on him and supplied him on her visits to his apartment with all the town and family tattle he needed to know.

Corinna had one sister, Hertha, who had also married young; to a mellow, good-looking and very courteous young man called Rudolf, who possessed a farm way over in East Prussia, in the very east of what was then the German Empire. She had gone off to live with him there nearly forty years ago and the couple had one daughter. Corinna kept in close contact with Hertha per post, with the two siblings enjoying a regular exchange of long letters. Her sister was her best, though geographically very distant, friend, as well as her confidante. If they ever had anything very private to discuss, then Hertha would write back in French, in case Georg one day took into his head to go prying in her box of letters at the bottom of the bedroom wardrobe and have reason to be offended. As it happened, Georg never did. He did, though, detest Hertha with a passion, and always had done. He had known her briefly as a young man, while courting her sister and being treated to no small degree of acerbity on Hertha's part. The two had thus enjoyed a mutual loathing for a while until Hertha married and moved off. Georg was over the moon the first time he heard that the husband-to-be was from East Prussia. "I would have liked him all the more if his farm were in Windhoek, but even so, that will do just fine," he once commented. As it turned out, a number of complications arose and Hertha never was able to make the long trip home to her native Lüneburg to visit her sister, though she promised to do so on repeated occasions.

The Hartmann family had never been greatly interested in discussing politics; and nowadays, recognizing its highly conflictive nature in the current climate, even less so. Corinna actively avoided all talk on the subject wherever she could. This modus operandi was partly inspired by Georg's deep-felt hatred of Adolf Hitler and his NSDAP party which, since 1933, was no longer something to joke about. From the moment that Hitler had first began to gain serious notoriety (beyond such loud gimmicks as the *Bierhalleputsch*) and political acknowledgement, Georg had immediately felt not just a deep-seated distrust and dislike of the man, but also a terrible foreboding fear that he could one day rise to be someone. At that point in the late twenties and early thirties few, if any, had taken him seriously. But Georg had always harboured a bad feeling about the "screaming Austrian and his nasty moustache", as he used to say back in the days before it became dangerous talk.

Once evening at a family gathering for Ernst's eighteenth birthday, he had polished off several glasses of *Obstler* schnaps. In this inebriated state he launched into the story of a man at the local church (*St. Marien Kirche*) with whom he had spoken just after the Great War. The Hartmanns were Catholics, their families coming originally from the Pfalz, and had at that time still been regular churchgoers. Said person that day at church, Georg had explained, was an ex-priest who had served in the hospitals near the front as a chaplain for the soldiers. He had even given last rites to adolescents, and to family fathers who had then died right there in front of him. That was what made him different, Georg had insisted: "He knew the horrors of the trenches, and of course he was Catholic, like us. So after the service some of us were chatting away together, we began to talk about the war and the things we had seen. He came over and was very compassionate and said how brave we had all been. He said a lot of very supportive things. But then he said that we should always keep on our toes because this could all happen again. One of the men there laughed and said he didn't think so - a fat stupid thing, he was. But the ex-priest persisted in what he wanted to say, he said to beware because the war would be forgotten in a few years. A new generation would grow up, but they would do so without fear of the war because they would think it was just old history. Those that were little boys now, they would be the young men in a decade who would not take heed of the tales of their uncles and father who had survived. They would not be interested, they would not listen, and that way they would not learn. And the ex-priest said, a man will rise up, and people will listen to him and they will be as if hypnotized by him. This man will shout and wave his fist at the sky, and the people will love it. And then another war will come, only bigger, louder, more terrifying this time. There will be flames in all directions, with the horizon itself on fire, and the graves will stretch out in long lines, and people will wail and scream, and there will nothing but destruction and endless dying! In the end it will be in a simple stable, just like the stable where the Three Magi first beheld the Boy Child Jesus Christ, that the German people will gather together again. Because that is all the space they will need! Those were his words and I can still hear them as if it were yesterday."

Georg's tale was heard out and later taken with all the merry dismissal that the rest of his drunken ramblings were. But when that fatal day came on 30th January 1933, when the leader of the NSDAP party Adolf Hitler was announced on the radio as having been proclaimed *Reichskanzler*, Georg cried out, "That's him! That's the one!" Nobody had a clue what he meant until he began to relate the old tale from the man at church again. Georg was triumphant at first, but then despondent with the weight of this prevision.

In the following months and years such talk became increasingly dangerous and Georg was instructed by his now older children, and by Gisela in particular, to keep his tales to himself. "Martin and I have a home and children growing up, Papa," Gisela had told him to his face while her mother looked nervously at the floor. "We don't want them to be afraid to come and visit their own grandfather because he rants like a madman. Or have to tell them that he has been sent to one of those concentration camps for a month."

With such an example, the other siblings found their natural lack of expressing interest in politics confirmed. They formed their own opinions internally but were resolved to keep them out of the way of public discourse. With time however, politics started to infringe so much into daily life that it became increasingly difficult to dodge the subject with grace and diplomacy. It became a difficult game to say the right thing even when saying nothing.

Inge was the least interested of all. Her major ambition in life was to have children. This she considered to be the greatest role in life for a woman and hoped to make her own contribution to the act of motherhood as soon as possible. That same summer she was passing by the St. Marien church one Sunday when she saw a confirmation service about to take place. A group of children were gathered in front of the church: the boys in smart blue suits with tie, the girls in white dresses with lace ruffs around the neck, wearing white gloves and carrying little bouquets of lilies-of-the-valley. Inge found the scene adorable. She remembered herself at that age and in just such an outfit; and she imagined them all in a few years' time, stepping out into life to discover the glory of existence in this bright world, and their good fortune in growing up in such a wholesome society and in times of peace and plenty.

Likewise she doted over Gisela's three children and admired what she saw as her sister's natural maternal talent, in which she achieved the perfect balance of discipline with friendly interaction. This would be a template that she wished to use herself once the time was ripe. Inge's education had been very basic. She had completed her corresponding level at the *Volksschule*, graduating with satisfactory grades in the courses of the fundamental subjects: German, handwriting, *Heimatkunde* (local history and geography), and arithmetic. She had then left school in 1931, at the age of fifteen and with the minimum of educational qualifications, and gone straight to work at the chemical factory beside the *Saline Lüneburg* (Lüneburg Saltworks). She had stuck that out for two years and was over the moon to be offered a job in a bakery and cake-shop by a friend of her mother's; not so far from her home and much more pleasant work. There she had first set eyes on Horst and got to talk to him while he was fetching a box of cakes to celebrate a colleague's birthday. Both had felt the spark of mutual attraction and, just under a year later, they had married. Now Inge was looking forward to starting her own family and thus fulfilling the great ambition of her still young life.

By the end of October that year, just as had been the plan, the Landecks handed over the complete set of keys to the *Gasthaus Sonnenschein* and moved out for good, heading off to Brunhilde's cottage out in Adendorf and whatever living conditions destiny was to throw at them there. On the same weekend, Martin and Gisela moved in with their children and all the basic belongings.

The Landecks had possessed neither the financial resources nor the breath of vision to modernize their business, liking it the way it had been for generations. And so, as with many homes and even businesses at this time, the Gasthaus was still run on gas, even the lamps. This was to be changed immediately. Horst's brother Wilhelm, a trained electrician by profession, came round with a workmate over several weekends and they wired the entire building up from top to bottom. Gisela and Martin had to take out a credit to pay for this intensive work but they were sure it was an important step forward. They were open-eyed with amazement when Wilhelm and his colleague showed them the sockets they had fitted into the walls and explained some of the many technological possibilities now awaiting them on the horizon. Gisela had heard from a friend of a neighbour who had bought herself an electric iron that could be fitted into just such a socket as they had installed, she had said; that seemed to be her first objective, along with one of the refrigerators that were apparently now very popular in America. Martin in turn seemed more interested in the thought of electrical lighting all through the house and above all a radio with an electrical connection.

Gisela was fascinated by the idea of cooking every day in the restaurant kitchen and eating every day with the family silverware as if it were her own, which to all intents and purposes it now was. Here in the Gasthaus she saw the opportunity for a residency that was both congenial and profitable. She said to Inge, "The first thing I am, I mean, we are going to get done, is to give the mural on the restaurant wall a lick of paint. It has become very pale and faded over the years, and I know just the person who can do that for me at a good price."

She nodded with pursed lips as her eyes scanned the restaurant, already planning replacements for the dull light shades and a new stove for the kitchen. "New and better times are coming and we have to be ready to make all the appropriate changes."

52

Chapter 4

November brought good news when a gushing beaming Inge announced her pregnancy. Horst told her he was the happiest man on earth and could not let her hand go the whole evening. Gisela was overjoyed and began planning the hand-me-downs: "Only if you want to, mind! You don't have accept them. I will quite understand if Horst is too proud. Although in all seriousness, the prices they charge for the little shoes, it is outrageous. And you need a new pair every year. I still have the old wickerwork perambulator I had for Katrina and Siggi, if you would like it."

Corinna was of course thrilled and even the habitually acidic Georg was a bundle of merriment. Gisela had already given them three beautiful grandchildren, whom they adored; due to his disability Corinna, like Gisela herself, doted in particular on "poor little Erich." Now their own little Inge, the youngest of their children, would be giving them even more. "How quickly you go from mother to grandmother. How painlessly and effortlessly," commented Corinna with a wistful sigh.

Gisela had been born in 1909 and a year later Corinna had given birth to a further child, Ernst Hartmann, now twenty-six. Following Ernst's birth, Corinna had suffered two traumatic miscarriages and a stillbirth before the war, and had regarded the birth of her final child Inge, in the midst of war-time famine in 1916, to be little short of a miracle. Now their own children, or at least the girls, were married and bringing them grandchildren into the world; a world that was so very different to the one they had grown up in. Radios, airships, motor cars now a common sight everywhere; even telephones and electrical lighting. It was hard to keep pace in such bewildering times, hence all the more need to feel part of the traditional rhythm of generations coming and going that they had always known. That was what most gave her comfort in her mortality, more so even than her religious beliefs: that one day she and her husband would inevitably slip from this vibrant buzzing world, while Gisela and Inge, perhaps even Ernst one day, would become grandparents themselves and impart the same values, the same traditions, to the next generation. With that security of continuity came, as her priority, the safety and wholesome upbringing of the little ones, now entering and negotiating this increasingly complex world of often fraught but nonetheless fundamentally happy German life. That they should have a better childhood and life than she ever did, was what most made sense to her about the concept of life itself.

The following May 1937, on a blustery springtime Friday, Inge's first child came into the world. Inge had reached the estimated 42-week limit but still there was no sign that the baby inside intended to leave his protective mother. A further two weeks passed until finally her obstetrician Dr. Schwenter decided that it was time for her to be taken into hospital for the birth to be induced. It ended up being a long and difficult labour for the first-time mother. Nearly seven hours she struggled to push her child out into the world. For the last and most intensive half-hour she heaved and sweated and cried out to everyone's growing nervousness until finally a boy emerged. For Horst it had the enormity of the coming of Christ: his own son had arrived, he thought with awe, a male heir. He could barely believe his eyes nor his luck.

The baby was a delicate little thing: "Definitely on the small side, only two kilos exact," whispered Gisela discreetly outside to her husband. No sooner was he out into the fresh air, however, than he began to scream with all the fullness of his lung capacity, to the delight of those gathered round.

Horst and Inge had been ruminating over both feminine and masculine names for the last three months, but with a touch of superstition felt reluctant to fix themselves on any particular name, much less divulge their considerations to others in the family. "I want to see the child born healthy first before I start giving him or her a name," insisted Inge. The names of the children should be kept strictly out of discussion's way until after the child was born, they strongly felt, though could not resist secretly musing upon numerous ideas.

Now that this very moment had finally arrived, they found themselves unready for the momentous decision; although there was one name that did seem appropriate for the boy, Horst had stated, and that was Adolf. Gisela's husband Martin, who had arrived in the first hours after the birth to congratulate his brother, heartily agreed. Indeed, as it arose in a later conversation, one of Inge's colleagues from the bakery had borne a child last November and he had been christened Adolf. It was a solid and traditional – not to mention hugely popular - name that, they felt, was of good standing and that would later open doors for the boy. Inge herself was not so sure at first, keenly feeling the political connection, but was later swayed by group pressure. Eventually, all those who had assembled in the hospital, on that and the following day, were in full agreement with the choice and began planning the gifts and necessary articles for 'little Adolf', as he was suddenly known. (The only exception was Georg - as was to be expected - who found the whole idea to be ridiculous to the point of offensive, and did not get round to going to see his grandson until Inge had returned home and Adolf was already a week old. Nevertheless, he learnt with time to ignore all the negative associations of the namesake and came to love the boy.)

Meanwhile, the baby himself was feeling his way through his first days outside of the womb in this strange new reality. Following an initially prolonged wailing session, that in its sheer length and intensity had started to make one of the nurses uneasy, he had finally snuggled in between his mother's breasts and piped down for a few hours.

The christening was quickly organized by Inge's industrious sister and thanks to Gisela's presence of mind and persuasive manner when discussing the matter with Pater Mäder, the priest from the St. Marien church, they managed to arrange a time and date that was manageable by all at such short notice. It turned out to be a warm fresh sunny Saturday and for Gisela it was the perfect day to bring both the respective families together again, an event that had not taken place since their wedding the year before, only this time at the *Gasthaus Sonnenschein*. There Gisela arranged a sumptuous buffet and spared no cost, eager to show off to both families as well as spoil her sister and brother-in-law and new nephew.

Gisela and Martin hosted the event, helped by their older two children while Erich sat in a corner with his crutch and was pampered by all who passed by him. The grandparents Georg and Corinna arrived in very elegant attire, clearly desiring to make a special show on this day despite their meagre income. Georg, although he had quickly accustomed himself to the boy's chosen name, had looked to be going apoplectic upon hearing it read out with the ringing tone of the priest in the church, and went a worrying shade of reddish-purple. For the rest, he was unusually quiet that day, as well as being under strict instructions by his both his daughters (he took little notice of his wife) to stay well away from both alcohol and politics. Their son Ernst came later and, not being of a sociable nature, stayed close to his parents and mumbled some sparse conversation with them.

Martin's parents Volkmar and Anna Landeck were also invited, at Gisela's bidding and above all so that she could show them the freshly painted mural on the wall as well as some other improvements and alterations that she had undertaken at the Gasthaus. They nodded with approval and proffered some appreciative comments, though neither felt well that day and they eventually left early.

The two older men Volkmar Landeck and Georg Grün had no mutual partiality nor respect and were clearly mistrustful toward each other. Politics played an important role in this antipathy, with Volkmar being an open NSDAP supporter and signed up Party member, while he correctly suspected Georg as being virulently anti-Nazi. As did religion, for the Landecks also held a fundamental distrust of Catholics. For the sake of their families, though, they maintained a tacitly understood concordance toward each other on such occasions which, they both hoped, would not be all too frequent.

Horst's parents attended, coming all the way from Uelzen and driven there by Horst's older brother Karl-Heinz, whose wife excused herself as two of the children were sick at home. Horst's sister Marianne came, along with her husband Manfred and their two children Johann-Christian and Emil; as did Horst's younger brother and favourite sibling Wilhelm, together with his girlfriend Ann-Kathrin. Also in attendance was Paul Schönbeck, a lanky firefighter colleague and friend of Horst.

The last arrivals were further members of the Landeck family, Volkmar's niece Edeltraut Bohlen, together with her husband Bernhard and two of their four children: Eva, who was very friendly with Gisela and Martin's eldest daughter Katrina, and Roland, now twenty-one and serving in the military.

Between the baptism in church and the feast afterwards, the whole day went off without a hitch. They all shared in the great happiness brought to a radiant Inge and Horst, relished in the general joy of seeing the symbol of that union blessed under the eyes of God, and in some cases found it moreover very appropriate that the child was carrying the name of the Führer who was leading the land to better times. But whatever one's stance on the boy's name, or rather namesake, nobody could have wished for a more perfect moment.

Gisela and Martin still didn't have a gramophone player so they borrowed one from the neighbour to provide some music. His - very extensive - collection of military march music in vinyl records did not seem the most appropriate sound for the occasion, so they declined his offer and Corinna brought round a selection of her French chansons instead. Throughout the buffet she took care of the order and changing of the records, and was delighted to be of service. While her husband wasted no time in locating the drinks, Corinna chirped, "Oh, it is on occasions like this that I wish my sister Hertha could have made it, to be here with us!" as was her custom at any important family gatherings.

There was a smart buffet, already partly laid out by Walter the chef at the Gasthaus together with a hired waitress, for when they all arrived. This included numerous and varied canapés, boiled eggs and potato salad with sprinklings of parsley, a selection of basic seafood dishes, two quiches, and plates of cheeses and hams lined with a few baguettes. Beer and wine flowed freely, too. Dessert was *Apfelstrudel* with cream. There were numerous vases of flowers all around, spraying out an abundance of bright colours to further cheer the atmosphere; the nearby florist Christiane Zimmer had done very good business that week with Gisela.

Now embodying her role as gourmet and fête hostess, a vocation for which she felt a natural calling, Gisela wanted to avoid having clumps of families hanging together and tried to mix up the guests as much as possible. This produced some initial awkwardness but with the flow of alcohol the crowd found increasing self-confidence talking to near strangers, most of whom they had parleyed with at the wedding the year before anyway. Soon the mumble of conversation rose in volume. It became quite a loud din, a sure sign of success to Gisela, and she headed to the kitchen to see how Walter was coping.

The women were caught between admiring the newborn and admiring the spread. Both were immaculately presented. Horst's mother Elisabeth helped herself to some *Schmalzbrot* (bread and dripping) with herrings, her favourite dish which Horst had quietly requested just for her, and she couldn't stop saying how delicious they were. The women began to remember a few years back to the early 1930s, when the poverty and the inflation had driven them desperate and made it so difficult to put a bit of decent food on the table.

"Day after day of just potatoes and bread", sighed Marianne, "I remember that well. We were glad for a bit of butter." Everyone knew that as she had married a farmer and lived out on the land, this had not been the case. All the same, she liked to fit in.

"I remember going to *Metzger Duncker* [butcher's] in the Bardowicker Straße," said Gisela, who had returned from the kitchen with two trays of assorted vol-au-vents to keep her mother Corinna happy with her favourite. "And if you were a little charming with him, he would reach under the counter and sell you a head and lungs of mutton for 20 Pfennig. Sometimes that was all you had in your purse. Or all he had on offer. The kids were little back then but they hated it. Siggi would retch, poor love, and Katrina always looked like she might start crying. Still, they got it down them in the end. It's the discipline that counts."

The older women went further back in time with bitter memories that stretched all the way to the Great War. "Around the middle of the war there was one year when there was literally nothing to eat. Nothing at all, except turnips," Anna began to recount.

"I remember it well!" joined in Corinna. "We called it just that: 'the turnip winter'."

Anna gave her a fleeting look, a little piqued at having her contribution interrupted and embellished on by another. She continued undeterred, "Just turnips - morning, noon and night. So you had to find different ways of eating them. Turnip bread, roasted turnip, boiled turnip, turnip soup. But in the end, there is no difference. I have never touched one since, not in almost twenty years now. I would give them to the animals before I would eat another one myself."

Elisabeth, having polished off most of the *Schmalzbrot* and just leaving a couple of slices for the others out of politeness, said, "We used to grow tomatoes in the little garden by our house. But some of the local people would steal them at night. In the end we had to pick them green and hide them away to get them to ripen elsewhere. There is no respect where there is hunger."

There were plenty more tales of food shortages and post-war inflation that the women were eager to chime in with, especially from the safe distance of such a varied and tasty buffet.

At the same time an incipient, mostly masculine, group had also started to gravitate around Edeltraut and Bernhard's son, Roland. Encouraged by his mother he had launched into a few tales about life in the military which was naturally a hot topic at the time. The men were keen to hear about the training of the next male generation, and it did not take long for the conversation to take a political turn. Roland was asked by his father Bernhard to tell the story of the sacked teacher at his old school – the *Johanneum Gymnasium* college - and so repeat the same story that he himself had related to Volkmar just two weeks ago in the car. Bernhard wished in this way for the old man to have it from the horse's mouth this time, as well as promoting his son's activities and status to the others in the group.

As Roland began to quietly explain the course of events, he soon attracted, to his initial nervousness but growing self-esteem, a larger group of listeners, mostly the middle-aged and older men and numbering nine or ten.

"Ah, yes. That was a couple of years back, in my last year at the college. Must have been 1935 then. Things have been much better cleaned up in the meantime. The problem was that there were still some teachers around left over from the old times. And the way they conducted themselves, really, you would think you were back in the Jewish Weimar Republic. Dressed in a slovenly style, had no sense of classroom presence or discipline, had no instinct for the times having progressed. And above all they had simply not captured the notion of what was now needed to be taught to the students. So there was this old fool, Janenz was his name, taught Latin and history. That was all he was interested in. Talked as if the world had not changed in centuries. And one day he set up this long tedious translation from…from Quintilian it was, I think," he waved dismissively, "or whomever, can't even remember the name. So we decided not to do a single sentence and later we excused ourselves by saying that this was because we had been attending our sessions at the Hitler Youth and had more important things to do that week than his stupid translation. So he went straight to the headmaster and tried to kick up a stink. The next day I led a small group of us to the headmaster's office where we soon put him right about what was the issue at stake and what our priorities were - the same priorities the country as a whole had, too. Additionally, I reported the incident to our Group Leader at the Hitler Youth. In any case, the whole business must have been quickly resolved because within a week Janenz was fired."

"Serves him right," said Volkmar. "What a silly old fool."

"Fortunately, his type was more of the exception. By then most of the new young teachers were strictly loyal to the Party and had strong political convictions of their own. Which was perfect for us, because the idea is naturally that you learn from your schoolmasters."

"And the curriculum has been greatly improved upon as well, I hear," commented Bernhard, delighted at his son's ability to tell the tale and hold the limelight.

"Exactly," nodded Roland with both filial duty and genuine enthusiasm. "Right away in 1933 the ministry had started to examine the traditional subjects and started to look for better ways of communicating the material. For example, mathematics. At first some were saying that you could not alter the teaching of mathematics, that mathematics was a purely objective language and had always been taught the same way and with the same priorities for centuries. That is of course absolute nonsense. So there were changes made with course material and the differences were notable from the start. For example, instead of abstract and pointless calculations, more real-life concerns were brought into play. We were taught to apply mathematics to everyday concerns and in that way were able to grasp the world around us far more accurately. When you actually sit down and calculate the time it would take for our country to theoretically make all the repayments insisted upon by the Treaty of Versailles, which is a number closer to infinity than it is to sanity, or the birth rate of Germans compared to that in other less advanced nations, then you start to get a better perspective of how the subject is actually supposed to be applied. The same can be said of various areas of scientific study too, such as biology. We were one of the first years at our college to actually study racial theory. It was fascinating, I loved every minute. Finally, things began to make complete and utter sense. And naturally we were given a very different approach to the study of history, one that was oriented around the history of our people and the specific problems that have historically faced the German nation. All of this had to have upmost priority. It would have been a crime to let a few bumbling old teachers interfere with that. It would have been like slowing down or impeding progress itself." Roland had become very worked up by his expressed ideas, which he embraced with all the passion of youth and expressed with a precocious sense of self-assurance. But he had begun to lose a few of the listeners' comprehension by that point, although the majority understood at least the gist of the speech.

"Well, I for one am very happy for you, Roland. You do us all proud and are a shining credit to your generation. Your late grandfather, my dear brother Joachim, would have applauded every word. It is such a shame he cannot be here to listen to these magnificent tales. But at least we can all rest assured that young men like yourself will one day achieve so much in the world," said Volkmar, with the emotional pride of an old man in decline and as if conversing with his own favourite grandson. "And not just for yourselves, for the whole nation! Therein lies our future." A ripple of nods and murmured agreements emanated out through the men around him. Some of them men raised their glass as if to toast to "the future", the words sounded so noble. There followed an awkward pause as no-one was sure how to follow that brief eulogy.

Roland's mother Edeltraut, who had drifted away from the group of women upon realizing her son had become a centre of attraction, felt that pause keenly and feared the conversation might ebb. Her voice came through from the back to relate how there had been visits recently by members of the military forces to the *Johanneum Gymnasium*, to show and explain some of the aspects of their various professions to the youngsters. "Last week there was a visit from a group of sailors who have been stationed on a submarine. They were telling the students about the different types of work they have to do, the different challenges they face. For instance, they have to learn to manage the controls in the dark, just in case there is an incident while underwater and they have no lighting. It all sounded fascinating. It is quite a world unto itself, what our military have to prepare themselves for." She wore her hair in a bun and would gently push it up from the back when she felt she had made an important contribution to a conversation.

Horst's older brother Karl-Heinz, who smoked profusely, lit up another cigarette and felt it was incumbent upon him to say, "That is precisely the way to get our young men interested in the military and in serving our country, of their own free accord and without any coercion. And this young man's bravery and common sense is an example for us all." He shot a warm look in the direction of Roland, wishing to gracefully bestow a commendation on the youngster outside his own family circle as well as clearly signal his own patriotism.

"Exactly," agreed Volkmar, having swallowed a small pie and now being free to talk again. "It is all very well and good that the *Wehrpflicht* (compulsory military service) has been brought back in, with which I am in complete agreement of course! But I do like the idea of the boys taking an *active* interest in military affairs, of their own accord. Makes real men of them in the end."

Bernhard lit up a cigar and said, "There is a lot of military investment currently going on here in Lüneburg. Very impressive. The Schlieffen barracks for example have been modernized to receive recruits for Luftwaffe training courses. And there are the new Scharnhorst barracks, too."

Wilhelm said, "Yes, I have a friend who works in a construction firm and he was telling me about Scharnhorst. That was completed last year and he says they have done a very good job there. All the electrical installations were up-to-date, all fitted out with the most modern equipment. Really tiptop." Approving nods and murmurs all round.

But judging from the flow of the conversation - and it was the women who noticed this, though they didn't utter a word – none of the men seemed to see the enormous elephant standing in the middle of the room. What were all these military preparations for, if not for actual practical application? But it would be a queer person who would ruin such a joyous occasion as a christening to pronounce that silly and theoretical word 'war'.

Nonetheless, the conversation trundled on through its usual political and military topics. A few recalled seeing Hitler when he gave his one and only speech so far in Lüneburg, in 1932 on the MTV-Platz in the Uelzener Straße.

(The dictator had been in good form that day and worked the crowd up to a frenzy as usual, with his masterful control of the art of the gradual crescendo. Near to the climax, however, the sound had cut off and most had missed the final spurt. It was suspected there were communist KPD-members among the technicians but these were early days still and no-one was arrested.)

The men also talked of the recent Hitler Youth parade on Am Sande; Roland had been involved in the organization of the event and namedropped some local Nazi bigwigs that he had met, including Telschow himself. Georg couldn't resist a comment at that point and told how Telschow was famous for liking a drink or two and was often seen propping up the bar in various establishments. But he sensed the lack of interest from the others and left his commentary at that.

Edeltraut jumped in and mentioned that the *NS-Frauenschaft*, a women's institute aligned to the Nazi party, had opened a new office in Lüneburg and how she had become a member. With both her daughters in the BDM, the female counterpart to the Hitler Youth, the whole family were now proudly part of the National Socialist project.

Paul Schönbeck had a friend who was an airplane pilot currently serving in the Condor Legion and he had recently taken part in operations in the Spanish civil war. Martin was an avid reader of military aviation magazines and his ears pricked up at the mention of this. He tried to get all the facts he could out of the fireman, who in turn only had a few anecdotes and vague references to offer.

Roland listened, nodded, smiled. He lapped up the attention when it was paid to him; he observed the others closely and silently whenever someone offered their opinion. He had a detached, clinical manner to him, like a doctor observing a ward full of sick patients, out of purely scientific interest; but the men liked him immensely. Except Georg who, even apart from his politics, found him unbearably smug. Georg himself said little that day and more than once caught Gisela looking at him intensively, seeming to glower and warn him to be on his best behaviour.

In another group, sitting by the buffet on the other side of the restaurant, the women and some of the men were crowded around Inge, who held Adolf in a blanket in her arms and looked adoringly at the cherubic face. He had behaved well all day and was now fast asleep, she was relieved to see; having woken them twice in the night before with hefty bouts of screaming. Horst was dizzy with the fatigue of combining long shifts of work with partly sleepless night; and though even more taciturn than usual in company, he could not have been happier than when he looked on and smiled at the baby's face.

Gisela meanwhile was calling for her daughter Katrina who was supposed to be helping her out with hosting the guests but seemed to have vanished all of a sudden. She was informed by Edeltraut, who had detached herself from the group of men in order to fetch more wine for herself and her husband, that Katrina and Eva had gone off to buy themselves some ice-cream in the town centre.

"With what money?" asked an indignant Gisela, forgetting her social grace for a moment. "We have food enough here to feed an army."

Edeltraut coolly responded, "I gave them some, I hope that was alright." She found Gisela's frugality vulgar at times and smiled inwardly when the other woman hurriedly said, "Of course, of course! Everyone loves an ice-cream when the weather is nice."

Gisela was keen for the ceremony to be an all-round success and so had bitten her tongue. But she made a mental note to give her daughter a good ticking off later on when everyone had gone home. When she was a girl, the children had helped out at home and there were always little jobs to be done. She did not like this modern way in which children went about their own affairs, independently to their parents' instructions. It was not a promising feature of the new generation, she felt, and she did not intend to tolerate it in her own house.

Edeltraut went on to ask – in her typically amicable but at the same time insistent manner – if they couldn't listen to something in German for a change. Corinna smiled over at her and replied, "Of course, of course!" She enjoyed her occasional moments of mischief in life and, just to spite Edeltraut, proceeded to play a few records by the (Jewish) *Comedian Harmonists*; in German, naturally.

Away from the political deliberations of the men, the other women were pondering on the baby's facial features. Marianne opined that Adolf had his mother's eyes, Ann-Kathrin that they were more like his father's; while Corinna – always keen to never take sides - decided to agree with first the one and then the other. A similar process was undertaken with chin, nose and ears and the conversation seemed to have no limits; at which point Anna nudged her husband and the two engaged in a beaming round of goodbyes before Bernhard got to drive them home.

Gisela was delighted with the convivial atmosphere and fussed around everyone, making sure they all had enough to eat and drink. Later that night, she commented to Martin that the buffet had gone down very well all round – everyone had complimented her - and that the organization of such 'regales' could be a further business venture for them to offer at the Gasthaus. She quietly concluded to herself that this was something that Volkmar and Anna had never delved into, and saw in it great possibilities to prove herself as more than worthy of her role as manageress.

After the christening there were all manner of items to sort out for the new addition to the family. As promised, Gisela was able to provide almost everything for her sister, from baby clothes to the "elegant" beige wickerwork basket perambulator that she had wheeled her own three around in. Horst would have personally liked to have been able to purchase more new things for the boy, but knew that at that time they couldn't afford such luxuries at that point in time. The pram alone was 25 Reichsmark and since the honeymoon and the move to the new apartment, they did not have a pfennig to spare. The hospital costs for the birth had also been higher than he had imagined: next time they should go for a homebirth, as everyone else was doing nowadays.

In any case, he concluded, there was at least stability in the land now - something you could never take for granted - and, once old debts were paid off, there would be more money in his pocket; all the reason in the world to look forward to a bright future ahead. Adolf was about to herald in a challenging but invigorating new phase in his and Inge's life, of that he could be sure.

Chapter 5

Four days later, on the Thursday of the week following Adolf Grün's christening, another religious ceremony was held in Lüneburg. This time the location was the synagogue, located on the corner of Reichenbachstraße with Am Schifferwell in the north-eastern part of the town centre. The occasion was the wedding of a local couple, both in their early twenties. The bride, Felice Wunderlich, was the third child and second daughter of Adam Wunderlich, an accountant and native of Lüneburg, and his wife and homemaker Ruth. Like her mother, Felice was short and slim; an unimposing and shyly very attractive young woman, with large almond eyes and long thick pitch-black hair that she had recently had cut, as requested by her mother, to a more "modest" length. The bridegroom was Issachar Beim: gangly, bespectacled, with a slight nervous twitch, looking permanently stunned as if still amazed that his destiny had led him to stand here today beside such a beautiful woman. The synagogue's resident rabbi, Moshe Liebowitz, conducted the ceremony, assisted by his nephew Jakob.

The Lüneburg synagogue was a striking and fascinating brick building. The exterior consisted of an impressive central dome surrounded by gabled rooftops and elaborated with a series of turrets. Attached to one side was a small tower, likewise crowned with dome and turret and the front entrance was magnificently adorned with its large arched entrance and matching window surroundings on both the ground and first floors. The first stone had been laid in 1892, in a small ceremony in which then Rabbi Gronemann emphasized in his speech the special support and financial backing received from the Lüneburg municipal authorities as well as many citizens of the town, both Jewish and non-Jewish. This support also included letting the sale of the grounds take place at a lower than standard price. The notable and noble edifice had, ever since its inception, attracted acclaim and positive comments from locals concerning its stylish architecture. It was an ambitious structure that was looking forward to a long and prosperous future; despite the Jewish community only consisting at that point in time of around 130 members, there was seating for 100 men on the ground floor below and for 100 women in the gallery above. Upon its completion in 1894, it was inaugurated in a long anticipated and much talked of ceremony, attended by a host of visitors including representatives of the imperial and municipal authorities, provosts, civil directors, master craftsmen, press reporters, together with a large number of curious observers. The event was quite the talk of the town that year. The first prayer in the newly opened synagogue was carried out in honour of the Kaiser, his wife and all the imperial family.

The Jews of Lüneburg saw themselves as fully integrated and analogous members of the broader German society, like-minded and on an equal footing with their non-Jewish neighbours. When war broke out in 1914, the sermons held in the synagogue referred to the "Jewish warriors" of the army of the German Empire, and encouraged its male members "to go to battle, unflinching and undaunted, with faith in God!" against the enemy, which many did. But towards the end of the 1920s, the ascendant national-socialist ideology began to consolidate its slow but sure dissemination through the population. With the establishment of a local branch of the NSDAP in Lüneburg in 1927, attacks became more open and more violent. In the night of 19th November 1927, as Shabbat began, the synagogue was damaged and desecrated; windows were smashed with stones, the swastika symbol was hung from a nearby tree, and painted on the ground near the entrance was the word '*Jude*' – Jew. From that point on, almost every year in October or November the temple was vandalized in some manner or other.

Those previous positive comments of admiration gradually gave way to voices of criticism and antipathy that seemed to find a root in mere peevish resentment. What had once been praised as a remarkably fine exterior, was now often classified as an eye-sore, an expensive architectural mess; what had once been a fine addition to the architectural variety and beauty of the *Hansestadt*, was now an ill-fitting and ugly blotch on the urban landscape. Likewise the community to which it belonged. It was disheartening for some, terrifying for others, how everything had changed from one extreme to the other in the space of a decade. Then, as the fateful decade of the thirties advanced, and especially with the *Machtergreifung* (literally: seizure of power) of Hitler in January 1933, so began the full desperation of the Jewish community. By the summer of 1937, it had shrunk to under 50 members. Those who could were, in most cases, planning their emigration; others went underground.

But even in the midst of intense terrorizing of a community, the strength of human spirit still rises to forge a bold route on traditional pathways. The Wunderlich family had announced the upcoming ceremony, delivered the invitations to the wedding and the reception afterwards at the family house, and prepared the event, meticulously down to the last detail, with defiant bravery. Adam's wife Ruth was plagued with nightmarish visions of groups of SA thugs breaking through the door of the synagogue on the day of the wedding and wrecking the ceremony; but she kept these fears to herself so as not to burden her husband or daughter with them, and kept her mind busy with organizing the modest banquet after the ceremony. This was planned to be held at their own home; primarily due to the difficulty in finding anyone willing to rent a public space to Jews for such an occasion, as well as it feeling more intimate, cosy and above all secure to be done that way. All those invited were to contribute to the feast in some way, with beverages and/or the preparation of recipes that they 'specialized' in, which made the event even more warm and personal. There were few such days of simple happiness in these dark times, and all those involved were determined to enjoy every minute with great intensity. As Joel Frey, a good friend of the family had rather darkly quipped, "As if it were the last wedding we would ever see!"

It was a fresh Thursday in late May with a sparkling early-spring sun matched by strong gusts of wind. The bride, the bridegroom, the invited friends and family members had all made their way quietly and furtively through the streets, hiding their smart suits and dresses under dull shabby coats so as not to attract any unwanted attention. Holding the wedding itself seemed an act of bravery, of rebellion even, but everyone had agreed that one should carry on as usual for important events. If ever there were an important, though infrequent, event in the calendar of the modestly sized Jewish community of Lüneburg, it was just such a fine wedding.

The synagogue was as full as it could have been that day, which did not amount to many souls. In recent years much of the former community had chosen to leave, through ostensibly sudden decisions and plans that had nonetheless already been quietly fermenting ever since the day of that dreadful news back in January 1933. All the same, the attendees did not wish to allow the gloomy progress of Jewish-German relations through this period pull them down spiritually. As the Rabbi had commented during the service, "when one has something so wonderful, so subliminal to celebrate, as the formal acknowledgement before God of the love between a man and a woman, one steps outside of the current affairs of that particular land, or that particular decade, no matter how much trial and tribulation has to be faced, and one enters into that realm of eternal human life where the background is that very love, and that love is the meaning behind our very existence." The service went perfectly, without a single hitch despite the nervous state of the bridegroom. All eyes were smiling at the smart young man and his beaming veiled bride. The prayers were spoken by the rabbi and repeated by the audience; the vows were uttered, the bridegroom broke the cup under his foot, the kisses were exchanged. A growing cacophony of happiness rose up around the couple as the congregation surged forward to surround them in a multitude of good wishes and expressions of tenderness.

Following the service, many of those attending had already begun to make their way as planned to the Friedenstraße, where the wedding reception was to be held at 17:30 that afternoon at the Wunderlich family home. The family stopped to exchange some words with others as they got back up into their old coats, heading back out on the street in subdued gladness and with cautious attention. Samuel Adelsohn, who was the synagogue's accountant and head of the committee for administrative affairs, had been buttoning up his jacket and taking his time to prepare to go. He was keen to talk to some of the men who had gathered at the back of the temple, as he watched them slowly assemble.

First of all, though, he had to pay the young man responsible for the wedding photography, Daniel Kaplan. Kaplan was a tall swarthy young man in his twenties, originally from Frankfurt but a resident since a few years in Lüneburg, who had kindly agreed to be of technical assistance in the shooting and processing of said photographs. He was asking for a bare minimum and Adelsohn guessed that that fee requested was enough to cover bare costs and pay for the next few meals. Accordingly, he paid him a little extra, out of his own personal and sorely depleted funds. He liked Kaplan's upbeat personality and generally irreverent attitude, which he found refreshing. He held the young man in high esteem despite Kaplan's alleged sympathy towards communism. (This was actually an error on Adelsohn's part; Kaplan had often mixed closely with communists though without adhering to those politics himself; through this contact, however, the reputation had stuck). This was an economic and ideological stance that Adelsohn – himself a liberal conservative – was very wary of. Exceedingly well informed about the inner turmoil and purges, even famines, that had taken place in the Soviet Union, the only thing that made Adelsohn more uneasy than a Nazi, was a communist. He considered both ideologies to be two sides of the same dirty authoritarian coin; only that the Nazis' hatred of Jews was more unabashed and violently honest. Likewise, he regretted Kaplan's clear lapse from the religion of his forefathers, if his attendance at the temple was anything to go by. Adelsohn blamed his political ideology for this, knowing that communism sat ill at ease with religious belief. But those were his private thoughts, and they did not in any way dim his general and open respect for Daniel Kaplan. Indeed, he could not help but admire the young man's easy-going self-confidence and accompanying brash mouth, though simultaneously not considering this attitude to be wise. In such times as these, Adelsohn deemed prudence and discretion to be essential virtues. He was all in favour of chutzpah per se; but one could easily be too daring for one's own good.

"Here you go, Herr Kaplan" he said, dismissing the photographer's objection to the sum being more than they had agreed upon. "Thank you very much for finding the time to come today. I appreciate that it is not always easy at such short notice. And here is some advice from an older man who has seen more than a little of life: take good precaution when you are out and about and make sure you do not get involved in any unnecessary trouble. History rewards the bold, but life rewards the cautious. That is the best way to get through these times safely."

Kaplan grinned and thanked him again, and it came as no surprise to Adelsohn when he heard, a couple of months later, that Kaplan had been arrested and imprisoned for insulting a group of SA brownshirts outside the department store *Fein & Günstig*.

While Avrele Korn, the shamash, went around the interior sweeping up and putting items back into place, and with Kaplan paid and departing off to the wedding party, Adelsohn made his way over to the back of a group of men who had assembled near the exit. They were locked in discussion.

Adelsohn had come to some unfortunate, even unpleasant, conclusions within the framework of the recent accounts he had prepared for the committee to go through in their next meeting. As that would not occur until August, and the matter seemed to him most pressing, he wanted to introduce at least a broad outline to a topic that they would later have to analyse in more details: namely the probable unviability of the continuation of the synagogue.

First and foremost, the disconcerting fact known to all: the constant haemorrhaging of community members in the last few years, in the wake of Hitler's sudden and shocking rise to power and his subsequent rain of blows against them. According to his rough estimations, as many as three-quarters of the Jewish community that had been living in Lüneburg just a decade ago, was now gone. Many of those few, that were still hanging in, were contemplating the same decision which further added to his general sense of hopelessness. Secondly, this exodus was compounded by the endless stream of new discriminatory laws emanating from the German central government. They appeared with alarming frequency, as if churned out of a factory on an endless conveyor belt. They worked against them with legal guile and on a myriad of levels, from the freedom to sit on a park bench to the freedom to marry the person of one's choice, but in particular they were aimed at the execution of professional and commercial activity. To put it short and simply, there were very few persons left to pay for the upkeep of their grand temple, and those who were left were increasingly short of funds. There would be a very tough decision ahead, and he did not wish to use any fulminating vocabulary out of place or before time.

He had sought Rabbi Liebowitz's ear on this subject, but the holy man seemed unable to take in the full reality of what was taking place around them. As Adelsohn had half expected, he was more interested in seeing in the words of the Torah how God would resolve this situation; and the pedantic world of material accounts meant little to him in comparison. It never crossed Adelsohn's lips, and it would be unthinkable for him to do so, but he desired so much to suggest that it was perhaps not God who would have to ultimately provide a way out, but rather the tough and resilient nature of a people who were historically not unused to feeling the rough side of human hostility. This was reflected in the quick-thinking and adaptive approach taken by many Jews in Germany's current political climate. It was this mindset that was allowing many of their community to achieve their goal at present and that amounted to one basic movement forward: to get out and away from Germany.

Rabbi Liebowitz was a tall figure who had once carried an erect, almost imperious presence. In recent times his posture had become more slouched, his hair had streaks of grey appearing, and the tightened skin on this face made him appear gaunt. There were bags under his eyes where his nights were robbed of sleep. Nevertheless, he maintained his habitually good-humoured disposition; though with a new element in his persona in the form of a subconscious but insistent nostalgia, a need to allude incessantly to times past and absent friends. He spoke gently in this moment, hands behind his back and swaying slightly on the spot where he stood, feeling contented amongst good friends and confidants with nearly all the synagogue's executive committee gathered around him.

"And so another beautiful marriage and hopefully, if God so wills it, soon there will be a beautiful birth to celebrate, too." He looked around the walls of the building as if they could and would talk. "So many people who have passed through that entrance and sat here in this space where we are now, so many who are no longer here. Do you remember Dr. Zelinger? The dentist with the miracle hands, they called him. I can testify to that - he was indeed an accomplished professional."

Joel Frey, short and plump with frizzled black hair and a perennial smile, chuckled heartily. "Of course, who could forget Dr. Zelinger? That man saved my sanity on more than one occasion."

Schlomo Rosenfeld, standing tall and slim beside him, agreed. "He was first-class, exceptionally gifted. That is an example of the professional talent that we all now sorely miss."

Rabbi Liebowitz related, "I remember, it must have been nearly ten years ago now, I was just beginning to take over the functions here from Rabbi Glück, and I had the most terrible toothache. So I asked Rabbi Glück and he said that none less than one of the best dentists in the whole of the region was a regular member of our community. I can hear him now as he said it. "His reputation extends well beyond Lüneburg and people come from quite a distance to consult him, so we are very fortunate that God had seen fit to put such talent among us." And he said that I should speak to him the next day, for it was Shabbath and he was sure to come to the synagogue to pray. He only came once a week but he was like clockwork, arrived at exactly the same time. He always sat in the same spot, a little further towards the back. So he gave me an appointment for the following week and what a relief it was when he located the abscess and was able to fix that for me." He sighed with fond recollection and added, "You know, there is little physical pain that is worse than toothache."

Nathan Süßkind, a young and enthusiastic committee member with a faculty for encyclopedic memory concerning people, said, "He lived in one of those beautiful old gabled houses on Am Sande. A big apartment on the second floor, I was there a couple of times. The dental practice was located in the Lünetorstraße, just over from the Alter Kran. You could see the river, and willow tree and the houses by the river, from the window in the corner."

Rosenfeld said, "Yes, I remember his practice very well. With the woodland paintings of birds and animals in the little waiting room. My wife said he had holy hands. She still suffers greatly with her teeth and gums and the dentist she went to after him is not nearly as good. Oh yes," he sighed, "his was an exceptional talent."

Rabbi Liebowitz continued, "And not just a great dentist. He was a very solid member of the community. Always willing to help out. Very generous, reliable too. He came from an old and traditional

Lüneburg family. Oh, it was a sad day when he told me that he and his family were all going to emigrate."

Adelsohn nodded in agreement with the Rabbi. "He was a very generous man alright. So charming as well. What am I saying, he was generous? He *is* generous! This is sad how we end up talking about people in the past tense, as if they were dead. I would not be surprised if he is not getting on better than all of us, doing marvellously well for himself. Emigration can be an uncertain game but if anyone deserves the very best, he is certainly one of them."

There was a pause and Lion Marienberg came over, after having been conversing with the shamash, and joined the group. He was an elderly, white-haired man with a pale, round, and ever-serious face. The Rabbi mentioned whom they were just speaking about, and he said, "I believe he left a few years ago."

Süßkind said, "Yes, just a couple of years after the *Machtergreifung* of Hitler. It was fully understandable. He could not stand the pressure. Those SA thugs started boycotting his practice right at the beginning. In a very insistent, very thorough manner. More so than in most cases, as if they were making a special beeline for him. I heard they even identified which civil servants were patients of his and put their names on display in show cases, to publicly shame them. Within a few months, most of them no longer dared to go there. Many just cancelled appointments on the spot. He lost a large section of his patients in just a couple of years, which was all the more maddening because he was so highly professional and everyone knew it too. It was terrible what they did to him. What they have done to so many of us."

Frey said, "You know, he was so active and keen to keep the community life going, that after the boycotts began he even offered use of his house for some little musical and theatre performances. We went to one of them, with string quartets by Haydn and Mozart. His wife prepared the refreshments and it was all quite superb."

"That must have been back in 1933 or 34," said Rosenfeld. "The ministry had just called out for the boycotts that spring. I remember that well because Dr. Baylin was badly affected too. The last I heard of him, he had moved to Hannover to be with relatives there. Yes, it has been a terrible business with these people, with ...," he stopped short of mentioning specific words or names, as if fearing to invoke the Devil or at least catch his ear. "And it is only getting worse."

"When exactly did Dr. Zelinger leave?" asked Marienberg.

Süßkind answered, "About two years ago. Yes, it was just before my nephew was born so it must be around June or July 1935. He went to Palestine in the end. I remember him showing me a copy of the passage. He was heading to Haifa. Wise decision. There is a lot of demand for doctors and dentists out there now."

Rabbi Liebowitz said, "Then I am glad for him. I am sure he will be just as admirable a member of the community over there as he has been here. And I am very sure that they will rejoice when they find out his profession upon arrival. Doctors and dentists, those are the kind of people that a community always needs." He still recalled with a shudder the toothache that first brought him into closer contact with that much-missed professional.

"I hope so!" said Frey with a light laugh. "I do not think he was especially looking forward to it. He only speaks German, nothing else at all. And he has his stiff character and his orderly way of doing things. I am not sure how he will fit in over there. But then again, he has a charming wife and she is very sociable and speaks about four languages all in all, so she will look out for them and help ease the difficulties of moving to such a different culture."

Süßkind said, "You mean Dafna? Of course she will! I know her sister Esther very well. It was she who told me that Dafna had already completed the Hakhshara. She could not wait to leave and take their children away."

A heavy pause followed such a painful but understandable statement. "Oy veh," sighed Rosenfeld and it was a sentiment that they all shared, even though they approached the question of the future ahead in such different ways. That enormous question for all of them, a question that some had only partly or reluctantly faced up to, was if and when they themselves would also join the exodus. It was an enormous step: to give up everything you had ever known; go through an arduous legal battle to gain a minimum of financial compensation for all that you had ever had; and embark on that uncertain journey to the distant destination of a foreign land and culture. In this way the question became more an assessment as to whether one's situation would improve, or at least remain static, or then again perhaps worsen. It was a huge gamble and one that they were all now forced to evaluate.

The rabbi said, "I often think of those who have left. They are always in my thoughts." After a pause, in which all nodded and looked down at the floor, he continued, "And then there was Kaminer's older daughter, Stefanie."

"Ah yes!" said Frey. "Such a charming young lady. Whatever happened to her?"

"She is in London now, I hear," said Rosenfeld.

"In London! That is wonderful to hear. I remember her mother telling us that she had finished training college, and with excellent final grades, and had gone on to work in a secretarial position in the operations department of an import-export company. In Hamburg, if I remember correctly. She loved the job and was so good with languages. She spoke fluent French and English, her father told me, and even some Dutch. She was always on the phone to other countries: France, Belgium, the Netherlands, America occasionally," said Frey. "Ah, so she ended up in England. Well, that is wonderful to hear."

"You see, I always stress to young people the importance of international languages, and there you have it. They give a person such mobility, open up new horizons," commented Marienberg with gravitas.

"It is amusing that the ladies seem in general to be more advanced in that area than we men are," pondered Rosenfeld. "The reports I often hear, including these two just now, usually confirm that observation."

Frey considered making a quip here about the high level of women's verbal fluency already being achieved in the mother tongue thanks to constant practice and then just transferred to foreign ones. But then he refrained as he recalled how much his own wife enjoyed a long and hearty gossip and felt the comment out-of-place, given the circumstances. "So, she managed to get her visa very quickly, then?" he asked instead.

Süßkind laughed cynically. "She had to! Did you not hear what happened?"

"Ah yes, you mean that nasty incident with the police," said Marienberg, nodding knowingly.

Frey and Rosenfeld, as well as Rabbi Liebowitz, creased their brows, to which Süßkind explained. "The Kaminers, her parents, have a second house in Harburg where she lived for a while before the director had a purge on the staff. No Jews or other undesirables. She got sacked of course but managed to find work in Hamburg. Everything is much more anonymous in a big city so she moved up there. But one of the tenants from the Harburg apartment was not paying the rent at the time, and there was a bit of a dispute between the Kaminers and him. He knew her whereabouts and in the end he took a grudge against the whole family and denounced Stefanie to the police. They soon found out where she was working and she had a visit from the Gestapo - within a week! They got her at first for not having formally registered her address with the local authorities."

Frey shook his head, "They don't waste time."

Süßkind continued, "It often starts with small things like that. And they also made the accusation, this came shortly afterwards, that she was gathering together sensitive papers and documents in preparation to have them all sent out to other countries. All completely made up of course, but all the same, they searched her apartment and had her placed in protective custody for two days. I heard that her family were shocked about what had happened and were worried sick."

"Must have been a very traumatic experience for them," said Marienberg, shaking his head.

"Naturally. So that was the moment she decided it was time to just leave, however she could manage it, by whatever means, with no further ado," said Süßkind.

"From Hamburg?" asked the rabbi.

"No! Too complicated and too close to home. Especially with her now having a police record there. Apparently, so I heard, she got a train to Cologne and stayed with a friend, waited for two weeks until she could sell all the jewelry she had, then went from Cologne to Paris, Paris to Calais, over the Channel to Dover, and on to London. So she was out of reach of the Gestapo within the month. She is a very enterprising young lady. Now she is trying to organize a visa for her parents and sister to get over too. She has even organized a place for them to stay once they arrive and everything, but they seem to be dragging their feet," concluded Süßkind with a sigh. Again, this phrase caused a round of gloom-laden glances and internal reflections among the listeners.

"It is not easy to just pack up and leave everything you know and love around you," said Rabbi Liebowitz finally.

"I do not speak a word of English. I do not know what I would do in London," said Rosenfeld with a shrug.

"It is a very big city and could be dangerous for a young woman on her own," added Marienberg. "If we got the chance...," but he corrected himself upon recalling something his wife had said to him that very morning, and said instead, "When we get the chance, we should wish to emigrate to Palestine."

"I am sure one can get by perfectly well in Yiddish there," said Frey.

"That is precisely what I have heard," confirmed Marienberg, with a note of satisfaction that his line of thought had been sensible all along. Now retired, he had spent a long career working with clients in Warsaw and Lublin, also sometimes in Prague and Krakow and Budapest, and was very fond of speaking Yiddish. He and his wife were in the process of weighing up the linguistic and cultural considerations that accompanied the various destinations that Jewish emigrants were heading to.

"How long has Stefanie been in London?" asked Frey.

"Nearly a whole year now," answered Süßkind. "She left last year, just before the Olympics Games in Berlin. In July, I believe. Things were a little more relaxed on the borders for a while, with so many tourists booking passages and heading over."

"The Segals have gone too. Just this month," said Rabbi Liebowitz. "They visited me just a couple of weeks ago to say farewell and to excuse themselves from further attendance here at the synagogue. In fact, I think they must be in Hamburg by now, waiting to get their ship. They said they had their tickets, but as Paul said recently, until you have boarded and the ship has set sail, you never know for sure. And even then, you still don't know for sure."

"I was just thinking of the Segals, seeing as they did not come today," said Adelsohn. "So they did manage to get that visa to Australia in the end?"

"The visa, yes, but not to Australia," said Süßkind.

"I thought that was where they were heading to, what with both sons already settled there," said Adelsohn.

Süßkind expounded this change of destination. "That was the original plan but in the last minute the visa application fell through. You know how it is, some minor technicality or other. They were considering Palestine, to where another of their sons had already emigrated some years back, or also the United States where they have a daughter. Furthermore, one of Judith's sisters lives there as well. In the end they decided for America." The group looked visibly pleased, nodded and murmured, "Good luck to them," etc.

Süßkind continued, "Their daughter lives in California, and Judith's sister is married with family in Chicago. So they are going to New York first, that was the best route they could find at short notice, and then they will have to decide whether to go to the sister's or the daughter's. Judith wants to go to Chicago but Paul is inclining more towards California. I think he prefers the better climate they have there, and prefers living with his daughter to living with the sister-in-law and having the whole family squeezed into a small apartment there."

"I hope Paul gets his way then. I have heard that Chicago is quite violent in some areas," commented Marienberg, taking his notion from movies he had seen with his wife. "California on the other hand sounds wonderful. *Ach*, if I were a younger man…" But he left the sentence unfinished, finding it pathetic.

Frey said, "From what I heard they are simply glad to be getting out. Judith is a very sensitive soul and suffered greatly when the Nazis started all this boycotting nonsense. She was so proud of the bookshop she ran. It all weighed down heavily on her. Seeing people, she knew so well, look nervously in the shop window and then pass on by without even going in. She said, why don't they just come in and say '*Guten Tag*' even if they do not dare to purchase anything? I remember seeing her get grey strands in her hair within a year. I never imagined a person could age so quickly."

Rosenfeld said, "And there was the added pressure connected to the sale of the house. They say Paul was called in to talk to some big fish at the police headquarters, for whatever reason."

"They do not need a reason to cross-examine you," Frey shook his head with glum resignation. "With us, they can be prosecutor, judge and jury."

"Exactly," said Rosenfeld. "He was there for hours and came back home as pale as a ghost. The poor souls, they will be heading out penniless. They barely had enough for the tickets. Although all their children abroad were ready to pay whatever was necessary, should the authorities decide to take their last Reichsmarks off their parents. Adam," (he referred to Adam Wunderlich, the father of the bride that day), "was involved in the matter, as their financial adviser. I can imagine it must have been a monstrously difficult process. It always is, whoever you are and whatever your fortune."

Upon hearing Wunderlich mentioned in this context, Adelsohn had looked up from the ground at him and made a mental note.

Marienberg shook his head. "It is impossible now to make a sensible decision. Every month a new law is brought in. It is like living in a house which is comfortable enough, and in any case it is all you have never known, but suddenly the walls have started to pull themselves inwards. Every week a little more, squeezing the rooms smaller and leaving you with less and less space. We, my wife and I, keep telling ourselves that there must be a limit somewhere. A red line where you just cannot humanly go any further. Perhaps we have yet to see it."

Rosenfeld said, "Maybe it is like the stock market, though. People always panic when the moment is wrong, sell up at a poor price and then regret it afterwards. Investment can be one prolonged state of regret if one is not careful, and these days life is an uncertain investment. The key is to be confident in bad times, cautious in good times." He was the only member present who actively traded on the stock market, which made his metaphor unclear for the others.

Adelsohn desired more details in order to better evaluate the situation with regards to the dispossession of properties belonging to Jews; for his own sake as well as for the sake of the continued running of the synagogue and with it the heart of this community.

Furthermore, he wished to know, and hopefully be consoled by, the fate of the Segals, these old acquaintances that he had always liked and admired. He had been a regular customer and the closing of said bookshop had caused him great sadness. "Please do explain what happened to the Segals' properties," he directed himself to Rosenfeld. "You were talking before of Paul being put under pressure to sell."

Rosenfeld replied, "Yes, he was. It was a terrible business. First the book burnings, then the boycott actions. For Judith, it was particularly painful. Apart from the bookshop, there was also the upholstery business which was originally her parents' business. Her sister and one of her daughters were running that. It also went bust due to the boycotting and in the end it was all more than she could bear. When Paul got hauled up for a visit to the Gestapo, that was the absolute limit for her. I heard they threatened to send him to Sachsenhausen. In the end it was the same tactic as with the Kaminers: endless monitoring, threats, insults, raids, wearing you down. So now they too have sold up."

"Who, the Kaminers?" asked Marienberg who had drifted off.

Rosenfeld looked mildly irritated by the question. "The Segals. I just said, they owned the upholstery place which Sarah ran and Angela, their daughter, was also working there. But Adam knows more about the details. He was very close to them. You should ask him when we get there."

"I have heard they are going to introduce a *Judenabgabe* (special levy on Jewish fortunes)," interrupted Süßkind.

"*Quatsch*! (rubbish!)" snorted Marienberg with near indignation, though more out of fear than derision. "We have enough problems as it is, without more baseless rumours."

"I am just relating what I have heard and I heard it from a good source," retorted Süßkind. "A very good source, in fact. Don't reject these things so offhanded. You have to keep an open mind these days. And the way things are going, I would not doubt it for a minute."

Rosenfeld said quietly, "He has a point, Lion."

"And for when is this all supposedly planned?" asked Marienberg.

"Nothing concrete has been decided yet," said Süßkind.

"You see," said Marienberg. "This is what I am talking about. If we start to believe every single rumour that is uttered and passed around, we will end up chattering about ghosts haunting the streets like frightened little girls."

"I have read some details on the subject too," announced Adelsohn, with an unusually grave tone. "One article said it could be as high as 15% or even 20%. To be placed on all Jewish fortunes over a certain minimum amount, and that amount will most surely be a very low minimum. Perhaps even as little as a few thousand Reichsmarks."

Another pause ensued as the new rumour acquired a ghastly tinge of inevitability.

Frey laughed and gave Marienberg a hard hearty thump on the shoulder. "Don't worry, Lion. It's just a rumour. By the time Count Lutz and his ministry get around to ratifying it, it will be 50% but you can pay it in monthly rates."

Süßkind laughed along too. "And by that time the Social Democrats will be back in power in any case!" The group chuckled along with the joke, even Rosenfeld. Grim times call for even grimmer humour.

Frey snorted, "Or the Communists!" to which Rosenfeld said with a grin, "And they will tax you 100%, so by that point, who cares?"

Rabbi Liebowitz, uneasy that the conversation was throwing out overtly political references with such gay abandon and loud voices, reminded everyone that the wedding banquet would soon be commencing over at Wunderlich's house. The men buttoned themselves up and then filed out into the street in the still bright but now windy late afternoon. They separated out a little along the way so as not to be perceived as a larger group, even though their number was only eight, and they talked in subdued tones to remain inconspicuous. All the same, they were easily recognizable as Jews to even an idle or disinterested eye, and well known as such by many neighbours; so as usual they caught glances from the odd passers-by that were sharp and acrimonious - foreheads creased into a frown, eyes narrowed to a scowl. They crossed the town centre and headed towards Wunderlich's house in the Rote Straße; up the cobbled streets, partly defiant, party fearful.

Chapter 6

They arrived around ten minutes later at Wunderlich's apartment in the Rote Straße, passed through the front door and hall, where they were greeted by the newlywed couple, and on to the spacious living room round the back of the house. The already sumptuously laid out tables of food and refreshments, that the Wunderlichs had prepared in advance, were further augmented with each arriving guest. People were moving around in their smartest suits and dresses, chatting and laughing and exchanging pleasantries, some deepening together into more intimate conversation but all looking relaxed and at peace in a way that they rarely did when out in town. Coming in from the intimidating world of the open street, it was like passing through into a different dimension where the innocence of merriment and casual banter were palpable in the atmosphere. Where worries had ruled the roost during the week, there was a concerted effort here and now to sedate them for the duration of this marvellous feast that celebrated a bonding between two special people. Adam Wunderlich, the father of the bride, greeted them all as family, with warm hugs and constant hearty patting of backs.

In this expansive back room, the furniture had been taken out to create all the possible floor space for the guests. Tables lined the walls, piled up with plates of delicious traditional dishes; the sight and the aroma were a godsend to everyone. There were stuffed peppers and stuffed cabbage with both mincemeat and rice. A silver tray of fish followed them, including a small dish of smooth *gehakte herring* (chopped up herring) and plates with filets of *Pannfisch* and *Matjes*, all fresh from Hamburg and adorned with lemon and sprigs of parsley. There were two large tureens of soup - chicken soup and a rich creamy pumpkin soup - placed next to a bundle of fresh loaves of challah bread and a basket of bagels. Next came three plates with a good few dozen *varenykys,* plus two more piled up with *latkes.* There was smoked salmon, salads, two dishes of *gefilte fish* (that Rosenfeld's wife Hannah had made for the occasion, it being her famous speciality), a bowl of chopped liver, and lavish plates with tongue of beef and pastrami. Beside them came two heaped dishes of rice with wheat, a large jar of freshly made *chrain* (courtesy of Frau

Marienberg) and a dish of falafels. At the end of the impressive display stood a large brisket, fresh from the oven and still steaming in a bath of meat sauce, with generous dishes of potatoes and vegetables beside it. With the deserts still to come there seemed to be enough food for at least three times the number of guests, and Wunderlich could not have been a happier man.

Adelsohn, however, wished to inform himself more comprehensively concerning the sales of the properties of the Segals, and with good reason; time not being on his side, and with numerous issues still to be sorted out, he knew he would have to broach the subject that very day. He had already put the topic to one side for too long in the run-up to the wedding, but any further delay would only tempt fate. He needed to be best informed as to the hurdles that would lay ahead concerning the continuation of the synagogue and how best to prepare himself to meet them. He was already aware of the dire financial straits of various members of the community, both exiting and still present members. In addition to that came the question of the continued well-being of the community as a whole; if they were to be denied even this last meeting place.

Adelsohn located Wunderlich, who was in the lounge with his wife welcoming the last of the arriving guests. After the initial greetings he got to the point. "Adam, this is not the most appropriate of moments, but things have become very pressing and I wanted to know if you would mind me asking you some details about the Segals and the sale of their properties." Wunderlich looked downcast. "Listen, Adam," Adelsohn continued, "I know this is not a good time to speak about these things. It never is. But I have been so sick with worry this week, I can hardly sleep. I do fear that time is running out so very quickly and I need to know some details urgently so as to be able to better orientate myself. I'm sure you understand what I mean."

Wunderlich nodded, placing a hand on Adelsohn's arm. "I understand." He looked around him and saw that the families and friends were intermingling. "Come through here, into my study. We can talk without being disturbed." As they moved into the side room, Adelsohn could not help but let his eyes linger on the white rectangles placed randomly along the wall, indicating the positions where pictures had once hung. Wunderlich second-guessed his thoughts and answered, "I am selling off all the artwork I have. Gradually though, one after another. It is the only way that we can get by."

Adelsohn hypothecated that one of the precious pieces in this collection, which Wunderlich was always so proud of, must have gone towards the wedding costs. He was right: it had paid for champagne and wine (Wunderlich had clearly splashed out), a decent amount of the food, the exquisite bridal dress, the service, the gifts of jewelry for the young couple. The sacrifice pained Adelsohn on the one side but it was Wunderlich's wish that they all came together today, to celebrate not only the wedding but also the continuation of life. This celebration, in such destructive and desolate times, was all the more an essential act for the parents of the bride.

"Things are not going well at the temple, I gather," said Wunderlich, closing the door.

"That would be an understatement. These are such desperate times, I have no words to describe the situation. We are literally heading straight towards bankruptcy. We are going through a rapid and ongoing loss of income from donations. The overheads take what little there is, even though those overheads have shrunk considerably in some areas. Especially in salaries. I work for free, both the shamash and even the rabbi now do as well, even though they have no other sources of work and I owe them both three months of back payment. I do not know what they can be eating in their households – bowls of fresh air and rainwater perhaps?"

"Rabbi Liebowitz looked so tired and gaunt when he came in just now. I suspect he is badly undernourished, although he would never mention it. Plenty of others are too. You know, that was one reason, I have to admit, that I encouraged my daughter to marry now and not later on after they have emigrated. I mean, I also wanted them to arrive at their destination as a decent, married couple. But it gave me the perfect excuse to put on a big banquet and invite everyone we know, make sure that between the feast and the leftovers, which should be generous, at least we will all be full for a good few days."

Adelsohn nodded and chuckled. "When we are going through times of prosperity and abundance, the first thing we forget is that there is no greater joy than a full stomach. To think how well we lived in those Golden Twenties. Now, not so much."

"Very true. So, tell me about the accounts."

"There is nothing to tell, Adam. Only that there is barely enough money coming in to keep a cow-shed running, let alone a community building of that size. Unless there is some marked improvement, and I have to admit that I currently have no idea in which form that would take place, we are looking at a financial abyss straight ahead."

"Everyone is leaving, Sami. People say "Next year in Jerusalem" at the Seder and they mean it. No, I fear there is no way back. Nearly everyone is either gone or going."

"I know."

"You said yourself, way back last year at Yom Kippur, how frustrating it is that we cannot even complete a minyan anymore, without bringing someone in from outside."

"Exactly. But when we could not, I still managed to find someone in Hamburg. We just had to pay the train fare and a few expenses. But now I cannot even do that, I have to rely on charity. In any case, what kind of community is it when you cannot even put together ten Jewish men for a service? That is pathetic. But I cannot bear to think that the end is near. I will do anything to try to salvage what we have. I just need to better understand how to face the situation, and which are the obstacles that need tackling."

Wunderlich made no remarks initially, ruminating until he said, "You still have hope. That is remarkable. I think that most of us have lost that hope, if I am to be honest with you."

"I have to have hope. If I do not, what should replace it? I cannot live in despair, so I choose hope instead. But I wanted to discuss something more mundane, just to inform myself. As I said, I need to grasp the full extent of the problems we are facing. And they were talking, back at the synagogue just now, about the Segals."

"Aha. But you know they are on their way to America. I told you that."

"Yes, I was aware of that. But it concerns the sale of their properties."

Wunderlich lowered his voice. Even here, in his own room, surrounded by his own people, who were moreover making enough din to hide the sound of a shouting match, even here he felt somewhat nervous discussing the subject. "There is precious little to do. The authorities now have the legal and financial framework so well covered, it is frightening. It is really better not to take on any difficult legal battles with them because you are going absolutely nowhere with that. Quite the opposite, you would just attract needless attention. You would ultimately have the whole power of the state up against you, and no-one wins against the state. Bear that well in mind."

"Then give me a better idea of exactly what I am up against."

"The Segals had two properties. Their house where they lived together with children, and a further property on the Lauensteinstraße, just behind the *Liebesgrund* park. The first one, their home, had an officially appraised value of 30,000 Reichsmarks. But we Jews now have to sell under the appraised value and can only ask for 80% of that. In this case, moreover, when the authorities were processing that figure they decided that the assessment basis should be not the appraised value but rather the unitary tax value, and that was 20,000 RM. So you're left with 80% of *that* sum, and that's only 16,000 RM. Then the buyer, this well-positioned party member called Braun, made an official request to reconsider the value of the property due to its year of construction, with it being an older building in an *alleged –* I stress that word - state of disrepair."

"But there is nothing wrong with the house. It is a little old for sure but they have always taken excellent care of it. In fact, I think there were some renovations carried out on it a few years back."

"There were, there were. The building is in very solid shape, all things considered. But there was nothing to do. Braun only had to pay RM 12,000, as opposed to RM 30,000. You see what I mean now? But for the Segals, that was just the beginning of the ordeal. First, they subtract all the fees from the authorities and the due taxes. Then that amount goes into a frozen account at a foreign currency bank in Hannover. Any access to it requires a huge amount of paperwork plus authorizations from various offices; none of which are in the least bit cooperative, naturally. So in the end, Segal was only able to receive a monthly allowance of RM 200 from the sales returns from his own home! By the time they have paid out a quarter of that, they will have brought out some new law that further reduces the sum." Wunderlich shook his head and laughed cynically. "My God, how we underestimated them. These Nazis are legal and financial experts."

"And the second property, the one in the Lauensteinstraße?"

"That went even worse. Segal had bought the grounds and the premises not so long ago, in 1931, back then when Hitler seemed like just a silly bad dream. But, of course, by this point now he also needed a quick sale. I think he was openly forced into that. I know he had a lot of hassle from the authorities. The final amount of the sale of the property was also sharply reduced, and furthermore a letter was sent by a neighbour, to *Gauleiter* Telschow personally, claiming that Segal's land was suffering from subsidence and that this had adversely affected an outer wall of her property and caused major damage."

"That does happen to some of the grounds, due to the saline." Adelsohn felt duty-found by objectivity to admit the fact.

"Of course, of course, we all know that, but those are gradual geological changes. How strange that a little plot of Jewish land not only suddenly sinks all on its own, but is also responsible for dragging everything around down with it too." Wunderlich raised his eyebrows. "*And* it happens to do that right now."

"Yes, I was just thinking about how the defence would work out in such a legal case."

Wunderlich laughed. "What defence? After the usual taxes and fees were subtracted, the amount left over was held by the finance office. Segal got a letter saying that, as there was a noted intention of his intending to leave the country in the form of an application for a visa to emigrate, he was obliged to state this damage claim in the original paperwork, because the sales revenue must be put on hold until all outstanding taxes and damage claims had been paid out in full. So by the time he was ready to leave, he still had not seen a single Reichsmark. If I recall correctly, I think they even informed him that _he_ now owed the municipal authorities an amount of money for the legal processing of the sale and the claim. The injustice of it all! - and probably not a modest amount either. But he is gone and I do not think he will ever set foot in Germany in his life again. Even if there is a return to some kind of normality here, which I very much doubt. Subsidence? You have to laugh. You know, I hear about things that are going on and sometimes I would be happy to see this whole town sink into one big hole in the ground."

"But this is all quite scandalous. How do they justify this kind of action?"

Wunderlich had brought out two glasses and was preparing to pour brandy into both: he looked questioningly at Adelsohn to confirm if he partook, to which Adelsohn nodded. "It's this *Reichsfluchtsteuer* (capital flight tax) of theirs. It has been in place for some years now and that is the devil in the detail. Initially they wanted to dissuade anybody with any money or assets to their name from leaving the country and taking it all with them. Now they are exploiting it to the full and stripping the Jews of everything we have. Knowing full well how desperate most of us are becoming to get out as quickly as possible and under whatever conditions. The thing is the Nazis want us Jews gone, packed off, vanished from sight. Overnight if at all possible. They want us to just sell up and get out, that is the long and the short of it. But they are equally afraid of capital flight. So they have created this endless labyrinth of legal and financial tricks to make it practically impossible to take with you any mentionable amount of your fortune. I have seen people stripped of almost everything they own, having to leave the country with just a few hundred marks in their back pocket. And that is all they have then to support a whole family and start a new life in a foreign country. Not to mention the money required to obtain visas and buy ship passages in the first place. If the Nazi party could achieve it, and I do not doubt that they will at some point, they will have the Jews leaving the country penniless with just a shirt on our back and a suitcase with underwear and a toothbrush, little else. You know, nearly everyone from round here whom I have seen emigrate in these past few years, and I have seen plenty, has to some extent, or even completely, been dependent on family members, including very distant family, to get them over. Either that or charities and other such organizations. With the legal tools we have left at our disposal, it is getting almost impossible to arrange or obtain anything without at least some help from the outside. If you have family abroad, wonderful. If not, you are in serious trouble. And with each passing month, things are getting worse."

"No-one could have imagined it would go this way," said Adelsohn, though instantly doubting his own words, finding in them an excuse rather than a factual statement.

"No, we should have seen this coming. We were such fools! Even here in this backwater Telschow was already stirring up trouble, working his way up in the Party lists back at the end of the last decade. I remember well in 1928, 1929, around that time, long before Hitler came to power, hearing about what he was writing in the *Niedersachen Stürmer*. All those articles about the inexplicably high number of Jewish lawyers and Jewish functionaries and Jewish doctors. It was an obsession of his even back then. Now he and his sort have real solid power in the country. Absolute power, some say. You know yourself, you don't have to look at the horizon to know that a big storm is coming. You can feel it, smell it, sense it. It is never a great surprise. How could we be such utter fools?"

"This is still my home country, when all is said and done. I fought in the Imperial Army in the war. I was wounded, I got a medal."

"That means nothing now. Nothing!" hissed Wunderlich with thinly disguised contempt. He himself had not fought in the Great War and was tired of listening to what he considered to be the dangerous naivety of other Jews who assumed that their role in that war would somehow bring them special treatment; an acknowledgement for the sacrifice they had once made for their country. The times had changed, irrevocably and unrecognizably - of that he was certain. "Look around you, Sami. Open your eyes. Keep in mind the boycotts, the endless bile in *Der Stürmer* and those other rags, the Nuremberg laws just a couple of years ago and the constant tightening of legislation since then. Remember, Sami, and I quote: 'A citizen of the Reich must be of German blood or of Germanic origin'. You are not a citizen of the Reich, you are not a citizen of Germany. This is not your country anymore, not our country anymore. It was, but it is no longer. That statement alone should have been enough. *Mein Gott!* - why were we not paying attention at the time? Why is it that in that moment when politics becomes essentially relevant, all we do is stare out of the window at any random passing distraction. Why do we see flames in the distance but still pretend that everything is in order? And even after Nuremberg, we are still standing here in this town talking to each other about this subject with the underlying serenity of two old men quietly playing dominoes in a bar. Every month there is a new humiliation! It is like a locomotive that is out of control and stocked up with coal, heading faster and faster to its doom. Believe me, nothing will get better. Nothing! Everything will get worse. If you know what is good for you, you will sell up. Sell everything, grab whatever you can get for it, be thankful for small mercies and just get out."

"I have my responsibilities - you know that, Adam. I am on the executive committee of the synagogue. I handle the accounts and carry out many of the administrative tasks. I have done for years. It has always been my greatest joy, one of the most precious and humbling areas of my professional work. I get next to nothing from it in monetary terms and that is the joy of it. Working for nothing and being glad to do it – how many people can boast of that? To be part of the synagogue and responsible for its continued running as part of the community…"

"I…," Wunderlich began; then more forcefully, cutting through the flow of confessional anguish, "I am sorry to have to interrupt but you keep talking about 'this community' and 'this community' is disappearing before your eyes. Sadly, but undeniably 'this community' is becoming history. That is a hard fact to face up to, but we must face up to it nonetheless. We cannot continue in a fantasy world. It has been dwindling for a good few years now. With nearly every passing month it is a little smaller. And with good reason."

"So you are advising me to give up and shut up shop? Just like that?"

Wunderlich searched for the appropriate words to respond with, but Adelsohn added, "Adam, perhaps I am not expressing myself correctly. That was not meant to come across as outrage, and it was not a rhetorical question. Nor am I judging you, nor asking you to defend your words. I am merely asking you as a person in whom I have complete trust. Clinically, objectively, I am asking you to give me your advice. Is that your advice?"

Wunderlich swayed his head and the words stuck in his throat, but he was able to express the brutal truth. "Yes, that is what I am ultimately saying. No, not 'just like that', because it is an enormous decision to make and a terrible thing that I am saying. But in this case, you, we all … have no choice." He splayed his hands in resignation. "How much of the mortgage on the synagogue is left to pay?"

"Over 3,000 Reichsmarks."

"And how much do you think the value of the grounds would be?"

"This was why I was asking you before about Segal's experience. It all depends on the value it has, but that value is *volkswirtschaftlich gerechtfertigt* (justified according to the national economy)." Adelsohn sighed. "Just reading those two words gives me a headache whenever I see them in print. Apart from the fact that they are a contradiction in terms. You instantly know that whatever comes after the world '*Volk-*' (people's) in the paragraph, it will always mean an endless series of complications. Some meaningless new laws brought in just now on the whim of the little screamer, all dressed up with '*Volks-*' this and '*Volks-*' that, and suddenly you have less rights than a dog."

"Yes, that is the problem in Europe these days. Wherever you see a *Volk*, there is trouble ahead."

"So, as you were asking, I imagine the land would be worth around 18,000 Reichsmarks. Although I am sure they will find countless reasons to push that price down."

"You do know," said Wunderlich with a kindly but sad smile, touching his arm with compassion, "that the building itself, the synagogue, is now worthless. Being … what it is."

"I know," Adelsohn nodded.

"So best to just arrange with a notary the sale of the grounds, sign the contract, and walk away. Nothing more," said Wunderlich.

Adelsohn swallowed through a lump in his throat. "You have worked with Schuster, the master builder, before."

"Not personally, no. But my brother has, and I am familiar with him and his way of doing business."

"How much do you think they will charge to demolish the building?"

"I imagine around 2,000 Reichsmarks. Perhaps a little less. You will need to apply to the town council for a license to have the demolition carried out, so there will be those fees to bear in mind as well. As well as all the various taxes levied on us Jews which are, well, they are what they are."

Adelsohn closed his eyes for a moment as he felt them watering slightly; opened them and looked on with bitter resolve. "Of course they are."

Wunderlich said, "Sami, dear Sami. As if we have not known this day would come. And if we did not know, we should have." He poured them a couple more glasses of brandy. "You know, my eldest daughter Jana was the first to cotton on and the first to go. By the end of 1933, the very first year of this nightmare, she had already cashed in her savings, had her visa for Palestine in her hand, and was ready to book the ticket. I can still remember her and Ruth telling me. Naturally, she had confided in her mother first. Completely understandable. So she calmly explained to me the where and the when and above all, the why. She had read *Mein Kampf*, she told me. Every last word on every page. I just thought of it as some revolting little book by some low-class Austrian nobody who was notorious for hating Jews, nothing else. Why should I pay any further attention to that? As if the world were not already full of people who hate Jews! But no, she was calm and collected and said to me that she knew that if the day ever comes when that man ever gets into power, then it is all over for us. And she was right! The most important things in life to know are who is your enemy and where he is right now. And so then, to everyone's great surprise, he did indeed come to power, and off she went soon after. By the beginning of the following year I got my first letter, postmarked from Ramla, telling me how well she was settling in," he laughed, wiping his eye. "Maybe I am wrong but I always think life must be so tough out there, and yet she always sounds so happy."

"Yes, your daughter was right all along," said Adelsohn.

"She was, she was. I just wish her stubborn and slow father had come to the same conclusion at the same time. I might not be in such dire straits as some. But all the same, I am getting ready. We have waited far too long already. Even if things did not get any better, they could not get any worse. And I am now slowly getting used to the idea that not only <u>can</u> they get worse, much worse, but that they undoubtably will, too."

"I sometimes think that those of us who are staying and soldiering on, we are living in the same illusion as Helene Mayer when she was competing at the Olympic Games. Remember her? She even gave the full salute, arm raised up high in the air, at the medals ceremony."

Wunderlich nodded. "It might seem as if we are being vaguely tolerated, but that is not the case. And they know it is not the case, and we know that it is not the case, but somehow this strange theatre drama goes on and on."

Adelsohn looked forlorn. He sighed and drank another gulp of brandy.

Wunderlich stood erect and breathed in deeply. "Yes, it has all been a ridiculous case of self-denial. I admit it. The benches in the *Liebesgrund* park suddenly had little signs with '*Nur für Arier*' (Only for Arians) screwed into them. Even in the playgrounds in the schools, by the sandpits, the same little signs. What kind of mentality would segregate children – little children! - and indoctrinate them to think that their own classmates are different to them? You really cannot stoop any lower. To my everlasting shame I ignored all that, and much more. But now I have seen the light; or rather the writing on the wall. And now my other daughter Felice is married to a wonderful husband as well. Who would have thought it ten years ago, that she would be giving her heart away to the youngest of the Beims? Haha! But seriously, Issachar is a good lad. I like him a lot, you know, although he does not have much in the way of common sense. None of them do in that family. But he adores Felice and he is an honest man, and a hard worker when all is said and done. He is also very eager to be emigrating with her as soon as possible, so I could ask for no more. Apart from the jewelry, our wedding present to them will be two tickets to the United States. For them to get as far away as possible. Even the madman himself will never get that far. They will get a ship from Hamburg to London, then London to New York. All the paperwork should be ready within the next month or two. Once they have that sorted out, we can buy the tickets immediately. Thanks to Herr Felix Nussbaum this time," he pointed a satisfied nod at a painting on the wall of a man sitting, head bowed, on a dock with a sailboat behind him. "I already have a buyer." Adelsohn found the picture morbid and foreboding, and could not imagine it selling for much. "Then they will be off to happier shores. That just leaves Ben, and Ruth and myself. We will be next - hopefully next year!"

Adelsohn smiled and they toasted, "Good luck! I shall miss you so much. But you know I always wish you and Ruth and your family the very best, in everything. My thoughts will be with you all."

Wunderlich put his hand on his friend's back. "The important thing for us all is to be loyal and honest to one another and get through this dreadful affair in good health. There will be a future, a long long future for us, with another temple to worship in elsewhere in the world. It is not like all our millennia of traditions are coming to an end just because of what these few thugs are up to here at the moment. But we do only have one life and we have to take care of our family and friends, wherever they are in this big wide world, and also take care of ourselves, if only for their sakes," he finished with a laugh. "Let us leave this topic for today, Sami. Let us go out and enjoy some of the delicious food that this, our small but resilient community, has prepared for us. Enjoying the evening, enjoying being together, and being there for one another. Another day may tell another story. But let this one be a simple and merry one and let tomorrow bring whatever it sees fit to and we will face it with a shrug. Alright?"

Adelsohn nodded and gave his friend a brief but tight hug. They opened the door of the small study, were swept away into the bustling joy of the guests outside with plates and glasses pushed into their hands.

"Gentlemen, you must try the varenyksy I have made. I probably should not say how good they are, but they simply are," said Frau Levitzki, the best friend of Ruth, catching the two men almost immediately with her huge and disarming smile and verbose charm. She handed them plates and insisted that they both took a good helping from the table beside them. "Those have a cheese and herbs stuffing, those have potato chunks and caramelized onion, and those at the end, that are a little darker, those are the sweet ones with cherry. I always like to make all three varieties but you know how things are nowadays, it is not every day that I manage to find all the ingredients in the shops." (She really meant "afford the ingredients, full stop", but like everyone she rephrased her tribulations to make them sound harmless.) "I am so proud of myself that I could manage to make all three this time!"

Chapter 7

The small town of Lüneburg was situated in the north-west of Germany, around 60 kilometres - or half-an-hour by train – south of the busy port of Hamburg, the nation's second largest city. It straddled the river Ilmenau, a tributary of the river Elbe; that wide and much traversed river which passed through Hamburg on it way on to the North Sea and so gave that metropolis its economic lifeline.

Lüneburg had enjoyed a long and prosperous past that was still reflected in the attractive architecture that lined the streets of its town centre. Along with Hamburg and other nearby maritime towns and cities - such as Bremen, Lübeck and Rostock - Lüneburg was a Hanseatic city. During the mid-1200s, around two hundred towns and cities along the North and Baltic seas formed a commercial alliance to protect their mutual mercantile interests; settlements now stretching from modern Belgium and the Netherlands, through the length of northern Germany, on eastward to Poland as well as up north to Denmark and Sweden. This Hanseatic League would eventually last for four centuries in total and play a major role in northern European shipping and trade. It was a loose alliance but nevertheless exercised considerable economic might and offered protection against pirates or the military maneouvres of nearby states.

But by the 17th Century, the twilight had set on this alliance. The Thirty Years' War (1618-1648) was a brutal conflict, the most deadly that northern and central Europe had seen thus far; killing off, amongst others, around a quarter of the German population. It had a devastating effect on the whole economic infrastructure in that part of the continent, including trade and commerce routes, and rang the death toll for the Hansa pact. The final Hanseatic day took place in 1669, in Lübeck, and after this it was disbanded. Later on, national interests would in any case supersede this defunct 'union of ports.' (Nevertheless, in more modern times some efforts have been made to bring this traditional old league back to life; since the 1980s namely, in an attempt to recover some of that old cross-border merchant spirit that once accompanied this most unusual alliance of cities.)

Though not a port as such, Lübeck's close proximity to Hamburg and the North Sea, together with its position on the placid

Ilmenau river, had afforded it entrance into the league. It therefore prospered greatly in the late Middle Ages thanks to the wide-ranging commerce that the Hansa facilitated. This was its zenith of wealth and opulence, when it rose to become one of the most important commercial centres of the entire league thanks to its excellent communication routes to the surrounding areas. But after those heady days there came a gradual decline that was further exacerbated by its inability to keep up with the industrial impetus starting to rise in the late 18th and 19th Centuries. Its old sources of finance – salt production, mercantile trade between regional areas by inland transportation of merchandise by barge and boat – left it out of the running in the new industrial markets.

But modernization did finally come, slowly but surely, to this neck of the woods. In the second half of the 19th Century the railway arrived, connecting it in a new way to surrounding cities. The town also became an administrative centre, with its finances boosted by government funds. The 20th Century opened in Lüneburg with the construction of a teacher's training college, a large general hospital (plus a sanitorium and a mental asylum), a slaughterhouse, and the most visible and admired structure of all, the *Wasserturm* - a lofty water tower with the cylindrical red-brick tower stretching up from a majestic base, worthy of a castle and complete with ornate turrets. (It became an immensely important structure, instrumental in the storage and supply of water in the town for decades, but was outdated by the 1980s. It still exists to this day in the form of museum and viewing platform from which the general public can look out on the surrounding area.)

Companies began to settle in the area, finding ample employment among the inhabitants of both Lüneburg and the circumjacent scattered villages. The *Lüneburger Eisenwerk* (ironworks) opened up in this period, as did producers of furniture, of plywood, a bone-dust and glue factory, and a large cement factory. The town was growing fast by now, having increased from just under twenty thousand inhabitants in 1871 with the establishment of the German Empire, to nearly thirty thousand by the mid-1920s. But all the same, Lüneburg remained somehow stuck in the past; a quaint though still very handsome relic of bygone times.

To the south and west of Lüneburg sprawled the extensive ranges of the *Lüneburger Heide* (Lüneburg Heath). This expansive area of heathland was sparsely populated by farms or settlements, consisting instead of endless acres of hills and valleys, forests and woodlands, streams, footpaths, and the locally famous rolling meadows of *Besenheide* or calluna. This distinctive species of heather bloomed in vivid shades of violet from late August through September and gave the area its idiosyncratic late summer image. The ground itself was sandy and offered only a few agricultural potentialities. The most popular was the grazing of sheep, with the wool trade being traditionally one of the principal economic activities of this region.

The town of Lüneburg itself was also surrounded mostly by heath and thick woods. Standing up at one its highest points, the aforementioned water tower, one could see a huge expanse of green, of all imaginable shades, dotted with just the odd cluster of roofs. Its location was thereby relatively isolated and rural, with the area only containing smaller villages and the nearby town of Winsen, roughly 20 kilometres to the north. After that, continuing northwards, came the edge of a mass of towns and municipalities that had once been situated on the periphery of the urban giant Hamburg but had since become incorporated districts of that city.

Lüneburg possessed a snug and pleasantly intimate town centre, sitting around a kink in the river Ilmenau, precisely at the point at which the river briefly split into two arms. One of these arms continued straight along and was hugged to the east by incoming railway tracks and Lüneburg's principal train station, slightly separated from the main bulk of the town; the other arm curled round closer to the actual town and widened out at the point where merchandise brought in on barges that had once been unloaded by the *Alter Kran* (old crane) on the reloading point here. Despite centuries of disuse, this wooden harbour crane still stood aloof - somewhat majestically and somewhat forlornly - as a tourist attraction, positioned on a stone wall beside an expansive weeping willow that hung in a display of proliferous branches reaching down to the river below. Around it stood rows of medieval houses and commercial buildings that had once formed the first port-of-call for the goods entering by fluvial transport. This area was known as the *Wasserviertel* – the water district.

(With the end of the Hansa League, the previously robust state of the Lüneburg finances came to an end as the previous heady influx of profitable goods such as herrings and cereals had dried up. This part of town therefore fell into disuse through economic decay and its buildings were not modernized nor replaced, thus retaining their old architectural styles; centuries later that aspect would ironically give it the flair and nostalgic beauty to bring back economic attention, this time in the form of tourism.)

This western arm of the river then curved out to run through the town centre before the two branches re-joined a few hundred metres later and the Ilmenau continued its course into the Elbe; which it did near Winsen, where the waters became part of that majestic riverway that would go on to flow through Hamburg and drain into the North Sea.

The town itself lay on a salt dome, which was the original grounding factor behind the town back in the 9th Century. The salt was sieved out of the salt works built there and sold as 'white gold' in the surrounding area, the trade of which eventually brought it into contact with the growing commercial port of Lübeck and so contributed to its ascendant prosperity. Later, in the times of industrial development, the old saltworks went into disuse and became instead the site of the newly founded chemical factory. But the effects of the salt dome lying under the town were still felt long after the mining has come to an end, due to the subsidence caused by the old underground pumping of water in order to extract the salt.

The *Altstadt* (historical centre) of Lüneburg was a compact network of narrow and slightly crooked streets, mostly lined with simple brick buildings bearing the standard triangular roofs. Also very numerous were the gabled buildings that had belonged to the mercantile class: both the crow-stepped gable, in which the triangular roof was formed through rising squares, shaped like stairs, that ascended from both sides to meet at the top in a central square; as well as the Dutch gable, with its rounded dome surrounded by flourishing curved sides. This frequently used mixture, coupled with many medieval beamed structures, gave the town a more relaxed feel, closer to Dutch or Flemish urban style, than some of the more typically Prussian towns of the region. Adding to the idyllic charm was the Ilmenau river itself, clean and sparkling as it wound its way through the landscape.

The central point in town was called *Am Sande*, a wide cobbled street and traffic junction that formed a spacious open square for both commercial activity and festivities. It was lined on all sides by towering rows of well-maintained gable roofs in a rich myriad of different forms and colours: some in deep orange tones and reddish brick, others gleaming white, a few in diverse shades of grey with intricate cream motifs. In the background loomed the distinctive tower of the *St. Johannis* church with its large and simplistic, perhaps somewhat awkwardly lumbering, patina-green turret, which sat atop a red brick façade displaying an ornate clockface. It was not far behind the *St. Johannis* church that rose in turn the famous water tower.

Am Sande had always been an important central point for many parades and celebrations, as well as more solemn ceremonies such as the funeral processions of important inhabitants. This was the case, for example, with the local SPD (social democrat) politician and newspaper editor Johannes Lopaus in early 1933. With the spread of power of the Nazi party in that decade, it was bedecked with the typical plethora of swastika drapes and flags, and was the scene of marches and other martial displays by the SA, the Hitler Youth, and other associated groups.

From *Am Sande* stretched out in all directions a series of slim roads lined with shops and other small businesses, forming a labyrinth of tight passages along which the townsfolk had trodden through centuries. A central artery for pedestrians and traffic, and running perpendicular to *Am Sande*, was the long *Bäckerstraße* (Baker Street), both the initial *Kleine* (small) and the following *Große* (great) *Bäckerstraße*. After traversing three blocks with all its sideroads, it reached the open square called the *Marktplatz* (Market Square), featuring the *Luna-Brunnen* - a fountain with the bronze sculpture of the moon god. The *Marktplatz* was a large square, sometimes used for public meetings, and at the back of it stood the *Rathaus* (town hall). This was so nobly built that it seemed more a small castle than a mere administrative building. Its elaborate baroque façade was plastered in stunning white and adorned with rows of small figurines leading up to the elegant balcony and clock-face. This façade was then topped by a two-tier tower in the form of a rounded octagon; within this tower, crowned by a golden weathervane, porcelain chimes pealed out a different melody three times a day, making it a popular attraction. Some distance behind the town hall, to the west of the centre, rose the sharp green tower of the town's principal church, the St. Michaelis.

At this junction with the *Marktplatz*, the *Große Bäckerstraße* became the *Bardowicker Straße*, named after a neighbouring district. Here were located a number of important businesses, including Lüneburg's star among shops: the department store *Fein & Günstig*. The *Bardowicker Straße* ran straight on to the farther northern side of the historic town area, hedged in on the northwestern side by the *Liebesgrund*; this was an open park area formed in a natural cleft in the ground and accessible by walking down the stylish steps installed at its few entrances. With its generous clusters of trees, it offered ample shade in summer and was a favourite spot for the town's inhabitants to enjoy a leisurely walk or find a quiet place to talk among the climbing roses and blue wisteria. It was also on a small street on the outer edge of this *Liebesgrund* park that the Gestapo would open their local headquarters, as throughout Germany, in order to be able to monitor the town more closely during the war.

Before getting as far down the *Bardowicker Straße* as the *Liebesgrund* park, the wanderer might have instead turned right to the east and headed down a small but busy street called the *Lünerstraße*. Directly behind this street was located the *St Nicolai* church, the third of the town's three evangelical churches which, together with the water tower, dominated the town's skyline. The narrow *Lünerstraße* comprised a series of shops and other small businesses that went the short route down to the first arm in the split of the river Ilmenau; there the visitor could step out into an open area where popular riverside restaurants boasted rows of dining tables and displayed plant-boxes densely packed with colourful flowers. At this point the name was modified to *Lünertorstraße* (the '*Tor*' signifying 'gate') as the street then headed off over a short bridge by the ostentatious baroque façade of the *Kaufmannshaus* (merchant's house), directly looking over at the *Alter Kran* back in the heart of the water district.

After crossing the river, the walker would come a few metres further to a perpendicular dissection by a throughway called *Am Schifferwall*. If one were to turn left at that point and head in a northly direction, it would lead in a brisk two-minute walk to a quiet corner where *Am Schifferwall* met with the wide *Reichenbachstraße* heading out of town; here on this quiet unassuming spot was the site of Lüneburg's synagogue. But if instead one carried straight on, then another bridge would lead across the second arm of the Ilmenau to continue along the *Lünertorstraße*, heading away from the historical part of town and approaching the area of the railway station and marshalling yards and, beyond that, several clusters of modern brick residences and administrative buildings. A little further on was the location of the army barracks which were growing in size and importance by now in the late 1930s, as part of the NSDAP drive on military spending.

Returning to the *Marktplatz* and the town hall, there was directly on that corner a further important street that ran parallel to the *Lünerstraße*, so also down to the river Ilmenau. The first short section of this street, directly by the *Marktplatz*, was called *An den Brodbänken*. The '*Brodbänken*' referred to the exterior benches that lined part of the street and upon which bread was still sold out in the open air to passing customers as late as the mid-19th Century, though after that it still remained an informal and familiar meeting place for townsfolk to gossip and exchange information. After passing by the first block, it reached a small junction with the perpendicular *Finkstraße* at which point its name was then modified to the *Rosenstraße* for a further block. It was on that short middle stretch of road, the *Rosenstraße* (Rose Street), that the *Gasthaus Sonnenschein* was to be found, the guesthouse with restaurant where Gisela and Martin had just taken over the management and were running at this point in time.

After this it then merged into the street *Am Berge* (running parallel to the *Finkstraße*) on a curved corner. *Am Berge* was an important central street and became home to the NSDAP branch office in the 1930s. It was also at this time the home of Arnold Schilling and the temporary home of his friend Daniel Kaplan.

All around the crisscross pattern of streets in the centre were a variety of businesses, including among others: the delicatessen shop Albert Maurer, the hairdresser Marlene Rempel, the florist Christiane Zimmer, the book store Dittberner, the furniture dealer Hugo Meyer, the greengrocer Herbert Madsen, the spirits and wine dealers Kloß & Stiller, the fish and seafood stall Erna Sultzbach, the hardware shop Urlacher, a small art gallery called Stolle, the notary Wolf & Sons, the sewing machine and fabric dealer's Oberbossel, as well as the spanking new bicycle and motorbike store Paul Jahnke, featuring all the latest accessories and doing excellent trade already in its first year of business. It was here, in this latter business, that Gisela and Martin would buy a bicycle for their son Siggi for his birthday the following year; a small luxury to spoil a child in those good economic times of the late 1930s. Gisela was a regular customer of Madsen's greengrocery as she liked his fresh fruit and vegetables and appreciated his professional and respectful tone; as well as of Christiane Zimmer, whom she knew from school and with whom she used the familiar 'du' form. There she would buy floral decorations once a week to adorn the restaurant. She gave Kloß & Stiller a miss, however, privately opining that their wines were overpriced and of poor quality, preferring to shop around elsewhere.

The bakery and confectionery, where Inge was employed, was situated further out of town, well over on the other side of *Am Sande* and away from this central town area; in the old *Lindenstraße* in the southern area. This was perfect for her as the apartment that she and Horst were renting was also situated in that area, in the street *Rotenbleicher Weg*. Not so far away lived Inge's parents Georg and Corinna, likewise in a modest and dingy apartment.

Here in this part of the town, some of the street names had been changed to adapt to modern vices, with the age-old titles that stemmed from the natural world being surrendered to political gestures. In this way, the *Gartenstraße* (Garden Street) had become the *Paul-von-Hindenburg Straße,* the *Finkenberg* (Finch Mountain) the *Horst-Wessel-Straße*, while the *Lindenstraße* (Linden Tree Street) had been renamed the *Adolf-Hitler-Straße*. Nonetheless, under the surface of this crude rebranding remained the old natural order. For centuries now, stretching back to the Middle Ages and Lüneburg's glory in the Hanseatic League, the town had been home to a multitude of linden trees, flourishing all around the town. They imbued the air in spring through their freshly aromatic white blossom. They brightened up the town in summer with their dense lime-green leaves that shone and rustled in the breeze. In autumn they stood in soft shades of yellow and orange, awaiting the late northern winds to carry them off. In the winter months they stoically stood through frosts and gales, until in spring the cycle resumed. (Those changes in the street names proved to be evanescent and once the Reich was over, far far sooner than the thousand years initially foreseen, those same streets would return to their former titles and the trees would carry on blooming each year as if nothing exceptional had ever happened.)

Chapter 8

It was a bright Sunday in the early June of 1938, a day of strong sunlight with intermittent cooling breezes. On this perfect day for enjoying the exercise of outdoor activities, many Lüneburgers had embarked on long walks in the surrounding fields and grassland to take in the fresh summer air. Some of the more well-to-do townsfolk took their motorcar down to the Lüneburger Heide area of heathland, to explore there the woods and hills, go swimming in the rivers and lakes, or picnic on the wide meadows redolent of heather that within a couple of months would erupt into vivid purple blooms.

On this charming Sunday Inge brought her second child into the world, shortly after midday. This time she had opted for a home birth on the advice of Gisela, who told her how the previously neglected custom had now become popular again. "Most women are having their children at home these days," Gisela assured her sister. "It is considered more proper and more German, and apart from that it is also much cheaper." Inge also took up the recommendation, dropped during a conversation between two customers at the bakery, of hiring a very amiable local midwife in her fifties, Frau Klaußner.

When the big day arrived, everything went perfectly - to Horst's immense relief. Inge's water broke and she lay down in bed at midday. Frau Klaußner was immediately contacted and was at the apartment within quarter of an hour. The labour was much shorter and Inge - by now more experienced and aware of the different types of pain that her body would have to expect and bear during the course of the childbearing - was able to give birth in a far more relaxed state of body and mind. By the time that Doctor Schwenter arrived, the baby was well on the way. After around three hours of hard work and she smiled up victoriously from the pillow. Another boy! – cheered Horst, biting his fists with the excitement.

Frau Klaußner washed and handed the swaddled baby back to the mother and wiped the beads of sweat from their brows. Doctor Schwenter packed up his utensils, wished the mother all the best, shook hands with the father, and was on his way. Horst would share many a gleeful conversation that week with family, friends and near strangers, too; as eager to spread the good news as most others were to share in it. There was little more innocently enjoyable than the accumulation of data concerning the birth of a baby, with each newly acquired detail more precious than the previous one. Particularly in times when the news commonly disseminated, here as everywhere in the Reich, was often so edgy, sometimes downright frightening.

A name for the boy once again gave cause for some discussion points. There were grandfathers to consider: Georg and Konrad were fine names indeed. There were names that evoked heroic legends, both past – Otto and Friedrich – and ancient – Siegfried and Sigmund. Inge, in a phase of renewed interest in her Christian faith, was uncomfortable with the recent fad of what she considered to be an unhealthy interest in the old Germanic pagan past; though at the same time seemingly ignorant of the roots of her own name, or those of her siblings. She opined that the name should be spiritual, traditional, and clearly Christian, as would befit a respectable couple.

Inge's brother Ernst, on the other hand, had been openly delighted with the first child's name (though principally to spite his father, knowing how much he hated Hitler) and additionally felt there was no reason for not showing some traditional Germanic pride. He suggested 'Burkhardt', at the thought of which both Horst and Inge privately shuddered.

Horst's younger brother Wilhelm had become somewhat of a film enthusiast and a regular visitor to the smoky confines of the popular cinema 'Schaubühne an der Neuen Sülze', together with his sweetheart Ann-Kathrin, where they enjoyed ditzy comedies and smoked and kissed. It had been recently renovated and even had a Wurlitzer theatre organ playing at the matinee showing. Wilhelm also liked a good war film and managed to get Ann-Kathrin to go along with him to those as well; in the more serious dramas though, he was rivetted to the screen while she got quickly bored and let her mind wander. He had taken of late to the films of war hero and ace pilot Karl Ritter, whom he described as "a gentleman and a warrior". They had recently seen the Great War dramas 'Unternehmen Michael'[1] and 'Urlaub auf Ehrenwort'[2], the latter recently premiered and both directed by Karl Ritter, which had thrilled him with patriotic pride.

---

[1] Operation Michael
[2] Leave on Word of Honour

"What about Karl?" he suggested. Karl Ritter - fighter pilot, war veteran and hero, film director; or Karl Dönitz, supreme commander of the *U-Boot* (submarine) fleet; or the immortal *Karl der Große* (Charles the Great). Martin heartily agreed, as did his father Volkmar during a visit to the Gasthaus: "You can't beat having the name of a fighter pilot. Those men are the new Teutonic knights on horses, shining in their bright armour!"

In the end, they settled for the obvious and simple solution that appeased all opinions and preferences. A name that was both wholesomely Christian and at the same time paid tribute to the country's current leadership and Germanic pride: thus the child was baptized Joseph, with a wink to the earthly husband of the mother of Christ as well as the widely respected Minister of Public Enlightenment and Propaganda.

With the birth of Joseph, who soon proved to be just as loud, difficult and demanding as Adolf, Inge realized that she would probably have to give up her job at the bakery in order to devote herself to her role as a mother. She did not wish to rely any longer on the kindness of relatives – at least on a regular basis - to take care of her two babies. In the weeks directly after the birth, while Inge was receiving maternity leave payments, she and Horst discussed the issue on numerous occasions and went through the arithmetic, taking a piece of paper to match salary on the one side with expenditure on the other. The resulting twin lists of numbers were, as expected, not very promising.

Horst was in favour of the idea of his wife staying at home to take care of the children, which he felt to be the traditional role that a woman should fulfill. Inge for her part also perceived the necessity of this role but was anxious about the dramatic drop in their disposable income that would entail from this. After the four weeks of maternity pay, during which she would get roughly half of her salary, she would receive no more money from the state and they would have to make do with Horst's salary alone. His job was secure, but not especially well paid.

Inge broke the subject to her mother and sister only. Shortly after and through an immense stroke of luck, at least for Inge and Horst, there arose a rental opportunity on the Rosenstraße, and only two doors down from the *Gasthaus Sonnenschein* itself. In this house the first two storeys belonged to an insurance company, while the third storey had been rented out for years to a childless couple. This couple, middle-aged and Jewish and with no other family in Lüneburg, was in the process of emigration abroad and would be vacating the apartment in the very near future. Gisela had got wind of this opening before the apartment was even announced to be vacant, and she had jumped at the chance. Using the good relations that she was building up with the neighbouring buildings on both sides of the Gasthaus, she managed to persuade the owner of the apartment in a single informal meeting and so secure the apartment for her sister and brother-in-law: "my sister is a mother of two little children and her husband is a fire fighter, both very respectful citizens and always punctual with their payments." The wife of the owner knew Inge from the bakery and testified to her husband that she was a pleasant and honest young woman; and, she added, unquestionably Aryan.

Gisela's idea was that she, or rather the current account of the Gasthaus, would contribute towards the rent (she originally offered to pay half, but Horst insisted on it being no more than 30%) in exchange for some assistance from Inge with the running of the Gasthaus and her taking care of all their children where necessary. The apartment, though the same size as the last one, was cheaper too; and being so close to the Gasthaus they could all eat together in the evening and so save further costs, Gisela pointed out. She was now fully involved with her business, which in turn left her precious little time for her family, but in this way she could at least bring so much together under one roof.

Gisela had calculated that if she coordinated the work at the Gasthaus between herself, Martin and Inge, and shared the looking after of the five children between those three plus Horst when he had time off, then they would all get by much better than before. Moreover, Gisela planned to bring their mother in on the plan, to help out too; Corinna would be delighted to have an excuse to get out of the house more often and in this way they would all get on marvellously and Inge could have all the children she wanted to. Gisela reckoned with their compliance but intended to wax both her mother's and sister's ear lyrically on the subject, just to be sure.

Additionally, she would have no need of hiring any extra staff, avoiding the costs involved as well as the bringing of strangers onto the premises who might not be trustworthy.

It was a bold plan; so much so that she kept it to herself and merely said she thought it was more logical to have the family closely knit together, now that there were more youngsters around. Gisela also organized the men to move the couple's furniture from the old apartment in the Rotenbleicher Weg up to the Rosenstraße; a short distance but involving some awkward and bulky items. This again was a wonder of planning and manipulation, of four male members of both families plus two firefighters, and a showcase for her natural managerial skills.

So by the summer of 1938 Inge and Horst were well settled into their new lodgings almost right beside the Gasthaus. They were very content to be there, finding the apartment much more comfortable and convenient, not to mention sunny, than their previous abode. Inge had hung up a picture in their bedroom – a tacky little painting of a cottage in a field with *Häuschen im Grünen* ('little house in the green') written below – making the room feel snug for her. She planned new heavy curtains with a floral design for the next year when they had saved up for the material.

Gisela was convinced of the effectiveness of the arrangement; something which she commented to her husband with well-chosen frequency, to gently though firmly hammer the point home and so justify the costs of helping to pay Inge and Horst's rent.

Gisela in turn soon got to see on a daily basis the natural maternal skills of her younger sister, who was by now effortlessly taking care of little Joseph and thirteen-month-old Adolf as well as Gisela's own three. Gisela considered her sister a naturally maternal figure, possessing – unlike herself - remarkable patience with all the children. Katrina and Siggi adored 'Tante (Auntie) Inge' and she equally loved to be together with them all, managing to instill harmony in a group of children of such varying ages. Inge was easy-going but the children respected her all the more for it, recognizing her fundamental good nature and calm constant temperament. Gisela recognized the usefulness and common sense in the set-up and how much pressure it took off her, and she was more than happy for things to continue this way forever.

Inge did occasionally hint at her desire to return to work at the bakery at some point - although the notion was not realistic at that point in time with Adolf and Joseph still so young; mentioning that she was missing her customers as well as the routine of going to work in the morning. This was not viewed well by Gisela who saw it as neither conducive to her own carefully formed plan nor to the general well-being of the whole family.

"There is no reason in the world," she said to Martin one evening, "why she should not have another two or three children and then we can all take care of them together. Actually, I like the idea of having so many nephews and nieces. I heard that the Führer himself has said that the important thing for a German woman is her family and her children and her home. It makes absolutely no sense for her to think of returning to work if she is at that stage in life when she feels she ought to have a larger family. It is better to bring children into the world while you are still young." Gisela, though possessing no interest in the Party or their politics, knew that invoking _his_ name was a sure way of backing most arguments. Martin – half listening and half drifting off into sleep in the armchair- mumbled his acquiescence and Gisela considered the matter settled. It would thus appear to Gisela with the sense of a prophecy intuitively confirmed when Inge announced the following spring, first to Horst and then to Gisela, her third pregnancy.

In the meantime, the Gasthaus had become a common meeting place for most of the family members who lived in Lüneburg or the surrounding areas. It had a warm back room where there was always cake and coffee, and Gisela was eager to make her new 'hotel' as inviting and comfortable as possible, not only to the paying guests but also to her own flesh and blood. There was even a Sunday roast lunch for the family sometimes, that Gisela and Inge organized together and made sure everyone was fed to the brim. She liked the idea of her home being a central point for family connections, even for those – such as Edeltraut – for whom she had no natural affinity but rather had to work quite hard on the friendship. It was worth it though; Gisela knew from experience that all people had their usefulness at some point and that maintaining good family relations was key to securing assistance and support with those chores and adversities that life often put in one's way. Bernhard was an engineer in a well-placed and well-remunerated job at the *Eisenwerk* (ironworks) in Lüneburg, had a new Mercedes, and was on good terms with the mayor's office, for instance, all of which impressed Gisela. Also, their daughter Eva was good friends with Gisela's daughter Katrina and often came to visit.

Volkmar Landeck had become a regular guest, enjoying the comfort of the back room where he could sit beside his older son and read the newspaper. Anna, suffering from an increasing variety of pains for which there seemed to exist no remedy, came only very rarely. She loved her son dearly but had little time for Gisela, whom she considered to be a highly capable manageress and wife but an irritating daughter-in-law. She preferred instead that Martin came to visit them at his grandmother's cottage in Adendorf from time to time, and was glad to see him on those occasions.

With living so close to the Gasthaus and working there part-time, Inge became an almost permanent presence, together with her two children. That a third child was on the way made Gisela look forward to what promised to be a budding extended family. Horst was more recessive and reticent, enjoying more the privacy and quietness of his own home as well as time spent exclusively with Inge and their sons; but he and Gisela had a good relationship, forged on mutual respect, and he came and went as he wished and was always welcome. Other semi-regular visitors included Georg, who looked forward to seeing his grandchildren as well as being treated to a few rounds of *Vollkorn* schnaps by Martin; and Horst's brother Wilhelm.

Gisela's own children were at this time learning to play the violin and she had the ambition that they should also proceed on to the piano, as soon as she and Martin were in a financial position to purchase one. The back room, she felt sure, was large enough to accommodate it without problem. Her husband was silently but bitterly against the idea, imagining with all due foresight the din that another - and this time far more powerful - instrument would produce; as if it wasn't bad enough already with two screeching violins.

Katrina and Siggi, now 12 and 11 respectively, had both been learning for a couple of years already but had made only modest progress. Possessing only a modicum of natural musical talent, they approached the task in hand with more obedience to their mother than actual enthusiasm. Gisela however was keen to show them off at family gatherings, where together they would thrash out well-known classics such as *"Kein schöner Land in dieser Zeit"*[3], *"Guter Mond, du stehst so stille"*[4], or *"Ave Maria"*. The audience sat through the performances with a mixture of endurance and mirth, usually laughing come the end and asking which pieces had just been played. This reaction nettled Gisela but she never let it show and just chuckled along instead.

Their teacher was Herr Korn, a gentleman in his fifties who lived nearby in the street An der Münze. Gisela was delighted with his work, despite the children's meagre progress, feeling that music-making gave the place a touch of culture; or at least, it would do so once the students had become more proficient. However, a thorny topic arose some weeks after the christening when Edeltraut happened to call round just as Herr Korn was leaving. Though glacially polite to the man himself, she turned on Martin (Gisela was absent in that moment) with scorn to inform him that not only was their violin teacher a Jew, but to her knowledge closely connected to the local synagogue, too. Martin stammered his ignorance on the subject, and later passed on the information to Gisela. Gisela coolly replied that she did not see any problem in that. The children seemed happy enough with their teacher, his rates were both reasonable and had not increased since he had commenced working with them, and more to the point she liked the man, whom she found always pleasant and polite towards her. This was the principal issue for Gisela, who had no interest whatsoever in his ethnicity nor religion. "He even tips his hat when he greets me or bids farewell. That is the sign of a gentleman. I cannot remember the last time a man did that to me, apart from Herr Korn."

Martin was not at all content with the matter though, especially when his cousin repeated her concerns a couple of months later. Once

---

[3] No Country More Beautiful in These Times
[4] Good Moon, You Move So Quietly

again, he approached Gisela and she responded by digging her heels in even harder, a trait she had picked up unconsciously from her father. With effort she had come to like Edeltraut well enough, as much as Gisela was capable of liking anyone outside of her own closest family, but greatly resented the woman interfering in her own family affairs. It also seemed to confirm what her father had often said, namely that those with strict political convictions were often just out to cause trouble wherever they could find it – and the National Socialists above all. Ideology was at this time in Germany more fervent in its dogma than religion had ever been, and far more self-righteous. Thus Gisela put her foot down and Herr Korn continued to come to the house and teach the children as usual, blissfully unaware of the family intrigues running behind his back.

The final straw came, however, when her father-in-law Volkmar also brought up the subject with them, explaining that such close contact with Jews was not only degrading to his family's reputation, but more importantly could harm their business if people found out and took exception to the fact. The first argument - as regards to the 'family reputation' - seemed absurd to Gisela, and actually made her laugh; but the second, concerning a detrimental effect on the Gasthaus as a business, sat with her and started to make her reconsider her stance. All the same, she did not wish to have to dismiss Herr Korn and staved off the decision for some time while she mulled over Volkmar's statement.

Fortunately for her, the issue resolved itself without her having to intervene. By now they had reached the late autumn of that fateful year for Jews and Herr Korn informed her, after a rushed and harrying class one Thursday, that this would be his last visit as he and his wife were leaving Lüneburg. (He did not mention where to, but Gisela later heard that they had left for France and from there were hoping to make it across the Atlantic to Canada.)

He thanked her for her kindness and patronage in a formal little speech that touched her heart. She, in turn, gave him double the amount for the class plus a handsome tip; partly out of pity for his difficult situation, partly out of relief that he himself had resolved her dilemma. In the end it was a loss for no-one, as the children were thankful not to have to continue with regular music lessons, while their father and extended family were equally thankful not to have to follow their progress.

Chapter 9

Lüneburg and its surrounding rural area were able to resist the widespread economic crisis and political chaos of the aftermath of the First World War far better than many areas of Germany. There were none of the hefty street fights commonly witnessed in Hamburg and other large cities, nor the Spartacist uprisings of Bremen and Berlin with cries of revolution; no coalminer strikes as in the Saarland and Ruhr area, nor attacks on business offices or mass releases of prisoners as was happening in many parts of the country.

On 9th November, following the German capitulation, the old Kaiser Wilhelm II had abdicated and fled to the neighbouring Netherlands. In this way the former German Empire came to an end and the Weimar Republic was proclaimed in its place. But among the conservative nationalist sections of the population, the demands of the Treaty of Versailles were a sharp thorn in the side. The reparation payments strapped onto Germany by the victorious Allied nations, and insisted upon in particular by France, were unrealistically high and caused great discontent among the population. The scene was ripe for political discord followed by economic crisis.

In the post-war turbulence there were continual clashes reported between communist groups and the *Freikorps*, a paramilitary militia consisting mostly of war veterans; even to the point of numerous assassinations. In 1920 there was an attempted coup d'êtat in Berlin and a crippling general strike. Alone in the *Ruhraufstand* (an uprising in the industrial Ruhr area in western Germany) there were around 12 million participants. The Minister of Finance (Matthias Erzberger) was assassinated in 1921 along with the Foreign Minster (Walter Rathenau) in 1922; in both cases by extremist right-wing groups. The war was over but the situation in the ruined land was far from peaceful.

A few years later in 1923 there would be another coup, called the *Bierhalleputsch*, that emanated from no less than a beer hall in Munich; it was quickly suppressed. This crack of the whip was carried out by a political wing calling themselves '*National Socialists*' and, though a complete failure, the attempted coup brought the group and its leader, an Austrian war veteran called Adolf Hitler, to wider public attention. Hitler himself was accused of high treason and sentenced to five years imprisonment, although he actually served only nine months and it was during this period of prison time that he penned his notorious autobiographical manifesto '*Mein Kampf*' ('My Struggle').

Hyperinflation was another feature of this early post-war period of the Weimar Republic. Prices rocketed up to unfathomable heights which decimated entrepreneurial endeavour and middle-class savings and threw the economy into complete disorder. The exchange rate for 1 US dollar rose in just two years from 14 Marks in July 1919, to over 76 Marks in July 1921. This, however, was only to be the beginning. By the following July 1922, the rate stood at 493 Marks and in the next six months leading into January 1923 it had reached no less than 18,000 Marks. From then on, the figures spiralled completely out of control through the rest of 1923. By July, it stood at a million Marks for a single dollar; in October, 5 billion Marks; on 7th November, 680 billion Marks; on 11th November, one trillion Marks; and on 15th November, 4.2 trillion. Paper money was virtually worthless, to be shunted around in wheelbarrows. Alternative currencies arose in which private companies or municipal authorities issued their own *Notgeld* (emergency money). The black market flourished like never before and was often the only way to obtain certain goods. In many towns and cities soup kitchens were organized for the needy so that people had access to at least a bowl of soup and a few slices of bread each day (by the end of the year a small loaf of bread was costing 200 million Marks).

There are innumerable anecdotes from the period, such as that of the woman who absentmindedly put a basket packed tight with banknotes to one side for a moment, only to turn round and find the basket stolen but the banknotes tipped out on the pavement and left behind. Or the couple who sold their property with the intention of emigrating to America to escape the economic chaos. The sale went through successfully but by the time they had finished off the final paperwork, caught the train to Hamburg and gone to buy the ship passages to New York, the money from the sale of their house was no longer enough to pay for the tickets. They returned to their hometown, penniless and now homeless too.

But the crisis came to an end by 1924 and a semblance of normalcy returned to the country. Lüneburg began to bloom in this period. It had even become a hub of regional administrative bureaucracy as one of the six regional centres of the province of Hannover, then part of the *Freistaat Preußen* (Free State of Prussia), the largest and politically most important state within the newly founded republic.

Now came those precious years of political stability and economic boom from 1924 to 1929. With the *Goldenen Zwanziger* – the 'Golden Twenties' as the decade was referred to in German - came the great industrial expansion and an economic surge for the nascent Weimar Republic. Millions of new homes were constructed, fresh business ventures sprang into life, the nation's infrastructure was vastly improved at all levels, great technological advances were made. Berlin in particular flourished and established itself as a global city and metropolis renowned for its cultural and entertainment value, forging links to its kindred-soul New York by cruise liner and air ship. In 1926 Berlin erected the first traffic lights in Germany and a spanking new radio broadcasting tower was inaugurated; in the same year the civil aviation company Lufthansa was founded. In those sparkling years of the late 1920s the movie industry and other forms of artistic creation experienced a rush of creativity.

It was sadly to be a short-lived roar of activity, with the infamous Wall Street Crash in October 1929 ushering in a global economic crisis that would hit Germany particularly hard. Companies went bankrupt en masse and the old ghost of unemployment returned to haunt the land. Many couples and families were ruined while others found themselves navigating a precarious job market or simply living in bottomless poverty and begging. In Lüneburg as everywhere, the distant crash was felt intensely and the number of those out of work and in need of social aid rose sharply.

The then ascendant NSDAP (*Nationalsozialistische Deutsche Arbeiterpartei* – National Socialist German Workers' Party) did not easily find foot in Lüneburg at first. In the surrounding rural area the population remained faithful to the *Landbund*, a union of farmers and small- and medium-sized businesses with a conservative, German-national outlook. In the town of Lüneburg at the municipal level, the dominant parties were the left-wing SPD (social democrats) and KDP (communists). However, by the late 1920s the NSDAP did commence to expand its presence there. The war veteran and former police officer Otto Telschow figured greatly in the political development of the party in this area. He was a thick-set brute, with the air of a mobster and sporting a Hitlerian moustache. Soon he could be heard around town giving vitriolic speeches in which he raged against Jews, freemasons and communists.

(At this point, and as if already foreseeing their future power, the NSDAP had begun to divide up the country into their own regional subdivisions, called *Gau*. Telschow came to control the *Gau Ost-Hannover* - Gau of Eastern Hannover - with its capital in Lüneburg. This designation would become official later on in 1937, with the Nazis by then firmly in power, and Telschow had his years of fierce campaigning rewarded when he was, as expected, conferred the position of *Gauleiter*, president of the *Gau*.)

A further factor in the growing influence held over Lüneburger society by the upstart NSDAP came with the retirement in 1930 of Dr. Friedrich Corssen, the chief editor of the popular local newspaper the *Lüneburgschen Anzeigen,* after 38 years in the position. Up until then it had remained a right-wing liberal publication; but now sharp winds of change were blowing. Under a new and far more radical editorial control, it moved firmly into the area of national-socialist oriented journalism and reported on the growing strength of the NSDAP party in an uncritical, softening manner.

In towns like Lüneburg, as all across Germany, the NSDAP was already starting to gain the manifold votes of semi-skilled tradesmen and unskilled workers, lower and middle-level civil servants, as well as retailers and other small businessmen. Soon it would expand its popularity among the ranks of the police force, the judicial system, and teachers, too.

1930 was a key year for the Nazi party at a national level in the German federal parliament election. It rose from an insignificant 2.6% just two years previously in 1928, to over 18%, and became the second largest party with 107 seats, just trailing behind the SPD (Social Democrat Party) with its 24% and 143 seats. In East Prussia, the NSDAP was the most voted party of all. For the triumphant NSDAP leader Adolf Hitler, the game was on.

There were to be two more free elections, those in the July and November of 1932. In both the winner was Hitler's extreme-right NSDAP. The moderate parties were losing foothold while the extreme-left KPD was doing increasingly well. No political consensus could be reached in the factious parliament. Eventually, following a series of cloistered negotiations led by the conservative DNVP (German National People's Party) and leading German businessmen, the parliamentary president Paul von Hindenburg appointed Adolf Hitler as the Chancellor of Germany.

This occurred in January 1933 and with it came the event known in German history as the *Machtergreifung* (literally: 'seizure of power'): that fatal moment in politics that would ultimately result in the dismantling of the previous democratic structure and its transformation into a centralized dictatorship. The Weimar Republic – the quirky political experiment that had been in place since 1919 – was now definitively over. The Nazis moved with such astonishing speed and legal agility that they had already made huge advances in legislation by as early as May of that same year, including the first of what would be many anti-Jewish laws.

Within this new political reality, local papers like the *Lüneburgschen Anzeigen* were able to go on to take an openly and unabashedly pro-Nazi stance. Meanwhile, in the wider population there was little opposition to the growing dictatorship among a people that was without work and going hungry. The number of unemployed in Lüneburg was situated in 1925 at around 600; by the end of December 1929, following the Wall Street Crash, it was up to 2,000; by early 1933, that number had hit over 6,300. Soup kitchens were opened to feed the poor and a *Wärmehalle* (warm shelter) was made available to protect the homeless from the -20° of cold with frost.

It was in this framework of poverty and hardship that people looked the other way when the violence began to occur. In early March 1933, following the complete closure of power by the Nazis, the hoodlums of the SA and *Stahlhelm* groups, as well as Nazi-friendly members of the police force, commenced their tactic of terror. They ransacked the homes of political opposiitors and beat them up, occupied buildings belonging to trade unions or other left-wing associations and wrecked the interiors, raided the editorial offices of media outlets that were antagonistic towards the regime and threatened their employees, destroyed equipment and articles belonging to these groups or businesses, burnt countless documents or seized whatever could be used as 'incriminatory evidence'. Sometimes whole sections of streets were cordoned off so that numerous offices and homes could be thoroughly pummeled without interference. Newspapers and magazines that were critical of the Nazis soon disappeared from circulation, leaving only regime-friendly reading material available.

This was all part of a process called '*Gleichschaltung*' (literally: 'co-ordination' or 'synchronization'), whereby control of all aspects of life was established in a totalitarian form throughout the country - in political power at all levels, whether national, state or municipal; in the press and media, in the judicial system, in education, in art and culture. Obedience to the ruling ideology became a prerequisite in many walks of life and people were sacked from jobs or thrown off apprenticeship courses merely for not conforming to the politically correct position.

Already by May the Nazis were celebrating their first book-burnings and there soon arose an entire culture of cancellation of authors and other artists holding undesirably contrary viewpoints. Classic artists of old who were now popular with the state – such as Wagner, Beethoven, Schiller - were celebrated with great pomp and enthusiasm; undesirables such as Gaugin, Mendelssohn, Meyerbeer, disappeared into obscurity. Contemporary artists who wished to succeed were required to fall in line or forced to emigrate.

Parallel to that citizens were cajoled, even coerced into showing respect for the new masters. For example, May 1st had been the *Feiertag der Arbeiter* (Workers' Holiday) for many years but now, under the Nazis, it became the *Feiertag der deutschen Arbeiter* (German Workers' Holiday). On this day it was expected that you raised your arm and gave the salute "Heil Hitler!" Open and public refusal to conform to this custom could easily land a person in prison. And from prison some were sent on to one of the newly built concentration camps, a growing feature of the new dictatorship.

The Nazis were already infamous for their use of martial and extrajudicial forces such as the SA to threaten and even terrorize all political opposition. The *Reichstag*, the German parliament building, curiously went up in flames the next month, in February. The incident was attributed to a young Dutch communist (who was swiftly arrested, tried, convicted, and then executed by the beginning of the following year) and served as an excellent excuse to tighten political control over the population under the pretext of protecting civic order. In an atmosphere of authoritarianism and stern control - and following a winter of poverty, hunger, and cold - Germany was once again sent to vote in federal elections in March 1933. With the elections closely monitored by the Nazis and the opposition intimidated by violent repression, Hitler swept up nearly 44% of the votes. Together with the conservative-nationalist DVNP allies he now held sway over 52% and commanded indisputable power. As part of the accelerating dictatorship, the other moderate and left-wing parties were then outlawed and their leaders and prominent members either fled abroad or were arrested and imprisoned. The DVNP itself was absorbed and dissolved by June, having outlived its usefulness. There would be no more multi-party elections again for many years, not until after the end of a world war.

The concrete effects of Hitler's rise to power were immediate. Already by March 1933 Joseph Goebbels, the 'Minister of People's Enlightenment and Propaganda' and principal inciter of the persecution of the Jewish community, was calling for the boycott of Jewish professionals and businesses throughout the whole of Germany. The SA (*Sturmabteilung* – literally Storm Department, the brutal and thuggish power arm of the Nazis) along with other paramilitary organizations such as *Stahlhelm* (helmet of steel) plus the youth indoctrination programme the Hitler Youth, were all utilised in the following years to intimidate the population and enforce the boycott. In the framework of this anti-Jewish drive, the premises of the Jewish-owned stores suffered regular campaigns of threats of violence and its clientele was publicly vilified.

In the case of Lüneburg, at least during this early period, the effects were more mildly felt. Ironically, this was in great part down to the attitude of *Gauleiter* Telschow. Telschow was a firm, indeed fanatical Nazi ideologue; but disorder and anarchical behaviour were anathema to him, especially in the form of wanton physical violence, and he was very much against the idea of "wild pogroms." Telschow was also a smart agitator and in his keenness to avoid chaos and disorder in regional and municipal politics, he was able to maintain strict control of all that was happening in the area. There was nothing of importance that did not first pass across his desk for personal scrutiny and then either rejection or approval; and that was the way he intended to keep things.

Indeed, following its opening salvo of frank and brutal hostility towards political dissenters, Jews and other 'undesirables', the NSDAP party at many levels came to the conclusion that the brutal face of the SA would not facilitate a rational way forward in those initial crucial years. The state continued its legal machinations without remorse, naturally, and the Jewish population in particular felt itself stripped of more and more rights with each passing year.

Now that the NSDAP was legitimately, or rather unquestionably, in power it wished at first to wage a war of charm abroad. This would go on to include one of its propaganda highlights in the form of the hosting of the 1936 Olympic Games, both Winter and Summer. Politicians such as Telschow had recognized the negative effects that would be produced by foreign media reporting of wanton violence and talk of this issue outside of Germany. His attitude was certainly widespread and would be reflected in some major political adjustments of that time. The following year of 1934 brought the purge of the higher ranks of the paramilitary SA, right up to the assassination of the commander Ernst Röhm himself in the infamous *Night of the Long Knives*.

(Needless to say, by the end of the 1930s, with the invasion of Poland and the subsequent acceleration into a global conflict, all thoughts of maintaining internal calm and wooing foreign powers were strewn to the wind. The NSDAP was by then free to show its truly belligerent, and ultimately genocidal, visage.)

In Germany's judicial system the Party also moved with unprecedented speed to take control of all key positions. Innumerable party-faithful lawyers used the corruption inherent in the new dictatorial structure to gain access to and secure positions of power.

Whereas there had been only four NSDAP-member judges in total in the whole of Germany at the beginning of 1933, by 1938 the percentage of judges who belonged to the party had risen to no less than 54% of the country's total.

Similar dramatic increases in positions of influence and power were taking place not only in the judicial system but also in education, the press, culture and ultimately in commerce, too. The pattern was always the same, in which opponents and dissenters were removed from their positions and replaced either by the old and trustable party-faithful, or by a new young generation of dynamic and ambitious climbers who were quick to recognize the potential gains to be made on a personal level and adapt accordingly to the new political and ideological environment. The higher positions of power were held by a small elite and often interconnected national with regional or even municipal government, such as was the case of Telschow himself who officiated as both *Gauleiter* for Eastern Hannover as well as a member of the central *Reichstag* government. In this way, the central control of power by the NSDAP could be effectively pushed down through society and then firmly maintained at all political levels and in all regions throughout Germany.

There was some minor opposition to the rapidly tightening grip of control by the NSDAP party. One such case was the *Arbeiterkulturbewegung* – the 'workers' culture movement'. This had originally been set up to promote folk music and people's theatre, along with art, sport and rapport with nature for the working classes. These groups, which encouraged free thinking and were based on liberal philosophies, stood in stark natural opposition to the control-obsessed NSDAP. They made some initial and brave resistance that was naturally crushed. Their premises were occupied and later legally confiscated and taken over; any further sign of insubordination was subjugated to harsh punitive measures. By September of 1933 said organization had already been disbanded. The members had got off light in comparison to others, though. Important figures from the communist or social democratic parties – those few who hadn't already fled into exile as soon as Hitler took control - were being systematically rounded up, beaten black and blue, and carted off to confinement in the network of concentration camps which had begun to open up all around the country.

In no time, any form of dissent whatsoever, any refusal to comply to the quickly self-organizing NSDAP structures, had become a perilous and even potentially life-threatening undertaking; a factor which facilitated the grip of the dictatorship not only on the population's movements, speech and acquisitions, but also their deeper psyche.

The high point of the Nazis' institutional presence in Lüneburg came in April 1937 within the framework of the *Groß-Hamburg-Gesetz* (Greater Hamburg Act) of that year. In this bill the nearby town of Harburg was absorbed into the area of Greater Hamburg, leaving Lüneburg to rise to become the capital of the *Gau* of Eastern Hannover in its own right. With this came a considerable increase in the presence of party functionaries, as a substantial administrative structure moved its premises from Harburg-Wilhelmsburg down to Lüneburg. With this also came an increase in the presence of systems of surveillance and repression, which was later intensified when the regional Gestapo office was also moved directly to Lüneburg in the summer of 1940. This office would become directly responsible for the monitoring of any signs of defeatism or resistance to Nazi ideology among the German population in the area, which included the arrest and sometimes execution of political opponents and dissidents. Furthermore, it also became responsible for the monitoring and deportation of all Jews from Lüneburg and nearby Winsen.

But even before this point, the authorities' control over whole sectors of the population had become highly refined and was functioning ever more efficiently. The Jewish population in particular found themselves restricted by more and more stringent legislation with each passing month. Between the constant increase in legal obstacles - that saw them segregated, rejected and outlawed at every professional and civic level; the increasingly strong police presence breathing down their necks; and the widespread social rejection by large segments of the population, the Jewish community came to recognize the sheer implausibility that their existence could carry on as anything even remotely recognizable from times before. Already the numerous laws that the NSDAP had been continually firing off since first coming to power in that fateful January of 1933, were making the normal lives of most Jews near to impossible.

Nearly all Jewish professional and commercial activity had been, or was in the process of being, eliminated by the gathering momentum of the so-called *Arisierungprozess* (process of Aryanization). In the framework of this 'process', Jewish owners of homes and businesses were coming under extreme pressure, which ranged from verbal threats to physical violence, to sell up and leave the country as quickly as possible; always assuming, of course, that they were successful in obtaining the necessary visa to move abroad. The often sluggish movement of paperwork around the world's embassies and consulates became a Kafkaesque labyrinth for many; despite hundreds of desperate applications and forms, together with diverse payments of fees, it still proved futile.

These continual, always highly disadvantageous, changes in legislation through the years, infringing deeply on their personal freedoms and rights, entered into all aspects of Jewish life. In the case of the synagogue, further changes in its taxation status in March 1938 made it clear that the continued functioning of the temple would no longer be financially feasible. This came in the form of the 1938 enacted '*Law concerning the legal relationships of the Jewish cultural associations*', which established that Jewish communities lost their status as public bodies and were thus liable to pay both real estate and wealth tax. It may have seemed to outsiders as a relatively minor change, but for the impoverished and powerless community members it was the proverbial straw that broke the camel's back. It would be simply impossible to find the funds to pay for yet another heavy tax duty. With much sadness and regret all round, but a clear sense of fate having decided and sealed off the way, it was considered as the only viable option that the grounds of the once so fine and noble temple standing at Am Schifferwall Nr. 5 should therefore be sold off.

The grounds were sold off at a minimum price that was then further reduced in an addendum to the sales contract the following year in the name of the Jewish community of Lüneburg. This sale was administered by the municipal Chamber of Industry and Commerce, represented by its president who – as one could see coming - was a high-ranking functionary in the local branch of the NSDAP. The final amount, following the reduction of outstanding fees on the mortgage, was eventually transferred to a blocked account in a foreign currency exchange bank, access to which could only be gained through the joint authorization of both the tax office in Lüneburg as well as the supervisory board of the chief financial director's office in Hannover. Thus, within a labyrinth of (highly uncooperative) financial bureaucracy the money was safely kept by the authorities. That same year the order was given to tear down the building itself, with the costs to be deducted from what little remained in that blocked account.

The final service in the synagogue took place on 23rd October 1938. In the following week, the local master mason commenced work as per instructions on the demolition of the building. He charged 1,500 Reichsmark for the job. It would mark the end of a community that had lived in the town since the 13th Century.

Around a fortnight later, when the savagery of the November *Reichspogrom* broke out during two nights of wild destruction, the still standing synagogue was spared the destruction that so many others throughout the Reich were suffering, due to the simple fact that it was no longer Jewish property.

There was a clumsy attempt by some youths to get a fire going inside the premises, with a bundle of wood, straw and paper soaked in petrol; but this was quickly put out by the fire service and some neighbours, with the accompanying comment that the building "no longer belonged to the Jews". By the time that the war had broken out, the building had been fully demolished and from then on only existed in pictures, photography and memories.

Chapter 10

It was on November 8th that the announcement came through abruptly in the press and radio concerning an assassination attempt that had just taken place in Paris. Like many in town, Inge and Horst, both busy that day, picked up snippets of news between jobs and errands. They heard something about the German ambassador to France having been shot at, in the centre of Paris, by an enraged communist and Jew. There was a flurry of initial reports in which some of the details varied from one source to another, particularly those that passed along the traditional route of word of mouth. By the evening, however, the flow of information had stabilized and clean clear facts could be discerned. It was not the ambassador that had been shot at, but rather a high-ranking diplomat at the embassy, a man called Ernst vom Rath. The most striking – for some people both appalling and yet oddly thrilling - aspect of this piece of news lay as much in the would-be assassin as in his victim. Then the gun had not been simply fired by a Jew, they pointed out; but by a Jewish *boy*, an adolescent barely seventeen years old. Meanwhile, the condition of the wounded German diplomat had been classified as critical.

Volkmar Landeck was sitting in the back room and was naturally up-to-date by the time Inge passed by to visit her sister at the Gasthaus that evening. "Vom Rath, Ernst vom Rath," he reeled off with a familiarity as if he knew of the man from before. "Yesterday at the German embassy in France. Right under our noses! Shot him a point-blank range apparently. Nasty, very nasty. It does not look good, although they have not said much about his condition. Poor man! There is no law and order these days, no security. You could just walk out to work one morning and bang, it is all over. And the Jewish pig is just a kid, just seventeen. Can you believe it? A little nobody, a fleck of dirt! And not just any Jew, not even a French Jew. No, he is a Pole. And he was living until recently in Frankfurt. They wonder why here in Germany we want to get rid of them!" he thundered from his armchair. "Of course we do, who would not?"

Horst's long day at work had drawn to a late close and he returned to the Gasthaus at nine o'clock for his evening meal to find Gisela rather than Inge waiting for him downstairs in the kitchen, wringing her hands by the stove. She looked tired and over-challenged. She told him not to worry but that Inge was sick and had taken to her bed. She had come down with a fever, as had little Josef, and both mother and baby were recovering in their bedroom. They had called the family physician Dr Zimmermann and he had been round to their apartment already, prescribed some aspirin, said it was a mild flu that should have run its course in two or three days. Adolf seemed unaffected and was playing with her own children upstairs in the Gasthaus. Corinna was also there and looking after them all together, while Gisela herself was cleaning up in the kitchen after, she admitted, a busy evening. Martin had gone out drinking at his local pub *Pons* with some friends.

Gisela insisted that Horst ate here first before going over to the apartment, as she herself had other tasks still to be finished off and wanted to clean up the kitchen for the night. He gulped down his food and when he got there fifteen minutes later, he found Inge in good spirits but pale and occasionally shivering, with beads of sweat hanging on her forehead. Baby Joseph was fast asleep in her arms, snuggled up against her chest. He wiped Inge's forehead and neck with a handkerchief before kissing them. He grimaced and stuck out his lower lip in mock sympathy, grinned and gently stroked his wife's hair, head and neck, looked at Josef with paternal concern while Inge repeated what the doctor had said. She was pale and her voice hoarse. Horst nodded, said he had already spoken to Gisela at the Gasthaus. He lay down on the bed beside her and spent some time with his wife as they engaged in a short and whispered conversation to avoid waking the babe; brief phrases of everyday matters, nothing of news or current events.

The town slept relatively peacefully that night, apart from a drunken old pensioner stumbling home and shouting in the streets; and an angry and equally drunken exchange, not far from *Pons*, between some vehemently pro-Nazi workers and a couple of colleagues known to be not politically aligned to the Party. As the night and the following day progressed, this generally contained antagonism grew and burgeoned, like a river swollen by sudden rainfall that had overreached its banks and was starting to grab at everything beside and along it. It was a furious whirl of currents and eddies that took in many disparate subjects, from war to employment to communism to business to national destiny to territory to crime; but it invariably centred around the role of '*the Jew*', in the clouds and shadows of an uncertain future, that the assassination attempt seemed to have triggered.

This poisoned stream was swiftly growing in strength throughout the land. It became an uncontrollable brute force that fed off its own toxins - existing naturally but requiring precise intervention in order to produce the required virulence - that were replenished by a cynically observing political leadership and its servient media. A self-fulfilling juncture had been reached, in the midst of this perfect storm, to give many the chance to not only scream out the bile and hatred from the bottom of their stomachs, but further to set free all the deepest darkest impulses that had been hitherto held - tied and bound - by the rules of orderly civic conduct. These rules were now set to be breached and cruel fantasies to be liberated.

In such a general atmosphere of mutual conformation, together with the necessity that many felt to clearly define a common enemy, it was an effortless task to set the rage to hop from one head to another like a parasitic flea.

The next day was a festive holiday of the highest Nazi order: the day of remembrance of the attempted (or, as increasingly few now dared to utter: the failed) Putsch by Hitler in Munich in 1923. There were festivities all over the land which included the swearing in of new SS recruits from the seemingly endless ranks of young men eager to join up. The Führer himself had travelled to the south that day to preside over a commemorative ceremony in the *Hauptstadt der Bewegung* – the capital of the Nazi movement. Thus in Munich that night, the ideological rulers gathered to pay homage to the "martyrs of the movement" who had died in the 1923 Putsch attempt, as did officials and the Party faithful all across the Reich.

As the evening progressed, and in the middle of these solemn festivities, there exploded like a well-aimed grenade the news that, despite all the best medical attention that anyone could have possibly received, vom Rath had succumbed to his wounds and had been pronounced dead. There was a sense of inevitability in the information; everyone knew about the gravity of his wounds. But after this final confirmation there came a reaction of such rabid proportions that it seemed only blood would quench it. All but the very naïve thought otherwise. What did, however, take many by surprise, was the rapidity with which the authorities reacted. And furthermore the extremely organized manner in which they reacted, as if this spontaneous anger had been well rehearsed.

The assassination was to be the spark that ignited a whole explosion of shock and fury, of vitriolic resentment. It was considered from above that there was clearly the collective sense of a need to somehow avenge the murder. The mechanisms, that had been waiting for just such an opportunity to arise, lost no time in going to work.

As the news was announced, Goebbels promptly gave a prepared speech (he had expected vom Rath's probable demise that very day) at 22:00 in Munich before the assembled party elite at the Putsch anniversary celebrations. He expressed, with his characteristic verbose spite and wagging forefinger, the outrage of the German people, and stated that anti-Jewish actions were self-evident and "to be expected". Further to that, a veiled threat against those who might be tempted to come to the aid of the victims: "No-one should stand in the way of the *Volkszorn*" (the fury of the people).

The well-oiled chain of command sprang into action; orders were passed on to initiate and, most importantly, give a free hand to violence for all. This fury was to be discerned, the Nazi leadership was quietly adamant, as coming first and foremost from the common man. Once the initial barrier of civic law had been broken down, they felt, this was more often than not the case.

Telephone lines were hot as the go-ahead was given, for more than a few had long been reckoning with an event of this nature. The ripples caused by Goebbel's words expanded out from Munich with terrifying speed. In no time, there were anti-Jewish riots taking place in all major cities, under the approving eyes of the Nazi elite and their governing authorities. Disturbances, lynching, burning, arrests, verbal and physical attacks – they spread like wildfire to even smaller towns throughout the Reich. As the night progressed, all across the Reich hell broke loose.

In Lüneburg the message was moving through town well before midnight. Prominent local Nazis and other higher-ranking NSDAP members had met in the *Schützenhaus* (meeting place for associations of marksmen and other gun enthusiasts) that evening. As the news seeped through, first the conformation of vom Rath's death and then Goebbel's unambiguous speech, an atmosphere of general outrage had formed. This soon spilled over into the streets, as the mood flowed out on the shouts of those leaving the *Schützenhaus* as well as many who had followed the news at home on the radio. More precise instructions from above were simultaneously passed on to the police force and to all local administrative headquarters of public services and utilities. Within barely quarter of an hour, SA brownshirts and other Nazi-affiliated activists were attacking Jewish businesses. Behind them came that usual useful beast, as hoped and expected – the crowd: sometimes hateful, sometimes ignorant and easily misled, sometimes simply in search of popular activity. Curious at first, but in many cases increasingly eager to join in with the orgy of destruction.

The local police station was put on maximum alert as to the probability of hefty disturbances but, as with the fire station, was instructed that under no circumstances was it to interfere with the sequence of events taking place. Instead, it was let those events run "their own natural course". Its role was to be purely passive and observatory. Additionally, a delegation was sent from the *Geheime Staatspolizei* (Secret State police force - generally shortened by Germans to 'Gestapo') to observe the proceedings and ensure that everything went according to plan.

At this point in time, the Gestapo centre that was responsible for the Lüneburg district was situated in Wilhelmsburg, to the south of Hamburg, and the officers arrived in military motorized vehicles that evening to make a detailed report of the events. One of the head officers was a man in his thirties named Eberhard Ritter, who had been in his position for four years by now and was longing for just this kind of action-packed night in order to see how the line of "passive tolerance and deliberation", as he referred to the current treatment of Jews by the broader population, could be crossed for once and for all. He was of the opinion, as many of his ideological stance, that once that line had indeed been crossed, there would be no going back. He would also end up receiving a promotion and transfer to Lüneburg itself in the near future.

The mayor of Lüneburg was a young career politician called Wilhelm Wetzel, in his mid-thirties and already the local *Gauamtsleiter für Kommunalpolitik* (head official for local community politics). He was a fierce anti-Semite and had been a signed-up member of the NSDAP since the beginning of the 1930s. He immediately contacted the heads of the police force and all emergency services, giving notice to the police that they were not to intervene or offer assistance in the presence of any attacks on Jewish property, businesses or persons. These orders were also reinforced by two local NS functionaries - *Kreisleiter* (chief of district committee) Heincke, and Schmitt, a young civil servant from *Gauleiter* Telschow's office - who themselves headed straight to the town centre to watch the attacks first-hand and make sure that the police followed their instructions.

(Some seven years later, upon being interviewed by the occupying British forces on the subject of their involvement in the Jewish Progrom of November 9th and 10th, commonly known as the *Reichskristallnacht*, both admitted they had been present that night and had witnessed the destruction and assaults taking place. However, they maintained that they had both gone out merely to "stretch their legs" after a long day in the office, had worn civil clothing - which had indeed been the case, as was testified by others - and had not represented any public office during these hours; instead they had merely observed the events taking place as dozens, perhaps hundreds, of others had too, all quite powerless in any way to hinder the thugs. As Heincke, without a blush of shame, would put it during the interview: "Who in his right mind would place his hand between snarling, fighting dogs?")

One of the first in Lüneburg to bear the brunt of this *Volkszorn* ('fury of the people') was the small shoe shop belonging to the Weingarten family. This was located in the little lane Bei der Nikolaikirche that ran by that church. The family lived above the shop on the first and second floors and were alerted by the din of an approaching mob, consisting principally of SA members who upon arrival pounded the shop below with a hail of stones. With all glass smashed, they poured gasoline and set light to the business inside. Furniture and stock flared up in incandescent flames while a further storm of stones impeded any theoretical attempt to put out the fire from the back of the shop. Seeing the hopelessness of the situation, the family had meanwhile managed to escape through a back passageway and fled to a hidden spot on the nearby Baumstraße, to wait in the shadows in hiding. They sat there in deathly silence until the very early morning, when the riot had calmed and most people had gone home.

Long before that, a few people put out the fire that had been set, though not in order to save what was left of the smoldering business but rather to avoid having the flames jumping over onto surrounding buildings. This would become a common scene throughout the whole of the Reich. Firemen stood atop their ladders and watched on in apathetic inactivity while Jewish houses, shops and other businesses, and most frequently synagogues, all burnt down. They held limp dry hoses that would only eventually come to use when adjacent buildings or upper floors looked to be threatened by spreading flames. One example in Lüneburg was a small cigar shop over in the Oedeme district, known to be in Jewish ownership, that was ransacked. The goods were all stolen in this case, either for personal consumption or a later sale. After this the premises were set on fire, although the owner was able to subdue the flames sufficiently to keep them in check. The emergency service was notified by said owner, who then had to watch how the fire engine and crew arrived only to stand observe the situation inactively, offering neither assistance nor a single comment of consolation.

Back in the centre, another Jewish family - Herr Unger, his wife and three young sons - were all forced to flee their home around midnight when its windows and those of their bookkeeping office directly below also received a storm of bricks and stones. The mob broke into the building and began to throw chairs and documents from the office on the first floor. The fleeing forms of the family were recognized by some others who were marching up the Bardowicker Straße in the opposite direction, in order to catch sight of the spectacle; they spewed out the vilest insults, even at the children.

A general practitioner, Dr. Tiberias, ventured out in his natural doctor's desire to see if he could assist any of the wounded. He was soon recognized and caught by one of the marauding mobs that had sprung up like spontaneous packs of wolves to roam the streets in search of victims, both human and material. He was dragged into a dark side alley and brutally assaulted. He was stripped of his shirt and undershirt and his body hair was singed with matches, while the men taunted him and threatened to set him on fire. In the end he was beaten and finally kicked to within an inch of his life. Not a young man at 59, he managed to drag himself somehow back to his apartment where his nervous wife ran down to assist him, still limping and bearing cuts and bruises, back up to the apartment. Within three weeks they had sold up and were gone.

Joel Frey, who had been a guest at the earlier Beim and Wunderlich wedding, was also nearly lynched as he crossed the square Am Markt on his way back home from a late-night meeting with Rabbi Liebowitz and their friend Schlomo Rosenfeld. He and Rosenfeld had parted ways after crossing the Bräuserbrücke bridge, with Frey heading innocently up the Baumstraße and turned into the central Bardowicker Straße, despite the fracas clearly resonating in the air. He was soon spotted and jeered at, and had to grab his cap and flee with great speed and agility to shake off a small section of the mob that had broken off in order to pursue him. He got away, breathless and luckily with only a fright. His friend Rosenfeld managed to make it home safely but was verbally accosted in the street outside his home by two couples of older women and men from the same apartment block where he lived.

Not so lucky was Leonard Kuperstein, a former student of veterinary medicine and then hopeful émigré-to-be in his early twenties, who was also in the area around Am Markt that night. He had tried to intervene in the wanton vandalism taking place in and around a dry cleaner's that was thought (as it turned out, erroneously) to be Jewish owned. He often frequented the business and knew the staff well. He addressed two police officers posted there and begged them to put an end to the destruction. These rudely rebuked him and as he stepped closer inside the building, to try to reason with some of the ring leaders, he found himself surrounded, and was beaten. During this assault, his head struck against a cracked shelf in the building interior. Unconscious, he was dragged out onto the pavement and left there. He was later declared deceased by a team of ambulance men who arrived in the early morning to check if anyone was to be found lying around the streets. Though it never came to light, he had survived the actual beating and fall, but at a later point someone had taken advantage of his prostate state to aim some hard kicks at his head, and these had ended his life.

Much of the Jewish population, such as the Wunderlich and Süßkind and Beim families, or Samuel Adelsohn and his wife, had hunkered down in their homes. The atmosphere had already been electric since the day before and they had sensed a possible storm coming upon hearing of vom Rath's death; though none had anticipated the sheer strength nor viciousness of that night's tumult. They listened nervously to the commotion outside; prayed for mercy; made some effort to barricade the front door as best they could, or at least block the entrance with furniture, in case the mob tried to enter their building. Some, especially those living further out of town or in quieter sideroads, did not even find out the full extent of the destruction until the next day. They slept through the night to wake up in a different country, as they slowly came to realize.

All across town the hatred, both blind and blinding, was extending out like a communal psychotic madness. Sometimes the attacks were random and spontaneous but generally they followed a consistent pattern. They were led by the notoriously violent local SA thugs in their pristine brown shirts, often half-drunk, along with the quieter but more sinister NSDAP functionaries and officials, including SS paramilitaries and boyish Hitler Youth members. These were all passively supported during the pogrom by the police force and other municipal workers under strict orders not to interfere. Behind them came the crowds of typical townsfolk, enchanted and fascinated by the torment, dragging behind them their pent-up hostility towards Jews to let their resentment warm and flare up in the nightly chaos until they found themselves capable of those atrocious deeds that until then they had only dreamt of. Bringing up the rear came those passive onlookers who were genuinely shocked by but also extremely interested in seeing what was actually going on, the

Schaulustigen (gawpers). Wherever there was a blazing building, there was a brute to take pleasure in watching it burn down.

This pattern was a replication of what was happening throughout the entire Reich, including Austria. The main attacks had been carried out by the usual extremists, together with a loud but still very much minority segment of the town's population; but they more than made up for their sparse numbers through the fever and intensity of their hatred. Wherever Jews were known to live, stones and bricks and other heavy objects were lobbed through windows, sometimes bundles of fiery rags doused in petrol were thrown or fires strategically set. Some Jewish men were attacked and severely beaten, while families fleeing the horror, escaping from burning or smashed flats, were hurled at with insults or objects. Even small children were not spared from verbal abuse or flying spit.

The department store Kaufhaus *Fein & Günstig* (literally: 'Nice & Well-priced'), situated on the corner of Am Markt and Bäckerstraße, was one of the most emblematic businesses in Lüneburg and widely known to all as having a Jewish proprietor. The business, which had first opened its doors in 1932, offered a wide selection of goods such as clothing, fabric, pens and stationery, sweets, and general household items, including many chic products but all at affordable prices. There was a large variety of fresh groceries available, which customers could pick out themselves and assemble together in their baskets before paying, back then a novel concept, and a snack bar on the second floor that was very popular with both customers and the stall holders from the surrounding markets.

The store had been a tremendous success at first, until the Nazi Party came to power at which point SA activists began standing by the shop front. They occupied themselves with distributing yellow stars and inflammatory leaflets, taking photos of and intimidating would-be customers, holding up banners in the faces of passers-by that read, "*Kauft nicht beim Juden!*" (Don't buy from the Jew!) – and many former clients carried on walking.

With Lüneburg being made the capital of the *Gau* of East Hannover in 1937, the vigilant eye of the local NSDAP became ever sharper. The Schwartz family who owned the store, acutely feeling the pressure of the rising animosity that the Nazis were managing to stir up, and aware that things could and would only get worse as the months progressed, left almost immediately for Hamburg and the relative anonymity of a large sprawling city. The family head, Abraham Schwartz, continued to come to work every day on the morning train, however tough the times were proving to be, in order to oversee the business into which he had invested so much time and energy and hope.

The actual material damage in this case was ultimately less in terms of overall destruction than that inflicted on many other stores and businesses in the town. They were nonetheless considerable and carried the unpleasant stench of an escalating hostility. Windows had been smashed and merchandise dragged out, to be either looted or soiled; shop window mannequins and items of inner furnishings, that could be ripped out but were of no further use, were set alight out on the street. They flared up early in the night, with the mannequins in particular radiating a grotesque glow. The flickering light projected onto the surrounding facades of the central street, like a hellish show.

Some of the riot spilled down the Groebäcker Straße and accumulated around the square Am Markt, where *Fein & Günstig* was situated. Whistling and shouting, many were watching with grins the wrecking of the department store. One of the more brazen members of this group, riding high on the thrill of vandalism, was Cousin Carsten. He had left home that evening at around 21:00, after hearing of the developments on the radio and listening in on exchanged comments in the stairwell of his apartment block. He made his way to the centre, looking for trouble to watch and, perhaps, to participate in. At *Fein & Günstig*, which he always avoided – in his own words – "like the plague", he joined up with the gathering crowd, sensing that there would be fun to be had. As the first stones and other objects began to fly, he grinned and looked round for something for himself, his eyes alighting on a hacked piece of wood from the store interior. He picked it up and aimed it at a window on the first floor that had got through the first barrage intact. It struck and knocked out a pane of glass, forcing some closer to the building to step back and shelter from falling fragments of glass. He raised his arms in victory and gave a triumphant shriek.

The drone of hate rose in pitch and again the department store was pummeled with any hefty or sharp object that came to hand, including its own rubble, before some of the more audacious onlookers forced their way in and started to vandalize and plunder the extensive ground floor interior. Others contented themselves with observing with spite and schadenfreude how a successful business, that had been boycotted for several years, was now finally lain waste. Despite the size and ugly mood of the crowd, no fire was laid inside the premises. This was later said to have been due to the swift intervention of two of the town councillors, who contacted the police and, in a secret deal among themselves, arranged for any further damage to be kept to a minimum. "Just enough to give them a decent scare", one of them had apparently said. "Enough to frighten them off."

At the same Abraham Schwartz was arrested in his home in Hamburg, dragged out before a screaming family, and later sent to a prison not far from Berlin. During the week he was forced to spend there, heavy pressure was put upon him to sell the premises and business with immediate effect. The whole Schwartz family had been naturally terrified by the events of those two vicious nights. Eventually, and in the case of Abraham himself just in the nick of time to escape a second deportation order to a concentration camp, the family was able to obtain tickets and visas to enter the United States, to where they promptly fled at the end of November. The store was later 'aryanized', as so many businesses and other properties were in Germany: snapped up by shrewd buyers, usually with good connections to the NSDAP at local or national level, and then later re-opened 'under new management'. In the case of *Fein & Günstig*, by the very councillors who had ensured that the property was not too badly damaged that night.

The atrocities committed that night were innumerable: the endless savage beatings and even killings on the street, the arrests and deportations, the terrifying storm of verbal abuse and bullying suffered by families who then lost their homes and livelihoods; the manifold buildings – religious, educational, commercial, domestic – that were destroyed. But it was not only the actual violence that shocked. It was the sudden release of a deep-seated rancour that so many ordinary citizens had ostensibly been harbouring with augmenting intensity. It extended beyond the usual subdued hostility that many had already showed thus far, such as the refusal to speak to Jewish neighbours or let their children play with Jewish classmates who had once been good friends. Rather, it was the manifestation of an acute loathing that had crossed the boundary from regulated discrimination and entered into hitherto unknown terrains of civic violence. It seemed for some that the time was now suddenly ripe for a candid and unguarded revealing of their inner malice.

If any Jews had still held hopes that broader German society might resist the fundamentalist antisemitic ideology and the fuming ramblings of their political leadership, then these hopes were now dashed. More and more things were now being openly stated, including in the course of daily discourse, concerning the Jews that lived and co-existed among the general population; things that had often been thought but not clearly expressed, as if they had laid dormant until this point. These demonstrations of contempt for Jews were increasingly backed up by the media and arts in all their forms: movie pictures, books, cartoons, newspapers, radio broadcasts – they put up a united front in which abusive language and concepts were not only tolerated, but readily preferred. The mechanisms employed by the controlling authorities of the NSDAP had been waiting for just such an opportunity as the *Kristallnacht*, and they would lose not a minute in going to work. Those who had been reluctant to join in the malevolent tirades, were either tempted by group pressure into acquiescence or cowered into silence. Among the non-conformists, few were willing to risk their own well-being to stand up for moral principles; especially as it meant not just putting their own existence, but also that of their family, on the line.

"*Juden raus, raus nach Palästina!* – Jews get out, go to Palestine!" Inge heard the chanting as the unruly group passed by below. She felt half-delirious between the fever inside her and the clamour outside on the Rosenstraße. To make matters worse the monotonous repetition of this word 'Palästina' - she had never fully understood where it lay nor what its significance was – which made the whole brawling yet more bizarre and unnerving. She would have dragged herself out of bed, weak as she was, to part the curtains and gaze out of the window, to see with her own eyes the sight behind the din. But Josef slept on, blissfully unaware of the horror raging outside, instinctively snuggling up tight against his soft warm mother while his tiny body battled the virus spreading inside. She did not wish to disturb and wake him, so she listened for some minutes and, still feverish, drifted back to sleep.

At a national level the one particular building that was consistently a favoured target of the mobs' attacks was unsurprisingly the synagogues. All across Germany and Austria they were burnt in their hundreds while the gawpers looked on; some amazed, taking in the details with large silent eyes as if hypnotized by the flames and unable to intellectually denounce the depravity; others grinning and even openly cheering, lapping up every second; others still who were negatively shocked but at the same time consumed by curiosity as well as being afraid to interfere.

In the case of Lüneburg, the burning of the holy temple was not executed as was the case in so many other areas. The synagogue was situated just outside the main town centre, on a prominent spot by the river that could be approached from the street along a short paved path. Along with Lüneburg becoming the capital of the *Gau* of East Hannover the previous year, during the legislative changes occurring in 1937, the Jewish community had soon experienced the harsh ascendant antisemitism on their own doorstep, as the presence of NSDAP came closer to home. There had been a notable increase in vandalism, such as the smashing of windows or the appearance of swastikas daubed in white paint. Comments – some loud and directly threatening - were directed against the community, first and foremost from official sources such as the mayor's office or the *Kreisleitung* (local district administration). A growing sense of hopeless dismay set in deeper still, especially among people such as Samuel Adelsohn, with feelings ranging from quiet resignation to despairing abandonment. The synagogue's committee for administrative affairs had unanimously agreed to try to sell the plot of land upon which the synagogue had stood earlier that same year. The synagogue itself had naturally proved to be unsellable, but they had entertained no hopes of that anyway.

Sensing that only worse was to come in these times and this nation, the regular worshippers had emptied the synagogue of its treasured items – the Torah, the small library of books, precious drapes and ornaments – and hidden them at home. Their fears were prophetically well-founded. On this night a group of SA thugs entered the inner chamber to vandalize what they could find worth destroying, and to prepare to set fire to the whole building. But the true damage had long since been done, and irrevocably, for the building was by now an empty husk with most of its community scattered around the globe, never to return.

Just before they could get the blaze going, they were located by passing prominent NS functionaries who had second-guessed the probable plans of the younger and more zealous members of the Movement. These duly informed them that this was not necessary as the building was "no longer under Jewish control". The youths left swiftly, heading off to look for some fresh target, and the cold bare synagogue remained intact.

Nevertheless, and as the local Jews had already suspected, they would eventually be forced to tear down the building themselves, stone by stone, in order for the sale of the grounds to be legally binding. The grounds were then sold at a presupposed meagre price, well under any real market value, and taxed into a near worthless amount, to be held in practically inaccessible accounts.

Meanwhile, over in the street Am Berge, Arnold Schilling had been alerted by the noise outside to the events escalating on the streets. Together with his apartment companion Daniel Kaplan, he had imagined such a scenario in the wake of vom Rath's shooting. They had reckoned with the diplomat's likely death and the resulting reaction, not only from the Nazi leadership but also the wider layer of both extremist and casually antisemitic Germans. Listening to comments often dropped in shops and cafés and other businesses, it was impossible not to suspect that the worst was to come.

With a realistic sense of protection, Schilling told Kaplan that he was under no circumstances to leave the atelier. Kaplan was a signed-up member of the SDP (Social Democratic Party) and had furthermore been arrested in March of the previous year. He had been charged with causing 'Landfriedensbruch' (breach of the peace) during which he had "verbally insulted and physically attacked" a couple of SA recruits in their late teens (said youths had been handing out anti-Jewish leaflets outside *Fein & Günstig* and harassing people who wanted to shop there). Although the so-called "physical attack" transpired in court to be of a harmless nature, his Jewish ethnicity hindered his defence. After his arrest he was sent to KZ Sachsenhausen for four months, followed by a further two in Dachau, and upon returning to Lüneburg he had gone underground and was now staying incognito at Schilling's apartment.

Meanwhile, Schilling had ventured out to examine the situation up closer. With his own political background as a communist, he was used to keeping a low profile himself, thus staying away from large groups of crowds as well as police officers. The times were long gone when he would talk openly in public of his admiration for Ernst "Teddy" Thälmann and the KPD. He made a long and detailed reconnaissance walk around the whole town centre, slipping between groups of people and observing the worst hit buildings. He soon realized that there was absolutely nothing to be done. He had a small camera on him and on a few occasions was able to surreptitiously take some photographs of the damage; always with the utmost discretion to ensure that no-one observed him in the moment. He returned home at around 2:30am, having assembled a good idea of the extent of the damage and the principal targets of the riots, looting and assaults. (The photography would later be passed on to contacts he had in the German underground resistance, and from there sent to sources in the foreign press where they were published.)

In the very early hours, some isolated noises still raged but the town was generally quiet. Most people had not left their homes that night; some had looked out the window in horror. But the next morning they all encountered the full picture of the devastation as they walked out on their business. For the very early risers, pacing down the streets before anyone from the authorities had been able to come and clean up, it was a stupefying sight. The baker Norbert Weiß, for example, lived further north and away from the centre in the Langenstraße, well behind the Liebesgrund park. As usual he had gone to bed early and slept heavily. Now he looked in amazement as he walked at 5 am in the pre-dawn darkness by the *Fein & Günstig* store in the town centre. Some isolated fires were still burning around the city. There were sporadic plumes of smoke in the air that eerily caught the last light of the streetlamps. The pavements were littered with rubble and broken glass. Random items such as clothing or pages of books or toys lay around, abandoned. A few hardy autumn songbirds had begun to sing in a new day about to commence.

He continued on more quickly, his thoughts racing, when two blocks further down he smelt an acrid stench of burnt leather and other substances. Turning briefly into the side-street that ran by the church, he saw a similar site outside the burnt-out remains of the shoe shop there. At the front of the disaster, and with perfectly calm manner and gait, Frau Weingarten was picking up what was left of the stock and carrying it back inside, while her husband swept up the shards of glass, that were once the shop windows, into a heap. Weiß watched in silence and disbelief, aware, as many were, that Herr Weingarten had been a much-respected citizen; a fierce patriot who had been highly decorated in the Great War for services to his country. Weiß stared involuntarily at the scene and found no words to express his confused sentiments. He saw Frau Weingarten stoop over to pick up a smashed old clock, an heirloom that had hung behind her on the wall as she attended to her customers. She began to sob bitterly and he might have approached her in consolation, had not her husband looked up in that instant and caught his gaze. Herr Weingarten's stern face revealed no emotion, no anger or fear: it was an expressionless mask. Weiss felt intimidated by the situation and, reminding himself that he was already late for work, he nodded dutifully and hurried on without further ado.

Soon many others were also passing by on their way to work. They too experienced the same surprise, even stupor, but no-one stopped nor uttered a word to the tragic couple, still quietly clearing up the mess that had once been their livelihood. One person, a bus-driver surnamed Francke, later told his wife how he had found the scene horrific and wished in hindsight that he had gone up to the couple and said something to them, but that at the end of the day there was nothing *to* say. His wife did not know whether to agree or disagree, feeling her emotions caught between an intense sense of pity for the Jewish couple she knew well on the one hand, mingled with her still smouldering anger at the assassination of vom Rath on the other; a murder that she considered to be undeniably political in nature and indicating the beginning of "more extremist activity". In any case, and already having enough on her mind, she did not wish to debate this issue with her husband, and did not mention it again.

In the aftermath, many mixed feelings were experienced by the broader population; through astonishment, horror, shame, sadness, apathy, or the feeling of an exaggerated but understandable 'retribution'. There were many Germans – a broad majority of the population - who were in full and firm disagreement with the brutal nature of the attacks; but only a very limited number who felt indignant or brave enough to speak out about it in public. Most who are lions in their dreams, are hyenas come daylight. It was moreover for some as though a natural phenomenon, foreseen and half-expected, was taking its due course; one may just as well have defiantly stood up to the incoming tide of the North Sea during a storm, as to have contested the fury being lashed out at the Jews by the Nazi administration. The sense of righteous justice having been meted out was shared by too many in positions of political, economic or mediatic power to permit any semblance of protest to manifest itself.

For a small but increasingly visible minority it was a moment of extreme excitement to see this humiliation of the Jewish community; to see those considered to be an insidious enemy within, as much an existential threat as any nation they had ever combatted, to now be receiving their just deserts. These people would soon open up and become inured to notions of the cruelest atrocities that would have been unthinkable but a few years before. As the political and ideological leadership of the country had predicted and hoped, the moral floodgates had been opened; anything and everything was now possible.

There were a few brave voices that rang out in defiance, but all too few and these were quickly suffocated. Two girls of seventeen years, for example, spoke out at their school in Lüneburg the following day when the subject duly though briefly arose. They warmly criticized the attacks, even going so far as to refer to "depravity." Their teacher argued back, with equal heat, but the girls stood their ground; at least at first. She eventually threatened them with a thinly veiled accusation of 'treachery' (a loaded term for such young souls) to the Fatherland, telling them that there would be a report sent to the director that week concerning their insolent behaviour. In the course of the week they also received strict reprimands from their own parents, who were either incensed at their insubordinate attitude or terrified by the possibility of repercussions.

Such open criticism was generally exceptional. The local newspaper, the *Lüneburgsche Stadtanzeiger*, reported how the assassination of vom Rath had led to an understandable and justifiable reaction of anger - "in our otherwise so peaceful Niedersachsen" - against those (in plural, despite a singular assassin) who had committed this heinous act. The paper was also quick to point out that, despite the due anger felt by the crowd, the owner of *Fein & Günstig* - "the Jew Schwartz" - had been temporarily taken into police custody for his own safety. It also cynically added that although the store's windows and some of the furnishings had been smashed, from the contents of the store itself "not even a shirt-button nor a trouser-belt had been stolen". (Upon release Schwartz boarded the first train back to Hamburg where, in the harbour area, he obtained all the pertinent information concerning tickets for ship passages leaving for New York, even before heading home to his family's apartment. As soon as the visas had been issued, three weeks later thanks to a close friend and useful contact in the German embassy in the US, he purchased tickets on the first available voyage out and the whole family left for good.)

What was not mentioned in the newspaper was that a further eight local Jewish residents, all male and all holding prominent positions such as lawyers, company directors and businessmen, were taken into custody but not released. They ended up, together with a further 30,000 local Jews, in the *KZ* (concentration camp) Sachsenhausen. There they underwent weeks, in some cases months, of extreme maltreatment, incessant abuse and humiliation, death threats, near starvation. They were harassed and bullied into agreeing to a quick "sale" (which easily amounted to more loss than gain) of properties and assets, thus "encouraging" them to leave the Reich as quickly as possible. In the absence of these family heads, the frightened relatives immediately began a desperate race to obtain visas together with ship or rail tickets. They attempted to raise a minimal amount of money by selling off everything they possessed at ridiculous prices, while at the same time paying off the costly compulsory levies and taxes that the Jewish families were forced into in the wake of the *Kristallnacht*. Sometimes the sales did not produce enough for the escape, leaving families impoverished, homeless and more vulnerable than ever.

A few days later, vom Rath's body returned adorned with splendid wreaths to Germany, in a small black locomotive bearing a boldly painted white swastika on the front of the engine, flanked on the way by numerous gatherings of Hitler Youth, SA brownshirts and uniformed SS, who stood smartly and solemnly in line. They looked on in fierce silence as the small train with the cold but now warmly influential corpse chuffed past. The coffin was taken on a political tour of Aachen and Cologne before the occupant was finally buried in his home city of Düsseldorf. It was a widely broadcast ceremony in the cathedral there, filled with the pomp of patriotic speeches, flaming torches and swastika drapes, and a wealth of Nazi nobility headed by the Führer himself. Speeches were passionate and the man's death was heavily weaponized.

Inge later caught some of the news and felt uneasy at what she picked up, but did not wish for these events to penetrate her mind too deeply. She brushed the issue aside like an unpleasant cobweb hanging by her face. She had enough to occupy herself with, she reminded herself; between household bills that did not balance; her two children and the worryingly sickly nature of the second; plus the financial concerns that Gisela seemed to almost relish sharing with her as if the manageress were relieving herself in this way of a part of the general worry. Inge knew by now that the running of the Gasthaus was overboarding Gisela, but also that her own financial security and that of her family depended on its success.

She heard of the devastated businesses, of the names of some of the departed, of similar events in other towns and cities throughout the country. She perceived but she did not react. She saw some days later the broken windows and wrecked interior of *Fein & Günstig*; and she saw the charred remains of the little shoe shop near the St.

Nikolai church, that were being repaired as she walked by. She passed by the usual *Stürmer* display box, glanced at the angry posters and accusations, registered the bold caption that always made her shiver, '*Die Juden sind unser Unglück* - the Jews are our misfortune', but placed a barrier between this bleak reality outside and her own attempt at creating a harmonious domestic world for her family inside.

The night before, Volkmar and Martin had briefly talked of the possibility of another war; albeit as a distant and theoretical concept. She felt unnerved by the events unfolding, felt that the destiny of her family and herself and all those around her was becoming dangerously precarious, while she sought to keep it anchored on solid ground.

Inge would have drifted on in that bubble but two weeks later she saw Arnold Schilling during a visit to the printers, *Druckerei Fiedler*. He was talking, in hushed but heated tones to Herr Fiedler, owner and manager of the business, but she went over to speak to him all the same. Considering the plethora of patriotic bunting hanging out in the front window, and some inside too, she felt it wiser to greet with "*Heil Hitler*", unusually for her. Both Schilling and Herr Fiedler were brusque in their response, clearly not in the mood for idle chatter; she was practically sent packing despite her status of customer. She turned round and quietly left, making as furtive an exit as possible in order to save face. She was quite hurt, feeling the loss of the friendly atmosphere that she had always known and enjoyed there.

Nonetheless, she returned some days later and saw Schilling there again, though this time alone. Again, she was treated in an icy and off-handed manner, although in the end she put this down to his being busy and not wishing to be bothered at work. She asked instead after the normally kind and friendly Herr Kaplan who was nowhere to be seen for a long time, now that she thought about it. When she mentioned his name, Inge was met with an obfuscated reply from Herr Schilling, one that gave so little information with such a minimal use of language that upon returning home she could no longer remember a single word of what he had actually said.

Chapter 11

Although Inge did not actively seek him out again, in the following months there came two further encounters, as was to be expected in a small town. One occurred on a cold wet day in late January, when Schilling passed her by on the street. He acknowledged her presence but merely nodded before briskly walking on. She put that down to the miserable weather, in which no-one would wish to stand around bantering, and the damp atmosphere that had contributed that week to colds and flus in quite a few people around her.

But then again, on a crisp bright February day just three weeks later, their paths once again crossed and he once again showed her the cold shoulder. She had stopped in front of him, forcing a brief conversation, but the greeting he gave her was merely a few short, snipped phrases before making an excuse and moving around her in a wide berth. There was something clearly amiss and she lingered for a while, watching his retreating figure and wracking her brains for the reason that could have caused this rupture in their normally friendly relationship. The inquietude nagged her all day and continued to occupy her mind on the succeeding days too, following her round while she completed her chores in the cold and silent rooms of the Gasthaus.

She determined that she would have to get to the bottom of the matter if she were to have any peace of mind. She wanted to at least find out what she ought to apologize for, although she was unaware of having done or said anything in the world that could have possibly caused such offense. She decided she would go to his workplace at the *Druckerei Fiedler* printers once more, but stop briefly and try to arrange a private conversation with him.

Inge felt an inevitably unpleasant confrontation ahead, but she accepted without further ado her guilty part in the matter; her need to seek reconciliation was overriding. She acknowledged that this would only come through a conversation that she herself initiated and in which she visited him of her own accord. That Thursday Gisela and Inge had a heavy cleaning day at the Gasthaus planned, taking advantage of the absence of visitors. Corinna had come at noon to pick up her grandsons, whom she doted on, and take them to hers for the afternoon. Inge left the Gasthaus shortly after she had finished tidying up the restaurant area, at around 14:30 in a moment in which those around her were either absent or occupied. She reached the nearby printers in the Zollstraße in five minutes with a brisk nervous pace. There she entered and waited for a customer to be served, before asking the young sales assistant after Arnold. She was informed that Herr Schilling now only worked part-time, on Mondays and Wednesdays. Inge dreaded having to spend the weekend mulling over the issue at home and thought it might be a wise move to simply visit him directly at his abode. She had an inkling that he lived close by.

"I understand," she said. "To be honest, it was more of a private issue in any case. Doesn't he live just round the corner on the next street, Am Berge?"

Inge was in luck and the woman replied, "Yes, that is right. Number 3."

"Perfect. I can see him there. Thank you so much."

She walked two streets away and located his apartment block, seeing by his surname on the bell buttons by the entrance door that he lived at the top on the third floor. The entrance door was open, with someone upstairs being in the process of bringing down a number of goods, so she decided against pushing the button. Standing there, she nervously scanned the street and shops around, just in case someone she knew might catch sight of her. She had nothing concrete to fear but by now any activity or behaviour that had the slightest covert touch, automatically made her nervous and wary. She looked around as if examining the contents of the nearby shop windows, saw no-one she recognized and, in one swift stride, entered the building.

She climbed the stairs to the second floor and, while tightly gripping the banister, caught a sliver of wood on a rough section of it. She felt a sharp little scratch inside her skin. "Just what I need!" she cursed. She felt it was set to be a tough day. Though still confused as to Schilling's attitude towards her, she expected to receive a sharp reprimand from him, for whatever reason.

She rang but there seemed at first to be no sign of life. She rang again and still there was silence; but she decided to persist in her wait, thinking he may have had to rush out for some unanticipated reason and would then be heading back home. And she would be waiting outside his door for when he did. Her mind began to wonder off in idle speculation when she was momentarily startled by a scraping sound coming from the door. A couple of locks could be heard to click round and the door eventually opened to about thirty centimetres. Schilling stood on the other side, unshaven and frowning in bewilderment at the unannounced and unexpected visitor, saying nothing. Inge beamed at him and asked if she may come in, that there was a little something she wished to discuss in private with him. He said nothing, simply stared at her with a cold look. Feeling the sliver smart in her finger, she involuntarily raised her voice and snapped, "Really, I have no idea what I could have possibly done for you to treat me in this manner! It is starting to get very upsetting for me!"

Schilling, who wanted under no circumstances for heated and above all loud words to be exchanged on his doorstep, where they would echo throughout the stairwell, swept open the door and quickly ushered her into the entrance hall.

The door closed behind her and she had reached her goal; she stood in the apartment, finally face to face with Arnold Schilling. He remained doggedly still. In an uncharacteristically forthright manner, she said that she had come to ask him what she could have said or done to so offend him. He was taken aback at first and merely shrugged. She began to expound, narrating their last few encounters and his cold reaction, to which he mostly gave her sullen monosyllabic replies. She did not give up though, persisted in her speech, citing their previous friendly relationship. In the few longer sentences that she could squeeze out of him, he referred to her as Frau Grün and used the formal 'Sie' (for 'you') to address her, which further provoked Inge. She ignored it at first, until on the third usage she snapped. Please, she implored in the end, if he would just say what was on his mind and have done! Why he was speaking to her in this formal manner, as if she were a complete stranger? It was obvious that something was very much amiss and she only asked for an explanation so that at least she could know where she had gone wrong; and for her to duly apologize or at least offer an explanation. She had known him for so many years from around town, ever since they were children, and had seen him regularly as a client at the bakery, she stammered. She was in turn a fairly regular customer at the printer's shop, who always paid punctually, who had recommended his work to family and friends, who always put in a good word for him.

"And now to top it all I have a splinter in my finger and it is starting to sting!" she cried, worked up under charged emotions that seemed to bring her to an unusual irritability at times.

"Come in and sit down there," he said, indicating a chair at the end of his short hall. "I'll fetch a tweezer to pull it out." He took care of the offending object, removing it and even applying a little alcohol to the puncture in her skin to disinfect it.

She thanked him and gave him a disarming smile, that missed its mark, and repeated the reason for her coming. He further avoided the confrontation while she further pushed for an explanation, until through sheer exasperation he eventually barked, "Frau Grün, are you really that blind?" He looked about to give her the opportunity to respond until common sense and caution caught the better of him. He sighed and gave a terse shake of his head. "It is better that you go." He moved to stand up and accompany her to the door.

"Please, please. I really do not understand the whole situation. Please help me understand, I beg you!" She was becoming loud again; he flapped his hand in the air and shooshed her. She repeated, quieter and calmer, "I beg you."

The phrase came across as extraordinary in his ears, with an innocent purity so out-of-place in these times of intricate complexity and codification in all that was stated. He paused in his intention of getting her to leave. She repeated "please," and Schilling nodded and took her through the hall and into the living area, which functioned as his work area. A central oak table was home to a messy and nearly permanent pile of prints and scattered photographic equipment; a bookcase nearby seemed to house, on top of the actual books, a good deal of paperwork accounts, also in chaotic bundles. On the walls were clusters of photographs, some stuck around in uneven groups, others in neat rows. On the floor she noticed groups of sealed cardboard boxes, with addressed labels on the top and large numbers scrawled up the side, that seemed prepared to be delivered to a customer.

Inge took in her surroundings for a moment, then spoke first. "Arnold, first of all, could we please use '*du*' again like we used to. And please call me Inge. We have known each other for years and you always have. I really want you to understand that I have absolutely no idea what I might have done to anger you but you must believe me when I say that whatever it is, I earnestly regret it and wish to have the opportunity to apologize and make good in any way I can. So please call me Inge again, I would appreciate it so much."

He nodded with a brusque, "*Wie du magst*," (As you wish) - at least, as she had requested, he had returned to the informal '*du*'. He added, "I just ask of you that you do not make any scenes in public, like the one just now. Nothing dramatic or loud. Especially here in the stairwell. Remember, neighbours listen and they are the first to discuss and report anything that appears to be a little out of the ordinary. These are complicated times that we are living in and what I most want to avoid is giving people any reason at all to talk about me."

"But all I want to know is why you are avoiding me. There is nothing suspicious about that."

"Everything is suspicious to those who have a low view of humanity. However simple the matter. People will talk, and when that talk is then spread around town, it quickly becomes distorted."

Inge said, "In a small town like this, people will talk anyway, about everything, whatever you do. That is their way."

"That is true. But as long as they have absolutely nothing concrete at all to work on, I can live with that. But in the moment that people hear how you and I are having a loud discussion, then numerous ears will try the follow the conversation and make out the source of our disagreement."

"And that is a mystery to me!" she exclaimed. "Arnold, we used to be on such friendly terms. Especially after the wedding and those beautiful invitations that you designed for us. The whole family said how wonderful they looked. I recommended you to everyone I spoke to. And now you are so cold and distant and obviously I must have done something terrible to upset you, so all I ask is that you can explain it to me. Is that too much to ask?"

Schilling was exasperated and flared up. "Are you trying to tell me that you are not capable of perceiving what is happening around you? Are you really that blind? Sorry for having to express myself this way, but there is no other." The pause hung heavy in the air. "All these things are going on around you and you act as though you cannot see nor understand them. As though all these monsters were invisible. Seriously, you have not noticed that certain incidents have happened to certain people, that things are not the same as they once were?"

"But what has changed?"

"To begin with, some people are no longer here among us. Some people have disappeared, some businesses have burnt out or been closed down."

Inge looked at the ground and reflected; she pondered on the events that had taken place during the *Reichskristallnacht*; she recalled the cheeky smirking face of Daniel Kaplan, who had worked with Arnold at the printer's and whom she had liked a lot. She had not seen him in a long while and she began to form a connection. "You mean about…you are referring the Jewish question?"

He looked incredulously at her. "The Jewish *question*! What question could there possibly be? Can you hear yourself, is that what you really mean?"

She shrugged in incomprehension. "It is just a phrase that people say. When they talk about the Jews."

"But what question is there?"

She looked flummoxed for a moment and stuttered. "I cannot say that I know exactly. It is not something that I have studied in any depth."

"But you must have some kind of opinion. Everyone has opinions these days."

"I know what I read in the newspaper or hear in the radio. Or see."

"See where? As far as this Jewish question of yours goes, there is nothing left to see. They have even torn down the synagogue."

"Yes," she admitted, blushing. "I know about that. I did not think it was the right thing to do, but then again I also heard that they sold it themselves and gave the order for demolition themselves too."

"And why would they do that?"

"How can I know that? I am not a Jew."

"I think you do know why. I think you just choose to ignore the truth."

"I did not know that you cared so much about religion," Inge retorted, defensive and fully aware of the hollowness of her statement.

"I do not. I am an atheist."

Inge's eyes widened a little. No-one had used that word - which sounded so finite - personally to her before, although some in her new extended family had little or next to no interest in Christian worship. Most believed in God, she knew, as some invisible and unfathomable entity in the sky. They had sung hymns at school. They still celebrated the birth and crucifixion of Jesus; had a vague notion of sermons by lakes, of water and bread turning into fish and wine, of the walking on water and other such miracles. People recognized the symbolism of a cross as one recognized the symbolism of a swastika, but nowadays there was often no great fervour in their faith. It was a matter-of-fact backdrop to their existence, unlike the more pressing issues currently occupying their minds. Far more relevant and in the foreground were the issues of politics and ideology, rather than religion. As relaxed as the subject might be, an open confession of atheist identity was still a rarity for Inge.

Schilling continued, "But in this case it is not simply about religion and places of worship. The synagogue was a community centre for the Jewish population here, as in all towns and cities here in Germany. That community has been steadily disappearing from among us for the last six years. People have been selling their houses, their businesses, their possessions at ridiculous prices. A major reason is that they are not permitted to work in most professions, or they have had their private businesses boycotted. So they have to leave. They are driven out, because of their race, because of who they were born as."

"But nevertheless, they still leave of their own free will. That is all I am saying," said Inge.

Schilling half-closed his eyes and sighed. "Why do you do this? – play stupid games like this? You know exactly what I am talking about. I know that you know. And you know that, too. Why would you take me for a fool?"

"I did not come here to be insulted. And I have never said that you are a fool."

"Then why did you come here in the first place?"

"I said at the beginning of all this. I wanted to know what I have done to offend you. I really have no idea at all what I have done, but whatever it is, I would like to apologize for it and clear the air between us. It pains me to have such bad relations with people I know well."

"And that is exactly what I am trying to explain to you! As I said before, a synagogue has been knocked down, businesses have been burnt down, and the owners are gone. And yet still you are insensible."

"Here we go with the synagogue again. Did you have funds invested in it? I know nothing about it! What do I have to do with the synagogue?"

"You voted for Adolf Hitler and his party, I imagine."

She stared at him with a bitter pout. "No, never," she finally admitted after a pause. "But that is to stay strictly between us. Don't ever repeat that. I do not want certain members of my husband's or sister's family to know. Or anyone really for that matter. I always voted for the Zentrum party, every time until the last elections in 1933. Because of my father more than anything. We are Catholics and anyway, as I told you, I do not really understand much about politics."

Schilling reconsidered his approach. He was beginning to find the whole issue so taxing that he wished he had never answered the door. "Well, that is something positive in your favour."

Inge made her stance clear. "Just because I did not vote for him back then, does not mean that I do not support him now. I do think that the Führer has our best interests at heart and works to help the German people, and I have voted in favour in the referendums. You can see for yourself: unemployment is far lower than before. There is not the inflation as before to worry about. People are more prosperous, and generous. Crime has dropped." On the last points she was mostly parroting comments she had picked up at the Gasthaus.

Schilling gave a cynical laugh. "That prosperity comes from the state investing in a huge military machine that is about to go to war at the first opportunity. Which will be disastrous for all of us."

Inge said, "If that is your opinion, I can respect it. We all have our opinions."

"Then what, returning to my previous question, is your opinion on the 'Jewish question'?"

"Why does everything always have to come down to the Jews these days? I hardly even know any. At most just a few, and none of them very well."

"Probably better than you think. But in any case, I do. And that is the reason for my repeated question to you."

Inge huffed. "I suppose it is the question of what the future will be like. Between us and the Jews. That is all."

"And what will that future be like?"

"As long as everyone is happy and working in the job and the place that best suits them, that is the important thing. Many Jews have emigrated to other countries with high standards of living, like America or France. I am sure they are just as happy, if not happier there. If they have better opportunities there, for working and living in general, then I do not see there being a problem."

"You really do not see how they were forced to leave? How do you feed your family if you are no longer able to even exercise your profession? How can you feel comfortable in your apartment if the neighbours hardly speak to you, if the newspapers say you are a parasite, if you run the risk of a beating if you bump into a group of drunks?"

"Yes, things were said and done that were unkind. Extremely unkind in some cases. But I still do not see what that has got to do with me. I did not make any of these decisions. I do not have the capability of understanding why these decisions were made. That is a matter for the Führer and his government and all the politicians. I would not have said or done the same things, that is true. But I cannot change what has been decided by those above. All I can do is to try to be a law-abiding citizen and help to ensure that Germany remains a safe and prosperous place to live in. I just want to bring up my children to have good health, and a good education, and to have the possibilities of good life in a country that they can be proud of and where they will be successful. That is all I want and all I can do, nothing else. Surely you must understand that a mother always thinks of her children first."

Schilling did not answer, and Inge continued. "I know what many people are saying and doing, but you know…," she looked around uncertainly, as if fearing that the very sloped wooden walls of the old loft apartment might absorb and store her words. "You know that I have never said nor done anything to antagonize anyone, including any Jews. I have always tried to treat everyone with respect. I have never prejudged anyone because of their religion or their race or anything like that. I was very fond of Herr Kaplan, for example. I thought he was a charming and very decent person, and I know that he was a Jew. If I had ever treated anyone unfairly or grossly, for whatever reason, then I would certainly want someone to point it out to me so that I could learn from those transgressions and have the opportunity to apologize. I am not afraid to admit my mistakes."

Schilling remained silent. Inge did not know what more to say but neither did she wish to leave. She desired the right moment to arise in which she could express the right words: the words that she was sure would both simultaneously explain her own stance as well as close the hostile distance that had formed between the two. Her eyes, moving round the apartment, settled on a section of the wall that seemed to be devoted to a photographic exhibition. The theme was sport, athletics to be precise, and therein she was suddenly struck by familiar images. So much that she instinctively crossed the few steps over to that section of the wall to examine them closer. "I hope you don't mind me looking at these," she said half-apologetically as she stood before them. "It was just that I recognized them. They are from the Summer Olympics in Berlin, are they not?"

"That is correct," affirmed Schilling.

She peered closer and saw a muscular blond man supporting himself on parallel bars, legs clasped horizontally together while his solid arms held him up erect in the air, the handsome masculine face looking straight ahead with an impassive, almost indifferent gaze. Beside him, a Javelin thrower caught in the instant of preparing to launch the spear, one leg heavily bent with foot far behind, above it the arm with the javelin held backward ready to release the energy to propel the object; the whole body in its contortion a representation of built-up energy waiting for the moment of a controlled burst. Her eyes trawled across a series of photographs of athletes caught in crucial moment of physical exertion, as well as other images from the Games including a cameraman bent over, aligning the camera on a tripod to hold the shot; and three women athletes at a medal ceremony, in which alone the woman at the back collecting silver had her arm raised in a Hitler salute.

Inge gazed at it for a moment. "You cannot tell what any of those women are thinking. They have no expression on their faces, hardly a smile either. But you _can_ tell they are thinking a lot. Is that not strange?" she mused, moving on across the collection. Further on was a shot of the jubilant crowd at the Games, men waving arms in ecstasy while in a row below them a group of smartly dressed, middle-aged women with small hats and tight curls smiled bashfully into the camera. Then came a photo on a busy street in Berlin, of two white statues of naked women running, strong and strident, one holding a modest olive branch up in the air. Behind them, pedestrians walked by or stopped to stare. "I do not remember seeing that," Inge commented.

"That was a sculpture on display at the Pariser Platz. There were a lot of art shows and displays on at the time in Berlin. I think they were desperate to impress the visitors. Either way, too many gimmicks to really take them all in."

Inge looked at a photo of the Friedrichstraße in the central district, with its historic Prussian buildings displaying masses of bunting with swastikas, the image filled with pedestrians shuffling past, behind them the dense traffic of cars and the odd bus. "I remember that very well," said Inge with a chuckle. "I mean, I do not know if it was exactly that street and exactly from that angle, but I remember the atmosphere. The crowds, ah yes, from all over the world they must have come. The noise and the *Tamtam*, it was so exciting. And all the many vehicles. It was like the whole city were constantly in motion. As if it never got to rest, not even for a moment. The strange part of a big city though is when you are walking down the street and you realize that no-one here knows who you are. They have no idea about you at all and they do not even care. You could be anyone and they would just walk on by. So different from here! In a way, I liked that sensation, even though it was strange to think about it. I suppose, sometimes it is gratifying to be able to melt into the crowd where no-one can know who you really are." She turned to Schilling, who was also looking intently at the photography collection, wrapped in recollections of discussions with the author of the photos. "So, you were in Berlin at the same time, too?" she asked.

"No," he answered. "I wish I had been. These here were all taken by someone else. By a colleague."

"I see. Well, they are very well done. They certainly capture the feeling of the event. For a moment, I could almost feel that I was back there again." She sighed. "It was a marvellous experience. I can only hope to live it again in some way, one day."

Schilling shook his head. "I am afraid that such moments as these only ever happen once. They are doomed to singularity. You can only enjoy them while they last, then cherish the memories afterward. What is lived, is lived, and then over."

It seemed a strange comment of his, Inge felt. A little senseless really, as if the very capital itself of a country would not be capable of holding out its arms to its people again and welcoming them in the same fashion. Many things changed, she knew; people died and were born, family constellations changed, businesses came and went, technology was always improving. But there were some things, she was certain, that would stay the way they were forever; a grand city like Berlin unquestionably being one of them.

She made no comment on this but recalled something else that had been on her mind, that she had been meaning to address. "By the way, as I mentioned him just before, it occurred to me that I have not seen your friend Herr Kaplan in a while. I remember that he was very kind to me when we first placed the order for the printer's to do the photographs of the wedding. We talked about Berlin, and the good places to go and the things to look out for. That was just three weeks before Horst and I went to Berlin on our honeymoon but I never did see him again. I enjoyed our chat so very much that I wanted to tell him all about my visit afterwards." She frowned and looked back up at the photography. "That must be well over two years ago. Where does the time go?"

"I thought you knew what had happened to him," said Schilling coldly.

"No, I have no idea. Truly, I haven't," she replied urgently, fearing there was bad news to tell and beginning to understand Schilling's insistence on discussing the Jewish question. "Is he alright?"

"More or less. Seriously, you do not know?"

"No! There is so much going on in my family of late, and with the baby crying morning, noon and night, I barely have a moment to think for myself."

"Daniel, Herr Kaplan, was arrested and sent on to a concentration camp. This was a while after your wedding. He was sacked from the printer's shop first, then arrested some months later."

Inge looked at him agape. "And why did they arrest him?"

"He insulted, so to speak, the group leader of a bunch of those disgusting SA thugs that were handing out their flyers outside *Fein & Günstig*." Schilling was using a deliberately provocative language in order to gauge the reaction from Inge and so to know whether or not it would be wise to continue. He had always felt instinctively at ease with her, despite some of her crasser blunders today, but he wanted to double-check all the same. She maintained a concerned and angry frown. "You know the ones I mean? The Brownshirts, Lutze's gorillas. Those groups that stand outside the shop windows and go up to people who look like they might be tempted to go inside, to harass them."

"Yes," she said quietly. "I never liked them. Very rough, very uncouth people."

"A group of them were selling copies of *Der Stürmer*, right there by the entrance. And doing the usual intimidation tactics to make sure hardly anyone went in. In the end, one of the sales assistants from *Fein & Günstig* had to come out and ask them if they would move on, and naturally they refused. As it happened, Daniel had been going by just in that moment and ended up getting into an argument with the group leader. Just a kid too, probably barely twenty. Daniel told him he should find a job and work for a living instead of "rubbing shit in people's faces." Things soon got loud and angry. He gave the boy a sharp push that knocked him over. The others moved in but Daniel stood his ground and all they could do was bluster and threaten. You know Daniel. He is tall but not well-built or especially strong. But he has nerves of steel. So eventually the police were alerted and they turned up and put him in 'protective custody', as they call it. He sat there for a month in prison. After that he got sent to the concentration camp in Sachsenhausen."

"That is so terrible! And for how long?"

"All in all he was locked up for just over six months in two different camps. He did not get out until April last year."

"Six months imprisonment! Just for an argument with someone about a silly magazine. That is frightful. And where is he now?"

Schilling hesitated, not having intended to reveal nearly so much thus far; but also not having prepared a plausible lie nor wishing to unveil the reality to someone whom he regarded as a well-meaning but hopelessly deluded person. He considered a pretense of ignorance to be the only suitable answer. "I don't know." After a further pause, he added, "Safe, I imagine."

Inge read into the pause and began to form an idea as to Daniel's likely whereabouts and Schilling's role in this, as well as satisfying herself as to a probable explanation of Schilling's strange behaviour towards her. She soon convinced herself that it was not hostility but rather extreme caution that had driven him to shut her out. She had no intention of confronting him on that matter and saw best to play along for the time being. She felt she had grasped the truth, or at least most of it.

"I see," said Inge. "Well, at least I understand a lot more than I did before I came here."

"You do?" asked Schilling.

"I think I do, yes."

"I am asking because there are people who are being treated like animals, Inge. You are aware of this, aren't you?"

"You have said 'like animals'. Those are not my words."

"You think what happened to Herr Kaplan was appropriate?"

"Of course not."

"Or even worse, what happened last November."

"I have already said that I do not agree with all that has happened, nor the things that have been said and published. As to the November night you are referring to, that night I was in bed with a bad case of flu and looking after my eldest son, who was sick with the flu as well."

"Adolf?"

"Yes. I said, my oldest son. I only have two boys."

"And the younger one is called…?"

She paused before answering and found the pause horrendous, as if she would have reason to be ashamed of her own son. "Joseph," she eventually said. "He is still a small baby, just eight months old," she added.

"Inge, I have a lot of respect for you but I feel you are not being open and straight with me. I feel you know what I am talking to you about, but you do not seem to want to admit it, or even discuss it. It is like you were pretending not to understand what I am trying to say."

"Perhaps you have to be clearer."

"Perhaps that should not be necessary."

"Let me say this much," said Inge, seeking a clear route through this thick and potentially hostile terrain. "We are not politically minded people at home. I am certainly not, nor my husband either. We just try to get by as best we can. Without casting judgment or aspersions. We try to treat everyone fairly and we try to do what is best in life. For ourselves and for the people around us. For our families, and our neighbours, and the… community." She involuntarily dropped out that word that she found so inane.

"For the Reich."

"And naturally for our nation as well. Who would not wish the best for their own country?"

"That would depend on their intentions."

She smiled. "You are talking in riddles again, Arnold."

"Then let me be clearer. Have you ever asked your husband where he was that night, when the mob was smashing up people's homes and setting fire to shops? Have you asked him why he was stood at the top of a ladder and doing nothing while someone's livelihood was going up in flames, right in front of him? That is his job, isn't it – to put out fires?"

She was astonished, her primary reaction being near outrage that her husband and not herself should be the cause of strife: "So all of this is because of my Horst? What nonsense! Horst has always done his job. He is proud of his work. All his colleagues and his superiors speak very highly of him. I know that for a fact!"

Schilling waved his hand dismissively. "Oh, Horst and a thousand others. This policeman, that fireman, the other one next to them. A whole land of idle eyes and silent mouths. But seeing as we have brought up the subject, in Horst's case, I specifically watched him standing on a ladder, just over from a Jewish lawyer's office while it was burning inside. He and all the rest of them, his colleagues as you call them, they all did absolutely nothing. They were firemen who were standing there, watching someone's business slowly burning down to cinders. The work of years, gone in minutes. They only intervened when it was looking to spread to the other buildings around. But what am I telling you here? I imagine you know more about all this than I do."

"I...I don't think that was the case, to be precise," she stammered. "It couldn't have been."

"I tell you, I saw it with my own eyes. And why wouldn't it be the case?"

"Horst is absolutely committed to his work. There is no possibility of him deliberately letting a building burn down. Absolutely none."

Schilling smiled, "Why don't you ask him?"

Inge assured him that she would. She wished him good day and left with a brusque farewell, more born of her own insecurity than any show of defiance to the accusation.

After she had left, Schilling returned to the atelier window where he continued to examine the street below form his vantage point. At the same time, Daniel Kaplan opened one of the two inner doors, that of Schilling's bedroom where he had been hiding, and entered the main room. Schilling looked over at him to acknowledge his presence, then turned his attention back to the scene below.

Kaplan crossed to the window and stood beside him; also watched the street and its movements, head kept slightly away from the glass so as not to be seen by anyone looking up or across by chance. He too followed Inge's figure as she left the building and moved across to the pavement on the other side of the cobbled street, heading briskly along Am Berge on the way back home.

"Interesting woman," Kaplan murmured.

Chapter 12

Kaplan continued to scan the street below, watching the pedestrians come and go and the odd vehicle shunting around at the end of Am Berge street. He eventually commented, "That was very poignant, I thought. The way she mentioned me like that."

"She did seem touched by your memory. Do _you_ remember talking to _her_?"

"Vaguely. I always tried to be nice to all the customers. Even the ones that I could sense were thinking 'Jewish pig' inside. I always put on a smile. That is probably why I went so wild that day at _Fein & Günstig_ when they arrested me. All those gritted-teeth moments pent up inside, it was bound to boil over at some point."

"She knew who you are, but it did not seem to bother her in any way."

"Not all Germans are raving Jew-haters. In fact, I even think in the final analysis that the majority are not. The trouble is more how many of them simply swim with the current. They just want a comfortable life and let someone else do all the thinking. That was probably what happened with her husband. He was not going to go against the flow of the river that night and make a scene that might cost him his job."

Schilling said, "I regret now how I treated her in the past months. You cannot blame someone for the behaviour of a relative, even a spouse or a son. "

"Despite her evasive manner when you were talking, and her obvious obedience to the state and the Party, I do not think deep down that she is a bad person at all. In fact, she is very sweet in her own way and would probably be willing to help out." Schilling didn't answer and Kaplan continued, playfully thinking aloud rather than uttering any solid statements of intention or consideration. "I wonder, if she knew the actual situation and understood what was really going on. And naturally if she could be completely and utterly trusted. Not likely to blab."

Schilling looked over and shook his head. "It is not about whether she is a good or bad person, or sweet or malicious, or kind or hateful. Or even if she is trustworthy. It is about survival and survival here comes with being inconspicuous in public, and in being cold and unemotional towards everyone around you. She could be the most wonderful being in the world but if she does not know how to lie convincingly, she could be the most dangerous person in the world for us. Everything is based on deceit these days. And hiding. People hiding their thoughts, people even hiding themselves. Communication is now about undertones and innuendoes and only telling a partial truth. And that is not her way. She is an honest and simple girl."

"I know."

"Things are not what they once were. Everything has changed and everything is continuing to change. By the month."

"I know, Arnold."

"Yes well, you of all people should know that."

"I do, I do. I have learnt my lesson. As you yourself have said, six months of hard lesson."

After a pause, Schilling went over to the central table in the atelier, sat before some photos lain there and began to browse through them. He said, "Trust is not easy these days, Daniel. People are living more and more in fear. It is natural that no-one is willing to take any risks, and that people think of their families and themselves first. Even losing your job could be a minor disaster for some families."

"I wonder what her family is like - do you know them?" asked Kaplan, still standing by the window and observing the street.

"Not very well. Her husband is a firefighter called Grün. Their families are pretty modest as far as I know, no-one special. She has a brother who works at the *Vereinsbank*. She and Grün have a little apartment together, right beside the *Gasthaus Sonnenschein* which her sister runs together with the brother-in-law. So there might be some money there. It was passed down to him by his parents but I have heard it is her sister who rules the roost."

"*Sonnenschein*," mused Kaplan. "Isn't that the big brick building on the Rosenstraße, about halfway along, opposite a little boutique?"

"That is the one."

"Yes, I know which one you mean. There is something I have never liked about that place. Not that I know anything about the current owners."

"Her sister's husband is called Landeck. I do not know his first name but his father, the former owner of the Gasthaus, is Volkmar Landeck. I think he used to be a councillor."

"Landeck, Landeck", Kaplan pondered. "Mm, I think I know who he is. And if it is him, he is quite the Party enthusiast."

"His niece works at the *Städtisches Klinikum*, in trauma surgery. She is one of the head nurses, I believe. Bohlen is her married name. And I know she is heavily involved with the *BDM*, does voluntary work there as an instructor."

(Schilling actually knew a good deal about Edeltraut Bohlen, and more than he was letting on. He had a naturally inquisitive nature and viewed the meticulous recollection of information regarding the town's population as being of vital importance to his existence in its current form. He had attended a few of the local *Judenauktionen* (Jews' auctions) out of curiosity, in which the property of fleeing Jews was auctioned off, invariably fetching attractively low prices for the local vultures. Strangely enough, it was habitually the most fervent Nazi that was happy to bid and buy up the goods that had once belonged to the 'enemy'. Schilling had recognized Edeltraut and Bernhard at a couple of these auctions, where they had acquired furniture and jewelry; they never showed any interest in the artwork on offer, which was viewed as 'decadent' by most attendees.

All the same there seemed no point in mentioning this subject, with its sickly and parasitic nature, at this moment in time to Kaplan; and moreover, he did not want to stain Inge's family any further, aware it could only reflect badly on her.)

Kaplan laughed out loud. "The *BDM*? Good grief! - can you imagine me having an accident and waking up to find that angel of death assigned to my bedside? And she would be the kind to sneak a look in the hospital pajamas before injecting the patient with an appropriate dosage of medicine. Ugh - no thank you."

"I think she would have already guessed as much by your name alone without having to proceed down to your penis," Schilling laughed, knowing the sexual vanity of his friend. "Seriously, though. I do not know a lot about the family. Maybe we should not presume too much."

Kaplan shook his head. "From what you have told me so far, it does not look very promising."

"It is a rather distant family connection from her to the old ex-councillor and the nurse. Even siblings or parents can vary very widely on political and ideological stances."

"Yes, but it is that Landeck connection that I do not like. His son is her brother-in-law after all. And if she lives right beside that Gasthaus, then she and her sister must be quite close. What is the connection of Inge to the Gasthaus? Perhaps she and her husband have a financial stake in the business, or perhaps she even works there."

"I have no idea, but I can find out. From the sound of things, she would like to keep the friendship with me ticking over in any case."

"She may want to commission some work," said Kaplan, and leant to an angle to get a better look at the street below. "That is Brunner down there, Christian Brunner. Works at the *Alte-Raths Apotheke* [chemist's]. He used to live next door to me when I first arrived here and we were always quite friendly. At least until the Nazis came to power. You know, he just stopped talking to me, almost from one day to the next. I could not believe it. He would even cross the street just to avoid walking up to me and having to ignore me to my face."

Schilling reflected inwardly, upon recalling that he had done the same with Inge, but said nothing.

"And I never really did understand why," Kaplan continued. "Is that what politics can do to a man? Alter his whole being in that way, send him on such a radically different course. You know, he had such a good character. He was a really decent person inside. Generous, thoughtful, altruistic. It must have been so powerful a force to change even a man like that. How we underestimated it all, yet the signs were clear. Here in a shop window suddenly appeared a bunch of little swastika flags, then another. The Wissler's stationery shop, an insurance office in Bardowicker Straße, the butcher next door. When the printers hung up his Nazi bunting in the window too, I realized why I had been fired." He stared out at the street below, watching the comings and goings which began to take on the rhythmical movement of foraging ants. He felt distant, apart from this very land that he had grown up in; and yet, much as it terrified him, he was reluctant to depart from it.

Daniel Kaplan had come from a humble background of working-class Jews from Frankfurt. His father, Samuel Kaplan, had been employed as a warehouse worker at the *Karstadt* departmental store; his mother had been a housewife and brought up seven children. Daniel completed his education up to the level of *Abitur* ('A' levels) in a top *Gymnasium* (high school) in Hannover and dazzled with excellent marks. Enthralled by the field of photography, he had gone on to complete further studies in this growing specialist field at the *Städelschule*, the renowned institute for visual art in Frankfurt. From there, he went on to complete an apprenticeship with the popular magazine *Das Neue Frankfurt*. His work thus far had, for commercial reasons, concentrated on photography of architecture and landscape. His passion though was for portraits and he hoped eventually to set up his own business in this field.

All plans were cut short by the Nazi's inexorable rise to power and the subsequent gradual upheaval of the Jewish community there, including his own family. His father, along with some other Jewish colleagues, was abruptly fired from *Karstadt* in March 1933, in the wake of the election result. As early as May that year there were the first anti-Jewish riots. Reading the writing on the wall, most of his direct family had soon packed up and managed to emigrate to Palestine within eighteen months.

Daniel himself had resisted what he regarded to be pressurized expulsion, feeling fully German inside and knowing he would have no affinity whatsoever with what he strongly suspected to be the stark, arid, and perhaps unpleasantly primitive surroundings awaiting them in Palestine. He had heard of Schilling's atelier in Lüneburg in late 1934, through the friend of an old classmate. He and Schilling arranged to meet up informally, in the bar *Algier* which was notorious for being a covert meeting place for left-wing and other anti-Nazi clientele, including agitators. Schilling, fiercely anti-Nazi and with communist leanings, was both impressed by the young's man obvious talent as well as feeling a deep sense of pity for the harassment and discrimination being suffered by him and countless other Jews. In his own circle of acquaintances and colleagues there were cases of acute hardship that he was personally aware of. He offered him a part-time unofficial job as assistant, modestly paid but with the prospect of commissioned work once he had gained more of a name for himself; as well as discreet accommodation in the tiny apartment adjoining the atelier. For Kaplan, it seemed to be the perfect set-up to bide the time between the current wave of political anger and a hopefully brighter future. Moreover, he found Lüneburg itself to be a charming and inviting small town and was happy to move there in the spring of 1935.

At first, he had felt confident that his gut feeling of optimism had been well placed after all. He had even travelled to the Olympics Games in the summer of 1936, stayed in Berlin and taken innumerable photographs for a project: pictures of officials, athletes, tourist visitors, shopkeepers, everyday Berliners enjoying the general fuss and international attention, all in natural poses and unaware of being photographed. His work showed clear talent and Schilling went on to publish and sell the project as a photobook, with reasonable success too and it made a healthy profit for both the young men.

In the space of just a few years, circumstances had rapidly deteriorated. Nothing had improved politically, while in all areas of life things had got far more difficult. Then came the incident outside *Fein & Günstig*, with the ensuing arrest with rounds of beatings and kidney punches, followed by six months of hard labour in Sachsenhausen and Dachau. Such was the hatred for Jews, at the bottom of a long pile of undesirables, that he was staggered by what he experienced. Finding himself released, he returned to the sanctuary of Schilling's apartment. Some months later came the *Reichskristallnacht* and with it another sharp slap in the face and a final wake-up call. From that point onwards Kaplan decided to lie low and left the apartment only on rare occasions. He stopped taking care of his appearance and one day, in those last months before the war, he saw how he had ceased to be that self-assured and dashingly handsome former self. Fear and anxiety had made him curl up inside himself; he walked hunched over, his hair and upper face hidden under the shade of a fedora, his lower face tucked inside the upturned and full collar of a trenchcoat, despite the mild weather. He engaged in no more idle chatter at the grocer's or bakery and his formerly outgoing personality was reduced to a fearful stony silence. All the same he was determined to weather out the storm, however hard it rattled at the window. With an unbridled, some might say foolish optimism, he was sure that Hitler's reign would be ultimately a short-lived one; that the threatening horizon ahead would break into a clear sunny normalcy once his German neighbours came to their senses and realized that they had in fact signed a contract with the Devil. It had taken time for him to ascertain that that contract was Faustian and without an opt-out clause; that it would probably have no termination outside of the twin extremes of total subjugation of all else around it, or total destruction of itself. For war would come, must come - of that he was now horrifically sure.

Schilling went to the kitchen to fetch a couple of apples and returned over to Kaplan by the window, giving one to him and biting into the other. "Do not spend so much time looking out. You never know who might look back up."

Kaplan turned round to his old friend and turned his back on the window. He said, "There is a very thick line between discretion and paranoia, we need to respect it." He grinned at him before biting into his own apple.

"Even so," muttered Schilling with his mouth full. "In these times paranoia is not an unhealthy attribute. Have you never had that sensation that someone is looking at you, like a prickling on the back of your neck, and you turn around suddenly and someone is doing just that?"

They munched in pensive silence. Schilling returned to the table and Kaplan moved back a step but turned round to look out the window again, unable to resist following the diurnal scenes below. Schilling began turning over the pages of an album of photography depicting winter rural scenes and wildlife in the snow.

Kaplan looked at the waning apple with tooth marks and said, "What I would have given at Sachsenhausen for an apple. On so many occasions."

Schilling looked up and said, "I can imagine," then shook his head. "No, what a stupid thing to say. Obviously I cannot imagine."

"Sometimes I spent whole hours fantasizing about food before I went to sleep. It became an obsession. At least until the rations were reduced even further and I felt real hunger like I had never felt it before. That is one of the reasons I am getting so scared, Arnold. I am so scared of it all happening again, only for even longer. Next time will be much worse, I know it will."

"That next time is precisely what we are trying to avoid," said Schilling softly.

"But there will be a next time. They are starting to take people away for any reason they think up. That last time I was stupid. Opened my mouth when I should not have. Made it easy for them. But now! They are demonizing Jews at every turn. What on earth have we done to deserve this level of scorn? It is monstrous, but more than monstrous it is simply incomprehensible."

"The Nazis need a *Feindbild*, the image of an enemy. A concrete image of someone toward whom they can get the population to level their anger and frustration," said Schilling. "And where there is no enemy, then one must be created. At a domestic as well as an international level. Jews are a convenient scapegoat. They always have been."

"You do not think that the situation will improve in the slightest, do you? Be honest."

"No, no, I do not," answered Schilling morosely. "There will be war before that happens."

Kaplan lowered his eyes in resigned sadness; sighed, considered. "All Jews are trying to get out of Germany by now, you have said so yourself."

"Those that can, they are doing so. Those with clarity of vision and judgment, with opportunities and connections, with the financial means, and the young. The tough ones and those with clout, they are going or already gone."

"And the fervent Zionists, too."

Schilling laughed. "I cannot see you going out to the countryside to spend so many months in a Hakhshara, Daniel. And with your very skeptical view of religion, that is not really going to work out so well for you. Unless you are willing to unashamedly lie and forsake beliefs, which we all have to do in the end when the situation calls for it. Survival is never built on principles. Perhaps you should consider it as a remote option at least."

Kaplan grinned back. "You know, I hardly understand a word of Hebrew. Can you imagine me trying to keep up with all the songs and story-telling like I was back in school again? Ha! Even if that were an option, and I fear it is becoming much too late for that in any case, I would not be seen as a good candidate for *Alija*. Apart from which, they are often turning those ships heading to Palestine away. The British are becoming stricter about their quotas and how many they are willing to let in. No, I would end up in Uganda, or Mauritius, or wherever it is they are trying to get rid of us. That is, if I were lucky."

"You get too easily gloomy and depressed, Daniel. One minute you are king of the world, the next you see no way out. I have heard that Adam Wunderlich is leaving soon. He has visas for his wife and daughter and himself, and they have managed to purchase a passage to New York for all three. I know for a fact he sold the last of his oil paintings on the quiet, to pay for it all."

"I am glad for them," he said. Then, after a pause, "They know there is no time to be wasted, and I should have known that too!" he snapped impatiently as he joined his friend at the table. "People are selling everything, at no matter what price. Selling possessions at give-away prices; losing fortunes, small and large. Selling up and just getting away to wherever they can: America, Canada, Palestine, France, England, Australia, Argentina, you name it. Wherever in the world that is offering a possible refuge. And it is not just the heads of large families. I have heard of single young men, even women, with good or average salaries, saving up, sorting out visas for siblings or parents, managing to make the leap. It is an exodus."

"We have been through this before," said Schilling. "You have a criminal record. You have known and recorded political views as a Social Democrat. As if being Jewish were not problematic enough in itself. There is no legal way you will be able to get out of the country. There is no official route out for you. And if they catch you trying to leave illegally, you will be arrested and there will be no second chance."

"I would never reveal where I have been staying, you know that. Even under torture."

"That is not the point. And that is not the reason I am saying this! I am simply trying to appeal to your common sense."

"So, the only option is to stay here in hiding, like a mouse between the skirting boards? Hardly ever leaving this apartment, living only between the shadows and the dark."

"For the time being, I would say yes. Yes, that is your best option. Perhaps your only option."

Kaplan said, "I wonder how long this will all last."

"A thousand years if you believe the propaganda." Schilling pursed his lips and looked mischievously over his glasses.

"Aha," smiled Kaplan, putting his chin in his hands and smiling again at Schilling. "Perhaps that is not irony. Perhaps that is what you really think. This whole Reich, this great Aryan *Großdeutschland* (Greater Germany) run by a hysterical Austrian. That it has the potential for a long-term future?"

Schilling looked on in thought, then shook his head. "No, I believe it is ultimately doomed to be an ephemeral regime. I like to think that at some point, in the hopefully not too distant future, I will live to watch it collapse in on itself. But then again, at this precise moment in time, it seems so firmly-rooted, so well-established, that I cannot see how. And most certainly not, when."

"First, Austria; then this 'protectorate', as they are calling it - Bohemia and Moravia. For them it is a dream becoming reality. Year by year, this Reich of theirs is getting bigger and stronger. Hitler has them all on a leash, you know: Chamberlain, Daladier, probably even Stalin too. Mussolini, he has by his side, sitting to attention like an obedient Rottweiler. He leads them all round the garden, makes them dance to his tune. He is a clever bastard, is Adolf. I will give him that."

"That reminds me. Be careful when you are listening to the radio, Daniel. Always keep the volume down to a minimum. I know the walls here are quite solid, but all the same, if any of the neighbours think they can hear you listening to the wrong frequency, they would report it to the police in an instant. The other day it was quite loud when I came in."

Kaplan nodded. "Of course. I am sorry. I will be more careful next time."

Schilling took up another photo album and began nervously flicking through the pages.

Kaplan said, "You know, it is only a matter of time before they want the Polish corridor too. This is not going to end with the Sudetenland. There is no way that it can. How can they even think it will?"

"I imagine it is more about hoping than thinking," answered Schilling. "The British, the French, everyone - they want to avoid war at all costs. So far, it has worked. The agreement was only made last autumn and since then we have had six months of near perfect harmony. Many are saying on the street that Hitler has everything he wants."

"Apparently the Poles want Slovakia."

They both laughed, bitterly and unintentionally. In such times of great geopolitical shifts, that could lead to the most surreal statements and ambitions, there was little left to do but to laugh.

"You know," said Kaplan, after a while, "That must be the reaction of Hitler when all these territorial queries come in. He and his generals and his ministers, they must fall about laughing."

Schilling said, "Maybe it is all true what they are saying. Maybe he is content and has everything he wants. Maybe he really has no intention of moving forward any further."

"No," Kaplan shook his head. "It is what I was just saying, it is the Polish corridor that is on his mind. They are always talking about Danzig on the radio. In those official broadcasts from the Party. It is like an obsession. Connecting back to Danzig and East Prussia, making the Fatherland whole again."

"But it does make economic sense. I mean, from a simply objective, mercenary viewpoint."

"I do not think that risking another major, possibly global, conflict makes much economic sense," retorted Kaplan.

"It does if you win. That is why countries go to war in the first place. And Hitler has been investing in armament since he came to power. There is no point in investing in a business and then being too afraid to try out your goods."

"Sometimes I wonder…," began Kaplan, but stopped. When one thought of Hitler, one always wondered what was really on the other side, behind the impassive wall. He was difficult to comprehend, but very easy to love or fear.

Both were silent for a moment. Schilling said, "Far be it for me to state the obvious to you, but if you thought it was difficult to leave the Reich now, imagine what it would be like if war really does break out."

Kaplan nodded grimly, "Near to impossible." He swung his legs round and got up, idled once more over to the window to watch pedestrians and their routines below. After a while he commented. "The worst thing, well, one of the worst things, is not knowing whom you might be able to trust, even just to a certain extent, and whom you never could. Whenever I have been out on the street which is, as you know, very rarely now since Sachsenhausen and Dachau, I look at some of the faces passing by. Not staring, just quick glances. Taking in as much information as possible before looking back down at the pavement. And in that face, I wonder how you can tell if they are a potential friend or foe. Is there something in the turn of their mouth, in their eyes, the way they are looking around them, their clothes, their voice? How do you tell who are the ones who really follow their Führer all the way? How can you see someone's loyalty to a regime in their face? Or their hatred of you?"

"You can eventually. But you need time and some degree of intimacy. People are experts at hiding their true emotions. Instinct teaches us distrust."

"And fear of the other. It is strange, but the Nazis fear us more than anything. It is almost like a phobia for them. Very tribal. In fact, I think they fear us more than we fear them."

"It's about more than just fear," said Schilling. "For the Nazis, the Jewish question concerns their sense of purity and their disgust at the impurity of others. They are trying to base their ideology on the notion that they are a pure race, and that with that purity comes goodness. So, they depict Jews in contrast as dirty, as corrupt and conniving, parasitic, and most importantly diseased. They state that this disease is potentially contagious. If you work with Jews, or finance them by buying their goods, or let your children play with them or - heaven forbid - socialize with them or marry them, then you too will be soiled, you too will be infected. This is how they direct their propaganda. To bring out that deep-rooted disgust that lurks in all people, that disgust of filth and impurity. To provoke an automatic reaction of repulsion, as in the way a person instinctively fears a rat or a cockroach. Because they are dirty and they spread disease. It is that same feeling of revulsion. There is an old saying that evil can only see evil all around it. That is what makes it evil in the first place."

"And you can see that revulsion in someone's face? Because I can't."

"I think I can. I have tried it out a few times. You only have to say the word 'Jew' and people react instinctively. You see in some that furrowing of the brow, the way the lips turn down slightly. There is an involuntary tightening of the frame. Sometimes a sharp intake of breath through their nose. Even if they say nothing, they look like they are preparing for a conflictive situation."

Kaplan widened his eyes and chuckled. "I can tell you are a born photographer, Arnold! You have an amazing visual sense. I envy you."

"I have also had the luxury, not being Jewish myself, to talk about Jews openly to people around me. That is a luxury that has given me the opportunity to observe."

"All the same, it is a magnificent talent. And what do you say when the subject comes up, I mean, of Jews?"

"Usually something vaguely negative, without being specific. Something that will remove any potential suspicion that I might be too sympathetic and thereby a suspect person."

"That is the wisest thing to do."

Schilling considered a recent incident. "Frau Dorf, who works at the bakery, said a few weeks back something about her Jewish neighbours leaving. To be precise, she said her neighbours had already left last month and when I asked why, she said, "Well, they are Jews, you know." That in itself was the whole explanation. But the shrug she made, her body language. And the tone of voice: "*Juden*", falling sharply in pitch, in that deprecative way. There was a woman standing right behind me, who is a good friend of one of the neighbours in this apartment block. I said, "Everyone gets their just deserts in the end," and Frau Dorf was handing back the change by that point anyway. It was ambiguous, and all I could think of to say. I turned round to go and saw how the neighbour's friend was nodding in agreement. But it was that resigned, wistful look, with raised eyebrows, as if to say, 'Well, what can you expect?' She smiled at me as I went past her. I know it was the right thing for me to say but I did not feel good when I got home. I could not help but feel cowardly myself, angry with them."

"In their case it was primarily comradeship. Both Frau Dorf and your neighbour are aligning themselves to what they consider the right cause, the just cause. They are parroting the words of the Party in public to show they are all on the same side. And of course it was the intelligent thing for you to do. That woman will perhaps repeat the incident to your neighbour and your neighbour will know that both she and you are on the right side too. Do not chew this over in your mind for another minute. Neither of us want the Gestapo knocking on the door here one evening. But what I am wondering is, and I understand that you were being deliberately ambiguous, do you believe that could be true?"

"Believe what could be true?"

"What you said there, that everyone gets their just deserts."

"Of course not! It was just a phrase to pass time in an exchange of words. It has no meaning." Schilling looked bemused for a moment. "Although under communism we all would, *that* I can say. In a positive, not brutal way. But with the system we have now, it is the complete opposite. True value and merit sink to the bottom, while all that is vicious and ugly floats to the top."

"No, I meant something different. I meant that perhaps the Nazis will get their just deserts."

"You mean, if they go to war?"

"Exactly. You said before that would be the only scenario in which the system could change; in which the Nazis might lose power."

"A major war, like the last one?"

"They are preparing for one, Arnold. I am convinced."

"I know what some are saying. But I prefer to think that is all just bluster. That is Hitler's way. Shouting, blustering, threatening. Then just plodding on, business as usual."

"But what if he is not blustering this time? What is he does trigger another international conflict?"

"If that happens, then this time it will be much worse. The weaponry is so much more advanced. It would be a massacre of huge proportions in the end. Unimaginably so. Of civilians, too."

Kaplan paused to consider. "I think he wants two wars. An internal one and an external one. The internal one has already begun: the political opponents, Jews, artists, other undesirables. The external one will follow on soon enough."

"And where and when will this take place?"

"When, I don't know. But mark my words: he wants the Polish corridor back and he wants Danzig." The falling twilight had started to darken the world beyond the window; there outside, the shadows of buildings were stretching along the pavements and streets. Later Kaplan said, "You know you were telling me how Braun's operation in Hamburg had uncovered some stolen passports? Do you think you could falsify a passport, with my details, and take a photo of me to insert into the document?"

"Depends what kind of passport. It would have to be a language in Latin script of course, not Cyrillic or anything different."

"I was thinking, Italian."

Schilling considered for a moment. "I should be able to, yes. I have a contact that sells blank German *Ausweise* (ID-documents), and passports, too. He would probably know how to get an Italian one."

"How much?"

"Well, a blank German *Ausweis* comes in at 10,000 Reichsmark."

Kaplan whistled softly. "Good business, eh."

"The best. War always has good commercial benefits. Especially where subterfuge is involved. Why do you think I became a communist?"

"Arnold, I don't have ten thousand. Nowhere near that amount. And you know that."

"That is not an insurmountable problem. Remember, I work in this field and can pay back in kind. I have good contacts to the black markets in Harburg and Hamburg, plus I still have a stack of *Lebensmittelkarten* (food ration cards) from a friend in Harburg and they are worth a small fortune. Do not worry, I can sort this out for you. I will need a little time but I will take care of it."

Chapter 13

If she had hoped to clarify her thoughts and clear her conscience through the unusual measure of visiting Schilling at his apartment, Inge could not have been more mistaken. Once back home, she was far more plagued with inquietude than before heading out. She heated up the kitchen stove, chopped and peeled some vegetables, finding at least some calm in these activities from the tossing storm of confusion in her head. Gisela had been upstairs in the guest rooms, dusting them down and cleaning the bathrooms; she came down now that it was time to prepare the evening meal for the family. It was a quiet time for visitors, both to the hotel and the restaurant, as typically in February. The weather was shifting to heavy rain outside and they could hear the initial tinkle of drops turning into a harder downpour; that would further impede potential diners from leaving home and might leave them with little more work that grey evening.

Gisela came into the kitchen and told Inge that Adolf, Joseph and Erich were with their mother Corinna. She would bring them round at six so that they could all have the evening meal together. Katrina and Siggi were attending their new NSDAP-organized evening groups, *BDM* and *DJV* respectively.

"I have peeled enough carrots and potatoes and the chopped onion is over here," Inge told her.

"Perfect," said Gisela. "I will get started with the beef now. It should be ready in an hour and a half." She frowned. "You do not look well. Is everything alright?"

"I thought I might just go over to the apartment and have a lie down for a while, before everyone arrives. Horst should be home soon too."

"Yes, of course. Everything here is under control," her sister insisted and sent her off.

Inge left and, after walking the few metres up the street and going up to their apartment on the first floor, was able to rest for nearly half an hour before Horst arrived. Still laying on the bed, she explained the arrangements and began to enter into all the details in a dull voice: where the children were, what she had chopped up for dinner, Gisela preparing the beef, when the meal would be ready, how her mother would be coming at six. As she finished the list, she got up off the bed and stood up.

It was a strangely banal monologue, her husband thought, and he noted her downturned lips and cold manner. He frowned and came towards her, softly asking what the matter was. He made to hug her, as he always did whenever he saw his wife looking weary or upset, but she moved nimbly away from his open arms and took a few steps round him until she was standing on the other side of the room, in front of the dresser. "I will be direct. Horst, is it true that you did nothing that night to help those people and put out the fires?"

"What night?" asked an incredulous Horst.

"You know what night!" she answered, raising her voice and making him grimace in bewilderment.

"I don't, Inge. I swear I don't," he repeated his innocence, beginning to find the whole questioning deranged. "What on earth are you talking about?"

Inge breathed in deeply to try to calm herself, knowing that she had difficulty expressing herself when under emotional strain. She paused to clarify her thoughts as Horst looked on in mystification. "I am talking about last November, after that diplomat got killed in Paris. You must remember, when everyone was out on the streets, and shouting and throwing stones. Throwing stones at the Jews' shops and houses. When they smashed up *Fein & Günstig*. They even destroyed Frau Weingarten's little shoe shop and set fire to it."

"Well, what about it?" he frowned, moving from baffled to defensive as he caught her line of accusation. "What has that got to do with me?"

"Horst, that poor couple was completely ruined. They are in their fifties and with no chance of rebuilding their lives. I heard about it afterwards, about all the things that happened. But I thought they were just the usual people in town who are always kicking up a fuss. You almost expect something like that from that kind of person. But I never imagined that you would get involved in that kind of plundering and rioting. How could you participate in something like that? How could you be so heartless?"

"I am not being heartless. And anyway, that was all a long time ago. Bad things can happen, Inge. In general. It is not my fault when it happens in public like that."

She paused for a moment before responding with, "I know what you did that night. Or rather, what you did not do."

"What do you mean, *you know*? What is there that you could possibly *know* if you were lying here in bed with Joseph, with both of you down with a fever?"

"I… know what happened. I found out today."

"What did you find out? And from whom?"

"That is…that is not what this is about. I am just asking you the question. When those riots and assaults happened last November, and some buildings were on fire too, is it true that you stood there and did not do anything to help?"

"Inge, you are not making any sense. Stand where?"

"On the ladder, of course!" she near screamed, frustrated by the difficult direction of this conversation and unaware of how the previous pattern of denial between herself and Schilling was being repeated. "For heaven's sake, Horst, why are you doing this to me? You must know what I'm talking about?"

At the suggestion that he might be causing her distress intentionally, he paused; in that pause a look of shame rose that was perceivable by a flush in his face.

"At least you can remember now," she commented quietly.

He waited a moment, chose his words. "It is not easy to talk about things that happened so long ago. And it is even more difficult to explain to someone who was not actually there. But it is very easy to say afterwards what should have been done and what should not have been done. It is easy for you to judge when you were absent."

He moved towards her again and this time she did not try to dodge his embrace. "Oh, but Horst…," she sighed, her hands raised as little fists, lightly hitting his broad chest and letting them slip down it as he drew her to him. "Ever since we first met, you have always told me how proud you are of your job, of what you do."

He brought up a hand to rub her shoulder and back gently. She looked over and saw them standing in the long mirror, her body held close but her eyes staring in frustration.

He said, "I am too. I have always been proud of my job. That is no lie."

"You always said how you see your job as an activity that keeps people safe. That keeps the town as a whole safe. You said that the people here can always rely on you and your colleagues to be there for them when they are in danger, and that every town should work like that. That is what you said to me when we were first courting, before we even married. That was one of the things that made me fall in love with you. And now it all seems so false."

Horst began to speak but stopped at the opening "*ich*" (I) which ended in a guttural cadence going nowhere; he was fully aware of the nature of his wife's accusation and had no excuse to offer. He would not make matters worse by pretending to be ignorant of the affair or condescending to her.

She continued, "You know, I know more about that night than you think. Later on, after I had got better and was out and about, I heard plenty of things that people were saying, relating to each other. I listened in on people talking sometimes, including in the restaurant or when I was shopping in town. Of course, you do not pay that much attention. It is just idle talk, after all. You listen, and you think about it, then you get on with your jobs and what you have to do. Because life goes on. I heard how they called Frau Levitzki a '*Judensau*' (Jewish sow) that night on her way home. And her daughter Rebekah, too. The girl is only nine, Horst."

She moved out of his embrace and went to sit down on the bed; he joined her, taking her hand in a clasp. She looked ahead, recollecting and beginning to realize the enormity of what had taken place on that savage November night that seemed, in but a few months, to already be falling into obscurity.

"I heard how they chased the Unger family down the street. Apparently they put the apartment up for sale and left two days later. And I have never heard anyone say a bad word about the Weingartens. They were nice people and I used to say '*Guten Morgen*' (Good morning) to Frau Weingarten every day on the way to the bakery if I saw her, and she would always greet me back. Even after the Führer took over and people started ignoring the Jews, I still said it. More quietly, less conspicuously, that is true. And she understood and did the same back to me as well. But we still greeted each other all the same."

Horst shrugged. "Things have changed. Things are different now."

"Things might have changed but you can still say '*Guten Morgen*' to a person passing in the street. We are not savages."

"You know full well how people feel about Jews these days. They cannot all be wrong."

"I know and I do not pretend to understand the situation fully. I suppose the Führer may be right when he says that they have too much power in banks. Maybe they do have financial control over us. Perhaps that is a big problem that needs to be solved somehow. But it is one thing to think something and have an opinion, and it is another to call a little child something so horrible and ugly like that. And it is a terrible terrible thing, and furthermore a sin, to destroy a person's livelihood for no reason, to smash the windows of a person's home and business and set fire to it."

"That was all months ago. Three months at least, perhaps four. You have never mentioned any of this before," he said, his tone of voice now returning to defensive dissension. "You have just said that you have known all along what was going on, and yet you have never brought up this subject before."

"Because I thought they were other people who were doing it! Strangers, people I do not know. Or want to know."

"So, it would be alright then to just let it happen, if it were others?"

"You are twisting my words around. Don't do that, Horst! Just tell me, is it true that you just watched the fires burn without even trying to put them out?"

"It was not a case of just watching fires burn. You try to simplify everything but the situation was more complicated than that. We were given strict instructions from above not to do anything."

"Who gives instructions *not* to do anything? From whom did these instructions come?"

He splayed his hands. "All these questions? My God, Inge, I have no idea from whom. I am being honest with you. I do not know why these instructions were given and I have no idea who ultimately ordered it. They were instructions that were passed down. I suppose first to the head of the fire department in Lüneburg, then to Hans Lenz, my supervisor, you know Hans yourself, and then to the rest of us. Everybody did the same, not just me. All I know is that that is what we were all told to do! To stand back and not interfere."

"So it was Hans Lenz who told you not to do anything?"

"Of course! He was the one who passed on the instructions in the first place," he said with raised volume.

She creased her brow. "That does not sound like him."

"No, it is not like him," the phrase faded into a quiet tone. Her husband was being forced to uncover some uncomfortable truths and was wary of being overheard. "But that is the way things happen sometimes. These are things that are outside of our control."

"We could control them if we would ask questions first. Even if we just asked, "Why?" That is our problem, Horst. We do not ask questions. If I had not asked Herrn Schilling today…," she cut herself off in the unthinking flow of words.

"*Ach so*, it was Schilling who you all this! Schilling from the printers, right? Of course he would, the communist. Why did not you say so at the beginning of all this? When I asked you. Why hide things from me?"

It was a pointless game of pride and principles, of cancelling the debt of dishonesty against the other player's account, but they kept it up. "I think I told you at the beginning but in any case, as I said, everyone was talking about it and it does not matter anymore who told me what, and whether today or yesterday or back in November. What matters is what happened."

Horst rubbed his eyes. "Where are Adolf and Joseph?"

"I told you already: they are at my mother's, together with Erich. She will coming round to the Gasthaus with them shortly so that we can all have the evening meal together. I even told you what we are having."

He sighed, irritated by his wife's sulk. "Good, then let us talk this through so that you know everything that there is to know. Probably at the end you will understand more than any of us, Inge, and then you can explain it to those of us who actually had to stand out there that night. So, at the station that afternoon we were told that there may well be an emergency situation that night, although there were no concrete details yet, but that it would probably happen either that night or the following one. In any case, very soon. And we were then told that, if that were the case, then we were expected to stay on duty the whole night, probably until four or five in the morning. Due to exceptional circumstances. Nobody was saying much about it but we all knew that it was because of this vom Rath, the ambassador that the Jews had shot in Paris. And everyone knew that if he copped it, then all hell was going to break lose. So at about half past ten, there was an important telephone call come through. I do not know from whom exactly, but I think it came from Munich. Paul Schönbeck, he took the call and he mentioned Munich. And after he had put down the phone, he said, vom Rath has died. Just that. Then there was a telegram sent to all public sector services, including us, and it confirmed that he had died. It went something like, "tragically and despite the best care, including from the Führer's physician himself, in a local hospital, blablabla." It was very official. And then everyone started talking at the same time. The director of the Fire Department came in shortly after, Herr Wagenknecht, and he said that this vom Rath had been shot dead by a Jew, a young and vicious Jew, and that it was normal that we should expect a lot of angry retaliation that night from people in town. Because after all this was an assassination of an important person. I do not recall the exact words anymore, but what he said was that this was a terrible crime and that it needed the…the corresponding punishment. That was _all_ we were told. Then we were informed that the orders came right from the top, from the _Gauleitung_ itself, and these same orders were to be given out all across the _Gau_ of Eastern Hannover and in many other parts of the country as well. In towns and cities everywhere. And they were that _under no circumstances whatsoever_ were we to interfere in the 'rightful anger of the people' - those were Herr Wagenknecht's exact words - and he said that we had 'to let things take their natural course'. To be there but to just be on stand-by and not try to stop people from expressing their anger."

"But you did at least try to put out some of the fires, didn't you?"

"Yes, if there was any danger of the fire spreading to adjacent properties, then in that case, yes, we were to intervene, I mean, to extinguish that fire."

"So you only let the houses and businesses of the Jews burn?"

"Exactly! That is exactly it!" At this point, Horst mistakenly assumed that this was the detail that would pacify his wife.

"But that is terrible, Horst! First, you let those people suffer and then you helped other people out, right in front of them, in their faces, so they could clearly see how much you hated them. To stand there on purpose and do nothing when one family is suffering, even though you can come to their aid and have all the means at hand to do so, and then finally only step in to help because other properties nearby _might_ have caught fire too."

"It is not the case that they _might_ have caught fire - they _would_ have caught fire! That was why we were there. And we did put out quite a few blazes that evening, I can tell you. I didn't get home in the early hours of the morning for nothing!"

She sighed and rubbed her head. She was aware that her husband was not seeing her viewpoint but she did not have the energy to argue further.

Hearing her silence, he continued in a subdued tone, "Perhaps it was not right what happened that night. When you sit down and think about it, all quiet and rational. But in that moment it was the only thing we could humanly do. There were windows smashed everywhere. And yes, I suppose there were some people laying fires in the interiors of buildings. I never actually saw it happen but they must have been. People were shouting out all the time, shouting insults. Or hurling things like stones and bricks. But apart from that, I never saw anyone actually got hurt. No-one was beaten up or physically attacked in any way. At least, not that I saw. And yes, tempers were high. These things happen when people get angry. They do what they do. There were also a lot of people just protesting and those were mostly peaceful protests too. You know, Inge, sometimes you just have to let these things happen."

"I think this is more about you, than anything else." She was close to tears by now. "As I have said, I know you were always so proud of your profession. Of the good you have done with your work, for our town and for the people who live here. So, knowing that you stood on the ladder and deliberately did not do anything to help people, when a fire was burning in front of you, it seemed so wrong somehow. It does not ultimately matter if they are Jews or Christians or whoever they are. You are a fireman and if there is a fire, you are supposed to come to their aid. This was a situation of violence, Horst. I am not standing up for the Jews as such. I am just saying they are people too and in an emergency situation like that, you have to help other people. A doctor cannot just say, this person is sick but I will let him die because he is a Jew. I would not do that. It would be unthinkable."

"But I have already told you why I did what I did. These were exceptional circumstances. Yes, of course I am proud of my profession, of what I do every day at work. I always have been. I still am. Maybe on another occasion I would see things differently," he said, though simultaneously considered that this was probably not the case. "I know what you are thinking. You think, any reasonable person would say that they should not have destroyed other people's property. But these are not reasonable times. Anger is not supposed to be polite and peaceful. In any case, they are destroying property, which can be replaced, so that is not violence. Not really."

"I also heard that the Jews had to pull down their own synagogue."

"To be honest, Inge, I do not care that much about synagogues. You know, if people do not want a synagogue in their community, perhaps it should not be there. That is all I am saying. In any case, people will do what they do."

"Horst, that is still not the right attitude to take in this kind of situation," said Inge, but did not wish to explain further.

The discussion had become pointless, they realized, and their arguments meandered aimlessly. They were both debating the issues in different directions, neither listening nor finding common ground. Inge sighed and cupped her chin in one hand, looking straight forward at the picture of flowers on the wall. She so hated disputes, and had gone from one toxic confrontation to another and ended up pleasing no-one. Were it not for the fact that at least she now understood the complete scenario and how even her own family were involved, she would have regretted ever visiting Schilling in the first place. She felt it was futile to continue. She was not capable of articulating rational arguments against concepts that Horst had thrown at her, such as the "rightful anger of the people" and the "corresponding punishment". Furthermore, she sensed these were not typical elements of her husband's vocabulary, and she was right: he had been quoting his superiors. Yet coming out of his mouth and presented in this compelling way, they seemed to become vaguely coherent statements that made sense and yet didn't. That outrage might descend into violence, that was to be expected in the wake of a heinous assassination. And yet the thought of people she knew being assaulted - and on top of that older, peaceful citizens of the town who had never until now caused the slightest disapprobation, suffering in such a manner - jarred heavily in her. She had already eschewed her own inner reprobation and shied away from the glaring facts for the past few months. Her conscience now pained her and begged questions that she did not wish to answer any more than her husband wished to answer hers. At the same time, she most certainly did not to wish to openly step out of line, as far as her patriotism to her fatherland and the necessity for obedience to the regime dictated. Much less so with her husband employed in such an important position of responsibility, plus two small children to take care of and perhaps another one on the way. Therefore, she decided to close the matter, at least for the time being. She saw how pained her husband was, and did not wish to distress him further.

She abruptly said she had a lot to do and couldn't leave Gisela working alone at the Gasthaus for too long. Also, her mother would be arriving with the children any minute.

Neither wishing to prolong the discussion nor to show any direct forgiveness toward Horst for his inaction that night, she merely said, "No point in us arguing over this all evening. Like you said, it is all in the past now. We have enough to worry about as it is," before giving him a slack hug and a light kiss, leaving the room to head downstairs.

Though she was now silent, over the next few weeks the subject rumbled on in the background of Horst's mind, like the low and intermittent rumble of distant thunder. At work, he had not uttered another word to his colleagues concerning that toxic November night since the week it had occurred in, nor had anyone (at least, not in his presence) brought up the contradiction of purposefully holding back assistance to the beleaguered victims. But he had been aware at the time of the ignoble nature of standing half-way up a ladder and holding a limp hose in his hands while a fire raged directly before him. Despite all the reassurances the following day from his superiors as to the moral certitude of their actions, he himself had not fully come to terms with it and had hidden the facts in a pile of scattered justifications that did not fully convince but, nonetheless, served to suffocate any internal unrest. He had trusted in the passing of time to ease his conscience, and it had. That is, until Inge's abrupt and unexpected confrontation had dug up the subject and dragged it loudly back into his world.

Once again he mulled over the events, and additionally things that were being increasingly expressed against the Jews in general, at work, on the street, in his family. The mood seemed to have shifted from contempt and mocking to full-blown malignancy. Notions, that would have once seemed almost horrific but now carried a certain nonchalance, were more commonplace. He had heard that month at a bus-stop how a middle-aged man had said to another, "You know, if all the Jews in Germany fell over dead tomorrow, I would not lose a minute's sleep. All they bring are problems for us all." Frau Meininger, who worked in the telephone centrale at the fire station, had gossiped about how her sister and brother-in-law were looking for a new place to live and viewing an apartment the next day with a view to purchasing it. A very nice property indeed, wonderfully central, right on Am Sande. She stated in a matter-of-fact way how it had just recently become vacant because some Jews had been living there but were now gone. Her younger colleague had looked impressed and asked how much they were asking; her eyes widened at the uncommonly reduced amount. Excellent price, a real bargain, she nodded glowingly, especially considering the good location.

There were other comments overheard too, from various sources, and Horst felt obliged a couple of months later to resume the topic with his wife. He decided to wait for the right moment which came on a warm day in early April. He had the day free and Inge had worked in the morning at the Gasthaus and had been given the afternoon off. Horst had managed to secure a lend of his supervisor Hans Lenz's motorcar for the day, as a favour for all the overtime that he had put in of late. He suggested to Inge that they could go out for the day with the children to somewhere nice in the Lüneburger Heath, to enjoy the warm sun and clear blue sky that were reigning that spring week. There would be room for the children in the back of the car and they could take a picnic. Inge was delighted and said it almost felt like a second honeymoon. "You know, we have not been anywhere since Berlin!" she chuckled in the best of spirits.

They rode out of town and passed the sporadic neighbouring villages and long stretches of woodland. As they drove deeper into a section of the heath, they saw a well-built blonde shepherdess by a flock of grazing sheep in dark shades of grey and brown, the rams with their idiosyncratic curled horns. A German shepherd dog jumped up into her arms; she was stroking it as they drove by and she waved at the car. Inge waved back and asked Horst if the dog was there to round up the sheep. He said no but that they still used the big dogs out in the countryside to help protect against the odd roaming pack of wolves. Inge went pale and said she had no ideas that there were wolves in the area. Horst grinned at the little fright in her eyes.

Now driving on a rough dry mud track, they found a spot to park the car and continued on foot. It was a short but invigorating walk in the fresh breeze, perhaps just ten or fifteen minutes as Inge did not wish for them to distance themselves too much from the borrowed vehicle. The view from the path was breathtaking, looking across the wide meadows of heather, dotted with small trees and bushes, and rolling down to a woodland area further on. There were songbirds and bumble bees, and the air was fresh and filled with the aroma emitted by the flowers and heather, and the pine and juniper trees. Eventually, at Horst's guidance, they reached a quiet spot at the edge of some trees by a small pond, where they sat down with the children and spread out the picnic. This was a place Horst had known well from his youth when he had come with a couple of friends, including Paul from the fire station, to strip off and splash around in the shallow water in summer. It was a nostalgic but welcoming sensation to return here as a married man and father.

The fresh spring breeze had strengthened during the course of their outing and it filled their hair and flickered around their bare arms and necks. They sat down under a tree, kissed and stroked each other and embraced as best they could with Joseph snuggled up tightly between them. Adolf stumbled round the immediate area, inspected grass and stones and the odd creature that passed his way. Inge complained to Horst about some recent guests who had left the room in a dirty state after a three-day stay, and said she thought Walter might be an alcoholic. Horst talked about his parents and siblings: his mother had not been well of late and he commented on some interfamilial bickering among siblings caused by her illness and the need for external assistance.

After the bread and cheese, they were quiet for a while, enjoying the sensation of the sunlight and the cooling wind on their skin; watched the clouds being pushed relentlessly across the sky, one cluster after another; enjoyed the near silence of the children, well-behaved and undemanding for once.

The peace was perfect but Horst was itching inside and felt the time had come to quietly relieve himself of pent-up doubts and address Inge's previous accusation. Inge was thinking about the hours she was putting in at the Gasthaus and how she thought she might ask her sister and brother-in-law for a small rise in salary. She was calculating how much it might be appropriate to suggest, and whether they would be open to the idea, considering that the business seemed to be doing well, plus the amount of effort she was investing into the Gasthaus. It seemed only fair but she did not want to sour relations with Martin and worried that the discussion with them might become confrontational. She was umming and ahing as to how to broach this difficult subject back home, while Horst remained taciturn.

Eventually, Inge picked out an apple and began to bite into it. Joseph woke and she rocked him gently, glad that he did not begin to cry. Adolf was sitting nearby with a captured bug and seemed keen to pull it apart. Horst felt this was a good moment to address the subject and his new line of thought.

"You know that day when we had that row in our room, I mean, that discussion we had, a few weeks back now, about the night when you said they saw me on the ladder and that I was supposedly standing still and not trying to extinguish the fires that were burning. On that night back in November."

Inge frowned, mentally in a different place, before cottoning on and then waving her hand dismissively. "Don't worry about that. That is all water under the bridge." She spoke hurriedly and a couple of chunks of apple fell from her mouth. "Oh, I am clumsy." The day was so beautiful that the last thing she wished for was to bicker with her husband.

He persisted. "Even so, I have been thinking about the things you were saying to me. Perhaps you did have a point. It was just I heard recently how the Beim family, the ones who had that warehouse over in Winsen and were corn merchants, well they have all left now. The whole family went together, I was told: the old man, his wife, two younger sons and a daughter. The two older sons had already left, had emigrated away. I know they had a small office up in the Hindenburgstraße because it was plundered that night but there was only a small fire and it was put out before anything could come of it. It was rented and the owner was down there quick because the neighbours were scared a fire would spread, which was understandable. Then I found out they had their own apartment up for sale but the price they were asking for it was ridiculous. It is a great big apartment, very up-market and right on Am Sande. Must be worth quite a lot really. It didn't make much sense somehow. It all seemed a bit …", here he struggled for the right word before alighting on, "unjust. I mean, to sell yourself short like that."

Inge had been able to gulp down another bite of the apple. She shrugged, "I suppose they wanted to get out as quick as possible. You cannot blame them for that. I would do the same if people around me hated me that much."

"No, but what I mean is that they're going to make a big loss on the apartment. They must have sold so cheaply because they *had* to."

"Yes, I suppose they must."

"That is what happened to the Weingartens as well. After you mentioned them to me and how you used to say 'Guten Morgen' every day to Frau Weingarten, well, I did a small check. They left almost straight after what happened, after their premises were burnt out that night. I mean, of course they wanted to get out. I understand that. People were angry, especially after what happened, and were taking it out on them. And it wasn't their fault, of course. But I was thinking, it did not seem right to lose so much money just when you were leaving your hometown behind and moving somewhere else, somewhere new and strange. Just when you need that bit of money to make a new start. And all that just because you were disliked. It is one thing talking about big financial wheelers and dealers, and all the Jews who are bankers and financiers and the such like, but I know these were just normal people with a small business, like your sister too. It would be like us being forced to move away and go to another town, or even country, just because Gisela and Martin had a major row with the neighbours, and the neighbours took it out on us, and we did not have any choice."

Inge was still munching. Horst pondered, "I mean, I don't know if that is a good comparison. This is about who they are, not what they said or did. I can see now that it was not right what happened to them. But then again, I was also thinking that perhaps in the long term it was the best thing for them."

Inge murmured, "Exactly. Who wants to live in a home that could go up in flames at any moment? I know I would not want to. I would want to move somewhere else as well."

Horst felt that sting but let it go. Inge in turn regretted her sharp words. Both remained silent for a while.

Horst sensed the circuitous nature of their discussion on abstract issues such as political opinions (in contrast to their harmonious interaction concerning pragmatic and day-to-day issues); noticed that once again they did not seem to be able to connect on this level. Sometimes, he thought, it was with Inge as if they were both speaking the same language but only half-understanding what the other was saying, then being left with the wrong end of the stick, and taking that out of context to boot. He had desired the opportunity to express his doubts about himself and his behaviour, to be open and frank about any remorse he had experienced or was currently exploring. But most of all he had wished to confront his wife's accusations from that day, only to now find that she seemed to have borne a grudge and was unusually acidic in her choice of words.

Inge for her part wished more than anything else to comfort her husband and ease over the words exchanged that sour day. Regretting her last sentence, she changed tactic and tried to smooth the conversation. "I was talking to Marianne and her husband Manfred about this just last week, when they passed by the Gasthaus to say hello. Manfred said that the Jews are going to be offered resettlement in the east very soon. In a huge part of Russia, with plenty of space for farms and houses, and also some more land in a part of...", she frowned and paused for thought, "of the Caucasus, I think he said. Or the east of Poland? Yes, it must be Poland, not Russia. Anyway, it is going to be a government programme, an official one, and once it comes into operation it should work out very well for everyone, and especially for the Jews. I had not heard of it before although apparently it is quite common knowledge, but of course no-one wants to see the positive side of anything. It is such a gloomy world at the moment and people are so suspicious of everything. It is almost as if they only _want_ to see the bad in everything," she sighed.

Horst shook his head as if to clear it from the strangeness of this unexpected change in Inge's mental course. He said, "If they are all in a better place now, then at least that helps to clarify things. Also, some of them went to Palestine and probably the land and properties are much cheaper there, so they could afford to sell their properties here at a lower price," he mused.

"Yes, exactly," she answered, vaguely.

Inge had felt a strong pang of injustice at the mistreatment of others, whoever they were, and still found the topic unsettling. But this was not the time or place, she considered, and was irritated upon having the subject re-opened like an obstinate wound. With her children around her, and she exhausted from so much work of late, now having an afternoon off in this splendid corner of nature, she certainly did not wish to discuss racial politics or have to think about Palestine or any such distant topics and far-off places. More than anything because she herself had something weighty on her mind, some information that she wished to share with Horst, and that greatly overshadowed the affairs of other people.

Ever since they had arrived at the spot by the oak tree, she had decided that this would be the perfect moment to share her news. But

Horst was already sullying the moment with his talk of the *Kristallnacht* and his deliberations about the fates of those affected. She would sweep away this gloom like the wind swept away clouds; she would make the sunshine twice as bright. She leant forward and said, "My love, I have to tell you something. Something very important, and personal."

He frowned. "Is anything the matter?"

"No, no! Nothing's wrong, nothing at all. Just the opposite! I thought this would be a good time to tell you. With us having some time to ourselves, and it being such a beautiful day," she laughed.

Horst was mystified.

Inge raised her shoulders girlishly and told him that she was pregnant. He asked several times, "Really?" - if she were totally sure? She related how she and Gisela had gone to the doctor and he had confirmed the pregnancy just yesterday. How many months? - her husband wanted to know. Four - and they hugged, carefully around Joseph, and kissed. Adolf, alerted by the animated mood of his parents, came over and hugged them too. Horst took Joseph in his arms to give his wife a break. She laughed, stroked Adolf's head which was buried in her shoulder and underarm, while Horst did a quick calculation. "So the baby is due in September?"

"That is right. Early September," she said, bursting with glee and pride. "Imagine that, our third child." She covered her cheeks with her hands. "Three children, imagine that!" she gasped.

She patted her hips smartly as Adolf detached himself and went to hug his father, who gave him his favourite sweet, a liquorice that he had been planning to treat him to later. They talked for a while, filled to the brim with future plans. Eventually Horst gave her Joseph back, stood up and rubbed his hands together, feeling both ecstatic and agitated, "Come on, we have to head back."

"Already?"

"Of course, we have to have a toast for the baby. I'm going to raid Gisela's cupboards and open the finest champagne she has."

"Horst, you know they are funny about anyone helping themselves to the stock. What with Walter and, I mean…"

But Horst wasn't listening. "I have the feeling that this year is going to be a wonderful year for everyone. I have had that feeling all along. And now I have been proven right!"

Holding the babe tight, she struggled to her feet while her husband held her arm. They began packing up the picnic things in a sprightly mood. Inge tried to get Adolf to help out, but the little boy was more hindrance than help with his stubborn refusal to conform to his mother's instructions, preferring to take his own erratic and illogical methodology. "No, Adolf. Do not put the dishes there, you will crack them. And be careful with that knife!"

Joseph had now woken up and begun to cry, and they went back briskly to the car with the children and drove home. Horst was still jumping for joy with the news of Inge's pregnancy. The spring sun, with its annual call to life and growth, had already cheered him and now, about to become the father of three children, he felt that life was finally beginning to make sense.

The homecoming was less sweet than imagined. No sooner had they given the car back to Hans and returned home, Horst found his sister Marianne, heavily pregnant, waiting for him in a dark quiet corner of the restaurant, with a coffee and some cake that Gisela had provided her with. She asked him to sit down and by her downcast face and dark clothing, he second-guessed the bad news she had brought with her. Marianne held his hand and told him that their mother Elisabeth had passed away that afternoon, in her house in Uelzen. "They think it was probably a stroke, but the doctor will have to confirm that," she said.

Inge consoled her husband; he promptly left with Marianne to meet up first with their brother Karl-Heinz and then all drive on together to their father's house. Inge then shared the news of her pregnancy with Gisela. Her sister was overjoyed and commented, "Isn't it strange how one life leaves and another one arrives."

Chapter 14

Gisela's children were progressing well through the school year; with the slightly above average grades that she had stoically expected, and the very positive comments concerning good behaviour that she had fervently hoped for. That was something for a mother to be satisfied with and at the same time reflected on the whole family.

At the school Lüneburger *Bürgerschule* that Katrina and Siggi were attending, the curriculum had changed in recent years to aptly reflect more modern times. Education, they had been informed in a letter sent out to all parents, was not simply the mere acquisition of facts; but more importantly the attainment of the critical analytic powers necessary for children to understand the wider world and those weighty and germane issues that surrounded them. For this reason, and following clearly laid down governmental guidelines, the school had set about introducing a new pedagogical methodology. This included the use of revised textbooks, in order to give traditional subjects more cultural relevance as would befit young Germans. They would thus be able to better understand the world around them and would be better prepared for the challenges that lay ahead.

Martin had not even read the letter back then - though he had heard some fleeting comments about the contents from others - but he had been in full agreement with the school's policy. Gisela had read the letter, though she had found nothing either particularly commendable nor especially reproachable in the idea. The primary goal was that the children should be able to achieve a reasonable competence in basic educational disciplines and could then expect to find employment with those acquired skills upon leaving school. How the skills were acquired was of only passing interest to her. Like Martin, she had a basic trust in the educational authorities and had in any case felt slightly intimidated by both the verbose style of the letter and its references to 'governmental guidelines'.

No such official communication had come through from the primary school where Erich was studying, the *Heiligengeistschule*, but new textbooks had been purchased and were in widespread use. Moreover, there was now a flag ceremony held every morning to instill in the children a sense of patriotism.

Gisela was sitting with her two sons in their private back room at the Gasthaus one evening in the early summer of 1939. This was a medium-sized room, just round the corner from the restaurant and adjacent to the kitchen, which served as a living room for the couple and their children. It was still furnished with the once sumptuous but now old and faded relics of Gisela's parents-in-law, something she planned to remedy once she had put enough money to one side. The ensuing bonfire after the new furniture came in was something she was quietly looking forward to.

The previous week she and Martin had received the end of school year reports on the children. Gisela, curious to see what exactly their offspring were studying, had decided to go through their homework with them. It was a Monday, the day on which the restaurant closed for its *Ruhetag* (day of rest) each week. After a rush of weekend guests, out to stroll round town or enjoy the abundant nature on the nearby heathland, there was only one couple left staying and all the corresponding customer service had been completed, allowing Gisela and Martin to relax with their children. For Gisela, such days were of vital importance, the bonding moments of the family.

Also present in the room with them, sitting opposite his son Martin and reading his standard weekly source of news - the *Norddeutscher Beobachter* -with an occasional sigh or tut, was Volkmar Landeck. These days Volkmar took each and any opportunity to escape from the domestic environment in which he was psychologically bullied with frequency by his wife and elderly mother-in-law. A visit to see his family and to check up on the running of the Gasthaus was always a convenient excuse to leave for a few hours, as well as fulfill his own familial responsibility toward the next generations. His late brother's son-in-law, Bernhard Bohlen, would later drive him back home to Adendorf, by which time the two women in his household would hopefully be either going to bed or simply too tired to say very much.

Siggi had turned eleven and was going twice a week to the DJV meetings ('*Deutsches Jungvolk in der Hitler Jugend*' – 'German Young People in the Hitler Youth'). It had been his father's idea originally, though one which he himself had come to thoroughly enjoy. His big ambition now was to join the Hitler Youth itself once he reached fourteen, which seemed at that moment to be an eternity away. His father comforted him, "Don't you worry, son. Those few years ahead will just fly by. Just try to think about other things in the meantime - time always goes by quicker when you're not counting it."

Erich, their youngest child and heavily mollycoddled by his mother, was struggling with the homework set for the mathematics class. Gisela was eager to help him out, aware of the vital importance and general application of the subject in so many branches of work, including her own. He was still just eight and learning basic arithmetic; at that moment working on an exercise that required him to add together the costs for various items under the title '*Ausrüstung für die Hitlerjugend*' (Equipment for the Hitler Youth).

The pupils were instructed to calculate the complete costs for a single Hitler Youth member, and after that for two and three further children. Having covered addition, subtraction and simple multiplication in numerous lessons, this exercise was to be completed as homework by the next class. Siggi, with the pleasure he had at the group meetings, would have loved such a puzzle; but for Erich it seemed somehow unpleasant, as if evoking worrying associations. Gisela glanced at the sum in the book: Shirt - 5 RM, Shorts - 8 RM, Cravat - 3 RM, Armband - 1 RM, Boots - 15 RM, Belt with buckle - 3 RM, Insignia badge - 1 RM, Shoulder strap - 2 RM.

"That's an easy one," she assured him. "You just put the different prices in a vertical line, like this, and then add up the last column. See? So, in total that makes 28. You write 8 there and carry over the 2 into the column before it, always working from right to left. Then in that column you have 1, from the 15 for the boots, plus the 2 you have carried, that's 3 in total. So, the grand total is three eight, thirty-eight. Now, wasn't that easy? You could have done that easily too, I'll bet," she smiled with encouragement but he looked dolefully back.

His father was reading *Der Adler,* a bi-weekly magazine centered around the exploits of the Luftwaffe and a favourite read of his, full of heroically adventurous stories and glossy photos. He rustled the magazine, sighed and looked over in irritation. "You have to learn basic arithmetic Erich, you know. You'll never get on in life if you can't add up a sum."

"Yes, Papa."

"Adding up is the easiest part. Then you have to subtract, and multiply, and divide."

"Yes, Papa," he repeated, looking nervous and futilely adding, "This week we learnt how to subtract at school."

"Your mother and I won't always be able to help you. We have enough to do, as it is. You will have to work these things out for yourself. Learn to be independent and do things for yourself." He resented the exaggerated attention that his wife paid to the handicapped child, feeling it would weaken him further still by removing his will to fight on despite the setbacks that nature had dished out to him. This world was made for the strong, he firmly believed; weakness had to be overcome.

"He will be fine," his mother returned. "Probably it was the type of exercise that was not appropriate for him. We will do a different one instead. So Erich, let's try another. '*Fahrrad mit Zubehör*' (Bicycle with accessories). This one looks nice. Shall we try it?"

The child nodded and wrote the list in a vertical column as instructed: Bicycle – 50 RM, Lamp – 4 RM, Tyre pump – 1 RM, Pannier – 2 RM, Dynamo – 5 RM, Kilometre counter – 2 RM. His mother was looking round the room, mentally planning which items of furniture would be the first to be thrown out and replaced once they had the money, when he tugged at her arm.

"Sixty-four Reichsmark", he said softly.

She briefly inspected the page, stroked his hair, "That's right, my love! That's exactly right. And you did it with much bigger numbers, too. Now, let's continue the exercise. What about two sets of 'bicycle with accessories'?"

Moving into the hundreds' column this required more concentration but was also achieved by the lad in a fairly short space of time, to the immense relief of both mother and son. Gisela announced her son's correct answer to her husband and father-in-law with all the ostentation of opening the Olympic Games.

Martin Landeck said nothing until they had calculated up to three sets, whereupon he rustled the magazine again and said, "And you have studied how to do subtraction too, you said?"

"Yes, Papa. We learnt it by calculating the Führer's birthday."

Martin was genuinely intrigued. "Really, how does that work?"

"The Führer Adolf Hitler was born on 20.4.1889. And we have to work out the Führer's age on the date today and also the Führer's age on," he looked at his textbook, "on 30th January 1933, which is the day on which he became Chancellor of the Reich, and also on the 3rd of August 1934, but I cannot remember what that day is."

Martin was himself mystified about the significance of the latter date. He looked round approvingly at his wife and muttered in her direction, "They are certainly getting them well trained while they are still young. Good to see the school direction knows what it is doing." Then louder to his son, "And how do you work that out?"

The little boy shook his head. "I did not really understand when they explained it, Papa."

Gisela stepped in quickly. "He can do smaller numbers just fine but it is still complicated for him with numbers in the thousands."

Martin did not wish for any defeatism in his family. "Imagine we are calculating your age. It is now 1939, so you put that number at the top, and underneath you write the year you were born in, so that is 1931. And you subtract the one at the bottom from the one at the top. That will then show you your age. So, how much is that?" He returned to his reading material and waited for the answer. Volkmar had started to drift off and was snoring softly.

"Eight," answered the boy after a while in a dull tone, not calculating and finding it a strange exercise when everyone knew perfectly well how old he was.

"Exactly. Now, to calculate the Führer age, you would write 1939 at the top, just the same, and underneath the year he was born in, so 1889. And then subtract the one from the other. Do you understand?"

"Yes, Papa."

"Good, then you can do it."

Erich nodded nervously, wrote down the figures and looked with dread at the calculation in front of him. He subtracted nine from nine to make zero but was at a loss as to how to subtract eight from three. To his horror, his mother has stood up sharply and gone to look out of the window at something that she thought she had heard. "I could have sworn there was someone out there," she said over from the window. "If those kids of the neighbours have got into the back yard again, there will be words." She glared out angrily but saw nothing.

The atmosphere became edgy for the children as Erich scratched some numbers and wished that something dramatic would happen to break the tension they found themselves in. Siggi glanced at his father and grandfather; saw one asleep and the other engrossed in a magazine. He leant over to Erich's notebook and quickly scribbled in '50' beside the equation. Gisela, returning to the table, caught the rapid movement. Both she and Erich looked at Siggi with repressed smiles, marvelling at the speed and ingenuity of the trickery. If the truth be known, Siggi himself had not arrived at the figure through mathematical calculation either, but rather had heard Hitler's age mentioned at school during recreation recently.

After a pause, Erich mumbled, "It is fifty, Papa."

Martin had meanwhile begun to get caught up in a story in his magazine and looked over with creased forehead. "What?"

"The answer is fifty," the boy said, louder and more clearly, waking Volkmar in the process.

"Good, very good," he nodded. For the sake of fairness he looked over at Siggi, who was now again deeply embroiled in his own page of calculations, and said, "And what about you, son? Why don't you read out your exercises for your mother and Opa Volkmar to listen to?"

Following a quick glance at his mother who gently nodded, Siggi begrudgingly read them through. He was still struggling with the final exercise but hoped to gain time by reciting the previous ones. "The first one I could do. It was about the colonies that Germany has lost due to the Treaty of Versailles and we had to calculate the areas of land and the population of those areas. That one was not difficult."

"And what were they?" asked Martin.

Siggi looked intently at his notebook and read the list with monotonous tone. "East Africa - 995,000 km² and 7,600,000 inhabitants. Southwest Africa – 835,000 km² and 103,000. Cameroon – 790,000 km² and…"

His grandfather Landeck interrupted, fearing it might be a long and tedious list. "Well, that is all in Africa. What about the more important areas?"

"Then we had the areas of the German Reich that were also lost due to the Treaty of Versailles. East Prussia – 37,800 km² and 2,100,000 inhabitants. West Prussia – 25,500 km² and 1,700,000 inhabitants," the boy continued through the exact losses in both territory and population in the previously German areas of Poland, Silesia, Schleswig-Holstein, Rhine Province and Alsace-Lorraine. Volkmar let him finish this time and was thoroughly indignant when he reached the end. "You see, you see! Just what I always say about that damned stitch-up. And does it say to whom they were all lost?"

"Yes, Grandpapa."

"It does? Let me have a look there," said Volkmar, indicating for the boy to bring him the textbook. The grandson got off his chair and walked over, nervously guided the old man's eyes with a forefinger as Volkmar muttered, "Let me see now - Poland and Lithuania, Poland and Danzig, Poland, Poland and Czechoslovakia, Denmark, Belgium, France." He gave Siggi his book back and said angrily. "No wonder people are saying the things they are. It is a disgrace. A disgrace, that is what it is."

Gisela sighed. "I do not know if this material is really what the children need to learn. In my day we did general sums. With sacks of apples and herds of cows. Or sheep and wool, things like that.

"No, this is precisely what the children of today should be learning!" Volkmar contradicted. "Precisely this. It is the best possible way to understand the problems that we are facing and the situation that we find ourselves in. And additionally they get to learn mathematics too. I think it is a wonderful educational programme. Much better than all that silly stuff with apples and… and… sheep." There was a pause following his outburst and the only thing to be heard was the repeated contemptuous muttering of "Sheep!" some seconds later.

Gisela did not care to enter into an argument with her father-in-law and remained silent, though internally still quite prepared to defend her boys if necessary. Fortunately the door-bell rang, announcing the arrival of Edeltraut with her daughter Eva. She had evening meetings at the hospital to attend on a regular basis and would typically leave her daughter with the Landecks for a couple of hours, Katrina and Eva being good friends. Later her husband Bernhard would come to pick up their daughter, as well as drive Volkmar back home. Edeltraut was of the opinion that she got on well with Gisela, with whom she had what she viewed as a solid and productive relationship: namely, one of dependable usefulness. Gisela in turn tolerated her as best she could and always made sure to put on a bright face in public.

Edeltraut Bohlen, née Landeck, was the daughter and only child of Volkmar's brother Joachim. They lived a little further out of town, in the outer district of Bockelsberg. She worked as head nurse in the 'Trauma Surgery and Orthopedics Department' of the *Städtisches Klinikum* (general hospital); while her husband was a high-profile engineer at the *Lüneburger Eisenwerk* (ironworks). Apart from their son Roland, they had two daughters: Leni, who had finished her initial training course as a nurse and was currently training for field work to support the military, and Eva, fifteen and at school. Despite the slight age difference of three years the cousins Katrina Landeck and Eva Bohlen had formed a strong bond. This arose partly through Eva being considerably younger than her siblings, five and six years respectively, who were now young adults and training for their future. The friendship between the girls was additionally forged by the close family connection held between Joachim and Volkmar, their respective grandfathers, right up till Joachim's passing away five years earlier.

Eva had progressed the year before from the JM (*Jungmädelbund* - League of Young Girls) to the BDM (*Bund deutscher Mädel* – League of German Girls), the latter being the feminine branch of the Hitler Youth; her family was proud of her excellent progress both academically and socially. At twelve Katrina would have to wait further two years for that same advancement, which caused her feelings of anxious impatience and great envy towards her friend and cousin.

On the whole Katrina was achieving mediocre grades at school although in one particular subject – general science - she was making very good progress, to the point that her teacher had commented in depth on this in the last general appraisal of the students emitted by the school. Gisela was impressed while Martin was only mildly interested, feeling that the correct and appropriate role for his daughter would be in helping out with the family business, or perhaps at most studying for a modestly positioned and traditionally feminine profession.

Edeltraut was brought into the back room by Gisela; she greeted the assembled family with her characteristic stiff smile and formally asked after everyone. Martin mentioned the boys' homework tasks and Volkmar voiced his own personal approval of the system involved.

Edeltraut could not agree more with her uncle. "I know, they have such well-designed and appropriated courses these days. Eva uses similar texts at the BDM meetings when they learn about Racial Awareness. But I really like the idea of combining the social message with a mundane subject like mathematics. Quite brilliant. Do you have that last exercise that you were showing me on you, Eva? Find it, dear, and tell them what it said."

The girl obediently produced her textbook and fumbled after the page. "It was here, on the exercises with percentages: 'In Berlin the percentage of Jews among the following professions is as follows: among doctors – 48%; among social and welfare doctors – 68%; among lawyers – 54%; among theatre managers – 80%. What can we deduce from that?' But Mama, I have not prepared my exercises on this question yet. It is for next week so I still have time."

"Of course! We only wanted to show them what you were doing," smiled her mother, who turned to the others and added. "Such interesting statistics. It certainly does make you think, doesn't it?"

Gisela nodded and smiled in response, though she missed the intended point of the statement and personally found the statistics to be very impressive in favour of the achievements of Jews of Berlin. In fact, she was surprised to hear that kind of positive rhetoric used by the BDS and in a manual issued by the government itself. Volkmar, on the other hand, had made the anticipated deduction; as did Eva, and the following week she would read out a highly-lauded work on that very topic with a little help from her parents.

Edeltraut continued, "There is a school theatre production of Schiller's *Wilhelm Tell* coming up soon as well, which I will be helping out with. There will be two performances held at the beginning of next month and I do hope I can count on your presence on one of them!" she cawed at the group. "So important for the children to immerse themselves in the classics of Germanic culture."

Gisela creased her brow, "But wasn't Wilhelm Tell Swiss?"

"Germanic, Gisela. I said, Germanic," Edeltraut reminded her. "And Schiller was from Württemberg." (Ironically, *Wilhelm Tell* was to fall out of favour with the Nazis later on; the audiences constantly clapped in all the wrong places, whereupon the text was discovered to be dangerously subversive after all. It was definitively cancelled in 1941 when the Führer forbade its performance in the Reich).

"Yes, all in all I find the revised curriculum to be such a great improvement on the old one," continued Edeltraut. "They do a lot more sport than before, a lot more physical exercise. A healthy body houses a healthy mind! I was at a school meeting last week and saw them training on the front field, all moving together in unison. It was an impressive sight." She sighed dramatically and smiled at Gisela. "They are so lucky these days. It is like a breath of fresh air. You know, it was not so well planned when we were at school."

Volkmar nodded from his chair and commented, "Well, that is the future for you. It should always be an improvement on the past. Otherwise, we would all be heading backwards."

Everyone nodded and agreed, and Edeltraut looked at her watch and said her goodbyes. Katrina and Eva went upstairs to look through some albums and compare their latest handcraft creations together, while the boys finished off their homework in the intimidating presence of their father and grandfather.

Much to the boys' relief, once Gisela had left the room to inspect some items in the kitchen closet, the two men began talking in lower tones to each other and appeared to have lost interest in the boys and their sums.

"Eva is a fine girl, you know," commented Volkmar to his son. "She will be an excellent companion for Katrina. Just the kind of solid influence you would want. I know they are still young but that is exactly the time for them to start to get a clear mind about what lies ahead." Martin simply nodded and grunted an agreement, by now bored with the topic of children and desiring to continue with his magazine which as usual had captivated him.

Volkmar continued, "The whole family are doing very well these days. Edeltraut is now head of nursing in the traumatology department, although she has only been there two years, and you have probably heard that Leni herself is training to do field work as a nurse. And Roland [Eva's brother] is only twenty but what a plucky young man he is becoming. The pride of the family. Already wide awake in life, aware of how things need be done in future if this country is ever to stand tall and proud again. Did very well in the Hitler Youth, you know. He was promoted right up to Senior Cadre Unit Leader when he was only sixteen. Making great strides in the military now. They even talk of him moving into SS ranks. He has always had it in him, you know. That kind of thing lies in the blood."

He returned to his newspaper, sensing his son's lack of conversational involvement. Some minutes later Inge and Horst entered with their two young ones. Gisela was expecting them and came back through to the room carrying a tray with coffee, returning for a second with chocolate cake and plates. "Where have you been?" she asked her sister.

"We just went out for a walk in the park. Horst wanted to enjoy the sun before he heads off to the night shift."

"Night shift again?" said Gisela.

Her brother-in-law nodded. "One of the colleagues has been off sick this week. Gastroenteritis, I think they said. So I am standing in for him as well as doing my own shifts. I have been working flat out now for nine days in a row."

"*Ach du meine Güte* (goodness gracious), you must exhausted, both of you! Let me take care of little Joseph," she said, taking the baby off him and telling her visibly pregnant sister to sit down in the armchair beside Volkmar. "You should not be exerting yourself so much," she chided, which puzzled Inge as she was working her usual hours in the restaurant and still helping to clean the rooms upstairs as well.

Gisela, in her unavoidably pragmatic way of interpreting the world, considered that the duties that she had assigned to her sister were bordering on the acceptable, and that any *further* exertion would therefore be extremely unwise. For her, Inge had more than enough exercise as it was, working at the Gasthaus; without the unprofitable activity of 'walking in the park'.

"I will be fine," her sister smiled with a handsomely flushed face.

"How many months is it now?" asked Volkmar, who had been kept up-to-date on multiple occasions and still had no idea.

"Six months," said Inge back. "The doctor said the baby is due in early September."

Volkmar smiled at her with mild interest. "You look very well."

Martin said, "I expect you will want a little girl this time."

Inge laughed. "I am fine with either. As long as the child is healthy, that is all I ask for."

"Of course, of course," Martin said hastily, feeling that he might have said something amiss. He had only tried to be sociable for his wife's sake and now wished he hadn't bothered.

Volkmar added, "Then again, with two little boys already, which mother would not wish for a little girl to keep her company?"

"That is true," said Inge, not thinking so but wanting to keep the old man happy.

Gisela was rocking Joseph in her arms while Adolf stumbled around the room, inspecting Volkmar and Martin, who both paused to pamper him for some seconds. He then headed for his mother with a frown and a petulant look, like a storm about to break. Inge lifted him onto her knee and said softly, "No, no, no. There is no reason to cry, is there?"

"What is the matter with him now?" asked Gisela, always happy to cradle Joseph now that her own children were getting too big to caress and pamper.

"Nothing," laughed Inge. "He has little fits, that is all. He is alright one minute, as right as rain, and then suddenly he gets all worked up and has a little tantrum. Don't you, Adolf?" she grinned and stroked his cheek and patted his head, smirking and giggling until he followed suit. She eased back in the chair, taking the child full into her bosom. "I have worked out the trick, though. I catch him just before he is going to have a tantrum, and then I play with him and stroke him, and I laugh and he laughs too. Before you know it, he has forgotten why he wanted to have a tantrum in the first place. They are so funny like that, the little boys."

"If only it were that easy once they are grown up," quipped Gisela dryly and everyone laughed.

"I think that one was meant for you, Martin!" said Volkmar, always glad to see another man as the target of jest. Particularly in view of the fact that he was famed for receiving psychological abuse from his own wife, and was painfully aware of that fame.

Martin grinned, made a grimace, and returned to his magazine.

Horst commented on how delicious the cake was. "The best one I have ever had." He added in a low tone over at Gisela, to tease his wife, "Much better than the stuff she used to bring home from the bakery. You must have a secret that no-one else knows, Gisela." Inge gave him a playful slap on the leg.

Gisela, very flattered, smiled, "The best butter to use is Walhorner Butter. That makes all the difference. And Calba chocolate is the other trick. If you can get it of course. It is not always available and never cheap when it is, but it cannot be beaten. We serve it as a desert with whipped cream and the clients never cease to sing our praises."

Volkmar asked how old Adolf was, to which Horst replied he was two. It was noted by the women, and was embarrassing for his son Martin, that this question had been asked and answered on so many occasions already. "Joseph is one in two weeks' time," added Gisela. "We must have a little party for him."

"Time flies," nodded Horst. "Seems like yesterday when we got married, doesn't it?" he said to his wife, winking and squeezing her hand.

"And little Adolf was walking all the way through the park?" asked Gisela.

"Not all the way," said Inge. "I had to pick him up and carry him for a lot of it. But he can do a lot of metres on his own and he does not stumble hardly at all. He fell over nasty once today, though. He grazed his knees a little on the gravel, see there," and she pointed to the now slumbering boy's legs, dangling over her own. "You should have heard the rumpus he kicked up when it happened. He screamed so much, I thought everyone in the park must be looking at us."

"He certainly has got a good pair of lungs on him, that much is clear," remarked Horst with a wide grin, standing by Inge's side and stroking Adolf's hair as he looked for a nearby surface to put the plate down.

"But apart from that fall, we had a wonderful time. The fresh air and exercise have done us all good," said Inge. "They shall sleep well tonight."

After a moment of contemplative silence, they said they would be on their way home. Gisela saw them to the door before clearing up and heading back to the kitchen.

"Bernhard is coming earlier today to pick me up," commented Volkmar to Martin, once the others were all gone. "He should be here any moment now. He has a Mercedes, you know. The new model. 170 V, it is called. Much more comfortable than the last one. He says it's a great improvement, too."

"I saw Roland the other day, bumped into him in the street. He was on leave from the *Wehrpflicht* (military service)."

"Yes, I knew that. Bernhard told me that he was at home for two weeks but I did not like to ask too many details. How did he seem? I have not seen him in months - he must be very busy."

"The same as ever. Doing well apparently. He has been posted to Berlin and has been doing intense military training with motorized vehicles, including with tanks. Sounded impressive."

"Yes!" said Volkmar with gusto. "I heard all about his training. Isn't that great news? We had such high hopes for the lad but he has exceeded our wildest expectations. Truly an honour to his family. He had already completed his first *Wehrmachtdienst* (military service) last year when he was just nineteen, as a rifleman, and he showed such promise that he stayed on to further his training. That is why he is currently in Berlin. They have a specialized training course there and he has already joined the SS *Verfügungs-Division* (VT-division). Very fine men in the SS, you know. They are going to have an important future ahead of them, mark my words. Well, it was either that or the Luftwaffe, and I think he has made the right choice."

Here Martin placed his magazine on his lap and perked up to the conversation at the sound of the word "Luftwaffe". The new generations of military aircraft that were appearing was something that fascinated him greatly. He spent many a happy hour poring over pictures of the Heinkel He 111 and Dornier Do 17 bombers, the Junkers Ju 87 Stuka dive-bomber, the fighter plane Heinkel He 112, and especially his all-time favourite: the beautifully sleek Messerschmidt Bf 109. Though his technical comprehension was limited, he loved to read again and again through the technical data, even learning some of them off by heart for no reason in particular. He had just been reading in detail about the new Focke-Wolf 190, the *Würger* (strangler), that had successfully completed its maiden flight; his eye had spent time enjoying the details of the impressive frame while his mind imagined it soaring through the air and on into battle.

Like other men of his time, Martin felt it advantageous for his country, and thereby for himself, to avoid being drawn into any large terrestrial conflict that might be brewing; envisaging endless labyrinths of dark damp trenches infested with rats, as he had heard of in the last great war. But the Luftwaffe might be something else, he pondered. To the ordinary man it offered romantic visions of air pilot aces, fast speed, and invincible spins of power. "That does sound very interesting, Volkmar. And I am very glad for him. We shall have to have him over for a meal and a chat some time."

"I always knew he would do well for himself. Do you remember at little Adolf's christening, how he told us about how they got rid of that pesky teacher from the school, when he was still in the Hitler Youth?" Volkmar let out a laugh that began to develop into a longer cackle before being cut short by a hacking cough. Martin returned his gaze momentarily to his beloved magazine until the old man had recovered use of his throat to expound on the topic. "That was a story. Oh yes, I remember it like it were yesterday. Actually, I was thinking of that incident while the other boys were doing their chores in mathematics. I really can see now just what he meant at the time. Ah yes, the story of the Latin teacher, that was so funny. Shows what a plucky young fellow he was. Always very strident and resolute, he was. Very clear about his future direction, even at that tender age. But he had it in him, you see. It was in his blood. You cannot hold them down when it is in their blood." He then sighed, "These could be difficult times ahead, you know. We need all the young men with the best possible military training if the worst comes to the worst. I mean, you can never know what will happen next. We live in complicated times."

Eventually Bernhard arrived and, after a brief greeting to the whole family, during which Eva and Katrina came back downstairs, he picked up his daughter and drove a tired but enthused Volkmar home.

Gisela sat down beside Martin to do some darning that had been pending for a couple of weeks. She sighed contentedly, "A nice day today," as she worked her way up the sock. "Things are really starting to fit into place at last. I just hope the rest of the year stays that way."

Chapter 15

The town knew that war was coming. There was nothing concrete to be discerned as yet; but they keenly felt it, sensed its approach. War was gathering on the horizon like the billowing dark grey clouds of autumn thunderstorms. It seemed unfathomable, frightful, but somehow at the same time the only sensible option left open. On the one hand they judged themselves powerless to stop it and, especially in the case of the older townsfolk who still vividly remembered the Great War that had ended just one generation before, they greatly feared its potential. Yet at the same time they welcomed it. There was a bloodthirsty anger brewing in large segments of the society that could only be stilled by revenge. They heard of their people being maltreated in eastern areas of Europe where they formed the ethnic minority; in particular, in Poland. They knew (and even the children had calculated) the continued economic strife that the Treaty of Versailles had placed on them. They were forming an increasingly overriding conviction of being historical victims; a people that had been grievously wronged, so often in the past, and that the time had come for justice to be served.

Many perceived the war's ineluctable passage ahead (gleaned from the constant flow of references in radio broadcasts and press communications that seemed to be whetting the public's appetite, preparing them for the idea of military action); others discussed it obsessively. For those more critical, or simply more cynical members of the town's population, any honest and fearful comments were only to be made in hushed tones. Even when made in private, opinions were whispered lest the children should hear and repeat what they shouldn't. Outwardly, in public, only the most ostentatious shows of patriotism were morally permissible. Anything less would have been tantamount to treachery and that did not simply entail social, or even familial ostracization. Anti-war activism was curbed with harsh punitive measures, with concentration camps being built at lightning speed.

There was in general, though, a very positive support for the direction their country was moving in, principally because the media, since 1933 firmly under the Party's thumb, was churning out what the political and military elite wanted the population to hear, and omitting anything which interfered with that narrative. With heavily controlled newspaper and other media sources being their first and foremost reference to what was happening in the outside world, the Germans were dished up an alternative reality that no-one had any reason to doubt. Those who did doubt, did so at their own - not inconsiderable - risk.

Inge and Horst were present on a few occasions when political topics arose in the company of others; for many like them, the subjects brought up were passed round the group like a hot potato that no-one wants to hold for too long. Ultimately, they saw political discourse as divisive, even among close families, and in their own case a potential threat to their marital harmony, a lesson they had learned in the wake of the *Kristallnacht*. The only time the issue was subjected to prolonged discussion was in connection with Inge's aunt Hertha, who lived in a small town in a rural part of East Prussia; that happened with a certain regularity, whenever Inge's mother had received a letter from her. Otherwise, they had plenty to keep their thoughts occupied, between work and bringing up two lively and very small children. With the spring announcement of Inge's pregnancy, family was the dominant topic that year.

Gisela likewise was very occupied, in her case not only with children but also with the running of the Gasthaus and restaurant. The main thoughts that she entertained in terms of politics, international or domestic, were concerns that a conflict might adversely affect business. Martin was taciturn, though more out of ignorance on the subject and apathy for political discussion. He made some sporadic comments, but generally parroted other family members and said nothing that everyone did not already know (outside of fussy technical data pertaining to war planes). One night in late July he hinted that war looked "inevitable", having heard that adjective used by Volkmar the day before. Gisela retorted, "You had better hope there is no war coming in the near future. That would have a terrible effect on the number of visitors. It would drastically reduce the number of inland tourists, and practically wipe out the foreign guests. Who is going to come and visit us if we are at war with them?" Martin looked perplexed when she spat it out like that.

His father Volkmar Landeck was far more relaxed on the subject and dismissive of talk of an international conflict. Moreover, being no longer in business himself and comfortably retired on savings, he did not directly perceive the threat to commercial interests in the same way as his daughter-in-law. Nor would he be called up to fight, should the worst come to the worst. Retirement had given Volkmar the privilege of viewing current affairs through the binoculars of theoretical principles and moral stances, rather than more pragmatic concerns. He listened to the radio, joined in with the discussions, enjoyed the heat of passionate debate. He placed his complete trust in the Führer and his decisions, and was sure the Führer would do what he had always done so far: stare out the other man and make him look away first. "He is too canny for them all," he chuckled. "He could call their bluff again and again, and they would still come back for more."

He held the British Prime Minister, Neville Chamberlain, in particular contempt; noting with great (albeit contradictory) satisfaction and a sense of justice the agreements reached for ethnic Germans in the Sudetenland area of Czechoslovakia, while at the same time noting that the British and French had ultimately been weak and let themselves be intimidated. All of which delighted him. His low opinion of the other European powers was confirmed in March 1939 when the Führer decided to occupy the whole of Czech territory and establish a protectorate there, far exceeding the agreement reached the year before in Munich, while still holding on to 'peace in Europe'. This made perfect sense to him and confirmed his own views; he repeatedly stated throughout the summer of 1939 how the Führer wanted to simply restore the German Reich to its former dimensions by retaking a few pieces of territory that no-one was especially interested in. The Führer might gradually take some more in the vast East of Europe, for good measure, and that would be the end of this great game. When the moment was ripe, Hitler would stop and be contented; but when precisely that was to happen, no-one could guess. Volkmar would say all this with the frail conviction of a fortune-teller reading a palm, "He is brilliant, utterly brilliant." Volkmar was also of the opinion that his age imparted him a special wisdom that rose above the views of younger news enthusiasts such as Cousin Carsten or Bernhard. His vanity would have been so happily pampered if they had acknowledged his sagacity more often, but sadly for Volkmar this was not to be the case.

Carsten was also a warm follower of the Führer and the nationalistic, militaristic direction that Germany was taking. Since four very instructive years spent as a member of the Hitler Youth up till the age of seventeen, he had been a firm and passionate believer in the principles of National Socialism, the tenets of which he felt he was grasping more with each passing year. His overt passion on the subject had caused the occasional clash at home with his family. Carsten's parents – 'Uncle' Robert (as he was known in Lüneburg) and his wife Gretha – held more of a *bürgerlich-konservativ* (middle-class conservative) stance in politics. They had at first greatly distrusted the NSDAP, which they viewed as radical and dangerous, and they disliked the frenzied aura of Hitler and the loud, thuggish, Jew-hating crowd that followed him. They had voted for Hugenberg and his national conservative DVNP party right up to the last free general election in March 1933, but had then seen how Hugenberg had gone on to give the new regime his full support after all. Eventually, like many traditional and patriotic conservatives, they had resigned themselves to Hitler being the best of the worst, which in any case was all there was on offer. They voted for Hitler's plan to re-militarize the Rhineland in the 1936 referendum, like the vast majority of Germans. With time they even warmed more to the Führer, especially with the economic upturn and reduction in unemployment, issues that lay closest to their political hearts.

Their son Carsten, the oldest of five, was not only far more directly enthusiastic about the Nazi Party but he also possessed a strong internal need to proselytize. The long and tiring conversations that the extended family, friends of the family, and even neighbours were subjected to, did not make him very popular at home. Furthermore, he had shown some deeply worrying signs of having the tendency to eventually become a first-class snitch. He had on several occasions reported to his father suspicions of unpatriotic conduct and comments amongst people they knew, much to the surprise and uneasiness of both parents.

Robert himself was very aware of the new and ardent political beliefs that were flourishing in the country, and that formed part of his basic mistrust of the Nazis in the first place. There was a case that Robert knew of, that had occurred a couple of years previous back in 1937, in which a 14-year-old boy in the neighbourhood had been tempted by a local SA group to report any irregular activity to them, with the promise of a new bicycle as a reward for any incriminating evidence. The boy had taken the offer to heart and, of all people, had reported his own parents for writing and printing anti-Nazi 'propaganda'. Both mother and father were found guilty and sent to prison, from there later taken to a local concentration camp in Fuhlsbüttel. The boy found himself all alone in the world and, for the record, without the bicycle. Naturally, no relative wanted anything to do with him and eventually he ended up being sent off, with just one little suitcase of clothes, to an orphanage. It was a haunting tale and although Carsten's family had absolutely nothing to hide, it still provided bitter food for thought, especially with regards to the oldest son.

It was almost a relief, his own mother commented to a friend (though she did not mean 'almost'), when he moved down to Lüneburg to work for the *Deutsche Reichsbahn* railway. His four siblings in Hamburg were delighted.

Once settled in Lüneburg, Carsten was soon back to his evangelical ways but he had little luck with his more distant family there. Those who were already strong supporters of the NSDAP did not need to be lectured to by this little *Grünschnabel* (whippersnapper) about the state of the nation; those who were not, listened politely and made a mental note to avoid the young man where possible in future. Nonetheless, in the back room of the Gasthaus he felt very much at home. Fed by Gisela, who flatly told him she wasn't interested in politics; and sitting between Martin, who liked to quietly concentrate on his magazines in the evening, and Volkmar, who held the same opinions but preferred to listen to political discourse on the new radio. Occasionally Volkmar had to hush the lad if it looked like he was about to open a monologue.

Gisela might have been unwilling to discuss politics, but in a way she had slowly warmed to the idea of having Hitler leading the nation - at least so far – and that was down to a single factor. Like Robert and Gretha, she had actively disliked him at first: the loud rants and the melodramatic rhetoric had put her off. She had no interest whatsoever in ideological issues such as the need for purity in the German race or the recovery of long-lost territories in the east of Europe or in south-west Africa; about such things she really could not care less. Moreover, there was something basic and animalistic about the Party that further irritated her. From the thuggery of the Brownshirts to all the speeches about strength and Germanic potency, she had felt an instinctive antipathy to this obsession with physical perfection and power. Her own third child Erich was severely handicapped, having suffered from polio as a boy, and she doted on him with all the maternal adoration in the world. Sometimes she could not shake off the feeling that her little Erich did not fit into the ideals that the Nazis considered eminent in their Weltanschauung, and the sensation that they might wish him harm.

Married to Martin, she had noticed with time how pro-Nazi many of her in-laws had become and accordingly never entered into any political discourse; she had always avoided such topics or eventually turned the discussions into harmless chatter about the more mundane issues in their lives. Volkmar, as Bernhard and Edeltraut too, had just assumed she was a little slow intellectually and left her in peace. And with the arrival of her children, Gisela then had all the subject matter she needed to fill any conversation. Now that the children were older, the management of the Gasthaus also fulfilled that purpose.

Gisela merely wanted to see the economy improve in general, with more jobs available, more products in the shops, and more money in men's pockets; and see the old problems of mad inflation brought under control. Furthermore, she considered it vital that there was law and order in the land, and thus an end to the political tension and violence that had plagued the country since the republic had been formed. Even those like Gisela who did not actively follow politics, could not help but hear of the fights, the riots, the assassinations that had plagued the shaky Weimar Republic.

Hitler, on the other hand came across as the classic Strong Man, one who had things firmly under control; that was something that Gisela could mentally latch onto (in this sense, she was very close to Horst and his standpoint, although the two never discussed such issues and so never found out about the cognitive proximity of the other). Gisela considered the running of a country to be akin to the running of a business or a family: one needed tight control of finances and personnel, a firm grip on everyday management issues, and above all a strict sense of *Ordnung* (order). *"Ordnung muss sein"* (there must be order) was not just a German cliché but indeed a common phrase of hers, that she used to instill this notion in her children and, when necessary, her husband too. Once a society had achieved this perfect state of *Ordnung*, she felt, everything else would soon fit into place. All the same, her inner satisfaction with the country's direction under Hitler was something she kept to herself - especially when visiting her parents – and would in any case soon be dented by the Führer's increasingly bellicose intentions.

Seeing the intensity with which political opinion had started to capture people's conversations, Inge's side of the family had in general come to be much more cautious with that particular theme. It was an open secret that her father Georg loathed Hitler with a passion and always had. (He and his wife, both Catholics, had traditionally voted for the centrist party *Zentrum* – and Georg referred to the Nazis as "heathens".) Since the *Machtergreifung* of 1933, and following advice not only urgently given out by his family but also a potentially hazardous situation cognized by himself, his once prominent rants against the politician had waned. Nowadays he preferred to say nothing outside of the most intimate family: that meant blood family only, and not in-laws like the Grüns or the Landecks. Even Horst he did not fully trust. There were some sporadic moments, invariably when alcoholic consumption was in play, when he would let loose a flow of vitriol against the dictator and all those who supported him. But by now these were few and far between. He had heard of enough people receiving late-evening visits from the state police, and even some who had done time in one of the newly mushrooming concentration camps, for him to express himself too carelessly. When he was unable to hold his tongue any longer, however, the old misanthrope turned out to be one of the few who had fully comprehended what was actually happening in the land.

One evening earlier that year, in March, Inge had gone round to visit her parents with the children and was chatting with her brother

Ernst in the front room while Georg was sitting as usual by the fire. Corinna was sitting by the window, taking advantage of the meagre light to mend her husband's shirts and humming along to chansons playing on the gramophone. Ernst had served coffee for himself, his mother and Inge, while his father downed a couple of schnaps with the crackling firelight on his face. Inge rocked the pram with a sleeping Adolf with one hand, while she cuddled up Joseph to her chest with the other.

"You know what I think about all this. *Dieser...dieser böhmische Gefreite* (This...this Bohemian corporal)," Georg began contemptuously. Ernst looked at his sister and grimaced while she smiled back, both fearing a heated sermon was on the way.

Georg took another gulp of liquor. "This Bohemian corporal is not going to be happy until there is a war. And not just any old war, oh no. No, no, no. A major conflict; a global conflict, even. That is what he really wants. He is a warmonger if ever I saw one. You can see it in that glint in his eye." None of those present were aware of any glint, but said nothing.

Georg continued, "He will go too far, and England and France and Russia and all of them will come for his head. But that is what he wants, the old fool. That is exactly what he wants. You will see, there will be war again. And soon."

"I don't know if war is in anyone's best interest, Papa," said Ernst.

"Then what is all this military spending in aid of? *U-Boots*, airplanes, tanks – there is no end to it all."

"Sometimes the reason a great nation has to arm itself, has nothing to do with war and conquest but rather is precisely in order to assure peace among other nations. Someone has to step in and take the initiative when everyone else is bickering and divided. And furthermore, it has to be said that this has been an enormous boost for our economy," said Ernst. "We can all see how much better off everyone has become since the Führer has been in power."

"But that doesn't answer my question. What do you do with all those machines you are producing? Just let them sit idle! No, no, I don't think so. He is plotting and planning. He is up to something."

"He has a very high reputation abroad," said Ernst, who normally did not care to argue with his father, but on this occasion felt it right to put the record straight on the Führer and negate his father's constant attempts to malign the man. "And with good reason. He is a strong man, and people respect a strong man. Foreign leaders especially, and that is precisely what our country needs in these difficult times."

"I do not see strength when I see Hitler. All I see is anger, and anger is not strength."

"But look at what the Reich has become. Last year alone we had the *Anschluß* (annexation of Austria) and after that were able to sort out the issue of the Sudetenland," persisted Ernst unabated, addressing his uninterested sister and mother, too. "There were a lot of reports published last year, I have read many myself in the *Niedersachsen-Stürmer*, written by journalists who are actually there on the spot in the Sudetenland and could see with their own eyes what was going on. It was a dire situation, with a lot of hostility from the Czechs towards the Germans including verbal and even physical attacks. No-one was really standing up for the German people over there, just Konrad Henlein and his party. We got the *Münchner Abkommen* (Munich Agreement) last September and suddenly people were sitting up and realizing, *THAT* is the way you get respect in this world. Even the Czechs have realized that the other powers are all on Hitler's side. Britain and France have given him everything he has asked for, and happily so. Since then, I have read the Czechs have been very subdued. Hence, problem solved."

Georg did not possess the geopolitical background to argue with his son, nor the desire to calmly debate a matter that he felt so viscerally. "Everything is so extreme with him. Everything is so loud and furious. I do not like someone wagging their finger in my face and talking to me like a teacher talks to a child. And they only gave him his little piece of Czechoslovakia because no-one could care less about it."

"Papa, it is about standing up for what is just and right. For years now the SDP - and the communists first and foremost! - have been running this country and its economy and its people into the ground. Now, finally, things are starting to look up, so of course support for the Führer is so strong. Everybody wants something they can be proud of. It would be unnatural not to. People are tired of bad news, they want something positive in their lives. And it is not just the Führer that is bringing about this change. You have to admit there are some fine people in the party. Competent and courageous people who are looking to make a positive change and are working hard to get things done."

"Like that old drunkard Telschow, I suppose," grunted Georg.

Ernst spread out his hands in exasperation. "He says what he thinks. And he believes in what he says. What more could you ask of a politician?" He also found it a bit rich that his father should express that sentiment while working his way through a bottle of *Kirschwasser* schnaps, though he bit his tongue.

To the women's relief the arrival of Horst, coming to meet up with Inge and the children and take her home, put an end to that line of conversation and Corinna fussed around them both and dispelled the debate.

On another occasion, Gisela and Martin came to visit bringing their three children with them. Georg was in an irritable mood and, aware that Martin was *hitlerfreundlich* (siding with Hitler and his ideology) on the one side but lacking in intellectual depth, he decided to pick a fight by flatly deriding the Nazis as the family sat round the table. Martin showed all due respect that he held for his father-in-law, which in turn was forged on the back of the even greater respect he had for his wife, and took the spars and needling of the old man with a nod and chuckle to avoid any deeper disagreement. When Martin did offer up any comments, they were the usual standpoints that all Germans of whatever political persuasion shared anyway: the injustice of the Versailles Treaty and the sheer impossibility of paying back the astronomical reparation payments demanded, the return of Saarland or the Polish Corridor to Germany, or the loss of the German colonies in Africa while the French and British still held on to their own numerous territories. It was evidently hypocritical to many, and Martin repeated the old colonial cliché about Germans deserving *their* "place in the sun" too. Georg, who remembered his own late father using the same expression many years ago, did not contradict.

Gisela took advantage of the lull and launched into a full-scale report about the latest refurbishments at the Gasthaus, the progress of her children in their studies, and an amazing array of banal details about little Adolf and Joseph. Alone the fact that Joseph was now teething became a conversational filler in its own right, and Corinna was eager to know all the details.

After Gisela and her family had gone, Corinna chided Georg softly in an unusually candid moment for her that was occasioned by her own existential fear. She knew that Katrina was good friends with Edeltraut's daughter Eva, who in turn was in the BDM: talk got round so easily between young girls. "Just be careful what you say when we have people round to visit, Georg. Just stick to normal, general topics – comme il faut. Not politics. And you should not talk so openly and critically like that about the authorities, and especially not in front of children. They are the first to repeat that kind of talk and they do not even know what they are saying."

Acidic through the drink, he retorted that it was none of her business what he said or whom he said it to - he would speak his mind wherever and whenever he deemed necessary. However, he did take inner note of his wife's words and procured to be more careful in public. Fortunately for the whole family, he only ever drank at home or on very special occasions. There was no chance of his blathering away thoughtlessly in pubs, as some other men did.

But however much Georg tried to aggravate those around him, he did at least give them food for thought: would there really be war? That spring there was the feeling in the family that war was something that might occur at some point, but that nonetheless had to be taken in one's stride. For most, war lay somewhere between a heroic sacrifice for the sake of the future of the German people on the one hand, and a sadly necessary evil on the other. This was the type of view expressed by such people as Ernst and Martin, or many colleagues of Horst from the fire station, or Horst's brother Karl-Heinz and his wife Ilse. They regarded war in the context of a chiefly defensive conflict. Should the country be attacked, by any of the (many) enemies of the Germans, then there would be no other option but to go to war. In this context a German military reaction would obviously be completely justified. They found the militarization programme that Hitler had launched to be highly commendable and prescient, then in this way the country would be prepared for the worst.

Those who more meticulously followed the words of the Führer, whether out of love or out of fear, had been given strong hints at the beginning of the year already. In January 1939 in Berlin, Hitler clearly uttered in a speech the words 'world war'; into which, he claimed, nations would be plunged due to the machinations of "international finance Jewry", and furthermore that this would then lead to the total annihilation of the Jewish race. Two major upcoming plans were thus exposed for all to hear, that would later come as a surprise to many.

Plenty of townsfolk of more fervently nationalistic persuasion - like Volkmar, Carsten, or Edeltraut - went even further. They supported a more radical approach in that the launch of a pre-emptive strike would also be justifiable against any perceivable threats, including against the great military powers of Britain and France, if need be. But all these people still clung to the idea that the most likely outcome of any major international friction would ultimately be a peaceful one. The odd military clash here or there perhaps, but nothing that would last more than a few weeks and certainly nothing that Germany would not emerge from in an even better position than before. Among the older population, who were naturally fearful of war, there was a trust in the Führer's ability to control the international community and play them off against each other wherever necessary.

With teenagers and young adults, however, devotion to the Führer was much more zealous and was often mixed with a thirst for conquest and revenge. This young generation, that had grown up in the twenties and thirties, had had no direct contact to war outside of the tales of father and grandfathers. Many had been sufficiently brainwashed by the controlling ideology that they followed the new military enthusiasm with blind obedience. They had been taught in school and the Hitler Youth that the Germans had been the rightful victors of the last great conflict but had been betrayed in the ultimate moment by the *Novemberverräter* (November traitors), a coalition of quitters and turncoats: Social Democrats and Bolsheviks, academics and artists, a weak bourgeoise, timorous politicians, and in particular Jews and other avarice-driven bankers. While the soldiers of the German Reich had stood brave and tall, ready to continue fighting, to give their all for their nation, the Kaiser himself had beat a hasty retreat to Holland while cowardly politicians had stabbed those young men in the back. Hitler, wounded in a gas attack on the battlefield, had allegedly wept his heart out when news of the capitulation came through.

To deepen the convictions and military prowess of the next generation, the Hitler Youth engaged incessantly in parades and mock manoeuvres. The high point came in September of 1938 when a Hitler Youth event consisting of just such military displays culminated in the marching into the city stadium of 80,000 boys and young men in tight formation to spell out the name of Adolf Hitler on the grounds, in an extravagant show of devotion to their idol. There, to clamourous cheering and applause from the young party faithfuls, Hitler gave a memorable speech in which he told them that they would one day rule the world. They had no reason to doubt his words.

These boys were also being drawn effortlessly into an atmosphere of casual violence that was exemplified by the behaviour of the SA. By the peak of the savagery witnessed in the *Kristallnacht*, they had started to take violence for granted, seeing it as a means to achieve what rightfully belonged to them. There was compulsory military service in effect and many had completed the training; fired up by the establishment, they were itching for a fight already. Little excuse would be more than enough to willingly enter a scenario in which they would engage in armed combat to the death with the supposed foes who threatened their country and ultimately their families. Some were furthermore being drawn deeper into the ruling ideology and the ranks of the SS, where they would also receive a select training that would undermine all basic principles of humanity and prepare these pliable minds for atrocities that, they were clearly being told, they may have to commit some day for the sake of Führer and *Vaterland*.

It became increasingly apparent to many that everything was about to be pitched in a final struggle for control of their destiny, and for the survival of the German people. They were prepared to meet that challenge, to lay down their lives where necessary; for in the case of defeat, they would be swept aside and wiped out in any case. Faced with the magnitude of such a threat, there was next to nothing to lose and so very much to gain.

It has to be said that no-one at this time was content about the German-Polish border as it had been set after the Great War. Even during the tumultuous times of the Weimar Republic - when different political parties were continually at each other's throats - the loss of the eastern German territories, that had been 'robbed' and 'handed over' ipso facto to Poland, was one of the few points of unity in an otherwise fragmented and very unharmonious political arena.

Reports began to seep through of attacks on German civilians by Polish nationalists. The media was quick to cover these alleged attacks and so stir up a blaze of public outrage in favour of its political patrons. The Nazi propaganda unashamedly fomented the nationalist sentiment, incited the population to wrath and a willingness to violence in the face of a heavy flow of negative stories. The idea had been carefully honed of the German people being demonstrably under existential threat by an enemy force: that weak, inferior but nonetheless pernicious Slavic *Untermensch* that was keen to see its old archenemy wiped off the map for once and for all. Now it was ever sharper and more discernible. This existentialist threat they faced was laid open and raw before them, shown in countless newsreel stories and printed in countless newspaper articles. As was naturally to be expected, the German population reacted accordingly. Faced with such horror, more and more of them opened themselves up to the necessity of crushing the enemy before it had the opportunity to annihilate them.

Throughout the summer of 1939 more and more details of alleged atrocities against Germans were covered by the media, reaching a peak in August with the reported murder of Germans in Kattowitz and other Polish border towns. Hitler reacted swiftly to these reports with spontaneous meetings and furious speeches held throughout the Reich. He attracted huge crowds, was passionately cheered and applauded wherever he appeared.

And besides, asked many, and were backed up by 'indisputable' historical reference: what was this 'Poland' anyway? A rough formless shape consisting of land hacked off from the territory of other civilizations, to be sewn together like some hideous modern Frankenstein's monster. This issue – this very questioning of the existence of a nation - was openly discussed, from the halls of civil service buildings down to the history lessons at secondary schools. It was brought into living rooms by young students who casually referred to a war, the horrors of which they had never experienced first-hand.

A typical example of these thought processes being explored in school classes happened in Lüneburg in the early summer, just before the holidays, at the Johanneum, the prominent *Gymnasium* (high school) there. It appeared in lessons imparted by Herrn Münster, the recently graduated humanities and philosophy professor: "It is important to bear in mind that, from a historical perspective, Poland is barely recognizable as an actual modern state," he told the attentive students. "It was already split up over a century ago and divided between Germany, Austria, Hungary and Russia. To all intents and purposes, it should have been long since dead." He concluded that it had only reappeared in the wake of the treacherous pact forced onto Germany in 1919, a creation brought to life by the victor nations as a punishment for Germany losing a war that it had never actually lost. This creature had been reanimated, reactivated, brought to life from nothingness, to be transformed into a puppet state whose sole goal was to frustrate German progress and unity. The whole situation was completely unreasonable and reasonless. "How should a mere concept lay claim to any rights if it does not truly exist?" he argued. "How can you kill something that is already dead?"

Toward the end of August there came for many the missing piece in the jigsaw that seemed to fit effortlessly into place. It came with the brazen announcement of the non-aggression pact that was to be signed between the Soviet Union and Germany: the Molotov-Ribbentrop pact, named after the country's respective foreign ministers. This was a mutual agreement between these two great powers that effectively divided Poland into two parts; a western half that would inevitably fall under German control, and an eastern half that would be left for Stalin to administer as he pleased. This deal had a clearly specious allure and yet – as so often happens in politics – it appeared to be a firm and attractive solution for the time being.

With that, the way forward looked clear. Germany could gobble up its half of Poland and the hitherto eastern expansion would halt there. As expected, there was indignation and even threats of war from Britain and France, who had ostensibly declared their intention to stand by Poland in the event of a German invasion. But their will to actually defend it with any kind of solid military action seemed unlikely, given their track record so far of acceding to all the Führer's demands. In that way, a bloody international war would be avoided and in its place would transpire a minor military skirmish with a technologically weak nation that would be over in no time. Germany would recover its lost territories and furthermore obtain a large chunk of *Lebensraum* for a whole new generation of settlers. Expansion was deemed both the necessary and natural way forward for Germany; for that which stops growing, eventually rots. Had not other European nations already cut their way into the world in the shape of vast empires, taking endless swathes of land in far off continents: the Portuguese and the Spanish, the French, the Dutch, and above all the British? Even Italy had had its chunks of Africa. This time it would be the turn of the Germans, to both recover and then expand their might. It would bring in a new historical era in which the Führer would be further confirmed in his track record as a giant among both statesmen and warriors. A modern hero for modern times.

There was widespread optimism for this seemingly plausible outcome; yet still something nagged at the minds of some Germans and made the approaching clouds of war all the more dark and threatening. Had it all been planned all along? There was something that didn't add up. The swollen military-industrial machine had provided so many with so much employment and manufactured so much weaponry: tanks, fighter and bomber planes, destroyers, submarines, armaments and ammunition in huge quantities – all ready for action. The conscription and armed forces were training an entire youth. The bunkers and air raid cellars being constructed in all cities and major towns, in case of aerial bombardment; the mass deliveries of gas masks to the civilian population. The fierce and grandiose language in the radio, the notion of a battle of titanic forces, plucked from ancient sagas and legends. The tense feeling that the political elite was preparing for a major showdown that must surely extend beyond Warsaw. The cheery and uneventful summer, the calm before the storm.

A stable and warm late August was bringing a pleasant summer to an end, and the mood was buoyant throughout Germany. Meanwhile in Berlin, a secret plan, that had thus far been referred to under the codename of Operation Tannenberg, was being hatched. The operation had been organized within the Gestapo and was the brainchild of Reinhard Heydrich, a high-ranking SS officer and director of the Gestapo and the Security Police, together with his deputy Heinrich Müller. Since 8th August they had been planning a series of fake military provocations along the German-Polish border, designed to act as ammunition in a propaganda war at home that would flare up at the same time as the German military operations. These incidents would be carried out by trained members of an elite taskforce taken from the *Sicherheitsdienst* – part of the SS security service. Already in the weeks before, the German press had been carefully preparing the wider population for the possibility of an upcoming military conflict. Now, solid evidence of the stark necessity to take action was to be delivered.

Around three hundred young men had been chosen from the ranks of the *Sicherheitsdienst* and taken to a specialist training school in Bernau bei Berlin, a small town around ten kilometres to the north of the capital. The prerequisites demanded of the candidates were a top level of physical fitness, a good to excellent command of the Polish language, and a firm commitment to absolute silence concerning their activities. As a disguise, the school was officially labelled as a fencing school; and indeed fencing, boxing and other fighting sports, together with gymnastics, target practice and general combat training, were part of the programme that the men underwent in those three August weeks. The object was for these agents, disguised as Polish military units, to launch minor, simulated, and newsworthy attacks on German *Dienststellen* (government institutions), that should appear as perfectly realistic and plausible from the outside.

Several targets were chosen and, as the month drew to its close, the faux sabotage crews struck at various pre-arranged points on the final day of August: a customs house on the German-Polish border, a forestry building, a small and unimportant railway yard – all came under pretend attack. The final highlight of the drama came in the evening at 20:00 at a radio transmission tower in Gleiwitz, beside the German-Polish border. A group of seven of the best trainees - organized in the week before and driven up from Berlin that very day - dressed themselves up as Polish soldiers and seized the tower by force, surprising the unsuspecting German civilian employees. The men spoke only Polish, both to the terrified German technicians as well as to one another. Holding the crew at gunpoint, they gave a strongly anti-German announcement in Polish which was sent out through the radio transmitter. It all took just thirteen minutes but was a very convincing show. Once the mission was complete, they disappeared into the dense night, leaving behind just a few random corpses of local German political prisoners, killed earlier that day and lying around with disfigured faces. This was to give the impression of a gunfight having taken actually place that very evening, with German casualties.

Together with details of the other incidents, this was the news that was sprayed out onto an unsuspecting German population that balmy late summer evening.

A few hours later there came an announcement from Adolf Hitler, in the early hours of 1st September 1939 in his idiosyncratically angry abrasive tone, through the NS-Rundfunk radio channel: "Poland has on this night, for the first time on our own territory, opened fire with regular troops." The speech climaxed in the now legendary words: "*Seit 5:45 wird jetzt zurückgeschossen* - Since 5:45am we have been returning that fire." Among all the untruths and disinformation was also the small fact that this had actually happened one hour earlier, at 4:45am.

Meanwhile, further to the east the German warship *Schleswig-Holstein*, until then inconspicuously awaiting orders, abruptly slid into the Danzig Bay. She anchored there and proceeded to launch a heavy fire attack on the Westerplatte, a long sandy peninsula which lay in front of the Danzig's actual harbour and was the site of an important ammunition depot of the Polish army. The nearby city shuddered as the shells thundered into the depot. The small army garrison guarding it, barely two hundred soldiers in total and only armed with machine guns and rifles, possessing not a single cannon nor tank, was utterly taken by surprise. The men were sleeping in their uniforms that night, as was the custom in these uncertain times, but nothing had prepared them for the sheer force of the bombardment that came out of nowhere.

People in Danzig itself were shaken out of their beds in astonishment as it roared fiercely in the bay not far from the harbour. For the Polish citizens of the city, it was the terrifying signal of the beginning of a bloody conflict lying ahead. For the majority ethnic Germans living in Danzig, however, it had all the exciting feel of a liberation campaign. They perceived that they were finally to be freed from the Polish yoke by their Führer and their countrymen.

At almost exactly the same moment, in the dark early hours of that fateful morning, the small town of Weilun in central Poland was suddenly attacked from the air by a squadron of German Stukas. The town was a nondescript settlement in a quiet rural area, of no possible military nor industrial interest, making the attack quite incomprehensible. The confused, dishevelled townsfolk ran for cover as quickly as they could. The planes divebombed for hours in repeated waves, reducing much of the town to rubble and killing several hundred civilians. Meanwhile, all along the German-Polish border, *Wehrmacht* troops set about removing boom barriers, fences and other impediments. They poured almost unhindered across the collapsing frontier. In total, 54 divisions – with almost 1.5 million men and over 3,000 tanks – would overrun the border to commence the occupation of the neighbouring land.

As all throughout the country, the news spread round Lüneburg that Friday like wildfire. People rushed from one house to another to tell family members, friends, neighbours this latest bulletin, in case someone had still not heard. Although partly to be expected, it was an astonishing event all the same. People gathered together around radios to catch the latest developments. There were few signs of enthusiasm; the mood was more subdued, even among those who were otherwise quite loyal to the Party.

In the evening of the following day, 2ⁿᵈ September, Inge Grün was heard upstairs in her apartment, crying out with the pain that the sudden contractions, though still relatively light, were now causing her. Horst was on duty that Saturday but Gisela had fortunately been passing by and appeared just in time to assist her. Greatly concerned at the pain her sister was visibly in, she immediately called for the midwife.

Frau Klaußner arrived punctually and Horst had rushed home as soon as he was notified at work. He was by her side the whole time during the birth, holding her hand tightly and kissing her, a constant flow of encouraging words as the night set in on the window behind them. Frau Klaußner told him he should go downstairs and get some rest, but he assured her that he was used to being up all night. It was not an easy labour this time, as it had been with Joseph. After midnight the baby's head began to move down the channel as the contractions became much heavier; decidedly painful and ripping inside her to make her scream involuntarily. The neighbours had already been warned that this could be a long night. It was not until three o'clock in the early hours that she finally gave birth. Dazed, she heard the sex of the child, once again a male, from the midwife. But after kissing and hugging her newborn in delight, she could not help drifting off and eventually fell into a deep sleep, completely exhausted.

Horst took the child to his chest and looked worried, but Frau Klaußner assured him the reason for his wife's pain and discomfort and the long labour most probably lay with the child's considerable size, coming in at 2.75 kg. It seemed, as Horst himself thought when he gazed at the babe, an unduly fat and big-boned child compared to the first two.

The name had already been decided, which Horst passed on to the hospital administration the next day when he came to visit his wife. It had been a difficult decision at first, with so many possibilities open. In the summer they had visited Horst's father Opa Grün (Konrad Grün) in Uelzen a few times, in the wake of the death of his wife. The widower was by now close to seventy and deaf as a post, though showing no other signs of physical weakness. He was mentally affected by his spouse's passing, about which he talked incessantly; and complained that he never saw his children, to which Horst felt frequent twinges of guilty conscience. He, like his siblings, had neglected his filial duty.

Inge and Horst had taken Adolf and Joseph with them, still babies in a double pram and a sight that softened the elderly's man heart and invigorated his tongue for the rest of the visit. Old times were discussed without end, as if he were desperate to relive a past that was starting to disappear in the midst of his wife's death, his increasingly absent children, and his own failing memory. He talked long and candidly about his life, while his son and daughter-in-law listened faithfully and even the children behaved.

Elisabeth and Konrad Grün had had six children altogether. Four of them had survived into adulthood, and the two that had died in infancy were a subject that Horst had never entered into much in conversation, apart from the barest of details. It was then, during one particular visit in July, that Inge came to get to know so many particulars about the siblings of her husband, both those living and those who had passed away.

The Grüns' first two children were Karl-Heinz and Marianne, both now married and with their own children. The third child, named Hermann, had died of pneumonia in the same year as he was born (1910). The following year had come Horst himself, and in the year after that his "little" brother (as he had always viewed him), Wilhelm. The sixth and last child Hildegard (1914-1917) had died as a child, suffering from enteritis with diarrhoea, exacerbated by malnutrition in the war years. Inge had secretly inclined in favour of Hildegard, among a small group of names she was considering for her own child's name if it were to be a girl. She found Hermann very suitable too, she said, and Horst smiled and wiped away a tear. Thus, both Hermann and Hildegard were deemed the perfect names for their yet to be born offspring. The families were informed and passed kind and appropriate comments. Except Volkmar Landeck, who was drunk when he heard and cackled about the choice of name for the boy and referenced the minister and head of the Luftwaffe. He even quipped about how the family was soon going to resemble a fine parade of Party prominence, in name at least; though he refrained from doing so in the presence of Inge or Horst. Gisela kept the overheard comment to herself, partly out of embarrassment, and partly so as not to cause her sister and brother-in-law any unnecessary irritation.

And so early on Sunday 3rd September 1939 a boy came into the world, to be the last of Inge and Horst's children, and he was named Hermann Grün. Two days later, France and England declared war on Germany in response to its invasion of Poland. With this declaration, the international conflict officially commenced, although to all intents and purposes it had already long since done so.

Chapter 16

Gisela and Martin were looking ahead at a dreary late autumn and early winter, with a massive drop in bookings compared to the same period in the previous year. It was never a good season for their usual clientele: neither businessmen nor tourists. In the wake of the newly developing war, most of the paltry few bookings made in the summer had already been cancelled. Although the general mood in Germany was optimistic and positively charged, with oft broadcast scenes of the successes of the Polish campaign in the news, it was still felt to be an unwise time to be spending idle money on unnecessary luxuries. Tourism now smacked of frivolous indulgence when young men were risking their lives for the Fatherland in foreign countries. Foreign bookings had almost completely dried up; those from previously well-represented nations such as the Netherlands, Denmark, and naturally France and Britain, were all gone.

In this bleak scenario, a booking for four separate rooms for visiting military officers for an entire working week in late November came as a godsend. The reservation was received with great excitement and swiftly confirmed in early October. The prerequisite was that the men would have the hotel to themselves and no-one else would be staying. Martin and Gisela had no objection to this pre-condition as the hotel was looking to stay empty that week in any case. Shortly before the visit, the name behind the booking request turned up in person, in the form of a visit from an SS officer, *Hauptscharführer* Ritter. A tall blond and strikingly handsome man with cropped hair and chiselled square jaw, he was received by Gisela and her husband on the Friday of the week before the other men were due to arrive.

He arrived punctually, in black uniform and cap; was arrogant and high-handed in his tone and gestures. The couple listened in silence and mentally noted the details he wished to discuss appertaining to the reservation. Breakfast was to be included and he left a list of what should be on offer. He also wished to inspect the rooms beforehand and inform himself of the bathroom facilities. He trusted that they were strictly adhering to the *Verdunkelungsverordnungen* (black-out regulations) as issued by the authorities, with all windows, entrances and other openings to be adequately covered up at night to make the town invisible to enemy aircraft. Gisela hastily assured him that all the rooms had been correctly fitted out and that they upheld all the required standards, and that it would be a pleasure if he or his men were to carry out an inspection whenever they saw fit.

Ritter nodded approvingly and pointed out, in a gentle but weighted reprimand, that there were no portraits of the Führer to be seen on the inner walls, and that the national flag was barely featured on the outer walls either. Gisela assured him that the portrait – which she privately intended to borrow from her father-in-law - was being cleaned and would be ready by Sunday for when the *Herrschaften* (the gentlemen) arrived. All amenability, she assured him that the appropriate flags would be purchased and draped in time for the gentlemen's arrival. With her lack of political sensitivity, she had not had an eye for these details. But she learned quickly. Her husband was later put to work on organizing copious bunting featuring swastikas which he hung over the exterior; a practice that quite a few businesses were now imitating.

Ritter's sentences were so sharp and clipped that he left the impression more of giving martial orders rather than discussing accommodation in a guesthouse. The men would be arriving on the Sunday evening of the following week, he informed, as guests of the *Staatspolizeileitstelle* (state police central office) in Hamburg, and he made a generous down payment on the spot. In addition to the accommodation, and also to be invoiced to the same office, the whole group would be dining in the *Gasthaus Sonnenschein* restaurant on the Thursday evening at the end of their work week. Again, the men were to have the place to themselves on that evening. There would be six diners in total. He himself together with his subordinate already had their own accommodation organized in Lüneburg, and would be attending only on Sunday, to welcome their comrades to the town, and on the Thursday for the evening meal. He also asked that, although this was to be a perfectly regular visit from government and military officials with no reason whatsoever for secrecy, that nonetheless some basic discretion be exercised in terms of idle talk among neighbours and acquaintances concerning the visit. The country was after all at war and vigilant enemies were a standard element in any conflict. The couple nodded in complete obedience and much awe.

The men arrived in uniform and sharply punctual on that Sunday evening and checked in. During their entire stay they consistently gave the 'German greeting' and dutifully received it back from everyone at the Gasthaus. All were seemingly military men and most from the SS, varying from two young officers in their twenties up to the senior officer *SS-Sturmbannführer* [Major] Ackermann. He was a short and weasely man with greasy greying hair, a thick Berliner accent and a belittling manner toward all those at the Gasthaus whom he interacted with. Although the younger men were friendly enough, it was to everyone's relief when they all left promptly after their early breakfast in the morning and were not seen again until late in the evening, and all week that way. Preparations were made in advance for the Thursday dinner in the restaurant and Ritter studied a suitable menu, including the accompanying alcoholic drinks, with Gisela and Walter. The men would be checking out on the Friday morning; though not too early, Ritter made clear.

That Thursday a persistent drizzle fell for much of the day, from late morning until well past sunset at 16:30 and dragging on into the early evening. Inge would naturally be working that evening. She had breastfed Hermann at home already and left some more milk in a bottle with Corinna, should he get hungry again. Corinna was happy to spend the evening at their apartment, with Horst for company whom she had always liked and was in any case far preferable to her husband as a conversational partner. Inge left them at around 19:00 and headed over to the *Gasthaus Sonnenschein*. Martin had also offered to help but Gisela had told him, in quite direct and frank terms to his face, that he would only "get in the way". She said she could best handle that evening with Walter in the kitchen and Inge serving in the restaurant. She would then coordinate between the two and keep everything in check. He was thus sent upstairs to his room "to read his Luftwaffe magazines", as if a child, and he was very happy to follow his wife's instructions.

At around 19:30, the men descended one by one, still in their smart black [Hugo Boss] uniforms that Inge could not help but find uplifting and which made her feel patriotic. She thought, if people ever had their doubts that the country might not be properly run, then they would be swept away by a sight like this one. She observed closely the crisp granite-grey fabric, the four large pockets and eagle with spread wings, the neat row of buttons down the front, the tight shoulder straps, the smartly brushed down dark grey trousers, the tall well-polished black boots. It was a sight that invigorated the room; a very appealing mixture, she found, of masculine charm and stylish authority. Upon entering, they nodded in greeting at Inge, and stopped a moment to admire the busy hunting image. Ackermann made a brief compliment as to artistic taste before sitting down and requesting the wine list. The others also took their seats with stiff, militaristic formality.

She informed Gisela and Walter in the kitchen, once all the six men were assembled, that drinks were ready be served. Gisela, coming out to greet the guests and assess the seating arrangements, was also impressed by the uniforms.

After a brief perusal of the wine list, Ackermann asked Gisela to recommend a dry wine, a "good solid dry white", he insisted; he wasn't keen on sweet. Gisela suggested the Gunderloch Riesling 'Rothenberg', a "noble wine among all the many fine wines from the magnificent Rheinhessen", and the men acquiesced. Inge was impressed to hear her sister speaking in that manner. Gisela returned like a shot with a cooled bottle, presented it to Ackermann, then returned swiftly to the kitchen to let her sister serve the wine and exchange some idle chit-chat with the youngest officers about the weather and the sights to be seen in Lüneburg.

After the initial pleasantries, the men were put at ease by the wine and wound down deeper into their own conversation while Inge faded into the background, merely responding politely to requests. The mood moved from formal to relaxed within the first quarter of an hour.

Inge, and through her Gisela and Walter too, soon found out more about the background to this meeting and the whole week's mission. It partly concerned an assessment report that was being drafted for the role of Lüneburg in a variety of functions in the Reich: its suitability for some and unsuitability for others. There was a brief referencing of the *Kinderfachabteilung* (pediatric department) of a local hospital and the transportation of a certain number of children there for "special treatment"; but this subject was rapidly changed whenever a third party entered the room and in this part of the conversation the guests were overtly hushed and discreet. The use of the marshalling yards at the railway station for the displacement of military vehicles and the issue of the moving the local *Geheimpolizeistelle* (Gestapo HQ) from Hamburg to Lüneburg were, on the other hand, more openly discussed.

"And for when is the move planned?" asked Ackermann of Ritter, who was set to have a directorial position in the new subdivision.

"Next summer, if all goes according to plan," answered Ritter. "That will then be the centre of operations for the whole of the Eastern Hannover *Gau*. We will probably be in the Julius-Wolff-Straße, a little further along the Bardowicker Straße from here, behind that large park."

Ackermann nodded pensively. "Your department is currently stationed just to the south of Hamburg, is that right?"

"That is correct, in Wilhelmsburg. It is not so far to come down here but I think the move will be very positive all round. From a geographical viewpoint it is much more centrally placed in the district. And from the little that I have seen of the town of Lüneburg itself, it strikes me as a very scenic place to be posted. Nice surroundings, the people are kind and helpful. Good-hearted people, as one so often finds out in the provincial areas."

"You won't miss Hamburg, then?" smiled Ackermann.

"I am originally from Hannover. I have only been working for a couple of years in Hamburg. It has its flair and its charm, that cannot be denied. But no, I have no special attachment to the city. I will be happy enough to move on."

"Yes, that is one of the good things about war. You get to travel around, see new and different places," Ackermann commented without any irony. "Often one has no idea where one will be posted to next. All part of the surprise, is it not? I mean, look at Huber here," said Ackermann, indicating the gaunt Austrian sitting beside Ritter, and Huber nodded and grinned wryly.

The conversation soon picked up on that topic, as everyone had a hometown to talk of. Their raucous din filled the room as if a whole wedding party were present. In her role as discreet waitress, Inge was a picture of charm and alacrity. She thoroughly enjoyed the evening, shuttling between the kitchen and the restaurant (otherwise empty apart from the three connected tables with the officers), bringing in the courses, passing lightly through the hall and over to the tables, weaving in between the happy hungry soldiers, checking how full the glasses were, pouring the wine, hovering in the background, listening in on the comments exchanged. Once the first of the two main courses had begun, she took a seat at the edge of the restaurant and silently monitored the table, on hook for the slightest request from the men. She listened at first to every word of their conversation, understanding some contexts, more uncertain as to the contents of others. But after a while, the discussion moved away from concrete events in the war and more into the realms of ideological positions and geopolitical musing; there her thoughts wandered and she found herself thinking of Hermann and what her family would be doing this year for Christmas.

"You really think the war will be over by Christmas?" asked Fürstenfeld with a tone of curiosity, elbows on the table and weaving his fingers together before him to strike a serious pose. Ernst Fürstenfeld was the second youngest present and very overweight, practically obese. Though in his mid-twenties he had enjoyed a steeply rising career thanks to high connections in both the Party and the army that his family in Gelnhausen, with its strong military tradition, held. Aware that he owed his position more to influence than to blunt achievement thus far in the conflict, he was always eager to prove himself, whether in the field or at meetings; and he was naturally sycophantic whenever he felt it would score points with superior officers.

To this Franz Möhring, a squat muscular man in his thirties and a close colleague of Ritter, chortled cynically. "Of course not, who is saying that?"

The Austrian Otto Huber was a wiry, middle-aged *Oberleutnant* (on the way to becoming an *SS-Obersturmführer*), with haggard face and receding hairline, and a lugubrious voice and disposition to match them. He lit up a cigarette and answered, "Everyone, apparently. It is a common expression. I have heard it too, that "we will be home by Christmas"."

"By Christmas?" Ackermann spluttered. "What do they think this is, the Olympic Games? Two weeks of running around and it's all over? By Christmas, ha! We only began the Polish offensive in September."

"It does of course beg the question, in that case, as to whether the German population really is mentally prepared for a longer war," said Huber calmly. "If they think, and there are apparently plenty who do, that we should just carry out the basics that were already discussed in the early part of this decade: take in Austria and absorb the whole of Czechoslovakia, take back Alsace-Lorraine from the French, free the Danziger Hinterland and take western Poland up to the border agreed with the Russians, and then basically leave it at that, well, in that case the war would be very short indeed. In fact, it was practically over before it started."

"That stinks of small-minded provincial thinking, if you ask me," said Ackermann, allowing the combination of good wine and such a short war to make him feel indignant. "In Berlin we are putting breadth of vision over simple historical reclamation."

"It should be clear by now that more territory than that would have to be taken," said Eberhard Ritter, seated beside Ackermann, his only superior among the men. "Significantly more. The Führer has spoken and written extensively of the need for *Lebensraum* in the east. We require industrial and agricultural self-sufficiency. We need to have access to our own oil and other essential raw materials. We need to be able to feel our own people and not be reliant on other nations. Don't these people even listen to what is being said in parliament or take the trouble to read the press?"

"Apparently not", mumbled Ackermann through a mouth half-full of pork.

"Some of them think this is all basically centred around Danzig and the Polish corridor, nothing less and little more," said Möhring with a wry smile. "But they might be pleasantly surprised to find themselves drinking vodka out of whores' shoes in Moscow in two years' time."

Ackermann roared with laughter and, taking his lead, the younger officers Fürstenfeld and Gustav Giering cackled like hyenas. Giering was an unctuous and enthusiastic junior officer, who had gone from excelling in the Hitler Youth to being an ambitious NSDAP-party member; he knew that this evening he was in the company of much bigger fish and was therefore mostly silent.

"You have a roguish sense of humour, Franz," said Ritter, often sharing his colleague's view of the world.

"The pact...", began Fürstenfeld. He had wished to push forward a serious observation at this point but suddenly stammered to find the right words.

"A pact is a pact for as long as it is useful," interrupted Ritter tersely, though still grinning at Möhring. "That is its nature. After that point it is best dissolved, swiftly and unilaterally."

"You youngsters have so much ambition," said Ackermann, referring to Ritter and Möhring and wiping the laughter from his eyes. "Well, you also have so much to look forward to."

Ritter shrugged, "When one's ambition is boundless but one's sights are realistic, there is much to be won. That is how I see our current position."

"Apart from which," added Möhring. "You can trust the Ivan as much as you can understand him. Either we stick in the dagger first or he does. Simple as that."

"All the same, I think you will find that he is going to be occupied for a good while yet." Fürstenfeld lowered his voice, having now found his moment and excited at the opportunity of being able to impart military news, hot off the press. "I have heard from intelligence sources that it is very probable that the Bolsheviks are going to invade Finland."

"And?" said Ackermann, his large palms extended outwards, his face a grimace of being unimpressed.

Fürstenfeld smiled smugly, "That could turn out to be a big mistake. They are not familiar with the territory, which is considerable in size. It looks like an easy win for the Soviets at first glance but voices are saying that they could easily become mired down in a lengthy and difficult conflict. Which would considerably change our hand when it comes to negotiating."

No-one had much knowledge of nor interest in Finland, and there was a brief pause until Huber asked Ritter, "If you had to estimate the length of this war, taking into account all of the required territories to the east of the Reich that have to be taken, how long would you say we are talking, more or less?"

Inge was still attentive to the conversation at this point and would have loved to have heard the answer so that she would have a fixed date that she could treasure and keep. Impressed as she was by the radio and newspaper tales of victory, and now seeing these smart uniforms close up too, she still did not wish for anyone in her family, and first and foremost Horst, to be called up. The dark tales of her father rattled in her head. However glorious this conflict would be in comparison to its predecessor, there still existed the risk, however small, of German soldiers getting in harm's way. But she was called off and then held up in the kitchen, while Walter prepared the next dish. By the time she had returned, the conversation had turned in a new direction. Huber was explaining how the deliveries of food, post and other goods to the soldiers were effectuated.

She passed round the table and softly placed the dishes before two of the men, returned to the kitchen. Gisela was delighted by the 'niveau', the quality, of the company, she was telling Walter by the stove. Inge took more plates to the tables, topped up the glasses with wine and went to fetch another bottle.

"As the saying goes, an army marches on its stomach. Never a truer phrase was uttered. You only have to look at the disaster of Napoleon facing Moscow to see that. For myself, I personally feel an indescribable sense of comfort knowing that we have a man of the standing of the Führer in command of our young men. Someone who is not simply a tactical genius but also a man who cares for his people, who cares about the lives of those young men out there risking everything, a man who cares with all his heart. For the soldiers, for the nation, for all of us. Secure in that knowledge, I almost do not care how long the war takes."

"If the war does become lengthy," Fürstenfeld was musing, hoping to impress his senior colleagues with his analysis of the art of warfare although unwittingly offering up some - albeit mild and indirect – military advice for the Führer, tantamount to blasphemy and indicative of a tongue over-loosened by wine, "then that might eventually become a drain on the domestic economy. Which I would think makes it all the more essential that we the military ensure that victory is always swift for us and crushing for the enemy. We cannot allow another war of attrition to wear us down and make us vulnerable like last time."

Ritter, his attention momentarily distracted as he watched Inge's figure passing round the table, sat up sharply and turned back to the conversation, shook his head. He was intensely irritated by this talk of "like last time" from so young a mouth and so dim a mind, and said bitingly, "There will be no war of attrition here. That is the strategy of the Führer and shows not only his greatness of thought on the one side, but also his _own_ military experience from the last war. He was a soldier, one of us. He fought on the front himself, he risked and nearly had to give his life, he knows exactly how things should be done this time. The Blitzkrieg will be our saviour: short, sharp, and utterly terrifying. If the war does extend beyond its initially estimated period, you will find it does so because of the vast new area opening up in a rapidly expanding Reich."

"And no-one should let the soldiers fighting out there worry about the length of this war," said Möhring, looking for a moment intently at Fürstenfeld. "Not now that we have the right people in power and are able to root out the traitors and defeatists in our midst. No, this war will feed the economy like a hearty bucket of slop feeds a pig. The industrial demand that is created by every new battle that arises in the East, by every town that is bombed, by every cleansing of the weeds that infest our internal civil structure, by every new square kilometre that we conquer and obtain - all this will all bring with it the most glorious stimulation for the economy. Demand creates production, and the demand for expansion will fire up the domestic economy. Furthermore, every fresh territory conquered brings with it a whole package of requirements to fulfill: laying down newly tarmacked roads, the construction of new buildings to replace the damaged ones, creating an infrastructure of German public workers to ensure that law and order are upheld in annexed lands. Can you imagine the employment created by the factories here back at home, working twenty-four hours to keep the supplies going for all of that?

The contracts pouring into automobile companies, dockyards, ammunition factories, furnaces, motorway and rail constructors, chemical plants. It is almost a shame you cannot have war without end."

"Full employment and pride in one's work and in oneself, that is the secret to a successful society," said Ackermann. "Work not only gives a man money in his back pocket; to pay the bills at home and buy himself a few beers, although that is obviously fundamental too. Especially with large families to take care of, which is exactly what we are hoping to see in our nation. That is all very, very important. As the saying goes, the devil makes work for idle hands. But moreover, work and full employment are also of such an essential nature because they give the population a sense of purpose. They give men pride in themselves. A man without pride is as worthy as a dog: he just idles around town all day, hoping to catch a bite here or there, a chop that somebody has thrown away, scratches his back somewhere, pisses somewhere else, sits down at the end of the day to lick his balls. He is pathetic, useless. He is living merely in order to wait to die. Worst of all he is completely dependent. When a man is proud of the work he is doing, and proud of his family, and proud of his country, then and only then is there an end to suffering. No more anguish, no more fear, no more anger or discord. Pride and purpose: that is all you need to give the people, and they will love you forever more. And that, gentlemen, is precisely what we need to give back to the German people."

"Take nearby Hamburg, for example" said Ritter, as his senior stopped talking to drink his glass empty and re-fill it. "Even up to 1932, 1933, the port was still suffering horrendously from the economic crisis. There were still around 120,000 unemployed men in the sector, all desperately hoping for work in an economy that was going nowhere. Hamburg's economy had been let to sit idly on a single base: that of global commerce. And following the Crash of 1929, that commerce had of course drastically sunk. The shipyards were bleeding jobs. Blohm + Voss had laid off thousands, and then thousands more. But when the Führer and the NSDAP came to power, they immediately fulfilled their promise of making an example of Hamburg to the whole of Germany, showing how to successfully implement government stimulation in a weakened sector. Since then, orders for military equipment and vessels have flooded in from the *Kriegsmarine* (the *Wehrmacht* navy). Submarine construction is currently proving to be a highly successful business operation, for instance. By 1936 alone, tens of thousands of those unemployed men were back in work and the rate of new employment has continued to improve with the passing of each new year. As the Führer himself has said: If there is no work available, then you have to create it."

"And these are the very working classes that before had been voting for the Social Democrats, or even the Communist Party. Suddenly they get to feel first-hand just how much having the NSDAP in power has improved their standard of living," said Möhring. "We have even made the 1st of May, the day of the worker, a bank holiday, as a sign of respect towards the working man. Hence we say: 'Honour the worker and you honour his work'."

"Yes, I remember when the Führer came to Hamburg this February, for the launching of the Bismarck," recalled Huber. "A fine ship indeed. A warrior of the waves. There were huge crowds with everyone cheering, it was a heart-warming sight. People I spoke to said that they could not wait for the next time he comes. It is a shame that he has not as yet had time to, but I am sure he will find time when things quieten down."

"Gainfully employed people are hopelessly happy people. What more could you ask of your leaders than guaranteed financial security and physical safety?" Ritter said. "It is as simple as that. And within that security, that safety, the people then find their true freedom. If you have no worries, then naturally you are free. That is partly why our high military spending has been such a perfect solution. The material wealth of a nation, plus its sense of physical security, its safety from potential enemies and predators: that is what decides its destiny. That decides whether it will progress forward and prosper, or whether it will ultimately fail and fall by the wayside. All that is necessary is to create the ideal economic conditions and set the ball rolling. The markets will take care of the rest so long as the government is guiding that side of the economy sensibly. Work creates wealth, and wealth creates work. The cycle feeds itself and unemployment drops like a stone as a result. Which in turns has the added advantage of giving the government free reign to concentrate on issues of higher standing. Those things of political or visionary importance. Principles, morality, culture, purity - the standards that a society sets and maintains."

"That is how to maintain a healthy society. Once you make sure that your society is healthy, and keep it that way, there is no reason it should not continue on so for centuries, millennia even," Möhring waved his hand in a grandiose manner in the air.

"And how is that best done?" asked Fürstenfeld, with eager eyes keen to show respect, although inside he felt he knew the answer already.

"I grew up on a small farm," related Huber. "There was always work to be done, always some little chores to be found. When the crop was growing, you had to pull out the weeds. You are not going to have a fine and uniform field of wheat if every random seed that passes by and drops there by chance is allowed to grow and thrive. So, backbreaking though it is, you regularly pluck them out. You protect the field from vermin and parasites, otherwise it will be overrun with pests and once the grain starts to grow, they will be ready to steal it from you. In large numbers. Even the smallest and most innocent looking mouse is ultimately predatory when it comes to food. So you make sure that vermin is exterminated. You prepare for storms, which are inevitable and unstoppable, but with awareness and solid preparation you can limit any potential damage. You listen to the laws of nature and take good care of the land which has been naturally given to you but which still requires your constant vigilance. That way, by harvest time you have a fine field packed full of waving golden heads of wheat."

"Then you employ the finest young wenches in the village, blond and sturdy with plenty of '*Holz vor der Hütte*' (buxom; lit: wood in front of the hut), sit back and watch them sweat away under the sun while they reap your just rewards. That is the life that you will want to live!" bellowed Ackermann, gulping down the rest of the wine in his glass and reaching out to the bottle. He drained what was left and ordered Inge to fetch another, smiling at her behind as she walked out. Ritter took that in during a glance.

When she returned, Inge heard how the conversation had shifted back to the war. After serving and taking her place again, she listened in with interest.

"Everyone knew France and Britain would declare war," said Fürstenfeld, who was sounding increasingly tipsy. "It was obvious. But they will approach that decision with the same firm determination that they did at Munich last year, and what will be the outcome? Abso-lutely nothing." There was a sprinkle of laughter. The brazen accomplishments of Hitler at the meeting in Munich, with the sight on newsreels of Chamberlain returning home with his promise of "peace for our time", stepping from the aircraft to wave the tatty piece of paper to an applauding crowd of English journalists, was still a cause of great mirth for the officers.

"If France is taken, Britain will soon follow," said Möhring. "The British might enjoy crushing small tribes in Africa and mad barbarians in Asia, but they will not want a run-in with a new and well militarized Germany. Do not forget, they lost last time. Were it not for the *Dolchstoß* (lit: 'stab in the back', a popular conspiracy theory among Nazis) the map of Europe would have already looked very different twenty years ago and we would not even be having this discussion."

Huber said, "I agree with Möhring. The British will not stomach a second major conflict in the space of just a few decades. But the wisest thing might be to avoid a direct confrontation. Appeal to their sense of chivalry. You do not step on my lawn, and I will not step on yours."

There was a mumbled agreement and Inge was called momentarily to the kitchen. She returned to fill up the wine glasses, heard them talking of America and soon began to lose interest.

"But perhaps if Britain were to enter the war, America would too. They have their special friendship, speak the same language," argued Fürstenfeld.

"They might speak the same language as the Tommys but America is fundamentally a land of German settlers. There are whole states - and the states they have there are vast, immense - where Aryan blood dominates," said Huber.

"If it might have once been the case, it is not anymore," contradicted Ritter with a slight look of disdain. "America has become over the decades one huge egregious mongrel. The Germans there intermingle with Italians, the Italians with Poles, the Poles with Spaniards, the Spaniards with Mexicans and with primitive indigenous peoples, even with negroes. The only ones who keep themselves to themselves are the Chinese. It is a complete mess. There are large Jewish settlements and many of them intermingle too. Furthermore, some negro servants actually bear children from white farmers. They have been doing so since the days of slavery and continue in this manner to this day. No-one in America knows their background anymore. A surname is meaningless. So your last name is Schmidt? Your mother could be an Italian and her mother a Pole and her mother a French whore who married a half-Jew. Nobody would be any the wiser."

Huber replied, "Perhaps that is the case in the bigger cities like New York, which I have from reliable sources is a sewer of sin, sodomy and racial intermingling. But out on the plains to the west, and in the rural northern states, the people still know their roots, have a strong sense of history, of ancestry."

"I have an uncle who lived in Texas for five years. He said that everyone knows their place there. The white man, the brown Mexican, the black negro, each to their own. They are strict about who mixes with whom," Giering piped up in an unusually solemn voice.

Huber said, "Yes, I have received the same information from an officer I knew who was familiar with southern states in that country, like Mississippi and Alabama. Not only have they always had separate schools and churches. They even have separate toilets, separate drinking fountains, separate park benches. Furthermore, it would not only be morally unthinkable but is legally forbidden for whites and negroes to marry. The Americans were putting great importance on racial purity long before we introduced the Nuremberg Laws. No, you can say what you like about them, but they were already years ahead of us in the application of racial policy. We have only recently managed to introduce a broad-reaching segregation of Jews, for example in hospitals and schools and doctor's practices. For the Americans this is second nature. In fact, there is one area in which they do not have separate facilities for the negroes and that is simply because they do not exist, namely negro libraries. Thus, reading of the written word in works of cultural import is retained for use by white Americans only. Brilliant, simply brilliant."

Ackermann had been quiet and brooding, but now said, "I am sure they have both positive and negative sides. Most nations, like most women, can be both beautiful and ugly depending on the lighting and the angle you are looking from. All the same, I feel the Americans are ultimately not to be trusted, whether in business or politics. An American would always put America first, always, and with that, American commercial interests. As for conflict scenarios, they would not, and could not, overreach themselves and engage in a long-term conflict against the Reich. This time the outcome would be very different."

Huber said, "Nonetheless, it must be said that they are moving forward quickly in many technical areas. Making very solid advancements in chemical fields, for example. Plus, their mass production is highly impressive. Ford is a genius without doubt. Then there is the sheer size of the nation and the potential army that could be conscripted out of it. Should an American military force, hostile to the Reich's territorial ambitions, be considered only a mild threat? And what if, for example, they joined forces with the British military as, and let us not forget this, they did in the last conflict?"

"There is no reason to even contemplate the possibility. What strategic interest could America possibly have in Europe?" said Möhring.

Huber continued, "What if the Jews begin to pressurize their government? You yourself have often said that the Jews have considerable influence on financial and political institutions over there."

"Oh, they have other problems to worry about. Do not worry about that," said Möhring.

"Like the negroes rising up!" guffawed Fürstenfeld and a round of laughter flamed up. "Now, that would be a battle worth watching!"

"After that monkey Owens won four gold medals, who knows? Perhaps they will want a slice of power after all," smiled Huber.

Ackermann was still chuckling at the thought of uprising. "Ha! - America will never give the negroes an inch of power. They would have far too much to lose."

"What is all this talk of America, who cares about America? No-one is interested in that country. Mark my words, in twenty, thirty years most people will have forgotten where it is," insisted Möhring.

Ackermann expressed a wish for a cognac to accompany his cigar, and Fürstenfeld raised eyebrows around him when he said he would join him in a swig: "I'm so sick of the lousy bottles of Sliwowitz, it's all we get at the moment," he whined. Inge rushed to the kitchen where a hectic search was launched through the cupboard containing harder spirits until finally a bottle of Hennessy was located. "Tip-top", nodded Walter in approvement, making a mental note as to where the bottle had been kept. Appropriate glasses were also not at hand and had to be frantically dug out.

"We have to do things proper," mumbled Gisela, as she carefully trawled her fingers through the inside of a deep dark cupboard, finally identifying the right form. "You can't offer second-best to people who have class."

As Inge returned to the room and handed Ackermann his drink, she heard Ritter saying to Huber, "Don't worry about the Jews in America. Start worrying about the Jews here in Germany and the rest of the Reich. That is where the real problem lies. I would rather take on the whole British Empire than have a dozen of those treacherous pigs living in the same town."

"I assumed most had already left," said Ackermann, indicating to Inge to give those who wished a glass of cognac too, then leaning back to puff on his cigar. "After the success of the *Reichskristallnacht*."

Ritter replied, "Many did, but plenty did not. Or could not. It is more complex that just getting the Jews to leave. If all the Jews had got up in 1933 and sold up in one coordinated move, Germany would have been bankrupted the very next day. That has been the problem all along, as correctly identified by the Führer and those around him. They have always had too much power. They have had unlimited financial means and, what's more, at an international level. They could decide whether we sank or swam. And they did."

Huber added, "Exactly, and that is where our current policy comes in. The Jews do not simply get to run off and take our wealth with them. No, they get up and go alright, but they leave that wealth here where it belongs, where it should be. The legal planning and implementation of this has been a masterstroke of the Führer and the party. Everything has been thought out and carried through with the upmost care and down to the last detail." He tapped on the side of the head. "Our leadership knows exactly what it is doing."

"So when will they all be gone?" asked Fürstenfeld with slurred intonation, feeling the effects of the alcohol.

"That may take a couple of years yet," responded Möhring.

"We are already working with maximum priority on that issue," said Huber. "I would personally estimate that parts of the country could be *judenfrei* (free of Jews) by the end of next year, 1941 at the very latest. We should take good note of how this is currently being put into operation in Vienna. *Obersturmführer* Eichmann is doing a magnificent job there."

"Austria will be a leading light in the new Reich and in the new world order. That must make you proud," smiled Möhring.

"It does, it does."

Ackermann chipped in, "I don't want to sit here drinking all on my own." He turned to Inge, "Young lady, bring us a bottle of your best German *Sekt* (quality sparkling wine). These gentlemen have good reason to celebrate. We all do."

Inge returned after a while, accompanied by Gisela nervously clutching a magnum like she feared she might drop it.

"This is Delsecco Perlwein from Rheinhessen", she stated with the grandeur of presenting a royal guest.

"Wonderful! Let's knock down a glass to celebrate our Führer's swift victory in Poland. Let me open it." Obligingly smiling, Gisela and Inge stood back and let the men take over. The cork shot out to a spontaneous roar after the pop, the six glasses were refilled in foaming and laughter.

Ackermann hoped there would be many more victories to come which they could drink to. The atmosphere was increasingly jovial and the men were charmed by the attention of the two sisters, with their fair complexions and humble good manners, not to mention the munificent flow of alcohol. They began to chat in smaller groups and pairs. Ackermann, now bleary and struggling to follow any of the conversations, let his eyes linger freely over Inge's breasts and reflected on how both she and her sister had been top-notch hostesses for top-notch officers. He was fundamentally a simple, brutish man: good-looking Aryan women with large breasts serving and caring for military officers and troops in conquered lands was a basic part of the vision of the great Germanic future that he saw ahead.

Gisela re-entered. "I'll just leave this bottle there and you gentlemen can help yourselves as you wish. It is our little gift to our brave soldiers," she said obsequiously. The bottle was of a schnaps that had come in a bulk deal from a local supplier and she had a further four bottles in the back that had been collecting dust for a year. She gave Inge discreet instructions to begin tidying up and trusted it wouldn't be long before the now raucous men finally headed for their bedrooms.

Feeling fuddled, Ackermann peered at the bottle beside him. "Damned good stuff, you don't get that every day on the front," he laughed with his drinking spirit now fully aroused. Fürstenfeld, hammered as well, was bold enough to show his impatience in insisting that the drink was passed around the table, saying that a glass of good German schnaps would be the perfect end to a perfect evening. And nearly the end of a perfect year, he added hastily, relating how he would be spending the Christmas period in the conquered and now almost completely subdued Warsaw, together with fellow officers from the 14th SS-Leibstandarte Adolf Hitler Division. Although the city was fully under German control, he added, there was still much "cleaning up" to be done.

The bottle went round the table and was liberally poured out, the men inspecting the label bearing 'Traditional Enzian Schnaps from Linz, 43% vol', and two clusters of blue gention flowers.

"It is good for the digestion after a meal. It comes from the Oberdonau in Austria," Inge mentioned as she glided neatly round the table and swept away some plates and the breadbasket.

"As does the Führer," Ackermann beamed at her as she walked past him and smiled back.

The men knocked back the first shots. Ackermann cried out, "Excellent!" and repeatedly banged the table, the others following suit. "Another round, I tell you! Who is with me?"

Inge was taking the last items from the table to be cleared away, leaving just glasses, bottles and ashtrays. Happy that everything was tidy, and somewhat intimidated by the heated though merry tumult that was flaring up, she retreated out of the room, feeling that her presence would not be required much from now on. They were all well dined and well oiled; she merely had to wait for the gentlemen to finish the last drunken stories, perhaps the odd song, and then she could finish the last of the tidying up. She went to the kitchen where Walter was leaving to go home and Gisela was heartily scrubbing a final pan, to exchange some observations, before going to sit out in the connecting hall not far from the entrance to the restaurant. She brushed down her skirt and waited quietly, invisibly, for the men to finish and leave.

"So, where do you all see yourself in ten years from now?" asked Ritter abruptly, looking askance at Ackermann.

"Ha! In ten years? Mm," he mused. "Where indeed?" A pause. "Good question!"

"I'd be happy to live in a pub with a half-decent restaurant like this one. Free food and booze all day, every day. And some nice ladies to come and visit afterwards to finish off the evening with style," Giering guffawed, opening his mouth widely to reveal some broccoli still stuck in his upper gums. They all laughed along, as well-oiled company does, though no-one as enthusiastically as he himself.

Ackermann appeared to be still considering, searching for the most appropriate reply for the company of men. He glanced up at Huber, smiled and nodded and raised his eyebrows at him to answer instead.

Huber clicked his tongue, looked up diagonally at an imaginary spot on the ceiling, before replying. "I would return to Tirol, I think. Somewhere near to where I grew up. Perhaps Kufstein or Innsbruck - a small and pretty town with some good restaurants and a nice view of the mountains. From the balcony of my parent's house you can see green meadows in summer and snow-covered peaks in winter. I would want a young wife and two children, perhaps three, or even four. Yes, four."

Huber appeared to have finished, albeit abruptly. Eyes passed over in idle curiosity to Fürstenfeld, who in turn seemed to have become suddenly timid, as if afraid of revealing too much about himself or of giving the wrong answer. He bumbled around a few words, some barely coherent; in the end merely stated that he really didn't know, he hadn't thought that far ahead.

Möhring also revealed no specific details but gave a short but meandering speech about the great honour he felt in serving the Fatherland so far, his love of his comrades and the duties he carried out, the inspiration produced in him by the wisdom of the Führer, the sense of rebuilding a great Germany, and finally his hope that this would all continue to be the case far into the future, in whatever capacity that would be most suitable for him and most profitable for the greater good of the Reich and the German people. "I will simply let destiny carry me along on its wings to its chosen destination. That strategy has worked out very well so far," he concluded with a nod and a smug smile. It was a tremendous speech among soldiers but seemed, for all the noble words, to be completely out of place. It had quite dampened the mood.

There was a momentary silence that was broken by Ackermann's deep voice gently sawing the air. "At my age, I would like to see myself enjoying a peaceful retirement. Where exactly? I am not sure. I was born and grew up in Potsdam, then studied in Berlin and fought in the Great War, and since then I have continued to live and work in Berlin for many years. Nowadays, with my current duties, I find myself travelling so much around the country that I sometimes wake up and have to think for a moment where I am. So I suppose I would welcome a quiet, secure retirement. Perhaps in a small town, certainly nothing big and noisy. I was stationed for some years in Zossen, about fifty kilometres to the south of Berlin. That was back in the days of the Reichswehr. Very pretty little town, very pleasant atmosphere. Somewhere like that. There with my wife, my dog, having some occasional visits from my sons and grandchildren, enjoying a morning stroll after breakfast, around town and through the park. Something like that. And you?" he looked across at Ritter.

Ritter looked taken by surprise. He was so absorbed in listening to the others recounting daydreams, that he himself had socially requested, that he had forgotten he would also be expected to share in his aspirations. It took some moments and a thorough clearing of his throat before he was ready to expound. "I have to admit, I suppose, when I think about it, that I've never thought about it, and the strange thing is, now that I do think about it, I cannot grasp any image. I cannot see any landscapes from a balcony or imagine where I might be strolling in the morning. All I can see is the battlefield," and he chuckled wryly.

"Perhaps we will still be fighting in ten years' time," offered up Giering and then immediately blushed.

But Ritter had grasped that thread. "You may have a point there, young man. Who knows? As we were saying before, some think this will all be over by Christmas. Obviously it won't. Not this Christmas, not next Christmas, nor the one after that. The Führer has great plans, ambitious plans, that we should feel proud to be part of. Very big plans."

"That is true," nodded Huber.

"Perhaps it is better not to wish for a clean, swift victory. Perhaps that would prove to be deceptive. I do know that all that you achieve in life, you have to strive for. Nothing falls from the sky. Everything you obtain is the result of your drive and your determination and your sweat. Sometimes your blood. No great task is accomplished overnight. The Romans knew all that many centuries ago. And they fought for centuries, too. I think our conquests will be immense, magnificent. But those conquered lands will have to be successfully settled, will have to be farmed or used for industry. New urban centres will arise, new schools, factories, garrisons will have to be built. It will be a," (he spread out his hands with grandeur, his eyes glinted, he seemed to be talking to the room as much as to those around him, and the silence was dense), "a vast, expanding Germanic Reich. A project of purity, of dimensions unheard of until now. It will be the ultimate masterplan of mankind: the greatest, most prosperous, most moral and noble empire in the entire history of human civilization. So," he said, returning his hands to the table, "to return to your question, Sturmbannführer Ackermann, I would have to admit that I see myself in ten years right here where I am now: fighting for our future."

Ackermann was thrilled. "Finally!" he bellowed. "Finally, a realist among us. After all our fairytales, all those confessions of us soppy dreamers here, finally we have heard the words of a solid, gritty realist. I like that! I really do like that," he exclaimed and banged the table with his fist.

A roar of jingoistic energy and uncontrolled joy, a hail of cries of "Heil Hitler!" and in the midst of the thunderous din, in which all seemed to be shouting at once and as one, a final round of schnaps was poured to finish off the evening appropriately. Glasses clinked. The moment for philosophizing was over, indulgence could resume.

This jolly mood was brimming with energy at first, with Gisela and Inge fearing that they may have to wait around until well into the night. But after a quarter of an hour of bawling, physical tiredness started to numb the men's frames. They yawned and fell increasingly silent, until one by one they announced their departure and clumsily rose from their seats. They stumbled up the stairway in a final half-hearted round of singing. Ritter and Möhring, seemingly the least inebriated, ordered the bill form Gisela. After a brief perusal, Ritter signed at the bottom and told them to have it put on his invoice. Möhring politely complimented the hosts on the excellent food and atmosphere that had made for such an excellent night, and bade them good night. Ritter did likewise, his smile and eyes lingering a little longer on Inge, who smiled back with innocent charm.

"Hopefully we shall be able to repeat the occasion in the near future," Ritter purred. "Thank you again and good night."

Once the restaurant was clear, Gisela and Inge scurried in, flung open the windows and tidied up briskly. Within fifteen minutes the room was returned to its former neat pristine condition, with just a few grey waves of cigar smoke still hanging in the chilled air. Upstairs there was heard a couple more rough choruses of song, before silence finally set in. By the time Gisela was heading upstairs to her bedroom at the top of the house, she could only hear the odd bout of loud snoring coming from the rooms.

Chapter 17

To Gisela's extreme satisfaction the visit by the SS officers turned out to be highly successful as a promotional tool for her business. The general opinion of the guests concerning both food and the accommodation had been unanimously full of praise, an evaluation which was swiftly passed on to further circles by word of mouth; a rating amplified by the important and influential position that some of these men held. The Party's natural manner of using the verbal relaying of information clearly functioned well, and in this case the result was very positive. Clientele picked up, despite the normally modest level of income to be expected in these autumn months, when carefree summer spending on tourism had come to an end and more frugal preparations for winter and the upcoming Christmas were being made.

The next year 1940 brought the restaurant a continued boom, when more affluent townsfolk sought to escape from the gloom of war in an evening out with wine and good food and friends. But as that war bore on, the commercial activity of the accommodation of the Gasthaus began to wane. It was rarely full, and sometimes disturbingly quiet. It was booked out for the official visits by military officers or functionaries, invariably thanks to the publicity or direct intervention of Eberhard Ritter. He had furthermore hinted that they should adorn the Gasthaus with a more lavish show of patriotism to achieve better results. They went out and purchased good quality and expensive swastika drapes which were hung from the third floor windows, and adorned the Führer's portrait in the hall with streams of the German flag colours, as well as buying a new frame and giving the glass a good clean. But however much they tried to please, these visits were still relatively few and far between for Gisela's liking.

The Polish campaign was barely over and increased hostility was being clearly shown from France and England, nations that were neighbouring and threatening and that would eventually have to be subdued if life was to go on as normal. This was not the moment for the frivolous luxury of tourism, while Lüneburg had on the whole only modest strategic or political importance for the Party and any meetings that may arise.

In the midst of this overall downturn came an announcement that briefly provided a much-needed moment of glory and commendation for the family. Inge was nominated for, and eventually awarded with, the very desirable *Mutterkreuz* - the Mother's Cross, the colloquial term for the 'Cross of Honour of the German Mother'. This was a huge honour and came most unexpectedly of all to the prize winner herself. It was a new award that the Party had created to instill a sense of pride in "Aryan mothers of large families", basically serving as a form of strategic encouragement for women to have numerous children. Inge had by now brought three children into the world in three years and there was of course all the hope in the world for women in general, from the Party at the highest national level, that this number might go on to be augmented in the near future. Moreover, in this particular case the names of the children had delighted all those participating in the decision, who saw in them a deep-seated loyalty to the Third Reich.

She received the award that September, just after the anniversary of one year of being in direct military conflict with the "enemies of the German nation." The ceremony was short but Inge and Horst were very impressed with the speech, and keenly felt the glowing praise. The officer in charge noted that while some in the world were furiously intent on trying to destroy the German homeland and its people, others, such as the brave patriotic mothers gathered here, were defying that destructive fury by creating new life: there had never been a clearer concept of the contrast between good and evil. Horst was touched by the use of the word 'brave' which, bearing in mind the fear and pain his wife had gone through with the first birth in particular, he felt was an apt description.

It was additionally noted during the speech that two of the three children had come into the world in the safety and comfort of their own homes, which in itself was a commendable act of heroism. It indicated the level of selflessness that was to be ascribed to the modern German mother. The hospitals and clinics were for the sick and the wounded, after all; the home birth, accompanied by the top-quality levels of care afforded by the excellent physicians and midwives of the Reich, was now the favoured option.

Despite the state accolade and all the familial attention, the birth of this third child presented a problem to the Grün family's financial resources. Their spending capacity had always been relatively tight and much of the money they had initially managed to save in their first year together had now been used up by the rearing of three children. Although their rent was low, thanks to Gisela's contribution, their combined income was also exceedingly modest. Relatives had helped out continually - old shoes and items of clothing along with the two prams they now possessed that were passed down from Gisela's children - but they were finding it hard to make ends meet.

Now that she was simply helping out her sister and being paid in cash and under the table, as opposed to receiving an official salary, Inge had no legal right to state benefit such as maternity leave. Doctor's bills accumulated in the winter of 1939/40 when a spate of coughs and flus struck all three children, little Hermann in particular being badly affected. Horst began to feel restless in the apartment, spoke of a desire to leave Lüneburg and head further afield once the war was over. He had, more than once, wondered whether they might not end up heading out to the east some day, to those lands that the Führer had promised them all on numerous occasions. These were idle and very premature speculations of his, Horst himself was aware of that much, but he entertained them sincerely nonetheless. Inge was inspired by the idea, at least in theory, although her notions were mostly romantic and involved the fancy of having a large house with lots of land, as she had seen in the cinema film *Vom Winde Verweht* (Gone with the Wind).

She mentioned the subject to her mother on one occasion, when they were with the children together. Corinna was positive about the idea, as she tried to be positive about all the ideas that her daughters shared with her for the sake of keeping a good atmosphere. She added that she was sure her own sister, Inge's aunt Hertha who had lived in East Prussia for most of her life, would be delighted to help out her niece in any way she could if they were seriously considering a move out towards the more eastern realms of the Reich. Quickly regretting having broached the topic in the first place, Inge then asked her not to mention the subject to anyone else, as it only concerned conjectures and "silly thoughts" and that she had promised Horst to stay silent for the time being. Inwardly, Inge would be very reluctant to have to leave the protection of the ever sheltering and assisting care of her elder sister; something she had got used to through the years. In any case, as Horst himself had clearly stated, nothing at all could be decided until the war was over for good.

Outside of a couple of notable exceptions, the budding conflict produced little great emotion in their family. It had had to be reckoned with and was absorbed into their psyche with a certain resignation to the inevitable. The only very harsh critic was of course Inge's and Gisela's father Georg Hartmann, renowned as that traditionally ceaseless critic of the Nazi party and the Führer, though pressurized by his children into a tense silence on the subject so as not to further arose the ire of neighbours and other busybodies. But all the same, he had lost none of his inner passionate hatred of Hitler, and that yet another - clearly long - war was now intensifying, incensed him greatly. One December evening his daughters came to visit their parents in their cramped apartment; Inge laden with three little children and Gisela with Erich, Corinna busying herself by organizing refreshments for everyone. Georg sat by the crackling fire, sipping on his beer and taking the occasional gulp of a *Vollkorn* schnaps. Outside, a long session of strong rain had set in and the room dimmed, marking the strong orange glow from the nearby open fire on his face.

"This is just the beginning, this mess in Poland. You will see how they will all head off soon, all proud as peacocks. And their mothers and wives and sisters proud, too, because the boys look so smart in their uniforms. Off to fight for the Fatherland! We swallowed the same old tale, too. Exactly the same one. God Almighty help us, for people never learn. Even with all the documents and books in the world in which it is all written down and explained, even with photographs to show the truth; people still never learn. War always comes back to tempt them, like an old vice that they just cannot give up. It always heats them up in the end, like the flush of a race or the thrill of a bet.

Yes, it is all fun and games until you actually get there and see what is waiting for you. Then you noticed how deep trenches were - three, even four metres deep. With ladders up the side for getting up, or back in quick. And a rotten place to live. Always damp, sometimes knee-high in water after heavy rain like what we are having today. Muddy, filthy place it was, like living in a sewer. Everything smelt of rotting, of decay and disease. It was cold so you huddled up in your uniform to keep warm but your body was always crawling with lice and you knew they were sucking at your blood, slowly eating you up. How disgusting is that? Rat everywhere too. Millions of them. They are the true animals from hell, they are. When they paint those pictures of hell, they put fire and flames and molten metal and thunderbolts in them, isn't that right? That is because they are painters and they do not know what hell really is. In hell there are just rats: that is all that is needed. I have seen rats eating the body of the fallen, out on the fields in front of your very eyes. You couldn't get to the bodies to bring them back because of the machine gun fire all around, so they just lay there. For weeks on end sometimes. The rats did not take long to get at them. You might catch a glimpse of that, of them gnawing on a body - perhaps on someone you knew, someone you had talked to recently, and then you would look away and hope you could forget what you had just seen. But you never forget. So the rats ate the dead, and the lice ate the living, and that was our life in the wet and the cold.

You couldn't hide food anywhere because the rats would get at it in no time. So any food you had, you had to eat straightaway. So then of course there was nothing left. And the hunger came. Long, long days of hunger. We were so weak and weary in the end. Suddenly there came the decision to go to battle. We were told to prepare ourselves. Stood there waiting and waiting for the final command, for the big moment. Like waiting forever it seemed, a silent forever. We were all scared to death, scared shitless we were, but no-one would admit it.

We shouted when we went over the top, shouted out loud and fierce with all our lungs could give. Roared, we did, and the officers thought that was a good way to intimidate the enemy. But we roared because we were scared. We shouted out in fear and we rushed on into the machine gun fire. As long as some made it across and could take out the enemy posts, that was all that mattered. You never knew if you were going to get taken out, or get through. So you shouted out all your fear, your frustration, your hope, your anger. It helped you too, shouting. You shouted through the bullets and you only stopped when you got into action behind the enemy lines. Or if you dropped, of course.

What madness was that?" he looked at the women, who sat in silence, not daring to interrupt the old man's tale. Inge was thankful that her boys were behaving and listening, while Hermann was sound asleep.

"You wouldn't think such madness could exist, would you? Women sitting by a warm fire, drinking coffee and eating cake, why would you?" He drank his beer. "But they were so enthusiastic about the war in 1914. Everyone cheered as whole groups of young men went off to war, marching by in the smart uniforms, could not wait to get the trains to take them to the front. Nobody was thinking of injuries and death, heavens above no! Nothing could be further from our thoughts. I was a young man at the time, just twenty-four. We had only been married a few years," he said to Corinna, who simply nodded. "And you were just a little toddler, you could not have been older than five," he said to Gisela, who smiled back. "And in the street everyone clapping and cheering. Although I remember at home, some of the older people were not so enthusiastic. The grandparents of the boys had lived through other wars, against Austria, against France. But the youngsters couldn't wait and their parents were proud as punch. In one class of *Abiturenten* (high-school/'A' level graduates) in town we heard how all nineteen had joined up and gone off to war, nearly all at the same time without thinking twice about it after their young teacher had given them such a stirring speech in class. They thought it was going to be an adventure, the poor idiots! And you know, in the end only two of those nineteen came back.

We all marched off, so gallant and tall. Everyone was proud of us and I think that made us feel we were invincible. Oh, they all came to see us off. Girlfriends waving frantically, mothers smiling. There was even a band playing. We were smiling too because we wanted to do them proud and show the world what brave men we were." He paused and looked down. "I think we were all very brave, looking back. Both the ones who came back and the ones who didn't. The ones who didn't were even more brave because in the end they gave everything. Afterwards hardly anyone cared. The war was lost, people just wanted to return to normalcy. Within a few years, it was like nothing had ever happened. People would talk about anything, about normal things like clothes and apartments and money. Even songs, or fashion or movie theatres. Air ships! My God, what they talked about, the most frivolous of things.

And we the simple soldiers, those who fought and saw hell in the face, who came back with ruined bodies and minds, we could have talked about the war from morning to evening. The fog, the damp, the mud, the gas, the bullets, the barbed wire, the rats, the makeshift graves, the random conversations with random brothers in arms who came and went and talked and died, the shrapnel and the lost limbs, being half-deaf after a shelling, the frostbite, and the typhus fever, too. That went through whole companies of men like an invisible beast from hell. We had fever and chills, and could not feel our limbs, we got red spots and went delirious. Many died of it.

Afterwards I could have talked about it for hours, about all these things. To anyone who would listen. It was a whole way of existing unto itself. Unique and terrible. It seemed like the only thing in life that could possibly matter. What could be more important than that battle with death, in so many forms? Of course you think it matters to everyone the same as it does to you, but that is not the case. No-one really wanted to hear too much. Especially as the years went by. A little here and there perhaps, to be polite, but not really.

You go off to war thinking it is the right thing to do. You think you are saving everyone around you, saving everyone back home, and that this is the only way of doing it. You think the war is righteous, and even glorious. But it is all a lie, all a trick. It is not glorious. It is not righteous. It is just hunger and cold and rats and death. That is all it is."

Gisela, worn down by the depressing monologue, one that she had already heard a good few times, interjected, "But you told us once about Christmas in the first year out there. How the men stopped fighting on Christmas Eve, and called a truce, and sang and drank together. Do you remember?"

"No, I don't remember that. I wouldn't want to either, even if it did happen. There is nothing good about war to remember. And it is dangerous to try to. This is why people go to war in the first place - because they forget. One generation goes through hell; and instead of the next one listening to what they have been saying, or trying to say if only someone would listen, no, they just carry on as before. They talk about other things, trivial and banal things. The women are the worst because they have had no idea what is out there in the first place. And that is how people forget, how a nation forgets. It is all one big con-trick, that is all that war is. A lie and a ploy to make you feel proud and brave, when all that is waiting is a cold dark horror. That is all there is to remember."

The three women looked down in silence, knowing the best option for them was to let him speak it all out, which he did every two or three years or so.

"In any case, our Herbert never got to see Christmas, did he? He was mowed down by the bullets in November 1914, in the first year already. In the Flanders massacre. I was not even there. I was stationed down south at the time, near to the French border. But Herbert was in the army further up north, near Ypres. They were hoping to beat the Tommies and the Belgians, outflank them and get up as far as the North Sea. That would have won them the war, they said. But there by Dixmuide, the officers misjudged the military presence of the French. They were useless old men, the generals. Brought back out of retirement, clueless to the last about how to fight a war. These weren't the old days of the Prussians fighting the French, with officers prancing around on horseback and waving swords. These were new times, different times. But they were too stupid to realize. They sent those men into battle. Old men and young men. Farmers, workmen, students. It was a hopeless battle. Running across turnip fields in the open, easy targets for enemy fire. They were blown to pieces, shot down like animals. Days of futile slaughter, all for nothing, and tens of thousands killed in the last battle.

It was all in the newspapers. They printed all about the heroic deeds of those brave men. That was where my parents first found out about the battle, although they never imagined at the time that they might have lost one of their sons in it. But they were so proud of the German army, even when the letter arrived saying that he had been killed. That is what the war does to you. It makes you feel proud, makes you feel fortunate. Even when you have lost that which is most important in your life. It makes you delirious. It clouds your mind. And that is what you are seeing all around you now. That stupid pride."

He put down his drink and laid his hands over his chest. "I remember Herbert, I remember him every day. You know yourself, Inge, when I asked you to put flowers on the memorial in Berlin, back when you went to the Olympic Games there. You would think everyone would remember. But the politicians and the businessmen, they come along with their mad ideas. Their wicked ideas. And the whole process starts up again. And even the mothers think their sons look dashing in the uniforms, and everyone claps their hands in glee and they all say, "This time it will be different, this time it will be different!" But it never is different, it is always the same. And again they send out the men and the boys, out into the distance, off into the cold mud, all for nothing. *Ach*, these National Socialists, these idiots! Why do people even listen to them? Who in their right mind would go to war against the rest of Europe? We have learnt nothing from the past even though we know it off by heart." He mumbled some more phrases of incomprehension at the current state of affairs in his country before closing his eyes by the fire and eventually drifting off. The women rose quietly so as not to wake him, moved the rest of the visit and their own conversation to the kitchen.

It seemed though to Inge for the first time that perhaps her father had a very valid point to make. This was her first encounter since the outbreak of the conflict with such strident anti-war sentiment. She had never thought about the topic before, having only known peace and always listening to her father's rumblings with patience but indifference. And, as Corinna reminded them, these rants of their father were issues that stayed at home and went no further. For all his blistering talk of the ignorance of women, Georg Hartmann was very lucky in that he could rely on the discretion of his wife and daughters. His daughters were married into families that would have deprecated, or even been shocked and angered by such talk. They knew full well that their father's words were not to be analysed or discussed any further.

Thus mentalised, Inge and Gisela returned home to concentrate on those things that were important around them. They had children to take care of; they had families with all the worries and intrigue that these inevitably brought; they had to measure money carefully - Inge to make ends meet and Gisela to balance the books in a business that was facing new challenges. If they talked about the events taking place in Poland, it was more like curious gossip than the doom-laden references of their father, sometimes little more than background music for idle moments. In turn, the official news coming through to them in the media was transmitted as chirpy and encouraging. The message that clearly rang out from the Ministry of Propaganda was undeniably true: all was going well and they were in good hands under the Führer's control.

That year Horst made an *Adventkranz* (advent crown) to be placed in the Gasthaus on a table at the front of the restaurant. They had often had them as children, though modest little affairs that they bought at the Christmas market. This year he decided to craft it himself, to make it bigger and better than ever before. He carried out his project with such secrecy in their apartment – slipping it covertly under the bed whenever his wife came in – that it was a major all-round surprise when he produced it at a pre-Christmas family gathering at the end of November. Attached to a wooden board was a round garland of fir-tree twigs sporting thick green needles, this being adorned with conifer cones, little silver painted wooden stars, slices of dried apple, sticks of cinnamon, aniseed stars, and most riveting of all for the children, four large red candles at each corner. When it came into view there was an elated applause and cheering, that made Horst blush and Inge clasp her hands to her mouth and feel pure love for her husband. Host told Gisela, as he presented it to her, that it was a gift from him for everyone at the Gasthaus to share in and for the children to enjoy. Gisela was overwhelmed, and very impressed by the solid construction, and told him he was the most wonderful brother-in-law that anyone could wish for in the world.

They placed it on a table at the front of the restaurant for all to see. Inge explained to her boys with a soft voice and pointing finger that they would light one candle every week on the four Sundays leading up to Christmas. Adolf was two-and-a-half and stood by the chair, supported by his father, chuckled and nodded with a big grin; while Joseph, at just over a year, and Hermann, barely a few months old and sitting on his mother's lap, looked on with big eyes, mystified. Gisela then passed round mugs of *Glühwein* (German mulled wine) and there was a round of songs. She looked at her children and thought how perfect a piano being played by them would have made the moment, and made a mental note to get their music lessons started up again once the war was over.

On the 6th December was St. Nicholas and this time Opa (grandfather) Volkmar had brought some presents with him. Gisela's three children and Adolf gathered round the old man, while Joseph and Hermann watched on from a distance in their parent's arms. "We have to decide who is a good child, and who is a naughty child!" declared Volkmar with a mock regality that grated slightly on Gisela's nerves. To boot, Anna was making one of her rare visits and had been scrutinizing every last inch of the ground floor since her arrival. It turned out that all the children were good and they lined up to receive their giftbags with each getting a tangerine, an apple, and assorted *Plätzchen* (small German Christmas biscuits). Simultaneously, Horst gave Joseph and Hermann a biscuit each to keep them occupied.

That same week they had all gone together as a large family to the stalls mounted in the *Marktplatz* where they had bought gifts and decorations, drunk *Glühwein* and eaten *Lebkuchen* (little ginger cakes spiced with cinnamon and lightly covered in chocolate). The atmosphere in the fresh cold was wonderful and they had laughed and joked and gelled like never before. Even Corinna had got tipsy and started kissing Georg in giggly pecks.

The next day they put up a Christmas tree in the Gasthaus; a tall dense spruce that Wilhelm had managed to get cheap from a young friend of his who worked out in the woodlands in the Lüneburger Heide. It was decorated in a vivid mêlée of glass baubles and glitzy streams of tinsel bought at the Christmas market. Around it on the floor, on some old wine crates, they had created a nativity scene on straw, with Mary, Joseph and child, shepherds, cattle and sheep, and the Three Kings arriving. This was all crowned with a big silver star overhead, made from tinfoil folded over cardboard that Adolf managed to steal and sneak off with at one point in the Christmas weeks; this earned him a telling off and a slight smack from Horst, who hated to have to do it but felt some discipline was crucial for the children's future.

It was a busy month, especially at the restaurant, and they closed the doors to the public on the 23rd with a heart-felt relief that a month's hard work was behind them. There would be little more custom over the festive period, with empty pockets throughout town, so they would open again on January 2nd.

On Christmas Eve Gisela and Inge put together a fine Christmas evening meal in the restaurant, helped by Corinna and Edeltraut, and the families came together and ate and drank like kings. On a smooth white tablecloth covered in scattered twigs of fir and cinnamon sticks and little golden stars, the places were neatly set with serviettes, silverware, wine glasses and the best china plates and dishes of the house. A large roast goose – stuffed with orange, apple, and onion together with thyme, sage, cinnamon, and rosemary - lay in the centre of the table, surrounded by tureens heaped with vegetables, piping hot red cabbage, roasted potatoes and sweet chestnuts in honey. Cooled white wine flowed from the kitchen without limit. For dessert Gisela had dreamt up something special, at Walter's suggestion, which were dainty glasses of assorted fruits - raspberries, blackberries and black currant - covered in quark and mascarpone and with crumbled *Spekulatius* (spicy German biscuit) sprinkled on top plus a sprig of fresh mint. The children gobbled them down, mint and all, with huge grins of relish and cried out for more, which touched Gisela to the heart.

Afterwards they sang '*Stille Nacht*' (Silent Night), '*Vom Himmel hoch, da komm ich her*', and some other Christmas favourites by the tree, before it was time to unwrap the presents lying on the *Gabentisch* – the table next to the tree that the children had been eyeing up the whole evening and waiting for the songs to finally end. There was a bicycle lamp and horn for Siggi, for the new bicycle he had received for his birthday; matching poetry albums for Katrina and Eva to write their thoughts in, along with a pair of little porcelain dolls; a whole set of tin soldiers, artillery and tanks for Erich (that in later war years would end up on permanent loan to Inge's children as they grew older and took more interest in war than their cousin); and a knitted scarf with matching gloves and woolly hat for Adolf. Hermann got two pairs of red and white knitted socks, which were waved in front of his bemused baby-face, and Joseph received new little shoes, which he snatched at eagerly.

Corinna oohed and aahed with each opened gift while Inge said with great satisfaction that it was the most generous Christmas she had ever seen. "It is so nice to spoil the children!" she later laughed to her sister. Both silently recalled their own childhood Christmas in which there had barely been enough money for the Christmas dinner, while presents had been luxuries for children from better homes. This further enforced the satisfaction in the women's mind that their children were living through better times than ever before, which in turn was for them the rudimentary reason for life and for living.

Edeltraut commented on how it was strange to think how her Roland, who some time back was a little boy playing with them at Christmas, was now far off in the east taking part in the Polish campaign. "They grow up so quickly," she sighed and there was a glistening in her eyes among all the sparkles of tinsel and other Christmas decorations as she thought of her distant son.

By eleven o'clock, the children were being settled into bed upstairs, with Inge's three staying overnight as they did on special occasions like this; while Martin's side of the family had wished everyone a 'Merry Christmas' and gone home in a cloud of contented and well-oiled banter. Inge stayed to look after her babies and keep a general eye on the Gasthaus, while the others headed off into the chilly night to St. Marien for the midnight mass. "And to think it almost snowed," said Gisela on the way. "That would have made it an absolutely perfect Christmas!" Everyone was in full agreement there.

The next day, the 25th or the First Christmas Day, at the Gasthaus the two sisters Inge and Gisela together with husbands and children spent the day between snacks and games. Gisela and Martin had a good collection – including *Halma, Im Zeppelin um die Welt* (In the Zeppelin Round the World), *Mühle* (Nine Men's Morris) – Martin's favourite, and the Nuts memory game with different kinds of nuts hidden under beakers and shuffled around for the others to guess. Gisela always had misgivings about the *Zeppelin* game ever since the

1937 disaster, but it had become such a firm favourite of Siggi's that it was always dragged out for a round or two. Siggi would say how he too would travel away one day, and Gisela was somehow sure he would.

And so Christmas passed with great cheer and left happy memories in its wake. The war, a few months old, was a distant and mostly relaxed event that was almost entirely providing for good news pouring out of radio sets and cinema news, chattered through the beer halls and bars and restaurants, in schools and universities, in shops and around market stalls, in workplaces and in private living rooms and wherever the subject arose, there was only a fundamental optimism to be perceived. The Polish army had been resoundingly crushed, in a few weeks no less. Relatively few in the *Wehrmacht* had fallen in battle; most had not even heard of any families with casualties. Those who did unwisely quote the official statistics concerning the dead, were considered as killjoys at best, treacherous at worst. And those few German soldiers who had fallen, had done so with all the valour and honour imaginable, to such an extent that it was viewed as almost an enviable way to go.

In this atmosphere of hearty and joyful satisfaction, many families in Lüneburg spent possibly their happiest Christmas of recent years, or for years to come. For Horst and Inge, it was a memorably beautiful couple of weeks, and a moment to reflect on how much life had improved for them in just a few recent years. Inge had brought three children into the world, all healthy and hungry, and had received a special award that ultimately came right from the Führer himself together with all the praise of the nation. She had never imagined that motherhood could be a heroic act and the thought filled her with a warm pride. She loved her husband more than ever, and both were very content with the living and working arrangements with Gisela and Martin, with Inge comforted in the knowledge that her sister would always be near in times of need. The Gasthaus in particular offered Inge a strong sense of security and appeared to her as a solid step upon which she walked, in what might otherwise have been precarious times. Both her and Horst were so perfectly happy with their lives and the family environment that they could only wish and hope for many more years of similar good fortune.

Chapter 18

"What a year this has been! What an indisputably wonderful year!" *der Vetter* Carsten (Cousin Carsten), as he was popularly known, would exclaim at the end of 1940. Who could argue to the contrary? If ever in history one had had good reason to feel proud to be German, everyone around him agreed, then this was surely that moment. All thanks to the genius of their Führer, and Saviour.

Cousin Carsten, the eldest son of Horst's uncle Robert, was a big-built young man with wavy brown hair, dull blue-grey eyes, and a cynical cackle of a laugh. Carsten had moved to Lüneburg two years ago, after finishing school with standard grades, where he had obtained a position with the *Deutsche Reichsbahn* (German national railway company). Trains were always his great passion since a boy and currently he was employed as a ticket controller at the main railway station in Lüneburg, with hopes of promotion to higher things in the coming years. He had just turned nineteen at this point and, like many young men of the era in various nations, held a great fascination for both technological gadgets and modern geopolitics, in both of which areas Germany had been making impressive strides in recent years.

Carsten had been precociously following the Führer's progress in international politics ever since those awe-inspiring Olympics Games of 1936; when Germany made the world sit up and take note, with an unquestionably impressive hosting of the event terminated by a crushing victory in the medal table. Already an eager member of the Hitler Youth, he discerned in the wake of this sporting event the symbolism revealed of the clear and manifest destiny that awaited his nation. He was a strict adherent to the prevailing ideology in all its facets. Although he had never actually known any Jews himself, he held a low opinion of the 'race', considered them two-faced and treacherous (he had refused to speak to the members of a Jewish family in his apartment block upon discovering their ethnicity). Likewise those nations of Slavic ancestry, and in particular the Russians, whom he suspected were quietly plotting his country's downfall, despite whatever dubious pacts they may have put on the table. He clearly discerned the Führer's policy for rapid territorial expansion and loved the tricks and turns that the statesman employed to outwit his foreign adversaries. When war broke out - as he had expected it eventually would, for he knew there was a limit to how much one could achieve through patience and good will alone - Carsten was in his element. He went to the cinema regularly, first and foremost to see the pre-film newsreel and secondarily to see a suitably patriotic motion picture, of which there was no shortage for a public hungry for nationalistic pride.

With eyes wide in intense concentration and raised heartbeat, he would watch the large white capitals letters of *Die Deutsche Wochenschau* appear before the German eagle. There then came a stirring trumpet call as bright searchlights flooded over a background of shimmering shades of grey. He lapped up the *Front-Berichte* – the reports from the front – and absorbed with encyclopedic memory the endless list of the Reich's battles, always resoundingly yet also heroically won, as if victor and victim were one.

The battles were presented as a narrative, with extensive and immaculate film coverage. Here a German destroyer took on and sank a fleet of ships, there the German heavy artillery took out a pocket of resistance, and all the time Stuka bombers dived and blasted the enemy. The reason these images were being filmed and brought back to the homeland, the audience was informed, was to show the German people, sitting in cinemas throughout the nation, just what the brave sailors and airmen and soldiers of the *Wehrmacht* were accomplishing. Thanks to the camera teams working in close coordination with the troops, embedded in the regiments and shooting film live beside them during battles, the audience had the sensation of almost being there on the front themselves; of seeing through their own eyes the challenges and risks that the soldiers faced on a daily basis, of living the battles through them.

It was, back then, an innovative medium in warfare; a craft that the Germans were finely honing, and Carsten couldn't get enough of it.

The middle-class was enjoying a much-welcomed return to material prosperity and hankering after the latest technological gadgets, which were capturing the nation's consumerist imagination. For his birthday, and prompted by the adolescent's quiet insistence to his mother, Carsten's parents had bought him an *Agfa Billy* camera. With this state-of-the-art acquisition, Carsten had the intention of photographing anything of peculiarity or noteworthiness that might be of interest to the state. (Although it must be said that he enjoyed capturing family moments too and took some of the few family photos taken of these years at the Gasthaus, including of Inge's and Gisela's children.) However, those noble intentions did not extend at the beginning much beyond endless pictures of trains arriving at platforms. But the war was still young; there was time for all manner of adventures to come his way.

He lived in a shabby little single-room apartment, rented on the Dahlenburger Landstraße, which corresponded to his starting salary at the *Deutsche Reichsbahn*. His outgoing costs were generally quite low, allowing him to put aside some money each month with a view to fulfilling his consumerist desires. The new technology fascinated him so utterly that, with a credit taken out thanks to Gisela and Inge putting in a good word with Ernst at the *Vereinsbank*, he was able to treat himself at the beginning of 1940 to a '*Volksempfänger*' radio. This was a large solid wooden radio receiver framed in a surrounding of dark-brown wood and displaying a soft beige gauze in the centre to emit the sound. Even for someone like Carsten with his modest income, it had not been overtly expensive at 75 *Reichsmark* new, and was proof to many of how successful the new government was in its economic policy. He calculated that he could pay off the credit in a single year if he was duly thrifty. It was partly thanks to this thrift that the family got to see more of him, when Horst began to invite him round to the Gasthaus to eat with him and the rest of the family. Gisela, always respectful of her brother-in-law, was happy enough with the arrangement, and treated and fed him as one of her own.

So Carsten was delighted with his new radio and the whole universe that it seemed to open up for him. It was certainly a serious, adult world for youth of his age, and that excited him. Rumours abounded as to how one could even tune in to international stations, such as the infamous BBC, on a radio receiver such as the one he possessed. That was of course considered as a highly illegal act by the authorities; these channels were referred to as *Feindsender* (enemy broadcasters) and met with Carsten's disapproval. In fact, a young plumber who had come to his apartment one day to inspect the water pipes in the flat, saw the bulky object and joked on that very subject. He received such a stern reprimand from the pompous young ticket inspector, one that sounded like a veiled warning, that the poor man remained silent for the rest of his visit and fearful for the rest of the month.

In any case, Carsten did not have the slightest curiosity to find out the veracity as to whether one could listen to adversarial transmissions or not. For him, his own national news was the one and only definitive version; more than ever in times of war, when malicious enemy propaganda must surely abound.

The *Volkempfänger* radio formed an essential part of his connection to the turbulent world of the conflict; so distant and yet, at the same time, so close. Carsten had listened regularly before to the *Großdeutschen Rundfunk*, the official radio channel of the Party. Once the war had kicked in, he had the radio running night after night. He enjoyed the complete show: the march music, the reports from the front, and the *Wunschkonzert für die Wehrmacht* – the concert of requests from the German armed forces, which featured many of the then popular music stars. Between the *Wochenschau* in the cinema and the news on the radio, he was happily up-to-date with the latest developments in the war. He was also more than willing to lecture all those around him on a daily basis with regards to the information that he was now accumulating, whether or not they showed any great interest.

It was through the *Deutsche Wochenschau* and *Großdeutschen Rundfunk* radio station that he followed the entire Polish campaign, that lasted but six weeks and had the sensation of being a clean and utterly crushing affair; like a bold but undemanding first movement of a symphony. Poland was neatly portioned into two by Nazi Germany and the Soviet Union and everyone took the slice that corresponded to them. Back in August, before the commencement of the Polish campaign, the Führer had already signed a non-aggression pact with Stalin and it seemed to Carsten quite logical that both would share with mutual accord the spoils of war. All the same, like many others he had the feeling that this would not be the definitive end of the matter.

Martin Landeck had already bought a radio back in 1937, a second-hand model from the company *Sachsenwerk*. It was a big lumbering wooden box that sat under the window of the back room of the Gasthaus and annoyed Gisela no end, who found it to be an unnecessary expenditure in increasingly hard times and one that furthermore got in her way.

"You do not clean up the rooms or dust the furniture, that is part of the problem!" she said in explanation to Martin of her antipathy to the object.

Her husband had purchased it at a reasonable price from a neighbour, who in turn had originally purchased it around four years before in order to follow the Olympic Games, but had in the meantime moved onto a modern and more slim-line model. Like Carsten, Martin also liked to listen to the never-ending flow of details of the *Wehrmacht*'s advances, which that year were coming in fast and furious. Sometimes he liked to just sit back and imagine the ominous Stukas diving in on the scattering enemy below. Volkmar, a regular visitor, had been absolutely delighted with this new acquisition, especially as he had previously encouraged his son to make the purchase in the first place. It was thanks to the radio, he said, that he was able to keep up with what was happening in the wider world and so be fully abreast of the latest military developments. He also related how when the Führer spoke, it was as if he were speaking directly to him out of the box.

Volkmar was not alone in this feeling and it showed part of the forward thinking of the Nazi party in their usage of modern technology. For innumerable Germans, there was a new, intense closeness of their leader's presence thanks to the high production levels and affordable prices attached to this increasingly popular invention. It can be safely assumed that the Führer equally appreciated the proximity he had to people like Volkmar and Martin and Carsten and the many millions of others like them, all at low cost and with zero displacement required.

This near spiritual presence to their Führer helped to give much of the population a strong sense of purpose in moments of doubt; it communicated a sense of acute euphoria and self-confidence that could rouse men and women in seconds out of apathy or fatigue. Not all were so touched by the master's voice, however, nor the glory of war. Gisela would often despair of so much news in the evening and, if finding herself alone with her husband, would change the channel to something lighter. Reports of German soldiers invading yet another new land would be replaced by the jolly sounds of dance orchestra numbers such as the evergreen classic *Ein Freund, ein guter Freund* or the recent film music hit from Marika Rökk, *Ich brauche keine Millionen*. To this music she sat down at the table to do some darning or sewing, tapping her foot while her husband returned to perusing his magazines with a light sigh of frustration.

It was through this medium that in early April 1940 the German people were informed how their troops had landed at numerous seaports in Denmark and Norway in order to "protect the neutrality of these nations". Newsreels in cinemas later showed how the soldiers had prepared for their entry into these countries the night before; it was fascinating material and came across as though they were screening a thriller. Stirring classical music introduced the rousing speeches of the Nazi leadership and the feats of the *Wehrmacht*: the *Festliches Präludium* of Richard Strauss was a favourite, as was *Les Préludes* by Franz Liszt.

Arriving at the port, the troops swiftly disembarked and stole through empty streets of Copenhagen in the early grey light, unnoticed by the still sleeping civilian population. The spearhead proceeded on to the Citadel which was quickly captured and brought under German control. A small fleet of aircraft from the Luftwaffe passed over the Danish capital and dropped tons of leaflets in which the capital's population was informed that the German troops on the streets were purely there in the role of protecting Danish neutrality during this difficult international crisis; that they were to be viewed as friends in times of need and not occupiers. High-ranking officials, including the German ambassador and a lieutenant-general from the German Supreme Command, then "negotiated" with the Danish government, who immediately ordered the Danish army not to attack any German troops. Faced with the size and might of the occupying force, not to mention their reputation elsewhere, there was nothing to be achieved: it was all over before it had begun.

By this time it was early morning and Copenhagen awoke to find itself under German command. German military vehicles, topped up with troops, sped unhindered through the city while curious bystanders gathered around. There seemed to be no noteworthy signs of hostility. Indeed, some Danes waved their hats as the German jeeps sped by; although – as even Carsten had to admit - the crowd was clearly not imbued with the same enthusiasm as had been observed a couple of years before on the streets of Vienna. But even so, assured the news its audience, the city continued on calmly with its business as usual. The king went on his daily horse ride through the capital, people bustled on their way to work, commerce kept up its busy pace. In the following days all communication routes around the country were brought under German control: naturally first and foremost harbours, railways and airstrips. Weapons, ammunition and supplies were swiftly brought into the land. All coastal areas were secured, thus ensuring that any invasion of the country would be quite impossible. Not only increased security for the Reich - the radio and newsreels proclaimed in snippets that rang out in tune with the then German psyche - but also much-needed security for a small, vulnerable and ultimately friendly nation.

On that very same April 9th, German troops also landed further to the north of Europe in Norway, likewise occupying the country in order to "protect its neutrality". Luftwaffe transporter planes such as the Fw 200 Condor, packed with jocular white-uniformed parachutists sharing laughter with the camera teams, wielded their way over the immense glacial mountainous interior. As with Copenhagen, Oslo was to be taken in the early morning hours as dawn was breaking. In a bay close to the capital, a fleet of Luftwaffe seaplanes landed, ready with weapons and supplies to be delivered to the incoming troops.

The first victim of this campaign, a British fighter plane that had been nosily circling an airfield close to Oslo, was soon shot down. The Luftwaffe landed in force and from there the troops swiftly overran the capital. Machine guns, heavy and light artillery, and flak guns were all swiftly brought into position in strategic coastal areas, ready to defend the country against any incoming attacks. There was some light resistance, said the newsreel, in a fortressed area near to Oslo, which was quickly eliminated in an aerial attack. Also, a pocket of resistance in Trondheim was reported. But these were the paltry exceptions and not the rule. With astonishing speed a series of strategic ports stretching round from Oslo right up to the key northern port of Narvik had all been brought under German control. The nation could now be protected against any possible British invasion (which indeed and true to plan was attempted soon after, though successfully repelled; by June, peace reigned once more in the Scandinavian nation).

Furthermore, Norway was an enormous but woefully underdeveloped country, Carsten had learnt from the news and effusively passed on to others. Its length was mind-boggling: if placed in central Europe, the *Wochenschau* had showed on a map, it would stretch right down from the top of Germany to the very bottom of Italy, from the Baltic Sea to Palermo. Alas the Norwegian government had paid insufficient attention to the communication requirements in their own land but now, thanks to the new German presence, the network in this formidable terrain could receive a much-needed improvement. Already the Germans had commenced the construction of a first-class road connection between Oslo and Bergen and months later a Norwegian brass band inaugurated the completed street, trombones and trumpets proudly blaring as the first cars cautiously made their way along the icy route. Communications were especially important to the Germans in the north of the country, where vitamin-rich fruit could be more easily brought to troops facing a long winter ahead.

The few major cities that Norway had were all firmly subdued and, to the great credit to their nation, people in the rural north had also rapidly accepted the presence of German troops; as showed in the numerous images of Germans buying goods in local markets with Norwegian children in arms while posing for photos. Some were even shown learning to milk cows as the bemused locals looked on. In Oslo, tight military formations marched around the central Stortorvet Square, while distinguished fighters were publicly awarded the Iron Cross. The news reports left the audience assured that the brave men of the *Wehrmacht*, far from home and fearless of death, were defending the railways and ports (that led to the vital Swedish iron ore mines) against military attacks by the British armed forces.

This was all very neatly and swiftly accomplished, spectators such as Carsten found. But once one danger had been ticked off the list, another soon arose to take its place. Such is a world in which foes abound. Following on from the brilliant and snappy capture of land in Poland to the east of the Reich, a vulnerable flank lying to the west became the next object of attention. This came in the form of the Low Countries and northern France, through which a susceptible and unguarded Germany could easily be attacked by her enemies. And the enemy, everyone knew, never slept.

It was an indisputable fact that over six months earlier, already on 3rd of September, France and Britain had declared war on Germany. Even though Germany had never expressed the slightest hostility towards those two nations. Thanks to said precociously belligerent declarations, they were officially at war and had been for months. At least, in theory. In reality, neither of those nations had so far undertaken any military action of noteworthy importance against the Fatherland. Nonetheless, there was every reason to suppose that at some point they may well do so. France alone, a bitter and ever vengeful neighbour with no less than 450 kilometres of direct border with Germany, had 110 army divisions at the ready.

Initially, following the sudden attack on Poland, civilians and even cattle in France had been evacuated away from the border zone with Germany. But the weeks, the months went by; apart from the odd and inconsequential exchange of gunshot, nothing much happened. Everyone was eager to keep the peace, brittle though it might be, and was anxious not to give the other side any opportunity to let the situation escalate out of the current one of tense peace.

"The Führer doesn't *want* conflict in the west, that is just the point," pronounced Volkmar one bleak February day as various family members of his had braved the glacial winds blowing outside to come to Lüneburg to the *Gasthaus Sonnenschein* and congratulate him on his birthday.

"What for?" he insisted, and was allowed to pontificate at length, it being his birthday. "We owe them nothing and they have nothing worth taking." Although war officially prevailed in the west, there seemed to be no great desire on either side to actually fight it there.

There was (very unofficial) talk that German and French troops were exchanging food supplies with one other, mutually helping to achieve a level of pleasant variety in the military cuisine. There was even a rumour of German and French soldiers going swimming together in the Rhein, and more than once. There was the hope in plenty of German households that the war would consist of no more than the already successfully completed Polish campaign, and that a peace deal would eventually be struck with France and Britain. The Führer himself had already proclaimed, in parliament in October of the previous year, his desire to bring those two great *Völker* (peoples) – the Germans and the British – closer together, not only economically but culturally too. He had pointed out, and true to fact, that he had never made a demand that in any way threatened nor tried to infringe upon the sovereignty of the British nation, nor questioned in any way the existence of its expansive global empire. The German attitude seemed to be unquestionably friendly towards the Anglo-Saxon land. The obvious conclusion to be drawn, that there was therefore no reason for them to continue on this path to war, was answered by Britain with an icy silence.

The winter of 1939/1940 had been severe, with heavy snowfalls and plummeting temperatures. With the advent of spring, several divisions of German troops had returned from the successfully occupied Poland to be stationed in the west. There had then followed the occupation of Denmark and Norway; by the end of April, Norway had been brought under satisfactory control with all communication routes secured.

There were now two million German troops standing ready for operation on the western frontier.

Almost one month after the initial occupations of Denmark and Norway, on May 10th, a new series of offensive campaigns abruptly commenced. It had been announced by the Führer that the three smaller states directly to the north-west of Germany - the Netherlands, Belgium and Luxembourg – were being misused by the British RAF air force. They needed to be protected for their own good, as well as that of the Reich's. This situation would be rectified as part of a general invasion strategy for the western neighbours, termed *Fall Gelb* (Case Yellow).

In an unexpected surge of tank and infantry divisions, the *Wehrmacht* entered eastern Belgium, swiftly secured the bridges over the Maas and began to cross the river. Simultaneously, a brigade of parachutists, noiselessly brought over in covert glider planes, landed at and neutralized the heavily-built bunker fortress of Eben Emael. It was situated in the Albert Canal, with significant artillery and ammunition supply, and was manned by over a thousand Belgian troops. This had been the principal source of defense against a possible German invasion along the Maas river and the Albert Canal, which were supposed to have offered all necessary protection. The bunker was rendered inactive by the following day, May 11th. In the meantime, little Luxembourg had already been seized on the very first day of the invasion, taken over by noon.

Simultaneously on May 10th, further German divisions also invaded the Netherlands. The 18th Armee was already well positioned in the German border region of Münsterland and it started its march through the northern Netherlands with relative ease. Alone on the first day they had reached the immense inner lake of the Ijsselmeer; by May 12th the coast. The Dutch, expecting to stay out of the conflict as they had done in the Great War, were not in any way prepared for the sudden onslaught. To make matters worse, their allies were tied up with the synchronous invasion of neighbouring Belgium. To the south, German troops approached the vital Maas river, to which the Dutch reacted by blowing up the two important bridges by the city of Maastricht. Undeterred, the *Wehrmacht* simply set to work laying provisional bridges down beside them and on May 13th were continuing their relentless advance.

German troops moving up through northern Belgium also entered the Netherlands and met with little resistance. Eindhoven was taken with barely a shot. In Rotterdam, however, some initial resistance provoked the threat that the city would be bombed from the air if it did not immediately submit to German control. While the terms of the capitulation were being negotiated, a mix-up in the communication system occurred which ended in the Luftwaffe bombing the city anyway, on May 14th. The urban centre was flattened, tens of thousands of buildings destroyed, nearly a thousand civilians killed. That evening, the Dutch national radio station broadcasted the official surrender of the Netherlands to the German occupiers.

Back in Germany, the *Wochenschau* news transmitted daily scenes of the *Wehrmacht*'s advancing army and air force in Belgium, and how they were working in coordinated discipline to eliminate the fighting will of the enemy. The ring they had formed around the allied forces of French, British and Belgian troops in Flanders and northern France was being pulled in ever tighter. Once again, the much-feared Stukas led the way, gradually intensifying their raids: first bombing empty airfields to render them useless, then airports and planes, transport colonies, eventually small towns. They caused havoc, spread panic, and most importantly interrupted the enemy's flow of incoming supplies. Following up on these sudden and unpredictable attacks from the air, the German army rolled on ahead, meeting with sometimes considerable but never unbeatable resistance.

Adorned with grave classical music in the background - usually a symphony orchestra playing a pastiche mélange of Romantic era works with martial themes - endless scenes of devastation were shown to the viewers in the newsreels in cinemas all around the Reich. Fresh updates on battle news were regularly emitted by the radio channels all day. These audiences were in turn reassured that a retaliation in similar form over German towns and cities could be ruled out thanks to the highly competent and alert German air defense forces.

The *Wehrmacht* curled round to the south to cut through Belgium like a knife through butter. It bore down on the central Belgian town of Löwen, just before which a courageous but hopelessly outnumbered resistance force, including a small number of Allied tanks, briefly stood up to the German war machine. Artillery fire and tank destroyers took them out while infantry soldiers advanced forward, accompanied by the fearsome though unwieldy Panzer II tanks. They entered the outer boroughs where, in tough urban battles, streets were gradually taken one by one as the *Wehrmacht* troops advanced past piles of rubble and the odd abandoned bicycle; past houses with shattered front windows, warped iron balconies, facades sporting large gaping cracks; past the odd building with flames licking out into the street.

These ruins, the German news announced, were the result of the short-sighted and neglectful decision of the Belgian government to make its own futile contribution to an offensive war being waged _on_ Germany by the other western governments. Thus here, as elsewhere along the collapsing western front, the people of Belgium were unfairly paying the high price burdened upon them by the sins and the stupidity of their own government. And most sadly of all, the propaganda concluded, it illustrated the senselessness of bringing the battle right into the suburban housing areas of the population.

The German troops marched on and the swastika flag was seen fluttering down from yet another town hall.

In Brussels there had been little attempt at resistance and the majestic city could thus be taken unscathed, which was the preferred method of fighting, the _Wochenschau_ emphasized: warrior against warrior in noble battlefield combat, far away from unarmed civilians in urban areas. At least the city would have remained unscathed, had the departing French and British troops not callously blown up the canal bridges without even warning the local population; a criminal act that had damaged many of the surrounding properties. Once again, the ever-ready _Wehrmacht_ was at hand to help out the local population by building temporary bridges in their place.

Soon in German newsreels the Luftwaffe was seen flying over Antwerp where burning oil tanks, deliberately set alight by British troops after they had beaten a hasty retreat, were observed and disdainfully commented upon. They bombed the Belgian defense artillery and ammunition bunkers around the city, allowing the German troops to move in and overcome the fragile military opposition, soon overrunning the city. While German motorbikes, many with sidecars, sped towards the city centre, some light resistance was registered in the port area. This was quickly neutralized allowing large numbers of German troops to enter the harbour on large rafts and in dinghies, alighting and then spreading out through the city's cobbled streets. The centre was empty and desolate by now, its proud historic centre with towering classical structures, the central sidestreets with their intricate baroque architecture: all the buildings now stared gloomily down in silence. Not a soul was in sight, the newsreader proclaimed, as the inhabitants cowered away inside their homes to escape the terror of war that the English and French military had brought down upon their heads. The fires at the oil tank depots were extinguished with rapid German efficiency; and fortunately for the good people of Antwerp most of the oil reserves could be salvaged in the end. That was the true face of the so-called Allied assistance: "sabotage and wanton destruction!" In the central squares, the Germans had placed artillery and flak guns, ready to protect the city against any enemy attacks (from the Allied forces of course, for friend and foe had swapped places overnight). Behind them the flower beds, densely packed with tulips, waved in the spring breeze.

As the days passed, the last pockets of French and Belgian resistance were inevitably enclosed and disabled. The German army was efficiently bringing all of Belgium under control. Skirmishes and minor battles abounded until the Belgian hinterland was taken in a shower of steel and iron; Belgium then officially surrendered on May 28th. A German soldier held up his copy of the journal *Der Sieg* (The Victory) to the camera, grinned and jabbed with his finger at the splendid headline that so perfectly corresponded to the publication.

With the Allied forces concentrating their forces in northern and eastern Belgium, they had gravely misread the situation. The principal German offensive had been planned to head south all along: to take on France, their old archenemy, and eliminate her from the game as quickly as possible. At this point the German army split and the main divisions of troops and tanks branched off southwards. Losing in Belgium, the French had retreated and were shown to have made a ferocious attempt at a diversionary attack just before Sedan, near to the French-Belgian border. It nonetheless collapsed under the heavy weight of the German assault. The *Wehrmacht*'s artillery fired away relentlessly as troops and tanks smashed on through the crumbling French defence.

In the cinema where Carsten liked to view the military campaign, the city of Sedan itself was shown to be caught up between the two warring armies, and the narrator of the newsreel concluded that the French artillery had ultimately set fire to their own city. As streets of buildings burnt away, the music became more and more hectic, with swiftly flowing scales and jumping violins.

It was by now patently clear to all that by taking Sedan, and coming in from southern Belgium, the *Wehrmacht* had neatly sidestepped the supposedly invincible French wall of defense – the Maginot line. This was an immensely long fortification consisting of a concrete boundary crammed with bunkers, together with diverse barriers, weapon installations, living quarters for troops, and even an underground train system. It was a vast and very ambitious fortress stretching along the entirety of the French-German border. It had gone from being the pride of the nation to the last hope of an increasingly nervous France; now it was utterly useless.

The *Wehrmacht*'s mission was to thrust through the opposing forces in a strong marching advance, straight through to the continental coast of the English Channel. Images of German tanks rolling unstoppable through fields of green corn filled the cinema screens and hearts of the German people. In fact, in the case of the spearhead heading there for the frontal attack, it was moving along so quickly that the generals and officers involved often held impromptu meetings on the roadside; they simply didn't have time to prepare more formal surroundings. On May 20th, westward bound divisions had reached the coast, taking Boulogne-sur-Mer the following day.

The Allied defence was by now collapsing in disarray, confusion and hopelessness. Within days, whole divisions of French prisoners of war had been taken in the onslaught. Bedraggled they were marched along roads and mud tracks by fresh smartly-dressed German troops. Some walked arm in arm, many looked forlornly into the camera. Later the film showed German troops giving first aid to their defeated foes, carefully bandaging arms. The captured General Giraud descended from a German transporter plane and obediently saluted his German captors before disappearing into the back of a car. Long cinematic shots were taken of lines of prisoners of war, including many from France's numerous overseas colonies: "black, brown and yellow - what a colourful chaos!" chortled the narrator.

The conquest of France continued with images of the now familiar sight of squadrons of Heinkel He 111 bombers dropping their lethal load over railway tracks and on industrial plants. (Bomber planes was a topic that Martin and Carsten loved to discuss at the Gasthaus that year, while Gisela rolled her eyes behind them).

Convoys of tanks and other military vehicles ploughed on across the long roads of inner France, effortlessly destroying what little resistance they met *en route*, by which time the newsreel music had become positively upbeat.

In the north, Calais fell into German hands on Sunday 26th May and the hot news came rushing in – the last vestiges of the enemy forces were on the run! After that came the infamous retreat of the British from Dunkirk as they fled in panic across the channel, by any means possible, to flee the crushing German onslaught. Once Calais was taken by ground troops, the German marine also arrived. The small but nimble speedboats took on larger enemy ships with great courage and fortitude. They penetrated the French and Belgian canal ports and spread panic with their sudden appearance; were able to sink auxiliary cruisers, destroyers, submarines and transporters trying to flee to the English coast.

Meanwhile further south, the German war machine continued to roll on effortlessly in a lethal combination of tanks, infantry troops and diving bombers, overwhelming the last remains of the moribund French defence. By June 10th the *Wehrmacht* had reached the Seine and whole divisions of the French army had surrendered. So stood the German military front, gallant and glorious in the face of enemy powers who, right from the start, had "wanted, prepared and instigated this war." It was the courageous *Wehrmacht* that had been able to notch up victory after victory on its flag. "With this war, Paris and London had wanted to annihilate the German people. But thanks to our German *Wehrmacht* the historically deserved judgment has been enforced!" shrilled the newsreel.

By the sides of fields of dense lush vegetation, German generals typed their reports, to be sent back to headquarters in Berlin, in an easy-going calm under the benign late spring sun. In Paris, Pétain recognized that the attempted resistance to the invaders no longer made any military sense at all; that only continued bloodshed would ensue. He signed the ceasefire, or 'official capitulation', on June 22nd in a railway dining car in a field by a forest in Compiègne (and in fact in the very same railway dining car in which the Armistice of 1918 had been signed in Paris, that had confirmed the German defeat. Hitler had had it brought all the way to the remote field to better enjoy the French opprobrium with this symbolic touch). This capitulation came into effect three days later.

The victory had not come without a price, the news later informed, and no less than 27,000 brave German men had given their life; men whose ultimate sacrifice would not go in vain. A funeral march played as the camera panned over rows of makeshift wooden crosses with names and tributes etched in.

But that France, la *grande nation*, could fall so swiftly and utterly, tickled Carsten pink. Volkmar briefly forgot his place as visiting guest at the Gasthaus and he had not just one but two bottles of champagne opened in the back room to celebrate in style. The French had been thoroughly licked in only six weeks. How times had changed for the better! France, the nation that had humiliated them a couple of decades ago, in long weary months of endless shelling, of dark trenches and slaughter, of poisonous gas. Dreams of imperial glory all drowned in a muddy nightmare; and then to have that nightmare transformed into an immensurable wall of debt by the Treaty of Versailles. Now the horror had been reversed. Now it was the other one's turn to be humbled. It was a sensational victory and an even more splendid act of revenge. This was the tactic of the *Bewegungskrieg* (literally: war of movement, referred to by the Allies as the 'blitzkrieg') that showed the Führer's ability to successfully adapt and develop the fundamental rules of modern warfare. Moreover, it signified the penultimate collapse – Carsten opined – of a once great but now decadent liberal Europe, with the British soon to be the final domino to tip and fall. A huge parade was held in Munich, even featuring a visit from Italian leader Mussolini, to celebrate victory in Europe. The Führer was cheered with exultation by the crowds and declared to be the greatest warlord ever. Even Stalin sent his congratulations from Moscow.

Carsten adored to talk - tirelessly, mirthfully, meticulously - of the *grande défaite* that summer. Such was his genuine passion for the subject, coupled with his narrative talent and a good sense of timing in storytelling, that even his overbearing love of minutiae in repeated retellings of the event was enjoyed by some, tolerated by all. He told of the pride he felt at seeing, on the Deutsche *Wochenschau*, the scenes of German troops marching stiffly through Paris. A confused and raggedy crowd watched on in subdued and helpless anger in the French capital as the victorious army strode by, arms waving with energy, legs stomping with force; followed by yet more soldiers on bicycles and horseback, an illustrious parade. A seemingly endless division of troops marched somberly through the Arc de Triomphe and onwards, a biting symbol. Such humiliation was a feast for German eyes. Finally came the scenes of Hitler and his generals touring Paris in a brief, almost furtive, little visit; stopping off at the Paris Opera House, the Sacré-Cœur in Montmartre, Les Invalides and the Panthéon; gazing up at the bare, skeletal Eiffel Tower which, Carsten repeatedly insisted, looked truly unremarkable. This was the comeback from the undeserved and unjust defeat of just over two decades past. This was history finally starting to make sense.

For even to him, convinced as he was of the irresistible might of the German army, the short sharp victory had come almost as a shock, albeit a joyful one. France had not had a great military disadvantage; indeed, it had had a lot of good cards in its favour, not least of all its alliance with Britain. Together with that ally, it had had at its disposal more arms, though granted, less soldiers to use them. Furthermore it had possessed more tanks, though admittedly it had been weak on planes. What had marked France for defeat, Carsten insisted, was its inability to embrace modern warfare. Instead of organizing the tanks into fighting units, it had dispersed them among the troops in an ineffective manner. Instead of using the planes to strike terror onto the fighting front, as the Führer had wisely done, it had let them buzz around well within the country's borders in an incoherent mess. There had been no coordination between the divisions, no understanding among the officers, and ultimately no real political will to resist.

Carsten's conclusions concerning the swift and easy domination of France enforced his geopolitical worldview by confirming two simple truths: firstly, that other nations were ultimately weak, and secondly, that the Führer was a genius not only as a statesman but as a military commander too. And this genius was never more apparent in the aftermath. For just when Germany could have strangled and suffocated their western neighbour (as had once been their own fate), just when the opportunity for bloody vengeance had offered itself - that was when Germany and its Führer had chosen a different route.

One of mercy and, as if that were not enough, of kindhearted compassion. In this way the *Wochenschau* gladly showed regular filmed scenes of life after the capitulation. It was unquestionably a cheery sight to behold. The bustling streets of Paris were full of strolling smiling passers-by; restaurants were filled with clients; the women, famous for their fashion flair, were clearly just as elegant and well-dressed as their reputation upheld. In the wake of the invasion, the air was said to be filled with the scent of perfume and fine food. Shops and bistros and culture all flourished. Thousands of German civilians took advantage of the occupation to visit relatives in the Wehrmacht and experience the French capital first-hand. They toured the famous sights, listened to Beethoven and Wagner in concert halls (where celebrities such as Herbert von Karajan came to visit), and gorged in the fine restaurants. Just like the German saying, they lived it up '*wie Gott in Frankreich*' – 'like God in France'.

There were no bombed streets nor burning blocks nor cowering civilians to be seen here. The magnificent streets were fully intact, many with swastikas fluttering in the summer breezes. Industrial plants were not dismantled to be carted away; factories continued to function as before; the agricultural sector continued to be productive and was even able to contribute to the war effort by offering up a certain portion of their produce - at most reasonable prices, naturally - to Germany. Just as social and familial interaction were left to continue as normal, so were French commerce, industry, and agriculture. The economy should continue to prosper; merely under the watchful, but never covetous, eye of its masterly neighbour.

Though not mentioned in cinemas, Carsten had heard that the German high command had made the well-being and sense of security of the inhabitants of occupied France a top priority. The behaviour of the troops posted there was meticulously controlled and any deviations from strict instructions, such as engaging in theft, plundering or physically assaulting the civilian population, were harshly punished. Rape carried the death penalty. A distant though civil interaction was encouraged between German troops and Parisians; a blind eye was turned (at least on the German side) to the romances that inevitably arose. Meanwhile, under such a benevolent sky in the summer of 1940, no-one was openly addressing the thorny subject of France's Jews as yet, though for the German leadership it was certainly a matter in hand.

At the height of the summer the German military leadership, and in particular its Luftwaffe under Hermann Göring, turned its attention to a new target; a new feather that it intended to add to its cap and make its crowning glory: Great Britain. Even the previous English king who had abdicated, Edward VIII, was pro-Nazi and a great friend of the Führer and the *Vaterland*, Carsten had noted with a chuckle. How perfect an affirmation was that? - what higher friends could you possibly hope for? He related to Martin and Volkmar at the Gasthaus one day, while Gisela's children were doing their homework at the table, how the now Duke of Windsor had been sent out of harm's way by Churchill; all the way off to the Caribbean where he was to be made governor of the Bahamas. (Volkmar nodded with fascination at this information, checked that his grandchildren knew what and where the Caribbean was.) Carsten said with great confidence that he had no doubt he would return to take back the reins of power, helping to negotiate the terms of surrender in Germany's favour once the conflict with Britain was successfully concluded.

In July, the Wehrmacht Marine moved in for the kill and together with the Luftwaffe began attacking shipping convoys and harbours. This intensified in August, with attacks on airbases that resulted in wholescale devastation of British warplanes. But the conflict dragged on lethargically and no sudden breakthrough could be made. Something was amiss. For the first time, Carsten was unable to boast of any easy victories of import.

The strategy had changed, Carsten observed in the late summer. The necessity arose to start bombing more earnestly the urban civilian targets, i.e. residential areas. In this way, England would then be pummeled into a "soft target" that later could be easily taken by invading infantry troops backed up by tanks. In early September, a large raid of hundreds of Luftwaffe planes attacked London in a bombing orgy; soon this was to become a regular nightly event and over numerous cities.

Pontificating from his armchair Volkmar was confident, and Carsten couldn't agree more, that the end must soon come for England too, just like all the Führer's other victories. And with that, the twilight of the British Empire. Martin came into his own here, with lively displays of technical data about both bomber and fighter aircraft that the Luftwaffe was employing for the campaign. There was, for example, little about the advantages or disadvantages held by the German Messerschmidt in comparison to the British Spitfire that he couldn't tell you; and he would happily do so at the drop of a hat. When alone, he could spend the happiest of hours imagining those two fighting machines wheeling around the skies in spectacular dogfights over the green fields of England and the white cliffs of the English coast. Volkmar and Carsten in turn were more interested in and vociferous about who would flee where once the end result came. They envisaged Churchill beating a hasty retreat to Canada, and George VI escaping with his wife to India, or maybe even as far as Australia.

Edletraut had her own conjecture, which she voiced with a laugh one evening when she came to drop off Eva. "I think they will head up to Scotland and hunker down and defend themselves from there. They know we are not interested in taking Scotland." She kissed her daughter goodbye for a few hours, and concluded sententiously, "Even the Romans were not interested in Scotland."

Others in the family were more sober and pensive in reference to the outcome of this latest belligerent campaign, though still with that tantalizing sensation of the Reich powerfully rumbling on as an unstoppable locomotive.

Carsten adored the *Sondermeldungen*, the special announcements which were regularly reporting each new military victory. Alone the opening standard text, in its urgent and roughly hacked tone, thrilled his heart: *"Achtung, Achtung, das Oberkommando der Wehrmacht gibt bekannt..."* – "Attention, attention, the Supreme Command of the German Armed Forces officially announces..." No story, no film in the world could have filled his heart with such joy and fascination as this real-life, real-time drama.

He hung up a map of Europe on the wall of his small apartment and took to sticking coloured pins in it to indicate the advances of the Wehrmacht. He then coloured in the nations as they capitulated and watched the Reich expand like a huge swollen monster. Parallel to that he also kept a notebook in which he wrote down all the principal details of the Wehrmacht's military adventures: archived newspaper cuttings, made an ongoing list of the most important battles, and tabulated a summary of how many days it had taken to conquer each nation. It was an impressive list so far: Poland – 28, Denmark – 1, Norway – 62, Luxembourg – 1, Netherlands – 5, Belgium – 18, France – 43. That last entry was his favourite and he could stare at his notes and the map for hours, to savour each and every detail. The next entry, still to be completed, was Britain and he was fascinated to imagine what score it would eventually rake up.

As so continued the mood into the autumn; one of an optimistic view of the future and the sense that the security of the nation was in good hands. When a small raid by British bomber planes managed to get through to Berlin in a retaliatory attack, some isolated clusters of bombs actually landed inside the capital city's boundary. Eight people had been killed by falling stonework, stated the grim report, and the newsreels showed groups of Berliners gathering round those few hard-to-find craters, staring at them with curiosity.

There was a sense of action, but without any actual hazard. These were good times to be German; and the children in the Gasthaus perceived the warm contentment emitted by the adults around them.

One evening in late autumn the boys were playing in the back room. They were half-listening to an impassioned discussion between Volkmar, Carsten, Martin, Bernhard and Horst, concerning the eventual fate of the British forces and the likely moment the Führer had set for the invasion of the stubborn island.

For little Adolf, now over four and accustomed to deciphering the adult talk that went on around him, the subject nonetheless became a blur of words. It was quite impossible to make sense of the big words as the men in his family talked on and on about the foreign lands that had been invaded, captured, brought to heel. He captured little of the actual meaning; but the tangible excitement in the air, including the strength of the voices as the passion rose, made a profound impression on him. He sensed the urgency of the matter, he perceived the deeply-felt conviction behind the babbling flow of words. But most of all, he understood their love of the Führer, the man in the portrait in the hall who even bore the same name as he himself. He understood that adoration; for they loved the Führer, looked up to him, depended on him, in the same way that he loved his father too - as a distant but nonetheless commanding figure that hovered in the background but ultimately possessed more power than anyone, even his wonderful mother. The Führer took care of their daily needs, and thanks to the Führer there was plenty, and thanks to the Führer there was the hope of yet more to come. The Führer was benign and generous, although the Führer could be harsh and even choleric. The Führer lived somewhere in the sky, he assumed, and spoke down to the people through the radio. The people obeyed him because they loved and respected him. It was not hard for the child to comprehend the form of this reality, and even at his tender age he was doing the same as many a grown adult. The Führer was simply a demi-god.

Leaving his small brothers behind, who had snuggled up in the caring arms of Horst, Adolf went out into the small back garden space, in the gathering gloom. Above the town skyline, in the deep and darkling blue of the twilight, a cluster of ashen clouds hung, their undersides tinged to glowing vermillion by the fallen sun. A cool breeze wafted and caressed his face and arms. On those arms sprang up clumps of goosebumps as the coldness intensified. Undaunted he sat down by a small clump of seeding dandelion heads and plucked one, staring intently at its form. A rounded cluster of delicate threads connected each tiny unit to form an uncanny whole that was solid but at the same time, was not. Under the surface was visible a myriad of tiny stalks concentrating into a central mass of tiny brown oval seeds. He knew the form once the seeds were separated and took flight: that of a parachutist in reverse, not plummeting downwards, as he had seen in picture books how brave soldiers did into enemy territory, but rather leaping upwards, determined and boldly wheeling off to new destinations far afield. The wind plucked them out at first and tossed them into the air, but they seemed after that to possess a singular life-force of their own, controlling their own fate and choosing their own path across the surrounding meadows before being swallowed up by the distance, their ultimate destiny a delicious mystery to all who watched their trajectory.

It was always a magical moment, just before that great breaking out into the unknown. The woven cluster of seeds possessed the same mindboggling quantity and uniformity as the list of conquered nations that the adults had been reeling off. It came to Adolf in that moment that each seed was a nation: one was France, one was Belgium, another was Denmark, and so on; all joined together at the central hub that was his beloved German Reich. He perceived his own country as an extended version of home and parents, imbued with trust and warmth and above all security.

When all the tiny parachutists drifted off, he knew that there would be just the central light-green knot left over, fixed to the head of the stem. That was a fact that could be relied upon.

The flurry of parachutists was a wondrous sight to behold, and he wished he could be one of them. He drew in the fresh air to his lungs, then abruptly flung out his strong exhaling breath at the dandelion head. Before him he beheld a mass of nations explode upward in a jumbled, tangled blast of miniature white bouquets, which fled over the fence and away with the evening, each swirling and bobbing off to an individual and as yet unknown destiny in the burning dusk sky.

Chapter 19

During the first months of 1941, Horst had begun to internally weigh up the pros and contras of voluntarily signing up for active service in the armed forces. He had become acutely aware of the question of his own role in the growing conflict since the arrival per post, in the autumn of the previous year, of the infamous *Einberufungsbefehl* (conscription order) for both of Horst's brothers – Karl-Heinz and Wilhelm.

The war was already in the process of consuming its first and natural selection of young men just finishing their studies and those in their early twenties. It was now working in two directions: reaching up for older men, those in their late twenties and thirties; while simultaneously continuing as before to absorb each new year of fresh young men arriving at their late teens. The latter included even boys who had just completed their years with the Hitler Youth, and whose training there now seemed to have been a preparation for this day all along. What the population was not aware of at this point in time, however, was that there were ambitious plans afoot which would require an extremely large number of well-trained soldiers: the reasoning behind this would become apparent by the summer of that year.

Wilhelm and Karl-Heinz were both indicative of the former trend in age in which more mature men – often family men - were also being brought into the conflict. Wilhelm was a year younger than Horst; he was an electrician, single, and twenty-nine. Karl-Heinz was thirty-two, married and currently employed as a technician at the company *Fassfabrik Reichenbach,* involved in the production of metallic vats, barrels and drums. But those were footnotes for the authorities; the war was about to become insatiable and so would its need to replenish its supply of fighting men. Moreover, Karl-Heinz had crossed the path of a high-ranking NSDAP functionary in a heated, work-related dispute.

Both Wilhelm and Karl-Heinz had accepted the order to commence the Wehrmacht's *Grundausbildung* (basic military training) with an outward show of enthusiasm and calm bravery, expressing their unquestionable desire to serve their country now that the time had clearly come. It was logical they should: any overtly negative perception of this duty could only mean cowardice or disloyalty, unforgiveable sins for a German man. The letter with the dreaded *Einberufungsbefehl*, arriving by post in the form of a certificate-like paper with instructions to attend training at the indicated barracks on the date stamped, came as no great surprise. By November, both were gone.

Much of Germany was in military fever. There were frequent parades around town, when the Marktplatz or Am Sande would fill with jubilant masses, swaying swastikas, rows of men in uniform raising their arm high in the Hitler salute. Horst remembered well how he had stood, together with Inge, Gisela and Martin, outside the *Gasthaus Sonnenhaus* back at the beginning of the Polish campaign the year before, when a whole heavy artillery regiment had marched up the Rosenstraße on its way up to the Marktplatz. People had lined the streets to wave and cheer. Gisela and Inge had commented on how "smart" and "modern" they looked in their neat uniforms with boots and breeches, and the new model of *Stahlhelm* (steel helmet) which shaded the eyes at the front and curved down at the sides and back to cover the ears and neck.

Whilst there was some occasional - albeit publicly very subdued - melancholy within families at the sight of their young men catching trains off to training camps, there was no great sadness. There was still enough optimism, not to mention the general sense of duty to the Fatherland, to snuff out any regret or sense of loss. The young men's absence, everyone was sure, would only be temporary. The war was going well, the country still moving in the right direction, the former greatness of the nation would soon be regained: this was the general consensus that accompanied a constant flow of fruitful conquests abroad, at a relatively low cost to life to the German soldiers involved. Simultaneously, the war was also magnifying and spreading out into fresh lands where it was logical that more manpower would be required in order to cleanly subdue, and then maintain as occupied, these newly acquired territories. Even in the framework of the almost effortless military adventure so far, one needed to be prepared for some snags and unexpected complications, some resistance that was initially fiercer than expected. Greece and Yugoslavia were two such cases in point.

By this point, the notion of knocking out of the arena a fastidiously stubborn Britain had started to fade from the public mind. The fierce bombing campaign on British cities during late 1940 and early 1941 – that the Anglo-Saxons nicknamed 'the Blitz' (the lightning) - had ultimately failed. The British morale had not buckled under the onslaught of nightly sorties to bomb its civilian population in a whole array of different cities, including Liverpool, Birmingham, Manchester, Bristol, Plymouth, Cardiff, Glasgow, Belfast, Hull, infamously Coventry, and – first and foremost - London. The dog-fights in the air between the fighter planes of the German Luftwaffe and the British RAF, had seen the RAF holding the upper hand. The German Messerschmidt 109 was a masterpiece of engineering and aviation design but the British Spitfire had proved to be more agile and flexible in combat, not to mention being a defensive nightmare for the cumbersome invading Junkers 88 and Heinkel 111 bombers. Thus the many attacks had either been well repulsed by the RAF or well endured by the population. Even the royal family refused to leave London at the height of the bombing raids on the capital. Thanks to the stance of the Prime Minister Winston Churchill, not the faintest glimmer of a desire to negotiate, much less to surrender, was forthcoming. In Berlin, the plans to invade Britain by land were quietly shelved. It was decided by the Supreme Command that the conquest of the British Isles was one conflict that needed to be on ice for the time being; other issues were more pressing.

The Axis strategy had reckoned that, after riding on the wave of German victories in 1940 in the north and north-west of Europe, Mussolini's Italy would now do its part in the south, by occupying Greece and Egypt. This in turn would also give the Axis access to the much-desired Romanian oil fields.

But the Italian war effort was pitiful in German military eyes. Following the Italian army's initial bumbling and ineffective moves, the Führer lost patience and sent his Wehrmacht in to do the job properly. Hence began the Balkan campaign in April 1941, in which Germany quickly and ferociously bombed and invaded the Kingdom of Yugoslavia and the Kingdom of Greece. This was a military theatre that would involve Martin's younger brother Dieter, who had been serving in the forces since the outbreak of the war. He had fought in the Belgian and French campaigns, and was later stationed in Italy, from where he was sent on in April to participate in the newly erupted Balkan campaign.

The initial invasions were successful and local leaders in favour of the German cause were supported or enabled into a position to take power. But there was still urgent need to pacify hostile pockets of anti-German sentiment, arising in the form of guerrilla tactics used by local partisans. These posed a serious threat to the continued expansion of the Reich and directly threatened the homogeny achieved thus far.

Following their *Grundausbildung* training in late 1940, the two young men entered the armed forces and found themselves in action. Both men had been noted for their technical skills and given the corresponding posts. As an electrician, Wilhelm was sent to the north German island of Dänholm, near Stralsund, where he was to undergo specialized training to be part of a *U-Boot* (submarine) crew. Karl-Heinz was considered luckier when it was heard that he had been posted to Paris, known to be an excellent destination for a conscripted soldier; the absolute top destinations to hope for were Norway or the British Channel Islands, the latter being the cushiest possible option of them all. The two men, neither of whom had been especially pro-Nazi nor enthused about the war, aside from the usual everyday phrases about the injustice of Versailles or the 'Heil Hitler' greeting to public officials, began to write home with a mixture of fascination with the conflict and adventurous wonderment. They felt how they were finally part of something so much greater than anything they had experienced before, something that gave a new meaning to their lives. It was in this positive light that many families received news from their loved ones.

Whatever role the censorship of post may have played in their correspondence with the *Heimat*, the soldiers in general were obviously gratified by their newly acquired duties in service to the Fatherland. Moreover, there was a consensus among the general public that everyone should do their part, in whatever way they could, to ensure that Germany was victorious this time round. Another defeat, possibly even bloodier and more horrific in the aftermath, would be unthinkable. Civilian men all over town were coming under pressure to offer up their services voluntarily. In any case, the obligatory conscription was plucking up innumerable men every month; plus having the ranks of the Hitler Youth ever growing up and maturing into readymade troops, it had an ample crop to work with.

Horst's case was clearly quite different to the other men in his family and circle of friends and acquaintances who had been called up. He had a wife with three small children, the youngest just sixteen months. And more significantly, his position as a firefighter meant he was officially categorized as '*uk*' ('*unabkömmlich gestellt*' – deferred from military service). No-one, including his own relatives around him - and close relatives were often the first to encourage family members to offer up their service to the Fatherland and so avoid disgrace to the family - disputed this. He practiced a universally lauded profession that was furthermore, in the face of the growing threat of aerial bombardments, classed as an invaluable contribution to the war effort in itself.

Since the beginning of the conflict there had existed the strong fear in Germany that the enemy would try to attack the country from the air; now even more so with the increase in Germany's own aerial warfare strategy. The chief of the Luftwaffe himself, *Reichsmarshall* Hermann Göring, had promised back at the beginning of the conflict in September 1939, when France and Britain declared war on Germany following its invasion of Poland, that not a single enemy bomber would make it into German airspace. "If one reaches the Ruhr, my name is not Göring. You can call me Meyer (a very common German surname)", he had quipped. But despite this assurance, the fear of attacks had been greatly amplified since December of the previous year when the British air force had launched an ambitious, albeit largely unsuccessful attack on the city of Mannheim. The event had been angrily covered in the press and local councils. Those in areas of industrial importance, and other military targets such as large cities, had begun to make all due preparations in case their turn was coming. Air-raid shelters were being constructed throughout the country and measures such as artillery fire, Luftwaffe fighter planes, and other defensive actions were being made ready for the worst-case scenario.

This fear was soon to be confirmed throughout the country as the nightly retaliation bombardments emanating from a now very hostile Britain became bolder, more numerous and – as the RAF gained experienced - far more destructive. Lüneburg itself received its first attack in the July of 1940, in a very minor, though at that time shocking raid, when bombs fell on the airfield on the edge of the town and in the district Im Grimm.

Through his job Horst was a key worker in these defensive preparations; that went unquestioned by everyone. He himself though was not entirely happy with his role. While it could not be denied that he was already fulfilling his duty to his town and his family, there was still the nagging notion that others were putting so much more on the line; risking that most precious and unique possession that a man has, his own life, while he was perhaps living an easier and more comfortable option. He was without doubt - at thirty - at an age that could well be considered '*wehrfähig*' - capable of combat in terms of health and age. He knew full well that he had a robust constitution and rarely suffered from sickness, that he was physically strong and mentally adaptable. In short, that he was the type of man who would make a perfect contribution to military service. And to top it all, it seemed to him wildly unfair, almost indecent, that he would let his little brother Wilhelm do the fighting for him. "What kind of man would do that?" he wondered in his increasing moments of self-doubt.

He was unable to shake off the sense of his military fate, of having to join the armed struggle sooner or later. Like many he had thought, as he watched Germany march in rightful anger into a justified and imperative invasion of Poland, that those young soldiers claiming with exuberance, "We will be home by Christmas!", were to have been right all along. But as the conflict expanded outwards - to the north, to the west, now to the south-east - he had been more and more chafed by the sensation that this conflict was to be of major dimensions. Despite the flow of announced victories pouring in at a furious pace, he was sure that there would be a huge necessity of manpower to control and stabilize these conquered regions, as well as to take in any further territorial extensions. There seemed to be an inevitability to his presence on the battle front and he in no way wished to give rise, through inaction, to the notion that he may be evading active duty through either pusillanimity or a lack of patriotism, using his profession as a crutch.

His conscience continued to torment him until one day he addressed the subject to his wife. Inge was immediately and unequivocally against the idea and had a whole fistful of good reasons for her position. Apart from the obvious issue of the necessity of his job, she also reminded him (hushing her voice) that his duty was not only to Führer and Fatherland, but also to wife and children.

"There are already so many young men joining the armed forces right now, Horst. There must be more than enough out there to carry out all the military operations necessary. Our families have already given generously. Both of your brothers have been called up and are serving in active duty. I know of many men from town who are out fighting too." She lowered her voice further and whispered in a hiss, "We are supposed to be taking back what is ours, not taking over the world."

He told her not to speak like that again. It was disrespectful but above all it was dangerous. He suspected her father to be behind the words, but he was wrong in that assumption. Old Georg had come to the conclusion that caution trumped freedom of speech and had got into the habit in recent times of keeping his thoughts unto himself. He had been in part persuaded by the reprimands of Gisela. Having seen Karl-Heinz called up to war at his age and with children to boot, she naturally had fears that the scope of conscription orders could set its sights on Martin at some point, too: in that, she had correctly comprehended that there was no need to unduly aggravate the authorities through reckless talk that could easily have indirect consequences. It was a known fact that some of the previously more outspoken people in town had already been packed off to one of the fronts.

Inge emphasized her strict opposition to Horst's proposed plan during the following fortnight and sought to show how much she needed her husband in the raising of their children by arguing that she had plenty of work waiting for her at the Gasthaus. She contradicted herself, however, by also pointing out that due to the significant drop in revenue at the Gasthaus, Horst's salary was of greater importance to feed the family. He realized this the day after and angrily confronted her, "How come there is so much for you to do there when there are so few guests? Even the restaurant is doing worse than before. You should get your sister to give her husband a kick up the arse. Make him do some work for a change. Then you would have more time to spend with the children."

Inge burst into tears; Horst sighed and instantly regretted his warm words, though knowing full well he was speaking the truth. Later on, he tried to expound on the subject. "They are not babies any more, Inge. Adolf and Joseph could be attending a kindergarten if you would let them. Even Hermann is nearly two."

"Not until September!" she said protectively. "And I do not like that kindergarten we went to last month, nor the woman we spoke to."

"She seemed pleasant enough. A little stern, but quite pleasant."

"She talked about strict education in preparation for school, and how patriotism can never begin early enough. About boys becoming soldiers and girls becoming mothers. They are three and four years old, Horst. What a thing to say! Who in their right mind would be drumming politics into little children's heads? I found the whole visit horrible. I want my children to grow up being children. Just little innocent children." She shook her head. "In any case, a kindergarten costs money and we do not have enough. That is one of the points I have been making."

There were some more discussions on the topic; but each time, Inge lost her patience and ended up in a huff. Horst was his usual balanced and centred self, but was still giving his thoughts of joining up considerable weight and was less influenced in this by his wife than she gave him credit for. She in turn said nothing to Gisela, for she knew how much he hated it when the two sisters "ganged up on him" with what he viewed as tribal blood loyalty and very misplaced in the presence of a husband.

He once mentioned the brave youths of the *Langemarckschlacht* – the battle in which an uncle of Inge's, Herbert, whom she had never known, had been killed at a young age in 1914. She responded to this with lines taken from her father's last discourse on the topic, and surprised Horst with her bitterness to and questioning of the concept of heroism in war, and her anger at the necessity of war in the first place. Striking in particular had been her morbid attention to detail regarding the daily lives of the German troops who had fought in the Great War; her unrefined references to rats had almost shocked him. But still, he stayed firm in his own opinion.

Eventually, he took an inner decision and changed his tactic with regards to Inge. Instead of persuasion, he would resort to quietly breaking the news. He left subtle allusions to the topic over a series of days, until one Sunday he sat down with her and said that his mind was made up; that he had spoken to his supervisor and colleagues at work, and informed himself at the local office of the military authorities as to the bureaucratical procedure. Inge, knowing and – she had to admit - loving the quiet obstinacy of her husband, did not put up any more verbal barriers. She sighed, bowed her head and dried her eyes, nearly sobbed but held back, took the news to heart, having already suspected as much from the hints he had left hanging in the air in the days previously.

She found a quiet moment two days later and said she simply begged him to take care of himself and to never take any unnecessary risks; that a recklessly brave fool was a dead fool; and that he had a wife and three young children waiting back at home for him. He held her tight and kissed her repeatedly, saying that she was not to worry for a moment; he would be gone for a while, to fulfill his duty, and then everything would continue as normal. He stressed the notion of "doing his duty", and Inge took the repeated phrase to be a reference to an old argument of theirs over his duty on the night of the *Kristallnacht* pogrom. She had the sense that perhaps he wanted to make amends for past neglect.

When they made love that night, Inge experienced an even deeper desire for him and his body than ever before, feeling she had to savour these precious and sublime moments of intimacy together; that there would be a long harsh and lonely winter ahead.

Thus the irreversible decision was made and he volunteered to join the army in June. It was a decision both regretted and highly commended by his supervisor and colleagues. They were unanimously full of respect; a couple of men, including Paul Schönbeck, were openly awe-struck that a colleague would voluntarily offer himself up for military service. Two much younger and inexperienced colleagues had already been given their draft notice in the winter before, but for someone in his thirties and with three children to take the leap, it was clearly a matter of pride. His announcement, though outwardly praised, put some in an awkward predicament. Albin Schenk, a colleague aged thirty-five with two children aged ten and eleven and his wife working as a typist at the town hall, followed Horst's example six weeks later, having gone through a similar analysis of his own conscience and besides having been subjected to pressure by family members into joining up.

The last days of Horst's civilian life flew by with what seemed to him to be an unnatural swiftness. Hardly had he mentally prepared himself, already the time was up. He was sent instructions indicating the day and time that he was to present himself for duty, and informed that he had been assigned to the military training area at *Standort Wilkenburg*, just south of Hannover. As Carsten worked for the *Reichsbahn* (the national German railway), he had been able to sort out a free ticket for him, in First Class no less.

Inge woke up at six that morning to prepare him a generous pack of well-filled sandwiches, together with fruit plus some biscuits she had made the day before. He told her not to bother, that he could buy something in the station when he arrived, but she insisted. In any case, she argued, and already well-informed, as a trainee in the army he could get a mug of *Ersatzkaffee* (substitute coffee) at the station when he arrived, but for food and better quality drink he would need *Lebensmittelmarken* (food ration stamps). She began to pull open a drawer to fetch some out. He stopped her and kissed her, said he felt sure that her packed lunch would be enough for the first day and that he would be well fed at the barracks: the *Lebensmittelmarken* were for her and the children, no discussion about it. She gave him a long embrace and sobbed a little until he asked her to help him by not being sad, especially in front of the children. They made their way downstairs and then round to the Gasthaus, where the boys had spent the night with their aunt and uncle and where, at the front by the entrance to the restaurant, Gisela already had them smartly dressed and ready to say goodbye to Papa.

"I will miss you a lot, you know," Gisela told him, looking him straight and intensely in the eye, as was her custom when she was being honest although this unnerved some men. "And do not worry for a single moment about Inge and the boys. They will be just fine and we will all be together under the same roof." They had given up the apartment now that Horst was going to war, and Inge and the children would be staying at the Gasthaus which was by now practically empty for most of the time. "You come back soon, safe and sound."

Horst smiled back, nodded stiffly. "You know, one of the reasons I am able to go with a clear mind is that I know that you and Martin are always there for my wife and my children. That means a lot to me. I know I can depend on you as a sister and an aunt to look out for and protect our family, and I want you to know that you can also depend on me as a soldier to protect our nation."

Gisela seemed to have something in her eye and rubbed it; the sight of which amazed Inge, who never thought her sister capable of being so emotional. To hide her disposition, Gisela said, "Come and give your old sister-in-law a hug, you young fool!" and embraced him tightly, patted his back and managed to recover her composure. Martin came up behind her, shook Horst's hand and patted his back, and told him not to leave it too long before he got some leave and could come back and tell them all about the action out there.

He caught the train to Hannover and changed there for Wilkenburg, arriving fresh and full of patriotic zest before noon. He made his way on foot to the barracks where he presented his papers to the guard standing post at the entrance. The soldier, with a look of permanent disdain on his face, glanced through the documents before telling him to proceed along to the second block and then on to the orderly room of the battalion.

Arriving there Horst encountered a gloomy sergeant behind a desk lightly covered with some scattered papers. He was, to Horst's surprise, just putting down a bottle of beer.

"You're early," the sergeant said with a surly tone. Horst was taken aback by this very first experience with military personnel and had in that moment no idea how to respond. Following his confused silence, the sergeant harrumphed and demanded his papers, which

Horst dutifully handed over. The sergeant made a disparaging comment that, "the fidgety ones always turn up first." Then, upon seeing his age, profession and personal family details, the tone softened considerably. He told Horst that he would be in the 3rd B-Company, which was in Building Nr. 7 – "when you go back out of the building it's the second on the right" – and that he should make his way to the first floor and choose himself a bunkbed. "That is all for today. Everything else will be explained tomorrow."

The barracks were located on an expansive area with groups of red-brick buildings and open areas for training. Around the edge of the drill ground stood clusters of trees and bushes bursting healthy green in the bright early summer. A sign indicated that there was a swimming pool further on to the north of the grounds, and before that was the large central structure with the administration headquarters and the mess hall. On one wall he came across a sculptured stone relief of muscular German soldiers exercising and marching, which appealed to him as he saw himself reflected. Somewhere far ahead, way out of sight, an officer could be heard barking orders to subordinates.

Horst located his building and room, spick and span inside; still empty and solemnly quiet, with only some sporadic shouts coming in from the area outside, along with the echoes of his own footsteps. He located a bunk near the door and threw his belongings onto the top bunk, relieved that he could procure that place for himself; this being one of the reasons he had been anxious to arrive at the barracks early. He took out a couple of newspapers he had brought with him, the latest editions of the *Armee Nachrichtenblatt* and the *Deutsche Sport-Illustrierte*, and flicked through them. He munched through a portion of Inge's food. Within the next few hours, the first men began to arrive and make themselves at home.

From snatched threads of conversation gleaned from the rising number of men arriving during the afternoon, he realized that many were very young, between the years of birth 1918 and 1922, and that they had just received the customary draft notice for the Wehrmacht. The men who had been drafted up so far, from among the people he knew of in Lüneburg, had also consisted almost entirely of such youngsters aged nineteen and early-twenties. But that day there arrived some men like Horst, also in their late twenties or even thirties. At thirty, Horst was clearly in the bracket of older recruits with only three men in their mid to late thirties.

(At least that was the situation at this – still relatively early - point in the war. Within a matter of some months, and particularly by the late spring of the following year as the Soviet campaign started to get mired down, that age demographic would rise considerably. Officers who organized and conducted the training would be finding themselves facing more and more men now in their thirties, in some cases in their forties or even older. But all that was still to come.)

The fraternal comradery among the younger men that afternoon was instantly strong, with bonds forming in the first few hours. Particularly the very young – the eighteen- and nineteen-year-old teenagers – had trained with the Hitler Youth already and had a common outlook and preparation. They seemed to Horst to be universally imbued with zest and optimism. Carried along on youthful good spirits, they communicated in an easy-going manner with their fellow recruits, locating common ground and cementing acquaintanceships. Where there might have been the faintest hint of reluctance to serve one's country or undergo the stern military training ahead, it was carefully phrased or disguised under self-mocking humour or cynical resignation to the darker side of life's lot. All in all, the atmosphere was jovial and very positive. The young men clearly gave the impression of looking forward to the tasks ahead as they shook hands and exchanged "Hallo" and names.

Horst, more reserved and insecure, looked for companionship in the older men and made the acquaintance that day of Julius Fink, a short, stocky, and amiable plumber from Wiesbaden; and a man from a farming family in rural southern Bavaria, who was thirty-four and clearly out-of-place in the military surroundings. That evening Horst shared some of his immense provision of food, courtesy of Inge, with the men and so cemented the initial bond.

The next day they formed a line for a medical examination. There they were commandeered and shouted at: "Come on, quick, pants down, piss in that bottle there, breathe in, breathe out, open your mouth and put your tongue down, eyes wide open, wider, bend over and pull open your arse cheeks, stand up, you're done, move on out!"

Like cattle they were pushed past the military doctors, one by one. The barracks were depressing surroundings with the white-washed breeze-block walls and low roofs, more so to stand waiting in endless lines. Boldly printed signs such as '*Feind hört mit*' (The enemy listens) or '*Mit dem Führer zum Sieg*!' (With the Führer to victory!) abounded on the grounds.

Horst would soon come to perceive the fundamental military importance of standing in line, every day and for everything: for coffee in the morning, for meals, for clothing, for soap, for weapons, for documents, for all manner of examinations and checks. As Fink commented, "They say, for half of his life the soldier waits in vain." The men learnt to stand to attention when a senior officer entered the room: clipping their boots together, raising their arm and barking, "Heil Hitler!" For Horst this was an uncomfortable novelty. Like his wife, he might have occasionally mumbled "Heil Hitler" when talking to an official or at work, but otherwise it was not so typical for him. Now it was routine.

After the medical examination, the men were sent to line up in front of an officer where any special aptitudes or skills were noted. Horst was indicated to move across to an artillery unit. From there on followed the military *Ausbildung* training course, a mixture of general physical training and more specialist technical training in the area they had been chosen for. The recruits were registered and the group trainer *Feldwebel* (Sergeant) Pflüger, a dyed-in-the-wool Prussian officer from Berlin, who spat out his orders in deep Berliner dialect, went through the names.

One hapless young man, a shy mechanic from Cottbus called Hans-Peter, had the surname Mjesicy (it was later told round the barracks that he was of Sorb origin). Pflüger instantly took a dislike to this. He even bluntly asked the recruit if he was truly German and of Aryan blood, to which he stammered a nervous but resolute affirmative. Pflüger made Mjesicy repeat his surname, each time saying he was pronouncing it wrong and ordering him to get on the ground and do twenty sit-ups, to wait for him to utter another repetition of his Slavic surname before ordering another twenty, and so on for a good while. Naturally Mjesicy only knew how to pronounce his name the way he always had done and could not imagine what the sergeant wished to hear.

Eventually Pflüger grew bored and screamed at him as to how exactly he wanted to hear that name pronounced from now on, which was actually very similar to what the lad had been saying all along. He furthermore commanded the young man to speak German only, at all times in the barracks and no other language whatsoever, which came across as an astonishing request to a person who had never spoken anything else but German in his whole life. Although the other recruits recognized the ridiculous nature of this humiliation, and despite Pflüger mercifully not repeating the sadistic performance again, at the same time they felt a natural unease in Hans-Peter's company, as herds react when they smell an outsider. Mjesicy was basically ostracized from then on.

To another recruit however, Pflüger and some other training officers took a longer-lasting and more deep-rooted dislike. Oskar Schwitzke was a bespectacled and overweight young man from Bonn, just turned twenty and with a lonely and depressive disposition. He was clearly from the upper-middle class and socially awkward to boot; a slow learner who generally kept himself to himself and showed little natural interest in anything beyond what was required of him in this military environment in which he very reluctantly now found himself.

He was utterly out of place, to the point of being useless; but that was by now – in the summer of 1941 – less of an issue for the armed forces. Though physically unapt, he forced himself through the drills with all the stamina and precision that he could possibly muster. This naturally did not decrease the aversion that the professional military men felt towards him. Every second word that went in his direction was a synonym of 'fat' or 'stupid' together with an insult. Never was a single word of praise to be heard, even on those rare occasions when the unfortunate recruit really did excel. All he received was repetitive mocking. It was clear to many that this training ground – as a symbol of the whole political system itself - would be the ideal place for many an officer to wreak revenge on old enemies and settle old scores; not just political, but those of class too.

The posh and introverted Schwitzke was the perfect punching-bag for a working-class soldier who now had him in his power.

An excess of sit-ups or squats might have carried him off with an injury within a fortnight, and so an alternative punishment was thought up by Pflüger. Thus it became the highlight at the end of many a training session to have Schmuck climb up one of the nearby trees and for all to listen to his recital of a nonsensical text, hammered into him during the first weekend, to be uttered over and over again: "I, the fat idiot Schwitzke, a useless lump of grease, must sit here in the tree and wait to be fucked sideways by a panzerfaust, for ever and ever, Amen."

Having him scrub the latrines and corridors was another favourite ritual. On one occasion, when Pflüger got out of bed particularly bad tempered, this task descended in level to him having to clean the latrines with just a toothbrush, his bare hands and a bucket of water, instead of breakfast and tattoo with the other men. "Make them clean – so clean you could eat your breakfast off those surfaces, you *Drecksau* (dirty pig), because that is what you will be doing," warned Pflüger, although this was not enforced.

Horst watched the young man run round the training field gloomily, day in day out, stumbling through and over obstacles, trembling in fear at the daily rollcall, eating his meals silently and alone in the corner. The only vaguely humourful respite came when he got to handle actual weapons, whereupon he suddenly smirked with such apparent malice that the officers and recruits around him showed more fear in their eyes than Schwitzke had ever done.

Horst asked himself if he shouldn't reach out to the lad in some way, take him aside for a conversation at some point, try to offer words of comfort to him as an older brother might do. But he hesitated and eventually decided against creating any contact to a person who was increasingly disliked by most, hated by some. The recruits were eager to follow the examples set by their superiors and began to torment the lad. To Horst, the issue brought back uneasy memories of his inaction during that November night, now nearly four years back, when he inactively watched the property of Jewish citizens burn while they too were humiliated. On that night he had also sensed an inner moral obligation to act but had not done so, and he would follow that same pattern in this case. A deeply embedded and guiding part of his mindset told him that it was not wise to interfere until specifically ordered to do so by a superior officer.

Horst held the belief that the world around him was inevitably controlled by those with more capability and intelligence than he possessed and that therefore no actions from above came without some basic reasoning; most probably one beyond his own complete comprehension. He acknowledged that the reasoning behind the strict treatment would be to roughen the boy up, turn him into a tough soldier, and thereby increase his chances of survival on the battlefield. No-one was meant to do anything other than excel; in fact, one of the frequently quoted slogans in the Wehrmacht ran, 'The impossible will be carried out immediately, miracles may take a little longer.' The expectations for Germans troops were exceedingly high and everyone – both instructors and the recruits themselves - were more than aware that a long and difficult mission stood before them: the conquest of a continent, no less. This was a mission that would not be successfully completed unless they were all in peak shape, both mentally and physically. A favourite phrase of the training camp commander *Oberst* (Colonel) Eidinger, which he had had engraved and hung on the wall of his office was, read "*Gesunder Körper, gesunder Geist*" (Healthy body, healthy mind). It was inspiring to the men to feel how both states of toughness went together: with their bodies well-trained, their thoughts would be equally rugged, pure and cleansed of any slovenliness or degeneracy. And it was a clear fact that this state could only be achieved through the maximum of discipline.

That being said, and although sadistic actions were more the exception, Horst felt that there was nonetheless a needlessly harsh manner in which the officers addressed them, both within and outside of the training programme and in everyday situations. From his previous professional life, Horst himself was much used to hard labour in teamwork, frequently under extreme duress and in hazardous situations in which orders were bellowed out and men swore in anger, pain and frustration. However, once the task was complete, his experience was that of men returning to address each other with normal civic respect. He had not been mentally prepared for the continual aggressivity of army life, most certainly not for the obnoxious and often spiteful shows of power that some officers engaged in with alarming frequency. He had imagined finding much more brotherhood between officers and recruits, always within the restraints of rank of course, but instead he saw too much gratuitous humiliation. Later on, he would come to note the stark difference between the military comradeship on the front and the military interaction back in the *Heimat*. The latter, as was here the case at the barracks, was a world inhabited by petty functionaries, career-climbing bureaucrats, pen-pushers, and bullies. He noticed how some military slackers appeared to have found a comfortable niche there and were happy to be in an eternal position of staying put in the *Heimat* to train in more and more young troops; they were sometimes additionally protected by those of high rank in the Party. Horst suspected that group trainer Pflüger was such a case in hand.

With the company commander *Leutnant* (2nd lieutenant) Heck on the other hand, an enthusiastic Bavarian who had joined the NSDAP way back in the early thirties and was very politically opinionated, he found it much easier to work with. Heck took charge of shooting practice with various weapons – from pistols to heavy machine guns - and though prone to occasional bouts of loud impatience, he generally guided the young men through the exercises with equanimity and rectitude. This was a technical area in which Horst, much to his own initial surprise and ultimate pride, showed some natural talent. He was not a star among the group, but during the shooting exercises his results were well above average and foreboded well for the future, he felt. As Heck said to one of the men, "You won't be a sniper, but you won't be a quick corpse either." To Horst's relief, he noted how Schwitzke also showed an above average rating. After the fiasco of his general physical training, at least this was an area that he was proficient in. Even Pflüger found some good words for him when he found out, and the task of cleaning the latrines passed to other recruits instead.

Apart from the general physical training and the specific military training, such as familiarity with the different types and uses of weaponry, the recruits also received some limited classroom activity. They mostly studied Germanic history and tradition along with basic *Volks*-oriented themes, as many already knew well from their time in the Hitler Youth. It was naturally of fundamental importance that the men understood the depths of the culture that they were potentially going to give their lives for. Military topics covered in detail included topography and reconnaissance of terrain, map-reading, target detection, minesweeping, plus some basic first aid. They studied the various types of injuries they might suffer in active duty and how those injuries could impair or even end their performance on the battlefield. The types of shot wounds were analysed one by one, so that they would know immediately how to attend to injured comrades: *Durchschuss, Einschuss, Ausschuss, Streifschuss, Beinschuss, Bauchschuss*[5] and so on – the list seemed endless. Some recruits audibly gulped, a couple even retched, at finding themselves confronted with so many ways to suffer horribly and not even die.

Additionally, they were thoroughly taught the regulations of the Geneva Convention, the Hague Conventions, and all internationally accepted rulings governing the humanitarian treatment of prisoners of war, as well as of the civilian population in occupied areas. Heck noted cynically at the end of one lengthy double set of lessons on this topic, "At least there you have the theory."

Weapons training was unnerving at first for all the recruits. It revealed, with the direct brutality that only bare cold steel could achieve, that basic duality around which war was based - killing or being killed. The recruits were informed about and shown the personal weapons that would be issued to all troops – primarily a Karabiner 98K rifle - and told how their company, once sent to the front and actively participating in the conflict, would also have three HMG (heavy machine gun) platoons plus one mortar platoon. They were shown how the HMG's firepower could be amplified by using a gun carriage onto which the machine gun, with its rapid-fire release connections, was mounted, thus giving it a far higher performance in terms of sustained fire. Though hellishly impressive, this feature also required great amounts of ammunition. These had to be dragged around in boxes, each containing belts of 300 rounds, by those serving as ammunition bearers. Those troops would be expected to bear four

---

[5] * Penetrating gunshot wound, entry wound, exit wound, grazing shot wound, shot in the leg, shot in the stomach

such boxes, each weighing 17kg, when in action. The soldiers operating the heavy machine gun had to deal with a bulky weapon that became red-hot through constant usage. In case of malfunction, such as blockage by cartridge cases, they were trained to quickly disassemble and transport the heavy device to a new location at around fifty metres distance, reassemble it, likewise with maximum speed and precision, in order to resume shooting before the enemy had time to react.

When in active duty, the troops would be expected to carry a load that consisted of at least a gun carriage plus two boxes of rounds of ammunition in addition to the standard equipment, i.e.: rifle, gas mask, tent, bread bag, canteen flask with water, spade, knife, and clothing. This would reach between 60-70kg and would have to be carried on marches of up to 20 kilometres a day, whether under a burning sun or through snow or heavy rain. It was a daunting thought for Horst, though he seemed at the time one of the few that was actually considering the functional angle to this physical challenge.

That came to pass, though, in the third week of training. One morning a rumble of thunder and dark grey clouds accumulating on the horizon signalled an impromptu early summer storm. The heavens opened by midday and it poured for a couple of hours. Pflüger was all smiles and jokes, and the recruits soon found out why. Laden down with heavy rucksacks the men went on a long march through surrounding terrain, now a dirty mess. Rushing through energetic streams of dark water and falling face down, running along fields of deep mud with little sacks of equipment swinging from the belts, Pflüger screaming commands from behind. Occasionally he shouted out a short sharp series of, *"Auf, marsch! Hinlegen! Auf, marsch! Hinlegen!"* (Up, march! Lay down!). Dripping in the wet mire, including their hair and faces, they looked a miserable bunch by the end of the two-hour exercise. Later, as they stood in a line under the lukewarm shower, physically exhausted as never before in their lives but laughing and joking together, and Horst realized the tactic; the hardship formed the camaraderie, cemented the bond between the men. One day that bond would end up saving lives and overcoming enemy onslaughts, the trainers knew.

Horst soon learned the importance of never showing that you were even remotely as informed as the instructor. He saw time after time eager young recruits let their self-confidence carry them a step too far, only to be roughly taken down. You were simply there to learn and feel lowly, he realized; not to shine or show promise. He kept quiet about his own professional knowledge if the subject came up. He maintained an impassive front in the face of the whims and bilious tones of the officers, through the endless "*Auf, marsch, marsch!*", through the excesses of press-ups and squats that at times could bring you close to vomiting. He came to assume that the reasoning behind such tribulation was that when the recruits finally got to reach the front as soldiers, it would seem like heaven in comparison.

The duration of the training, as explained to them at the beginning, was expected to be three months. It was ultimately cut short to ten weeks following an exceptional announcement made on the cloudless turquoise sunny day of the 22nd June. That morning, once the recruits were up and ready, the training camp commander *Oberst* (Colonel) Eidinger arranged for a large radio to be carried out into the centre of the training area and connected up to an electricity supply by a couple of recruits. He wished for as many men as possible to hear the message that was set to be broadcast to the whole nation very soon. He seemed, despite a very guarded use of words, to have a good idea as to the content. Rumours abounded that Minister Goebbels had already read out an important statement concerning a new military campaign that morning at 5:30am, just as they were waking up.

Stern music, in a blaze of brass instruments, came out of the radio: soon they would get to know this motif as the *Russland-Fanfare* (the Russia fanfare). It extended into a brief orchestral pomp and then the Führer was announced. This time his voice was calmer than usual, lulling yet resolute, as he prepared the German people for some information that needed to be digested with the right amount of composure, approval and unshaken loyalty.

He explained how that very morning at 3am, the German Wehrmacht was forced to defend itself against a large offensive undertaken by Soviet troops. This action had taken place within the framework of the increasingly hostile and threatening presence of the Red Army on the border of the German Reich. It was in direct violation of all the responsibilities the Soviet Union had promised to assume, as well as being in contradiction to all the previous declarations of peace that had been issued. The German army had been forced into a defensive position by these belligerent acts of war, and therefore now found itself at war with the Soviet Union.

Apart from establishing this abrupt state of open conflict in which the Reich now (reluctantly) found itself, the Führer also took time to enunciate the fundament that was to accompany the military action. "The war against Russia," he said, "will be of the type that cannot be conducted in a chivalrous manner. This struggle is one based on ideological and racial differences and must be carried out with a rigour and harshness never seen before in human history."

With these words, the war now took a whole new direction. Its raison d'être was no longer centred around the previous rationale of purely defensive counteraction against the portentous threats of old enemies, nor the reconquest of areas of land that had been unfairly stolen in previous conflicts and rightfully belonged back in the Reich. Now it had morphed into something far larger, and horrifically meaningful; which was crucial if this announced expansion was to be convincingly justified by the leadership, to be then assimilated and accepted by the wider population. Most Germans did not wish to lose their only sons for so many acres of farmland out on the distant plains of Eurasia, nor the recovery of Alsace. But a brutal and dynamic menace to the existence of all of them; to their children, spouses, parents, siblings, neighbours, colleagues; to their culture and their very way of life - that was something to stir a nation into action and individuals into possible sacrifice. It was to be a titanic struggle ahead, this much Germany understood; of the proportions of classic struggles of good versus evil. It was to be a struggle between two completely opposing sides from which there could only emerge one victor, for the other side would suffer complete annihilation. It was to be all or nothing, triumph or death.

Thus, the troops listened to the radio announcement with a shivering sense of destiny. Their moment had come, their training had an existential purpose. After a cluster of further details concerning the

Soviet aggressions and German retaliations, plus some riveting words about the obvious necessity of victory, the speech ended and there was silence. The broadcast then continued with further relevant statements until the march music kicked in and Eidinger switched if off with a flick. "Good, so now the next step is clear," he concluded, wishing the stunned men a good day and ordering the same pair of recruits to carry the radio back to the officers' quarters.

The next morning the men ate their breakfast off the oval stoneware plates, jokingly named *Hundeteller* (dog dishes), in an atmosphere of excited expectation. All that which they had so far awaited, imagined and dreaded, had now been fulfilled. They were not merely to join in on an already hot conflict and help out comrades in need; they would be spearheading a new and hugely ambitious conflict that would – they felt uncannily certain – change the map of Europe forever.

As to whatever misgivings or uncertainties may have arisen, these were silently quashed. There was no time to waste; the game was on. Preparations for mobilization began that same day, including a curtailing of the original training schedule. The men were handed out their *Soldbuch* – the Wehrmacht soldier's ID and service book – and field-grey uniform, together with the basic equipment. Some could hardly believe the precipitous flow of events that overwhelmed them all.

The following day, Horst and a number of other recruits prepared to board the next train to the eastern front.

Chapter 20

It was a bright summer's day, not just in the barracks but throughout the Reich, the day the news exploded in the German media that the Wehrmacht was to invade the Soviet Union. It was announced in a trail of brazen glory that morning, received by tens of millions of civilians in the Reich as a bombshell newsflash. For some this came as a pleasant surprise, sparkling with acclaim and the promise of elevation, confirming a destiny that many knew must surely await the German people. It was for them a logical continuation of a series of military successes, possessing the same physical inevitably as a stone gathering speed as it rolls down a hill.

Others however took in the news with trepidation, bewilderment or even shocked dismay. Common, though rarely expressed, was the uneasy sense of the Reich overreaching itself in an unfavourable moment of a delicate balance of power. Those with a negative outlook of whatever intensity were wise enough not to express in public a single word of their fears or unease. That would have led to social and professional ostracization, or quite possibly a prosecution that could soon lead to prison or a concentration camp. Words could not be thrown to the wind as there were informers everywhere to catch them. Even to other close family members, individual doubts or rebukes were camouflaged in general jingoistic tropes. Condemnation of the military decision as being a folly was unthinkable. Mothers, fearing aspersions of disloyalty, which was considered tantamount to downright treachery, did not dare to express their natural desire to want to have their sons at home and alive and by them. Regret and anxiety were subdued at farewells, as their boys caught the trains to war.

Those who now wished to be freed from a war that was rapidly knowing no bounds, realized too late to what they had politically aligned themselves by casting those fateful votes a few years back. But hindsight is the most precious and thereby the most elusive gift, and so there was no option but to follow with apparent jubilation how that same war unfolded.

That very day, in countless barracks across the Reich, preparations for the immense invasion began. The *Marschbefehl* – the marching order - was issued nationally and within the following two days many divisions had boarded their respective trains and were heading to the front. On one of these sat Horst. He had just enough time to write Inge a letter before he left; she already knew the content before she had received it.

The train was basically a series of freight wagons, furnished with a couple of stools and straw on the floor, with a boiler in the corner for heating in winter. It was packed with men, the mood buoyant and raucous just as it had been back at the barracks when the recruits first arrived. There was a sense of adventure among the young men, as if this were a serious adult version of a school outing, with some clearly very excited about the upcoming prospect of their baptism by fire. Songs were struck up, including the *Die Wacht am Rhein*, a patriotic song from the old days of the German Empire:

"Lieb' Vaterland, magst ruhig sein,
Fest steht und treu die Wacht, die Wacht am Rhein!"
"Dear Fatherland, you can be calm,
Firm and loyal stand the Watch, the Watch on the Rhine!"

It was a rough manly din of a melody but with much emotional power for all those in the wagon. Cigarettes were passed round by those fortunate enough to have received some from proud fathers and other admiring friends and relatives. Cards were played, photos of anonymous naked women were passed round, jokes were told. The journey was long and some took a nap, despite the racket, in the thick straw laid out.

At the Polish town of Rzeszow, the journey came to an end and they alighted and were taken to the *Kommandantur* (garrison headquarters) there. An imposingly tall *Generalmajor* (General Major) Jentz greeted the troops with a perfunctory handshake and a concise, well-prepared speech that offered a grim vision of short-term hardship coupled with a glowing vision of long-term destiny. He made no bones about '*der Iwan*' – the Ivans, as they called the great Russian bear that they now had to bring down – being a formidable opponent. Well-armed, boasting an impressive number of troops and endless further reserves of men to call upon, this was not an adversary that would give up easily. They had to prepare themselves for a difficult and possibly longer, more drawn-out battle than the Wehrmacht had known before. This was not going to be like Poland, nor Belgium, nor France, nor Greece. Alone the sheer size of the nation would make its conquest a daunting task. But win they must, and win they would. So much depended upon it that there was no other option than to give all they had. Only that way could future generations of Germans live in peace and prosperity. More than that, even: in the face of the fierce Bolshevik threat to overrun all of Europe, at stake was the whole of Western civilization, and with it all that was ever great and good in history. All that depended on a German victory and this huge responsibility fell ultimately upon their shoulders. It would be achieved by their superiority: both moral and military. It was their courage, their competence and their determination that would bring this monumental, this critical mission to a successful conclusion. Without doubt, it was to be the most important military event in the entire history of the German nation, he concluded.

There was a general feeling among the men that this was indeed no hyperbole, but rather the plain truth and a gritty reality. They registered the high-flown language of the speech but fully understood the underlying tone of its message. After it had terminated, they prepared themselves to face the future with pride and optimism; found themselves basking in the hot tingling pleasure that precedes the great game.

Horst and others on his train had been assigned to the same company. This had just suffered a series of casualties and like all the companies in the *76th Infanterie-Division* it was receiving its *Nachschub* – human ordnance, the fresh supply of new troops sent to the Front to replace those who had fallen in battle. Most of the others in the company were relatively young but still experienced soldiers, having fought in the western campaigns in Belgium and France.

That evening came the handing out of weapons, ammunition and equipment. These were distributed in generous lots, which came across as a welcome contribution until the men realized this was because the platoons were undermanned, with just 20 instead of the usual 100 - 120 troops. Under cover of darkness, they began their first march towards what they were told was the *Hauptkampflinie* – the main battle line. From there onwards, the Wehrmacht simply had to advance as quickly as possible. They were to push through the territory, organizing attacks where they met with resistance, strengthening positions already taken, and preparing appropriate defensive measures in the face of enemy offensives.

The first few months were unnerving at times for Horst, but generally uplifting. In his company they followed in the path of the implacable rolling of the heavy German tanks; the *Panzer* Type II was particularly effective on the open Soviet plains. They blasted their way through line after line, aided by organized air attacks. These usually came in the form of a squadron of *Stukas*, the Junkers Ju 87 planes that were used to such great effect to dive-bomb the enemy. Horst made a mental note to tell Martin all about them when he was home next. Whenever they appeared they brought with them such a unique shock reaction, whether from military or civilians, that the mere sight of them caused the expectation of horror already, followed by that idiosyncratic terrible low scream as they dived in for the kill. The German military intelligentsia had noted, to their utmost satisfaction, how this tactic had struck such acute fear into the hearts of the Poles when the *Stukas* were employed during that campaign, creating exactly the desired psychological effect. Bringing up the rear after the tanks and the *Stukas* came the German foot soldiers in dozens and dozens of divisions extending outwards in all directions. The Red Army was pushed relentlessly backwards. In the south, where Horst's division was posted, they were well past Lviv by mid-July, about to pass Kiev by the beginning of September. By the end of October, they had passed Krasnograd and had nearly reached the Donez river, having thus crossed almost the entire Ukraine. It had been a mammoth achievement in an enviably short space of time.

The Soviet defense was considerable though, and the Red Army troops often put up a bitter fight, causing numerous casualties before eventually being taken out. Particularly feared by the Germans were their so-called *Stalinorgeln*, the 'Stalin church organs'. This was the nickname given by the Wehrmacht soldiers to the *Katjuschas*, the Soviet rocket launchers that were mounted on trucks, with the long metal rocket projectiles resembling the musical organ pipes of churches and cathedrals. These rockets were not a precision weapon, but rather were simply fired in large numbers in a general direction so that their splitters and shrapnel would spread outward in a large radius and destroy anything near around them. They proved to be a formidable armament when fired into dense groups of troops. Their constant wailing sound when fired, together with the immense explosive power they packed, soon had the German soldiers trembling.

But despite all the often deadly setbacks, the German war machine rolled brutally onward: unwavering, seemingly unstoppable. Sometimes the speed of the advance was so great that groups of Soviet troops were suddenly cut off and actually ended up caught behind the German line. This posed a considerable hazard for the Wehrmacht as these soldiers melted into the landscape, hiding in fields of barley or patches of high grass, to then open fire on the German troops from behind. Horst's platoon was snared by just such an ambush on one occasion in September. They were resting on a grassy area beside a field of sunflowers for a few hours, allowing some of the men to sleep with their rucksacks as pillows. Horst and another soldier, an *Obergefreiter* (lance corporal) named Giers, were conversing. It had been a long week of marching, with much terrain covered, and both had begun inspecting their sore feet to discover all the blisters on their soles. In the case of Giers, they were bleeding heavily and Horst commented on this, telling him how back home his sister had used *Apfelessig* - vinegar made from cider - to treat blisters.

Suddenly out of the sunflowers came machine gun fire, followed by a series of grenade explosions all around. The men threw themselves to the ground or ducked in cover, then returned the fire. They had been ambushed by the enemy but were able to encircle the field and take out the rogue Soviet platoon in less than an hour. All the same, there were two casualties on their side and a number of wounded, some seriously. Horst was the first to return to Giers after the skirmish was over and called over the accompanying *Sanitäter* (Medic), Sani-Klaus as they called him. He inspected Giers and diagnosed a shot to the femur which would mean a return transport back to the nearest clinic or possibly back to his hometown, depending on further examination. Horst and Giers found some humour in the attack after Sani-Klaus had gone on to inspect other wounded troops; at least that solved the problem of the bleeding blisters.

Another disadvantage of this rapid movement forward was the difficulty of keeping up with the advancing front. With the distance increasing, both new troops coming up behind to replace the wounded or fallen soldiers, as well as supplies, were frequently held up. The lack of food supplies that could arise through such discoordination became a major issue. Initially the commanding officers had taken a very dim view of any harassment or stealing from villagers; but as soon as the food supplies dried up, they began to look the other way. So, the troops would 'help themselves' to turnips, carrots, and onions from the fields, or confiscate the odd bunch of chickens or geese and organize a large meal. There were some initial inhibitions among the soldiers concerning the theft of livestock, especially when it was clearly causing distress to the peasants. But hunger overcomes all barriers, and the bar had already been set low on this campaign. The officers limited themselves to accepting the theft of agricultural goods but made it clear that the theft of any other non-essential goods, and most certainly the charge of any other greater crimes, would be punished; and where appropriate, harshly. Rape carried the death penalty. This level of relative morality among the regular Wehrmacht troops was maintained during the early period of the campaign; but soon sank in later years and especially during the final, desperate retreat.

In the late summer months, the weather became extreme. A heatwave settled on the vast open plains and they often marched during the day at nearly 40°C. Night-time, on the other hand, brought bitterly low temperatures, barely above freezing. The daytime's long lonely steppes were arid and bleak, the sun glared without mercy, the horizon was often lost in a non-descript shimmering haze. One lance corporal, who had served in the North African desert corps of Rommel, commented that he never imagined how being in Russia would be like fighting in the desert. They were covering up to fifty or sixty kilometres a day and though the fighting in their region was still relatively light, the bodily exertion was strenuous and left them exhausted. The tank chains whipped up huge clouds of heavy brown dust whenever they thundered on out ahead of the men. This dust settled on their sweating faces which in turn became a soft layer of permanent dirt.

Thirst accompanied them constantly and their canteens, the water bottles they kept strapped to their uniforms, contained nowhere near enough liquid to relieve their parched mouths and throats. The water in the few wells they came across was routinely undrinkable, and in some cases had been poisoned by the retreating Red Army. Despite that hazard being common knowledge, the mind-bending thirst drove some soldiers to drink water from dirty puddles that might appear now and again, simply unable to resist the sight of the precious liquid. This invariably led to serious stomach and intestinal problems, not to mention the danger of then fainting under a full-blown circulatory collapse.

In the face of such hardship, the commanding officers made a point of continually filling the men's ears with propaganda concerning the noble and epic nature of the battle that they were undertaking. They lectured long, with gravely earnest countenance and tone of voice, about the horrors of Bolshevism, which enslaved its people under the fearsome yoke of communism: a yoke so firm and tight that, once in place, it was near impossible to shake off again. In this way, the Russian revolution had lasted so long, despite the terror, despite the hunger and the poverty needed to keep it running.

And indeed, the people of this part of the world, here in the Ukraine, knew more about that than anyone. They had starved in their millions under Stalin, had been dragged off to the brutal gulags for merely criticizing the despot.

Realizing this, the troops soon began to see themselves not so much as conquerors but more as liberators. It confirmed everything they had been taught.

This motivating spirit and the optimistically held view of an inevitable, conclusive, crushing victory, hopefully with a minimum of casualties on their side, put a strong stride into the Wehrmacht's long and arduous marches. They continued to make great gains in the territory brought under control, at least until the end of the autumn months. By mid-November, a gradual change began to affect the land they were treading across, and the game changed considerably. There were long, persistent rains that left the ground soggy to the brim and barely passable. The heavy German tanks soon sank into the mud of the rough routes with no asphalt, while the men desperately struggled to free them. They were becoming more of a hindrance. The vehicles bringing up the supply of goods, most importantly ammunition and food, were also getting bogged down. Delays were increasing to a worrying level.

The weather chilled, the nights drew in, and in just a few months the Germans soldiers were starting to lose their sense of untouchable and fortuitous luck. Horst's platoon had been severely dented by the lack of any recent notable military success. Heavy casualties dealt a blow to comradeship with the constant loss of so many newly formed acquaintances. Dirt, discomfort, and hunger abounded. And to top it all, winter was approaching.

One morning Horst awoke to find the land around them had changed to white overnight. The sparse covering of trees and bushes were likewise powdered in snow. A stiff chill filled the air and the water had iced up. It was a foreboding sight and sensation, with the knowledge that much worse was to come.

They continued their advance but by now the terrain was far more difficult to cross. The Russians were in their element, it was clear, while the Wehrmacht was out of its depth. Encounters with the infamous Russian T-34 were terrifying, when they trundled impassively along the snow, the powerful 76mm gun occasionally swivelling round as if smelling out prey. The men watched from hidden positions, always nervous. They were formidable beasts, as the Wehrmacht was finding out to its cost, and more than a match for the German tanks, especially in complicated terrain in which its wide bands allowed to move more freely than the German tanks, which were often stuck in mud or snow. For the infantry they had become a nightmare too; horribly impervious to the men's anti-tank guns, with sloping armoured sides that deflected the shells with ease and sent German projectiles shooting off at sharp angles to let them explode harmlessly away from the tank. When this trick was identified and reported back to Supreme Command, German scientists worked frantically to discover the formula and copy it, but to no avail.

The T-34s could be taken out in extreme cases by risky and desperate manouevres, such as sneaking up with satchel charges that produced a timed detonation. The infantry men also constructed anti-tank trenches, used together with camouflaged heavy artillery from which to lay in wait and try to ambush the enemy with a variety of weapons. But it was a perilous venture, especially when ammunition was low and the number of effective strikes were limited. If a Soviet tank was not taken out immediately, it would become a vengeful beast. With their broad tank treads, almost double the width of the German Panzer equivalent, the Soviet tanks enjoyed significant freedom of movement.

Their powerful tank gun would fire at groups of fleeing soldiers and rip them apart. Horst once saw a man have his body cleaved in half at the torso; the top half sat screaming in a bath of blood and intestines in the snow for two or three seconds until his head slumped limp to one side. In some battles the tanks roared over the trenches, where soldiers would hide and hope to pass unnoticed. When this was not the case, the Soviet tanks would shunt over and over the trench, again and again with their thick tank tread like a wild infuriated animal, either crushing the occupants if the trench were too shallow or filling it with snow and packing it down hard if the trench were deep, thereby having the soldiers suffocate.

Eventually, with the winter intensifying and making movement difficult, at times impossible for both sides, the territorial lines were drawn all along the thousands of kilometres of Soviet front; a brutal stretch of land that marked where the *Wehrmacht* had managed to advance to, and where the Red Army still held out.

The German army set up their bunkers all along the front, in the better defended strips at about fifty metres apart. These housed three or four men, huddling down together to keep out the cold in holes in the ground. In no time, plagues of lice came out of nowhere, seemingly in their thousands, and infested the men's bodies under their sweaty clothes. The food offered little variation between the couple of meals of the day, and a warm millet gruel was not infrequently the only dish for days on end. This was accompanied by bread. Once the supplies began to dry up later in the winter, there was just some occasional sausage made from the meat of surplus slaughtered horses. Small home-made ovens of the most basic structure, usually just empty rusty old tin containers, fired by collected twigs, warmed up the men and their food. Warmly toasting chunks of stale bread topped with a sliver of sausage were one of the highlights of the day, appreciated as the most exquisite delicatessen. At the other end of the nutritional process, the sewage system was basic but effective: at the exit of the bunker the soldiers defecated onto their spades and flung the contents as far as possible out into the no man's land between the two lines.

As the two fronts began to set in, rigid and icy, it became clear that in these times of attrition the Russians were more daring and adventurous, not to mention better equipped, than the Wehrmacht. They would make occasional concerted attempts to break through the German line, sneaking in at night under cover of the first snowstorms, disguised in white camouflage covers so that their forms were only recognizable once it was practically too late. A few times they located and broke through gaps in the German lines, overran the guard posts and dragged the men off. But these minor attacks were ultimately ineffective; the Germans were well organized and quickly identified and defended these gaps, repulsing any attempts at further advances. Every cloud had a silver lining, for a failed Russian attack also meant enemy prisoners or corpses, which in either case could be relieved of their thick winter clothing. But how it despaired the German soldiers to see how much better the enemy was fitted out than they were! They acquired fur-lined caps, thickly padded jackets, heavenly-warm felt boots, all from the Bolsheviks. Many of those that survived that first Russian winter were uncomfortably conscious that they did so thanks to the high quality of Soviet garments.

Like his comrades in arms, Horst hated and dreaded the night guard duty, which extended from midnight until the first, now ever later, sign of dawn. Due to occasional Russian offensives, strict wide-awake attention and vigilance, plus the regular shooting off of flares, were all of vital importance. The men would turn round in circles, keeping an eye out in all directions as well as keeping their feet in constant motion. The latter was essential in order to avoid the slow freezing of the extremities that usually went unnoticed at first until it became a serious medical condition.

The sentry posts were armed with machine guns. This was the only weapon capable of warding off any enemy assaults for long enough until the rest of the platoon in the bunker had time to rush out and intervene with supporting fire. Apart from the machine guns, the principal weapons that came into play in such offensives were hand grenades, submachine guns and, in some situations, even spades. As machine guns were not always totally reliable once the temperature had dropped below freezing point, the guards had to be doubly careful and often carried a couple of hand grenades around with them, just in case. Horst would have one close to hand all night, sometimes touching it under his coat or even passing it from one hand to another, whenever he was spooked by apparent movement or sounds in the darkness.

The snowstorms intensified; by this point, neither side was budging. The offensive forays from 'the Ivans' became increasingly rare and brief. The fronts dug in deeper. Finally, a bitter winter settled around them, freezing everything it touched like some frosty demon. It came earlier than the men had expected and was wickedly harsh from the onset, with cold currents already sweeping in from mid to late November. By December the infamous Russian winter had firmly established itself in the icy fields and sharp eastern winds that cut through often scanty clothing. Woolen underwear was of poor quality and in short supply; the field caps and head protection offered inadequate protection against the winter; the cloth of the coats was far too thin, the gloves too delicate. The bare leather combat boots that reached up to their calves, cynically called *Knobelbecher* (dice cups), were never the right size and in any case left their feet feeling numb. Alone the wholly inappropriate clothing was causing numerous troops to be taken out of combat in the course of those long cold months. Apart from feet, other vulnerable parts of the body included ears, nose and, most critically, hands.

Freezing gusts swept in continually and without mercy from the endless steppes beyond. The initial rugged wild adventure had transformed into a difficult test of endurance; and from there, in a matter of just weeks, into a nightmare. Frost bite became a closely lurking threat, while infestations of lice a hideous norm. Hunger nagged daily at their stomachs. The delivery of supplies became an endless source of conversation and speculation, in which sadly all optimism was squashed by the obvious fact that they were being woefully neglected. But complaints were dampened and, in any case, cautiously expressed with regards to the audience. Nobody was fool enough to intensify their criticism or utter an ill-thought comment to the wrong person, thus running the risk of being reported and disciplined correspondingly.

Outside of purely military matters the conversations mostly revolved around home, women, and food. In this environment, there was little place for the luxury, or danger, of politics. And there was no-one in Horst's platoon to recount facts and figures, victories and heroic deeds, as someone like Cousin Carsten had back home. Which was just as well: the immensity of this endless nation, that the troops now found themselves stuck in, had no meaning. The horizon was lost in darkness by night, and by day too, with merely the dull whiteness of snow on the ground meeting the dull colourless shades of the sky, which passed through endless monotonous shades of white and light grey. In blizzards, which soon increased in frequency, there was nothing to do but hunker down, shiver, wait, and drift in and out of sleep in the bunker.

The Army Group South was stretched out over 600 kilometres of terrain. In the case of the Army Group Centre it was over 1,000 kilometres and still with no foreseeable takeover of Moscow. The Army Group North covered a further front of 600 kilometres, including a tenaciously held resistance throughout the long siege of Leningrad. The huge Russian motherland had absorbed these legions, these thousands of ferocious men, like a sponge absorbed water. The Wehrmacht was weakened and worn out, had no clear military objective, had no other option but to dig in for the winter and hold out as best they could. Considering that at some points along the front they were outnumbered three-to-one, that in itself was a commendable achievement.

Horst had yet another close encounter with a bullet one night while returning from collecting firewood. It had been several days since they had last been under fire and he had been lulled into a false sense of security. He began to whistle a melody, part of *"Sing,*

Nachtigall, sing", a recent hit from the singer Evelyn Künnecke, with his memory taking snatches of the text inside his head.

Sing, Nachtigall, sing
Ein Lied aus alten Zeiten,
Sing, Nachtigall, sing
Rühr' mein müdes Herz.
(Sing, nightingale, sing,
A song from the old times,
Sing, nightingale, sing,
Move my weary heart.)

He had first heard her sweet enticing voice on the radio in the back room at the *Gasthaus Sonnenschein*, resting after work with Inge by his side. That now seemed a world away and his mind had wondered off to better times as he approached the bunker.

Out of nowhere came a bang near his ear as a bullet shot close past his head, narrowly missing him. He flung himself forward the final few metres and grabbed up his machine gun that he had briefly put by side at the bunker entrance. He fired off several rounds at a clump of bushes around a small hill, over on the other side of the wasteland from where he suspected the shot had come. The snow flew up in a rage of little eruptions as his bullets raked the ground. There was a sharp cry from the other side, repeated a few times before silence returned. He assumed that he had at least seriously wounded the sniper and taken him out of action, but he did not approach any nearer to find out for sure.

Such incidents were minor, banal even in comparison to the major injuries or near-death encounters that many of his comrades were now suffering. Yet each such incident was slowly hardening Horst up like the gnarled wood of an old oak, gradually deforming him inside. He stomped through the brutal days, ceased to consider why he was there or what he hoped to achieve for his country. Reflections were the bearers of doubt and distress. To counteract this, he had let a dull fog descend on his mind, blunting all the sharpness and light of hope, dimming any clarity of future vision. Instead, he had come to follow a single guiding light which was the immediate future ahead: the next minutes, the next hours, at most tomorrow. His long-term hope became centred on one objective: to hopefully live another day.

There came but one moment of relief in that thick numbing cloak of military tenacity in attrition warfare, and that was Christmas. It was his first Christmas away from his home, his family, his town. The men instinctively pulled together to put meaning into the festive moment which in turn, they hoped, would put some meaning back into their stark existence on the front.

In an area about two kilometres from their little bunker they located a small cluster of fir trees and, as other nearby units were doing too, they trekked there in the week before Christmas and hacked themselves a short but stocky sapling that would fit in their little bunker. There was little to hang up on it; but one of the men had a few photos of naked women that he sometimes shared around, so he cut out one of the figures as the silhouette of an angel and they tied it to the top with some wire. They called it their '*Heilige Hure*' (Holy Whore), which most of them snickered at, and they would later drink to her health. Horst felt internally repelled by this action, finding it deeply disrespectful not to mention blasphemous, but he did not let it show. War makes men this way, he thought. Other than that, a few old spoons were attached and served as hanging baubles.

Thanks to the still efficient *Feldpost* (German military postal service), most of them had received some packets from the Heimat, in little cardboard boxes crammed with biscuits, cigarettes, blocks of chocolate, dried hams, well-packed jars of homemade jams, little bags of coffee beans, nuts, and plump red apples. These were shared around with those whose packets had still to arrive. Most of it was wolfed down that same evening by the famished men, used to days of gruel, and nearly all was gone by the end of the following day. These *Feldpostpäckchen* (postal packages, which in some cases were even donated by strangers for those soldiers who had not received anything) also contained Christmas cards signed by whole families, which were hung from the fir-tree branches and helped fill up the bare tree. From the generous stocks that the rear-guard troops had at their disposition, way back beyond the front-line, some items were sent on to the men in their bunkers at the front: candles, some cooking fat, and a couple of bottles of *Glühwein* that the men warmed up on the makeshift stove and poured into their battered rusty tin mugs.

With that they celebrated on Christmas Eve until well into the early hours, singing the traditional Christmas songs they knew from back home and happier times, with the sentry watch changed every two hours to allow everyone to participate equally. Fortunately, Ivan was quiet that night and not a shot was heard from the other side. The next day, it was business as usual and the 25th, the First Day of Christmas for Germans, was just another bleak cold day on the edge of life.

Into the next year, just as he was reaching deepest despair in the endless freezing dark of February, there came through the news that he was to be granted furlough from the front within the next couple of weeks. He borrowed a pen, obtained a sheet of writing paper, and wrote to Inge immediately to pass on the good news, while also stressing that he could not as yet give her any more specific information.

The *Heimat-Urlaubsschein* – the official leave pass to return home on holiday - came through out of the blue on the 26th February and was placed into his eager shaking hand by a grinning sergeant. On 1st March, while Russia still stood impassive and glacial before them, he and a few other men also granted leave were transported back with a military convoy to Kiev, and from there in a freight wagon to Berlin. Bedraggled but looking spruced up in his stiff uniform, people glanced at him approvingly, some even fondly despite his messy stubble and the heavy, musty smell of old sweat.

He changed trains at Berlin and continued on to Hannover, nodding off all the time in deep weariness, changing again there to finish the journey back in Lüneburg. He dragged his sore feet off the train, through the station, into the chilly wind blowing down the Bahnhofstraße; turned left into the main road Lünertorstraße to make his way to the town centre; glanced over at the familiar *Alter Kran* (Old Crane) and drooping willow by the cold flowing river, crossed over the bridge; turned a sharp left to pass the row of shops and restaurants by the riverfront, smelt the fried onion of evening meal preparations; turned right into a sharp breeze and the Rosenstraße.

In these last minutes of a journey that had seemed to know no end, from the white hell of the eastern front all the way across eternal lands to the familiar sight of his hometown with its cobbled streets and gabled roofs, he found as he marched up that final stretch that he could muster the energy to change his posture from a slouch back up to an erect and proud straight line, his gait from a trudge to a swinging pace. In a spirit of contained joy he reached the *Gasthaus Sonnenschein*, entered quietly through the front door and passed down the hall, encountering an amazed Inge standing with a dusting cloth in her hand beside the tiny reception area, who screamed for joy and ran to him.

Chapter 21

The town had emptied notably by the late summer of 1941, as more and more young men were called off to war. That very war - that many had assumed would be little more than a short sharp excursion into Poland to sort out the thorny issue of Danzig and the Polish corridor for once and for all - had now transmuted into a much more extensive and long-term issue. It was now the second anniversary of the Polish campaign and the conflict was not only ongoing but now firing off in all directions.

In silent, often concerned faces, in homes and at workplaces, could be read the dawning realization that the ambitions of the Führer were enormous. The vast Soviet Union, stretching far out into Asia in endless plains and steppes, was to come under the Reich's control, but how much of this mass? – up to Moscow, or beyond that on to the Volga, the Urals? Unless Moscow was to be taken in a sudden assault, Georg Hartmann mumbled quietly one night to his wife Corinna in their quiet, darkened bedroom, "then this whole thing could go on for years, decades even. This will be worse than the Great War." She nodded back with her mouth pursed in a frown. In private she was very concerned about her sister living out so far to the east, in such charged times as these. She had a pessimistic bent and if this new stage in the war proved as unpropitious as her instincts told her, then Hertha could be in the first line of counterfire. But she had learnt to keep her thoughts to herself; nowadays no-one dared say anything that did not extoll the necessity of conquering more land to the east, the famous *Lebensraum* that the people of Germany would require in the future in order to grow and fully prosper as a nation.

By this point, however, the war was not only about the Reich's expansion further out, whether westward or eastward. The Reich had also turned its claws sharply in on itself and opened a third and internal front. This group of enemies were the undesirable elements of society, that would need to be purged if the goals of the Reich were to be achieved: the traitors and the pacifists, the weak-minded and the infirm, trade unionists and communists, degenerate artists and homosexuals. But above all, Jews. Many Jews had already escaped, some forewarned back in the early to mid-1930s by the very rise to power of the NSDAP; others later intimidated by the growing ferocity of the boycotts, interdicts, and random attacks. A further segment of the Jewish population was finally terrified into action by the wanton violence of the *Reichskristallnacht* that was clearly a turning point in the persecution. But not all had been able to do so; and some had clung to the hope that a swing around would eventually occur, one that would dispel the necessity for such drastic action as leaving behind the one and only home that they had ever known.

Now in 1941, this final hope was clearly laid bare as a fata morgana. The local Gestapo police forces were working with full force and round the clock on the task of the deportation of Jews, combing towns and cities for all citizens of Jewish ethnicity and keeping meticulous records. Whole families were called up by letter, dispossessed of all they had, abruptly sent off to an uncertain fate somewhere in the east; never heard from again. The trains were rumbling off in an increasingly regular rhythm; reasons for not getting on them – such as being a Jewish war veteran, the child of a Jewish-Christian *Mischehe* (mixed marriage), or simply elderly - were slowly running out. Exact times for reporting in were given and those who came late incurred a savage beating at the hands of SS officers. Everyone was searched and money, as well as jewelry and other valuables, were confiscated.

The only route out was to go underground or attempt to flee. In the case of the former, either physically, if one could find someone with enough bravery and compassion, or with so much hatred for the Nazis that they were willing to risk their lives to help; or metaphorically, in which Jews attempted to melt into the background, to have their ethnicity become as invisible as possible – and considering the strict and thorough state of German bureaucracy, this was no mean feat.

Some Jews in Germany who were able to pass undetected – at least for a certain amount of time - by the state's omnipotent racial control. This could be achieved, for instance, through having fairer hair and complexions that appeared roughly 'Germanic' to the casual eye. Daniel Kaplan was not such a case. He had a swarthy complexion, with thick pitch-black hair and a healthy olive skin that naturally darkened in the summer sun; his arms had strong black hair and his eyes large deep-brown pupils that were adorned with thick black eye lashes and crowned by dense black eyebrows. He had to shave twice a day so that the naturally active facial hair, which extended down to his neck, didn't begin to form a dark beard and moustache in no time. He was a handsome man, tall and athletic, and easily caught the attention of passers-by. In the early 1930s, when he was just coming into his early twenties, he had cut a dashing and confident figure whenever he strode down the street. He had a good number of admirers, not only among those Jewish women in town considering possible future husbands for their daughters, but also plenty of 'Aryan' women too (plus a few Aryan men). But Daniel stayed romantically alone: he had no desire to endure a drawn-out argument with his father about marrying a goy, nor to endure the jubilation of his mother's wedding plans upon his deciding to marry a fellow Israelite either.

Despite his initial self-confidence, the increasingly harsh and methodical persecution of Jews and all things Jewish left him plagued with anxiety, until he finally decided to get out of the country with the outbreak of war. The violent entry of German troops into Poland in September 1939 had been the penultimate straw; the final one when he heard of the first forced deportations of Jews. But he found to his horror that a heavy curtain had already fallen around the Reich. Visas were nearly impossible to obtain for those without good connections, even then only at exorbitant prices. Falsifications were risky and controls were exhaustive. And the doors to other nations were closing around them. The surge of refugees had been enormous and many countries were putting up strict limits. The tragic tale of the St. Louis ocean liner had become common knowledge within the Jewish community by now and converted it into a terrifying fable on the insecurity of escape routes.

(The ship had set off from Hamburg in the spring of 1939, carrying nearly a thousand German Jewish refugees and heading for Cuba. Upon arrival in Havana, the ship was refused permission to enter the harbour due to last-minute changes in legislation. With no chance of its passengers disembarking, the St. Louis continued up the coast to Florida, where it met with a similar refusal from the US authorities. In desperation, it moved on and began negotiations with

Canada to allow it to dock in Halifax. The head of the Canadian immigration department, a racial purist named Blair, argued in favour of refusing the St. Louis entry and was successful. Having been turned away from Cuba, the US and Canada, there remained no other option than to go back to Europe, with the ship finally returning from its odyssey and docking in Antwerp, Belgium, over a month later. Although nearly 300 passengers were able to continue over to Britain, of the 900 original passengers over 250 would eventually be caught by the Nazis in occupied western Europe and murdered in the Holocaust.)

To increase the tension that Kaplan was experiencing, horrific rumours were beginning to reach the Jewish community as to the destination of the deportations. Schilling, naturally inclined to pessimism in all facets of life, which in this case turned out to be healthy realism, was brutally direct and told him he strongly believed the worst of these rumours - i.e., that Jews were not merely being transported to alternative settlements but rather they were being murdered in mass. Schilling also confirmed that the Gestapo were stepping up their search mechanism and were determined to locate every last single Jew.

The culminating point for Kaplan came with the suicide of a friend, Nathan Süßkind. He had known him from his sporadic visits to the synagogue, and had conversed with him the last time in great depth at the wedding reception held at the house of Adam Wunderlich. The Süßkind family was small and all had managed to emigrate to Palestine; but Nathan's permit to leave the country had been turned down by the authorities at the last minute with the premise that they wished to inspect his finances more closely. Nathan had insisted that his family went on without him and had stayed behind in the rented apartment. New legislation, introduced in 1939 by the Department of Resettlement, meant that as a Jew he could be evicted from rented property at a whim, which was precisely what happened in the winter of that year. Now faced with the double threat of homelessness and possible deportation, and psychologically beaten down by the widespread hatred in the town, he had followed the fate of many fellow Jews during this period and taken his own life. His suicide had in turn weighed heavily on Kaplan, who now more than ever knew he had to make an escape while there was still a realistic possibility, rather than risk being cornered by the Gestapo and so lose all control over his destiny.

After much discussion and analysis Schilling and Kaplan had both arrived at the conclusion that the only sensible way out at this point was also to be the most desperate and dramatic: fleeing undercover out of the Reich in a westerly direction, and preferably into southern, unoccupied France. They spent many hours discussing the topic in hushed tones, often well into the early hours of the morning with dark heavy curtains drawn across the windows; examining possible routes on maps, weighing up pros and cons, striving to locate the best plan. These were moments of despondency and great desperation for Kaplan, who keenly felt the existential fear of capture and deportation, being under no illusion as to what would then await him. It seemed at times that any plan was too daring, that a successful escape would hang on a hope and prayer. But the cooled though still extant remnants of his faith told him that may be enough; in this way his desperation was overcome and transformed into practical thinking.

Kaplan had been initially drawn to the idea of heading south-west and getting through the Swiss border and into that neighbouring neutral Alpine state. Schiller advised against this, however. Legally, it was nearly impossible to have all the requisite paperwork in order, which besides involved showing proof of possessing serious money. The border guards there were notoriously difficult to bribe ("the Swiss are even more *korrekt* than the Germans!") and with the few that were open to the idea, the costs were astronomical. The only theoretical option for them would be a clandestine entry. A contact he knew had attempted precisely that route and after several hours of walking along rural paths had successfully managed to sneak in through the 'green border', only to be arrested the very same day in Schaffhausen and accused of espionage by the Swiss authorities.

A further person, Jewish this time, had made this same attempt but lost her way among the labyrinth of trails and narrow paths along the border zone, eventually taking a wrong turning and almost running into a group of German Wehrmacht soldiers. In the end she had given up hope and returned back to Frankfurt in the train, having her (forged) identity card checked several times on the way home by inspectors. The whole journey had been fraught with heart-stopping panic for the poor woman; she had got back safe but a nervous wreck, as well as being broke and back to square one with her flight plans.

"The Nazis know that it is a popular escape route for people to try their luck at, so the random controls and checks heading down there are numerous," said Schiller. "We have to think one step ahead of the enemy and in that way try to do what they would not have second-guessed."

By the late summer of 1941 both Schilling and Kaplan, noticing that the Gestapo's web was spinning ever closer and tighter around those Jews still in hiding, decided to prepare for immediate action. A plan was hatched during several months and finally put into effect once all the pieces were in place. False documentation had been prepared by Schilling, the relevant contacts in the underground had been paid and provided with all necessary information. Some officials had been bribed in advance; others, Schilling had been assured by contacts with experience, would receive their part on arrival. No such plan was ever hermetic but the men took the greatest care to ensure that all possible, and especially hazardous, deviations from the plan had been taken into account, and that there existed at least the traced form of a plan B, should one be required. The precise day was fixed: it would be Wednesday 24th September.

An associate of a good friend of Schilling - a former dockyard worker, trade unionist and committed communist from Hamburg called Keller - would be driving. He was of absolute trust and had already carried out a handful of such operations. For the upcoming series of new operations, in which Kaplan was to be placed, he had been able to arrange a realistic cover in that he was allegedly involved in the removal of household furniture and goods belonging to the high-ranking manager of a shipping company in Hamburg. This in itself was partly true. Said manager, preoccupied by the possibility of British bombs crashing into his opulent villa in Altona, which contained a notable collection of Flemish art, had decided to have his expensive and unique furniture, paintings and other valuables transported to safe keeping. This job was actually set to take place in late October but the contact group had quickly created a number of falsifications, in this instance changing the destination on the corresponding paperwork to an address in Rosenheim, in southern Bavaria. They were hoping to carry out a series of three to five runs in total from northern destinations before the official move took place: this one from Lüneburg was set to be the second.

The idea was to make the journey look as convincing as possible to any random checks that might occur en route by inquisitive officials. Kaplan was to be hidden at the back of the van, sheltered by a plethora of what appeared to be valuable paintings and items of furniture. It was in fact mostly old junk and poor amateur art, but to the casual eye it should match the official inventory. Towards the end of the official journey, the van would go on to make a dramatic detour that would take it on to Mittenwald, just before the German-Austrian border. The plan entailed that the refugees would alight there and board an Italian farm truck, leaving the 'removal van' to go back to Bavaria to spend the night, and then eventually return to the north for the next run.

This plan had been some months in the making. Schilling had been active for some time in the forgery of documents and he had taken great care with the accuracy of the false Italian passports for his friend Kaplan as well as a second fugitive, who had also paid upfront and would be travelling with Kaplan. This man was one Dimitry Dolmatovsky: a Russian-German man in his early thirties who had previously been active in the KPD (Communist Party of Germany). Schilling did not know him personally but his name had been passed on to him by a fellow conspirator of Keller's in the Hamburg underground, who was also involved in the trafficking of people. Schilling had feared that Dolmatovsky might be a Soviet spy who had had his cover blown and was desperate to find an alternative route out of Germany. But he had the man's identity double-checked and it seemed certain that he was indeed in the process of defecting from the Soviet Union; with the war now flaring up on the eastern front, he was eager to head as far west as possible, preferably to Lisbon and then beyond. This was also Kaplan's intention and the double escape meant the costs involved could be covered.

Like Schilling, Kaplan had initially had a bad feeling about Dolmatovsky, but Schilling had already received half the payment upfront and needed that money to make up the price tag for the whole operation: human smuggling had become an increasingly risky feat, and so an increasingly expensive product on offer. Tales of betrayal abounded. At the end of the day, no-one was truly trustworthy, while people were forced to place their lives in the hands of people they had only known for hours. Desperation made for stories of both horrific tragedy as well as great heroism.

By late summer, the precise day and time were set and confirmed. A few weeks rushed terrifically past, the big day approached and, after a nearly sleepless night, Daniel Kaplan drank a coffee in the dusky early morning light and mentally prepared himself for his rendezvous with fate.

At first all went smoothly. Keller, complete with forged documentation, arrived punctually at 10am, as arranged, in the town centre in his removal van. Dolmatovsky, clutching on to two small suitcases of his only belongings, was hidden in the back of the van behind some stacked up furniture with framed paintings of fruit, flowers and other still lifes filling the front. The van parked on the corner of Rosenstraße and Am Berge. The street Am Berge ran a short stretch from north to south through central Lüneburg, parallel to the Ilmenau river, with the parking spot just two blocks away. This was beside the curved corner in which it met the Rosenstraße, descending from the town hall and the Marktplatz. The Rosenstraße ended there and Am Berge continued down a slight slope before turning back onto itself and becoming the Ilmenaustraße, then following the river all the way out of town.

This curved corner, on which just a decade ago horse-drawn carts had stopped to unload merchandise, had a scenic charm with its mixture of old gabled houses and more modern red-brick structures. It was a cobbled section of road from which one could glimpse the ornate town hall at the top of the Rosenstraße in one direction, and the Ilmenau river below in the other. In its central position it was actively visited for most of the day, with pedestrians crossing from one part of town to another along the streets that intersected there.

The atelier of Schilling was situated at the beginning of Am Berge at Nr. 3. From the front window of the apartment, Kaplan he had a sweeping view of the area around and below, which included aforementioned spot. Both men had been ready and anxiously waiting for a couple of hours, nervous as the moment of destiny was about to arrive. When at 10am sharp they spied how Keller's van was parking neatly on the side of the road, in front of the bakery at Am Berge 1, they reacted with a start. "He is here", whispered Kaplan urgently. "It is time."

The two men sauntered downstairs and out into the street. Kaplan carried a slim briefcase, his first piece of luggage. Schilling carried a scratched old wooden crate which bore black print about marmalade but actually held a cotton sack; this was Kaplan's second piece of luggage, with clothing, basic toiletries, ample food, and a few books that he could not bear to part with. Also inside the box, on top of the sack, was a large envelope containing Schilling's contribution of forged documents and money for the operation. This was for Keller to take out once they were all en route. The general impression was meant to be inconspicuous; no-one wished to awaken the idea of someone leaving town.

They approached the van and Keller wound down the window. Schilling smiled and passed the wooden box through the window to Keller, who placed it tight up beside him. At the same time Kaplan had casually boarded the van on the other side and now sat in the passenger seat, clutching his briefcase. Keller and Schilling exchanged a few last words, while Keller turned the key in the ignition and prepared to leave. The motor whined but did not start at first.

In that moment two pairs of people appeared, coming from two different directions. Kaplan, looking straight ahead with a hard beating heart, saw and recognized the first. Schilling, standing by the driver's door and finishing his last words with Keller, looked round instinctively in the opposite direction and saw the second.

The first consisted of two SS officers from the Gestapo HQ in Lüneburg: *Hauptscharführer* Eberhard Ritter and his immediate subordinate and personal assistant *Oberscharführer* Franz Möhring. They were immediately recognizable by their uniforms and large ostentatious caps. Furthermore, Kaplan had seen them some weeks before, walking down below the window along the same stretch of street. Now they were coming directly at him. He stared ahead at them, frozen in terror like a herbivore setting eyes on a known predator. The men were engaged in conversation but, as Kaplan continued to unintentionally and irresistibly stare forward, Ritter looked up and their eyes met. The two SS-men were conversing and strolling - around 20, 25 metres ahead, he estimated – and coming nearer. Ritter's gaze hooked onto Kaplan for a moment, and it seemed that Ritter's eyes lowered in search of a tell-tale yellow Star of David on his lapel or chest; in vain. Kaplan in turn looked down at the floor of the van.

At the same time, Inge was walking down the Rosenstraße with Adolf and they had just reached the corner. She had left Joseph and Hermann with Gisela that morning at the Gasthaus; both of them were being extremely ill-tempered and difficult to handle. They had already fallen out and had a brief pushing match in the restaurant in which Hermann, though only two but large for his age, had knocked over his three-year-old brother. He in turn had fallen back heavily against a small table and made it jiggle. A dish on the edge of the table had fallen off and smashed onto the floor. Joseph had started to howl, Hermann to stomp on the ground, Gisela to shout down the stairs. The whole uproar had exasperated Inge.

Adolf on the other hand had been unusually well-behaved that day. Though known for frequent tantrums, he had been quiet and attentive and when Inge asked, "Would you like to come with Mama to the shops?" he had smiled and eagerly nodded. She needed to buy groceries for the family and so was being accompanied by Adolf on their short walk.

Adolf was now four and a half, and increasingly independent. He had already started the classes at the *St. Ursula Grundschule* (primary school), the very same school that Inge and her siblings had attended as children; although in earlier pre-NSDAP times when it held the status of a Catholic institution. Adolf moved around the house with quiet but firm steps, curious but cautious. "He is such a reflective and watchful little boy," Corinna had once commented. "Not the blundering gust of wind that so many children are."

Today he clasped a medium-sized rubber ball in his hands, painted in stripes of white and primary colours; this ball was his new fascination. He loved to bounce and catch it, even achieving some simple dribbling with it, and could happily play in this manner all day.

Inge had told him to just carry it while they were outside. "You can bounce it when we get back home. If you do that on the street, it might bounce away and you will lose it," she had warned him. Weaving their way through the other pedestrians, they turned from the Rosenstraße into Am Berge. It was a bright pleasant morning, warmed with the last remnants of the old summer. On the corner was parked a van, and talking through the window to the driver of that van was her friend Arnold Schilling.

She smiled as they approached him, "Hallo, Arnold! How are you?" A stronger gust of wind in that moment threatened to take off her hat and she put up one hand to secure it, leaving Adolf standing free.

Kaplan leaned right down towards the floor of the van, as if to tie his shoelaces, and hissed, "Look ahead but carefully!"

Keller, from behind the steering wheel, glanced ahead and spied with a shudder the two SS Gestapo officers heading their way. He averted his gaze immediately, not wishing to attract their attention, and turned back to Schilling, who was now himself turning round to greet someone. Keller glanced into his rear-view mirror and saw a young woman with her little son close to the back of the van. He wracked his brains to think of the next move. It would of course be potentially disastrous for him to enter into any verbal contact with the SS men and he felt sure that one of them was staring at them. Keller had his alibi, his papers, but the mere possibility of a confrontation, with all the enormity of a possibly negative outcome, including not just questions appertaining to Kaplan sitting beside him but worst still a search in the back of the truck, electrified him. His turned his eyes down to the pedals, examining the clutch, the accelerator, the brake in turn, and again; waited with hot fear for the men to approach, and hopefully pass, his vehicle.

Keller then reached into his shirt pocket and took out his wallet, slipped his driving license out and examined it, eyes passing mindlessly over the familiar data, intent on finding an innocent-looking activity for the moments during which the men would pass by. They were walking on his side of the pavement and he knew he was temporarily but incorrectly parked. Would they even bother with the minor hassle of traffic control? His window was down and he listened to Schilling exchanging pleasantries with the young woman. An eternity filled every banal word they said and every second that passed.

The boy with her bounced his ball off the pavement and laughed, amused at engaging in his favourite hobby outside in the street. He immediately did it a second time and said "Mama!" Keller heard her reprimand him with, "Adolf, Mama is talking!" Keller looked ahead again, unable to resist the temptation of assessing the imminence of danger. Kaplan had likewise raised his head and was looking to the left out the window, towards the river. Both men knew that it would be unthinkable to just move off, with the SS officers now only ten metres ahead. In no time they would be beside the van. Keller's hand still grasped the driving license but was now trembling (though also from the double coffee he had drunk that morning) so he placed it back in his breast pocket, knowing that unless they were lucky and the men simply went past, his nerves might give the game away. Kaplan breathed in and made profound philosophical reflections in his head on the nature of survival, partly to pass the moments in a distracted mode, partly out of the fear of death approaching him; as inevitable and inescapable as the mythical grim reaper seemed to him these SS officers.

An abrupt change in the scenario came with the third bounce of Adolf's ball. With a chuckle he sent the ball down with extra force, out of curiosity, and it bounced back hard and at an angle that sent it chasing off down the road. Horrified at seeing his mother's prophetic warning about to come true, in that he would lose his ball between the tall crowds of passing adults and the huge urban landscape that towered around his little body, he set off after it. It bounced with some momentum along the pavement until it came directly into the path of Eberhard Ritter, who neatly caught it in a quick reflex. The boy continued running towards his ball, his face crumpled in further terror at the thought of the large man now holding his ball, surely about to keep it for himself. When he reached him, Ritter was grinning widely and holding out the ball to him, while Adolf was about to burst into tears. The boy held back, unsure as to how to proceed with the tall uniformed figure, and he and Ritter regarded each other for a moment.

Inge saw all this happen with a frown. She watched Ritter holding out the ball, and her son stopping just before him in confused hesitation, and turning briefly to Schilling said, "It has been so nice to see you again, Arnold, but you can see I must dash. We must talk again soon!" She hurried over to her son. Schilling smiled and touched his hat, turned back to look at Keller, visibly pallid.

Kaplan muttered to his side at Keller, "Get us out of here, now!"

Schilling nodded and stepped back towards the café behind him, instinctively retaining his large false smile. Keller turned the key in the ignition and this time the motor caught and began to hum. Schilling waved goodbye in an attempt to produce an image of normalcy.

Keller checked in his rear-view mirror and said, "Watch out on your side, make sure no-one is behind us."

Kaplan replied, "It's clear on my side" and was sweating as Keller shunted slowly out of the parked position and reversed a few metres into the Rosenstraße. He changed gears and there was a sharp yowl from the gearbox as he moved from reverse into first. Involuntarily he interjected, "*Scheisse*! (Shit!)" Kaplan stayed as motionless as a statue, as did Schilling who was still standing in the same spot and watching the proceedings with his nerves on maximum edge, not daring to glance over in the direction of Inge and the SS-men, preparing to quietly fade away. Keller battled with the gear stick for a moment until it slid into first, then automatically looked down Am Berge, as anyone would to check that there was no oncoming traffic.

Ritter was staring at the vehicle, though his eyes seemed to settle more directly on Kaplan in the passenger seat. Möhring had taken the ball from Ritter and was now offering it in a teasing manner to Adolf, who had by now realized that this was all a big joke and was jumping up and down playfully. Inge was talking to both men, quite amiably but with one hand placed on her son's back in instinctive protection. Ritter was still looking over her shoulder at the van and Keller could see Ritter's lips turned down into a grimace of puzzlement. Keller shifted his gaze ahead and drove the vehicle gently round the curve of Am Berge and down the few metres of slope to the riverside. Sitting upright in the seat, still and pale white as a marble statue, he drove round the corner with slow determination and continued along beside the river on the now Ilmenaustraße. He drove slowly, at around 25 km/h, not wishing to attract any attention until he felt secure that he was far enough away from any potential danger. After a couple of hundred metres, he turned slowly but sharply to the right, over the Altenbrücketorstraße; the bridge there which then opened out into the main street Dahlenburger Landstraße heading out of town. The more metres he drove, the more he accelerated. Once they were well out of the town borders, he put his foot down and hit 60 km/h, with his hands still trembling though he had calmed down. Only then did he permit himself to turn to his companion and grin with the ecstatic relief of the pardoned.

At the corner of Rosenstraße and Am Berge, Möhring had given Adolf his ball back and then heaved him up in his hands and pushed him up into the air, at which the boy giggled with delight. He rocked little Adolf a few more times up and down, then held him for a moment as the boy regarded the uniforms with an impressed look on his face. He reached out to finger a button but his mother, seeing this action and not totally comfortable with the situation, said, "Adolf! Don't do that!"

She put her bag down and held out her arms to take the child. Möhring laughed and placed the boy back in his mother's embrace, and Inge brought her son gently back to the ground. She firmly took his hand, squeezed it gently to implore the child to behave. She said, "Herr Ritter, my sister always says to send you her best regards if I should see you. It was such a pleasure and an honour to have you and your colleagues stay at the Gasthaus and we do hope that you will all bear us in mind should you have any future events planned. It was such a wonderful evening."

She heard a brief mechanical screech behind her but did not turn. Ritter seemed absent, looking over her shoulder at something behind her. There was something that did not quite fit, Ritter felt. The van in that position, the driver and his passenger (both dark-haired and foreign-looking); had it not been for the fact he saw Inge talking to a man whom he had seen talking to the driver at the same time, giving the impression of a larger social group, then he would have hailed down the van and made an on-the-spot inspection. Even now, as the van was shunting round and preparing to move off, his senses were still on alert as to something irregular about the scene. His forehead creased and his eyes narrowed as he searched for a solid reason for his instinctive suspicion, but none was forthcoming.

Furthermore, he had Inge before him, smiling widely with her pretty face and glowing cheeks; her well-formed body discernible for him under the autumn coat; looking at him with big blue eyes and wide smile, saying how she hoped there would be another visit. Distracted, he turned to look her squarely in the face and he lost the thread of thought concerning the van. "I, um, I have no concrete details at the moment about any further meetings here in Lüneburg. At least not with that particular group. But should anything be in the planning stage, I would let you know immediately so that we can make an advanced booking. We have been very satisfied with the service, so I would imagine we would be very happy to return to your sister's Gasthaus in that eventuality." He nodded at her and smiled, glanced back over her shoulder; but the van was long since gone. He shook his head as if physically brushing away an irrelevant thought.

Möhring said, "So your son is called Adolf. That is a good solid name. Is he your only child?"

"No" she laughed, turning to him. "Although sometimes I wish he were! I have another two back at home but they were naughty today, very naughty indeed!" she moved to a matronly voice as she took her son into the exchange. "So they are staying there with *Tante* Gisela and *Oma* Corinna, aren't they, Adolf? And if you continue to misbehave in front of these gentlemen," she addressed him directly with raised finger, "you will have to stay behind next time, too." She said that as a disciplinary strategy but she was very fond of going shopping with Adolf. He had such a precociously clever way about him with monetary issues, from coins and notes to the ration cards themselves, and she liked to help him add up the amounts and watch him pay the shopkeepers and hand over the coupons.

She looked back at the two men. "I won't keep you any longer. We have to get on with the shopping. Say 'thank you' to Herr Ritter, Adolf, for catching your ball for you." The boy obediently gave his thanks. The two groups bade each other goodbye; Möhring clicked his feet together and gave Adolf a military salute, both grinning at each other before waving goodbye.

Inge headed up Am Berge to the grocer. Ritter and Möhring turned into the Rosenstraße to head back to their HQ and continue the day's work.

In the meantime, the removal van had stopped briefly in a quiet corner of the rural area surrounding Lüneburg. Keller opened the doors at the back of the van and removed two of the paintings, allowing Kaplan to work his way through the carefully arranged furniture to get to the back of the van, where he crouched down beside his fellow escapee. With that important step completed, Keller speeded off down the main road and was soon turning onto the *Reichsautobahn* (motorway) to continue the long journey south.

They drove down the smooth asphalted motorway which everyone – no matter how skeptical or even hateful of Hitler - deeply admired; first past Braunschweig and Halle to reach Leipzig, then heading sharply south on the RAB 9 towards Munich. This was a long stretch that lasted nearly six hours but he took it in his stride. It was an unnerving experience with so many of the vehicles travelling in the opposite direction, and driving up toward them, being clearly marked military vehicles with Wehrmacht soldiers or SS troops, that howled and whizzed by. At one point, he was hailed down in a random check on the autobahn but this passed without incidence once his papers had been checked by the guard. Between the sunshine and the SS, Keller was now sweating profusely. He drove off, saw a clear patch ahead, and hit 100 kilometres an hour.

Upon reaching the Bavarian metropolis of Munich and passing through the traffic hub in the south-eastern district of Ramersdorf, nicknamed '*das Tor zum Süden*' (the gateway to the south), Keller drove on in the direction of the town of Rosenheim. According to his documentation, this was to be the final destination for the contents of the van. But at Holzkirchen there came a deviation from the route and instead of heading south-west to Rosenheim, he headed south-east first through Bad Tölz to then continue on westwards through Upper Bavaria towards the Austrian border.

The landscape became scenic at this point, deceptively idyllic among the foothills of the Bavarian Alps with the wide expansive meadows and distant mountains towering over the horizon. The van wound its way between the lakes Kochelsee and Walchensee, the early evening sun casting a golden hew around the alpine expanse. Just before Mittenwald, Keller veered off the main road and the van climbed chugging up a smaller route that headed towards some minor populations in the foothills. There, tucked neatly out of sight, Keller came to a halt and his passengers jumped out, to be hustled into a further vehicle that was parked and waiting for them. It was a battered old farming truck with an open back packed up with bales of straw, agricultural tools, and a couple of cages with noisily flapping hens. The driver, an Italian partisan called Martinoli with his notably pregnant young wife sitting beside him in the front, was primarily interested in collecting his share of the money from Keller, but there was a minor dispute concerning the amount agreed upon. Eventually, after various anxious hisses from the two anxious escapees, Martinoli and Keller were able to reach a compromise. Kaplan and Dolmatovsky were seated in the back of the truck while their few cases were hidden among bales of straw. They were given old coats to don and told to each hold onto a pitchfork, look stupid all the time, and not say a word unless absolutely necessary: in that case it would be mumbled German with Italian accent and both men indicated they knew the procedure in such a case of emergency. To complete the presentation, Martinoli passed a dirty rag over their faces to soil their complexions appropriately. He indicated that he was ready and took his fee - the money and a small clump of jewelry - plus two falsified Italian passports from Keller. The men parted ways with mutual grunts. While Martinoli headed off down toward the German-Austrian border, Keller slowly chugged back in the direction of Rosenheim where he would rest and stay the night at a farmhouse belonging to contacts from the network.

Martinoli's old truck was waved through the border, from bored officials on the German side to a young Austrian guard who superficially looked through the Italian passports, both real and fake. Martinoli explained in broken German that they had come from

Garmisch and that he was heading through Innsbruck back to his farm in Meran. They were waved on again.

They passed into Austria and did indeed follow the route that had been casually mentioned, first to Innsbruck and then further down to Meran. By the time they had passed by Innsbruck it was already nearly 22:00 and the dark mountains, eerily lit up by a near full moon, gleamed impassively down. Kaplan found great comfort in the sight of the jagged mountain peaks, finding the surroundings to be so very different from the endless flat grassy acres of central and northern Germany that he was used to. He felt he was getting more and more distant from the omnipotent presence of the Gestapo. But, as he then reminded himself in a sudden rush of superstitious agitation, he was indeed still within the Reich, and its tentacles reached far. They could still grasp out and catch him at any moment; the journey was literally far from over.

All the same, he and Dolmatovsky began to relax more after they crossed effortlessly the Austrian-Italian border, without even having to stop. Sometime after midnight they passed by Meran, in South Tyrol. As the city's name appeared on the road signs, Martinoli made a quip and all three laughed at the thought of actually going there. Meran, partly German-speaking, was widely known as a Nazi *Hochburg* (stronghold) and the last place in the north of Italy where they would wish to stop off at, however hungry or tired. Martinoli's wife even shuddered as they drove by.

They continued stoically through the night, crossing a large expanse of Italian Alps powdered with snow that caught the moonlight, watching the passing landscapes and saying little. Kaplan eventually fell asleep in the back seat and slumbered uneasily for a couple of hours. In the early hours they were still heading southwards and passed Rovereto, leaving the bulk of the mountains behind to head down into the fertile plains of the Po Valley region. They drove past Brescia and Coroma; by then the first lights of a new morning were scraping across the sky to the east behind them. The dawn was pushing away the comforting darkness in gradual strips of light - blue, mauve and grey - that then gradually radiated from a pale orange to a strong yellow.

At Tortona they left the main autostrada heading down to Genova and the Mediterranean and took a sharp westward turn that, in just over a couple of hours, brought them to the small town of Cuneo, on the far western side of northern Italy. "Almost there!" Martinoli reassured his passengers with a smile. They continued along a short stretch of road to a small village called Demonte, some twenty kilometres further. After chugging along an increasingly narrow dirt track, they arrived at a small and isolated farmhouse. With that the second stage of the journey was over. Here the group received food and wine and could rest and sleep for a few hours in some basic straw beds. In the late afternoon, Martinoli and his girlfriend got back in his truck and embarked on their journey home, taking the same route back.

Kaplan and Dolmatovsky were given over to their third companion, a humble villager and father of eight who said he was called Giuseppe. This was to be the cheapest part of the voyage, but by far the most strenuous. That night they headed out as soon as the first stars appeared in the twilight sky, trudging for hours behind Giuseppe who only uttered the occasional monosyllabic reply, up into the foothills, higher and along steep passes. Kaplan had the same sensation as first entering into the Alps back in Austria, and once more noticed how at ease he felt out here in this rocky terrain. The moon rose up on the horizon and passed across the sky through the early and middle part of the night, once again illuminating the dramatic surroundings of jagged rocks and impressive abysses in an iridescent bath of sparkling white and duller silver tones. At one point, they passed along a narrow mountainous trail between two huge rocks and Giuseppe mumbled in a low voice - with such unclarity that the men had to ask him to repeat - the great words of such life-saving importance: "This part here is now France."

They stopped a number of times on the route in order to rest, as the two urban men were unused to such physical strain. Giuseppe, old enough to be their father, silently waited for them to catch their breath before heading further on. As the morning light started to come down over them, they walked into a new day. They continued under the warm sun for hours; it later sank into a cool afternoon; after a couple of hours they felt the first chill of an evening breeze and perceived the growing gloom. Another day had set but by then they had reached their destination, a small hut just outside the village of Saint-Sauveur-sur-Tinee, where Giuseppe left them and disappeared abruptly without farewell. Daniel was incredulous that they had finally made it out of any last clutches of the Reich. He later recalled the perception of how he felt like an eel that has nimbly slipped through the hands of all its many would-be catchers and killers.

Here, utterly exhausted but at the same time jubilant, they stayed for a few days with a minimum of bread and cheese, to await the arrival of a further man and a woman; a couple who, like them, was on the run from Nazi Germany and had come down through a similar network of routes. The four refugees were eventually picked up by motor car and taken along the southern French coast, past Marseille and Montpellier, before covertly crossing the border into Spain at Cerbère. There, they were able to organize their own transport with the last of their dwindling funds. All that was left over was the minimum for payment of the last stretch and for a little basic food. They headed down through Spain toward their ultimate destination on the Atlantic coast: a small community of fellow refugees and pre-paid accommodation in Lisbon.

Chapter 22

For ten whole days Horst was treated like a king and fed like a goose before Christmas. Inge could barely let his hand go, and they kissed constantly as they hadn't done since Berlin and their honeymoon. Horst hardly went out at all but spent much of the time sitting with his boys and playing all the games that they could think of. He taught little Adolf to play a couple of card games and to bet on the outcome too, using some old *Notgeld* (emergency money) coins from the years of hyperinflation that they had dug up from a treasure chest of bygones that Gisela had in the cellar. The boy clearly had a quick and eager mind for the task. Joseph on the other hand was more interested in speaking and liked to form long meandering infantile sentences which enchanted Gisela and Inge. But he was also quite introverted in the presence of his father, seeming to feel unsure of him and more comfortable in the presence of women. Hermann was a mass of giggles and grins and charmed everyone who passed by him into talking to him and patting his head or stroking his cheek.

As expected, the days passed with the speed of lightning and already the moment to leave had arrived. The proud family gathered with smiles and tears at the entrance to the *Gasthaus* to see Horst off, just as they had done two months earlier with his brother Wilhelm, who had been able to get leave home to spend Christmas with the family. He had been on two long-lasting missions in the North Atlantic and had had a lot to tell. Horst had wanted so much to have seen his brother but was also thankful for small mercies in being able to come home at all in such difficult times. He heard about the quip that Wilhelm had made at Christmas, which made him smile: "A war broadens your horizons. We never travelled abroad in our family and now look at us." Apparently old Volkmar had been present but had not discerned the ironic humour; rather, he had nodded in enthusiastic agreement.

Hans, his old supervisor from the fire station, had turned out to see off his friend and former colleague too. He gave him a box of 50 Aitkah cigarettes, in a sturdy red and green tin box with '*Echte türkische Tabake*' (real Turkish tabacco) in large silver letters across the top. "But you know I don't smoke," said Horst with puzzled mien.

"I know that. They're not for you, lad," came the gruff reply. "They will be worth more than money once you're back on the front. Just don't bargain them all away too quickly. And beware of thieves: a war brings out the best, but mostly the worst in people."

His father Konrad, looking older and more ragged each time he saw him, had come all the way to Lüneburg for the occasion. He had stayed the night in the Gasthaus and was embracing his son the next day as if he would never see him again. Neither of them mentioned Karl-Heinz or Wilhelm going to war, as though that was all taking place in a parallel world, like a vivid bad dream. For old Konrad himself it was a bewildering time. First losing his wife, then seeing his sons all taken off to war. He had begun to reflect morbidly on past memories, especially of the children – Hermann and Hildegard – whom he and his wife had lost while still infants, and his own mother's death at that time, too. It seemed now, to the oft confused and aged man, as if those he loved were suddenly disappearing again, repeating the same cycle two decades later with a new war and an ineluctable sense of destiny.

His parents-in-law Corinna and Georg embraced Horst tightly in front of the Gasthaus; told him, under sad smiles, to take good care of himself so as to be home soon for their daughter and grandchildren. Gisela was misty-eyed and even Martin seemed concerned.

Volkmar arrived at the last minute, brought as ever by Bernhard in his car, and thumped him heftily on the back, shook his hand with stiff formality, and told him how proud he was of what Horst was doing for their Führer and their Fatherland. Horst would have happily skipped that message but it was part and parcel of the farewell ceremony. "We have to be everywhere these days," Volkmar concluded. "Dieter has been fighting on the Balkan front, you know. Damned *Macaronis* (Italians), what a useless lot, couldn't even capture Greece on their own. This war is becoming a thankless task for Germany."

Also among the well-wishers was Cousin Carsten, who looked sincerely morose. Horst had sensed soon after his arrival that the lad, with whom he had never had any considerable contact, was seeking an unusual closeness to him during his stay. He found out the reason why: Carsten had received his own conscription order, just a few days prior to Horst's arrival in Lüneburg. The young rail enthusiast, who had turned twenty the previous autumn, would soon to be off to a training camp near Frankfurt himself. On the penultimate day he had asked Horst what advice he would give him, but Horst had felt unsure as to his own capability or authority for giving a suitable reply. He did not regard himself as having any special wisdom to impart to another man: all that was to be known for a soldier-to-be was more or less common knowledge. Moreover, he did not wish to extend any advice that, in the wrong circumstances, might lead to misunderstandings and through that to misfortune.

He had said, "You will find out everything during your training, and from wiser and more experienced men than me, Carsten. Just be true to yourself and to your comrades once you are out on the front and you can do no wrong."

The following day of departure, Horst thought he saw a look of fear in the boy's eyes as he shook his hand and clapped him on the shoulder. He knew that Carsten was about to see the reality behind the show that he had been applauding and cheering for the past two years, and he doubted that this reality would in any way correspond to his expectations.

Horst caught the train from Lüneburg to Hannover, Hannover to Berlin. From Berlin, Horst headed with a rough, packed Wehrmacht train back to the front with a group of soldiers, most also returning from leave but plenty also heading out to the east for the first time. Those were enthusiastic young men, most barely out of school, all patriotically eager to do their bit for the war effort. Horst found their plapper tiring and kept himself to himself.

He lay on top of one of the lower bunks for most of the time, reading his magazines and pondering on the future. Some of the youngsters were sitting in a circle on the floor and playing a game of cards; another group of slightly older men beside them were downing beers and laughing, telling anecdotes from the front. The mood was rumbustious; one of men returning well-fed and mollycoddled from their families, but glad to be back among their comrades. If you had to fight out there in the mud and cold, then at least you had good company. At one point there was a serious lull in the discussion as the subject of frost bite came up. Horst looked up and listened in on the sharing of experiences and mutual advice. This fraternity between the men, he now saw, was a very different type of social bonding than that which men would normally have together. It went far deeper and explored those otherwise unknown or unspoken moments of extreme danger and existential fear. It had a primitive urgency, then conversation was a basic factor required for survival. He wondered if it was due to war that men had first begun to talk in depth to one another.

He thought how he had been glad to have had the opportunity to see his children: how they had grown up so fast, how well Inge handled them! Quietly strict in discipline, openly loving in care. His wife was clearly an excellent mother; plus, having someone sharp and practical like Gisela by her side offered him further comfort of mind. As the train chugged on, he closed his eyes and let his family pass before his mind's eye. Adolf was four going on five and quite the little man, developing his own infantile character which Horst found enchanting. He saw him as independent, stubborn like his grandfather, determined; but playful and observant too. He felt sure that his son would make him proud some day, perhaps even grow up to be someone of importance. Joseph struck him as a little strange, too demure and withdrawn into his own little world, but Horst contemplated that that was to be expected given the unusual circumstances of war and a now absent father. That would rectify itself, he was sure, once this whole conflict was over and things had returned to normal. He looked forward to the challenge of bringing up his boys to be young men imbued with all the respectability and responsibility that being a German citizen in today's world brought with it. And of course, last but not least, the apple of his eye, little Hermann; although, Horst smiled, actually not so little. Slightly chubby, mischievous with a hint of slyness, sturdy and good-humoured, only three as yet but already vivacious, full of energy and curiosity. The twinkle in the child's eyes, his contagious chuckle and manic antics: they all combined to melt Horst's heart. He deeply loved the boy, seeing so much of himself in him, from his prominent nose and hazel eyes to his fascination with model vehicles. He was still in seventh heaven that little Hermann had so taken to the model fire engine he had been given for his birthday last year. Horst had promised himself that he would try to get home leave again in September, to be with Hermann this time round for his third one.

Horst's heart ached to be back with his family while at the same time recognizing the overriding necessity of procuring a safe and livable country for that very family to live and grow up in. In that he saw an indisputable and weighty role as a good father to his children and an honourable man to his nation. The train swept on through the Ukrainian hinterlands, mostly now conquered, moving closer to the front. Horst dropped asleep and dreamt of his children and the buildings and streets of Lüneburg; he woke in the dim twilight, highly confused at first as to his surroundings. He then took in, with dismal familiarity, how he was back at the southern section of the front.

As the destination neared, some men began to shave in preparation, someone struck up a tune on an accordion, others shared cigarettes and stared out of the darkening window. They arrived at night and were taken further on in a motorized convoy. Horst heard the familiar military tone and vocabulary around him, and his hitherto resisting heart sank heavy at first. But all in all, the return to the war was less traumatic and more routine than he had imagined.

Back on the front, the spring offensive had begun. The winter that had frozen the advances achieved in the previous year and caused such general frustration, was now coming to an end. The ground was thawing, the air warming under a still weak but now visible sun. Soon the German troops were once more pushing forward and the Panzers were able to roll on undeterred, blasting down the opposition and with the troops moving up confidently behind. But within a few days, Horst could sense that the enemy had learnt from the errors of that previous year and were not retreating as submissively and unanimously as they had before. It often happened that German troops surrounded and successfully occupied villages, only to discover to their – sometimes fatal – surprise that neighbouring villages nearby held hidden large pockets of Soviet resistance. The Red Army seemed to have worked out that, while open confrontation with the well-equipped Wehrmacht, especially in wide open spaces, was not a wise tactic to follow, the hiding games that were offered to them in settlements, even of the most basic type, gave them much more room for stealthy movement and ambush.

In one such case in April, Horst and his platoon had spent the night sleeping in a peasants' farmhouse that they had taken over as they secured the village. It was an old ramshackle building with clay walls, rattling old windows and a few straw beds. There, with two young troops keeping watch, they passed the night with full stomachs and in deep sleep. In the corner slept a young couple to whom the house belonged, together with their young son.

In the morning, the men prepared to leave and Horst, who had been disturbed by strange dreams, had difficulty in rousing himself punctually. Eventually, the rest of the platoon was outside and ready to go while he was still dressing. He heard the platoon commander shouting for him to get a move on, then ordering a young private called Zipprich, who had just turned nineteen and arrived at the front two weeks ago, to go and tell him personally to get a move on. Seconds later there came a huge crash as the shot from a mortar smashed down close to the front side of the building. Horst threw himself instinctively to the ground as he felt the strong explosion, covering his head with his hands. Shards of broken glass burst out of the windows and scattered all around. His first thought was, and correctly so, that their presence there had already been known to nearby forces who were now attacking. Moments later he heard confused and panicky cries, followed by an uneasy silence.

Rushing outside, he immediately came across the body of Zipprich lying against the side of the house. His skull had been completely shattered by the force of the projectile and his head cracked opened in two halves, which in turn now hung at an odd angle from his neck. Blood and brain matter soaked in blood was splattered all around, including quite high up the outer walls of the farmhouse. Horst retched at first, then knelt down by him in an automatic but obviously ridiculous attempt to somehow help the fallen comrade. He heard the commander coming over and quietly telling him to get back as he knelt down to inspect the corpse. He closed the still staring eyes, now far wider apart on the splintered head, and gently removed the *Erkennungsmarke* (army identification disc), bending and snapping it in two.

Horst moved back slowly, brushing off a few pieces of shattered glass still stuck to his uniform. He had seen plenty of corpses by now but not, at least so far, one so grotesquely mutilated. He touched his uniform again and realized that those fragments of glass were all that he himself had received from the shot, despite being only two or three metres away from Zipprich. The horror sank in that the lad's death had come as a direct result of him being sent to tell Horst to hurry up. He concluded, with a shuddering guilt, that the incident was ultimately his fault but that there was nothing more to say or do about it. There was no absolution to be had, no sense to be made of yet another hopelessly terrible death. He would have no other option but to move on like a machine.

In the meantime, some of the other troops from the platoon had sped off in the direction from which they assumed the projectile had been fired, blazing machine guns as they approached their objective. But they found nothing, and only with time did the lack of return fire suggest that they had merely repelled the attackers to a safe distance. Horst told the commander he had got to know the boy well in the last few days and that he would make the habitual wooden cross to be placed at the head of the grave. This, he knew, would at least give him the opportunity to furtively beg forgiveness, in a frantic whisper, from the body about to go into the earth. The commander agreed and took advantage of those moments to prepare the report of the incident and to re-think the strategy forward. He took his time and so Horst was able to additionally scratch a rough "*wir werden dich nicht vergessen*" – "we will not forget you", as was often done after the deaths of more popular and well-liked comrades. (Ultimately though he did forget him, having no other choice in the matter; in such circumstances a man must look for comfort in the living and seek his point of reference there. In any case there would soon be more than enough tragedy to occupy their thoughts elsewhere.)

The commander came back from his communication with a stony face and told the men they had to burn down all the buildings. He said, there existed the probability that they would end up being used as shelter by any Soviet troops still hanging around nearby. This was an awkward moment as the action would obviously be a huge, if not fatal, blow for the peasants themselves. The commander repeated the order and the men set to work. Within some minutes the whole farmhouse, together with nearby stalls and huts, were all blazing away. The local couple now stood outside with a few belongings that they had been able to snatch up in the last moment, the woman clasping the boy to her chest. They looked on without emotion at the soldiers, to whom they given food and accommodation the previous day. Their cold hard stare bored through Horst, who had looked back in shame and caught their eyes. Behind them, the flames licked upwards to the sky. He shuddered but did not wait a second time to be told by the others to hurry up.

They moved on and Russia's plains stretched out impassively before them. There was an attempt to cultivate hatred for '*der Iwan*' in the army; when commanding officers repeatedly hammered in the officially sanctioned ideas of their negative racial traits, as well as their natural murderous intent, into their subordinates' minds. But left to themselves, the soldiers also found a good deal of natural respect for their adversary; the respect from soldier to soldier. They were quite sure that these Russian soldiers had as little interest in participating in the actual conflict as they did, and that they too were being pushed along by higher forces. They felt the pain when one of theirs was brutally taken out; but equally, upon killing, they knew full well the pain that would arise on the other side. Somewhere far away, a mother and father, perhaps a girlfriend or wife as well, would break down in tears. Horst, as a responsible father, would shudder at the thought of possible orphans left behind by the deaths of enemy soldiers at his own hands, while simultaneously wondering how Inge would get by in the case of his own demise. These considerations were nonetheless a brief and occasional luxury: there were two fundamental and guiding instincts among the men - the urgent necessity to dominate the adversary, and the equally urgent repulsion of the adversary holding any position of power over them.

Nevertheless, Horst felt the war was not only a conflict on the ground but also a conflict in the mind. He continually had to numb the fear of his own death, as well as numb his conscience concerning any unnecessary deaths that he may cause to others. Under the term 'unnecessary', he not only included the killing of civilians, of which he had so far not found himself directly guilty, but also of the very young soldiers, still adolescent boys. And he had killed the latter too many times to want to recall. He saw how many of the youngsters had not had time enough out fighting to come to a studied resolution that they would have to fight to kill, many times over. They seemed to him at times like saplings that easily bent in the wind, and he imagined that the Russian youth would be in the same position as his own young comrades. But he also understood the urgent voice in the young men's heads that was goading them on to be the strong man, to be the victor. They would be experiencing the same vivid emotions that he had: the same sharp heat of excitement in exchanges of fire with the enemy, the desperate need to come out on top, the awareness of how much – their whole lives – was at stake, and the desire to prove themselves worthy before the other men in his company.

He sought various strategies to process any later guilt felt toward the killings of adolescents. One was to consider the fight a noble cause, in which the German forces had to win in order for the forces of good to prevail. In this way, they would be achieving not only a victory for themselves, but moreover a victory for their adversary too, by ultimately freeing their families from the yoke of bolshevism. If Horst imagined that the Russians had little interest in fighting, he was convinced they had even less in politics. The country was vast, he told himself, and so they were merely pushing back the population so many hundred kilometres. And what difference could those casualties make within this immensity that swept out further and more monotonously than the sea itself? Once Moscow fell - as he had heard stated several times when back at home - it would all be over for good, and for everyone.

One night Horst shared his thoughts with a superior officer; the commanding officer of his platoon in that moment in time, *Feldwebel* (Staff Sergeant) Glatz, who would die three weeks later in an ambush. The men had spent the day advancing in close coordination. In the evening, as they sat round and shared a cup of vodka that the men were passing round, Horst unloaded his feelings on that officer concerning the killing of very young men. Glatz showed some comprehension for Horst's predicament but warned him to keep such thoughts out of his mind if he wanted to survive for very long.

"A good soldier is one who can kill automatically. Just kill without stopping to think or reflect," he stated in his calm voice, hand chopping the air like a meat cleaver with the gentle insistence that was his everyday manner. "You must not look at the enemy as a human being, just look at him as an object. An object that you have to knock out quickly before it knocks you out. Otherwise you have already lost the next confrontation before it has even begun. You just kill where necessary and move on without thinking about it – that is the only way. You need to be that good soldier at all times because if you are not, you won't stand a chance. A bad soldier is the one who gets killed."

In May, a small group of soldiers returned from home leave to suddenly find themselves posted further down to the south of the Russian front. They were sent to join the same division as Horst, which was by now positioned around twenty kilometres to the north of Slowiansk, in eastern Ukraine. One of these men turned out to be no less than Julius Fink, the Wiesbadner plumber whom Horst had befriended during the training session. The men hugged each other heartily upon recognizing the fellow recruit from way back then, and spent the rest of the day posted together on sentry duty. There they were able to engage in deeper discourse and compare experiences. Fink told Horst of some of the more shocking things that he had heard, of mass shootings that SS-units were carrying out in the wake of the conquests.

"So, the regular Wehrmacht pushes on through Russia while these elite troops, *Einsatzgruppen* (operation units) they call them, come up after, behind them. And sometimes they just massacre everyone, wipe out whole towns and villages. Men, women, children, the lot. Especially if they find one with a lot of Jews in it."

Horst was horrified by this information and said that he personally had experienced no such brutality. Quite the opposite, even toward the enemy prisoners there had been a sense of chivalry and respect, he insisted, and most certainly toward any civilians caught up in the warfare. He recalled the slight change of morality towards the villagers when the food supplies had been low, with the increased requisition of livestock and vegetables and other goods. This, he knew, could and probably should be classed as robbery. But beyond that, gruff and harsh though their attitude had been in the face of hungry and pleading peasants, it was nowhere near the levels of violence that Fink had just described. Then he recalled the burnt down farmhouse of the Ukranian couple with the boy. They had been left to fend for themselves without a roof over their heads. But still, he reassured himself, there had been no slaughter of civilians where he had been.

Horst was plagued for weeks by these thoughts until he increasingly came to consider that these tales may well be rumours, or merely the exaggeration of a single, very unfortunate incident. He could not reconcile his sense of pride in his country and the restrained way in which he and his comrades were liberating these foreign lands, with such tales of barbarity. Moreover, it made little tactical sense from a military perspective. Why on earth would the commanding officers send one line of men to push the front forward, only to waste their time sending a second group behind them with the sole purpose of committing sadistic and unnecessary mass murder. In the end, he decided it would be better to take Fink's story with a pinch of salt. He was glad and relieved to notice that no-one else was bringing up the subject.

Around a week later, the platoon commander requested that a group of men go to a nearby village to collect a supply of provisions from a deposit there. Horst volunteered together with Fink and a young soldier called Litze, who was eager to prove himself. There had been rumblings of thunder all day and an oppressive heat; the atmosphere was electric and ready for a storm. They set out under cover of darkness and, as expected, in the dark early hours a storm whipped up with driving rain and strong gusts of wind. They battled on through the gale and the night until they reached a railway line. Fink said they should follow the embankment to the right, but Horst insisted they instead went to the left, that being the south-westerly direction that would take them to their destination. The opposite direction, he argued, would only bring them straight up against the Russian front and into the jaws of danger. Fink relented and followed Horst's suggestion, who was now doubting himself and worried that his instinct might have failed him and that his error could bring both men into peril. There was no going back now, having stated his conviction with such fierce certainty and having overruled his comrade's suggestion.

After two hours of trekking onward they reached an area of dense woodland in the first light of dawn. There, on the edge of the forest, they came across a small wooden farmhouse. Smoke was coming out of the chimney; the occupants could be heard inside, preparing to start the day. Deciding to take shelter there and dry their clothes before they caught a chill, they crept up, coordinated themselves with machine pistols ready, and stormed the building in a flash.

Both shouted one of the standard Russian phrases they had learnt - *"Ruki verk-h!"* (Arms up!) – as they crashed into the room. The three inhabitants, an older couple and a young man, seemingly their son, started in shock and all instantly raised their hands. Horst and Fink advanced slowly, listening intensely for a moment to reassure themselves that no-one else was present in the house. Fink, who had expanded his vocabulary in the course of the campaign, added, *"Ty odin?"* ("Are you alone?"), to which the inhabitants nodded.

Still aiming their weapons at the three farmers, Horst and Fink spread out to inspect the room and adjoining kitchen. Now clearly hearing them speak together in German, the older man laughed and made a comment to his son, half in what sounded like Russian and half in German, namely that these were Wehrmacht soldiers. He asked the intruders if they wanted some cigarettes and a glass of vodka, to which they agreed following a mutual glance and nod that came with the instinctive sense that no threat at all was posed by these people. Quite the opposite, they were clearly being offered warm hospitality despite their own violent entrance into the peasants' home. They smoked the cigarettes, downed the first vodka, and gradually all those present began to relax. The farmers' raised arms had come down, the soldiers' weapons were pointing to the ground, there was a growing sense of amiability. Fink explained to Horst that these were probably supporters of the pro-German partisans, still covertly present in the area. Stalin had left many bitter foes in the wake of his purges, especially in the Ukraine; all with good reason to detest him and the state he stood for. These people in turn had viewed the invasion of the Wehrmacht as liberation from the Soviet oppressor.

After finishing the cigarette and glass of vodka, Horst offered up some of the horse sausage that he had on him. At that gesture, the old man ordered the woman to fetch some potatoes and the younger man was sent outside to milk a cow in an adjacent shed. While the mother cooked the potatoes, there was a dubious moment in which a heavy silence fell. Horst began to half suspect that the whole episode with cigarettes and alcohol was just a ruse, that the son had run off to betray them and a hoard of Soviet soldiers would burst in and spray them with bullets. But he decided to rely on an overriding sense of trust and disentangle himself from any paranoia; this instinct was eventually proved to be true and his fears only figments of the imagination. The son returned with a pail filled with fresh warm white milk. The soldiers handed over both their rations of sausage and some bread, and once the potatoes were ready and the son had come back again, this time with the milk, the woman was able to make a large pot of mashed potato. Alone the smell was glorious. Horst was amazed to find one of his favourite ever dishes served up in this, the most unlikely of places.

The food was all placed together on a large table and the five ate heartily, laughed together, and made some primitive but amiable conversation. Horst and Fink were furthermore able to dry their clothes by the fire, taking turns to sleep a couple of hours while the farmers went about their chores in the nearby fields outside. By the late afternoon, the German soldiers were rested and fed and felt generally whole again, grateful for a moment of shared resources and pleasant company in a land in which so far they had, for the most part, only known conquest and killing. Horst later hoped to the high heavens that Fink's stories were indeed just fabrications: by now he couldn't bear to imagine otherwise. They continued on their way, reaching the deposit before nightfall. There they stayed for a few hours and collected the supplies, before heading back to their camp with warm clothes for their comrades and a fresh spring in their step.

The offensive went on relentlessly. Festive or special days came and went. He noted them all internally but, like almost all the men, never mentioned a word. In June it had been Joseph's birthday, four already; at the end of July his and Inge's sixth wedding anniversary; in August, it would have been his late mother's birthday; in

September little Hermann would be three. Horst wrote regularly back to Lüneburg, mostly to Inge. He was careful to remember each and every date in his writings and to tell Inge to pass on greetings and best wishes where corresponding.

The German Panzer divisions swept on across the fields, clearing the way for the soldiers marching on up behind. It was a successful spring and summer campaign with much advancement made. The casualties were always shocking when someone you personally knew was abruptly taken out of this world, and especially when they were physically close at the time; but they were still within the limits of what could be considered acceptable. On good days, which were frequent, they were advancing on foot at 7-8 kilometres an hour.

The terrain during this time was perfect for the Wehrmacht's combination of tanks and troops – long flat plains with few obstacles between. On one occasion, the marching platoon found itself descending into an elongated valley, a noteworthy feature out on the otherwise monotonously flat steppes. Grassy hills flanked them on both sides. Striding along next to Horst were two young men, both just high-school graduates snatched out of their studies by the war. One was clearly a Berliner, with his distinctive accent. Instead of 'gut' (good) came "jut", instead of 'was' (what) he said 'wat'; plus the rough and direct way of speaking that sometimes seemed to border on rude but was clearly well-meant and offered to be taken with humour. Horst vaguely recalled some of those Berliner mannerisms from his brief visit as a tourist on honeymoon (way back in 1936 in those easy-going times of peace, now almost as if in another life). He had met quite a few Berliners as fellow soldiers, and had come to appreciate their fresh, unaffected and playfully sharp manner; which in the field of combat was the perfect method for communication between comrades.

The other young man marching beside him was telling his comrade about his family house in a small town called Enkirch, in the Moselle Valley. He had become very enthusiastic in details at this point, describing his hometown and its sloping hills that led down the Rhine, the carefully cultivated vineyards, the best of the many delicious wines that came from the area. In the midst of such an effervescent depiction, in which one could almost feel a warming western German sun beating down on the grapes, there was clearly a whimsical homesickness in his voice. Even the Berliner had become thoroughly enchanted by the story and was desisting from his habitual roguish comments.

There came a droning from the distance, gradually increasing in volume upon approach, and in very little time a Russian plane came towards them. As it flew overhead, they recognized it as being the notoriously formidable *Sturmovik* model and everyone automatically tightened inside. It changed its course, evidently preparing to dive into the valley, while the platoon commander screamed for everyone to take cover. They all flung themselves to the left and right of what seemed to be the course of the plane, desperately searching for cover where there was none to be had. They were like the proverbial sitting ducks, in the deep but open basin of land in which they were now caught inside. The plane dropped a single bomb, which fell among the troops in a spectacular explosion, and it continued casually on its way without turning back.

The bomb had fallen near the back of the group and not far from Horst, who was left temporarily dazed and deafened by the blast. As he struggled to his feet, he saw that the two young students had run almost directly into the unpredictable path of the bomb. The Berliner had lost a leg and moreover had multiple shrapnel wounds. He was screaming in pain as his comrades ran over to him to calm him and stem the bleeding wounds. The soldier from the Moselle Valley had been killed outright, with deep bloody wounds to the chest, neck and face. One of the burly older men had picked up the light body, which hung lifeless in his arms, to bring it to the company commander. On the way he suddenly fell on his knees to the ground, still holding the corpse, whereupon he sobbed into the young man's dead chest for a while. Later Horst found out that this soldier had a son himself, almost eighteen and expected to be called up soon, possibly next year. After another comrade had taken the boy's body away from him, the older soldier then began jabbering - his mind slightly broken - about the stupidity of their commanding officers; he rounded firmly on the entire Wehrmacht leadership, up to and including the Führer, with uncouth vocabulary. The commander told the others to make him shut up, one way or another, or there would be trouble. They managed to make him see sense for all their sakes.

Despite the best efforts of the medic and surrounding comrades, the Berliner died around fifteen minutes later, succumbing to his injuries. A further three dead bodies from the blast were also carried out of the valley and, once they had located some trees and were able to carve two more crosses, they marked the burial site of the men. There rested the remains of two students whose last snippets of conversation had been filled with vineyards and the verdant hills of better times. The commander took their identification discs.

On went the march until they reached and were able to cross the river Donets on pontoon bridges that another platoon in the area had already laid, a few days earlier. The tanks crossed first, blasting at the small pocket of Soviet resistance that had gathered on the other side. By the time Horst's platoon was to cross over, the Red Army had been scattered and they had no contact with the soldiers. Horst had feared the worse upon crossing the bridge, assuming the river – which seemed to be such a divisive point – would be heavily defended. He was half expecting a Red Army sniper to pick him out during the scurry across the wobbly structure, with him falling to be carried off by the smoothly running waters; or have a well-launched grenade explode nearby. He was immensely relieved to arrive safe and sound on the other side without encountering the expected armed resistance, thus allowing the group to stride swiftly on. At this point in the campaign, with good weather above and clear terrain ahead, progress was swift and generally clean.

In late July, the division found out about the upcoming attack on the city of Stalingrad that was planned: a major urban population centre in the direction of which they were already advancing. Another general came to visit the companies, one by one, and deliver a resounding speech. At the end of that month, Horst and his platoon observed heavy aerial fighting taking place in the direction of their next natural border: the wide river Don. They continued their march in that direction and found that the Luftwaffe had done a very effective job. Their platoon soon entered into that great arch which the Don followed round before it flowed off into the Sea of Azov. They ploughed on with considerable speed and hearts filled with optimism, taking out the opposition by now with a minimum of effort. *'Der Iwan'* seemed to be weakening somewhat; falling back even, they commented.

In the second week of August the first infantry divisions had fought their way through, crossed the Don, secured the area and erected the bridgeheads. The pontoon bridges were swiftly laid and the tanks, with troops close behind bringing up the rear, rushed across. They were subjected to numerous aerial attacks by Russian aircraft as well as the howling noise of the 'Stalin organ-pipes' as the *Katyusha* rockets smashed into the river and terrain around them. This Soviet resistance was short-lived and soon overrun. The Wehrmacht crossed the Don successfully and continued its unflinching course toward Stalingrad, that eminent city on the Volga that was about to become their next target.

By the middle of August, General Paulus, the commander-in-chief of the 6th Army, gave the order to attack Stalingrad. Down the dusty hills of the *Kalmückensteppe* hurtled the German army, tanks growling along the sixty kilometres from the Don towards the Volga. These arid plains were perfect terrain for the German tanks and greatly promoted their triumphant operation. As they came nearer to their target, the resistance from the Red Army became tougher and more embittered; but in the end they were hopelessly overpowered in the face of this adversary. The German infantry marched on behind with brutal precision towards the city, now in their sight. As a target it seemed helpless enough, occasionally sparkling from the distance under the summer haze. But to be on the safe side and protect the two flanks, the German command had instructed that armies of other Axis forces were to be employed on either side, to bolster the ensuing assault: to the north Hungarians and Italians, to the south Romanian divisions.

In the days leading up the attack, Horst had heard rumblings of discord concerning this strategy. It was common knowledge within the Wehrmacht that the Hungarian and in particular the Romanian troops were under-equipped and insufficiently trained, like most of the axis forces accompanying them in this mammoth task. They presented a clearly weak and potentially hazardous link in the chain of divisions securing the area. Horst heard that, despite these concerns being passed on to those higher up in the chain of command, the decision to organize the attack in such a configuration was to be left standing as it was; more than anything in the dearth of better plans. In any case, alone the 6th Army was reckoned to be one of the greatest fighting units in the entire Wehrmacht. The Führer himself had stated that the 6th Army could storm the very gates of heaven. Stalingrad could impossibly possess a stronger entrance.

After months of arduous marching forward across the steppes in the arduous heat, there was great assuredness in their hearts that the path to a clear and decisive conquest lay shortly ahead. They were now within reach of that symbolic city on the Volga, to which the terrible Bolshevik dictator had given his own name. It sat ahead of them in its innocent pride, straddling across the river at such a crucial point. And it was theirs for the taking.

Chapter 23

The first advancing troops came to perceive (for there were those who like Horst were still uncertain) an immense vision of destruction that had taken place just anterior to their final approach on the city. The German Luftwaffe had pounded Stalingrad mercilessly over two whole days of near constant air-raids, bombarded it into a hellish landscape of ruins and still blazing fires. Even from a distance the smoke and flames could now be seen, and the burning city lit up the night sky with a terrible incandescence. This excited many of the troops, awaiting their chance to sweep in on the maimed and now easy prey.

It was a truly catastrophic attack that few of the observers had anticipated. Stalin in turn refused to evacuate the city, insisting that the inhabitants dug in deep and that the city was defended down to the last man, woman, and child. The Soviet authorities soon spoke of 40,000 dead, most of them civilians, in the days following that first assault. The oil tanks on the banks of the Volga were badly hit; large black pillars of billowing smoke filled the horizon and acted as a marker point for the German troops during the day, indicating the ever nearer destination of their great mission.

Once this initial aerial barrage was over, the tanks and infantry moved in for the kill, reaching in less than a day the outer suburbs to the north of the city. Simultaneously to the south, further Wehrmacht soldiers drew up to the battered districts there. The ring around Stalingrad was slowly closed.

Although they did not at first appreciate the fundamental change, those wide open plains that they had so effortlessly conquered, were now behind them. A new and very different type of warfare had opened up. They moved through increasingly built-up areas with slow caution, for the enemy could be hidden in any random corner, ready to rush out and attack from behind when least expected.

The German commanding officers were keen to capture a strategically important point in the west, which they considered would offer itself as a great symbol of their ultimate destiny in controlling the city as well as offering an excellent viewpoint over the city: the famous Mamai Hill, which the Russians called *Mamayev Kurgan* but to the German troops was merely *Höhe 102* (Hill Nr. 102) on their maps. It rapidly became a tough, embittered battle. The Red Army were prepared to throw everything they had into its defence, surrounding it with barbed wire and minefields as well as protecting it with solid blazes of artillery power. The Germans responded with more heavy aerial attacks in the area around until finally the Soviets were beaten back.

The eventual conquest on 12th September cost numerous German casualties (in the final battle the hill was taken by thirty German soldiers in close-quarters combat, of whom only six survived), but it provided immense satisfaction to those survivors and the comrades who joined them at the top. From this magnificent vantage point the German division active in this area, including Horst's platoon, was able to look down on the metropolis that lay before them.

It was a twisted hellscape of blackened ruins, many still smoking. Most of the apartment blocks, especially those towards the inner city, had been heavily hit and were now merely shells of walls displaying endless rows of black empty window holes. Factories and other metallic structures lay in twisted contortions. All around, from the innumerable fires still blazing in many buildings, curled up columns of smoke that were wafted away and carried up high into the clear blue skies. The streets themselves were a mass of the fallen rubble and masonry from smashed buildings and general debris lying in a cluttered mess. In some cases, whole blocks of adjacent buildings had been utterly razed to the ground, leaving bare plots of earth filled with smouldering chunks of the residues of businesses and apartments. The streets were littered with burnt out vehicles and other scattered objects, making them at times complicated obstacle courses.

At the further edge, in the outer suburban areas where less damage had been wreaked, the men perceived with binoculars that the buildings were small wooden structures, often clustered together in little villages. After these, working inwards, came the industrial complexes with silos and chimneys, administrative buildings, factories, processing plants. Here, many were clearly badly hit with bombed out facades and smashed ragged cavities gaping upwards like open wounds. Looming in the background on the banks of the Volga were the oil refineries, some giving off thick black smoke following direct hits by the Luftwaffe in their thorough bombardment.

But it was the rows of bombed out skeletons of residential buildings, within and all around the central area, that most struck Horst and his comrades, leaving a clear impression of the complete and utter level of urban destruction that had been reached. This was the first thing that Horst set eyes upon when he reached the hill-top himself, as part of one of the platoons that had surged on up in the wake of the initial victory. His second thought, as he gazed out over the ruins, was the fear that one day this might also be the visage that German cities would present. Especially if the Wehrmacht's victory were not swiftly achieved. This frightening reflection helped to make him more determined than ever to carry out his mission to his greatest possible capability.

The men had already been scrupulously instructed in the importance of their capturing Stalingrad. This sprawling industrial centre and transport hub in the south-west of the Soviet Union, with its enormous oil refining industry, was vital for the continuation of the Soviet war machine, as well as the movement of supplies up to Moscow. Once it had been taken out of the game, then the rest of this once-mighty land would collapse as a lifeless sack. It would be, to quote a metaphor that one captain had employed while participating in a pre-battle speech to stimulate morale, like cutting the strings of a marionette. In this case, one whose strings were directly controlled by Stalin himself and which was furthermore the very namesake of that sinister puppet master. Coupled with the push further south through the Caucasus Mountains, aiming to capture the oil fields around Baku, this victory would make Germany truly invincible. It would not only deal the fatal blow to the enemy; it would additionally feed the German defence industry with oil for as long as it took to quell all local resistance and subdue the more distant enemies of the homeland, too.

They did not have long, however, to gaze upon the sight of the mortally wounded city. As they began to cross the hill-top and head down the other side on their way toward the centre, they were immediately greeted by heavy artillery fire. The familiar howling 'Stalin organ-pipes' sounded up, as rocket launchers began firing at them from the other side of the Volga. The *katyushas* soon thudded down all around, leaving a tired Horst dazed in the first moments. Julius Fink, who had been close to his side for the last two days, grabbed him by the arm and the two quickly found sanctuary in a nearby trench, though with barely enough room for both of them. Around them the deadly barrage of metal splitters whizzed off in all directions following each strike. Horst saw no fewer than four men caught out by these splitters; they fell out of the air in mid-run and collapsed lifelessly to the ground. In one case, blood spurted up high out of a vein in the man's neck as he lay on the ground, eyes staring upwards.

After the attack was over the medics were called, who rushed out of cover to attend to the wounded and certify the deaths. By nightfall, the *katyushas* quietened up and the platoon was able to continue its long slow march onwards. That march was indeed slow and was to become far longer than expected.

A week later Horst's platoon had reached the edge of the central district, but this advancement had come at a great cost to human life and especially on their own side. His company had been replenished with fresh troops in mid-August, just before the attack on Stalingrad, taking it up to around 220 men in total. Between the initial assault on the city and the penetration deeper into the metropolis, however, they had lost about half of those troops already in just over a month of combat.

At the end of that week the soldiers found themselves passing through an industrial zone that had been nicknamed the tennis racket due to its appearance from the air. It was a densely packed complex of rail tracks and factories that formed one of Stalingrad's major supply lines for manufactured goods. In the wake of a heavy aerial raid by the Luftwaffe, it had been reduced to a macabre jumble of buckled steel and huge chunks of bombed out concrete, within an area densely littered with fallen rubble. This unholy mess was furiously defended by the Red Army. The occupation of this space went back and forth between the Wehrmacht and the Red Army for several days in the midst of great bloodshed. In the end the Wehrmacht prevailed but the whole division had lost just over 750 troops by the end of the battle.

Passing through this jungle of twisted metal and smashed cement, it seemed a high price for such a paltry advance.

And this was to be just the beginning, a foretaste of battles to come. The slaughter became tremendous and ceaselessly ongoing. The German troops at all levels and ranks soon realized that their military advantage thus far, and the secret to their astounding success throughout Europe, had relied on the famous *Bewegungskrieg* (war of movement). While being very effective out on wide open fields in Poland or France, or the extensive plains and steppes of the Ukraine and Russia, it had no useful military application whatsoever here in the very different environment of house-to-house combat. The tightly packed urban area of Stalingrad, lying in a mass of ruins, had been converted into a deadly labyrinth in which the enemy hid, stalked and ambushed at will. The men were not in the slightest prepared for this class of urban battle, so very different to what they had known so far.

The previous tactics of the Wehrmacht had concentrated on the combined attacks of air force, tanks and infantry troops, which had worked spectacularly well. This new theatre of operations no longer allowed for coordinated attacks by whole divisions. Instead, in these dogged street fights among the rubble, the size of combat units was reduced down to platoon or group level. The battlefield had been greatly diminished and in turn the level of fighting had become closer, more personal; it was now fiercer and far more brutal. The Soviets were very conscious of the vital importance of holding Stalingrad and fought with a bitter resolution as they literally had nothing left to lose. Every factory hall and floor, every floor of every house, every pile of debris, every inch of every street, were all bitterly fought for. A few metres of desolate land were gained, lost, regained, and so on, while hundreds on both sides were dying every day for this. In this new urban war of attrition, the Germans quickly found themselves at a great disadvantage. Nevertheless, they struggled on doggedly and made notable progress.

It was particularly frustrating as the final victory here seemed so near: palpable, almost touchable. Most of the city centre was taken in those first few weeks, along with the waterworks and other utility plants. German troops had reached the banks of the Volga but were still unable to bring the entire length completely under control. The central *Roter Platz* (Red Square) had been taken, along with the very headquarters building of the Communist Party of the Soviet Union, from where the *Reichsflagge* (the flag of the Third Reich) was hung. These victories were shown in the *Wochenschau* news back home in Germany and watched by friends and family of Horst. They had the firm impression that Stalingrad's days were numbered.

The city was a graveyard of ruins, it should have long since surrendered. It felt and looked to be utterly eliminated, wiped off the map. There was first and foremost the massive destruction that the buildings had sustained. But also the streets all around were a mess of wreckage. Walls and fountains areas were charred and missing segments, statues were badly chipped or cracked, fences half-destroyed and leaning over. The air was full of fumes and pillars of rising smoke, stinking of pungent chemicals, burnt rubber, rotting corpses. They were littered with incinerated vehicles, chunks of rubble, twisted metal bars and bicycles, discarded furniture and other large scattered objects, abandoned bath tubs that had served as shields and so on, making them at times complicated obstacle courses. The interiors of buildings were all dirty and burnt, the floors filled with soot and the gaping holes of explosions, the walls peppered with bullet holes. It was a sheer miracle that people were still actually living between these walls and scavenging these desolate streets for survival. At night the skies were a gently throbbing reflection of the orange fires raging below, besmirched by thick choking smoke rising up from the endless battle.

If any place were ripe for surrender, then it had to be this mortally wounded city. But a full, complete liquidation of the enemy could not be achieved. One German officer commented that it appeared as if they were stomping time and time again down on a cockroach, only for it to somehow survive and nimbly rush out from under their boots. Even an area that seemed to be so firmly held in the hands of the Wehrmacht, had whole units of Soviet soldiers hidden within. Groups of them would suddenly open fire, sending everyone scuttling for shelter. In the ensuing exchange of fire, dozens might be killed on both sides until the German officers were – erroneously - sure they had attained complete control of an area once again. Then the pattern would repeat itself.

During a stretch of nearly two weeks in October, Horst and Fink were stationed in a large second-storey apartment that was serving as one of the division's principal headquarters in the district. The officer in charge of his company at the time, a stalwart figure called *Hauptmann* (Captain) Schopf, was running a rigorous operation to try to bring the whole of the district under complete Wehrmacht domination, but this objective was proving to be near to impossible. Scouting troops were sent out regularly on nightly stealth operations to relay back details concerning sightings of the enemy. Guards were strategically placed to secure all incoming routes for supplies. There were medics at hand, and discipline, especially on vital issues such as the distribution of food among the troops, was kept to an utmost degree so that the captain could count on a strong innate sense of moral warfare and mutual collaboration among the troops. There were Russian civilians still living in the area too, who were occasionally seen sneaking out of seemingly lifeless and battle-struck buildings to secure some food or water for their hidden families, and they were duly left in peace.

The apartment in which the soldiers were housed must once have been a plush affair, estimated Horst; perhaps belonging to a well-placed and culturally-minded functionary. It was large, with the central living room alone stretching out to as much as 200 square metres, and well-positioned facing out from the front of the building. This became the focal point for all operations, with contact through cable link to the central command in Stalingrad and some bunkbeds for the sick or lightly injured so that they could be monitored by the medics. Of the former owners there were still paintings, framed photos and even a tapestry hung on the wall, though plenty of the pictures had slipped down to be propped up on furniture below or standing on the ground; while the walls together with all the adornments were all blackened with soot. Bullet holes abounded and there was a yawning gap on of the sides of the building from a well-aimed mortar shell; this had been covered with a heavy rug hung over it. The furniture was damaged and covered in filth, although it served its basic function for the soldiers to have somewhere to park their behinds or place a mug or a gun for a moment. The piano was a smashed-up jumble that only produced a clinking din. All the surfaces were a black-brown mess, covered in plaster dust. The ceiling miraculously retained some of its old turquoise charm, a welcome touch of bright colour in the otherwise dim surroundings, though it too was besmeared with the blackness of burning all around.

Outside the building the *Stuka* attacks had done their worst. The immediate surrounding area was a twisted mess of masonry, cement and metal, cleared in some place to form makeshift squares and narrow streets through heaps of rubble. The troops installed machine gun posts by the two balconies that, in better times, would have looked out onto a pleasant sunny square filled with pedestrians and trams below; now it was pulverized, charred, and deathly silent apart from the occasional crackle of machine gun fire in the distance.

To the west of the building the *Wehrmacht* had the immediate district fairly well under control, but the buildings further to the east and south were a nest of Soviet activity. Occasionally a sniper's bullet would ricochet off the outer wall; only once did it actually pierce one of the windows to narrowly miss the captain himself who was shaving by a mirror on the wall. He started and cut himself quite deeply, while his men returned the fire in a mass of machine gun fury that was like trying to kill a mosquito with a clumsily sweeping baseball bat. The adjacent building, where they instinctively suspected the sniper, or snipers, were hidden, was peppered with bullets and the last two intact windows higher up exploded in a spray of glass splinters. Nobody knew whether they had taken them out or not, but they had a couple of days of peace anyway.

There were sporadic exchanges of machine gun fire with the opposing areas, or the odd grenade was launched, both from the vantage point of the upper apartments or from the street below; it all came to a few casualties on both sides at most. An actual advance to seize the area could not be achieved, while the Panzer support was occupied elsewhere and taking its time to arrive.

This was Horst's favourite period in Stalingrad, if favourite could be an appropriate word. He always had enough to eat and a place to sleep in one of the five cosy bedrooms in the apartment, together with the other men not on guard; there was an ample and undamaged bathroom at the back with a large marble bathtub where they could occasionally wash themselves in peace; and the captain was a fair and respectful man with an equable temperament and who was clearly keen to complete his mission with speed and efficiency and inspire a sense of optimism in the other troops. In the snarled confusion of the city, he radiated the sense of a solid base and clarity of objective.

(He even taught the men how to keep the lice at bay by mixing ash in with the soap. That was a novel idea and major breakthrough for many, driven to despair by the insufferable plagues; although of course the soap would later be one of the first supplies to run out and that was the end of the chemical relief. Even so, thanks to such details it became a pleasure to feel the respect owed to beneficent authority whenever they gave the customary smack of heels, salute, and bark of, "*Jawohl, Herr Hauptmann*!" – "Yes, Captain!")

This came to a brutal end one night when the Soviets managed to sneak in and then blast the front of the building with dynamite. The whole façade fell out into the jumbled square below, taking over half of the front living room, including the captain, with it. In the frenzied confusion, the surviving Germans who tried to flee the building were taken out by Soviet flamethrowers, lighting up the darkness with their twisting bodies in flames and filling the air with screams. Horst was sleeping in a back room at the time and managed, together with a group of other soldiers, to make a successful retreat through the yard area at the back of the building. They later estimated that around a dozen troops had made it out alive. By the next day, the Soviets had regained the ruins of that building and brought the back area under heavy fire, including with artillery; they were looking to regain terrain to the west once again.

Meanwhile, over towards the river area, on some days the Red Army was sending as many as ten thousand - albeit poorly trained and poorly equipped - soldiers into battle in boats launched from the opposite shore of the Volga, in an unrelenting counterstrike to retake the city centre. They landed and came forward in monstrous waves, screaming "Orahh!", jerking in quick spurts to zigzag around the hail of bullets that met them. They were wiped out in uncountable numbers, effortlessly peppered with bullets by the Wehrmacht, but still they came, day in day out, and were starting to wear down the Germans.

Fink said to Horst at one point, "You know, whoever wins this, we are both going to lose." It was a potentially dangerous thing to say; Horst, though in agreement, did not repeat it to anyone else. As time passed, the Wehrmacht was being slowly but surely worn down into dismay, exhaustion and even resentment towards an often absent and seemingly incompetent leadership. All that and with the notorious Russian winter looming not far ahead.

Precisely this torturous situation had been the Soviet plan all along. Stalin's advisors and generals were more than aware of the German advantage in open spaces and had thus intentionally created this radically new scenario in which they would engage the Wehrmacht once it had been first drawn into the city. Stalingrad had not been evacuated and so was still full of the civilians who had survived the aerial bombings, as well as it being packed with Red Army troops. Though horrendously scarred and seemingly moribund from the outside, Stalingrad was actually still a living breathing city, through which the shadows of men and women flitted day and night, all trying to survive from one morning to another as best they could. Like ghosts from another dimension, the Soviet troops also hugged the advance of the German troops, as if two separate realities were co-existing: the German advancement on the one side, and the continuing life of the city, with its shady Red Army hidden all around, on the other. Snipers were a constant source of concern for the Wehrmacht. The Russians, aided by civilians still holding out in the ruins, mastered the art of ensconcing among the wreckage and taking out careless or simply luckless German soldiers who might stumble across their path. Fink was killed in this manner toward the end of October. He was by then in a different platoon, and Horst found out about a week later. He could barely believe it at first and imagined the burly, good-humoured hulk in his mind for the rest of that day, wiped away the odd tear that formed when he recollected some of their conversations. That night he finally wept properly for the first time, out of sight and as hushed as he could manage. His uniform was a mess of snot and dirt and he felt more miserable than ever before since the Soviet campaign had commenced. But life and the war went on, and on the following day he had two near death experiences of his own, both in close quarter exchanges of machine gun fire, and so he left aside the memory of the cheery Wiesbadner to join the crowded choir of victims in the sky.

The Germans discerned their unpreparedness and disadvantage at great cost. They had no training for these primitive basic street combats. At first, the soldiers from both sides would be fighting with pistols and hand grenades. But as the ammunition was exhausted, they had to resort to the swords affixed to bayonets, or even knives and spades as weapons. This hand-to-hand fighting had barely featured in their training as it had not been envisioned as part of a battle tactic in any scenario. It was almost primitive to contemplate the proud German Wehrmacht fighting like Roman gladiators with century-old tools and weapons. But this was now the reality. Often it was more luck than training that was required for the younger men to survive. It was a new type of warfare for them and they came to call it the *Rattenkrieg* – war of rats. And so, in this manner continued the ongoing skirmishes and resulting dilatory progress for weeks on end.

Nonetheless, as October came to an end almost three-quarters of the city had been conquered and German troops filled those occasional central buildings that were still more or less standing. But then the Red Army kick-started back into life, pushing back in small advances and reclaiming territory that had cost so much time and so many lives. At one point Horst, having participated in the long drawn-out battle to secure the 'Tennis Racket' complex at the end of September, found himself posted there once again but one month later. It had been retaken by the Soviets and needed to be liberated again. The whole campaign was starting to resemble a recurring nightmare. There were moments in localized battles in which the Red Army held the cellar, the Wehrmacht the ground floor, and the Red Army again the upper floors; all of the same building. Now it was impossible to ascertain how much of the city had really been taken; in fact, sometimes it seemed as if there were no single spot in this ghastly broken tangle that truly and fully belonged to the Wehrmacht. That which had but a matter of weeks previous seemed so solid and easy to grasp, now kept slipping through their anxious fingers like liquid mud.

The Soviets defended the bridge heads with an intimidating ferocity too and were thus able to receive fresh supplies of food and ammunition, as well as new troops to replace the fallen. Try as they might, this was something the Germans were unable to control or stop. The densely packed nature of the front, in which both German and Soviet troops practically co-existed, made aerial bombings impossible. Even so, they did occasionally take place, in a last ditch attempt to clean out an area of great strategic importance, but naturally with the Luftwaffe inflicting disastrous casualties on their own troops.

This co-existence was so close that Horst and other comrades, hiding in rubble and ruined buildings, sometimes witnessed internal scenes between the Red Army troops. On one occasion he observed from a vantage point a loud argument between a group of Soviet soldiers and their commanding officers. It seemed to him that the soldiers were being pointed to move in the direction of an almost certain death in a hail of German bullets further ahead, and were pleading against this decision. To no avail, as two of the officers produced their pistols and shot the two principal dissenters dead. The other soldiers rushed out in shock into combat but were soon mowed down. Horst, surprised at catching and viewing the scene, had not participated in the volley that had eliminated them, but afterwards felt a deep sense of anger and sadness. He thought of the friends he had made, and mostly lost, along the way; saw how the other side suffered under the same desperation and was being forced to participate in the same futile madness.

As the mortar attacks had left the German radio communication system badly impaired, which further exacerbated their progressively fragile hold on the situation in the face of aggressive Soviet counterattacks, the Wehrmacht relied more and more on the humble *Melder* (running messenger). These were usually the youngest troops who ran, or if lucky rode on bicycles, from one communication point to another, to personally pass on reports and then return with the corresponding responses and orders. In the chaos that followed an especially bloody battle to take the steelworks 'Red October', a group of pale-faced fresh soldiers had arrived at the front together. They had just been through a short training at the very same camp near Hannover that Horst had attended and were nearly all eighteen or nineteen. "*Mein Gott, blutjung!* (My God, so very young!)" Horst muttered as he saw them and sighed with sadness. One of them was immediately put to work as a *Melder* and sent off to the army headquarters in Golubinskaya, where telegraph and telephone lines with connections to Berlin were installed.

In the absence of an officer of higher rank, Horst and another soldier instructed the young recruits in haste about the nature and form of the mission ahead (which sounded ludicrous to Horst even as the words came out), what to expect from the enemy, and what to watch out for. Horst could see these boys were evidently terrified out of their minds. During the training course they had been fed on a heady diet of heroic battles and victorious marches, all to a resounding militaristic music and images of young men hoisting their flag in far-off countries. This jumbled wreck of broken streets and shattered buildings that lay before them, in which the dead and the wounded were incessantly being carried off, at times as if on a conveyor belt, was not what they had expected to face; so swiftly had they been snatched from schools and colleges, rushed through a rudimentary training, to be then transported off to the front in trains and trucks. He wondered if they had even had the time, or the motivation, to contemplate their own deaths.

Afterwards they took positions and awaited further instructions. The new platoon commander arrived, a young sergeant, and began to consult with Horst as to the best route for another attempted advance. Horst was now one of the men with more authority, not because of his age but rather the length of time that he had survived: over two months already. In the meantime he personally knew of very few soldiers that were still alive to boast the same. The messenger boy had just run by a relatively intact wall and was heading towards the soldiers, who were crouching ahead behind a large pile of twisted metal. He was moving stealthily and carefully, clearly listening out for any tell-tale sounds nearby. But as he reached the men, a powerful salvo of machine-gun fire opened up from an angle they had not expected. The lad had just opened his mouth to say, "The Russians…" when the ground sprang up in bullet holes all around them. Horst was running for cover when he tripped and fell into a shallow but adequate shell crater. He turned round in the crater just in time to see the platoon commander also rush for cover but fall in a further salvo. The ground was meticulously raked by machine gun fire until he heard one of the new soldiers shout out the direction from which the shots was coming. Numerous German hand grenades flew in that direction and, following a deafening series of explosions, there was quiet again.

The young German troops instinctively sprinted forward to take the adjoining area that they had now cleared. Horst inspected the body of the platoon commander, a tall dark-haired man in his mid-twenties, and removed the identification disc with the Italian surname. Hearing a moaning sound nearby he found the young messenger, lying against the metal pile in the very same spot where he and the commander had been talking when the fire was first opened on them. He was in great pain and Horst was considering how best to lie him down while he called for a medic, if there was one to be located in this area. The messenger looked at Horst askance and tried to speak, but a heavy flow of blood came out of his mouth, his eyes rolled and then stared blankly ahead. Horst turned him over and saw the line of bullet wounds in his back that had cut him off mid-sentence. He returned him face up, closed the eyes and removed his identification disc too, now grasping two in his hand. He squatted for some moments, for some reason abruptly taken by these two new deaths, although he had already witnessed similar scenes on numerous occasions. But in this case he was conscious of the notion, yet again, that someone had died trying to warn him, trying to protect him. He felt the sense of endless blood being poured into an imaginary bucket, all in order to keep him alive, while he cognized that his life could surely not, under any circumstances, be worth so much sacrifice. Such inner perturbations had disturbed him in recent days, penetrated into dreams in which he was injected with the blood of the fallen and sent off into action, jerky like a wound-up toy soldier.

In that moment he heard the stealthily crunching footsteps of approaching fellow troops; another small platoon was creeping up to assist in the repulsion of this latest counter-offensive of the Red Army. Horst stood up hastily and said, "There are two bodies here, the others have managed to move forward." After inquiring after the platoon commander of these men, he handed over the identification tags to him before being sent off behind the previous group; to help them hold down another few square metres of dirt and debris for a few more days.

By this point in November, the troops were starting to realize that the city would not be taken in the immediate near future, almost certainly not that year. The artillery was hunkering down in miserable holes in the ground which made any serious firefight senseless. Moreover, winter storms would make any decisive aerial offensive, or even logistic support, next to impossible. With a clear change of strategy in the direction of the commands being handed down to them, the commanding officers on the ground settled into the idea of a defensive war of attrition for the foreseeable future, with priority given to maintaining control of those districts that they had already managed to conquer.

As if in answer to their conclusions, the *Oberkommando* (supreme command) of the *Wehrmacht* dictated the cessation of all counteroffensive activities such as the street and house battles that had marked the daily slaughter up till then. Instead, it was decreed, the troops should hunker down for the time being and concentrate on defending the front thus far achieved. In turn, the defensive flanks around Stalingrad should be reinforced to ensure that the enemy did not break through these points. This latter notion, however, never really came to fruition. The gushing streams of new German recruits, that were being taken out of all possible sources and spat out at such a fast rate by the military training programmes, were already being absorbed by the vast eastern front, which stretched out over five hundred kilometres from north to south through the Soviet Union. High casualty rates produced by now meaningless battlefronts like Stalingrad itself, meant that it was impossible to adequately cover with any kind of military logic and tactic such a far-reaching line.

The familiar biting cold returned that Horst knew so well from the year before. The same inactive holding of the front, the same endless stretches of gloomy days and long freezing nights, the same helplessness, the same hopelessness. Also, much that was familiar but now far worse: the icy winds penetrating their coats, the mortar shelling and powerful blasts of machine guns raking the ground around, the constant fear of snipers, the presence of rats: all had increased in intensity. But above all, there was a new element that had now entered the game for the first time: the creeping sense of defeat ahead.

Horst made friends, yet again. He was a thirty-something mechanic from Breslau called Tauber, who had five children back home and was worried sick lest they should have enough to eat that winter. He had lost both siblings, two younger brothers, in the war already: one in the campaign in Belgium, another on the eastern front, up by Smolensk in a major battle there that very summer. His wife Else worked in the administration in the principal hospital in the city and the punctual payment of her salary was vital for the survival of a now large family. She and the children had moved in to live with his parents, themselves now destitute in grief, as well as a widowed sister-in-law with two children. There were no less than eleven mouths to feed in one gloomy apartment. Tauber never expressed even a smidgen of complaint about his own life, so preoccupied was he with the plight of his family back home.

They had been comrades for nearly a week when Tauber received a huge downer. He had been promised furlough for the end of November, had even received an official paper marking down 25th November as the beginning of his leave. He was as excited as a puppy, a large strapping man jumping up and down in glee and then doing a sort of jig before the bemused figures of Horst and others in the platoon. They all laughed heartedly and gladly at the silly sight: there was so little to laugh about these days.

Horst, while sharing in the initial joy, had suspected the worst deep down inside. Sure enough, his fears were later confirmed: the official announcement came through, just days before the given date, that a general *Urlaubssperre* (a ban on all holiday leave) was now in effect. Tauber literally dropped like a sack when he heard the bad news. "What do you expect?" said Schegel, another new member of their platoon, gruff as ever. "We are trapped here. Haven't you realized yet? There will be no way out."

It transpired that the Soviets had recognized how both the Rumanian division defending the front to the north of the 6th Army, as well as the Hungarian forces to the south, were the weak links in the chain. They were not only lacking in equipment or any rigorous training, but most of all they did not possess the fighting spirit and sense of purpose that the German forces did. Like all the other Axis forces, they had quickly realized that they were fighting, and now losing, someone else's war. Hence the Red Army had organized a concerted and tactically perfect offensive to be launched against these two divisions. Their plan was to successfully beat their way through the front at these two points, then curl round in both directions to form a pincer trap around the German 6th Army in Stalingrad. Those always so proudly lauded troops would be fully encircled and helpless; the stranglehold the Soviets maintained around them could then be gradually tightened, like a slow throttling. That was to be the Stalingrad *Kessel* (cauldron), in which the men now found themselves, and there would eventually be, as Schegel had correctly foreseen, no way out for the vast majority of these troops.

It had been during this period of late November that Horst had written a long letter to Inge. It would be his penultimate letter home, but the final one to get through punctually by the field post service to her address at the *Gasthaus Sonnenschein* in Lüneburg. He told her how much he was thinking of her and the children, sent his deepest love to them and to the rest of the family, wished them all a Merry Christmas. He remained optimistic in the letter, against his realistic judgement, about his chances of getting furlough himself early next year. He neatly avoided any details that might be upsetting for them, which basically amounted to almost everything that had actually happened over the last few months. He also knew full well that the letters were controlled and that simply a realistic depiction of life on the front, never mind a long list of lamentations, would be censored and the letter would end up destroyed.

Above all, he did not wish to cause her any more mental anguish than that which she was already going through. And so he opened the letter with loyalist warmth, told of his valiant comrades and their concerted effort to conquer this city they were fighting in for Führer and Fatherland, of the advances that had been achieved so far, and gave a positive analysis of the situation with a view to an upcoming victory. After all that had been dutifully noted in the opening paragraph, he could relax and be more simple and truthful. He went on to express his love for her and the children and his great desire that they should all be together soon, once this part of the mission had been successfully completed. He said how much he was looking forward to coming home and seeing his boys grow up, and teaching them to ride a bicycle and to swim, in the beautiful lakes of the Lüneburger Heide. They would all picnic there as a family again one day. He asked Inge not to forget him but, before signing off, then wondered why he should express such a morbid sentiment. The ink was cast in that final cramped space of the only sheet of paper he had, and he was left feeling uncomfortable with this impetuously written and now regrettable ending. But there was nothing to do, the letter could not be written again and would have to go off with the next *Feldpost*.

On 17th November a storm started to brew during the evening; by midnight it had become a furious blizzard, with howling lashing winds and only pathetic visibility for the troops. For most of the soldiers on the eastern front, of whatever nationality, it was their first Russian winter, and it had arrived with a monstrous prelude. The men hunkered down as best they could and prepared for the long months ahead. Two days later the storm had lifted but a deep cold set in and froze them to their bones. It was at this moment in time that the Soviets launched their offensive to break through the Axis front.

They thundered through the northern flank, taking the land bridge from the Volga to the Don River with enormous strength and complete superiority in both manpower and material weapons. More than a thousand gunmen, backed by mortar and aerial attacks, fired into the northern flank in a storm of steel and fire, sweeping the Hungarian defense aside like rag dolls. At one point a wall of flames measuring almost three kilometres in length stretched across the front, practically wiping out whole companies. Then the Soviet tanks smashed through and finished off the rest.

The following day the Red Army also broke through the Romanian units on the south-western flank, likewise hopelessly outnumbered and in every way inferior, including in morale. Another massacre ensued as the Soviets prevailed. By 23rd November, the two Soviet forces had met up and entirely encircled the invading forces. It was all achieved in a matter of days. Three hundred thousand men, German and other Axis troops including Italians, Austrians, Romanians and Croatians, were trapped. They were hermetically sealed off, hiding in the hostile ruins of a broken city, thousands of kilometres from home, and with next to no more supplies coming through.

Tauber now understood why he would not be going home. And as the subsequent days went by, the others realized that this lamentable situation was now to be applied to all of them in the long run. Their new platoon had found itself stuck among the ruins of a tractor factory in the industrial sector, while heavy and relentless enemy fire ahead was slowing down their advance. The latest young *Melder*, who had been posted to their area in late November in the wake of their encirclement, had survived over a week already. That was a feat of great distinction which earned him much respect all around.

Herberg was his name - a sharp and nimble lad from Großendorf, a small town on the Baltic Sea; always with neatly combed blond hair, only nineteen but with the sagacity of an experienced soldier and the cautious instinct of a feline. He had achieved various levels of distinction within the Hitler Youth and the training certainly showed. His most treasured item, he related one afternoon, was his *Leistungsbuch* (achievement book) from said organization. Added to that, he had the most amiable and out-going character that you could wish for, outside of his frequent rants on race and his angry tirades against Slavs, Jews, and communists, that were too warm and passionate for the older, calmer, and more apolitical men. Horst had never grasped this concept of the 'international alliance between communists and Jewish bankers'; it was a conundrum that had made little sense to him before and was very irrelevant by now. Herberg, once he had learnt which topics to choose, enjoyed conversing with men like Horst and Tauber, who were for him more mature figures with more life experience for him to learn from. He was very eager to improve himself and advance professionally and was already planning a longer military career within the Wehrmacht, even into peacetime once the *Endsieg* (final victory) had been achieved, he related. He had an unshakable confidence in this fact. "The final victory is only a question of will. Our leadership itself has said as much," the teenager once informed them. They had no fitting reply to that.

Some of the other troops in the platoon, and in particular the younger ones, had sunk into a grim silence of disillusionment upon learning the news of their fate in the Soviet pincer; but the older men had a buoyant sense of human comradeship which naturally bred chat and social discourse. Having families with wife and children waiting for them back home, the older men were able to find recourse in the nostalgic visions of harmony that said families brought with them, even in darker moments. As Horst himself commented, in one of the bleak days of early December, "Thinking of Inge and the little ones is sometimes the only thing that keeps me going."

The chatter with Herberg was sometimes tiresome but nonetheless beneficial to the two older men in that it gave them access to information coming in from higher duty stations, which included frank discussions held by senior officers concerning the conditions being faced by the troops and the orders being emitted by the *Oberkommando* back in Berlin. Herberg loved to pass on everything he heard to Horst and Tauber, with a propensity for minute attention to detail and a remarkable sense of both memory and objectivity. In this way, the two men ended up finding out considerably more solid information than the other troops. Bearing in mind the extremely negative nature of much of this, they carefully selected what they passed on.

One important point they did learn, *and* decided to freely share with the others, was that the generals and other higher officers also trapped on the front were practically begging for an immediate cessation to the battle and an aerial evacuation of all troops. There were still two operable airfields, located in the surrounding villages of Pitomnik and Gumrak, and with a well-organized airlift by the Luftwaffe this would be perfectly manageable. The Führer had then emphatically contradicted them and ordered the 6th Army to entrench itself in preparation for the coming winter and to await further military assistance from the outside. Under no circumstances, Hitler had insisted, was Stalingrad to be abandoned to the Bolsheviks. The considered opinion at the *Oberkommando* in Berlin was that this latest offensive was but a last futile attempt, by an already mortally crippled Red Army, to try and take out the famed German army, and that it was an attempt that would be doomed to failure.

The perspective from the Stalingrad front was very different. There was a general awareness that the Wehrmacht simply did not possess the resources to secure the requisite amounts of fresh troops required to break the deadlock, seeing as so many were already wrapped up in other conflicts along the whole breadth of the enormous Soviet front. The officers trapped were acutely aware, and communicated this in great detail and insistence, much to the Führer's chagrin, of the failure of the supply chain to bring in the necessary food, ammunition and adequate winter clothing that the soldiers already stationed there would be requiring. They stopped short of saying that the men would soon begin to starve and freeze to death unless there was a radical change in tactics, but this was implicit in their reports. Still, the Führer stayed his course and insisted in strict obedience of his commands: there would be no evacuation under any circumstances whatsoever.

All this was freely blabbered by Herberg to Horst and Tauber, whenever he returned from one of his many daily missions passing information and commands backward and forward. It was a hopeless situation they were in. Sometimes they didn't know whether to thank him for such a candid transmission of facts or to wish he hadn't spoken in the first place.

December deepened and another brutal winter was set to descend on the men. From one day to the next, the temperatures plummeted and stayed consistently low, hovering between -15° and -20°. As predicted, supplies were now barely getting through. The oft promised and longingly awaited winter clothing never appeared, despite the radio reporting how back in the *Heimat* the citizens were busy donating, sewing and collecting from house to house. There were such bitterly cold days when the men would have given almost their very souls just for a fur-lined coat or well-padded cap and pair of boots. The last few tins of *Fleischkonserven* (preserved meat), a rough mixture of meat and fat, came to an end, as did the bread. The hunger that Horst had experienced in the previous winter was nothing in comparison to the sharp nagging pain that now ripped inside his stomach. It was incessant in its anger and the combination with the cold that made it almost unbearable.

The men had been scavenging for animals in the streets; but the pigeons were gone, there were no dogs left, and the few cats they spotted were sly to their tricks and almost impossible to catch. The sun was equally elusive; appearing occasionally in a weak milky film, devoid of warmth, before disappearing again. One day it hailed with a passion, the hard little stones of ice beating down on the ruins, rattling and rebounding all around them in the gloomy midday grey. It ceased as abruptly as it had begun. Some time later, a snowfall followed in great contrast, tumbling down in large ungainly flakes that filled up the air around. They whitened the streets and covered up the compact ice forming underneath, on the paths the soldiers had made along them, so that these became treacherously slippery.

Tauber and Schegel told Horst how they had recently spent nearly half a day stalking a cat and it had still got away. "At the beginning, when we first got here, they would come up to you, even brushing against your leg and meowing, looking for food. But now they have got wise. They do not come near you," Schegel sniggered bitterly. "I have seen the boys call "*Miezchen, Miezchen*!" (kitty, kitty!) but they just watch from a safe distance. If you do manage to catch one, then you have to smash its skull straightaway otherwise it becomes this incredible savage fury of clawing and biting. I saw a soldier who actually got so scratched he ended up badly injured because he was too slow. He was bleeding like he had been shot! Haha!" he laughed.

"What is it like, the…the meat?" asked Horst with the shudder inside of foreseeing a complicated winter ahead.

"Very tasty, and much more tender than we thought it would be," said Schegel, suddenly quite serious as he remembered the meal with fondness. "We had it in a soup with some pasta noodles that someone had found. We were half-a-dozen men and had two good hot bowls and more than enough bread, too."

They continued that day scavenging for firewood and perhaps an animal, a tin of food, a scrap of something remotely edible. The wind was icy, seeming to not only cut through to the bone but to the very marrow of the bone, as Horst imagined. At night, cowering in their shelters, they warmed themselves as best they could while the lice, also looking for warmth and food, multiplied on their dirty bodies.

Then, in the second December week, a surprise opportunity reared its head: Horst and Tauber were probably going to have a chance to escape from the deadly encirclement around Stalingrad after all! They hugged and jumped on the spot when they found out the news, could hardly believe their luck.

They were approached one darkening afternoon, after a meal from freshly arrived supplies, by the commanding officer of the company at that point, *Oberstleutnant* (lieutenant-colonel) Sämig. He opened the conversation by stating how he knew they were a mechanic and a fireman and thought them to be perfect for driving a small army truck on an assignment. One of his troops - a young staff sergeant and radio communication expert who had been awarded the Iron Cross for bravery - had been badly wounded during a mortar attack by the Red Army that morning. He had lost a leg and a lot of blood, and it was not clear whether he would make it under these conditions. Sämig seemed very eager to have him evacuated and handed them the requisite forms for the man to be immediately air-lifted out of the encirclement that the Soviets had created.

"There are only two functioning airfields, as I am sure you know," he said. "Namely, Pitomnik and Gumrak. Those are our two connections to the air-bridge and it is through those two aerodromes that we are receiving all the incoming supplies and also, in some emergency cases, evacuating the badly wounded. So your mission is to get this man to the airfield at Pitomnik and make sure he is placed onto one of the outgoing planes, with priority. The situation is rather chaotic there to say the least, as I am given to understand. So, you might have to be very…" He considered for a moment, "Let's say, persuasive. Or even insistent." Horst and Tauber both understood this to mean bribery and/or coercion. It was not clear with what exactly they were supposed to bribe someone but the men indicated their comprehension.

The rest of the details were as follows: Their official mission, should any officers from the *Wehrmacht* stop them to ask, was not only to put the wounded hero on an outboard flight, but also to pick up a large load of supplies, namely medical supplies for those few still operational field hospitals in Stalingrad, and bring them back to the city. The injured man's name was *Mäuschen* ('Little Mouse'), the lieutenant-colonel informed them with a straight face. "That is his nickname and that is what we have always called him." Only later did Horst and Tauber read on the ID forms that the man's surname was also 'Sämig' and they found out that he was a cousin of the officer. Hence his keen desire to help his severely hurt relative to return home.

There were expected to be several tonnes of supplies arriving that day, through a fleet of Ju 52s, but the veracity of these announcements was always touch and go, the officer admitted. "A lot of the planes are being intercepted by the Soviets and shot down. Further to that, a landing is often impossible due to bad weather conditions. So I have no way of knowing what exactly has arrived, but that is the information that I have been given." He then went on indicate, in a most roundabout manner, that he would have all the understanding in the world, upon finding that said supplies had not arrived after all, or perhaps even if they had, if the men were to simply board a plane themselves together with Mäuschen and "get the hell out."

He also warned them of the increasingly bleak and snarled situation at the airfields, where deserters were furtively amassing in large numbers and forged official certificates of injury were worth gold. Furthermore, the morale among the troops gathering there had plummeted to hopelessness and animalistic desperation. "They see death approaching and will do next to anything to try to break through the organizational structure and board the first plane out. We had a case three days ago in which a plane carrying injured troops on stretchers was already overfilled, and then a further number of uninjured troops managed to get on board too. When the plane took off, the stretchers all slid to the back and the healthy men tumbled after them. The combined weight suddenly transferred to the back of the plane and it was too much. The plane fell back vertically and crashed just after the airfield, no survivors. Bear in mind this kind of thing. If you see a very chaotic situation, with the pilots being harassed or soldiers trying to force their way onboard, you would be advised to look for a different option. And if there is no other way, then so be it."

He surreptitiously slipped Tauber a pair of gold watches, in case of any necessary bribery. He said, "Take good care of the lad, please. He means a lot to me and to my parents. By the way, I know you both have wives and children waiting for you at home. Think of them." With that, he loyally saluted with the 'German greeting' and led them to the truck that was waiting, with a barely conscious and moaning Mäuschen already loaded into the back on a stretcher. In the front, by the driver's seat, were a bunch of grenades to provide extra support for their machine guns, should they be spotted and fired at by Red Army patrol units.

The evening dark had fallen and they headed off, headlamps turned off so as not to attract the enemy fire. It was a wide road to Pitomnik and a light snowstorm had kicked in, filling the air with thick swirling flakes. They could hardly see the way and were thankful for a relatively well filled-out moon that was reflected in the snow and gave them enough visual assistance to stay on the road. Every now and again there was a jolt and a bump as they drove over something large lying on the roadside. It was only as they concentrated more closely on the route ahead that they realized to their horror that the forms lying around were the dead or dying bodies of *Versprengte* (scattered soldiers) from the Wehrmacht, and that they were rolling over. Horst was driving and Tauber beside him thumped repeatedly at the dashboard in front, in hot fury. "This damned mad war! Shit!" he yelped.

They finally arrived at the airport in the early hours and the scene was grotesque. Crowds of men had filled the area between the landing strips and the administrative buildings behind. Many were limping or clearly badly injured, and a large group were lying on stretchers, like Mäuschen. Everyone who could stand up straight was jostling and trying to get to speak to the few military personnel and medics organizing the flights. The racket was infernal between the noise of men and the planes; the atmosphere was one of high-level aggression waiting to explode. Even after months of battle, Horst and Tauber were taken aback.

They looked around and saw a number of Ju 52 planes being refueled and prepared for take-off at dawn, with supplies having been unloaded and injured men now being loaded up into them in the cargo space. But it was crystal clear that the amount of aviation available was grossly inadequate for the waiting soldiers, fervidly trying to leave and knowing this was the only way left. It was in most cases a matter of life and death and so arguments, even fist fights, were breaking out among the men as to who could board this time and who couldn't. The military units in charge there, and the pilots and crew of the planes, were all attempting to keep order as best they could, but the desperation and panic had made desperate beasts out of the men and the collapsing situation reflected this.

Horst and Tauber donned their white snow suits and helped Mäuschen out of the truck, taking him over to one of the supervising officials and registering him for an outboard flight. Mäuschen was delirious by now and they handed over his ID and medical documents and explained the urgency. "Look around you, everything is urgent," responded the official dryly. Tauber nervously fingered the gold watches in his pocket, never having bribed anyone in his life.

Fortunately a medic soon appeared and, after examining Mäuschen and flicking through the forms, he gave a nod and let Horst and Tauber carry the stretcher over to a nearby plane. There, they heard the pilot arguing with a high-ranking officer, a general perhaps and clearly in good health, who was trying to convince him to let him board the plane. An altercation between the two was clearly escalating, with the pilot insisting the plane was full while the officer moved in tactic from loud angry threats to a hushed attempt at bribery in order to secure a seat. Still the pilot refused. The volume rose and others began to gather around, seeing to try their luck. Horst and Tauber looked round and spotted another plane somewhat further along the snow-driven terrain, and they shuffled off as quickly as they could toward it. They had more luck and were able to have Mäuschen swiftly placed onboard by two waiting medics.

Once that part of the mission was fulfilled, they stepped back and looked at each other. Were they really going to try to escape by somehow boarding that plane or perhaps another one in the fleet? The air was heavy with the shouting of men, the roaring of propellers and engines. The howling wind had increased in intensity and the storm seemed to be budding into a full-scale blizzard. The pilots were obviously desperate to take off while they still could.

"We can't just stand here in the middle of the airfield!" shouted Tauber at Horst, and they looked at each other. The look lingered, despite the snow and the din and the frantic activity all around, until Horst had an epiphany. He had been in this situation before, some years ago in Lüneburg. Whatever the familial consideration, this was not the moment to put himself and his easy comfort first, when his whole vocation was supposed to be oriented around altruism.

"Do you want to try to get out?" he shouted back at Tauber. "You go if you want! Someone will take the watches off you and let you in!"

Tauber paused to reflect, but then shook his head. He would have happily left the supplies, which he assumed had not even arrived, but he wouldn't leave Horst here alone. If this ridiculous conflict had taught him one thing, it was the unconditional love for a fellow man, a fellow soldier, that only this near-death camaraderie held. Horst put his arm round Tauber's shoulders and led him away from the droning and whirring of the planes.

They found a military officer in charge of dispatching cargo, showed him the paperwork from Oberstleutnant Sämig, followed him over to the collecting point. They could see how some of the boxes had already been looted; food supplies, they presumed. They located the batch that corresponded to them – it had indeed been delivered, punctual and correct - and gazed at each other again for a questioning moment. They smiled grimly at each other and Tauber said, "You know, Horst, I do not mind being stupid. I can die happily knowing I am stupid. But not if I am a self-centred animal or a cheap crook. I am a soldier and a soldier should have dignity. If not, the war is never won, even if it is."

They shunted the truck over to the collecting point and loaded up the crates. Dawn was breaking and the first planes were coasting down the runway and, too heavily loaded, were whining and struggling to thrust up into the dreary winter sky. With a little weak early sunlight, they drove back to Stalingrad in good spirits and with the supplies they had been sent to fetch. They were fired at on the way but managed to dodge the attack and, reaching their old district, that still seemed impossible to conquer and hold down, they handed over the crates and kept the gold watches. They got a promotion for their pains. A general came to congratulate them for their bravery, shake their hands and tell them they were now to be considered as *Unteroffizier* (non-commissioned officers). Both Horst and Tauber thanked him and saluted back, looking grimly at the corpulent middle-aged man before them.

The rest of that December dragged on in a series of endless skirmishes. The front between the Red Army and the Wehrmacht was as blurred and indistinguishable as the horizon separating the cloudy sky and the snow-covered ground, and there was the sense of continually going backward and forward in fruitless relocations. Then the Soviets upped the game considerably and commenced an aggressive drive against the Wehrmacht's western flank, pushing deeper into the city in an attempt to jostle them right to the banks of the Volga. They blasted at the men with all the heavy weaponry they had; wave after wave of 'Stalin organ-pipes' were fired at Wehrmacht positions. Heavy artillery rained down on the dwindling front and smashed open many of the few buildings that had withstood the war so far. The Germans tried desperately to organize new lines of defense, often in the midst of icy winds and blizzards, but ultimately to no avail. Their numbers were weakened and so little was getting through, whether ammunition or food or medical supplies. Thousands of injured soldiers were dying in the makeshift hospitals through lack of staff or adequate treatment. With the intense Soviet attacks, the demand for treatment was at an all-time high. Antibiotics were lacking and there was barely any alcohol to sterilize with. Men were lying around with festering and untreated wounds, succumbing to sepsis or pneumonia, hyperthermia or typhus or an endless list of pathologies, though first and foremost to starvation. Gangrene was rampant, and those lucky enough to have located a doctor who was free and available to carry out an amputation, would go through it without anaesthetic.

The Wehrmacht fought on with feverish determination, worn down by frost and hunger, giving their all for a few chunks of stale bread, seeking shelter in holes in the snowy streets and buildings as they shifted from one collapsing line to another. This was partly possible because many still believed in the promise of assistance coming in from the outside, or even a possible full-scale evacuation taking place. Of course, it was never going to be the case and so, with the men assailed by cold, hunger, disease, and the constant ferocious Soviet offensives, the mass dying eventually began. Whole platoons withered away. The Germans found themselves pushed inexorably back into the dismal interior of the city, as the Soviets tightened the noose around them.

The situation was extremely severe in the outer districts where the troops were more exposed to the elements and where the Soviets were now nearly smashing through. Horst's platoon had been fighting near to the city centre, slipping from one bunker to another for sleep and shelter but had been spared the utter annihilation taking place further out. All the same, the conditions were miserable. The daily ration of bread was already down to just 50 grams a day. Rags were metaphorically worth gold; when found, they were ripped into lines that could be wrapped around the head, then the feet, changing regularly so that both received at least some insulation for a certain number of hours. That insulation was also necessary to stop the steel helmets from literally freezing to the soldiers' heads. Old parasites returned: fleas and lice became a horrendous suffering, prickling as they swarmed the bodies of the men huddled up inside their dirty clothes, desperately trying to stay warm. The pests bit through into their very sleep so that they fell asleep itching and woke again itching.

Horst's nights were hellish. In one recurring dream he stood aloft on his ladder back in Lüneburg, standing erect and proud in his uniform while the town centre burnt down before him. He held a hose in his hand but did nothing, watched people screaming and running away, trying to escape the flames. Some of them he knew, others he recognized as Jews, others still he instinctively knew from the dream that they were Jews. Swastika flags fluttered over the flames and further down the road Wehrmacht troops were waiting, ready to shoot down the fleeing figures as soon as they came nearer. He could see them running obliviously into the trap. Horst stood there passively, unable to move his legs, only able to observe in silence. His throat was clamped, he could not even shout a warning. He heard Inge pleading with him somewhere in the night, a voice without form, but he could not respond. He could only look ahead from his elevated height, over the smoking rooftops. The scene morphed almost unnoticeably and he was now standing on a hill, overlooking Stalingrad. He heard the natter of machine gun fire and felt sick to his stomach; woke up in shivers to find his empty stomach was churning, his skin itching.

Toward the end of the second week of December, *Melder* Herberg was finally caught out by a grenade which landed in an unexpected moment right beside him, just as he was passing on orders to the company commander, Feldwebel (Staff Sergeant) Bucher. Both received a full blast of burning sharp splinters close up and were killed on the spot. Tauber took on the task of writing a letter to Herberg's parents, as he had promised to do. He dutifully praised the young man's courage and skill as well as commenting on how it had been a pleasure to get to know him. He and Horst later agreed on how amazed they were that a messenger could last three whole weeks.

Chapter 24

It was 19th December and Hans Tauber had stated that very fact with great aplomb in the morning as the weak sun came through the slits and holes in the corners of the cellar. He was keeping track of time for them, penciling each day off around dawn and announcing it; everyone assumed that he was right and acknowledged the fact with a grunt or a sigh. It had now become a random, meaningless number. What was twenty as opposed to fifteen or twenty-two? Since they had found out they were not going anywhere, it no longer mattered to them, just as little as the nineteenth of December held any significance to the rats or other animals scratching out a bare existence in the winter ruins. As with those creatures, it was simply another day in which it would once again be decided whether this animal or that made it all the way through to the end; or whether instead they left their life behind on that nameless piece of ground at that nameless point in time. With the men it was a similar challenge as with the rats, with the singular difference that the men's mortality rate was far higher.

All the same Tauber insisted that in order to fight against the growing insanity, a condition which just such an attitude had begun to facilitate, it was all the more important to mark the spot and make it clear, and to be very aware of the fact, that today was the nineteenth. He tapped the wall with the pencil emphatically. Not the fifteenth, when they had passed through a long session of dull distant explosions, nor the twenty-second, which may or may not await them, but rather this specific day – the 19th December. This day was special because each day of life was special, Tauber stated. There came neither agreement nor disagreement.

They were hunkered down in the cellar of an apartment building near to the city centre. It had been quite a find in more ways than one for the platoon, with its stash of boxes of tinned food hidden away in one corner which had been located and quickly gobbled up in a few days by a dozen desperately hungry mouths. There was even tuna fish among the tins – the men thought they must be hallucinating when they first opened them up and smelt the contents. They also found a large bundle of warm woolen blankets that were greeted with the wide eyes of sheer ecstasy once they came to light. There were nooks and little spaces in the cellar where trunks and boxes of all natures were theirs to open up. It was such fine and gentle looting, they took their time once their bellies were full after the first round. Two whole days were spent rooting through the basement in hope of locating some treasure; this occupied the men's minds and brought them back a smidgen of hope, keeping them sane. They kept the cellar's hidden treasures a secret from other nearby platoons, only to ascertain in the end how limited those treasure really were.

The cellar had been in the process of being converted into a provisional air raid shelter for the occupants, before then being abandoned: hence those few hoarded treats and trinkets. It was bare but comfortable and mostly intact, even though considerable damage had been sustained by the building that had once stood above. It was a four-storey apartment block and grenades had smashed through higher up, completely destroying some of the apartments on the upper floors, while leaving part of the roof precariously intact and the ground floor still sturdy. During a later mortar attack, further sections of the higher floors had all tumbled down onto the street around, now just leaving a few sections of the upper walls and the almost complete but burnt-out shell of the ground floor. Despite these attacks, the cellar ceiling had not given way, although a small section of the far north-east corner of the ceiling was completely gone; this had been plugged up with a mixture of rubble and bric-a-brac from the cellar floor to keep the penetration of the freezing gusts to a minimum. A rough general coldness filled the air, particularly at night, but at least they were sheltered from the dreaded bite of the wind. By day, they had a reasonably good view of the outside area, especially when they climbed up to the first floor (the second floor had no stairs and was completely cut off) to check if the enemy had tried to sneak into the area.

They were in contact with other isolated platoons but there was little left to do except hold the area from enemy incursions as best they could. The headquarters company sent out messengers who relayed the latest state of the zone, gave the occasional order to fetch or locate supplies, carried out liaison with other companies in the area. But the chain of command was breaking down with each passing day, reduced to a series of occasional and desultory orders. The only real mission left was to simply hold on to the district in which they were located and stave off as best they could the ever approaching enemy. No easy task when the tanks and trucks barely had fuel enough to move; when the German machine guns kept jamming in the intense cold while the cleverly-designed Russian Kalashnikovs worked just fine. There were gradually fewer times that the punctual *Lagebesprechung* (military briefing) was called as there was so little left to discuss. In the end they fizzled out altogether. Outside the cold numbed most activity during the day. Night after night the frost fell over the silent streets and carried off any life it caught there.

There were seven of them in the cellar on this day of 19th December, all that was left of the company. Horst Grün; Hans Tauber; Beck, a dull nineteen-year-old with short black hair, still wide-eyed and innocent, firmly believing in the final victory and refusing to be crushed by despair; Westermann, a plump street sweeper in his forties from Hamburg, whom they affectionately called '*alter Fischkopf*' (old Fish-head) after he told them how everyone else did and how he had grown fond of the nickname; Schegel, the facetious and cynical Sudeten German and owner of a pawn shop; the quiet and solid Rohrbach with his prematurely grey hair, once a history teacher in a well-to-do private school, living in a large house on the Starnberger See, now a role model to most of them with his calm Christian faith and strength of character; and finally a hulking bear of a man called Pietsch who was down to muttering the odd phrase and quietly going mad in the corner.

There had been twelve soldiers sheltering there, up until a couple of days earlier when five of them, including their own platoon commander, were tempted by hunger and hopelessness to desert and seek a way out. They had decided to make a last-ditch attempt to break through to one of the two still operational airports and had left after midnight, thus contravening the official instructions to stay put. "Anything is better than rotting here in this hole," the commander, a lieutenant in his late twenties, had commented as he left. "Even death is better than this." The others had heard heavy machine gun fire about half an hour later, but that was nothing new. The five men never returned. Beck said he hoped they had made it; the others kept quiet and nonchalantly assumed they had died.

The Soviets advances continued and by now most field hospitals had been seized; the bed-ridden were shot and the others taken prisoners. Radio communication with the outside was increasingly difficult. Nearly all the horses had long been slaughtered by now and there was barely a piece of meat to be had anywhere. The hunger was further exacerbated by the biting cold. The men's stomachs screamed out during long phases as a little crisp bread and a spoonful of canned meat in heated water had become standard rations, apart from the occasional supplement of trapped rat that only Pietsch and Schegel would eat. Most rats though were too sly and quick for the benumbed men and managed to stay out of harm's way. Indeed, sensing that these large animals around them might well be on their last legs, offering a potentially huge carcass of meat, the rats seemed to have increased of late in numbers. At least if the nightly squeaking was anything to go by.

That was the case too in most of the buildings in the surrounding streets, where numerous platoons and individual men lay hidden in ruins and trenches and dug out holes. Westermann swore a couple of days later that one had bit at his foot in the night and now everyone was paranoid. Physically malnourished and psychologically listless through apathy, the men were living increasingly under the blankets which they tucked tightly around them whilst sleeping, although a small part of the head was always exposed. Beck was terrified beyond belief; it was a nightmare come true for him. He knew of a private from another platoon that had been bitten by a rat one night. It had taken a chunk out of his cheek. The other soldiers had come to his aid straightaway and put on a bandage, but a week later he was dead. His head had swollen up and turned black. Beck couldn't believe how toxic the little beasts must be. Tauber wondered out loud if they carried the plague with them. And so Beck, in terrible fear of gnawing omnipresent rats, asked Horst to always watch over him while he slept, which Horst faithfully did.

In the days leading up to Christmas, wild rumours sparked into life yet again, like a forest fire that keeps on re-igniting in some spot and refuses to go out. They concerned the imminent arrival of a relief force from outside the cauldron they were trapped in, to come to their rescue and create an air bridge to fly them out. It had been passed out on the street from one company to another, and the more it was repeated, the more it was believed. It seemed absurd to many, and more than just that – it was a cruel fata morgana in such times, like a tasteless joke. Yet the more absurd the vision that appeared, the more eagerly it was grasped. Even upon grasping thin air, for many it was still to be held on to.

Finally on 23rd December, and much to Horst's relief, several voices among the local ranks of officers were heard to extinguish the false rumours of evacuation for once and for all, as they sent the word around that it was definitively not taking place. The troops' instructions were to hold out as best they could and make sure that their district did not fall into enemy hands. The question as to how this was supposed to be carried out if they were near to starving and possessing only a bare minimum of ammunition, was no longer even asked. The whole series of incongruities seemed to be just a further part of this nightmarish labyrinth of senselessness in which they could neither win nor surrender.

That day Horst set about writing, as best he could move his fingers in the cold, a last letter to his family. Given the circumstances, he knew it was highly uncertain as to whether it would ever arrive. But he took the task seriously, told the others of his activity and where on his person to find the letter, should he not survive. He was desperate to tell his wife how much he loved her, how much he had loved her from the first time he had set eyes on her, and how – even though she would think him silly – he often recalled down to the last detail that most wonderful day in his life, when they married in church. He wrote how he would always go on loving her every minute of every day after finishing the letter. He sincerely apologized to her for each and every occasion on which he had caused her any distress or pain, whether with intention or unwittingly; asking her, in the case that he didn't make it through, that she would remember him as a flawed but faithful man. His loyalty - and loyalty was a concept that he had come to profoundly meditate upon in these last few painful months - had always been one hundred percent directed at his wife and his sons. Nothing else in the world mattered a jot in comparison.

Where he felt great pride in his life (and at that moment in time he felt so little pride, though he did not admit this to her) was in his marriage to a wonderful woman and equally wonderful mother of the most precious children a man could hope for.

Horst was desperate to open his soul and tell her the whole unadorned truth about how he now viewed the war and the events that had led up to it. He hoped (and later requested) that one of his comrades would personally deliver the epistle to her and thereby sneak it through any censorship controls. Hence he took the liberty to address the children openly and directly, telling Inge to let them see the letter when they were old enough to understand what he hoped to be able to accurately express.

He apologized for his absence as a father; and he apologized for the terrible and erroneous decisions that his nation, including he himself, had made. He wished them instead all the serenity, wisdom, happiness, and above all peace in the world for the future. He wanted to make them understand that there was no gain to be had, nor sense to be made, from destroying that which others had created with their own hard labour; that there was no place in the world for hatred toward those who thought or prayed differently; that there was no meaning to an existence in which a man had to kill just to stay alive. They should instead strive to achieve a different world from the one they had been born into; one in which they could learn to live in harmony with neighbours, whatever the differences, for their own sake and one day for the sake of their children. He was sure that day would come, he wrote, but it depended on them to create that future, guided by those nobler sentiments and attitudes that all people were capable of if they only made the effort. If there was anything to learn from his own hard lesson, it should be that his mistakes would lead to their enlightenment, and through that to their ultimate happiness; for he loved them more than anything in the world, including his life itself. And most importantly of all, he concluded with an exclamation mark, they were to take good care of their mother!

He filled the one sheet he had, on both sides, to the very full. Even though he was scratching away with clumsy and half-frozen fingers, it was still a remarkably well-formed handwriting and he was perfectly content with the letter once it was finished. There was among the supplies still a few envelopes left, so he was able to seal it up and place Inge's name and address clearly on the front. Relieved that he had been able to speak to her one more time, he settled back against the grimy wall behind him.

A little later, he talked to Tauber and their conversation inevitably turned to Christmas with the family, the times they had once known in the streets and houses in which they had once celebrated, which all now seemed more distant than the Moon. Horst confessed how much he had loved having the traditional fir tree in the house and how that was the highlight of Christmas for him.

In the evening, Tauber took advantage of a slight snowstorm to go on a scavenging foray. These storms always offered him cover and more importantly psychological comfort against his great fear of the rogue snipers who occasionally slipped through the crumbling front to take out any stray German soldiers from their hidden vantage points. First, he went to speak to an officer in a nearby bunker, who had nothing new to relate but was glad of a few minutes of idle conversation. On his way back, Tauber looked around to see if there was anything to be found on the streets. He only brought back some firewood but was delighted to find that one of the twigs resembled in its intricate form – albeit with much imagination - a miniature tree. He also had a big surprise for Horst for when he got back. Among the bits and pieces that he had hoarded away in the cellar, there were a little strand of red ribbon, dirty but still clearly red, and a shiny star-shaped stud that looked to have fallen off some garment. He had also located the week before a small green, elegantly shaped bottle, such as those he had seen in pharmacies, and put it to one side.

Once everything was prepared, he took his creation and placed it on the large makeshift table in the centre of the room, then called Horst over. He stood in front to hide it from sight, waiting until Horst was right beside it before revealing it all with a triumphant "ta-dah!" The strip of red ribbon had been wrapped around part of the twig, which was then placed in the little green bottle to keep it standing upright. On the top, the star-shaped metal stud had been secured and sat there neatly as the crowning glory. By its side, Tauber had placed a candle, their penultimate candle, on a small chipped old plate. Rays of the flickering candlelight were being caught in the surface of the stud, making it twinkle. It was a pathetic sight, of course, but at the same time the most wonderful Christmas tree imaginable. The other men also approached out of curiosity and all of their faces, even Pietsch's, lit up at the festive vision. They gathered round this twig in a bottle and contemplated it in silence and with solemnity.

That day, the soup was thinned down even more, making it by now practically heated up water. "At least we can rely on a regular supply of snow," said Tauber with a grim chuckle. "That never fails." The reasoning behind this thinning down was so that they could have a thicker soup for the following day, for the Christmas Eve supper, for which they would also use up the last sliver of horsemeat sausage. Afterwards they would go back to thinning down the rations further; but at least let this one special day, this holy day of every year, be allowed to offer something to look forward to, just as it always had done in whatever moments of scarcity they had endured in the past.

The next evening there was quiet on the eastern front and they were able to celebrate a Christmas service to honour the birth of Jesus Christ, the Son of God; which they did at midnight on the dot, sticking to their timetable with a feverish respect for punctuality. Even in these pitiful conditions, as someone commented, some virtues should still be upheld. Schegel had laughed cynically but at twelve o'clock at night they all rose in unison. Rohrbach, a deeply devout Catholic back home, was able to perform a remarkably realistic service. He used to play the piano and organ in peacetime, he told them, and had always helped out at the school's pre-Christmas service: thus he had a solid voice and natural musicianship, as well as being familiar with many of the prayers.

At the end of this expedient service they bowed their heads and worshipped God: both thanking Him for all that they still had, as well as supplicating Him for a prompt deliverance from this misery.

There followed a hearty rendition of *Silent Night* around the decorated Christmas twig, during which the men mustered up considerable strength and power of voice, helped along in the lyrics by Rohrbach's firm example. From the dirty stinking cellar under the ruins of an almost demolished apartment block, carried along in the flurries of snow outside, travelled the deep hoarse plaintive but still resolute strains of that most famous of Christmas carols, down the dark streets: "*Stille Nacht, heilige Nacht. Alles schläft, einsam wacht…*"

After that came thick soup with the last few lumps of horsemeat and extra bread. Plus, the pièce de résistance: Tauber had found a tin of peas a few days earlier and had saved it up for the evening's stew. In they plopped and it was all so dense and nourishing, it was heavenly. If only every day could be Christmas, sighed Westermann and everyone laughed and nodded.

Outside the temperature had fallen yet further that evening and hit -25°C. They should be grateful, Beck commented grimly. He told how he had heard how in the outer limits of the suburbs, where the Red Army was advancing rapidly and the soldiers were under heavy fire as well as literally starving to death, it had fallen to as far down as -35°C in the icy blasts of wind that swept in from the open plains. "Might as well just shoot yourself," rumbled Schegel.

Later they turned on the standard Wehrmacht radio receiver that they had dragged to the cellar upon first 'moving in', and true to expectations it still seemed to have some life left in the battery. If one thing in this whole hellhole was not going to fail them, then it was going to be good old reliable German technology, Horst laughed. They listened - with the surreal sense of taking part in a fictional movie - to a broadcast from the *Grossdeutschen Rundfunk*, the official German radio channel. A voice was telling their countrymen back home in familiar strident tones about the brave men of the 6th Army, still courageously holding out against the enemy in Stalingrad and fighting for the future of their Fatherland. The speaker painted a quaint and heroic picture of the front, it seemed, almost as if knights of old were charging into battle on a daily basis in gleaming steel armour. In any case, one that had nothing to do with this reality of filth, hunger, lice, cold, and endless waiting.

"Do they really believe all that tosh?" asked Tauber at one point, exasperated. The show predictably ended with *Stille Nacht*, where to everyone's sheer astonishment the speaker informed that it would be sung, no less, by a choir posted out near the battlefield, on the banks of the Volga. It was by then midnight back in the *Heimat*. The men stood or squatted down in amazement to hear this remarkable harmonious performance, so professionally accomplished and with dense orchestral accompaniment too; and all allegedly taking place not far from their bunker.

"Midnight mass on the Volga?" said Horst, shaking his head.

"That's just ridiculous!" spat Schegel, while Westermann whined pitifully, "They're lying, they're lying."

Only Beck had some comprehension for the specious show. "You have to believe if you are going to fight. And we are all fighting now, even back home."

Everyone was relieved when the battery pack finally gave out half-way through the carol and the radio receiver shut up for good. They returned to their positions and initially enjoyed the silence of the night that reigned outside. There were no mortar shelling, machine gun salvos or Stalin organ-pipes on that eve. But on the next day, on Christmas Day in the morning, they heard the sound of heavy artillery and machine gun fire coming from a westerly direction. The Russian bombardment continued relentlessly. The men slipped back into lassitude.

Two days before New Year, Pietsch got up and walked up the stairs leading out of the cellar, turning the corner into a small anteroom by the entrance on the ground floor. There he could be heard sobbing for a while. Nobody thought anything of it until suddenly he shot himself in the head. The other men rushed up as they heard the shot, and froze to cross themselves before the corpse. In the night, they took it outside and buried him under pieces of frozen rubble as best they could. Tauber once more proved himself to be a man always ready to create something out of nothing; he stuck a cross he had made out of a rotten floorboard, with Pietsch's name, rank and date of death etched into it with charcoal, into the makeshift tomb.

They were down to six now but still the soup thinned down endlessly. The men's bodies craved in vain for fat and sugar, if only just a couple of grams. Not only their limbs had become slow and clumsy but their brains too, sometimes as if even the process of thought itself was numb and stiff like their fingers. "How are we supposed to carry on when we just piss away whatever we eat?" said Schegel to the wall.

Horst had the presentiment that these were the men he was going to die with. How strangely random was this destiny, he considered as the feeling grew, and the way in which the final moments of this little group of souls would be drawn together by the inexplicable, inscrutable threads of fate, rather than in the caring hands of families or among the familiar voices of home. It was not even so much death itself that made him despair, but the misery of perishing here in this bleak trap of a basement, in a country in which he had only seen men kill each other, in which he barely understood a word of the language, in which everything was irregular and unfamiliar and ultimately painful. In these final days of the Stalingrad Cauldron he recalled often, through images and short clips of film-like sequences, his old way of life back in Lüneburg. He contemplated it with the bitter acknowledgment of just how much one unwisely took for granted in this ephemeral and unpredictable world.

They spent New Year's Eve listening to the sound of fierce fighting on the city periphery, heard the all too familiar wailing sound of the Stalin organ-pipes bringing in the New Year. Beck announced the exact point at which 1942 ended and 1943 began. "But in Germany, right? Not in this shithole," asked Tauber. Beck nodded, "In Berlin." Horst shivered and didn't care either way.

Later in the night there was a long pause in the shelling and Beck timidly suggested, "We could all make a wish. For the New Year."

Everyone laughed. Beck frowned at first at the mockery but joined in the general laughter as he caught on. "And what would that wish be, I wonder?" guffawed Schegel.

After a while, once the laughter had died down, Westermann said soberly, "The lad's right in a way, though. In this very moment I am only wishing for a glass of beer. I was just thinking, I could stay here forever if I could just have a last beer, just here, right now."

Rohrbach pondered. "Why don't we all tell each other our favourite meal and we could wish for that? This is, after all, a time for miracles and for faith."

Tauber shrugged. "Might as well. Anything to forget all of this."

Beck was now unsure about his own idea and said, "What if it makes us even more hungry? It might be like torture."

Horst laughed bitterly and shook his head. "Nothing could make me any more hungry. I have been so hungry for so long, it has become the natural way to be."

They mumbled in agreement; and so each shared a meal and wished for the others that they may enjoy that very meal again, some future day.

Rohrbach began, with his ever genial and lulling voice. There he sat in the dark filthy cellar, in the freezing cold and the stench, awaiting another round of the thundering of shelling from afar, and calmly began to paint his image in the air as if they were sitting in the plush set of a cinema film. "My wife makes the most delicious *Krustenbraten* (pork roast with crackling) with *Dunkelbiersoße* (dark beer sauce) and *Semmelknödel* (southern German bread dumplings), and that is what I would choose. The beer for the sauce is made with a König Ludwig dark beer, and I would have a bottle of that to accompany the meal."

Westermann nodded, seeing the beer swaying in the air before alighting before him. "Much of the finest beer in the world comes from Bavaria."

Rohrbach continued, "She would make some fried carrot and celery, and decorate the plate with some sprigs of parsley because, as she has often said, and she couldn't be more right, you eat first with your eyes. And then you slice the *Krustenbraten*, and dip it in the *Dunkelbiersoße*, and then you cut up the *Semmelknödeln* and dip them in the *Dunkelbiersoße*, and then scoop up a little spoon of vegetables and dip …"

"In the *Dunkelbiersoße*," laughed Tauber and Horst.

"Exactly," smiled Rohrbach. "Again and again till there is nothing left except some of the sauce and you would lick the plate clean if it were not for a sense of table manners."

"Oh, I would lick the plate clean alright," said Tauber with a sigh. "A thousand times over."

"And for dessert she would make a *Kaiserschmarrn* (Austrian fluffy shredded pancake with berry jam and cream)."

Beck, despite his earlier qualms, joined in with enthusiasm and piped up with the next contribution. He retained the detail, as introduced by Rohrbach, of a dish frequently prepared by a beloved woman in his family. "I would love to have some *Kümmelkartoffel* (potatoes in cumin), like my mother makes them."

Some of them laughed, bemused. "What's that?"

Beck laughed along too, but then they all became deadly serious as he described them. "She fries up some bacon and onions in lard, and then she adds the cooked potatoes to that. On top of that come salt and pepper, and then she sprinkles lots and lots of cumin, and it all fries up together. In the Rhineland that is quite common. And I would have two *Frikadellen* (large flat German meatballs) with it. No three. Four! And on the side of the plate a nice green salad. That would all be wonderful together!"

There was a pause.

"And the dessert? What about the dessert?" Tauber pressed him, eager for more details.

Beck had no idea and said spontaneously, with a childish grin, "Ice cream. Two scoops, I think. Strawberry and chocolate."

There followed a brief pause.

"I shall begin with a soup," announced Westermann with all the gravitas of a theatre director introducing a new production.

Beck clicked his tongue in frustration. "Stupid me, I forgot the soup."

Westermann looked at him. "Don't worry, son. You can have some of mine," and the men chuckled and grinned. "So, the soup will be a creamy *Kräuter-Flusskrebssuppe* (crayfish soup with herbs), and it will be followed by oysters with lemon." He paused and most of the men had shut their eyes and let themselves be carried away by Westermann's quiet voice and amicable Hamburger accent. "Six of them. I will squeeze the lemon on each of them, then eat out the oysters, then lick out the shells again to get out all the lemon and seawater. There is nothing like lemon and salt, together they are like magic. After that, I will tear off a big piece of the baguette, open it up and fill it with goose liver pâté. And to finish off, they will serve a raspberry froth with real raspberries at the bottom and whipped cream on top and in the middle of the whipped cream, some little lavender blooms sticking out. Actually, I think I will have two of them as they are not very filling."

"I did not realize our restaurant was going to be so up-market," laughed Tauber.

Westermann reprimanded him with a humourful tone but a straight face. "What, you think just because I am from the dockyards of Hamburg, I will be ordering fried herring and *Labskaus* (traditional beef, onion, and potato stew)?"

"Will Sir be having a cigar and brandy after the meal?" grinned Beck.

"You can give the cigar to someone else. But after I am done with the cheeseboard, I will have an Ahoi Rum first; then a beer – mm, yes, this evening I would like a nice cold Pils; and to finish I will knock back a couple of shots of Helbing Kümmel." His creased face finally broke into a smile as he looked at Beck. "That would go well with your mother's potatoes in bacon."

"Helbing Kümmel," repeated Beck, fascinated by the mention of his favourite spice. "I have never tried it."

"Oh my boy, my poor boy!" exclaimed Westermann with a wistful laugh. "If you have never had a Helbing Kümmel, then you have not lived. If we get out of this mess, and you come to Hamburg, I will take you for a night out in St. Pauli."

Beck's young face, with its smooth pale complexion, lit up like a flare in the night. "Yes, I would love that. Yes, definitely, after the final victory, we will go out for a night in Hamburg, *und die Stadt unsicher machen*! (and paint the town red)."

"I fear it already is," replied Westermann with a sigh.

"So, I will now place my order too," said Tauber. "I will also start with a soup, an oxtail soup would be just perfect. And I will share the baguette with Westermann. There should be enough to go round."

"Don't bet on it," rumbled Westermann.

Tauber smiled and continued, "With plenty of thick creamy butter on the bread. Then a *Rinderbraten* (German beef roast with filling) in *Rotweintunke* (red wine based gravy), accompanied by green beans and carrots and cooked potatoes. Then for the second course a *Schnitzel* done the Holsteiner way, this time with a salad. And the salad should include some fresh carrot, cut up in that special way so that it looks like a rose. Perhaps some French fries on the side too. Ah, and some mayonnaise to dip them in. For dessert something light, just a few stewed apricots with cinnamon sprinkled on top, for I shall be very full!" he said with wide open eyes and pursed lips in a mocking gesture of a higher class.

"You know what goes well with stewed apricot?" suggested Horst. "*Quarktaschen* (curd cheese turnovers)."

Tauber's voice continued with great aplomb. "Good, you have convinced me. Put a couple in with the apricots and cover it all in whipped cream and brandy. The Wehrmacht is paying after all. In which case, pour me a couple of glasses of *Asbach Uralt* (German brandy) at the end, to wash down the meal."

There was a pause until Schegel, lying back towards a corner and somewhat apart from the others, said with a harsh grating but weak voice. "I do not see the point of this stupidity. What is your intention here, to drive us all mad?"

"It is just imagining," said Tauber. "There is no harm in imagining."

Schegel coughed and sat up. "We are rotting away in this shithole of a city and you want to play at imagining things?"

"Like he said, there is no harm in it," affirmed Horst. "We might never eat or drink like this again. Let us enjoy it one last time."

Beck did not agree. "We will all get through this battle, comrades, and one day we will go back to our old lives and be able to enjoy all these wonderful meals. I *know* we will."

"Trust you to start an argument on New Year's Eve," said Tauber, turning to Schegel with contempt. "Just because we are having a bit of fun. Where is the harm in that?"

Schegel gave out a rasping growl, "Bah!", and coughed again.

"Perhaps Horst has something in mind," intervened Rohrbach with his soft and conciliatory tone. "By the way, I was wondering where you are from. I thought Hannover maybe."

Horst shook his head. "No, but not so far away. From Lüneburg."

Westermann cried out. "I know Lüneburg! I was there some years ago. On an outing with some men from work. It is a beautiful little town."

Horst grinned with delight. "Yes. Yes, it is!"

"We ate at this place called the *Altes Brauhaus*. Very good food and an excellent selection of beers. Do you know it?" the Hamburger asked.

"Yes, yes of course! In the Grapengiesserstraße. It is just down the road from the *Gasthaus Sonnenschein* which my sister-in-law runs with her husband. It is by the river - yes, I know it well. Imagine that! You saying that here in the middle of Russia! Oh, it really is a small world."

"If only it were," sighed Westermann. "If only it were. Perhaps then we would not be stuck in the middle of Russia. But never mind, tell us what you are having this evening. Enjoy every last image, every smell, every memory."

Horst contemplated. "I will start with asparagus spears in butter sauce. That is one of my favourite dishes."

"A fine choice," commented Rohrbach, nodding.

Horst said, "We get ours fresh from the *Pfalz* (Palatinate region). My wife and her sister always buy them straightaway in April, they get really excited just waiting for them to arrive. So that would be the starter. Then I would like the roast wild boar, with vegetables and roasted potatoes and lots and lots of gravy. After that a roasted pike filet, with parsley and little cubes of bacon, perhaps with some cooked potatoes too. Yes, all together."

"You are greedier than me. And the dessert?" asked Tauber.

"I once had something called the *Fürst Pückler* cake. Now that was a very fine experience," Horst said, but the others were none the wiser. "I would hardly know how to describe it. Full of creamy layers, with chocolate and fresh strawberries cut up. It was heavenly. Good, well, to finish it all off, I will have a few shots of *Nork Korn*."

"Aha!" cried Westermann. "I will join you in that, my friend! Ah, yes, such a good taste for cuisine and spirits that my comrades here have. Such excellent choices. This is turning out to be a fine evening indeed."

They savoured the thoughts for a while, until the Stalin organ-pipes fired up again for a renewed bombardment, including a relatively close strike that caused some flakes of plaster to fall down from the ceiling. The jolly restaurant faded away leaving them back in a silent dark cellar.

January progressed in a freezing void. The days passed with ever gnawing hunger and still they held out in their holes. They realized how they themselves had become no better than rats; these animals were all around them, eking out the same basic existence, and had become one of the few and most faithful companions left. No, they thought, there was little to distinguish them from the rodents. They too were scavenging, hunkering down, hiding and waiting, sly and cautious and guided by an ever functioning will to live that ticked over with strength and determination, as in all living creatures. They were physically below ground level, cohabiting with these most despised of all creatures (and Horst accepted now that terrible savagery had indeed been committed by the German army in its war of annihilation, that they too were despised like the rats and would be for long to come), behaving in the same manner and pursuing the same goal: bare survival. They had fallen so far that all that they could still say, for another day at least, was that they were functional and sentient beings. Without dignity nor aspiration nor meaning in their lives, but sentient nonetheless. Aware of changes: in dark and light, in the voices and movements around them, in the cold and the still deeper cold.

The little reserve of sausage was gone, as was the millet, and so they survived on the last pieces of bread they had, lumps so hard they were sucked for hours in all the little saliva they could muster. Not giving up and remaining determined, they kept their reserves down to strict levels of daily consumption, so their rations were reduced and reduced further to draw out these pathetic supplies for as long as they could possibly hold out. The soup was by now basically water and they had half a slice of crispbread a day. Westermann died at the end of that first January week, of a suspected heart attack. He had commented to Rohrbach that he had a known heart condition, although the doctor inspecting him in Hamburg had not considered it bad enough to hinder his recruitment. But the biting cold, the constant fear, and the weak physical condition that they were all in, had done their worse. He had complained of chest pains during the last days, then pains in his arm and stomach, and finally had not withstood a massive infarction. He was placed outside next to Pietsch.

Schegel had terrible frostbite and was clearly in bad shape. He was suffering in acute pain, his nose and ears blackened and deformed. Eventually he could no longer stand to have his boots on, despite the bitter cold, and begged the others to help him take them off. As they did so, they discovered the feet inside, withered and blackened, now just atrophied clumps. He cried for shame and for nearly an hour he continually swore at the Führer and all the generals and the other fat cats in the NSDAP, calling them every foul name he could muster up and wishing them all an eternity in hell for their stubbornness and blinding stupidity, their complete lack of understanding that had resulted in this maddening disaster. In the end, exhausted and purged of his hatred for the senior officers and political leadership, he slumped back into his little spot, mumbling a few incoherent phrases while some spittle occasionally dripped from his cracked lips. Beck offered him half of his own ration of crisp bread, dipped in some hot water, but he refused every offering or comfort from the others. Eventually they all went back to their own positions and sat in a heavy silence only broken by Schegel's sporadic ramblings.

The next day they heard from nearby soldiers that a demand to surrender had been formally sent by the Soviets to General Paulus who, following the strict instructions of the Führer to defend Stalingrad down to the last man and the last bullet, had rejected that demand. Some units had made desperate attempts to escape but were easily mowed down. One tale came through to the men, heard of by a nearby platoon and passed on, of how the commander of a whole battalion had tried to lead his troops through what he perceived to be a weak point in the Red Army encirclement. They were nearly a thousand men in total, mixed companies of Rumanian, German and Italian origin. The Russians soldiers had let them all pass and watched them take off in desperation towards the open snowy steppes. At that point a horde of T-34 had borne down on them, gunning them and crushing them in large groups under their tank treads.

The men also heard how there were next to no transporter planes getting through by now; a few days later the last one would fly out for good. They were definitively trapped, beaten; yet still they fought on. Especially the younger men who displayed a truculent fanatism that seemed inhuman at times. Years of methodical brainwashing during the twice-weekly militarist evenings at the Hitler Youth, which had successfully run the line between boy scout adventure and early army training combined with hard racist and political indoctrination, now all fulfilled its role. Hitler had known that once he had the boy, he had the man - it had been a principal tactic from the start – and this plan was now playing out perfectly. They believed unswervingly that the very existence of Germany was at stake, and therefore the only options were to fight or die. In this way, the death rate for young German men was between 30-40%, and for those born in 1920 it even rose as high as 41%. It was astounding just how many people a tyrant could eventually take to the grave with him.

The next day heavy fighting resumed in the outer areas of the city and the Red Army further tightened the pocket of men, with hundreds more Wehrmacht soldiers killed every day in this doomed attempt at defense. In none of the official messages received was there any mention of those German soldiers who were simply dying of cold and hunger with their supplies exhausted, but it was common knowledge that these casualties were vastly exceeding on a daily basis even those who were falling in combat. Sometimes, small groups of men could be seen sitting together behind heavy artillery, all frozen as statues. Starvation decimated the ranks. Everyone knew it was over, the battle was lost, perhaps even the whole war. Everyone knew, it seemed, except those in charge. And the Wehrmacht seemed to have been tricked. Even though it had occupied right up to the very centre for months, it had never actually taken the city. It had managed to pull open the gates of Stalingrad, but it would never pass through them.

On 12th January, another concerted Russian attack began in the outer line of the encirclement, which the men heard from their bunker. It was duly noted by Tauber, who was still keeping meticulous track of dates and events. Horst decided to leave the cellar for a few hours to scavenge out on the streets. The temperature has risen slightly, though still well below freezing, and gusts of wind were swirling up the snow. He had decided to take his chance, egged on by the chronic hunger inside.

He moved a few streets along, lumbering and combing the ground with his eyes, when he came out into an open square lined with the burnt and shelled ruins of buildings. He scanned the area and thought he saw something glinting a little further ahead, half-hidden in the wintry whiteness. He recalled the twinkling of the Christmas tree star that Tauber had crafted. Curious, he hobbled toward it and heard a shot ring out as he simultaneously felt a sharp hot pain in his belly. He reacted quickly, stumbling back whence he had come, and heard a second shot that ricocheted off a nearby wall. He continued with feverish haste until turning a street and feeling he must be out of range of the sniper. He heard a blast of machine gun fire from that direction followed by excited shouts, and assumed the sniper had perhaps been taken out by another nearby platoon. But as an uncontrollable dizziness overwhelmed him, he sensed that he was far from out of danger. Unable to stand any longer, he lurched over to the side of the street and knelt in the snow by the blackened side of a building. He saw that deep-red blood was dripping into the soft white below him, and fell back sideways.

Lying sprawled out among the snow-covered rubble, he fumbled with one gloved hand inside his shirt and felt around lower down, finding a small and acutely painful hole in his wet flesh around the stomach area. He pulled the hand back. The ragged remains of the fabric of the glove around his finger were darkened with blood. He did not have the strength to get back up; was as helpless as a baby on its back. The wind increased slightly in intensity during a further long quarter of an hour, dropping occasional flakes of snow on his face and body. It began to wail, plaintive but menacing, and more soft little shreds of cold fell on him, slowly melting on his whitened bristly face. He was going to be covered up eventually but there was a systematic inevitability to it, he felt: now it was his turn. After spending two summers and two winters of seeing comrade after comrade snatched away by the claws of death, now his moment had come, the moment that, in a way, he had perhaps been waiting for all along for. He knew all was lost, they all did; it was as if the end of the world were descending on them and crushing all that was to have been the Great Reich of a thousand years.

It was not just the fact that for the last surviving men in the cellar their own personal mission as soldiers had failed, but that a whole army, and to top it all the most famed and lauded army in the whole of the Germany, had utterly failed. Mired in defeat and humiliation, the men had a wider understanding of the colossal significance of their failure here on the cold banks of the Volga. Likewise, Horst sensed not only his own coming death but that of something far greater: this huge mad dream that they had all shared. He had been drawn into a swirling vision, he thought, they all had; and this was the result. It was easy now, looking back, to see the trail of absurd delirium that had led to this result, but at the time so sweet had been the hope that it had been impossible to resist. It had all been inevitable, he concluded, just like the fateful encounter and his falling here in this patch of snowed-under debris. He was close to grasping how he had unconsciously sought his own destruction.

With great effort he managed to remove the glove and slip his bare hand in below the shirt. He could now sense with his fingers more precisely and perceived how the blood was gushing out fast from his stomach, dripping down over both sides of his body, over and between the protruding ribs, giving his flesh and skin some last moments of warmth. The pain was intense, more than anything he had ever felt: a sharp stinging at a specific spot in his belly that then spread out and wracked through his whole body. Soon it would threaten to drive him mad. A stomach shot was not necessarily fatal but it was often bad news. He knew from bitter experience on the field how half the soldiers died afterwards and that swift surgical intervention was essential for survival. Now and here in these circumstances, in this dying city, there was nothing more to be done. And with such pain driving through him, it was better that way. He retracted his gloveless hand, left it lying limp by his side, felt it pass from freezing cold to numb and useless.

He did not make any last attempt to try to get to his feet and shuffle a few metres forward. It was unlikely, in this already debilitated physical condition, that he would have been capable of doing so. Rather he simply lay back and remained still; resigned, moving to the state where he was at peace with the world, letting his spirit and blood slowly leave him. He felt the odd flake land on his exposed face and closed his eyes, taking in these minute sensations which filled his sensory world. His mind, desperate to detach itself from the shooting pain inside, wandered to memories; to little scenes from his childhood, to his arrival at work on his first day with the Fire Department in Lüneburg, to the time he saved an old woman's life bringing her down from the third floor on a ladder during a fire, to the first time he saw Inge behind the counter while he was standing in the doorway of the bakery, to the wedding in the St. Marien church, to the honeymoon in Berlin, to the births of all three children, to the day he signed up to join the army, to the holiday last February back home with Inge and the children, to the moment the men knew they were encircled in the city and with no way out.

He heard a voice, then another; thought for a moment that he must have died and moved on to the next plain of his existence already. But the voices were familiar and he opened his eyes to perceive how Beck and Tauber were reaching over toward him, hands running over his body, moving inside his shirt and feeling over his skin in a last-ditch attempt to identify the exact position of the wound and so stem the flow of blood. He thought he saw Tauber crying and even felt a warm drop fall on his cheek, so very different in sensation to the snowflakes.

They were trying to animate him, telling him that everything would be alright, looking for the best way to lift him. Horst would have been content to die there and then in the midst of their futile motherly comforting, but suddenly he was gripped by an urgent necessity as he remembered his one last mission in which he must not fail. With the last reserves of energy he could muster, he flapped his left arm around and tried to concentrate on bringing Tauber's head down closer to him, desperate to indicate this to him with his clumsy limb. His friend understood and quickly knelt, thrust his face closer to Horst's.

"*Ta..ta..Tasche*," muttered Horst with supreme effort, his head shaking in cold and pain. "*In der Tasche* (In the pocket)", and he fingered weakly around the pocket in question in his jacket. Tauber unbuttoned it and reached inside, pulled out the scrunched envelope, instantly recognized the contents and the extreme importance of this creased and dirty little object.

"She will get this, I promise you that. Don't worry about it. But first we need to get you back quickly to the shelter and sort out this wound," Tauber assured him. For Horst only the first words had any meaning, and in this state of great relief and contentment, with a smile pushing up his blue lips, he began to slip out of consciousness. He summoned up the images of his family, of Inge and Adolf and Joseph and Hermann, and cast them in oval gold-gilded frames. They smiled back at him, safe and sound in the distant comfort of Lüneburg. He held the four images there and kissed them all. The gold frames glinted and they looked so happy that he himself could not have been happier.

The actual moment of Horst's death occurred while in transit back to the cellar, as Beck and Tauber were rushing him on a makeshift stretcher through the icy streets. Once they had got him inside, they realized that their assistance had come too late. He stayed below with them for some hours and Tauber wept on his chest, which he had pointlessly bandaged up after verifying he was dead, if for nothing then at least for the sake of dignity. Later he was carried out to the street to be placed beside Pietsch and Westermann, whose tombs had disappeared in the last few days under a new snow drift, leaving only the very tops of their wooden crosses peeking through. Tauber took off Horst's identification disc and kept it to one side. He did not want Horst's wife to find out about her husband's demise through a clinical letter from some faceless functionary from the Wehrmacht. Instead, he would hand over both items to Inge himself once he had made it back to Germany, and explain to her personally the final weeks.

Tauber spent two whole days laboriously preparing the next cross for Horst, this time ornately decorated with elaborate etchings and by far the most attractive one he had ever made in his two and a half years fighting in the Wehrmacht. Beck and Rohrbach commented that it was a fine work of art that befitted a fine man. They carried out a religious service and prayed, not just for Horst but for the whole of Germany too, and returned to the cellar to drag themselves through another stretch of days. Schegel was by then moribund and had not spoken in two days. He registered the news of another fallen comrade with a grunt.

On 22nd January, a second demand for surrender was rejected by General Paulus and the reaction from the Soviets was swift and brutal. They received orders to clear out the pockets for once and all and bombarded them mercilessly for hours upon end with heavy artillery fire. Explosions cracked all around without letting up for a single minute; later, as the Soviets progressed closer, the ground and walls were raked by wave after wave of machine gun fire.

Barrage after barrage of hot steel had pounded the area. It was divided up as the Red Army prepared for its infantry to sweep in, to seize and reclaim their land. Within a week, the Red Amy had combed through the whole city. They reached the district of Horst's cellar-mates who, in preparation for their expected arrival, had managed to mount a tatty torn white-ish flag on a stick of wood the day before and hoist it by the ground floor entrance. (They were fortunate to have had the awareness that there now existed only one contingency plan, and that was preprepared capitulation. Not all nearby bunkers did, and those still seeming to stay active were duly taken out by the Soviets throwing multiple grenades into the cellars and reducing the contents to a bloodbath.) Schegel had already died by this point and his body had been placed outside beside the others, likewise among the rubble.

As they heard the stomp of Russian boots approaching the building, Tauber, Beck, and Rohrbach left the hideout with arms raised. They walked out dizzily, clumsy on their feet through near starvation. The enemy soldiers brusquely searched them, angrily demanding in German, "*Uhren, Uhren*" (watches, watches) as they felt up the soldiers' wrists and removed with rough but effective dexterity their watches, one of the few decent spoils of war for these troops. Thdandeey never found the two that Tauber had hidden in his breeches around his genitals, and he hoped they would come in useful later on. The Russians told them to hand over any food they had, and were sorely disappointed to find that they had none left whatsoever, not even a crumb. The three German soldiers looked closer at their captors and discerned that these victorious Soviets were nearly as gaunt and starved as they were.

They were briskly marched off, together with thousands of others who were now leaving their hideouts and surrendering throughout the city, to be placed in captivity as prisoners of war of the Soviets. Most of them would never return alive to Germany; and of the three survivors of that particular cellar, only one would.

Chapter 25

Back in Lüneburg and much to Adolf's pleasure, heavy rains pounded the town, washing the streets in streams of water that swirled in eddies, carrying off scraps of rubbish and old dirt. He adored the rain and could watch it for hours, falling from nowhere and leaving the water to create a myriad of patterns on the ground below. For him, the weather was perfect: unpredictable and tending to stormy.

One Wednesday afternoon, Inge scurried back to the Gasthaus under the weak protection of her raincoat raised over her head, as an unexpected shower broke overheard. All around her, pedestrians were running for doorsteps and shop entrances as the rain lashed down. As she turned into the Bardowicker Straße, just before arriving home, she saw an older couple in their sixties standing together with a younger man, all smartly dressed under the downpour, on the corner of the Baumstraße. They had moved closer up to the side of the building, to seek there some minimal shelter from the rain. The couple were looking over diagonally at the entrance to the *Liebesgrund* park further down on the opposite side of the street; the man pointing and saying something to his wife, while the younger man – who looked to be their son - kept his gaze on the ground. Next to them stood a few suitcases. Inge glanced at them for a moment, uneasy at the sight that was so prosaic on the one hand, but at the same time peculiar. Her attention was also caught by the sight of the yellow stars they were wearing, a fact she registered before running on to reach the Gasthaus as quickly as possible.

This was the family Rosenfeld, who up till this moment had quietly lived their lives for decades in the back apartment of a two-storey brick building in the Salzbrückerstraße. Mordecai Rosenfeld had worked as a tailor for over thirty years, until the rise to power of the NSDAP and its position on the status of Jews, had seen him sacked, shunned, and seeking out a meagre existence with his family. The war came and he hid himself away from sight, having obtained through an old contact a commission stitching torn uniforms for the Wehrmacht. He had been very lucky to have had this activity, he often said; with that sense of luck that was always relative to the times and circumstances in which one lived.

Undoubtedly, he and his family had owed their immunity so far from the ongoing waves of deportations to this work. Also to Johannes Schmidt, the owner of a large sawmill and wood distributor and former town councillor. He had been a private customer of Rosenfeld and an affectionate acquaintance back in the "old days", as Rosenfeld fondly called those better years before. Having a keen and demanding eye for a well-cut suit, Schmidt had always been a keen admirer of Rosenfeld's fussily correct work and had found his company pleasant and stimulating whenever he was being measured and advised by the clothing expert. Despite being a *Vollnazi* (a total Nazi), he had kept the odd preferred old acquaintance among the Jewish community, as indeed many a *Vollnazi* did, to whom he wished – as exceptional cases – that no bad should come. His distant though firm hand had protected the family so far, but by this point the pressure of the ruling ideology was determined to crush all remaining Jewish life out of the towns and cities of the Reich. Lüneburg was to be no exception. The tentacles of the Gestapo extended everywhere and with terrific efficiency; they left no index card unexamined, no door unopened, and no list incomplete. And someone else would have to be found to stitch the uniforms.

The Rosenfelds were a family of three - Mordecai and his wife Leah, and their only child Schlomo. The latter was in his late thirties and professionally an investment banker and trader, although that route had been firmly cut off from him for some time now. He was of a deeply religious conviction, in contrast to his more secular parents, and had been a keen member of the synagogue committee before it had been sold and ultimately demolished. On sharply reduced incomes all three had weathered the times as best they could together. As late as 1942, with the war going at full tilt and the rate of deportations beginning to reach an ever-greater prevalence, Schlomo had made an application to the authorities for the family to move to Hamburg. There he hoped they would gain time by living anonymously in a large city, but this application had been promptly turned down. Now they had been officially informed that they were to prepare for evacuation to the east of the Reich, where work and housing would be waiting for them.

The seemingly innocuous and very formal letter had arrived last week. *"Sie sind vorgesehen zur Evakuierung. Halten Sie sich bereit mit je einem Gepäckstück."* ("You have been scheduled for evacuation. Be ready to leave with one piece of luggage per person"). Though not good news, it nonetheless seemed logical enough: after all, were not children being evacuated from cities in the wake of the bombings, too? His family had received a list of instructions, various forms to sign, and were given a precise time and place at which the police would pick them up. There they now stood, waiting for this inevitable next stage; in the case of the parents, still with the same stiff optimism that had accompanied them through all their previous brushes with the ever-changing laws. Mordecai and Leah were down-to-earth people who did not subscribe to wild conspiracy theories. They firmly believed that in the east there would be work – albeit it tough and menial at first – and housing – albeit basic – waiting for them there. It was a perfectly logical conclusion to arrive at. Everyone with a business needed cheap workers, that was a fact of life.

Schlomo, however, had a fatalistic view of the world and did not share his parents' naturally auspicious outlook. Instead, he had sunk in recent months further inside himself, brooding in dark thoughts. Though not completely convinced, he did sometimes fear that something more sinister was afoot; as did many Jews who had heard enough rumours to meditate on the probable reality concealed behind the distortions and excuses that the Reich authorities had hung up like theatrical decoration. The rumours were truly horrific and spoke of an endless murder that was unimaginable.

It was on this very same spot that Lion Marienberg and his wife had also stood just eight months previously; also with some belongings packed into a couple of suitcases and the rest of their belongings sold or given to friends to take care of. Their plans to emigrate, partly frustrated by the mountain of bureaucracy involved, partly frustrated by Lion's own hesitancy, had sadly come to nothing. There were three families there with the Marienberg couple that day in total, and they were all taken off together by a vehicle commissioned by the Gestapo. At the *Einwohnermeldeamt* (registry office for residents) in Lüneburg there was an official register of their *Abmeldung* (notice of departure) with the exact date and the exact

Zuzugsort (place of destination) noted as being Minsk. This entry had naturally been filled in by the authorities, not the Marienbergs. The couple had not been heard from since.

Schlomo knew all this, and it was since then that he began to succumb to the increasingly strong suspicion that those Jews being sent to Minsk – along with other destinations such as Riga or Lodz – may have been killed immediately on arrival. The first shocking revelations of some massive and terrible operation against Jews, taking place in the occupied east, had already been sneaked out through diplomats posted at the Swedish embassy in Warsaw. Newspapers in the US were also now reporting with frequency about massacres taking place, although at the same time other international sources, most notably the Red Cross, were not echoing this. For the broader population though, in wartime nothing got through to those only receiving German news.

Apparently, Thomas Mann had spoken on the subject in a broadcast on the forbidden BBC. But Schlomo had not heard it himself and there was no corroboration to be had from those directly around him, nor obviously any disavowal from the authorities either. He also told himself that even if this were the case, then this reality must be constructed out of the purest madness, out of the most inconceivable malice humanity had yet seen. He also knew that in war people had a morbid fascination with tales of atrocity and often related them for the thrill of horror alone. He could not help but wonder what people in the future would one day make of these rumours – and if they would ever find out what had actually been going on, what really did happen to the deportees.

For Schlomo's parents, it was clear that all that the 'evacuations' being organized involved transportation to the *Arbeitseinsatz* – work duty. Whatever his own misgivings on the subject, Schlomo himself had personally vowed to stay together with his optimistic and compliant parents, to the bitter end if necessary, and help them in any way he could. Even if he feared the worst inside, he was hardly going to try to flee alone and leave them to their fate; nor was he totally convinced of the horror he dreaded, that he could neither prove nor be sure of.

Two days earlier Schlomo had visited the '*Judenhaus*' (Jews' house), as it was nicknamed by those in the know, situated in the Grosse Bäckerstraße 23. There, two Jewish families were still unofficially living and offering hiding and assistance to the remaining members of the community in need. The neighbour, a tailoress who lived on her own, helped out as best she could. After dark, she waited for the signal from the Jews inside, in the form of a flower vase placed in the window, and then placed a covered tray of food just to the side of the front entrance to the house.

Schlomo had gone there to visit and say goodbye to his friend from the synagogue committee, Joel Frey, who was in hiding there in the cellar with his wife, after having narrowly evaded a recent Gestapo raid a few months before. Schlomo furthermore wished to relate how that their joint acquaintance and partial benefactor Adam Wunderlich had sent his best regards and said he would help out in any way he could: they only needed to contact him. He was in the meantime living in New York, together with wife and daughter, where they had all been reunited with their eldest daughter and son-in-law, now settled down and with a small business in Brooklyn. (It should be added that the Wunderlich family was forced to leave behind most of their belongings, as the move order documents were confiscated by the Gestapo and all items were seized, including the rest of Adam's admirable collection of art and most of his wife's jewelry. These was later auctioned off; the furniture was snapped up at cut-rate prices by local residents, while the artwork and jewelry was quietly put aside by Gestapo officials and other scavengers for their own personal sales.) Wunderlich's offer was generous to a fault, as was typical within the Jewish community, and he was clearly eager to help out friends from Lüneburg, by every means possible. But the obstacle course had become so difficult in these last years, there was little to be done.

"Dear old Adam, God bless him! Every time I hear of someone who has safely got through to the other side of the tumultuous river, it is like hearing angels singing," Frey had cried and clapped his hands in glee. Then Schlomo had told him of his own fate and that of his family; and that he had come to say goodbye. He had to watch with distress how Frey's joy deflated in seconds. "It is better to be honest,"

Schlomo said to him. "Although my mother is still very hopeful. She does not believe that any fate is sealed and in the evening always sees the stars first before the night sky behind." Frey's wife returned from helping prepare the food upstairs in the kitchen and the three prayed together.

The two days had passed since then and now the Rosenfelds were waiting together on the street corner, hoping to do the right thing by demonstrating cooperation. The shower of rain that had erupted out of the sky continued for a good while without letting up, but for the Rosenfelds there was no doorstep nor shop entrance that would open up to welcome them inside; that much they knew, so they huddled up against the wall. Mordecai's wife Leah had convinced herself, and was now in the process of trying to convince her spouse and son, that no-one would come that day, what with the weather having been so bad the whole time. They would end up schlepping their cases back home again and the whole silly drama with the police would start again from zero, she insisted. But she was wrong. The police did come eventually, twelve minutes late. By then the rain had subsided and the sun had come out through the dispersing clouds.

Just before the arrival of the police, the Rosenfeld family was joined on that corner of the street by a young woman in her twenties called Hannah Schulberg. She was Jewish but married to an 'Aryan' German, stationed with the *Kriegsmarine* (military navy) in Lübeck. His racial status and modest rank had protected her so far, but that safeguard had now ceased to offer any further protection. It was time, the local authorities had decided, to "clean up for one and for all in Lüneburg", as Eberhard Ritter had told his subordinates. This final and thorough campaign was to be carried out with maximum efficiency and to have no more 'exceptions'. "We are not going to lag behind the national standards being set elsewhere," he commented to an enthusiastic Möhring.

On their way to the prearranged meeting point - and this explained their uncharacteristic tardiness - the police had picked up an elderly woman who was practically bed-ridden and had been physically unable to leave her apartment; a sad state that had nonetheless also protected her thus far. She had been brought down from the apartment on an army stretcher and roughly thrown into the back of a small truck. After that job, the others were picked up and packed into the vehicle beside and around her. The elderly lady greeted those climbing in beside her with a teary smile and nod. As he regarded her lying there, Shlomo shuddered with cynical rejection of the thought that they were going to be given employment once they arrived at their destination.

Passengers and luggage were flung heftily from side to side as the truck sped off, taking its occupants to Hamburg. Once they had arrived there, they were transferred that same day onto a train that more resembled a cattle truck, together with many other Jews from Hamburg and surrounding areas. That train then set off punctually, well before sunset. As Schlomo had indeed foreseen, the ominous destination read: Minsk.

This ostensibly mundane but utterly brutal moment on the street corner, that did not even arouse the interest of most people passing, had been perceived but not comprehended by Inge as she rushed past in the pouring rain. She had not recognized the family specifically, who had in any case been living in a state of almost complete self-isolation for the past four years. She had simply seen them standing there in the rain, forlorn and half-hidden under coats and hats, among a disorderly display of luggage; and she sensed that something was very amiss.

These were not people that she knew on a personal level but she had noted the yellow stars sewn on their jackets and understood its significance. There had been something in that image, framed in her fleeting glance, that had greatly unsettled her. Her mind told her they were emigrating to the east to find work and be given housing, but she had an instinctive sensation that something in this plan did not make sense.

A seemingly inexplicable stomach complaint had accompanied her for several days and, together with a spate of dreary rain-soaked weather, this had kept her spirits down. She began once more to concentrate on confronting her more personally relevant challenges. At one point she considered whether or not to relate the scene to Gisela, perhaps just to mention it in passing and tell her how strange and unsettling a sight she had found it. But she estimated, and correctly so, that her pragmatic sister would have little time for "sensations" and dismiss her as being over-sensitive to the silliest of minor issues. And that in the middle of a war. Inge conceded to herself that perhaps she was, indeed.

Last November, Inge had received a letter with a very assured and confident tone from her husband, but something had rung warning bells. As with the sight of the Jews standing in the rain, she had that gnawing feeling again that something out of her grasp did not add up. The family had moved gloomily through the month and Inge had attempted to give her little children, Adolf now five, Joseph four and Hermann three, a glimmer of the upcoming Christmas season. But there was no real festive spirit to be had and no-one had their heart in it. Still painful for Inge was the memory of the miscarriage she had suffered earlier that year, when in May she had fallen down a flight of stairs and begun to bleed heavily. She had been taken into hospital and, following an intervention, Dr. Schwenter had confirmed the loss of the fetus in the third month. With Horst out fighting on the front, it had been heartbreaking for her to think that their joint child had been lost. She had gone through bouts of sickness for weeks afterwards.

It had been such a harrying and angst-laden year in general that by the time December had arrived, Inge was looking forward to seeing it end. One of the most difficult features was that she did not know how to address the persistent questioning of the children with regards to their father, in particular from little Hermann. He could pronounce whole sentences quite clearly by now and he understood a lot of them too; yet he seemed not so inclined to remember the content: "Where is Papa? When is Papa coming?" he asked at least once a day.

She patiently repeated her set response, "He is away fighting. He will be coming home when the war is over, which will be very soon. Perhaps even after Christmas."

Joseph, who loved Christmas, was more calculating and would ask, "How long is soon?" or "How long is Christmas in total?" Upon once being told by Gisela that it was twelve days, he said to Inge with a degree of sly reckoning, "So, if he comes back before the end of the whole Christmas time, then we can celebrate it all from the beginning again, only with him here with us."

Adolf once said with big eyes, "Herr Müller is fighting at war, and Herr Köhne from the next house. Onkel (Uncle) Wilhelm and Papa too. When they all come home, the town will be full!" He looked at her with a grin and for one bizarre moment Inge could not tell if she had detected irony in the infant voice. She shook her head to clear it from such disturbing thoughts and wished there were an easier way to explain "fighting" and "war".

For Christmas there was some clientele in the restaurant, including one large group meal organized by SS-*Hauptscharführer* Ritter, who was now becoming a quite regular visitor. He even enjoyed stepping in for a quick spontaneous chat at the Gasthaus reception on occasions, with Gisela or Martin or Inge, if he was passing by in the street and not too busy. Gisela commented that he seemed to feel very at home.

At the group meal the week before Christmas Day there were ten men attending in total, all from the newly opened Gestapo headquarters in the Julius-Wolff-Straße. They ate and drank well and moreover tipped exceedingly well, and Gisela was very grateful for the extra income. The only slight hiccup came when a couple of officers became inebriated and made some lewd comments directed at the sisters. Fortunately, Ritter was there to put them gently in their place, without spoiling the jovial atmosphere but to clearly avoid "any further embarrassment for the ladies". Neither of the women mentioned it afterward.

At New Year, the families came together for a meal and some drinks, but in a very subdued atmosphere. It had been made clear from the start that politics was a topic not to be discussed, nor contemplations about the course of the now long-lasting war either. Consequently the women said little outside of trivial small talk, and the men next to nothing. The children in contrast were chirpy and happy to steal the show. They did listen to the Führer's speech, though more for the sake of being able to say to others afterwards, in all honesty and with witnesses, that they had listened to the Führer's speech.

"For the fourth time now, fate has obliged me to give the New Year's speech to the German people in a state of war. In these four years however, the German people have come to clearly see that this

war, that was forced onto us, as so often in the history of Germany, by old enemies, does truly concern the question of our existence, or our annihilation.

The German people will, this time, be the last ones to leave the battlefield and they will do so victoriously. In this way, the new, long period of peace will be harkened in: a peace that we all long for, in order to re-build the community that is our nation, and thus express our sole and most worthy gratitude to our deceased heroes."

Midnight came and the New Year was gingerly toasted. There was one wish expressed inside more than any other: the simple wish that the soldiers - the husbands, brothers, fathers, sons, and uncles - could return home soon to the expectant hearts of their families. That was all they desired. Even peace was not wished for; for what could peace promise, in that tense moment, but merely an uncertain continuation? Nor was victory, then victory at what price?

By January it had become apparent, even to those with only the most casual geopolitical interest, that the battle currently being waged in and around the city of Stalingrad was to be decisive. It was mentioned incessantly, as was the presence there of the much-praised 6th Army. Although the Führer had had complete confidence in a resounding victory in the weeks leading up to Christmas, through January the announcement of that victory continued to drag. Rumours were spreading, which were being – albeit cautiously – confirmed in the press and the radio, that this unquestionable victory might not be on the cards after all. Even worse, there was talk of a retreat (though never a defeat, which would have been treacherous and, with the wrong judge in the worst mood, even punishable by death).

Inge encountered Eberhard Ritter in February while out on her way to the bakery up on the Hindenburgstraße. The bread was all sold out for the day at the place she habitually went to, the *Bäckerei & Konditorei Gürber* in the Zollstraße; even though they usually put a little to one side for her. So, she had taken a longer route up to the next bakery and there her path had crossed with Ritter's. They had greeted each other with formal cordiality and she had explained what she was doing in that more northern part of the town.

Speaking to her with the firm gentle authority of an older brother, he told her to explain to the staff that she was a friend of his, and in that case she could have as much as she had available on her ration card for that week. He furthermore asked if she had enough with that and said he could procure more for her if necessary. Inge was very grateful for the offer but declined it with her breezy smile and submissive nod of the head. Ritter was insistent and in the end she had to decline the offer a few more times, each time more politely but firmly than the previous one, before she was able to find an excuse and the determination to move on along the street.

Their paths crossed some weeks later, too. Inge had already dropped Joseph and Hermann off at the kindergarten where they spent the morning until noon. From there she continued on with Adolf to the primary school where he had started classes the previous autumn. She was waving goodbye to her oldest son, who was heading into class with great independence and without looking back, when Ritter suddenly appeared behind her, seeming to fill the air of the school entrance with a face grinning from ear to ear. He had a school inspection to carry out that morning, he explained and noted, what a coincidence it was that they should meet again. This time Inge felt actively uncomfortable, for there was something about his manner, the way he looked at her, and his choice of words, that suggested to her something different to a mere passing amiability that one would expect from acquaintances in a small town. To confirm her foreboding, he actually asked her if she and her sister would like to come out for a meal and a drink in town some evening soon. It would just be a formal occasion, he proposed, with his assistant Möhring coming too. "I was thinking that, after all the hard work you ladies have put in for my colleagues, and all you have had to put up with, it would only be fair if we could repay the service and give you both a much-needed night off. I am sure Gisela's husband would be in full agreement." It was here that it struck Inge as both odd, as well as tasteless, on Ritter's part that he had not even mentioned her own husband. Furthermore, his familiar tone and assumption that "Gisela's" husband would automatically agree. But he wasn't finished. "And if not, well, that would leave just you and me, and I would be in full agreement with that."

Inge nervously replied she would bear the offer in mind and definitely mention it to her sister, but that their days were so very full at the moment with so many jobs that she could not promise an affirmative answer. "Of course not," he said with an oily smile. "Think about it, that is all. And if you manage to find time, you know where to find me." He laughed, "After all, our address is on the letterhead of quite a few invoices you have in your bookkeeping." He tipped his cap and strode past her into the school.

This encounter and the clearly prurient proposal brought great distress to Inge. Not least because she assumed that she herself must have done something to attract his attention in this manner. She experienced an overwhelming sense of guilt, as if she had shown disloyalty to her husband, which she considered a terrible sin considering his status of missing in action while fighting as a hero on the eastern front. Knowing the importance that Horst always placed on family loyalty, she felt all the more wretched due to this illogical but, for her, unavoidable feeling of unfaithfulness.

Inge did not mention the encounter nor Ritter's suggestion to Gisela. To her great relief the number of days, on which she did not run into Ritter again, rose and rose. She had at first counted them off, convinced that he might be following her or keeping track of her movements. That was, after all, his vocation. But she noted two, then three weeks had passed, finally a month, and gradually with the passing of time she started to relax and trust that he had come to his senses and recognized his own error.

These first advances had been in every way repellent to her. What most infuriated her, was how she recalled the complete lack of acknowledgement that he made of her husband. She considered her husband to be of a higher status than those not on the front and thereby deserving of all the respect in the world. People like Horst were risking their lives "while others were warming their behinds in quiet civilian duty," as Gisela had once put it, in reference to another person who seemed reluctant to face the battle music. That Ritter would so outrageously court the attentions of a married woman, and one with three young children as well, she perceived as more of an insult to Horst than a threat to herself.

The issue came to a head in April, just as she was beginning to find comfort in the continued absence of Ritter from her life during a further fortnight. Martin had gone that Monday to see his mother in

Adendorf, who very rarely came by these days to the Gasthaus. Volkmar had also been staying at home in Adendorf for a while, having been laid up with problems with his legs while walking, in addition to the already increased back pains. He told his son, "I'm going mad here with those two around me all the time," and even at one point contemplated the possibility that they might be poisoning him. It was to be a long evening for an only mildly interested son.

It was approximately six o'clock in the evening and Gisela had been cleaning the outer windows of the Gasthaus that faced out into the street. She had finished and gone in to throw away the dirty water and put away the bucket and rag, before getting the children ready for their bath-time. Out of the back room came music from the radio; it was the evening of waltz music live from Vienna, occasionally interrupted by a jolly commentator describing the scenes of dancing couples before him, as the orchestra accompanied the evening show.

Inge stood near the reception, and Ritter breezily entered and greeted her. She smiled back, feeling very much on edge inside but able to retain an icy politeness in her manner; her posture defiant and erect, her chin pointing firmly upwards.

He said that he had not seen her in a while and hoped that she was well. She replied that she was well enough and that she had been very busy. He came a step closer and commented that they were busy people; he had just seen her sister cleaning the windows outside. "She should let her husband continue with the upper storeys on the outside, though. More of a man's job." He said he was free that evening and could help them out himself, if she wanted to fetch the ladder. (He had glimpsed Gisela's face in a second-storey window and assumed she was now doing the extensive job from the inside.)

Inge politely answered, "I am sure Martin will be happy to do them once he comes back from Adendorf," and immediately regretted giving out this information.

Ritter looked around. It was dim and quiet, the kitchen clearly closed for the night. He heard what sounded like the far-off sound of children playing upstairs. "You don't have many customers tonight," he said with an unpleasantly meaningful tone.

"It is Monday. We always close on Mondays. It is our day of rest."

"Shame. Though I would be happy to be a customer tonight for you," and he gave a mock bow. "To help keep up with the income. Don't worry, you will not have to fire up the stove. I shall not want anything to eat. Just a beer or two, perhaps a schnaps."

Inge still did not drop her smile, although it was now glacial. "I am very sorry, Herr Ritter, but we do not have permission to serve guests this evening."

He moved a little closer, still smiling. "I am the head of the local police force for the entire town and its surrounding region. I do not think anyone is going to object, and much less lodge an official complaint."

Inge moved a couple of steps backward and was already up against the wall. Ritter looked around him, sensing that the two of them were alone. "It has such a cosy, homely atmosphere, this place. I liked it right from the start. I could get to feel quite at home here." He continued steadily forward and in no time was up in Inge's face, his arms opening out as if ready to embrace her body. Both Ritter and Inge abandoned any pretense of formality or politeness; both stopped smiling.

"Stay well away from me. I am a married woman," she said with quiet firmness, her arms rising instantly to place a barrier.

Ritter pushed lightly against her upheld hands with the chest pockets of his uniform. He put a finger to his lips. "Shh," he said softly, the bulk of his body moving closer up towards hers, like a feline stalking. She felt an increased pressure against her hands. "I am very sorry about your husband but I am sure he died a hero's death."

Inge opened her mouth in disbelief and her hands trembled. "How could you say such a thing? What a terrible horrid thing to say!"

Ritter flinched back a little at the harsh reproach, but recovered with a casual, "It is better to get used to the idea sooner or later. They all did their best but it was ultimately a dismal failure."

"My Horst is missing and he has fought as a hero for the Führer and for the Reich. There is no failure in that!" she snapped.

"There is obviously 'a failure in that' when all that is left of an army surrenders to the enemy and lets itself be taken as prisoners of war. It is most certainly not a resounding victory, in anybody's book."

Inge had no logical argument to counter the bitter words, only outrage and a deep sense of hurt, and above all the sheer indignity of what she was hearing. "I think it is time that you went, Herr Ritter."

"I think you mean *Hauptscharführer* Ritter and no, I do not think I should be going anywhere. Do you think an officer of my rank takes orders from a serving woman?" He smelt her fear, as an animal does, and began moving closer again.

She cringed back in terror, more intimidated by him as an SS-officer than by him as a powerfully built man. As she took in the situation, she instinctively made a dash to her right, planning to run down the corridor and out the front door, onto the street. He caught her immediately with an arm and the left-side of his body and moved her to hold her firmly pinned up against the wall. She started to shriek but was cut off in shock as he slapped her face hard with his free hand. "We have had enough of these silly games," he said, and gave her another slap across the face. She felt him squeeze up tighter and, to her horror, realized that he was sexually aroused.

"For the sake of God, do not do this. I beg you, do not do this," she pleaded, her heart racing in panic and her head and arms trembling.

Ritter's face was directly up against hers. He snarled, "If you scream, or make any noise, or try any tricks on me, I can assure you that the result will not be pleasant. Neither for you nor for others - do not forget who I am. Do I make myself clear?"

She remained shaking, looking at him in abject fear but still hoping that all was not lost, that he would – upon seeing her clearly terrified - find the mercy in him to let her go. She had no concept of sadism and could not possibly conceive that this moment, of seeing her suffering and so acutely afraid, was immensely pleasurable to the officer.

He tightened his grip of her arm and cupped his free hand around her chin. "I think you understand. And I think you can also appreciate that I am not in the habit of being talked to in that kind of insolent manner." His hand moved up from her chin so that his forefinger began to play around her bottom lip, then sliding up further and beginning to enter her mouth enough to lightly feel, with the edge of the finger, her gums and the base of her front teeth. "So we can either find a nice place, somewhere out of the way, to lie down, or I will begin to make life hell. For you, for your useless brother Ernst at the *Vereinsbank,* who will end up near where your husband went, along with your equally useless brother-in-law who pretends to run this dump. Now do you understand?"

She regarded him in utter fear, still trembling and incapable of saying anything. He grabbed her and began to pound her against the wall behind her, with such sudden force she felt winded. "I asked you a question, I want a nod." She nodded, felt his hand move down to her throat and begin to press against her windpipe. "In that case," he said, "let us proceed to the restaurant to continue this discussion. After you." Ritter roughly turned Inge round, in a sharp single movement, to face the entrance to the restaurant. He pinned her arm behind her back and kept his hand clasped on her throat. He had pushed her only two steps forward when he abruptly came to a halt. She felt his grip relax.

Looking up, she saw just ahead of them her sister Gisela, starring at Ritter and gripping a large kitchen knife in her hand. There was a moment of complete stillness, until Ritter further relaxed his grip on Inge to the point that her trapped arm was free and his hand had left her throat and fallen down to rest on her shoulder.

Gisela uttered with simple and clear force, in a snarling voice that Inge had never heard before in her sister, "*Raus!*" (Get out!)

Ritter removed his hand from Inge's shoulder and stepped back and away from her. Gisela in turn made a step forward towards them, her eyes still fixed on Ritter and the knife pointing towards him.

"Get out," she repeated; more calmly, with greater clarity and contempt.

Ritter knew he had lost the match that day and regarded Gisela with near hatred in his one last look of defiance. "It would be in everyone's best interests, especially yours, if this were not mentioned any further. You can be assured of my silence concerning today's…conversation, and I shall expect yours in return. Good day." He turned and departed up the shadowy corridor until they heard the front door creaking open and the heels of his boots clicking on the cobbles outside; sharp footsteps moving off until they faded away. Gisela had already placed the knife down on the surface of the reception and rushed to her sister. The women embraced each other for a moment while Inge sobbed.

"It's alright, it's alright. He's gone and I'm pretty sure for good this time," said Gisela, patting her back.

While she was recovering from the shock, Gisela fetched them both a couple of glasses and a bottle of brandy out of the kitchen. "This will help us to calm down." She poured the drinks out. "Don't mention anything to Martin. He will just get worked up and not have a clue what to do."

Inge said she had been so lucky that her sister had happened to come in just in that moment. "No, nothing to do with luck," Gisela replied. "I wouldn't have even known what was going on if it had not been for Joseph. You see, I was trying to get them all to have a bath, but he didn't want to. So I thought I would take care of Erich first, who was already sitting in the water, but he is so difficult to wash, poor love, and then do Adolf and Hermann after him, who were both ready to get in. And with him being so awkward, I thought I would probably leave Joseph until tomorrow. But I had just finished with Erich and was helping him dry himself down, when in comes Joseph into the bathroom and said there was this horrible man downstairs who was hurting Mama. So I came rushing down, saw what was happening, and grabbed the nearest knife."

They knocked back a second shot and went back up to the bathroom, where both Adolf and Hermann were splashing noisily in the tub. Joseph was off again on his adventures somewhere in the Gasthaus. They had to call out for him to come to the bathroom so that his mother could give him a big hug and thank him for his bold intervention.

It transpired that he had been hiding in the shadows at the bottom of the staircase when Ritter had entered, and he had witnessed the whole scene. "So I went and told Aunt Gisela," he said with a proud grin. "Daddy said to tell Aunt Gisela if there is ever something wrong and you are not there. I thought it would be best to tell her," and between mother and aunt he was smothered in kisses while his brothers roared in play from the bath. Adolf was flinging heavy waves of water at his little brother but Hermann was once again close to tears.

"How they love to pick on him," Gisela shook her head, moving in to chide the older child, while her sister, still trembling, held on tightly to her vigilant and quick-thinking second son.

Chapter 26

The two women did not speak to any further parties about the attempted sexual assault which had left behind a deep mark of shock in Inge. She had never experienced such levels of violence before in her life, much less directed against her personally. Had it not been for the constant comfort and support of her sister, she would have broken down under the strain; particularly due to the self-blame she subjected herself to and the self-questioning of what she herself may have done to encourage him. She related this to her sister during the frequent but furtive conversations they had on the subject. As much as Gisela tried to point out the complete lack of guilt that Inge carried in the matter, it was no easy task. Inge was quietly convinced that she herself must have done something to initiate the chain of events that led to the assault.

Eventually, at Gisela's behest, they informed their mother about Ritter's menacing behaviour toward Inge, although leaving out the detail of the actual aggression. Corinna reaffirmed that her daughter was not in any way to blame and added, "This is the new generation of men that this country has produced. Your father says that all the time - that is *entre nous* of course. Violent thugs and vandals, and now in positions of power, too. It has gone to their heads." Both agreed that Inge would be wise to stay quiet on the subject due to the high rank in the SS that her tormentor held. The basic premise was the extreme imprudence, to the point of impossibility, of reporting the matter to the police: all three women acknowledged this sordid fact at the beginning of the discussion and had to accept it with bitter resignation.

In a later discussion, when the two sisters were alone, Gisela felt obliged to point out the possibility that Ritter might not have been dissuaded from his intention to sexually assault Inge on another occasion. They knew full well he had the power to order her to come to his own office if necessary, on whatever trumped up charges or suspicions that he wished to make up. It was as if living in a primitive society with the sheer authority that he held, both as a high-ranking officer and as a pathologically violent man.

Inge initially resolved to stay shut away inside the Gasthaus, not leaving for any reason. Gisela naturally agreed to assist her in any way she could; she took care of all the tasks that Inge had been responsible for before, including doing the shopping and taking her children to school and to the kindergarten for her. Furthermore, Inge did not wish anyone to know about the incident, including Martin. Despite her initial strong agreement, upon deeper reflection this posed a problem for Gisela, who had never lied in any major way to her husband and did not want to start now. While there had been a few white lies along the way, mostly concerning stock checks or matters of business, she felt this was a different area of far greater magnitude. Gisela therefore asked her sister to feign illness as the reason for not leaving the Gasthaus, and Inge complied. She told how she had acute stomach pains with vomiting to explain why she spent long periods in her room, which in turn left Martin very concerned for her health. He had been aware of her miscarriage the year before and began to worry about there being a connection. He was fond of his sister-in-law on a personal level, as well as recognizing the harmonious and hard-working side to her character that she brought to the household, and he wished to avoid any further calamity. He began to insist that she saw a doctor, saying that the costs would not be an issue if she had to see a specialist, while Inge assured him that that would not be necessary. It was just a minor stomach upset, she lied, that she had suffered from before and would eventually get over. Martin was not convinced, while Gisela and Corinna watched on in silence as the interaction became absurd.

After nearly two weeks, Inge quietly informed Gisela that she would return to her normal routine, including going out to do the daily shopping. She said that she had had sufficient time to mentally recover from the shock, which was not the case; and anyway, she told her sister truthfully, she did not want to spend any more time sitting around in her bedroom, letting herself become obsessive about the matter. It was not as if Ritter were going to attack her in broad daylight on the street, she argued, and Gisela agreed. "The sooner you are back on your feet the better. You will have to be defiant towards him, if you see him. Do not cower or look frightened. He is an animal, and an animal smells fear. And most important of all, and I want you to take good heed of what I am saying here: you have nothing, absolutely nothing to feel ashamed of. This kind of terrible thing happens every day to young women. It is part of the rotten side of the nature of people. Or more specifically, the nature of men. Do not let it get you down. You walk down that street with your head high and if your paths cross, just ignore him and look straight ahead. Here at the Gasthaus there will always be someone to keep an eye out. At least we are warned now and can be more careful about who enters during the day. I shall keep the back door locked too, just in case."

Inge nodded as her sister spoke and thought, "She is right but that is all so easy to say now in the calmness of this room, so very different to experience it with the anxiety of being vulnerable out in public." Nonetheless, she promised to take her sister's advice to heart and adjust her mindset accordingly. Within a week, her routine was back to normal. She looked over her shoulder more often, was nervous when taking Adolf to the primary school where she had once bumped into Ritter, but with time came fortitude and she felt she was recovering her old character to do battle with this new threat.

That is, until she saw Ritter again. Fortunately, she was on the other side of the Münzstraße at the time, heading home alone and carrying a basket with some potatoes and other vegetables she had bought for the evening meal, while he was intently staring in the shop window of a tobacconist and appeared not to have seen her. But even at that distance, she felt a huge wave of heat flare up inside her and her heart began beating wildly. She rushed on, almost pushing with force through the small cluster of people that had formed a clot at the corner of that street with the Finkstraße, in order to rush on home. She ran in sheer panic and had almost reached the entrance to the Gasthaus when she slipped and fell, dropping the basket and seeing how the assorted vegetables began to dance down the street. She ran after them, scooping them up as quickly as she could in hot trembling hands. She was finally able to limp up to the front door with what she hoped to be all the groceries recovered, though stopped once inside the front hall, to slide down the wall and sob in uncontrollable convulsions. Gisela was the only one at home at the time, and dashed down the stairs to find her still sitting on the floor and weeping.

Inge recognized how deeply the trauma had cut into her and how difficult the future now presented itself. Lüneburg was a small town and sooner or later she would run into him again; probably on the next occasion there may even be a verbal exchange. If she had reacted with such panic to the mere sight of him, how would she handle hearing his voice or having him near to her? "This can't go on," Inge said later to her sister. Gisela agreed, but was initially stumped as to a solution. Nonetheless, her mind rattled away on overtime, weighing up all the differing aspects of the dilemma, until she came to a reluctant but possibly workable solution.

Within her formula was her own personal assumption that Horst had indeed been killed in the infamous battle for Stalingrad, that was by now widely though quietly viewed by the German public as a resounding military disaster. This was naturally an opinion that she would not dream of even hinting at to her sister, who was still optimistic about his return and assumed he had been taken as a prisoner of war by the Soviets, but that this had not been correctly documented in the war-time confusion.

Although Gisela, like others, did not personally think this military débâcle would affect the overall progress of the war in any great manner, it was clear that it had been a great setback. There may well be a necessary restructuring of the armed forces ahead when more "useless Nazi pen pushers", as her father would have called someone like Ritter, were sent out to battle. In short, she was of the opinion that Horst would not be returning but that Ritter may well be leaving. But, she knew, all of this would take time.

With this framework established in her mind, she reflected that the best move for her sister would be to 'disappear' for a while until the dust had settled. She would tell her sister that this period could be until the return back home of Horst; while Gisela herself would regard the period as defined by Ritter moving on. She suspected him of being an ambitious creature, at least judging from his bravado of conversational spirit at the meals in which he had participated at her restaurant. She was surprised that he had already spent so long in a little provincial nest like Lüneburg, overlooking the fact that this was now the capital of the East Hannover *Gau*. But she felt confident that if – or rather, when - he was stationed elsewhere, she would find out immediately.

As this formula began to make perfect sense in Gisela's plan, she next pondered on where her sister could best disappear to, and there she was unsure. A solution to this presented itself when Corinna, who had been privy to some of Gisela's thoughts on the matter, began to hint to Inge herself about this being a possible route out of her dilemma. Inge was instantly taken by the idea and, with their mother's support, the gambit began to take form with rapidity. The three women discussed the issue intensely together, whenever Martin was not around, and Inge filled in the final piece in the puzzle with the destination: "Hamburg!" she exclaimed. "That will be the perfect place to wait for the war to end and for Horst to come home."

She expounded on her reasoning. "Horst has an uncle who lives in Hamburg, and this uncle has a high position in the police force there. He would be a first-class contact."

"Oh course!" said Corinna. "Cousin Carsten's father, Robert. A charming man, very serious – I have always liked him."

"Exactly," nodded Inge, becoming more enthusiastic with each passing second. "And I shall contact him and tell him, not directly, but in some way that he will understand, that I want to move to Hamburg for a short period of time until the waiting is over here at this end. And it will also serve, after the war, as a direct way to explain to Horst and the rest of his family what exactly was going on. Everything will be so up-front and honest."

Gisela warmed to the idea. "And it is not so far away. You can come down any weekend you like and spend it with us. We will pick you up at the train station. We can even do that in Bernhard's car so that you do not have to walk down the street. I will tell him and Edeltraut some silly excuse to explain your leaving. You can spend all the weekend inside with us. And if you do want to go anywhere, just to have a walk outside, then I will go with you and we will go arm in arm everywhere. Whatever happens, I will be right beside you."

Corinna, however, was not so convinced. Such a large city, and with the reputation that a major port had, and some parts of it could be dangerous. Where would she live, what would she do? It would be an anonymous existence in contrast to this small and protective town she had grown up in. She did not say as much, but Corinna could well imagine the elder daughter packing her bags and heading off with determined steps to a metropolis, though not the younger.

That was a major question that hovered over the plan: what was Inge to do to make enough money to get by? She was most certainly not afraid of hard work and she had instinctively assumed that the employment in question would be factory work, though that thought depressed her. She saw herself sitting in an enormous place the size of an aircraft hangar, in a long line of women standing before a conveyor belt, monotonously checking pristine shells and bullets for hours upon end, operating without emotion and like clockwork toys. But when she mentioned this notion, Gisela was quick to correct her. There were hundreds of different jobs for women to be involved in, why would she have to work in a factory? As far as Gisela was aware, that kind of heavy work was carried out by enemy prisoners of war that they brought over from the concentration camps. There would surely be an opportunity for something much lighter and less physically demanding for her sister, she told her.

What eventually clinched the deal was speaking to Uncle Robert himself. Gisela and Inge contacted Horst's relative by telephone, just on the off-chance and to sound out the idea to him. After all, he lived in the city himself and had a good idea of what would be proper and acceptable for a young woman in Inge's position. Though initially surprised by the idea, he was ultimately supportive. Inge also told him that she wished to help out with the war effort, and that struck a chord in him. He told how many young women, including married women like herself with husbands fighting on the front, were taking military training and helping out the Wehrmacht in a host of different ways. His sister was involved in the recruiting and training of these women and had a wealth of knowledge on the topic. While it was true that many women were also assisting in manual jobs, such as working in ammunitions factories, he did not deem this to be a wise idea or very suitable choice for a young lady of her standards. Inge blushed at the compliment, but had to admit to a lack of qualifications and relevant experience when he asked her a few basic questions about her professional career thus far. Even so, he remained confident that they could find some employment for her. It might be basic at first, but it was all a question of starting low and working your way up through application and determination.

There were a few more communications between the two parties until the plan was sealed and Uncle Robert said he would be on the look-out for an apartment-share for Inge, preferably with some young professional ladies who could help show her the steps on the career ladder.

It should be mentioned that Uncle Robert's enthusiasm for the idea also stemmed from a very different perspective on the war than that of someone like Gisela. Like many, Gisela readily believed the positive propaganda that was being pumped out in the press and media. She viewed the conflict as not set to last too much longer; a year at the most and then the enemy would give up and Germany would have won whatever it wanted (her mother thought much the same, despite the gloomy prophecies that her husband Georg frequently emitted). She had heard so much cheering throughout the previous few years, that the unease that came in the wake of Stalingrad, partly neutralized by the undying optimism of the daily government propaganda, did not fully register with its full potential. Robert Grün, in contrast, understood far better the significance of the defeat on the banks of the Volga than the others did. He would never have considered for a moment entering into detail about this with others, even his own family, and left his thoughts as very private conjectures. But he was aware that this was set to be a drawn out and immensely bloody conflict. Although he saw victory at the end of the tunnel, it was to be a long and wearying tunnel ahead. He had read certain classified facts and statistics, concerning the treatment of the troops and the provisions they had received, and was silently concerned that the elites had not grasped the basic necessities of the troops on the ground. He felt that the Führer had made a grave error in not evacuating the men from a pointless slaughter, and for the first time he acknowledged, again in complete and utter privacy, the weakness and capacity for failure of a man whom he had never liked but had at least come to regard as a brilliant military strategist.

And so, seeing a lengthy conflict ahead, he deemed it necessary that as many people as possible, including women, put their shoulder to the wheel and helped with the war effort as best they could. It was to be a decisive period ahead for the nation with no time for prim and proper notions of women only being fit for kitchens, nurseries, and churches. He fully appreciated and backed Inge's endeavour.

With this unequivocal support, the plan soon forged ahead. Details were discussed. If the worst came to the worst, and it would be an awful but possible coincidence that Ritter were posted to Hamburg, then the problem would be solved and Inge could return home. It was deemed unlikely that he would be visiting the city for another reason and, in any case, Hamburg was precisely the kind of large city in which one could easily hide, in crass comparison to Lüneburg and its charming but compact centre where everyone knew everyone else and paths frequently crossed.

Inge had initially resisted the sadly inevitable notion of parting with her children. She planned to look around for suitable schools and kindergartens in Hamburg for them as soon as she was informed of the apartment's address and district. The idea of leaving them behind was absurd, she had told her sister at first. If she had to go, then naturally she would take them with her. It was unmotherly to think otherwise. That was the place of a German woman, she argued; the Führer himself had said so on numerous occasions and moreover she had a medal to back that up. A true German woman bore children, looked after them, brought them up with a sense of morality and a proper education.

But here Gisela brought home to her the reality of a Germany firmly entrenched in a war rising in intensity and with an ever-widening *Heimatfront* (home front). Civilians, including their own children, were now as much at war as their fathers and uncles. Ever since the massive bombing of Cologne the year before, there had been a growing awareness among the population of the unlimited nature of wartime bombing. Every city was a potential target.

"There's no question about it, Inge, they have to stay here with us. You cannot be taking them with you up to Hamburg. Who will look after them during the afternoon when you are at work? In any case, children are being evacuated out of a lot of cities now because of the bombing raids. In Berlin the authorities are already doing that in large numbers - sending the kids to stay with families out on the land. Imagine that, living with strange families out in the countryside when all you have ever known is city life, poor things. Adolf and Joseph and Hermann will be just fine here with us. Mama and I will look after them well. You know how Mama loves taking them for walks. She thinks the world of them. They are always asking after Oma Corinna, it is so sweet! And like I said, any time you want, you just come and visit us and spend the weekend here, or a week or two. Whatever you see fit. We are just half-an-hour away by train. You can even come at night and leave the next morning if you are worried."

Inge eventually saw reason. Nearby cities like Hannover or Hamburg were not only likely targets for raids, they had already been attacked and may well continue to receive further bombardments.

While nowhere was totally safe, Gisela argued, they represented far more potential danger than a provincial town like Lüneburg with very little industry or strategic importance for the bombing campaigns. "Look at Essen and all those other cities in the Ruhr. They have been heavily bombed, it was all on the radio. They are industrial centres. They have strategic value. Even I know that. But there is next to nothing here to bomb. We are a small quiet town where people mind their own business." This wasn't quite true, as both Inge and Gisela herself were aware, with the very minor but nonetheless frightening bombing from August 1941 still fresh in their memory. But it was formulated that way by Gisela to stop the conversation heading any further in that morbid direction. Ultimately, they agreed that the plan they had crafted between them was the best possible solution to the current situation; a situation, they reminded each other, that must surely be transitory. At some point either Ritter would leave, Horst would return, or the war would end – hopefully all three together and very soon.

Nevertheless, leaving behind her boys was a strongly negative factor that left Inge saddened and doubtful. It seemed to her to be the only major obstacle in an otherwise smooth plan. But Inge also knew that her mother and sister were both excellent mothers and perfectly capable of taking the maximum care of her children. She knew it would pain her greatly to be away from them, and she was also unsure as to how to break the news to them. She became reluctant to leave at one point and requestioned the plan; felt she was abandoning her "babies." However, a stern conversation with mother and sister wiped away the last of her doubts and she accepted that her temporary move should not be further delayed. As Gisela said, once and hesitantly, "After all, Ritter might come back."

There was a heavy inevitability about the decision; it seemed the best of a series of bad options and the only one that made any sense. However distraught she would become in the following period at the thought of leaving her children behind, Inge was to be equally comforted at the thought that their safety would have priority. If major cities had become war zones, then obviously she would not want her children brought into that fray. It would be as ludicrous as having had them taken along with their father to travel the Russian steppes together. So much was clear to her and overrode her instinctive need to have her offspring near to her. Additionally, her trust in her sister's maternal skills was absolute.

The next step was to inform the children themselves, in a clear language that they would understand while at the same time pressing home the importance of secrecy.

One night, after they had their baths and were put to bed, Inge sat down with them. "Your Mama is going to have to go and help a friend with some work, so I shall be gone for a while." They looked at her seemingly baffled, so she continued. "I will not be gone for too long, but I have to go. And you will be here with Tante Gisela and Onkel Martin, and Oma Corinna too. So you will have all your family around you. Just as usual. Everything will be the same."

"Is this like when Papa went away?" asked Joseph and seemed to knock her out with his simple question.

"No, I will not be gone as long as Papa has been gone. Because I am not going as far away."

"Papa is in Russia," said Adolf, with a tone of strong confidence. "He is fighting there," he added. "In the war."

"In the war?" asked Hermann, understanding significantly less of the subject than his brothers who regularly lined up toy tanks and soldiers in formation lines and smashed them against each other.

"That is correct, but it is not so important now. I just want you to know that next week I will be going away in the morning but I will not return in the evening. So I will be gone for a few weeks. You must not be worried or frightened. Tante Gisela will take care of you like she always does. And Mama is fine, she is just helping out a friend."

"In Russia?" asked Joseph.

"No! No," replied his mother. "Not so far, not nearly so far. That is why I will not be gone for very long. But this is Mama's secret and you must not tell anyone. That is very important. This is just for us to know here in the family, do you understand?" They nodded, used by now to being asked by adults if they understood things that they had but a basic grasp of.

Inge put her fingers to her lips. "Not a word." They nodded. "If anyone asks where I am, you just say that Mama is helping a friend. And don't say anything else."

Joseph asked, "What is your friend called?"

Inge was flummoxed at first but thought a made-up name could not harm the story. "Maria," she said.

"Maria," Hermann repeated.

"*Tante* (Aunt) Maria?" asked Joseph.

"No, just Maria," his mother replied patiently. The boys took in the information and began to feel tired; there were no more questions.

She spoke to no-one outside the family about her decision to move. It was decided to keep the subject hushed up so that under no circumstances could Ritter get wind of the plan. In such a small town as Lüneburg, the rapidity with which gossip travelled was hellish, even with trivial issues and let alone with something of much greater import. She did consciously make one exception, however, and that was to go one last time to visit Arnold Schilling. She instinctively felt a certain comradeship with him somehow, though she had no idea why, and considered him to be an ally on whom she could count in future.

His apartment half-way down the nearby street Am Berge fortunately meant a very short walk from the Gasthaus, around three minutes if she went with a brisk pace. Though still feeling great trepidation as to the slim possibility of a chance encounter with Ritter, she decided that the odds were sufficiently stacked against that happening and so she would take the risk. She set out on the Thursday afternoon a few days before her departure was due to take place, hoping to catch Schilling at home. She arrived at the apartment block, swivelling her head in all directions to discern who was around her, rushed up the stairs and was in luck: he was at home. This time he let her in immediately and with a warm welcome and large smile. He seemed quite a new man, she thought, in terms of his disposition towards her; but she noticed how gaunt in the face he appeared and noted too how much thinner his body seemed in comparison to before. She did not wish to comment on the matter and put him in an embarrassing situation, but it was clear that he was eating very little.

"I have brought a cake with me," she said, now very glad to have had that foresight. "We can have a slice to see how it is and I will leave the rest of it with you, if you like." He nodded and thanked her profusely, making her wish she had brought two or three with her.

He prepared some coffee and they sat down at his worktable and talked. He had heard that Horst was missing in action and expressed his sincere sympathy. Inge was grateful for his words and felt that his affection was genuine. Whatever may have been said about the fireman the last time they had spoken, Inge felt sure that Schilling would not hold a grudge in the face of such deleterious circumstances. Schilling, in turn, was indeed saddened by the news. He was also of the opinion that Inge, though she herself seemed to not even entertain the possibility, was most likely already a widow.

Inge told him that she would be heading off to work in Hamburg in the next few days, in order to make her own contribution to the war effort. Also, she mentioned, to put some distance between herself and a person in Lüneburg who had been pestering her of late. She did not go into detail about the nature of the molestation, and she furthermore asked Schilling not to spill a word on this subject to anyone. She ascertained correctly that Schilling had compassion for her situation and for her need for total discretion. He even said that she could count on him to help her out with anything within his powers; she had just to contact him and he would see what he could do. Inge was grateful for the offer of support and she saw in Schilling's eyes that he was genuinely concerned.

After this was all established, Schilling went on to make a confession, feeling that it was a good moment for the two of them to trade more confidential information. He also asked her for total silence on the topic, and she nodded eagerly, glad to be in on the secret and beginning to get a taste for the whole game of subterfuge.

"I remember how the last time that you were here, you asked after a friend and ex-colleague of mine, Daniel Kaplan. You said that you had not seen him in a while and asked me to pass on *schöne Grüße* (your best wishes)." She nodded and he continued, "Well I did and, it is a long story, Inge, and quite complicated, you see, I cannot go into a lot of detail, at least not at the moment, but the thing is that he had to leave the country and that was going to be very difficult." Schilling heard his verbal clumsiness as he wondered how much he could and should tell this woman, whom he was instinctively fond of but did not know well enough to confide so deeply in. "The thing is, he left in the end, and I have recently received some excellent news. He has made it across the Atlantic, from Lisbon, and is now in Buenos Aires," he beamed.

Inge's eyes widened. "That sounds wonderful! And all the way across the Atlantic. Where is Buenos Aires?" she asked, stumbling over the pronunciation.

"In Argentina, in South America."

"Oh, that is wonderful!" she smiled with glee, then asked. "But why did he have to leave so suddenly?"

Schilling paused. "He was, I mean, he is a Jew."

She raised her head and nodded slowly, comprehending a little more of what had always been going on around her. "I understand."

"He also needed to get away from someone who was pestering him."

She paused before answering, taking in the enormity of the sentence. "Yes, of course he did. I never…I never thought about this kind of topic before. Not really. Perhaps I should have given it more thought."

"The reason I am mentioning this to you is that both he and I wanted to thank you."

"Thank me – for what?

Schilling gave the broad grin of satisfaction at finally being able to relay a piece of information that he had kept inside for so long. "You were instrumental in him being able to get away safely. Although you did not know it at the time."

"I was? And I didn't know?"

"No, not at all. Let me explain. It was a while ago now, back in the autumn of 1941. You probably do not remember the day. Daniel had organized some transport to pick him up that day, and that transport was parked at the end of the street, on the corner of Am Berge with Rosenstraße, not far from where your sister's guesthouse is. Everything was ready to roll when we saw that two officers from the…", (he lowered his voice, even feeling afraid in his own home), "from the SS were coming towards us. Perhaps you know or have heard of them - they work at the Gestapo HQ and are called Ritter and Möhring." Inge felt a sharp heat inside her face and hoped she was not blushing noticeably. Schilling in any case was continuing. "They have their offices in the Julius-Wolff-Straße. And just as they were about to pass by the vehicle - and they were looking like they were perhaps about to hold an inspection on the spot – well, in that moment you appeared. Out of the blue, with Adolf bouncing his ball. It all happened so quickly, but basically Adolf and you ended up distracting those two officers and it was precisely that which gave Daniel and his driver time to get away without any further ado. You might well have ended up saving their lives."

Inge sat with her mouth agape.

"You look a little shocked," said Schilling with a chuckle. "I just wanted to tell you the story in order to thank you. I am sure Daniel would want to thank you personally if he could. Inge?"

She was jolted out of her recollections. "Yes, it is just that I remember the day. While you were talking, the scene came back to me. I can recall seeing you standing beside a small truck that was parked on the street, and Adolf was bouncing the ball up and down, and I remember, yes, talking to the men you mentioned, I..." Her voice trailed off as she looked down and gulped, struggling with internal anxiety. She looked back up at Schilling and said, "I am so glad that I was able to help Herr Kaplan. You cannot imagine how glad I am that he was able to get away successfully. Please give him my best regards when you are able to communicate with him." She sighed. "I hope so very much that this mad mad war is soon over and things will return to normalcy. And that changes are made in the government so that people can come back home and we can carry on as we once did. That is all I wish for, if the truth be told."

Schilling had no intention of correcting her and saying that going back to that level of normalcy was by now sheer impossible; that the past way of living that they had all once known was already gone and, like so many people, it would never return. "Yes, you are right. Let us hope for that," he lied instead.

Uncle Robert had located an apartment, Inge found out from Gisela on arriving home. The next two weeks flew by, while Ritter was noticeable only by his continued absence from their lives. Inge found further internal strength and determination through the stimulation of the warming summer sunlight and was able to forge ahead with her plans.

The eve to the big day finally arrived and during the afternoon Inge packed two suitcases with clothing and a few possessions: family photos, essential documentation, toiletries, an expensive perfume that Horst had given her and which always reminded her of his smile in that moment, some jewelry, some basic stationery. She caught an early morning train at Lüneburg, on the Hannover to Hamburg line. Gisela went with her, and Inge waved her goodbye from the carriage before taking a seat on the packed train and firmly pressing down her neat skirt. She spent most of the journey thinking of her husband; what he was doing, what he would think of her travelling along in the train to the port city to the north.

She reached the destination station, *Hamburg Hauptbahnhof* (Hamburg main railway station) half an hour later, at around a quarter to eight. Dazzled by the crowds of people rushing by to the early morning trains, she descended and stood around with some insecurity at first. But soon she moved off and melted into the trail of people heading down the platform and converging with others still in the entrance hall. The station had been badly damaged during air-raids on the city and large sections of the roof were missing. It was partly cloaked with a thick camouflage covering, an enormous structure that straddled across much of the station and was painted asphalt black on its top, so as to resemble an empty space when seen from the air.

She found a corner of the hall that seemed more sheltered from the flowing masses and sat down to consult yet again her map and the instructions as to how to reach the apartment in the Borgfelde district. She went through the carefully annotated details she had added to Uncle Robert's basic information. At first, she felt nervously apprehensive; intimidated by the size of the crowds in the city that – unlike in Berlin - she was now facing alone, but she was also determined not to let her natural fear get the better of her.

She left the station and went outside to look for the tram stop indicated in her instructions. Out there in the open, she also realized how cooped up in the Gasthaus she had been the past few weeks, how pleasant the sensation of fresh air now felt. Even the natural elements were close, with a boisterous wind rushing down the Elbe river from the North Sea, carrying inland a distinct salty taste of sea on its gusts and now blowing strongly around the two Alster lakes near to her. Feeling increasingly confident of rising to meet this new challenge, she smiled under the warm light of the morning sun.

Chapter 27

Inge took the tram #17 from the *Hauptbahnhof* stop, got off at the Burgstraße; turned left with a brisk pace into that loud bustling street and took the first left to reach the more secluded Bethesdastraße where the apartment was situated. The well-connected public transport and its proximity to the apartment was an immediate plus point. Looking around in quiet awe she found the area very attractive, with its tall elegant buildings, its rows of elm and horse chestnut trees lining the pavement, offering shade and birdsong. The metropolis, that had been an open yawning of people and traffic rushing on their way when she arrived, had reminded her of the urgent haste of central Berlin. But here this port city had acquired, once out in the residential area, a busy but pleasant atmosphere. She walked down the street of her new home with an elated heart at the prospect of living here, if only for a while. So happy was she with this first impression, she could not resist adding up the infamous *Milchmädchenrechnung* (literally: milkmaid's bill), i.e. once the war was over, and once Horst had returned home, they might like to move here, to find jobs, to bring up the children in Hamburg, and so start a new life. Once the war was over, once Horst had returned home. Although aware that her daydreaming may be somewhat hasty - here, she felt sure, there would be well-paid work for them both.

Inge felt drawn to her surroundings and as she strode up the pavement her heart warmed instinctively, enjoying the mixture of sun and leafy shade as she progressed. She reached Nr. 31 and gazed slowly up the whole façade, stopped to study the ornate balconies scattered around the front of the building on different floors, up to the little crowning turrets atop. She rang the bell and there was an immediate buzz to enter – she knew she was expected. She stepped into the building a little nervously, passed by the rows of post boxes on the wall of the foyer, and crept to the foot of the staircase. The dark wooden steps were clean and well-polished, the staircase itself in good condition, and there was a vase of flowers on a small table near the foot of the stairs, giving off a sweet scent and creating a homely image. She felt immediately at home and proceeded to climb the stairs to the third floor with more vigour and self-confidence.

There were three apartments on the third floor. On the door almost directly before her was a bell with the names *Lenz* and *Witzigmann*, and beside it the obligatory fire extinguisher and bucket of sand, ready for war on the home front. She rang and a pretty young woman opened up and gushed that she must be Inge. So punctual, she marvelled, while she herself was not yet fully ready.

She chuckled and showed Inge into the front room, introduced herself as Lotte Witzigmann and explained she had had a long series of late shifts and now couldn't get to sleep until the early hours. "I only got up half-an-hour ago. Doesn't that sound awful! I have a late duty again today so actually it is just as well that way. So, this is the apartment, our temporary home," she waved expressively at the neat but simple front room; a small cluster of pictures on the wall by the sideboard with mirror, a table surrounded by four bare chairs, a sofa with a few scattered cushions. Lotte had long wavy blonde hair and was slim, though with a lean athletic build that radiated energy. Her effusive smile and natural loquacious manner attracted Inge from the start.

Still talking, she moved to the window; swept back the old red curtains and raised the heavy black blinds, letting in the rising morning sunlight. "The living room and balcony have a charming view of the street and they get some beautiful sunlight," she said, shielding her face from the glare. "Your room is on the other side - would you like to see it straightaway? I know I would!" she grinned.

Inge had placed her suitcases on the floor momentarily and now snatched them back up, smiled, nodded in shy acquiescence. Lotte showed her to her room with its plain but sturdy furniture: a large double bed, a wardrobe with mirror, a table and small desk with drawers by the window, a rug on the dark wooden floor. "It's a cosy apartment, well built, and the neighbours are very respectful. A few children around but not too many. That is so very important when you are working shifts. Unfortunately, they have such high-pitched yells when playing and do not understand the word silence. I do not know what I would do if I had any of my own!"

Once in the kitchen, Inge asked Lotte almost immediately about her job, keen to orientate herself professionally among the new women. The reply in this case was that she worked in the

Luftschutzwarndienst (air-raid warning duty). "We are the ones who throw you all out of bed in the middle of the night!" Lotte chirped gayly.

Inge huddled up her shoulders in glee (in unconscious imitation of Lotte's manner), thoroughly enjoying the warm spirit. She found herself beaming with the contagious humour that Lotte freely emitted into every room she entered and with which she infected every person she conversed with.

Inge said, "That sounds very..." and searched for a word with which to impress her new flat-mate; she stumbled on "glamorous" and immediately regretted it.

"Glamorous?" Lotte replicated. "Oh no, not at all. How I wish! But it is interesting work, yes. Would you like a coffee?" to which Inge lit up with a "Yes, please."

"And do take a seat," Lotte continued. "It is your home now, too."

Inge wished to know who had been living there before and Lotte explained, "Angela, another girl from our department. But she has been posted to Breslau and left last week. Good connections. That is one city they will never bomb," Lotte winked. "Actually, we were all in the same women's barracks together, but then in April there was one problem after another. First there was a small fire which was probably due to faulty wiring. Then some big plumbing and drainage issues. We made a huge complaint and the same day they found a large, unexploded bomb nearby, so what with this and that, they decided to just evacuate the place, until things were better sorted out, and we were all found temporary accommodation. So, Trudchen and I and the other girl, Angela, we ended up being placed here. Käthe was already living here, she had moved in a few days before us. She used to work as a pre-school teacher but now she is a full-time assistant with the Red Cross and has been doing a training course this summer at the *Allgemeines Krankenhaus Eilbek* (Eilbek General Hospital) near here. She is wonderful, such a sweet girl, from Thüringen, and she can sew so well. Knows how to alter or mend anything. I am sure you will get on well together. So then, Angela moved on to Breslau and they eventually told us a few days ago that a new girl would be coming. Which must be you!" She pointed at Inge in a pantomimic way, giggled and said, "Now, that was a nice surprise! By the way, how did you find out about the apartment?"

"My uncle, well, to be precise, my husband's uncle is employed at the *Reichskriminalpolizeiamt* (German police department for criminal investigation) here in Hamburg, and he said there would be a room free for a while. Just a temporary arrangement. I would have stayed at his apartment - they live near the centre, in Neustadt - but his home is full up with all the family and there was nowhere appropriate for me to sleep. So he said he would try to find me a room in an apartment share. And, well, here I am."

"I understand."

"I know I am so lucky to have been given this accommodation. And it is such a pretty apartment here, with lots of light. So well-placed in the city. The area was very easy to reach with the tram, coming from the main station."

"It is, isn't it? I love the area. This whole eastern part of Hamburg is wonderful to live in. Very nice type of people here. Normal, down-to-earth, working people. I feel so at home. In fact, I shall be sorry to go. I think I will be sent to Kiel in September or October, at least that is what I have been told. Although that can all change at the drop of a hat. I have lived in so many different kinds of accommodation in the last few years - that's the thing about the Wehrmacht. Once, the quarters we had were this lovely old villa in Belgium, I swear it was like being in another century. And when I was doing the training in Gießen, I had private quarters with another girl from the course, Else, in a large family home in this little countryside nest nearby, called Heuchelheim, with a middle-aged couple who cooked for us. We each had a big room with a huge old traditional bed, but the mattress was a sack of straw! And in the bathroom there was just a stool and a cast iron bath, not even a mirror. My God, it was very rural. Honestly, the places that I have stayed in, I could write a book. But I think my favourite so far has been this apartment. So sunny and cosy, just right for four working girls," and she gave out her idiosyncratic cry, which she released sporadically during her excitable relating: a soft gasping shriek during which she often bit her lower lip and huddled up her shoulders.

While sipping her coffee, Inge asked her what her job consisted of exactly in terms of duties and, though willing to talk openly, Lotte's mien and tone instantly became far more serious.

"You see, all aircraft entering the airspace of the Reich are closely monitored. Further along the Elbe, west of Hamburg, there is a small town called Stade and there we have an important radar centre, built into a bunker, which tracks and identifies incoming aircraft. All that information is sent on to an analytical centre in Cologne, and we receive from Cologne the information that is specifically relevant to our area and process it here at our headquarters. We refer to it as aircraft incursion. I work there as an *Auswerterin* (recognition and evaluation worker). So, we are all equipped with telephones, recording equipment, notice boards, and we are told the exact entry details of the incursion: the direction, height, number, and speed of the aircraft. Also, if the destination is known or suspected, and in that case the estimated time of arrival there. We have a large map on the wall and there, between the graticules, I register with markers all this flight information. That is how we present it to the officers. In the case of enemy attacks, they have to decide about the deployment of fighter planes or flak, where and when, and they pass on those instructions to the appropriate local command centres. Like I said, it is not glamorous, but it certainly keeps you on your toes. And I like that. I could not do with being bored at work."

"Have you always done that since you have been working with the *Wehrmacht*?"

"No. First I completed my training in Gießen and then it was well over a year later, when I was already working at a printing firm in Frankfurt, that one day a policeman came to our door and told my mother that I had to report in two days' time to the police headquarters as I was now *dienstverpflichtet* (required to report for duty). I had a heavy cold that week and got home from work feeling terrible, but still! - on the Thursday I had to go. I told them the next day at work about this and said, and very dramatically I thought at the time: sorry but I will probably be gone for a few months," she laughed. "That is now a few years ago. No-one imagined back then how time during a war could pass by so quickly. So, in that first week of training I had the enlistment formalities to complete and then there was further intensive training in Gießen, concerning aviation tracking. After that, my first position was an assignment in Cologne."

Inge took this all in and asked Lotte about her background, keen out of self-interest to orientate herself with the common professional routes available for young women of her background. Lotte was a mine of information and loved to talk. She launched into her life story with great aplomb, starting right at the very beginning as only the most self-confident can.

Lotte was from Frankfurt and had finished the *Mittlere Reife* (secondary school leaving certificate) at sixteen and gone on study a *kaufmännische Ausbildung* (commercial education course) at the *Höhere Handelsschule* (a higher technical college in Frankfurt). In her final year, she found out that young women were receiving more military-oriented training at the *Luftschutzwarndienst* (air-raid protection warning service), including that required to become a *Fernsprechermelderin* (telephone and telegraph messenger), and thought it sounded very interesting. "It was also an additional qualification that I felt looked impressive and only involved one hour of study every evening at a centre in Frankfurt. Plus, they even paid 50 *Pfennig* transport costs a day, which in itself seemed generous to a young girl. This was around 1937-8. I never imagined that there would actually be a war at some point! - let alone one in which towns and cities were going to be attacked from the air. Anyway, a year after completing the course I was enjoying a relaxing summer holiday with my family, near some lakes in the south of Germany, and when we returned to Frankfurt at the beginning of September, it turned out that war had broken out after all. I was called up and had to pack my suitcases after having just unpacked them!

Later, most of the work consisted of quite basic functions within the section called *Telefondienst* (telephone duty). We would all sit in a row, with headphones on and connected to a cabinet in front. We would be given theoretical information concerning possible enemy planes approaching, and we would just have to pass it on to the appropriate unit for them to activate the alarm system and the sirens. That is all it was: listening, typing down, and then calling the responsible *Meldestelle* (reporting office) to pass on the information.

Administrative centres, town halls, major industrial companies, police and fire stations, military headquarters, that kind of thing. All very basic stuff. In the early years, there was not much going on at all. I remember in 1940, in Cologne, there was just the one time when a few English bombers got through and dropped about six bombs on a local railway line. There was next to nothing going on, just little nuisance raids. Not like nowadays - now it is just madness with the enemy! I have a friend who lives and works in Cologne and she said last year was terrible. A lot of raids and at the end of May, a huge one. She got bombed out of her apartment and had to move in with a married couple she knows. So anyhow, back then at the beginning it was much more peaceful. We were mostly doing test runs of the alarm system to make sure the information flow was functioning well."

Inge sipped on her coffee, engrossed but at the same time with the sinking feeling that this was going to be well above her station and that she would probably end up in the ammunition factory after all. Nevertheless, she remained drawn to the tale and she encouraged – not that much encouragement was required - her newly-found acquaintance to continue with her curriculum vitae.

After Cologne, Lotte was stationed in Belgium; first in Brussels, later in Antwerp and Leuven. She had adored the country and even made friends among the women there. But only among the Flemish, she added, who usually spoke very good German, as opposed to the Walloons who only spoke French and hated the Germans anyway. There were often moments of antagonism with the Walloons in parts of Brussels: "The tram drivers did their usual trick a lot. You see, you had to get up on this step to get into the tram, and I would be standing waiting there, with other German women from the centre, and we were in civil dress but they recognized us anyway, then just as we were getting inside they would close the door so that we got stuck there and couldn't move. And we would shout out, and they would start complaining about us and cursing away in French. Just stupid things like that. I had no idea what they were saying. I have never felt much desire to speak in French, no more than was strictly necessary for the training and to get by. In any case, when on official business we were usually accompanied by Flemish guards. There were a lot of very German-friendly Flemish people there. When we were in Brussels, we women had very classy accommodation organized in this beautiful big town villa. It was almost like a luxury hotel. They even had a Flemish Waffen-SS volunteer group posted there to look after us, just in case. They were lovely men, very charming and correct, and used to guard the house all night. We ate so well there, I miss that. We would go out to the *pommes frites* stands, they were wonderful, especially in spring, and sit outside and have a midday snack. You could get hold of anything in Brussels, anything at all. Coffee, butter, cognac, even ice-cream. Chocolate was very dear, though. I once paid 12 Marks for a hundred-gram block. Lipstick, silk stockings too. And that wonderful perfume, the one in the little blue bottle, what was it called again?" Lotte struggled to recollect the brand, determined to grasp it. "Ah yes! - Soir de Paris. Oh, it was divine. All on the black market of course. Although as German girls we had to be especially careful about that. It would have been so shameful for us to get caught by the military police!" She let out her little cry of mirth, "Imagine how that would have looked! But we never were, thank God. Back at the villa, we had full board of course and it was first-class. In the evenings at the accommodation we always had soup, main course, dessert, and a glass of wine. The cook was this fat, sour-faced old Walloon who would not give you the time of day. She must have hated us Germans with all her heart!" Lotte tittered at the thought. "But her husband was Flemish and the caretaker of the building and he was always very pleasant to us. Our supervisor there was actually a nursing home manager by profession, had never even trained in the Wehrmacht. A very charming lady, from Düsseldorf, I think. She never wore a military uniform, only civil clothing, and was having an affair with one of the married bomber pilots who was actually twenty years younger than her!" Lotte found great hilarity in that part of the story and laughed abundantly. Inge, with her strong traditional views on the sanctity of marriage, was inwardly a little shocked but feigned a collegial smirk as best she could.

"I was only in Belgium for about six months but the time spent there did me the world of good. I learnt so much. We even got to fly in planes so that we could see what a landscape looked like from above and get a better instinctive feel for our job. The pilots were so kind and explained so much. We had a couple of trips over Belgium, once in a *Tante Ju* (Junkers Ju 52), and another time in a Messerschmidt 109 which is such an incredible aircraft. So sleek, so agile! And the pilots were always so good-looking. I was there for about a year and after that I was sent to Gießen to do further training. That lasted four weeks and after that I was in Aschaffenburg, then Stettin, and I have been here in Hamburg for about two months now."

"So many places," commented Inge with a dreamy sigh.

"Oh, I like all the moving around, it doesn't bother me in the slightest. And my fiancée is stationed in Italy, so it keeps my mind from worrying about him," she laughed and waved her wrist with a dangling silver bracelet. "That is a gift from him. It is even engraved with our names and the date of the first night we went out together. He has such a wonderful memory, more than I do!" she chuckled, then gave out a deep sigh. "But we said we did not want to talk about rings until after the war."

"You have seen so much of the world and done so well for yourself," said Inge, clearly impressed.

"Yes, the training and the promotion opportunities have been very encouraging. You can see how the government clearly invests in our future and you really do have the sense that you can make something of yourself through hard work and discipline. I am in a position now where I have been working with new trainees. Showing them the ropes, so to speak."

"You said before that you are the one that throws everyone out of bed in the night. Does that happen much here in Hamburg?"

"Actually, it has been quiet here these last few months. Thank heavens! But yes, there have been many minor raids on Hamburg so far, dozens even, but especially in the last eighteen months. Like everywhere in Germany. There was quite a serious one in March, but we were not here at the time. It is just something you have to get used to."

"We heard on the radio about the recent raids on Stuttgart and Munich. They sounded awful. We had some bombs fall on Lüneburg too, it must have been about two years ago. But only a few, nothing like the attacks you hear about on the radio. I think they probably dropped them on us by accident! They have built bunkers all over town and the air sirens sometimes go off but nothing ever happens. The planes always pass over and fly off somewhere else, so we have been so lucky so far. I mean, it must have been terrible what they went through in Essen last month. We heard there were fires burning everywhere and the whole city centre was destroyed."

"Yes, they were very badly hit there, unfortunately, like all the towns in the Ruhr area. Trudchen is from Essen and she was very worried about her family at the time. Obviously, the enemy is going to try to attack all the urban and industrial centres it can. That much is clear. They have never hidden that intention. Just last month they ran a major raid on nearby Kiel, also a military port, so it is naïve to assume they will not continue to try to attack Hamburg. It is simply up to us to defend ourselves against them as best we can, until the final victory comes. After all, that is why we were forced into the war in the first place. Because the enemy ultimately wants to attack us and wipe us out. If we do not defend ourselves, he will achieve that goal."

This was not a position that sat well with Inge, who was now feeling a growing distrust toward the authorities that ran her country. She decided to forge ahead with more practical questions that lacked political undertones.

"And if they do try to attack us here in Hamburg, I mean, while I am here, how will they do it exactly? Do they use poisonous gas?" The thought had terrified her, so she was keen for details.

"No - some people think that, older people, especially men who fought in the last war. But no, they are not using gas. There have been some rumours to the contrary, though, and all the bunkers are supposed to be fully equipped with gas masks and detoxication flues, just in case. In general they are using a mixture of high explosive bombs, incendiary bombs, and also what are known as delay action bombs. Those are particularly cruel. They are designed to stay in the ground and go off later, once there is an all-clear signal. They are hazardous for firefighters and other rescue workers. You see how cruel the enemy is? And they have these air mines, the so-called 'apartment-block busters'. Those are incredibly powerful, they can pulverize a whole house, complete with the cellar. Then of course there are the different incendiary devices including phosphor bombs, which are barbaric. There is no end to it. Sometimes I think it is a miracle that we are all here, safe and sound."

Inge pondered on that with a slow nodding reaction and considered how peaceful Lüneburg had been.

Lotte said, "Talking of that, don't forget to follow all the usual blackout measures. They are very strict here about that, and understandably so! Make sure all that after dark all curtains are drawn tightly to and pull down the *Verdunkelungsrollos* (black-out blinds) in all of the rooms. If any of us are working the night shift, you can go into our rooms to check that their blinds are down too. The important thing is that the apartment is always sealed off at night to stop any luminance getting out and being seen from above. We also have protective tape around the window frames. Herr Lindemann takes care of the front door of the building and the entrance area. And there are some spare *Luftschutzlampen* (literally: air-raid protection lamps - dark-blue painted light bulbs) in the kitchen drawer, if you need them." She paused and added, "By the way, Trudchen has the late duty today, she should be back at around half past two."

"Do you all do different shifts?"

"Yes, we have either early duty from 6:00 to 14:00 or late duty 14:00 to 22:00. Once a week we all have to do night duty, from 22:00 to 6:00 in the morning. I will be doing that the day after tomorrow, so please be quiet in the morning if you are in the kitchen or the living room. Same with Trudchen. She works with me. Oh, and Käthe's brother Klaus is due to be coming home next week. He is stationed in Yugoslavia and has an eight-day holiday due, so Käthe has asked us all to go out with him next Friday afternoon to cheer him up and have some fun. We have managed to change our duty shifts so that we could all go out together. You will come along too, won't you? - go on! I have never met Klaus before and Käthe always speaks so highly of him. She says he is very charming and handsome. She must think the world of him. I can understand that, I love my brothers very much too. I did not used to so much, when we were kids at home, but now they mean the world to me. I worry about them all the time, but at least neither of them are out fighting in the east. At least not yet! I hope it does not rain when Klaus is here. It is always so cloudy and drizzly here in the north, even in summer. So much nicer back home but there you go," she said. "They said in the radio that it would rain at the weekend and the beginning of next week, but I hope it clears up by Friday. So, you will be coming along?"

Again, Inge smiled and nodded her agreement, now somewhat exhausted by this burst of social activity with Lotte. Fortunately, Lotte had plenty to do that day. They sorted out some formalities concerning the living arrangements, including the payment of rent, water, electricity, and heating costs; the pooling of resources between the women with regards to their *Lebensmittelkarten* (ration cards for food) and Lotte promising to sort out a *Bunkerausweis* (identity card for access to the air-raid shelter) for Inge. In addition to that, Inge was told she ought to register with the *Einwohnermeldeamt* (registry office for local residents). "They need the information for statistical purposes, so it is best to sort that out as soon as possible."

Once on her own, Inge settled into her new room and, despite all the excitement caused by the first day, she slept soundly that night. More than anything, she was immensely relieved that the journey had gone so well; that the city had not intimidated her as she had thought it might, with her arriving alone in a strange place; that she had had next to no trouble finding the apartment; and that the other women had been so friendly and welcoming. So many of the worries and reservations, that she had been stacking up inside, were cleared away, leaving her with a lucent mind. The next morning, she heard the deep gruff call of a ship's foghorn coming over from the port and instantly felt at home.

That first week she became accustomed to the varied arrival and departure times of Trudchen and Lotte, who had placed a list of their shifts on a noticeboard in the kitchen, as general information and for the good running of the apartment. Trudchen came across as the more quiet and reserved members of the group, but with an underlying dominance in her character too. She had dark curly hair and a short, well-built figure, including a large bosom. Her character was rigid; weighty, with gravitas and an arresting presence that could cause captivation or even intimidation in the listener, but never indifference. They both wore uniforms to work, which Inge found aesthetically attractive and sometimes she imagined herself in such an attire. Theirs was a dark skirt with light grey blouse and a jacket decorated with eagle and swastika emblems, plus a pair of lightning bolts on the jacket arm and on the *Krätzchen* - the little service caps they wore - too. They looked so smart and professional leaving the apartment in their uniforms that Inge was often envious.

Due to the military women's irregular shiftwork patterns, Inge found herself spending more time with Käthe, who worked regular times during her training. It was with her that Inge located all the nearby shops and places of interest. These included two well-stocked grocery stores, the best bakery, a friendly butcher, the newspaper kiosk, the laundry and dry cleaner and, last but certainly not least for Käthe, the local hairdresser. Käthe was in her early twenties, an attractive young woman who saw war as no reason for a woman not to take care of her looks. She herself had blonde hair, though darker and more voluminous than Lotte's, which she rolled inwards at the bottom with a side-parting on top: "à la Greta Garbo, don't you just know," Lotte had already quipped about her hair. Indeed, Käthe was a huge fan of the cinema and a mine of information regarding its stars and divas, whether American, Scandinavian, or German.

She proposed in the first week to take Inge to the hairdresser and insisted that she would pay for the session too. Inge chose the very practical but nonetheless stylish *Entwarnungsfrisur* ('all-clear signal' style). Women with longer hair had it combed upwards and tied in place in little wavelets on top of their heads; the upsweeping style was named after the phrase always said once the all-clear signal came, after a session spent in the air-raid bunkers: "*Alles nach oben!*" – "Everything up!" Inge, who until then had worn her hair plain, simply combed down, was congratulated that evening on her "glamorous" new look by the other women. Lotte said that Hamburg was obviously doing Inge the world of good, and the four women, in fine spirits, opened a bottle of wine.

Käthe was an easy-going young woman and Inge quickly bonded with her on most levels. As Lotte had already mentioned, she was a fervent patriot and had nothing but high words for the country's leadership and high hopes for a short, sharp, and above all prompt victory over the enemy. It had not been Inge's custom to say "Heil Hitler" much in greeting, but she now found herself copying Lotte's persistent example when out shopping in her company. This action left a mildly unpleasant taste afterwards, in view of her recent critical feelings towards the Führer and his minsters and generals; but equally she had no intention in the slightest of rocking the boat with regards to harmony at home.

On her fourth day there, she decided to clean the apartment, both to show off her good will as a flatmate as well as to be able to thoroughly sanitize her room. She always bore in mind the solid German advice that her mother had instilled in her: trust is good, control is better. She took the rugs and small carpets to the balcony and beat them soundly, cleaned the walls in the kitchen and bathroom, made all the mirrors in the apartment shine, mopped the kitchen and all along the wooden floors in the living room and hall. In her bedroom, she used a fresh bucket of water, gave strong strokes all along the floor, especially under the bed where she knew dust and dirt accumulated, and dug in with great vim in the corners of the room. She took a washing rag and got down on all fours, wiped around the legs of the bed and thoroughly cleaned its underside, and carried out the same procedure with the wardrobe.

She was wiping near to the wall when something seemed to come loose and detach herself. Fingering the still mostly hidden object, she felt that it was paper and cautiously pulled at it. It came out without too much tugging, and she found herself with a small but compact green notebook in her hand. Fascinated she opened it up and began to turn the pages, soon realizing that she was in possession of a diary. It began in the summer of 1939 and seemed to consist of sporadic entries, roughly one every few days; sometimes just a few lines with attentive numerical details, such as times, prices, or other digits. In other entries there were short paragraphs that, as she passed her eye over a couple of random examples, looked profounder and more confessional. She flicked through to the end, noting how the writing became smaller on the last pages, and saw the final entry near the end of the book, dated from September 1942 and followed by about ten blank pages. She picked herself up and placed the book inside her suitcase, having an instinctive sense of keeping her find to herself for the time being. She continued her cleaning and by the time she was finished that afternoon, Käthe had returned home from the shops. The training nurse was struck by the work that the new girl had done so sharply, and voluntarily as well. "The girls will love you, they hate cleaning," she said with a grin. They had a coffee together on the balcony while the sun fought to push its way through the occasional gap in a thick covering of slow-moving cloud.

That night in her room, she perused her find, reading excerpts here and there in more detail. She ascertained that the author of the diary was a young man who: had turned twenty in 1940; had originally wanted to study German literature at university but was now forced to consider other options, without having any real idea as to what; whose frequent references to *"wir Juden"* or *"uns Juden"* indicated his family was Jewish; who was horrified by the war but felt it must end soon with a German victory so that Hitler and his "military machine" would be appeased. Once, he spoke of emigrating to either Argentina or Palestine; but above all he simply wished for a swift end to the war that left the Germans full and content, like a tranquil lion after a large meal, and therefore leaving him and his family in peace.

Inge did not dare to read the final pages in any detail, beyond glancing at the dates. In fact, the more familiar she became with the young man's persona, which rose gradually out of the words like a ghostly figure out of the dark, the more a shudder of guilt crept over her. She thought at first it was the guilt at reading without any given permission the private thoughts of another person. But she sensed that the guilt went deeper. The diary left her feeling uneasy and, desirous to continue basking in the comforting sensation that her (once potentially traumatic) move to Hamburg had brought her, she did not read any further in those first weeks. She told herself it was not right to pry and snoop in another person's personal world and placed the small plump book among her private possessions, hidden away from sight.

Two days later, however, she did ask Lotte if she knew anything about the previous owners of the apartment. Lotte answered that, to her knowledge, it was a government-owned building that had been taken over by the Wehrmacht. As far as she knew it was normally used as temporary housing for civilians from large companies who were working on projects connected to military concerns. A group from the chemical company I.G. Farben had been living there for some months and had left that spring and vacated the apartment. After that, Käthe had moved in, followed by Angela, Trudchen, and herself; and now Inge. In the case of Lotte, Angela and Trudchen, their presence as Wehrmacht assistants was an unusual and temporary set-up.

"But your uncle who works with the police will be able to tell you all about that. He will know much more than we do," she assured her. Inge said that was a good idea, she would ask him on her next visit, though she knew from the start that she never would. The subject never came up again, and Inge came to the (correct) conclusion that the Jewish family living there before had been deported and the apartment then expropriated by the local municipal authorities. She kept all this to herself.

The diary was not the only thing that Inge came across during what became her regular cleaning sessions. Tucked away out of sight, on the top of the shelves in the living room, was a board game – '*Luftschutz tut not!*' ('Air-raid protection is essential!') The box displayed an elegant German town street into which some bombs had fallen, both onto the road and into some of the apartment blocks. In the midst of this event was a scene of panic: two men watching on and flailing their arms, a mother and her children fleeing in terror, a horse rearing up and away from its cart. She opened the box curiously and found a Ludo-like game of advancing using a dice from one side of the board to another, through partly burning house rooms and explosive outdoor scenes. She thought what a remarkable idea it was: to teach children basic air-defense procedure through fun and games. The next day she caught Lotte and Käthe together in the kitchen, and asked if it belonged to anyone. They shook their heads and seemed to think it must have come from the *Luftschutzzentrale* (air-raid protection central offices). Lotte suggested that Inge took it with her to Lüneburg, the next time she was home: "It is for children to play with and none of us have children, so give it to yours."

Käthe's brother Klaus Würdig arrived, as planned, the following week. Käthe breathlessly announced this to the women in the apartment for several days on end. That Friday, he came to see the women and arrived with supreme punctuality at 16:30 on the dot, bringing flowers for the kitchen, perfume for his sister, and a little box of chocolates for them all. He was tall, his dark blond hair swept up, his warm navy blue-green eyes, the exact same colour as his sister's, sparkling with seductive charm. He had a well-built figure with broad shoulders and strong limbs and the beginnings of a paunch. Käthe commented on how smart and handsome he was in his uniform, a real lady's man; to which Klaus blushed and laughed and modestly dismissed his sister's "silly nonsense". His easy-going charm and general insouciance, combined with his good looks, produced admiration in the women, of which Klaus was fully aware. Käthe introduced him to her cohabitees with giggly enthusiasm; before them stood an amiable and clean-cut soldier with elegantly coiffed hair, whom they all thought looked more fit to star in cinema films rather than to fight on muddy battlefields. A glowing Käthe related that she had already received a few consecutive days of holiday approved from those that were pending, so that she would be able to spend more time with her brother. With everything well planned and everyone assembled, the five set off in good spirits on the tram to the city centre.

Leaving the main train station with its camouflage covering, Klaus led the way as they walked down the *Ballindamm*, a huge promenade of trees alongside the *Binnen Alster*, the smaller of the two lakes by the Hamburg city centre. It was covered with an intricate construction formed out of planks of wooden planks and wire, designed to attract the attention of would-be bombers and get them to drop their deadly cargo into the lake instead. At the end they turned onto the elegant *Jungfernsteg* avenue and continued their stroll down the busy pavement. Lotte nudged Inge; while the others were occupied with pointing and chattering, she indicated that "over there in that direction" was the house of Klaus and Käthe's mother and stepfather, nodding significantly. Inge did not feel it was the right moment to inquire further.

Strolling past the impressive rows of buildings that lined the inner-city streets, feeling carefree in the sunlight and breeze, it was a picturesque and enjoyable walk for everyone. After wandering through this central area, past shops and other small businesses, they crossed the Stephansplatz and stopped to stare at the stone and pink plaster palatial façade of the *Alte Oberpostdirektion* – the Old Post

Office Administration building – with its ornate corner tower. They headed for the nearby park area, deciding in a quick chatter to have a look round the *Niederdeutsche Gartenschau* area beside the *Wallgraben*. This was a small lake, more like an elongated pond, surrounded by flower beds and statues of rough-hewn white bears gazing impassively out at the water. They completed a perfunctory round and, seeing a large restaurant with a café area outside, decided to sit outside and take a breather and have some refreshments.

The area was crowded, full of people surging out to enjoy the warm dry weather and benign blue skies that Friday afternoon, following a grey week of intermittent drizzle. Somewhere nearby an accordion player was belting out some popular songs. A group of laughing young soldiers in uniform – at the end of their leave and about to head off again to the front, now an intrinsic image of typical life in a German city - was sitting together on the grass, chatting and joking and watching the crowd stream by. The odd uniformed officer walked by with an attentive young woman on his arm. Some older women were chatting nearby in a group; civilian couples sat around, some looked romantically involved. Groups of older men were sitting round tables, taciturn and drinking beer, also observing the crowds mingle past. The bourgeoise was clearly out in number too, smartly dressed in dapper summer fashion, eager to impress despite the summer heat; the men in casual and sporty suit jackets with wide-cut trousers, the women in sleek wedge silhouette outfits with padded shoulders, prominent lapels, and thin waists *à la mode parisienne*. But it was mostly the labourers who poured in from the port areas and outer districts, enjoying an invigorating walk on that pleasant Friday; occasionally greeting acquaintances as they passed by, women pushing prams and men holding children in their arms, stopping to chat and share gossip. The people of working-class districts to the east like Hammerbrook, Eilbek, and Barmbek, having finished a hard week in dockyards and factories, were eager to herald in the coming weekend with a leisurely walk in the sun among families and friends. Everyone of all classes knew of the dark but distant conflict in the east of Europe, a conflict clearly audible in the radio and visible in the press yet muted in the mind; one that was slowly unfolding itself to its full extent in the battlefields of the Russian campaign. In these moments it was far enough away, out on remote plains and steppes, to be semi-forgotten. Here in the lively, rumbustious streets and parks of Hamburg, the warm early summer sun blanketed out any deeper fears. Even Inge found here among the good company a few hours of respite from her habitual worries about the fate of Horst, and she was able to smile along with the others and share in snippets of conversation. She was enchanted by the crowds that bustled by and the sheer energy that the large city emanated, so different from the quiet and staid pace of life back in Lüneburg.

Käthe was giving Trudchen a running commentary on all the neighbours. The latter had asked her about the couple living opposite, who kept themselves to themselves, and the topic had blown up from there. Lotte had returned from the public bathroom and commented on how well Klaus looked and how happy he must be to be back home.

Klaus said, "You cannot imagine how much this place has changed for the better. In just a matter of a few years. I remember back at the beginning of the thirties. When our parents used to argue all day and night." He turned to include the others in the conversation. "Our father was employed in the port, worked in shipyards as a welder. Then the contracts dried up. First the export business and the mercantile side all plummeted, then the ship construction itself. It was like dominoes falling, one after the other. He got laid off in 1932. They had always had lots of petty arguments at home, rows even. You see, I love my mother dearly but she really doesn't understand about basic budgeting or how to run a household. She runs up bills without thinking. Whereas my father liked to have things strictly under control. Her way of running the household infuriated him. After he lost his job, things just went from bad to worse. I felt sorry for him. He became so depressed, started drinking too. I remember he told me at one point nearly half of the workers at the port were unemployed. I know now that even in the city as a whole the rate was still almost 40%. That is just mind-blowing when you think about it. Hard times, indeed. By then I had graduated in engineering and was looking for employment myself, so I could understand the frustration of the men there."

"But did he not have the right to unemployment benefit?" asked Lotte with a frown; she had little knowledge of the subject but was touched by the man's fate.

"Not really," Klaus answered with a cynical shake of his head. "The insurance paid a quarter of his previous wage for about six weeks, perhaps two months. After that he had to look for help from charities, just like everyone else. My parents barely had enough to get through the month, plus there were old debts hanging in the air, too. I think the crunch came one day, around a year later, maybe a little more, when he came home one day from the fish market. This was when they were living over in Altona. They have a famous *Fischauktionshalle* (fish auction hall) there where the local fishermen sell their own fresh catch to the general public. People turn up in the early morning, even in winter when it is dark and cold, to have a look round and chat to the neighbours, and try to get a bargain. There is everyone there: Hamburger housewives, merchants who sell the fish on to restaurants, revellers on their way home from St. Pauli after a hard night out drinking. And one night he had stayed away the whole night, went drinking somewhere with old mates from the port, I suppose. I really cannot imagine how, when we hardly had enough money for coal or to pay the rent. But all the same, he did that sometimes. So he staggered home in the early morning with some fish he had bought wrapped up in paper, said it would be perfect for dinner. And our mother swore it was old and rotten. It did smell, as fish often smells. Mama was screaming, "Look at the eyes, look at the eyes! They are white and cloudy, they have sunk back in the head. And the stench! I am not poisoning my children with rotten fish." She was screaming enough for not just the neighbours but the whole street to hear. She said he was so drunk and stupid he had brought home rotten food to kill them all. He started shouting back, saying it was not his fault and that the seller had assured him it was fresh that morning, and that it was not his fault either that there was no money to buy decent food. This massive row started about whose fault everything was, each blaming the other. I think he slapped her hard a few times and then stormed out. Anyway, that was the end of their marriage. I went to technical college, worked at NIEMO in Braunschweig for a few years, and then enlisted in the army in the spring of 1939. By the time the war broke out, it was the best thing that could have happened."

"I am so glad it worked out for you in the end," said Inge, relieved that at least someone had done well for himself out of the war.

Käthe, listening in from the edge, was grateful that the conversation had now moved away from their troubled family life, though also thankful to her brother for partly clarifying the topic for the others. She had been complaining to Trudchen about the woman on the first floor: common, with noisy children, her husband was bald and grumpy and never said *Guten Morgen* nor *Guten Tag* nor anything - so rude! Trudchen didn't have much to add to the subject and the conversation had dried up, whereupon Käthe now jumped at the opportunity of turning round to praise her brother. "He has been promoted, again already. The second time in a less than a year, this time to *Hauptmann* (captain)! Do not expect him to mention it though, he is far too modest for his own good. Look, you can see it on his shoulder patch." She reached over and fingered the collar insignia, describing the form and colours as her brother laughed and shrank away, as if being tickled. She sat back down, still blazing a triumphant grin.

Klaus blushed and looked down at the ground. Trudchen, with her sharp scent when it came to the falsities of human nature, quietly perceived that the modesty was feigned and part of a pleasing impression that he wished to create among the women. She began to take a dislike to him but would have died before she let it be noticed.

Käthe glowed, "Once the war is won, he will be addressed as *Oberst* (Colonel) Würdig - mark my words. Or even *Generalmajor* (Brigadier) Würdig perhaps."

Klaus laughed. "Käthe dear, let us get it over and won first, before we start making any big plans for the future."

"Then I am going to find him such a nice sweet girl, a real home-maker to settle down with here in Hamburg. They will have four children at least, each one as good-looking at the next."

"And we will all live happily ever after. In a castle, I suppose?"

"Almost! - a noble villa in Blankese. I can see it now. In fact, I am already planning what dress I shall wear at the wedding."

"No turbans or shawls, please!" laughed Lotte. "With peace we shall have proper fashion again."

"I can barely imagine the thought of being higher than a captain", Klaus said, nodding into the air in a sudden elated daydream.

In this merry buzz Inge naturally commented on how proud his mother must be and how wonderful it must be for her to have her son and daughter together at home. There was an awkward pause in which Klaus and Käthe exchanged an embarrassed glance. Inge connected the dots and grasped the weight of the fact that Käthe purposefully lived away from her own mother in the same city; even after the arrival of her beloved brother, she was still sleeping in the apartment with the rest of them.

Inge quickly added, "And I can see exactly what you mean, Käthe. Klaus is made to be a general at least. He has the air, the poise. He definitely has the look of a general." She felt a twinge of sadness inside, though. It was - amongst all that buoyant chat and the sunshine and the jolly crowds flowing past - a doubly difficult moment when she then found her thoughts slipping back to her still missing husband.

Klaus moved the centre of conversation away from himself and said to Lotte and Trudchen, "So Käthe was telling me that you both work in the *Luftschutzdienst*. That is such essential and honourable work you are doing for the future of our Reich. You must be very proud."

Trudchen raised her eyebrows. "We are, but I am curious that you are saying that. Most soldiers do not like seeing us women turning up for work."

"Really? I cannot think why."

"Oh Trudchen, you do like to stir things up," scowled Lotte, leaning on the table and sighing, before turning to Karl to explain. "She is referring to the fact that when we arrive at a new place of work, it sometimes means that some of the men already working there will be sent to the front. So, in that context our presence is not always well received." She turned back to Trudchen. "Anyway, I have only heard those comments a couple of times. On the whole I find the men very friendly, and happy for us to work with them."

"I have heard it said a few times. I supposed at the time I was meant to feel guilty for doing my job."

"In any case, the women are far worse!" exclaimed Lotte. "Especially the middle-aged ones. You know what they call us when they see us in uniform?" she rhetorically asked Karl. "Officers' mattresses! Can you believe that? So terribly vicious."

Trudchen laughed grimly and sipped her beer. "That is true. I heard it once when I was getting off a bus, in Gießen. I could not believe my ears."

"They say it all the time, even the young ones sometimes!" said Lotte in exaggerated outrage.

"Perhaps," suggested Klaus playfully, "they are worried about their husbands spending too much time with beautiful women like yourselves. I could understand that jealousy would play a role in their thought processes."

Lotte smiled at the compliment but persisted, "They might also like to stop and think that there is a war going on. Not everyone can spend the day only worrying about the shopping list and whether the children's nappies are full or not."

She mentally bit her tongue and dared not look at Inge, but fortunately Klaus was more interested in some technical details and he shifted the conversation. "So tell me, what are the bombing raids like here in Germany? I heard that Wuppertal was badly hit."

"That is correct," said Trudchen. "That was recently, in the last week of May. The damage sustained was significant, to say the least. Heavy use of high explosives to blow open the buildings followed by incendiary bombs to create large-scale fires inside, especially in the city centre."

Lotte was playing with a crack in the table but listening intently and adding her own material to the topic. Inge noticed how much more serious she had become now that the conversation had turned more specific in detail, and she wondered if Lotte might not be vying with her colleague for the attention of Klaus. He was indeed, Inge reflected, very good-looking and charismatic.

Lotte said, "They know that many urban centres are built up with narrow streets containing a lot of wooden structures. Those typical old medieval centres with wooden-beamed houses, which are charming for tourists to look at, but in the face of bombing raids are like dry kindling just waiting to ignite. The fire spreads rapidly and whole streets go up in flames. Furthermore, they have developed a new marking technique that we are just now starting to see being employed in raids. First, they send in *Mosquitoes*, which are outside of the Flak range and too fast for the night fighters. These drop coloured marking flares, in red and green. Apparently they look like Christmas trees coming down out of the sky so people are calling them that. That way, when the heavy bombers fly over the area, they can see exactly where they have to drop their load. They are blasting through buildings with high explosives first, leaving them open and exposed, with no roof or doors or windows, and then dropping incendiaries inside with the next wave of aircraft. The effect is devastating: a whole apartment block can burn out in no time and the fire quickly spreads to adjacent buildings. Additionally, heavy explosive bombs like the blockbusters are powerful enough to penetrate underground and shatter waterlines, which further hinders the emergency services in putting out the fires. Luckily casualties have generally been low so far due to adequate air-raid protection measures. But exposed urban areas, especially town and city centres, are becoming very vulnerable. They could be taken out in large numbers if the enemy persists with this tactic."

"I hear they want to re-build the cities better afterwards," said Käthe, eager to add something herself. "In a more modern and practical style for our new times. I believe the Führer himself has spoken on the subject."

"Not too sure about that. Personally, I like our old Hamburg just the way it is," said Klaus with a pained smile.

"Yes, me too," Käthe agreed, with her arm now entwined in her brother's.

Klaus dropped the volume of his voice considerably and glanced at Lotte and Trudchen. "We do not always get the full reports out on the front about what is happening here at home. I understand that, in terms of troop morale. But I get the impression, from what I have heard, that some of the air raids are getting to be very serious. Naturally, I get worried, especially with Käthe and my mother living here. I mean, theoretically it must be an important target for them."

"In the last few months, it is almost as if they have been avoiding Hamburg," said Trudchen, also speaking more quietly. "Sometimes whole squadrons almost fly over the city but then just head on somewhere else."

Lotte said, "In our department, a visiting officer claimed that it must be down to our strong flak defence. But after he had gone, others were shaking their heads. Someone even suggested the British are trying to lull us into a false sense of security."

"But how high is the actual risk of serious damage to residential areas?"

Trudchen said, "In our office we received a detailed analytical report concerning that recent attack on Wuppertal. This was in late May. There was a particularly worrying phenomenon that occurred in a part of the city during the bombing, namely in the district of Elberfled, near to the city centre, and extending in a north-easterly direction up to Barmen. This part is situated in a deeply cut valley. It seems the incendiaries were dropped there in such concentrated numbers that a massive fire arose. This was further exacerbated by topological factors, plus a concentration of older buildings. What actually occurred there is being termed by our experts as a 'fire storm'. The fire becomes so intense that it actually begins to suck in the oxygen out of the surrounding areas. Very strong, almost hurricane-strength winds are created, and these pull everything back into the central fire. The fire continues to rise in intensity and a positive feedback sets in, so in the end it can consume vast amounts of property. And naturally people too," she added.

Lotte commented, "Apparently, that was exactly what happened in one of our earlier raids in England, on Coventry. Although by pure chance at the time. But some of our intelligence officers think that the British military must have closely studied the effects and are now trying to apply corresponding techniques to their own bombing raids."

Trudchen said, "The problem is that with these intense levels of heat and such enormous blazes, this all reduces the efficiency of most air-raid shelters to nearly zero. The oxygen is literally sucked out of the bunkers and replaced by carbon monoxide and other toxic gases produced by the fire. Anyone inside does not stand a chance. They would be asphyxiated in a question of minutes. Further to that there is the question of the very high levels of heat. The only shelters able to withstand that level of extreme conditions are the concrete tower shelters."

"Like that big brick one over at the Berliner Tor?" asked Käthe.

"Exactly," said Trudchen. "By the way, the bricks are just the façade. Under that it is pure concrete. They have their own air supply with ventilation there, plus running water and strong steel doors. The concrete is supposed to be very thick. I doubt even a blockbuster could crack that."

"I was there on a tour a few weeks ago," said Lotte. "It is absolutely incredible, with a spiral staircase going all the way down deep to the basement. They say it is very popular. So of course it is always too full for everyone to use."

"Those are the exceptions," continued Trudchen. "Most people shelter in home-made bunkers in their basements. Even ones that have been purpose-built or reinforced with concrete are not going to withstand a major fire like that. The death toll in Wuppertal in May was well over two thousand. I heard the officers say they saw photos of whole long streets of apartment blocks, all burnt out. Just the charred outer walls still standing up. Nobody expected anything of those proportions. At least, not in a purely residential area and well away from any industrial targets."

Klaus took a long swig from his beer before pronouncing, "They have no pity, these English. Not that I blame them. In their position, I would not either."

"All the more reason for our proud Wehrmacht to finish off the enemy for once and for all!" exclaimed Käthe, raising both the volume and spirit of the conversation with a flash of general patriotism while reducing the actual content to meaningless civism. "Whether the English or the Russians, we shall defeat them all. On land, under water, and in the air!" She had found the previous exchange deeply disturbing, not to mention bordering on defeatist, and was eager to lighten and liven up the conversation.

Lotte said, "We should not forget that we have an excellent defence system in place in Hamburg. In fact, one of the best artillery defense groups in the whole country - over fifty heavy flak batteries, numerous light flak too, and excellent searchlight coverage. Plus first-class public shelters that could withstand even heavy attacks. That is to be expected - this here is the Reich's second city, of great importance in terms of industry and manufacturing, and, more important still, the U-Boot and military navy construction. Also, it is on a direct and easy path for aircraft incursions from eastern England. Of course the enemy will be eager to attack, and it is up to us to give them back a taste of their own medicine!" Lotte had become quite strident and everyone nodded.

Trudchen felt that they had probably said more than enough on this topic for one afternoon, and furthermore out in public too. One never knew who was sitting closer than one imagined, and perhaps listening intently.

"Don't worry," said Klaus. "Victory will come. And the longer it takes, the more glorious it will be." He himself was becoming uneasy at so much talk of war; when he had come home from the front precisely to get away from it. At the same time, he knew full well how irresistible the subject always was. He proposed that they went to the cinema and saw a film; something light-hearted to take their minds off the topic.

Käthe knew just the thing. "I have read that they are showing *'Altes Herz wird wieder jung'*[6] at the cinema *Schauburg St. Georg*. It is not far, in Steindamm, over near the train station, so it is on our way back anyway. Emil Jannings is starring in it. It is just the thing for us today: funny and romantic and light-hearted, and I have heard it is quite good as well. I mean, if you would like to go?" The idea was well received, and they spent the evening chuckling together in the cinema.

In the days following Klaus's visit, the women – Lotte and Käthe in particular - became closer to Inge, though Trudchen still remained somewhat distant, instinctively wary of new people. All the same, Inge struck them all without exception as charmingly rural, a little naïve perhaps, but well-meaning and hard-working and with a strong sense of cooperation, especially in the area of domestic chores. Even though their time together was set to be short - both Trudchen and Lotte were due to be posted elsewhere within the following months - there seemed to be a strong sense of feminine camaraderie

---

[6] An Old Heart Is Young Again

developing. An agreeable sororal atmosphere had flourished in the apartment, as opposed to when flatmates simply grit their teeth and put a brave face on getting on together, as Trudchen had sometimes experienced female companionship in the women's quarters of barracks.

Käthe had already asked Inge about her children back in Lüneburg and whether she missed them. Inge sensed that she was puzzled as to why she would leave them, albeit it in her sister's very able care, and come to work in Hamburg. Inge had prepared herself to dodge this potentially awkward subject with her pre-formulated explanation: namely, she wanted to help with the war effort but without bringing her children into a large city, and stressing the point that she herself had family in Hamburg. This point was however clearly feeble, to the point of being silly; with parents, siblings and three children in one town, hardly being comparable to some distant uncle figure in another. Käthe protracted the conversation by saying that she couldn't imagine having any children of her own and how much she envied those women who had been blessed with large families. Inge blushed and confirmed her love of her children, spoke with pride of her young sons, told Käthe their names and ages and a few character details, whilst also emphasizing her sister's very capable nurturing and educational methods in the process.

Inge in turn asked Käthe about her family. Käthe seemed relieved to be able to open up, finding Inge's easy-going manner conducive to a confessionary process that she had been internally desiring. In this way Inge quite innocently and naturally found out a good deal about her, considering the short time that they had known each other. Käthe told her a little about the divorce of her parents, a detail Inge had known already but was glad to have expanded upon for the sake of clarity; additionally that her father was a long-time NSDAP-Party member and had moved off to work in Berlin, after which her mother had remarried. Käthe had not seen eye to eye with her mother's second husband, which was the reason that she had sought her own lodgings and independent existence. She had applied at the *Arbeitsamt* (job centre) for a training course with the *Rotes Kreuz* (German branch of the Red Cross). This application had been immediately accepted and furthermore had allowed her to stay on in Hamburg, at least for the time being.

Unlike Lotte and Trudchen, Käthe showed little interest in travelling, although she had heard that many of the nurses were now being sent to the front to help take care of injured troops. She accepted the fact that this may well be her own fate with an unquestionable sense of patriotism. But she also hoped, despite the lack of encouragement that the latest war developments were giving them all, that the conflict would soon be over. The Führer himself had stated that much. She was keen to stress that she believed wholeheartedly in the word of the Führer, as well as the necessity for the war in the first place. Her own fiancé was stationed in Italy, and when the war was finally over they planned to marry and move in together into their own apartment. Perhaps in the Harvestehude district, she quipped with a wry smile, knowing they could never afford it. Either way, she trusted that Franz would manage to get a good position in an accountancy department. She was sure that those soldiers who had risked their lives for their country, would always get preferential treatment in civilian life.

On another occasion, Käthe made a further comment about her family in Hamburg that concerned her mother's new husband and made Inge prick up her ears. The statement seemed coded. Käthe mentioned feeling uncomfortable in the presence of the man, of preferring to meet her mother on neutral territory while not wanting to cause her mother any pain, considering "all that she had been through already". Inge took this as an indication of an abusive situation and that Käthe felt acute fear towards her new stepfather. This notion was clear to her when Käthe mentioned how, whenever she passed by the street of her mother's house, and even though it was the street she had grown up in, she would always made sure to take a side-street to avoid walking past the apartment. Käthe stated this while she nervously drummed with her fingers on the table, and Inge said softly, "I know exactly what you mean."

Käthe, who had heard only wonderful things of Inge's family, frowned, puzzled at such a statement. "In what way?"

"I mean, I understand what it is like when there is someone whom you wish to avoid," she said, hardly believing her own bravery at addressing the subject. She added, "Especially when it is a man who knows you. And who says things about you."

Käthe nodded slowly, before cocking her head and gazing at Inge with a triste smile. "Then you do understand me," she said at last.

Inge nodded vigorously. "I do, yes." She touched Käthe's hand, gave it a warm stroke, before standing up to wash the cups and plates.

Käthe, due to be at work in forty minutes, had no further time for conversation. But as she was leaving, she gave Inge a hug at the door and said how glad she was, indeed they all were, to have such a perfect person turn up out of the blue to share the apartment with.

She might have mentioned something about this later on, or simply spoke positively about Inge in general, for Trudchen seemed to drop her cool guard as well and began to open up. She arranged that Sunday for the two of them to meet up in the Hammer Park, which was not too far from their apartment. The weather had been warm and sunny all week and was expected to stay that way. Käthe was meeting her mother to go and see a film at the cinema, while Lotte was working the late shift. So Trudchen, wishing to take advantage of the good summer climate, asked Inge to accompany her. Inge naturally jumped at the opportunity.

They walked round the park until they came across a gelato stand where they treated themselves and sat down on the grass. Over ice-cream it seemed a good moment for Inge to find out more about employment possibilities for her in the city, as well as deepen her friendship with Trudchen. Inge sounded her out accordingly about her career. She already knew that Trudchen worked as a *Horchfunkerin* (communication intelligence worker) in the same *Luftschutz-warndienst* department as Lotte. "It must be such fun working with Lotte. She has such a lively and jolly character."

Trudchen smiled wryly. "Lotte is very different at work than when she is at home, or out socially. You would probably barely recognize her if you saw her on duty. She is deadly seriously and has the most incredible powers of concentration. She is like a machine. I admire her. I wish I could be so contained and concentrated. I think that is why she has had such a successful career." Trudchen went on to relate how she found the work and life in the *Wehrmacht* enjoyable, with its varied tasks and sense of purpose in life. Her job as a *Horchfunkerin* was to track radio signals on different frequencies, listening in with a headphone and jotting down what she heard. Generally, she would listen in on a typical frequency used by the enemy to send messages and simply note the information being sent. "They're codified messages, so you write down, I don't know, H_C_W_A_P, and it looks meaningless, but it is passed on to the code breakers for them to work on. I had to do a special training in morse code for that, but it is not complicated material. We also listen in on enemy radio stations, which is much more interesting, to take down any noteworthy items that they are emitting. Of course, always bearing in mind that they know that we are listening in, and so they codify accordingly."

"How did you get into this line of work?" asked Inge, quite fascinated by the idea of women doing something that sounded exciting and masculine.

"Not by the direct route that most take. I was working in a bookkeeping company, in Essen, but it was having financial difficulties and I ended up out of work. This was two years ago, so naturally I registered myself at the job centre. A person there said that the Wehrmacht was looking for assistant workers und that there was a place on a course in Düsseldorf. That was not so far away from home, and I already knew the city and liked it there. I had to do some basic tests in German and Mathematics. There was an essay in German and lots of dictations; and in Mathematics a whole set of puzzles to solve, plus these endless arithmetical exercises. They were not difficult but there were so many hours of them. I think in retrospect it was more a question of them testing your stamina rather than it being about the actual sums. There was a foreign language evaluation and my levels in French and English were both quite good, so that helped. At the end I had a psychological test with a visiting expert. Among other things I had to relate my happiest memory in recent years, he said, and I knew what he wanted to hear and told him the appropriate story.

After that there was a three-month training in Düsseldorf, which went well, and then came the conscription order. I was posted to Frankfurt, then to Lübeck, and since March this year I have been here in Hamburg. We were in barracks at first, probably Lotte has told you about that." Inge nodded. "We have also been working in coordination with the *Kriegsmarine* (Wehrmacht Navy) for some of the tasks, with the U-Boot operations. There have been some developments in British military intelligence concerning the codifying of information so there is currently a lot of activity in that department. That is the reason I think I shall be going to Rostock or Kiel by the end of this year. Perhaps earlier, in the autumn."

"That sounds so exciting, working with codes!"

"My work is more mundane than it probably sounds. I just take down the information, which has to be assessed by experts as the enemy knows we are listening in so there are constant attempts to cause misunderstandings or diffuse false information. I am working a lot with transmissions from Radio London at the moment."

"So you understand them when they are speaking in English? That is wonderful!"

Trudchen nodded. "We all have to speak English and French in my department. Speaking Russian helps too, but they have other women there for that. Do you speak any foreign languages?"

"Oh no!" laughed Inge. "None at all. We have never had to, not where I live." Inge had a thought. "And when you listen to the enemy speaking, do you hear things that surprise you, that you did not know about before?"

"Definitely," said Trudchen, lowering her voice. "Often it is very interesting to compare the information that you are hearing from them with the information that is being transmitted here in Germany on the radio."

"So, the news does not always tell the full story?" Inge continued, deducing cautiously.

Trudchen's eyes narrowed. "Sooner or later, yes. Well, generally. Naturally *we* get to find out everything first-hand. For instance, a few months back, in April, I was on night duty, and it was just after midnight when I heard about a major bombing that had taken place, over Essen. And I am from Essen, that is where my family lives. But the national radio station was not yet saying anything about it and I was so desperate to find out if my family was safe."

Inge put her hand to her mouth. "And were they?"

"Yes, in the end I got through and found out they were fine. No injuries, and their apartment block was untouched too. But I had considered getting the first train in the morning, I was so full of panic. Luckily I was able to reach, by telephone, a good friend who worked at a police station there. He sent a couple of Hitler Youth boys to the street and reported back that they had got through the night without any problems. 'Not even a scratch and the house still intact', I can still remember those words. But I could only do all that because I had the information and, most importantly, the contacts. I remember a girl from Berlin. She was worried about her family and was turning the dial until she hit a British channel to see if there were plans to bomb Berlin in the next days. But the *Spieß* (the sarge) came up softly behind her and he watched and heard everything. She went through a big disciplinary dressing-down, nearly got three days arrest, though in the end they decided to let it go with a warning. So, you have to be careful, you never know." Trudchen's eyebrows betrayed a frown. "I heard that you are related to one of the chief officers working with the *Kriminalpolizei* (criminal investigation department of police), is that right?"

Inge smiled. "To be honest, I do not know him that well but we are related in that he is one of my husband's uncles. It was partly his idea for me to come to Hamburg to find work here," she said, immediately regretting the final lie in the details and at a loss as to why she had bothered introducing such trivially false information in the first place. She was relieved to hear Trudchen move the conversation onward.

"And your husband, is he in the Wehrmacht?"

"Yes, that is right. He is fighting on the eastern front. The last I heard he was fighting in Stalingrad, but there was a big surrender and since that battle I have not heard anything else from him. I imagine it is difficult for the letters to get through if the Russians will not allow it." Inge noticed that Trudchen's brow furrowed involuntarily, and she felt a sense of uneasiness. She added, "So if you ever hear any information being sent out about that part of the world, be sure to let me know."

Trudchen gave her a melancholy smile and responded, "I would not hear anything directly myself. The girls in the Russian section cover most of the eastern front. But naturally, if something were to happen and I had anything of importance to pass on, I would tell you immediately."

"Thank you. I do worry so much. Constantly." She made an effort to contain herself. "Do you have anyone from your family in the war?"

"Two brothers and my fiancé. All on the eastern front."

"I see," Inge said. "How brave! Your parents must be very proud."

Trudchen gave out a cynical chuckle. "Yes, in their own way they are proud. I suppose you could say that."

"Hopefully it will all be over soon." She felt this was a good moment to pose a major question, for which she brought her voice down to a hushed tone. "Do you think so?"

Trudchen paused to find the right words. "It is very hard to say."

"And, do you think, they would," asked Inge, falteringly, "they would bomb Lüneburg? I mean, heavily. In the city centre."

Trudchen slowly shook her head. "I really cannot tell you whether they will or not. They might bomb anywhere at all tomorrow, but I would not necessarily know that until tomorrow. To my understanding, even the bombing crews of the enemy do not normally find out their destination until the same day." She saw a look of panic in Inge's face. "But I do not think the chances are very high of a heavy raid, no. It is not much of a major industrial or strategic target. Not like the Ruhr area, for example. That is why I always worry about my parents so much. And it does not have any political significance, like Berlin or other big cities. So I do not see that as being a strong possibility." She looked round at the people sitting in or walking round the park. "Here in Hamburg it is a different matter altogether. I would worry more about that."

"Have there been many air raids?"

"A lot, yes. But nothing very intense, nothing out of the ordinary. At least not yet. There was a large raid last summer. I think about three hundred died. I heard one of the girls in a bakery telling her workmate that a couple she knew, two friends of her husband's parents, were killed at home. And the son of these friends was due to return from the front, on leave. He suffered a major trauma when he found out. He was the only child and furthermore he did not even know where to go to stay - there was no house left either. The bodies had been buried in a common grave so he could not say goodbye to them." Inge's eyes had widened upon hearing this tale. "But do not worry," added Trudchen hastily, regretting her way of entering into such detail and finding her rough direct manner to be irreverent, considering Inge's meek disposition and obvious concern for her family. "There is a lot of bombing activity and you just have to be alert. Those large raids, like the one on Cologne last year, are definitely the exception, not the rule. As long as you get down to the bunker in the basement quickly, as soon as you hear the siren, there should be no problem. The problem comes when people dawdle around. Or do not take the warnings seriously and stay in their apartments." She laughed, unable to resist as she recalled a story. "My brother-in-law, he is from Duisburg, so not so far away from our family. My sister moved there four years ago to live with him after they got married. About six or seven weeks ago there was a big attack there. So, my sister told me how they had decided to stay in the apartment. She had not felt well because of stomach problems, and she was going to the bathroom a lot and did not want to go down to the bunker under the apartment block, where the neighbours went. And my brother-in-law, Herbert, had stayed with her in the apartment. When he heard the sound of the planes approaching, he wanted to watch what was happening, so he went up to the window and opened it. Suddenly there fell this cluster of bombs very close by and blew all the windows out and sent him flying back into the living room, right against a bookcase there, where he banged his head! Then more bombs started falling nearby and they both ran down to the bunker faster than they have ever run in their lives. When they got down, he was bleeding from cuts on his face and she made an awful stink in the bunker toilet with all her diarrohea." Trudchen's laugh tinkled again. "But she swore that next time she hears the siren, she is heading straight for the bunker. I had been telling her that since I started working in the Wehrmacht but she did not take any notice. Sometimes a shock like that is the only way to wake someone up." Then Trudchen remembered why she had laughed. "And the funny thing was, her stomach problems cleared up the very next day!"

Inge, not at all grasping her sense of humour, simply said, "I am sure if I heard a siren, I would not hesitate to go straight to the cellar. We have heard sirens a few times in Lüneburg but not that many and nothing much has ever happened."

"As I said, it is not an important target for the enemy. If I were you, I would not worry about your children or the family. As long as they follow the instructions they are given, there will be no problems. The children live with your sister, is that right?"

"Yes, that is right. Gisela, she is called. And she is very strict with them, makes sure they do as they are told."

"I was brought up in the same way too. To do as I was told."

"It is very important," nodded Inge. "You have to have discipline in a family. My mother always said, and she started to say it again after my children were born, she said: give me the child and I will show you the man. I never forget that."

Trudchen smiled. "Yes, I have heard that somewhere before. It is very true."

"That was the way that we were brought up and that is what we want for our children too. At least in our family."

"Do you have any other brothers or sisters, apart from Gisela?"

"Just my brother Ernst. He works at our local branch of the *Vereinsbank*. I am the youngest of the three."

"He is lucky that he hasn't been called up."

Inge blushed, feeling an old and ugly topic rear its head. "He has health problems and has a letter from the Wehrmacht that he is relieved from duty. It was all done officially."

Trudchen asked, to politely confirm her cohabitee's fantasy. "So, when your husband comes home, I imagine you will go back down to Lüneburg and meet him there, and probably then stay there."

"That is right. I imagine that would be what I would do," she answered at first but recognized it for what it was – a fantasy - and her voice began to tremble. She tried to plough on with the next sentence, although conscious of the lack of substance to it, and could just say, "That might be soon, because the last letter," before she broke down sobbing. A couple of older women sitting opposite looked over, while Trudchen moved swiftly to place herself beside her; shielding her from curious eyes, hugging her and stroking her back.

"*Ist gut, ist gut* – It's alright, it's alright," she murmured soothingly.

Inge was overcome and sobbed out her sorrow in hefty convulsions. Even Trudchen was taken aback, having underestimated the sheer mental agony that Inge was hiding away inside. Eventually, with the tears released taking part of the pain away, Inge was able to mumble a continuation of that which she wished to express. "It should be soon, because the last time he came home was February of last year. That is sixteen months now. And I have not heard from him since before Christmas. I got a letter dated 27th November, while he was still in Stalingrad, but since then I have not heard anything. No-one seems to be able to tell me anything. I have asked and asked at all the official posts but…," and she blubbered again, went on sobbing. With the second round of tears, she had calmed herself considerably and wiped her eyes, so the women picked up their bags and moved off, feeling freer and less observed walking back quickly down the busy Horst-Wessel-Straße to go home.

They walked in silence, with Trudchen locking her arm in Inge's until Inge said, her head still bowed, "Just so that you also understand, and it does not matter who he is, but there is a person who has been making life very difficult for me, in my neighbourhood. I did not want to bring the children here, and they are so happy at home with Gisela and her husband. And I have my parents there too. My mother helps out a lot and thinks the world of them. I felt they would better staying there, but I needed to get away. That was the whole problem. Gisela has said she will phone me the very instant that a letter comes from Horst. The very moment, but I…I have this terrible feeling inside sometimes."

Trudchen consoled her, as they walked along, with her close physical presence and by stroking her back, holding her hand tightly; trying without words, only touch, to inspire some optimism in the young woman's broken heart. She suspected the worst, being extremely well informed in comparison to the broader German public, as to the true extent of the military disaster that had commenced with Stalingrad and was still unfolding out on the eastern front. Even so, she also knew that there was always hope, at least until he was officially declared as deceased; there was also a slim chance that he had in fact been taken prisoner.

That evening all four women ate and drank together late at the apartment. Käthe had brought a bottle of wine and in the end they giggled profusely over silly things. Inge had recovered some of her old optimistic spirit and the atmosphere was very positive in the apartment.

After nearly three weeks, Inge travelled back to Lüneburg and was able to spend the weekend with her family and see her beloved boys once again. The conversation in the park with Klaus that day had set her thinking about burnt out houses and Hamburg's strategic status in the war; so she took the diary she had found, along with board game, back with her to Lüneburg for safekeeping there. She showed the board game to Gisela, who also found the notion commendable, of learning about war through games and fun, and she let the children have it to play with together. It soon became a firm and coveted favourite.

Inge chose to put the diary in a small metal safe that she and Horst had bought for important documents and money in cash, which was hidden away at the bottom of a dark cupboard space at the Gasthaus. There inside lay a photo of Horst and herself, and the jewelry she had received for her wedding, which she was keeping secure until her husband's return. The other photo she possessed of Horst, one taken of him together with her and the three children, was always tucked inside her dark brown leather handbag.

The weekend in Lüneburg passed in a flash. She barely had time to have a meaningful conversation at length with either her sister or her mother. Others in the family, such as Ernst, she did not see at all. But she slept well that Saturday night, happy that the arrangement was working out well and that Gisela seemed to have so effortlessly taken on a large family.

Inge felt she had barely arrived back home when she was already catching the early train on the Monday morning back to Hamburg. In a city infamous for gloomy rainy skies, it was even sunnier by now and the summer looked promising in both professional and personal gain. Within ten days, Inge had received details of a job that Uncle Robert had managed to organize for her.

Nothing special, as she herself described it in a telephone conversation with Gisela; just cleaning work at the extensive Hamburg Police headquarters where Uncle Robert was employed. But it was a start, and she was more than happy with that.

June progressed into July and the city became much warmer.

Chapter 28

The whole week had been marked by an exceptionally dry and persistent heat; the temperature was still rising that evening of Saturday 24th July. The air lay rigid, barely a waft of breeze. As the night moved in over the still sweltering city, distant flashes of lightning out over the North Sea were visible in the sky. The moon had filled out considerably during the week and by Saturday it was nearly round. Shortly after the lightning died down, it rose to radiate down through clear skies and cast a mystical light over the slowly slumbering port city. With the streets in black-out, its light reigned alone. It smoothed over the streets and filled them with grey-silver shades, softly glowed across the rooftops, slid under some curtains to illuminate the immediate floor around the windows in irregular shapes. It was the fascination with this intense mixture of shadows and tones of light, together with the discomfort at the lingering warmth, that had kept Inge out on the balcony where she sat on a small stool and drank a couple of glasses of water. Lotte was working that night, and Trudchen and Käthe were either in the bathroom or already in bed. There had been no plans made for the Sunday. Käthe would probably meet up with her mother as usual, somewhere in the city centre; Lotte would return from night duty in the early hours and go straight to bed; Trudchen had been assigned late duty that Sunday afternoon at the last minute, stepping in for a colleague who had called in sick.

The sirens had gone off that evening at 21:30. At that point in time, Lotte had already left for work, while the remaining three had dutifully made their way down to the cellar and entered the small air-raid shelter there. It was a tight two-room space, but with well-built concrete walls and ceiling that gave the occupants a strong sense of security. They had dragged themselves down the stairs and up again on several nights at the end of June; the sirens had wailed time and time again. Each time it had been just the British *Mosquito* planes which, aptly named, did little more than cause nuisance and help promote nights of anxiety and restlessness. They were very swift reconnaissance and light bomber aircraft, made of plywood and able to fly at high altitudes; as she had found out from her well-informed flatmates. They caused little damage as such, certainly not compared to heavy British bombers like the Lancaster or Halifax, but managed to set off the entire alarm system throughout the city. When occurring with frequency this could effectively disrupt the normal day-to-day running of the city. They had had about three weeks of relative peace since then, and she assumed that the irritating *Mosquitoes* had returned again that evening. At around 22:00 the all-clear siren had sounded; everyone had sighed and puffed and made their way back to their apartments, hoping for a decent night's sleep.

Inge breathed in the early night air and watched the street down below her. Under this moonlit night she appreciated in the soft silver radiance just how both noble and charming Hamburg was, with its long and magnificent streets, its rows of stately apartment blocks with often intricate exteriors, vermiculated along the ground floor; something that she now recognized as *Gründerzeit* architecture since having been first introduced to the term by Horst while on honeymoon in Berlin. Not just in the centre but also here in the worker districts, the fine buildings and apartment blocks seemed infinite in comparison to what she knew in her hometown, stretching for miles and cheering her heart with their majestic beauty. She reflected how strong was the beating heart of this grand city on the Elbe.

A clique of friends came out of a nearby building, headed off laughing and noisily chatting towards the train station. The bars at St. Pauli were open all night and, despite all the repeated warnings from the police and the military and above all the kindly and ever-concerned radio announcer '*Onkel Baldrian*', many Hamburgers continued to party out in town whenever they got the chance. With an increasingly uncertain future hanging overhead, hedonistic pleasure was one of the few things that made any sense; dancing and singing the night away behind the black-out curtains. Inge assumed that plenty of them would be taking advantage of the warm Saturday night air to liven up their routines. She smiled down wistfully at the figures passing by in the street, feeling her own romantic desolation while thinking for the others: "All the more reason for you all to binge through the night while you still can!" Only a few years back she herself would have disapproved of any indulgent behaviour during such a monumental event as a war; finding the attitude unserious, even disrespectful, given the circumstances. Drinking and carousing would have been unthinkable; while men were fighting abroad, risking and often giving their lives for the Fatherland, trying to make a better world for them all; while everyone else was making do with so little and at risk of losing so much.

But now she saw things differently. In the midst of war, more than ever, presided the necessity to celebrate life. She felt now more tolerance toward this inevitable need to fall into the hot emotion of festivity. Certainly if Horst had been there she would have liked to have danced and been merry with him too, laughed and smiled with him, made love to him. She grasped the emotional background to the laughter trickling along the street, the revellers' drive for simple pleasure. She felt how life was too unpredictable and short for prim composure - alone the frequency of the air-raid sirens here had taught her that much. She understood increasingly that the war was not only being fought out on the battlefields, but also in the very streets of German towns and cities, in the offices and the apartment blocks, in hospitals and shops and schools. The more she spoke to Lotte and Trudchen, especially the latter, the more apparent that aspect of daily life became; this was in turn strengthened by the sight of buckets of sand, rigid instructions, and fire extinguishers everywhere. She wondered how such horror had come to be acceptable; but at the same time was still unable to grasp the facet of this also being direct retaliation for a belligerent methodology that her own nation had already, and frequently, used as standard currency in this fatal exchange. It was one thing if foreign cities she wouldn't have known to find on a map were casually reported as having been bombed in a radio broadcast – whether Belgrade or Warsaw, Bristol or Hull; it was a very different affair when these cities were Cologne, Hannover, Essen or Bremen.

Most unnerving for her, however, was her recently growing and now ever stronger aversion to the Führer. The seeds of doubt had already begun to grow in her mind when she heard of the suddenly announced invasion of the Soviet Union; this military movement had directly led to the absence of her husband as well as other men she knew in Lüneburg. Perhaps, she pondered, her father had had more insight than she had given him credit for. She recalled the burning night back in November 1938, when she had lain in bed but the air had been full of hatred and shouts, and she thought of the little group of Jews, looking so sad and pathetic in the rain, that she had seen waiting on the street corner to be taken off: to where and what? People were now disappearing everywhere; out of her family, out of her vicinity, her town. This was not the nation's great destiny as she had imagined it.

She began not only to doubt that the Führer could be on the wrong track, but she began to suspect that he was dragging her people, in rage and dogma and endless secret plans, into a deepening war that was hopeless and brutal. She had come to reflect in recent weeks that this conflict could kill millions before it was over, for she could not imagine someone like the Führer simply calling it a day and looking for a peaceful way out. She saw an increasingly futile war ahead, not to mention bloody and painful, and she now feared for her children and her country.

She thought that evening of her three little boys; imagined Gisela and Walter in the restaurant, washing the crockery and cutlery, pans and glasses, cleaning up and mopping the restaurant, scrubbing the kitchen surfaces without her. Upstairs, her angels would be asleep already, unaware of what her mother was in this moment experiencing. She felt deeply saddened that it had come to this but also knew, as she began to circle the subject of her family and hometown, that the man who was responsible for this situation would surface in her head; and that she wished to avoid at all costs. So, she cleared her mind to concentrate on the present, on this warm silvery night in Hamburg, the weekend ahead, the handsome row of apartments with balconies looking directly over opposite her.

Absorbed in humdrum deliberations, she became sleepy but lingered on the balcony a while, not keen to return yet to the sheets that quickly became sticky with sweat. She reminded herself to ask Gisela to borrow the best cotton sheets they had at the Gasthaus, the next time she returned to Lüneburg. Although the restaurant business was still ticking over, all things considered, they now had next to no external visitors staying the night, so she doubted that her sister would have the slightest objection to that. Her eyelids drooped.

The air-raid siren sounded out again and she snapped out of her thoughts with a start. It must have been late, well gone midnight by that point. There was a bustle of movement somewhere directly below, while on the other side of the street someone somewhere shouted, "*Schon wieder, es darf nicht wahr sein!*" - "Again already, this can't be for real!" Further down the street, a woman frantically dashed out of one building pushing a pram, to disappear inside a doorway a few buildings along. Gradually there were more and more sounds of activity, and fleeting signs of movement in the moonlit street. For the second time that night the city was submerging itself – just in case.

The howling sirens continued and within five minutes Trudchen and Käthe were in the kitchen, in nightwear and thick dressing gowns, rubbing their eyes. "I don't believe this," sighed Käthe, and casually flicked on the radio.

Trudchen filled a glass under the tap and took a long swig of water, said with a grim smile but brisk tone, "Come on girls, Air Danger 30. Let's get dressed and get down to the cellar." Within a further five minutes the two were decently dressed, though still bedraggled, while Inge was relating how she hadn't even been to bed and had been drinking some water on the balcony. "I couldn't sleep", she chuckled. "Now I am glad I didn't bother."

At this point the siren had changed to a more urgent intermittent tone, that sounded at a frequency of approximately fifteen times a minute. On the radio, the familiar voice of '*Onkel Baldrian*' had been giving the usual air-raid instructions, as he normally did at night in his calm and reassuring voice. There seemed to be this time, however, a new edge to his voice; one of insistence and urgency that struck the women as uncommon. Moreover, he was emphatically repeating that a large squadron of enemy planes was directly approaching the city and that all citizens were to make their way *immediately* to the *nearest* air-raid shelter or bunker.

Käthe frowned, "Air Danger 15 already. That was quick!" and looked at Trudchen. She in turn looked puzzled and disappeared back into her room to quickly slip into her uniform. Inge had gone to her room to pack a little bag with her usual set of basic items; it was moments like this that she found Hamburg very tiresome.

"Come on, Inge. We have to go. Now!" shouted Trudchen, ready to leave and visibly nervous, her tone of voice clipped and martial.

Inge rushed out with a nagging feeling that she hadn't satisfactorily packed her 'little bag of essentials', as she called it, and the three left the flat to make their way – as Trudchen liked to say, 'with haste but without speed' - down to the cellar. It was almost full by then, nearly all the neighbours having dutifully though begrudgingly returned.

"Seems like the Tommys do not want us to sleep tonight," said Herr Lindemann, the house caretaker and local *Blockwart* (block leader) with his characteristic snicker. "Don't they know half of Hamburg does not sleep on a Saturday night anyway?"

The three women took their place, smiled comfortingly at each other. The door was closed, only for there to be a knocking as a neighbour arrived tardily. In that very moment, Inge was going through her bag to check the contents. She realized to her horror that the most precious item was not there. Furthermore, she recalled exactly where she had left it: the photo of her children huddled together with her and Horst, that she had placed on the bedside table upon returning to the apartment after the first air-raid siren that evening. "I have forgotten something, I will be right back!" she cried. Before her two companions could react, she had jumped up and pushed past the neighbour who was, in that very moment, coming in.

She raced up the stairs and frantically searched in her pockets and bag for the housekeys. She became nervous as she couldn't find them; then realized that they hadn't locked the door in the first place. "Oh, how stupid of me!" she whined and pushed the front door open, dashed to her bedroom. There she quickly located the forgotten photo and placed it carefully in her bag, tucked inside a folder of documents so that it wouldn't crease.

She considered for a moment if there was anything else of importance that she had forgotten in her rush to pack the bag. She found no reply to this urgent inner question, and so was moving back out into the hall when she heard a strange, distinctive sound, a deep rumbling outside. Unable to resist curiosity, she went through the kitchen, slipped through the heavy black curtains, and passed out onto the balcony, peering upwards.

The first thing that Inge noticed in the sky were a few wisps of cloud out towards to sea which were lit up in spectral white by the glowing moon, by now stunningly full and powerful. Most of the famous sites in Hamburg, including the churches, were hidden from view on that side of the apartment, but looking to the left of the balcony she could see all the way over to the steeple of St. Gertrud, pointing up sharp into the ghostly night. The sirens had stopped by now and up behind the church tower rose the first searchlight, slowly investigating, feeling its way across the night sky over Hamburg. It was soon followed by others. They swung round, sometimes overlapping, testing angles, stroking the dark heavens in search of its secrets. The first artillery guns were firing their test rounds over the Alster lakes. The din intensified as others around the city joined in, all boasting their combined readiness for combat.

The searchlights continued gently revolving around the sky, looking out for the tell-tale *Mosquitoes* which often buzzed high above, out of range for the artillery and too quick and nimble to be easy prey for the *Luftwaffe* fighter planes. That was a sound that she clearly identified, the distinctive whine of *Mosquitoes* overhead. But in the background there was still that very different noise, the sound she had first perceived in the apartment; a deep growling far-off, though increasing with each moment in intensity. In that very instant, the searchlights began to quickly move around the sky in sharp jerks, as if in a state of sudden panic and desperate to locate the intruders. But there was nothing there to see. The flak artillery let off numerous clattering rounds, which left in their wake fragile little wafts of smoke rising up over the skyline and a light ringing sound in Inge's ears. But they seemed to be firing blindly, aimlessly up at the sky.

A strange flickering radiance lit up her whole line of vision and with such intensity that she could clearly see the clock face on the St. Gertrude church tower. It was ten to one. The source of this light, however, seemed to emanate from the western side of the city. She was so intrigued by the celestial display that she forgot herself and ran through to her bedroom on the other side of the apartment, flinging open the window and sticking her head out; then grabbing the stool to stand on it and try to improve her line of vision. There she perceived that the light was not coming from a single source but rather consisted of a multitude of gently falling forms of light, all glowing in red, green, and white, looking like masses of gleaming Christmas trees. They drifted toward the ground on little parachutes, seeming quite harmless and creating an aesthetic light display that covered the whole city. The flak continued to fire off sporadically, coming from different directions, and Inge distinguished the different tones that came to her: some thundered far off, some roared, while others nearby made more of a banging sound. She saw a flak grenade explode high up, caught in the moonlight; first a burst of fire, like in a firework display, that turned into a light white cloud, before dispersing into the night sky. She stood there on the edge of the incoming raid, unable – against her better judgment - to take her eyes off the symphony of light and sound all around her, captivated by its strange unearthly beauty.

That initial rumbling sound was now a solid drone, far louder and like the deep tones of a church organ. She saw something on the edge of the sky and realized she must be seeing *them*, coming in from the west, indistinct shapes in the night sky but clearly in huge numbers, like a swarm of enormous insects. Dozens, hundreds, she couldn't tell: a mass without end, sweeping up the horizon and beginning to cross the sky with majesty and terror. Flak was being fired intensely at them, in ear-shattering blasts.

There came the screaming wail of the first falling bombs and the subsequent bright explosions, quite far off on the other side of the city. The searchlights still twitched around the sky but seemed unable to hold onto any of the aircraft above. The flak artillery fired off round after round, but as if at random into the solid sky. She saw the first buildings flaming up, heard another series of smashing explosions, and came back to reality with a jolt. "*Ach, du lieber Himmel*! – Oh, heavens above!" she cried, instinctively covering her mouth with her fingers, before grabbing her bag from the hall and fleeing out of the apartment and down the stairs. Above her the whirring of the bombers and the persistent yet pointless firing of the flak and heavy artillery was deafening. As something whistled down nearby and exploded with such force that the walls of the house shuddered, she gave a squeal of fright.

She was soon hammering at the thick iron door of the bunker, which to her immense relief opened up. An arm jumped out and she was dragged inside in a shot, while the door was slammed shut. "Where were you? We were worried sick!" hissed Käthe. Her stylishly parted hair normally framed a smiley carefree face, but now she had a different expression, looked almost ferocious in the dim cellar light. "I'm sorry, it was just…", stammered Inge but Trudchen was roughly dragging her over to a bench. There they sat in silence, Inge now pale with shock. Another couple of ear-splitting explosions sounded off nearby and a unanimous gasp went up in the cellar. The walls shuddered and a thick cloud of powdered dust, with plaster and other little particles, fell over them and filled their hair. The lights flickered. The three women huddled up closer and held each other tight.

For two further hours the bombing continued, wave after wave howling down. Despite the occasional fright when bombs smashed down closer to home, the explosions were mostly speaking dull rumbles in the distance. But those sporadic closer hits shocked the group of neighbours, making them cower in the shelter. They had never experienced a raid this long and intensive. During the middle of the bombing, the lights went out altogether. They sat stoically in the dark until Herr Lindemann, cursing, found the lanterns. There was the odd mumbled prayer, but next to nothing was said. Finally, at around three in the morning, after the bombing seemed to have ceased for a good while, the all-clear sirens could be heard in the streets above and there was a collective sigh of relief. The neighbours began to stand up and prepare to leave, brushing themselves down before leaving the shelter in an orderly fashion, with still heftily beating hearts.

The women rushed up to the apartment for a moment, to verify that there had been no damage and for Inge to leave safe her precious little handbag which she had clutched at in the cellar during the bombing. Additionally, Käthe changed into the white and blue striped dress of her nurse's uniform with white apron, though placing a long light-brown overcoat over the top and putting her uniform cap and neck brooch in a cloth bag to carry them beside her; she did not wish to be identified immediately, not until she had first seen her mother. With the telephone network being down, she was frantic to find her, so the three women headed out without further ado onto the street. They walked briskly up to the Malzweg, both Trudchen and Inge consoling the near hysterical Käthe as best they could.

They marched round the corner and entered the broad Bürgerweide, turning left to head towards the Inner Alster lake and city centre. Now they saw first-hand the bombs that they heard in the past two hours. All around, but particularly ahead of them in the centre and to the west of the city, were what seemed to be hundreds of fires. They heard the intense wailing coming from the overlapping sirens of ambulances, fire engines, and other emergency vehicles buzzing around the streets. Buildings were in flames everywhere ahead, and pillars of smoke were rising up into a sky that was now far dimmer than Inge had experienced it before, abandoned by the moon and filled instead with endless thick plumes.

Hordes of people were scrambling out from cellars and into the open, rushing off in all directions, stopping briefly to share information with others about the attack: a general incredulity over the scale of the bombing and, much more muffled, the abject failure of the *Luftschutzamt* (Air-Raid Protection Department) and above all the *Luftwaffe*, to adequately defend the city; the state of damage in various districts as well as particular buildings, both emblematic and local; the instructions concerning those who had to report for emergency duty at their local police, military, or Hitler Youth groups.

This informal communication network was gradually putting together a picture of the extent of the destruction together with its geographical form, thus enabling them to identify key risk areas that might affect their loved ones, their workplace, and other personally relevant facts. It appeared that the centre, in which just a few weeks ago the women had all promenaded along so carefree together, had been very badly hit. The famous gothic St. Nikolai church seemed to have been a principal target and perhaps even an orientation point for the bombers. A police officer they met on the way related that much of it had been blown up by explosive bombs or had caved in through the extensive fire that followed; the tower was completely burnt out and all around it lay the rubble of surrounding buildings, also taken out in the bombardment. He warned them to stay away from the immediate area as there was still considerable hazard through falling masonry. In addition, the air-raid police had noted the unusually high usage of heavy blockbuster and mine bombs, some of which had timing devices and might still go off at any moment.

The three women marched steadily on, coughing through trails of smoke and the pungent smell of soot and chemical fumes that left a bitter taste at the back of their throats. At first, the eastern areas they walked through had only been lightly hit. There was the odd bomb crater and a few damaged buildings. On one street, an explosive bomb had completely taken out an apartment block at the end of a row, cleaving it from the neighbouring houses and leaving a mess of rubble in and around a deep crater. Soviet prisoners of war from the local *Neuengamme* concentration camp, dressed in the familiar, faded striped-cloth uniforms, had been brought in to clear the rubble and carry off any corpses they found below. Fires were few there but, as they approached the Alster, they could see ahead on the other side of the lake how hundreds were raging in many different spots and at varying distances. Small groups of uniformed older boys from the Hitler Youth were running or cycling toward the centre, with instructions to report on damage and assist the rescue services. At one point they passed a bush onto which a number of strange glittering objects had landed, that at first seemed to be strips of tin foil. Inge had already noticed some of these lying around on the streets on their way down. Now she paused to inspect them closer. They were thin and very light strips, silver on one side and black on the back, about thirty centimetres long and three centimetres wide, lying around randomly all over the place and presumably dropped from the sky. Curious, she snatched up a handful of them and placed them in her jacket pocket.

They turned south towards Schopenstehl, the street where Käthe's mother and stepfather lived. Upon reaching the street their pace built up to a trot, but they saw to Käthe's tearful relief that there was negligible damage in the street as a whole, and that her mother's own block was clearly unscathed. The facades around it were likewise intact, smoke rising elsewhere behind them and into the orange-illuminated night sky. Now much nearer to the city centre, there was the more intense clamour of people running past. Fire engines and other emergency vehicles could be heard frantically driving around, sirens wailing, often finding streets blocked by rubble or bomb craters, screeching to a halt, revving backwards to search for another route.

While Trudchen and Inge began to process the enormity of the situation, staring in disbelief at the fiery skyline ahead, Käthe had rushed through the open front door of the block and encountered her mother Magda, descending the stairs. She hugged and kissed her daughter with unbridled joy, told her that both she and her husband, still upstairs and examining every inch of the apartment, were fine. Magda had called in on an elderly neighbour who had suffered a seizure in her apartment due to the shock of the nearby bombing, and she had stayed a while to comfort her until her family arrived. Now she intended to go to her brother's apartment behind the Sankt Petri church; check that he was safe and see what the damage was like there. Käthe gave her mother her overcoat for the journey, while putting on the neck brooch and cap from her bag. She was now fully identifiable as a Red Cross helper and intended to call in for duty straightaway.

The two women ran back into the open street. "Nothing is working at all, no water, no telephone, no electricity. It is a complete disaster," Magda said in passing, greeting Trudchen and Inge with a grim smile and nod. They heard shouts and then the roar of a collapsing building, several streets away but still loud and reverberating heavily. From the same direction came the cries of a woman screaming. The air here was notably thicker with fumes and noise, Inge and her companions sensed.

"They are saying the city centre was very badly hit," Magda commented. "I heard that in St. Pauli there are endless buildings on fire. Whole sections of the Reeperbahn have been wiped out and, of course, it was full tonight. Also, a lot of bombs fell in the west, especially in Altona. And in Eimsbüttel and Hoheluft too. I have never heard of anything like this, it is a total disaster." She hugged her daughter, saying "Take care, my treasure," and rushed off.

Käthe had spotted a Red Cross truck coming down the street and stepped out to hail it down. She jumped in the back and was whisked away, while Trudchen stated she would be reporting in at the nearest police station. Inge said she would go to her uncle's apartment in the Wexstraße, assuring her companion that it wasn't far and that she knew the way. The two marched briskly together to the end of the street and parted ways at the *Alter Fischmarkt*.

Inge walked all the way down the street Große Reichenstraße before heading up toward the centre, passing just a few blocks away from the Inner Alster lake, past the prominent *Rathaus* (city hall) which had taken a couple of explosive hits. In this area, the signs of damage were much clearer; smashed-up trams and tramlines, incinerated vehicles, bomb craters and burst pipes, damaged facades, fires everywhere along the darkened but now energetic night streets; some blazes were smaller but a few of considerable magnitude and filling whole buildings. Pavements were covered in shattered glass and lumps of other debris, smashed stonework and fallen plaster, shreds of burnt materials, torn fabric and smashed or smouldering furniture, ashes, dust and dirt. Some air defence volunteers cycled by on the street, young recruits that were locating and reporting damage. Emergency services were a blare of activity, frequent shouts could be heard and the odd screaming. Civilians darted past her on their urgent missions; others walked around aimlessly, having escaped from bombed-out buildings but still in shock.

She walked on, crossing two canals before turning left into the small compact Neustadt district, where she located her uncle's apartment block. The whole area was practically untouched, although the panic here was evident. In all directions there could be seen more distant towering flames and surging clouds of thick black smoke, billowing up into the night sky. Although none were nearby, and there seemed to be next to no damage suffered, the psychological effect was still strong. Inge was tense as she ran to the apartment block and rang the button beside the nameplate. Out on the balcony stood the figure of an adolescent boy, one of Carsten's younger brothers, who recognized her and called for her to come up.

She entered the apartment and ran into a near hysterical Aunt Greta. She was sobbing and relating how Uncle Robert had stayed with the family initially, but after the all-clear signal he had gone off to the *Polizeispräsidium* – the Hamburg Police headquarters – where he worked. This, she later heard from a neighbour, had been hit early in the night. She had no idea where he was and had no way of contacting him due to the telephone lines not working. There was no water, she wailed, and she now had a severe headache from all the noise and panic caused by the air-raid.

"I thought they would never stop!" cried the fragile Greta. Inge found herself hugging her in a tight embrace of consolation as if she were her own mother, although she herself could never remember having ever received the slightest familial attention from Greta before. Her four younger children, aged between eleven and seventeen, sat around looking numb and shocked. Greta recovered her state of mind in due course and announced to them that this was the final straw, that they would be leaving Hamburg tomorrow to stay with relatives in the countryside; up in Schleswig near the Danish border, "Where this sort of thing never happens." If it wasn't for their father holding such an important position in the running of the city, she would be off with them, too. She said it was almost a blessing that her Carsten had been called up to the army - "Poor boys out there, but I doubt they have it as bad as we do," she sighed.

Uncle Robert eventually returned in the early morning, just after half-past eight. He told how police and firefighting units were on their way from other cities in the region: from Bremen, Lübeck, Kiel, to mention a few of the points of support. The Hamburg Police headquarters itself, where he had worked for nearly three decades, had burnt down completely as a consequence of the bombing. The building had itself been hit by an explosive bomb but of greater significance had been the conflagration produced by several of the surrounding commercial buildings, which had spread to the police headquarters to make it a further victim of the flames. The severity of the bombing, with the large number of affected streets within a wide area, together with fire stations themselves being hit, among them the principal station in the Quickbornstraße, plus the lack of available water due to disruptions to the water mains, had all resulted in the fire brigade being unable to react to the massive demand. Furthermore, communication and organization by the authorities had been badly disrupted by the sheer magnitude of the raid. The bunker under the Hamburg Police headquarters had been encircled by a particularly intense blaze and could not be evacuated for several hours after the all-clear signal. It transpired that the fire department had also been unable to effectively put out fires due to low water pressure, partly a result of the widespread nature of the bombings as well as burst water pipes. If one of the enemy's strategies had been to saturate and overwhelm the fire service, said Uncle Robert, they had certainly achieved that objective, along with many others.

He mentioned that for the coming weeks, perhaps a little longer, Inge would no longer have a job, now that her workplace had burnt to the ground. The chaos left by this major attack was mind-boggling, he admitted, and he himself was not sure where he was going to work in the coming days. He had to report that evening to the provisional emergency office of his department which, it had been hastily decided, was henceforth to be located at the central command post of the *Ordnungspolizei* (Order Police) in the Feldbrunnenstraße until further notice. After that even he had no idea as to his workplace or duties.

He assured her nonetheless, with a kindly and sympathetic tone that she was much in need of, that he would find her another suitable position, "once things have begun to normalize again, perhaps within a month, if possible." She in turn clasped his hand, thanked him, and told him not to worry about her, that the important thing was that they were all safe and sound, and that she was there to help out in any way she could, whenever he and the police department needed her. There was little else for her to say in any case. In this topsy-turvy world into which the night had fallen - one in which thousands had lost their homes and all their belongings, and many their lives as well - any even slight regret from Inge's side would have been tasteless in the extreme. She was still aware though, that she still needed to work all the same, and produce the money required to live. Like Germany, she told herself, she would not be cowed by the stabs of fate: next week she would begin again to re-organize her life in the city.

About an hour later, following a round of hot coffee using water from their emergency supply, Inge finally headed back to the apartment, long after dawn in the early morning light. It was an eerie, still partly smoking, dirty yellow sky. The noisy chaos continued in the background, but the streets to the east that she passed through were quieter and emptier by now, though the city air was still laden with fumes which tickled her throat. She became disoriented and headed towards the *Hauptbahnhof* (main train station) to better guide herself, after which she inadvertently took a different and longer route home. She passed a group of people sitting and lying out on the lawn under the stars, beside a bombed out clinic; a ragtag bunch of the already sick and injured, now looking around in utter confusion. Glancing behind her, she saw towers of smoke still rising up from the city centre and beyond that too, billowing up and filling the horizon like threatening storm clouds. Later on in the now quieter streets she came across an older man, badly injured and bleeding down his upper right side including his face, who was stumbling along, deranged. He spied her and clumsily staggered at her with a screech, wildly waving his arms and screaming obscenities. Terrified, she ran off and, though not followed by him, became acutely scared on the final stage home. She stopped only to pick up, out of curiosity, one of a scattered bunch of printed postcards that she found lying around in the street.

When she reached the apartment, she was wide awake despite not having slept all night, pumped up high with adrenalin. She found it horribly dismal (she had taken it for granted that it was completely intact, despite all the destruction she had witnessed). It was empty and silent there, while somewhere out in the battered city her new-found friends were vitally occupied.

Trudchen appeared shortly after ten o'clock that morning, with much to tell but too worn out to tell it, as she herself put it, and made straight for her bed. Inge sat on the couch in the living room and eventually fell asleep there.

She was woken up shortly after 16:00 on the now Sunday afternoon by another air-raid warning. She groggily came to life just as Trudchen ran in from her bedroom, and together they headed for the cellar. It was a much shorter raid this time, barely twenty minutes, and no bombs fell nearby. When they got back inside the apartment, they found that Lotte had also returned. She related that a squadron of American bombers had just attacked the dockyard area and bombed oil tanks, ships, and U-Boots. They had hit the Blohm + Voss shipyards hard, where high levels of destruction had been reported. The raid had been aimed at the industrial targets, however, and residential areas had been almost completely spared.

"That seems to be the strategy nowadays. The British come at night and bomb the residential areas, while the Americans come during the day and bomb military or industrial objectives," Lotte commented in the living room, removing her uniform jacket and lying back on the couch.

Trudchen nodded. "I was looking forward to having Sunday off this week but now I can see I shall have the night shift again tonight. Busy times."

Inge yawned and said, "How can the people here get anything done when they hardly get any sleep?" She produced the postcard she had found on the street. "I found this on the street when I was coming home. Where is it from?"

Trudchen flushed in the face and snatched it from her. She said to Lotte, "More of those flyers were dropped by the British tonight. They never give up with their propaganda." Then turning roughly to Inge, "You must never pick these up or be seen with them. There is the death penalty for keeping these!"

"I had no idea!" protested Inge. "I am so sorry. How could I know?"

"It is not a problem this time, just do not do it again," said Lotte, taking the postcard to rip it up into tiny pieces and drop them in the rubbish can.

Inge rubbed her forehead and whined. "Everything is getting so complicated here. And frightening."

Trudchen came up behind her and stroked her back. "Do not worry, Inge, it is not usually like this. I have never experienced an air raid like the one last night. It has been exceptionally heavy." She turned to Lotte. "So, it looks like they have finally decided to go for Hamburg in a big way."

"It was bound to happen sooner or later," came the cool reply. Lotte was staring at the ceiling, running her forefinger over her lips, deep in thought.

"Nobody had any idea of anything planned until last night and by then it was too late. I would never have imagined anything of these proportions."

Lotte shrugged and simply said, "Me neither," still staring upwards at nothing until her eyelids dropped and she drifted off.

Compared to that hellish Saturday night, the rest of Sunday and Monday was more peaceful in the residential areas, though never still. Sirens sounded out during the next two days and often had them running to the cellar for a few hours. However, these raids were either the infamous '*Mosquito bites*', aimed at keeping the inhabitants of the city in a state of heightened tension and lacking in sleep, or they were part of the American day raids on the industrial plants and dockyard areas. The Americans attacked in large bomber formations on both Sunday and Monday, in broad daylight. Dense squadrons of the huge and frightening silver Flying Fortresses swept over the city. They were bombing the port and shipbuilding areas and, although the women and others sitting with them in the cellar heard the distant explosive booms, nothing fell near to them.

By Tuesday most of the fires in the residential areas had been put out, though dense columns of smoke still circled up into the sky at various points across the maimed city. Those who had lost their homes were being placed in makeshift accommodation or staying with relatives. One of the main power stations had been hit in an American B-52 follow-up day raid, so power was intermittent. Some children had already been evacuated in the fear that there may be more such attacks to come; dozens of extra mobile flak units were brought in to bolster the defense, should that be the case. Some dense columns of smoke still circled up into the air at various points across the city.

Following the attack from Saturday night, the information acquired from various sources was pieced together, giving Trudchen and Lotte at the *Luftschutzzentrale* (Air-raid Protection headquarters) a good overall impression of the scale of destruction, which they in turn passed on to Käthe and Inge at home. The air-raid had been officially classified as a major catastrophe, with countless buildings destroyed over a wide-sweeping area, in particular in the city centre and the western districts, they were told. The death toll was first estimated as standing at around one thousand, but that figure was eventually revised upward by a further five hundred, as more and more corpses were located under the ruins of buildings. The injured ran into many thousands; all undamaged hospital and clinics were hopelessly overwhelmed and all but the most serious cases were being turned away. Käthe said she had no overview per se of medical care, but that from the ground level she could sense that the overall situation was bleak.

The failure of Air-Raid Protection to resist the onslaught had not just been due to the sheer magnitude of the Saturday night attack - which had involved an estimated six to seven hundred enemy aircraft - but also due to a new camouflage technique that had been employed, and obviously with great success. This had involved the aerial release by the planes of many tons of small strips of aluminium foil, which had gently fluttered to the ground and, during their slow descent, had jammed the radars and made it impossible to identify individual planes. All that had appeared on the radar screens was a huge and meaningless blob, a mass of confused data that could not in any way be used to adequately counter the incoming attack. No-one had known where they were or where they were going. The *Luftwaffe*'s night fighters had been unable to locate and intercept the swarms of RAF bombers; the flak defense had been equally at a loss. Hamburg had ended up being an open target. On hearing this, Inge had gone to her room and come back with the silver strips that she had found on the bush and had kept for herself. Trudchen and Lotte examined them and affirmed that they were exactly the items that were to blame. Inge offered them up but they assured her that Air-Raid Protection had already collected hundreds, if not thousands, for closer inspection.

All the same, the increasingly ineffective role of German fighter planes as a defence mechanism was clearly a sore point. Lotte let slip a derogatory comment about "that fat useless Göring", at which Trudchen smiled broadly, though later she quietly admonished her colleague and told her to be careful about speaking in such terms in front of the other women in the apartment.

On Tuesday, Inge cleaned the flat thoroughly, including the others' bedrooms. The women were clearly exhausted and expressed their gratitude. Lotte and Trudchen had all their free days cancelled for that week and had shifts of duty each day; Käthe was likewise busier than ever. When their paths crossed, she told devastating tales of the injuries she had seen, feeling the need to share the experience with someone. As these tales also included children, Inge would have preferred not to hear, but all the same she wouldn't have interrupted for the world, recognizing her companion's need to express herself and work her way mentally through the experience.

Inge went out shopping on Tuesdsay and was able to put together the cheap ingredients for a solid meal of beef and vegetables. She had it ready by the afternoon and served first a portion for Trudchen, before Trudchen headed off for the night shift. She warmed it up a couple of hours later for Käthe and Lotte, who were returning home from early shifts. She enjoyed being busy and able to take care of her companions in this difficult time; there was something maternal in the set-up that stimulated her and helped her to come into her own.

Käthe and Lotte went off for a nap after eating, while Inge settled in for the evening, sewing some of the rips in the women's uniforms that had arisen during work. After two relatively quiet days now, she entertained the thought that the enemy may have finished their bombing schedule, which had after all been very long and drawn-out, and trusted that a tranquil night would set over Hamburg that Tuesday and bring a return to relative normalcy.

Chapter 29

Late July had brought unusually warm weather and by this Tuesday 26th the mercury had climbed even higher. For many it was unbearably hot and, to increase the general mood of irritation, the water supply had become limited and unreliable so that the possibility of bathing and washing away the sweat and grime was greatly reduced. There was next to no breeze and the sharp smell of soot from the attacks of the previous days still lay heavily over the city. Between the heat of the nights and the endless howls of air-raid sirens due to *Mosquito* nuisance raids, the atmosphere had become tense and edgy.

"Count your blessings, girl," said Käthe when Inge moaned about the sweltering weather. Some isolated columns of smoke could still be seen rising in the wake of the Sunday raid on the dockyards.

After the women had eaten and gone to bed, Inge washed up the dishes and decided to read a book. She passed her finger over the cover spines in the bookcase in the living room, mostly non-fiction books about general health, housekeeping, and cookery; all left by Angela. No-one had taken much interest in reading in the last couple of weeks. Inge had taken out a copy of *Der Hitlerjunge Quex* - being inquisitive due to the fame of the book rather than directly interest in the subject matter - that she had found among the titles. She had worked her way through about twenty pages by 19:00, at which time Käthe and Trudchen had returned from their nap, both still groggy.

Käthe had put in twelve-hour shifts on Sunday and Monday, and this evening she decided to visit her mother again, whom she had not seen since Saturday night and the bombing. Lotte was at work, so Trudchen and Inge were left alone in the apartment and Inge made coffee for the two. Trudchen eyed up the book title of Inge's reading choice, but left it uncommented.

Inge decided, upon returning to the living room with coffee and cake, that this might be an intimate and appropriate moment to speak openly to Trudchen about subjects that had been weighing on her. She had noticed certain things that Trudchen had stated or, more accurately, insinuated, and that gave her to believe that she could discuss these issues with her; issues that others might consider to be a breach of the correct attitude and morals. She had even sensed an openness to (fair and balanced) criticism of the authorities, which was refreshingly new for her. She plucked up the confidence to ask her this in this moment of coffee and cake. "Would you mind?" she put forward timidly. "It is so hard to talk sometimes, and I would appreciate talking to someone like you, who has seen a lot and understands such a lot."

"I am not sure I am up to either of those compliments, Inge, but I can try to answer honesty and fairly. Naturally, this conversation would be strictly confidential," Trudchen said, arching her eyebrows.

"Of course, of course," said Inge. "Total discretion. That is why I wanted to speak to you and just to you."

"Good, then fire away."

"About the war. When do you think it will end?" asked Inge.

For this starting inquiry Trudchen only had a cynical laugh. "You sweet girl, now that really is the question of all questions! For hundreds of millions of people, I imagine. And the answer is worth all the gold in the world." Trudchen shrugged. "What can I tell you? It will be over when it is over. That is all we can hope for."

"But it must end eventually."

"I suppose it must. But there is not yet a clear end in sight."

"So what happened at Stalingrad?"

Trudchen did not answer immediately but sought to find the appropriate vocabulary. "Stalingrad proved to be a very difficult military goal that was not achieved as quickly as it was hoped it would be. And the…the necessary retreat of our troops in the aftermath of the battle has been a set-back, strategically speaking. Perhaps even a … major set-back." She decided to abandon this oration and speak honestly from the heart. "Listen Inge, you have told me that your husband is still on the eastern front and was in that area, which is why I have not wanted to talk to you any further about the subject. I do not want to say something to you, out of idle speculation, that is then proved to be completely untrue. You would bear me a grudge, and quite rightly so."

"But I would prefer you to be honest. If there is bad news to be heard, I am sure that I can handle it." Both Inge herself and Trudchen knew that was a blatant lie.

"You know the bad news yourself. The 6th Army was encircled and entrapped in Stalingrad. That was in February. The battle was lost, and there were many casualties. Also, many men are missing. They may be prisoners of war of the Soviets, or they may have died in battle. In terms of individual fates, there is still a lot of uncertainty. It will take time until the status of all the troops who are missing or taken captive can be fully ascertained."

"I know. I know that part, it is just...," said Inge. "It is just, I need to know whether it might have all been... in vain. The battle, I mean."

Again, Trudchen forced herself to be cagey. "The retreat has been a big blow to the war effort. Some are even saying, although I naturally cannot vouch for that personally, I am just repeating what I have heard, but some are saying it could end up having a very dramatic effect on the future course of the conflict."

Naturally, neither would bring themselves to utter that dreaded word - "defeat" - which had as much power as a bomb itself.

Inge said, "Horst used to write a lot. Every month, even if just a few lines. I told him not to worry, to concentrate on taking care of himself. I have not heard anything from him since a letter I received in late November. And now it is July already. Sometimes I have weak moments and I fear the worst. But the only thing I can do, the only thing that makes any sense for me, is not to give up hope. Neither for him nor for us all. I mean, the war must end at some point, but then at least we shall have won the war. I need to have that hope. I need to know that however much we suffer, it will not have been in vain."

"Absolutely!" said Trudchen. "Hope should be the last thing we lose. And there is all the reason in the world to believe that your husband is among the prisoners of war."

"They do not know much about how our men are being treated. I have asked for details but every time I ask something, the answer is always vague."

"The truth is that no-one knows for sure. *Ivan* has never been very much disposed to freely giving out information. Not even to his own people, much less to a country with which he is currently locked in battle. All you can do is hope and, as I said, there is much hope to be had."

"If only I could receive one letter, just one, it would change everything."

"Of course it would." Trudchen felt this was the moment to push for information on a topic that still slightly mystified her. "But if you were at home in Lüneburg, you would receive that letter even more quickly."

"Well, our address is at my sister Gisela's home, at the Gasthaus she owns and runs together with her husband. She would call me immediately if anything came."

Trudchen also felt the moment ripe for a sharing of confidences. "Inge, be honest with me now. Did you come here to Hamburg for some reason?"

"Yes," she frowned, smiled awkwardly. "I have already told you why."

"No, I mean the real reason." She bent over and touched Inge's hand. "What you told me did not make a lot of sense, the more I thought about it. Forgive my intrusion into your private life but I thought this was as good a moment as any to ask. I mean, you and your uncle in the police force, I do not think you are that close. Whereas you _are_ very close to your sister. Not to mention your three little boys there."

"I would not bring little children to Hamburg. Not with the bombings."

"I know. But you would not really wish to leave them somewhere else either," she smiled.

Inge paused briefly for thought; decided to take the leap. "The real reason why I wanted to, needed to, get away from Lüneburg, is that I was being harassed by a man. Continually harassed, and violently so, too."

"A _Bonze_ (top dog) in the Party, right?"

"He does have a high position, yes. In the SS. He works at the Gestapo headquarters, which is now in Lüneburg. He is a wicked man, utterly detestable. I do not want to go into details but the situation has become very threatening for me, so that...", her eyes became teary and she had to wipe them, but she did not cry. "He said terrible things about the soldiers fighting out there. And about Horst. He even implied that I was already a widow. Such a horrible, evil man. Of course, if Horst came back, everything would be so very different."

"I know it would," said Trudchen and leant over again to pat her. "I understand what you are thinking. But don't worry, Inge. You are safe with us. You are far away from him here."

Inge held her arm, the women staying in close and restorative contact for some moments, until Inge said, "I think I could drink another coffee."

Trudchen laughed, "I definitely want another one before I have to go to work. The stuff they have in the *Dienstraum* (workplace) is undrinkable. Heavens knows where they get it from. Are you sure you should be drinking coffee? Will you be able to sleep alright tonight?"

"Oh, the coffee does not bother me. I can still sleep after a coffee or two. In any case, there will probably be another one of those *Mosquito* raids tonight, so I am used to waking up around midnight even if I do get to sleep earlier!" she laughed.

"We could have a little glass of that cognac that Käthe's brother left."

Inge nodded and dried her eyes.

She made the coffee and they continued talking. Inge was delighted that she had got the secret off her chest and found a confidante. "In these times it is so difficult to find someone to talk to," she confessed.

"I know, it is. You have to be so careful what you say. Even with people like Lotte or Käthe. I know Lotte well and she would never repeat anything she heard from me, but I also do not think she would approve of my saying certain things either. So I keep many topics to myself and we mostly talk about things that happen at work. Lotte is not especially political and certainly not close to the Party, more your typical German national conservative. Käthe however is _very_ loyal to the Party. She doesn't blindly follow everything, but she is very optimistic and sure the Führer and Dr. Goebbels are in complete control of the situation, that the war is completely necessary and justified, and that we must be prepared to make great sacrifices in order to achieve our victory."

"Back in Lüneburg we listened on the radio to the speech Dr. Goebbels gave in Berlin recently, about the total war."

"That's right, I remember that, earlier this year."

"You could hear everyone shouting and cheering. They all sounded so very sure of the coming victory and so joyful about the idea that we would keep on fighting, regardless of what happens. I… if I am honest with you, Trudchen, I am not sure where my country is going. Or what this 'total war' actually means."

"As far as I am concerned, we have been in a state of total war for the last two years already. I do not see anything new in that, nor can I imagine how we could possibly give yet *more* to the war effort."

"I remember when Horst and I went on our honeymoon to Berlin. That was back in 1936, when we got married. Imagine that, it has been nearly seven years! It is our anniversary tomorrow on the 27th July, but don't tell the other girls. Just our secret. Anyway, we went there to coincide the trip with the Olympic Games. We stayed in a very charming little pension called Hotel Funk. It was in the Fasanenstraße, not far from the big park with the botanical gardens and the Ku'damm shopping street. We did have such a wonderful time. I loved every minute. It was a nice bright summer, but not hot and close like it is here at the moment. Just warm and bright. The sky was a clear blue. You know, that was the first time I had ever left Lüneburg. The first time ever! Those were such good times back then. Things were starting to get better. There were jobs again after the crisis, and people could go into shops more often and treat themselves to nice things. Cousin Carsten, as we call him in my family, he bought himself so many gadgets. Things that I could barely have even imagined existing when I was growing up. Cameras and radio, and a neighbour got a refrigerator for the house! People were buying cars too - that was a very modern and useful thing to have. Everything was new and exciting. I thought it was the start of something wonderful and that the Führer would lead us into, well, into prosperity, which he did, but I thought it would be into a calmer, more stable prosperity. Then things changed, slowly. At least it seemed slowly to me. Perhaps I just did not notice what was going on. One day you wake up and find yourself in a strange world, and you wonder how you got there and why you did not see it before."

"And when did you first realize that things were not going as you thought they would?" asked Trudchen, probing.

Inge considered. "I think the night when they burnt down all those Jewish shops and homes, and attacked them in the streets. I mean, it was common knowledge that the government had brought in these strict new laws to make them separate from us. And many people, typical people in the street, really did not like the Jews and would not speak with them and refused to work with them. But that night things changed somehow. It was like a first hint of what was to come. I know that was in November 1938. I remember it well because my second boy, Joseph, was born in the June and was just a few months old. I was ill at the time and had been in bed for about two or three days with the flu. Joseph had got it too and I was looking after us both. So I was in bed, but I could hear it outside. When I later found out from other people what had happened, it did not seem right somehow. It was all so violent. Whatever the Jews might have done or not done, I do not know enough about that subject so I prefer to leave that to those who do, but whatever the case may have been, the way they mistreated those poor people was unforgivable. There were some people I knew and they looked so sad and broken down afterward. Most of them could barely bring themselves to talk to me again, now that I think about it. Not that I blame them at all. Personally, I never said anything about the subject, just listened to what others said, until a time later when a person I knew brought the subject up. It was just that there were laws and government instructions about what to do and what not to do. Things were so strictly controlled – well, they still are! It seemed like everyone was scared of maybe doing something wrong themselves, so that when someone else got caught, you were almost relieved it was someone else and not you, so you looked the other way. I know that doesn't make much sense but it was how it felt. I have to admit, it makes you feel guilty at the time, to look the other way, but in the long term it is more comfortable that way. You know, someone said recently, here on the stairs of the apartment block, that they are all working together: the international Jews, and the Bolsheviks in Moscow, together with the British and their air force. All working together to destroy us for once and for all. But I do not believe any of that. It does not even sound convincing."

"It is not at all convincing," said Trudchen, a touch icily. "Or true."

"And talking about the Jews," said Inge, now feeling emboldened to press on with her other doubts and queries. "I keep hearing that they are going to the East somewhere, to work on a project there, but do you know where? The East is immense."

Trudchen looked at her with intensity. "It certainly is," she said.

"If this is not a good topic for you, we can talk about something else."

"I do not have a problem with any topic, Inge. Just say what you think, I will no repeat anything to anyone."

"It is just that I saw some people one afternoon, some months back now, standing on the street corner together with their luggage. I think they were waiting for some kind of transportation. They were wearing the yellow stars like Jews are supposed to. But it all seemed very strange, the way they were going to be picked up. Not just strange, it was… sinister. Also, among the Jewish families in our town, so many have left so quickly. Their apartments and houses and businesses were sold very quickly and at a price that did not correspond to the true value. Even I could clearly see that much, and it is not something that I would normally notice. I thought that maybe they do not need so much money to start up again in this Palestine place that many go to. Then…," she lowered her voice and looked round over her shoulder.

"There is no-one else here," said Trudchen, softly and without emotion.

Inge snickered at her own silliness. "Of course. So then, some weeks ago, just after I had moved in, I found a little book in my bedroom. It was lying wedged behind the wardrobe in my room, on the floor but stuck behind one of the back legs. So I took it out and started to glance through it. It was a diary, the diary of a young man. I read some of it but I felt guilty about reading someone's private thoughts, so I stopped. I had already read enough to know that it belonged to a young Jewish man and that he used to live here. Right here in this very apartment, with his family. I mean, my bedroom must have been his bedroom. The last entry is dated September 20th last year, and I was thinking that the same thing might have happened to him as to those people waiting around on the street to be picked up. If they are being taken to a better place, why do they leave so quickly? Why are they reluctant to go? Why does the police always pick them up quietly, in little groups, even make them wait around in bad weather? I have heard they receive letters saying they must wait in a certain place at a certain time. It is strange how it is all done. In fact, there is a lot about this subject that does not makes sense." She had additionally wanted to tell Trudchen the story about Daniel Kaplan and his narrow escape from the Gestapo, but instinctively felt she would do better to leave that case unmentioned, at least for the time being until she was completely sure of her confidence and trust in her.

"Is the diary here? May I see it?" asked Trudchen, visibly touched by the story.

Inge blushed. "I took it home with me, when I went to Lüneburg last time, and left it there. I was going to read it all, but I did not get round to it." She considered, in the wake of the air-raid on Saturday night, that taking the book home had been a wise precaution. "Although I do not know whether I even should. There is perhaps private information within. And I am reading someone else's thought without them having given me permission to do so. It is not like when you buy a book that a person has willingly published."

"I understand totally. So, this family, the family of the boy, they lived here before us?"

"Yes, that is right. I even saw the number and name of the street mentioned. Plus some details. The crack at the side of the balcony, and the way the bathroom door keeps sticking. And about Herr Lindemann, the *Blockwart*. It seems there was this mutual hostility between him and the family. I read that Lindemann watched them closely and constantly asked them questions. Even impertinent questions. I think they were scared of him. And I know that Herr Lindemann is a very enthusiastic … man," she finished with a blush.

"The Party, and indeed politics and ideology in general, they are very important for some people," she said with careful formulation. "Personally, I am not a very politics-oriented person. I find the truth hard to follow in politics, I always have. And I find the whole bravado tedious to listen to. But I do love my country and I want to do my best to fight for it. Whether we like it or not, we are in this war now and so we have to give our all. For the survival of our nation, for the survival of all of us. That does not mean that I am in agreement with everything I see or hear around me. Some things may even be very… - how can I say it best? - there are unpleasant things that happen in a war, that is unavoidable, but there are also atrocious, terrible things, that go further than mere war. Naturally these cause me… distress. And so sometimes it is hard to actively follow a political or military strategy that seems to go… to go contrary to that which you have always believed in." She looked flushed for a moment and her words had faded into a state of confused agitation. She gave a quick shake of her head, as if to pull herself out of a spell, and ploughed on, "But whatever happens, my basic loyalty must always be towards the Fatherland. There can be no other way."

"So when you say that you are not in agreement with everything, what things exactly do you worry about, what things cause you this distress?"

"The increase in the bombings of our cities. A lot of people are dying, Inge, even children, and they are our future. There is also my family to consider, and not just my parents in Essen but also my brothers and my fiancé on the front. They are stuck in the ridiculous mess that this ridiculous campaign against Russia has become. Many will not survive it, I am sure, including people I know and some that I love. And yes, what is happening to the Jews as well. I never liked that part of the speeches and the political manifesto. And yet we all watched it happening, right from the beginning. I suspect deep down that the situation for them is maybe much more serious than we imagine it to be. They are taking away huge numbers of people in trains. But packed in, almost like cattle. As you yourself have just said: where to exactly, and why so many all at once? And furthermore: why do they all have just a little luggage, a couple of suitcases, when they have whole households like the rest of us?"

Inge said, "I have never thought about it in detail. Those are other people's lives and there is always something else for us to worry about."

"I think there must be a wide awareness among the general public, and acknowledgement thereof that something major is happening. Here in Hamburg, for example, the Jews are made to assemble on a regular basis over on the park by the Moorweidestraße, not far from the University Library. Like you were describing it in Lüneburg: they stand there in groups, wearing their yellow stars and waiting to be picked up. And everyone that goes by there, knows that something strange is going on, and yet no-one stops to discuss it. It is a strange state of secrecy when everyone knows there is a secret but no-one wants to know what it is."

"I suppose so, yes."

"I have heard some reports, well, to be honest they were more rumours, from people who have been posted out on the eastern front. Although I have no solid proof of anything and after all, any lowly private, like any simple sailor, can tell of dreadful things he has seen and exaggerate them. Remember, Inge," said Trudchen looking at her closely with narrow eyes, almost as if to intimidate. "This conversation stays strictly here. Normally I would not have said a fraction of what I have said today."

"Of course, of course," nodded Inge. "You know I have to be discreet myself. Now that I have told you all my secrets." They both had the sensation of willingly creating a mutual blackmail system; one they felt would never be employed but, due to its nature of potential mutual destruction, one that allowed both parties to feel more comfortable and loosen up in their budding trust.

Trudchen looked down at her now empty coffee cup. "As I said, I do not know of any actual details, and even if I did, I could not speak about it, but some are saying that they are being killed."

Inge's eyes widened. "All of them?"

"Many, yes. Possibly most of them."

"Why? How?" she gasped.

Trudchen shrugged. "Why did we bomb people's houses in London? Why is London now bombing us? At the end of the day there is no real sense to any of this."

"Are they shooting the Jews?"

"I really do not know, Inge. I have only heard rumours. As I said, I have no solid information, no photographic evidence or incriminating documents. I am merely repeating what has been heard from soldiers and others who have been fighting in the east. And people are now wary to whom they pass it on to."

Inge was still stunned. "But shooting so many people! It makes no sense. There must be work for the people out there to do, something productive. I don't understand the reasoning behind that kind of killing. If we are at war with the enemy, why are we killing innocent people?"

"In war almost everyone is innocent."

Inge shook her head. "No, it's not the same. Those poor poor people, waiting in the rain. Just standing there, waiting to be picked up. And they never had any idea what was going to happen. They must have gone off like lambs to the slaughter. Oh dear God, this is dreadful. This is so terrible, what you are telling me. Just shooting people dead like that for no reason!" she hissed, her voice quiet but feverish.

"Perhaps there are firing squads. Or perhaps they are killing them with grenades, in groups. As I said, I do not know exactly. What I do know, or rather, what I have heard from good sources, is that they are killing a lot of people in general, but especially Jews. Thousands, perhaps hundreds of thousands. There are special elite groups from the SS that are active in Poland and the Ukraine and Belarus and other parts of the east, and they are wiping out whole communities. And more than that, they have also built huge concentration camps, also further out to the east. Like the ones here, only these new ones are much bigger and have mainly Jews. And no-one gets out, no-one comes back. They are transporting thousands there every day by train, but the internal population size remains steady. So that must mean that they are dying inside, somehow. And please remember, you must not repeat a single word of any of this. Not to anyone at all. Not to Lotte or Käthe or your uncle or whomever, and especially not to anyone in your hometown, in Lüneburg. People in small towns gossip, and gossip spreads faster than fire. If someone in a position of authority overheard, they would surely come for you, and after they had got you to talk, they would come for me. With my position in Air-Raid Protection Duty that would automatically mean prison for me, maybe worse. Bear in mind that none of us can change what is happening, whatever we say or do. There are very high powers controlling this."

"No, no, I promise you I will not repeat a word," Inge shook her head in anxious tension. "You know I would not."

"Yes. I do. Otherwise I would not have mentioned it in the first place." She looked across out of the evening window and for a while they said nothing.

Inge said, "You know, next to no-one back home would believe me even if I said anything. There are so many rumours, it is possible to believe anything. People gossip, others even spread false truths deliberately, confuse everything. The official news, instead of helping, just makes the situation worse. You do not know whom or what to believe, so in the end you prefer to just not believe anything at all. Then you do not believe in anything. These are such mad times. You do not know whom to trust. Anyone could report you, even for just opening your mouth and saying the wrong thing, and you would disappear and be gone, as if you were never there in the first place. Nothing is solid, nothing is reliable. Even the Führer is a fake. I do not believe a word he says anymore, or what any of them say. They say one thing and then it is another. They said the war would be short and victorious, and now it is going to be long and full of death. This endless series of campaigns that are going nowhere. They said we would be happy and better off, and now we have rationing and live afraid. They said barely any bombs would fall on the towns, and now people are spending night after night in air-raid shelters while whole streets are burning. Nothing that we were promised has come true. And now this terrible crime with massacres of Jews, all for no reason. If what you are saying is true, then that is a crime that will never lie hidden. We will be hated forever. People will say we were savages. And they will be right, we _have_ become savages. We were told there would be a shining future ahead for us, yet all we have is hatred and evil and death. Everything is senseless. This is worse than the work of the Devil and yet we cannot stop ourselves. This war is like a bloody wheel that keeps turning round and never stops. With every turn, more and more die. Why could we not have foreseen all of this? Why did we place our trust so blindly? Why cannot we stop it all?" Her voice was trembling and seemed about to break under the weight of emotion.

"It is a little late for tears now, Inge. I suppose you have never read *Mein Kampf*, have you?" Trudchen asked. "Most people I have met, have not. More is the pity. I did not either. But now I know that these things you are talking of, the war, the hatred, the killings, they were already announced. Terrible events never appear out of nothing. They are years in the making. It is just a question of recognizing the signs."

"No, I never did read it", sighed Inge. "We have a copy in the Gasthaus somewhere. Gisela's husband was given it by someone. His brother, I think, or his father. But I do not really read a lot, not books, not since school. The one I picked up off the shelf today was the first in many years. I think I will enjoy reading it. Perhaps it will help me to understand what is happening, and why. I hope I will try to read more when this is all over. Try to make myself more informed, less trusting. It could be that has been the problem. When you trust too blindly, they take advantage of you. Trust should not be a flaw, but it is."

"It is not your fault. These systems are created by intelligent people for just that purpose. They use suggestive words and phrases and ideas, all with the sole goal of manipulating the rest of society. Before I started to work in the Wehrmacht, I never imagined how much could be said differently through the correct choice of words. Or hidden. Alone the euphemisms are endless. You know, for example, that when they say *Sonderbehandlung* (special treatment), it has nothing to do with a special treatment as you or I might imagine it, but rather it means 'killing' someone. So I imagine when the authorities talk of *Umsiedlung* (resettlement), it is not what it seems either."

"If what you have been saying here is true, then we have all been living the greatest of lies. We are living a trick, a swindle! And there is no way out now! Trudchen, what should I do? What are we supposed to do with our lives when we have been living a falsehood?"

"What we all have to do is to make sure we get through this conflict safe and sound. Then, after that, our next goal will be to not make the same mistake again. We have to offer a better future for the next generation. For the next coming generation, like your own children. Prepare a future that is more about simple prosperity and less about conquest. I would like to see a Germany that is respected and admired in the world, not feared."

"If what you said about these mass killings is true, I do not know if we will ever be respected or admired again. People will think of Germans and say we are all murderers. They will spit at us. Maybe it is better if we lose."

Trudchen now looked down in an intense and silent inner conflict: Inge had expressed, in seven simple words, the very doubts that had plagued her of late. On the one hand, she felt inside a strong hope for the survival *and* victory of her nation, for those two concepts were complimentary as far as she could see; but on the other hand there was also a nagging sense of shame when she thought of the horrors that still awaited them all in this prolonged fight, and the atrocities she feared had indeed been committed in the name of her nation, that would one day come back to poison any victory and haunt any new dawn.

That evening, once again, she ducked away from the awful recognition that her loyalty had been utterly betrayed, shied away from the fear that she was deceiving and consoling herself with excuses, and said, "Those are the unknown destinies that the future holds in store for us. In the meantime, all we can do is live and learn, and be honest to ourselves. Either way, I fear it is too late now for regret or self-recrimination." Trudchen got up to take the coffee cup back to the kitchen. "Just look after that diary and keep it safe back in Lüneburg. It might be the last thing that boy wrote. And if that is not the case, then it will have important memories for him. You have his name and former address. You might be able to trace him once this war is over, and give it back to him."

"Sometimes I wonder if it will ever be over. It already feels so normal, like all this here were just the normal state of things. I was thinking this morning about the sirens at night, and the *Mosquitoes*, and Käthe in her Red Cross uniform with those dreadful stories about the survivors she told us, and their burns and injuries - until I realized how normal it all felt. That was shocking! It feels so routine, so commonplace. I never imagined it would feel commonplace to be at war. How did we get used to it so quickly?"

"You would be very surprised at what people can get used to," Trudchen replied, and added, hoping to take herself and her companion away from dark thoughts, "Why don't we put the radio on? But not the news or *Onkel Baldrian* or any of that. Just something nice and easy to listen to. Please."

Inge nodded grimly. "There is a dance orchestra concert on tonight, from the Ballhaus Femina in Berlin."

"Absolutely perfect."

But both felt the shocking banality of stumbling from mass murder in one moment to dance music in the next in order to clear the air, but said nothing.

Käthe came home from visiting her mother at nearly 21:00 and chatted for a while with the two, until Trudchen left for work. Lotte arrived shortly afterwards from her late duty shift, but was exhausted and had little to say.

The song '*Die ganze Welt ist himmelblau*'[7] was playing softly on the radio and Inge was enjoying it, swaying her head a little from side to side. It was at around a quarter past eleven, just as they were getting ready for bed, that the telephone rang. Most of the lines had been working again since Monday morning and they had received various calls, generally from concerned relatives who had heard about the ongoing attacks. Inge had also received a call from Uncle Robert, who asked after her well-being and told her that their children had already been packed off first thing on the Monday morning to stay on a dairy farm near Denmark.

"God help them there, I think they will be expected to help out with the farming chores and that will be an unpleasant shock," he had related with a chuckle. His wife Greta was in bed with migraine but sent her best regards. He added that he would be in touch as soon as he had any positive news on the job front.

Shortly afterwards came another call. This time it was Trudchen on the line, calling from her workplace at the Air-Raid Protection central office. Käthe picked up the phone and the conversation was brief. She went pale and rushed to tell the other women. "That was

---

[7] The Whole World Is Sky-Blue

Trudchen on the telephone. She was calling from work and says there is a large squadron of British bomber planes detected and they look to be heading directly towards Hamburg. She says they must be using the tinfoil strips again because it is all one big mess on the screen, but it looks to be a major attack and we should go to the cellar immediately. Or better still, go to one of the big public bunkers." She whined, "So what do we do?"

Less than five minutes later, at twenty minutes to midnight, the air-raid sirens began blaring out the Danger-30 frequency into the night. The women were fully dressed again and discussing their course of action in the kitchen. All around them, the nocturnal bustle in the apartment blocks was cranking up. The block wardens began to do their rounds and check that the evacuation to the cellars was proceeding correctly, while Käthe tuned the radio channel back to '*Onkel Baldrian*'.

"The air-raid tower at Berliner Tor is not that far to walk to, but it is always packed full," said Käthe. "I went there once and had to stand up the whole time, there was nowhere to sit. And the toilet area was disgusting that night. I wanted to retch the whole time. Although they do say it is very well built and could even withstand the blockbuster bombs. It is right opposite the main fire station, which is comforting."

"We can't enter without a *Berechtigungsschein* (entry permit) anyway," countered Inge.

Lotte snorted. "I work for the Wehrmacht and have my *Ausweis* (ID) on me. Käthe is with the Red Cross. I would like to see them stop us!"

"I know a good one in the Harderstraße but that is too far," said Käthe.

"There is a large public bunker on the corner of Ausschläger Weg and the Süderstraße," said Lotte, thinking. "I was there once, it is very well equipped."

"But our own shelter is perfect," said Inge. "Herr Lindemann was telling me how it was built just a few years ago, right after the war started, and he was so happy about the air filters. At least we know the people there, they would not be strangers to spend the time with." In that moment, the *Fliegeralarm* (air-raid alert signal) sounded. Inge gasped, "Are they here already?"

Lotte said, "I would suggest staying here too. They could start bombing any moment now, and by the time we get to Berliner Tor, it might be too late."

They hurried out of the apartment as other neighbours were reluctantly making their way down the staircase toward the cellar. Frau Götz from the second floor was cursing the *Mosquitoes* that she was sure had returned yet again to drive them into sleepless insanity. None of the three women thought it necessary or wise to contradict her. Down at the cellar, they passed by Herr Lindemann who was standing at the door and urgently waving everyone inside. "Quick now, everyone! We can never know what is coming." He was so frantic he had even forgotten to greet with his habitual 'Heil Hitler'.

It was almost midnight and the cellar was full, with all the neighbours having reported in by now - twenty-eight persons of all ages, mingling around. The air was musty and smelt of sweat. Inge, Lotte, and Käthe gently pushed their way through to the second room, which was less crowded, and found a seating area for the three of them together. Some were saying how they were very sure it would be a minor or even just a nuisance raid; others however were petrified of the possibility of another major raid, perhaps one this time that would be directed at the east rather than the west and centre of the city. "They might come for us this time. Fresh territory. No-one bombs ruins," commented the recently pensioned Herr Bittinger with morbid gravitas, as he took his preferred seat by the wall. The three women said nothing and, in the absence of the sound of bombs so far, began to wonder if Trudchen had not passed on an erroneous evaluation and that it would be just a nuisance raid after all.

Around midnight, the heavy artillery could be heard coughing out rounds of shots, preparing itself for whatever the British were going to throw at them this time. The occupants of the bunker looked around at each other with the usual tinge of pre-bombing anxiety, though in general the mood was one of relaxed resignation to yet another few hours of night-time spent underground. Lindemann, short and chubby and with a bushy grey moustache, sat in intense observation by the bunker door. He had his arms crossed; was looking officious and feeling gloriously important. How he had learnt to love these raids!

Fearing the worst, the air-raid siren system seemed to have been over-cautious in its timing. Around an hour of waiting followed, filled with mumbled conversations and visits to the adjacent bathroom. The artillery had stopped, and people were expecting to hear the all-clear signal. However, shortly before one o'clock in the morning, the bombs began to drop from above. It seemed in the first moments a similar experience to the Saturday night, but soon the occupants of the bunker perceived how this time the bombs were falling, on the whole, notably closer. They came now in fast-following clusters that screamed and then thudded down with enormous might, to send shockwaves through the earth. Sometimes there were more distant dull booms to be heard, but abruptly others would smash down nearby, sending a hefty shudder through the solid cement walls of the bunker. There came the piercing howls before close hits landed; the occupants acutely felt the dramatic shockwaves and changes in air pressure that hit their eardrums. Time and time again they were thrown around on the benches, as yet another barrage came down in worrying proximity.

The tension increased with the frequency of the closer hits. Bombs were now whistling down, exploding in terrific bursts nearby, while the occupants were pummeled by the air pressure waves that seemed to pull the very air out of their lungs. The house shook with each hit. The light coat of cement dust, that had occasionally fell from the ceiling during the previous Saturday raid, had now augmented to smaller chunks dropping down, and there were a couple of disturbing cracks to be seen. Occasionally the sheer crash was so great that the walls heaved and it seemed like the ceiling would cave in over their heads. In one particularly close hit, everyone was thrown from the benches and landed sprawled on the floor in a heap. A dense cloud of dust followed down from the buckling ceiling and had them all coughing. The lights, which had begun to flicker wildly not long after the commencement of the bombing, went out totally. A couple of lanterns were lit up and they cast a shadowy light over the terrified group.

A middle-aged couple in the corner, the Flegels from the fourth floor, prayed in fervent whispers. There were only two children this time: a fourteen-year-old boy and a twelve-year-old girl of the family Schulz, sitting beside their parents on a bank. They were due to have left for a little village in southern Germany on Sunday, along with their grandmother, but the transport had been delayed and here they all still were, impassive and silent under the aerial bombardment. Wilhelmina Biel, a tiny middle-aged widow and school teacher, whimpered in the corner. The Geroth couple from the first floor, who ran a small newspaper kiosk together and were both in their late fifties, tried to keep their calm in front of the others, but they gave out sharp cries whenever the bombs struck close by. Among the people gathered, there was some shouts and many desperate cries as the bombing progressed through and beyond the first half-an-hour. In all minds lurked the very real worry that a *Volltreffer* – a direct hit - would finish them off. Many of the occupants of the bunker were mentally signing off and entertaining final thoughts, thinking of what had and what hadn't been done, and what should have been done, in their lives. Inge only had one thought: her promise to her children that she would return.

It seemed for those hiding underground to be lasting forever. For many it was becoming literally unbearable. Before the second bombing wave had even finished, they were noticing serious breathing problems in the shelter, not to mention the intense heat. One elderly man called Schenk had already fallen unconscious and was lying on one of the camping beds at the far end of the shelter, away from the door. Around him his wife and daughter were comforting and stroking him, though his likewise octogenarian wife could be heard painfully snorting as she tried to bring the air into her lungs. The air in the cellar was obviously far from clean and among the stinking fumes and the coughing, there began to arise a panic. In the dim lights of the lanterns, faces could be seen sweating profusely as the temperature continued to rise.

Herr Flegel broke the silence and gasped, "We have to get out of here. This is a death trap."

His wife and two men near to him nodded and expressed their agreement.

Lindemann was visibly shaking, now quite terrified. "Where is there to go to? It will literally be hell outside."

"There is hardly any air," said Flegel. "And what there is, is warm."

"I know that! Naturally the ventilator is not bringing in any fresh air if the power is out. Once the power comes back on, everything will return to normal."

"We should have got the version with the hand crank, I said so before."

Despite everything Lindemann was now beside himself at this insinuation of incompetency on this part. "We agreed in the majority to get the best model! We even took a vote. Why on earth are you bringing this up now?"

Flegel persisted, "We cannot stay here forever. There will be no air left. We are not going to be able to breathe soon. Whatever is out there, it cannot be worse than this."

Herr Bittinger supported him, "I would rather take the risk of dodging the bombs than suffocating here underground in the dark."

"Exactly. Who wants a coward's death here in the cellar?" said Flegel, emboldened and looking around him.

"We are talking about common sense, not bravery!" hissed Lindemann. "The bombs will stop soon. They have to, they cannot last forever. Nobody in their right mind runs out into the middle of a hail of bombs. Have you gone mad?" And as if to reinforce the caretaker's point, three bombs crashed down as he was finishing his speech, the second especially close and rocking the cellar.

"This bunker was installed only three years ago. Reinforced with top-quality concrete. It will hold, I know it will," Lindemann insisted.

"But we cannot breathe!" cried Schenk's daughter. "It is so hot already, and it is getting hotter. We are going to roast down here!"

"Even if it holds up, we will die of asphyxiation. Or worse, burn to death. I am taking my chances," snapped Bittinger at Lindemann.

Lindemann snatched the flashlight from the elderly woman sitting next to him. He stood up and went to the door, tried to open it. "Help me with the door then," he said. "It is your look-out if you are that stupid."

Flegel and Bittinger went over and the three men slowly forced open the heavy iron door with great effort. Both door and frame had been slightly distorted by one of the near hits as well as the rising heat. Outside they looked up at the staircase and entrance hall above, by now an indistinguishable mass of flames, the whole structure being consumed by a rapidly spreading blaze. They sheltered their faces with their arms from the heat and slammed the door shut.

Lindemann said in stone-cold fear, "It is blocked. The whole house is burning, and it is blocked."

A universal gasp arose from the occupants. For a moment everyone looked stunned, until Flegel said, "And what about getting through to the next bunker on the other side?"

Lindemann stared in incomprehension.

"Through the old *Brandmauer* (fire partition wall) right at the back of the cellar. It's not concrete, it's brick. We can get through that and then out. We just have to break it down!" bellowed Flegel. "What is on the other side?"

"To my knowledge there is a narrow gap before the next bunker, with a basic staircase structure there," replied Lindemann icily, piqued at this growing insurrection.

Herr Geroth came up behind them and wheezed, "If we knock through to there, we could get out."

"I suppose the tools we have are sufficient for you all to break through, if that is what you want," Lindemann admitted. "Although I still consider it futile and strongly advise against it."

Flegel and Bittinger ordered all the younger and middle-aged men to help them and grabbed the emergency tools, that were stored away carefully in a niche in the cellar: hammers, two sledgehammers, axes, pickaxes, shovels and spades, even a crowbar. They bashed away at a section of the wall until they were at the end of their energy and, as some looking on feared, the last of the oxygen. Lindemann was quietly thinking the same too and sporadically hissed, "You are mad, mad, all of you! You will be crushed out there, blown to pieces!"

Eventually a breach was made, and the men gathered more closely round it. They pounded away until a small section of the wall was knocked out, enough to squeeze through. Flegel called his wife over and they were the first to stumble over the rubble and out into a narrow dark passageway, with a rough-hewn cement staircase leading up the first floor of the neighbouring building. They heard the close sound of crackling and saw the ubiquitous yellow-orange glow. The air was chocked with fumes. They looked up anxiously before grabbing hands and making a run for it, up and away.

The portly Herr Schröter, a medium-ranked civil servant and devout NSDAP member, who had observed rather than participated in the bashing, was already close behind Flegel as the gap in the wall finally fell out. He roughly pushed past the others standing in front. "That is perfect then," he uttered and disappeared up the stairs and out.

More soon followed, including Bittinger and the Geroths. Behind them came Lotte, who had grabbed and pushed the two other women forward. "Flegel was right," she whispered to them. "We have to get out of here."

They rushed through the gap and sprinted up the narrow staircase under a shower of falling powder of plaster. Behind them came a few more occupants; all in all, over a dozen had dared their way through the exit by now. But another series of monstrous crashes, almost directly behind the building, shook the ground. Most fell backwards, both those on the staircase or those already up in the inner courtyard above.

Some people had been standing doubtful by the breached section, still wondering whether to follow Lindemann's advice and stay put, or whether to flee with the others. But the blast created by the last falling bomb was huge, a cry went up and a crush of rubble from above fell into the staircase and over the breach, sealing the gap back up. Lindemann and what remained of his faithful would have to weather the growing fires and put their trust in the bunker after all. The night air, entering for a short moment through the open gap, had at least given them a fresh waft of air, and with that the psychological hope of a respite, while the still falling bombs terrified them out of further attempted actions. They huddled back up near to their iron door to wait for an end to the attack.

Lotte, Käthe and Inge were passing just beyond the top of the stairs when the latest hail of bombs struck. They picked themselves up and ran out into the courtyard, where they found a multitude of shards of glass lying around. A man, hit by falling masonry and sliced by glass, was lying face up with open dead eyes. Inge screamed and they all ran out of the yard and through to the entrance of this neighbouring block. Here too the house staircase was in the process of being consumed by the fire and somewhere behind them, in another building close by, came the crash of whole floors caving in.

"Out, out, out!" shouted Lotte, and they rushed out into the open street. After a moment's hesitation, they instinctively shuffled further forward, away from the building behind. Behind them came a resounding smash that left their ears ringing, as their neighbours' entire staircase fell in on itself.

There they saw people fleeing in all directions. A few other groups along the street were scrambling out of buildings, having also sensed that the slowly unbearable cellars would become deathtraps. The women, still confused and unsure, moved further away from the pavement and out into the middle of the street, as they heard the sound of large chunks of the interior crashing down through the floors of the flaming apartments.

It must have been barely half an hour since the bombing had commenced, but so much had already changed in the once familiar street. Their first impression was of the way the façades of still intact houses on the opposite side were illuminated by a bizarre flickering blood-red light, as if thrown onto the house fronts by a gigantic projector hidden somewhere further on. The night sky directly above was also lit up with eerie bright orange incandescence, although the deeper heavens below and beyond that were still pitch black. Occasionally, a group of bombs fell somewhere close in the area, screaming randomly from above. They could see buildings in flames all around, in various degrees of intensity including, when they turned round, many of those directly behind them. Pausing for a moment to orientate themselves and decide on the best route forward, they watched the horrific scene unfolding around them.

Some buildings seemed untouched at first but were rapidly drawn into the general conflagration. They saw how fiery plumes extended outwards from the neighbouring roof structure of a building already burning. Once the flames had taken hold at the top, they reached down inside the shattered insides of that neighbouring block, victim of an explosive bomb, moving down from floor to floor, consuming staircases and interiors. They watched through shattered window gaps how the flames jumped from tables to sofas to curtains to bookcases, before dancing up high from the floor, nearly touching the ceiling. Eventually the fire could be seen licking out of windows at all levels, extending out into the street, greedy for more oxygen. It was happening everywhere, from all sides; entire rows of houses on both sides of them were clearly in danger of soon being ignited. There was nothing to stop this expansion and the fire threatened to ultimately become omnipresent, inescapable. Additionally, there came bursts of explosions followed by jumping bunches of sparks falling into the street, as if it were actually raining fire. Inge felt, this was what she had once imagined to be hell.

The next thing that struck them was a strange sound that they could hear, one that was neither close by nor far away, but somehow filling the streets with rising intensity. It was a howling, like the wind when loudly moaning around the house during a gale. Very soon there came sharp gusts of wind, blowing down the street and carrying masses of dancing sparks with them and a prickling hot wind; this all seemed to be part of that dreadful noise. They gripped each other and stood there in the middle of the street, unsure as to what to do or where to go next. Further ahead, a broken water fountain was aimlessly spurting up water high into the sharp air, while around it houses were starting to burn. In the direction of Malzweg, they saw flames creeping along roof tops, resembling red tulips that jerked and jumped. In no time those flames had penetrated into the next block, filling the rooms in surging fire that then began to snake out into the street. Further down the same street, high up on the fourth floor, Käthe saw to her horror how an old woman was out on a balcony, screaming for help. The flames came out of the apartment behind, riding up the back of her dress until she fell back into the blaze, still flailing away, and disappeared from view.

Interrupting the strange howling was the blasting of the artillery fire in the background. The flak was still hitting out at the sky above, but it seemed ineffective, as if firing away purely for the sake of it. Likewise the searchlights, which swayed around wildly; each constantly searching to find a target to trap, together with another, in a cone, and pin on it their hopes for a flak hit.

Through her work, Lotte was aware of how vulnerable and open to attack Hamburg was, thanks to the recent new developments in technology on the enemy side, as well as the lack of ability on her own German side to match those innovations. The tinfoil stripes that blocked the radar were just part of the growing threat to the nation's vast and heavily populated urban areas. She now saw theory put into vivid practice.

As Lotte took in the various sensory signals – the heat, the thundering blasts, the flickering glowing and gusts of sparks, the angrily moaning wind, the acrid smell of burning – she realized that her worse nightmare had indeed come true: a heavy bombing on the eastern side where she was living, and a total failure of the Air-Raid Protection services to adequately defend the city. They would literally have to run for their lives. Both in front and behind, fires had broken out on numerous floors of the housing blocks and flames were licking out into the street. "Get into the middle of the street," barked Lotte. The women moved forward. Following Lotte's example, they then broke into a careful run, picking their way through streets strewn with rubble, tiles, broken glass.

Instinct led them away from the source of the ghostly red light, that seemed to be coming from Malzweg. They headed eastward past Jordanstraße, which had multiple fires and was clearly badly hit, towards the crossroads with the broad Ritterstraße. They hoped to turn left there and head up to the junction with Hinter der Landwehr, then along the Mittel Straße up to Hammer Hof. At that point, Käthe said, they would end up by the Hammer Park, which even had a small pond and with so much green seemed to logically offer more protection than the densely built-up streets of the area. It should take around ten to fifteen minutes at most. Lotte added that if they crossed the park, there was a well-fortified public bunker on the other side on the Sievekingsallee; as long as the route along the streets leading there wasn't closed off by rubble or blazes, that would be perfect.

They moved on and had almost reached the first junction when they realized how ahead a strong wind was roaring down the street ahead, whipping down the sidestreets and around them. They arrived at the edge and saw how in both directions – both the Ritterstraße to the north as well as the Schwarze Straße to the south - the street was literally on fire. Clusters of sparks danced by all around them, sending them into extreme panic as some got caught up in their clothing. Further off, fleeting shadows were dashing in different directions in a disorganized scramble. They saw before them a couple of trees bent over by the wind while pieces of debris went dancing down the street, carried off by the force of this sudden gale. A man crossed the street closer to their line of vision, running away with difficulty from the inferno. Behind him came another man, though clearly elderly and without the same strength. The latter dropped onto the street and began to crawl forward until a rush of wind and sparks surrounded him and he collapsed prostrate. His body was jerking, between his own struggles and the wind pulling at it, while shards of glass rattled over and past him. The back of his coat and his hair began to catch fire.

The younger man looked to be making it with great effort across the street. But he slowed down before reaching the other side, decreasing speed as if in slow motion, his legs plodding until he seemed to almost sink into the hot tarmac. He too began to catch fire. A small group of four women had just come into view further down, running along the pavement on the opposite side of the street, also with great difficulty against the force of the gale. A seething gust came from nowhere and hit them head on, knocked them down like skittles and they fell lifeless in a row. Käthe screamed and Inge put her hand over her mouth and urinated in fright down the side of her leg; they turned away. Lotte shielded her face and continued to scan the way ahead in a state of disbelief, discerned how the metal tramline on the ground had buckled up into the air and snapped. Horror-filled, she joined the other women in beating a hasty retreat.

They ran back down their own Bethesdastraße, following the street straight ahead to stop this time at the junction with Burgstraße. They entered a few metres into it, but this route was now likewise blazing and the streets already filled with considerable rubble from collapsing houses. They continued the retreat towards their old home. The flames had intensified notably there in the short time they had been on the run. By now they were licking greedily out of the floors of many of the surrounding buildings, in some spots forming a gruesome obstacle course for anyone hoping to flee in that direction. Lotte consulted with Käthe and they agreed the best course of action was to continue in a southerly direction towards the canals. If that route was also blocked, then they would try to head west towards the centre and the gigantic Berliner Tor bunker.

They turned for a moment to look down Bethesdastraße, in the direction of their own apartment block. There they saw a few figures from houses further down running towards them. A middle-aged woman stumbled and fell, while her husband helped her back up and supported her as they continued to run through the heavily strewn pieces of rubble and around craters in the road. Behind them was another figure, a woman who was running closer to the right-hand side of the street and the starkly blazing buildings there. She had slowed down in exhaustion and one side of her coat had caught fire. She began to screech with a piercingly high pitch that rose over even the howling around. In a manner of seconds, she was transformed into a fiery torch. Through Inge's mind flashed involuntarily the image of the burning torch at the Berliner Olympics; she had thrilled to see the tongues of the flames in that moment, and now they were pure horror. Behind that woman came others fleeing, but some were falling already, brought down by the toxic fumes and intense heat. And so, another possible way out was impassable.

The streets around them were all gradually being consumed by flames, blurring into a mass of dancing yellow and orange, dirtied by the smoke that was billowing up into the night sky. Hot gusts of wind were frequent and came out of nowhere; a scalding air that reminded Inge of the opening of an oven. The burning of all different types of objects around them was so intense that she could taste it. "And the others, the others in the house?" gasped Käthe, pushing back her hair from her sticky scalp, her face grimy; she had not recognized anyone else from their block coming down the blazing street. The middle-aged couple continued their determined stumble onward, handkerchiefs over mouths, looking downwards to keep their eyes away from the growing heat around them.

The women headed southwards with even greater urgency. "Perhaps they got out on the other side," said Lotte, aware of the devastating bomb that had struck not far behind the building but saying something for want of giving an answer to the visibly distressed and frightened nurse. They ran down the narrow Elise-Averdieck-Straße, that was burning but still passable. Struggling against hot gusts flinging sparks and debris, and the surrounding heat in general, they turned left and eventually reached the intersection of Borgerfeld Straße to the left and Hammer Landstraße to the right, where the splendid corner buildings were starting to flare up.

There they crossed over the intersection, instinctively heading away from the chaos behind them which seemed to be crackling ever more ferociously. A few blocks along, over on the other side of the street from them, they saw a group of firemen. Some were attempting to help a group of people out of the cellar exit at the front of a house that was burning above. The survivors were coughing and spluttering, as they struggled out of what was supposed to have been their sanctuary but had instead become a perfidious underground trap. They scuttled off in all directions, looking for a way out of the growing inferno, but they became rapidly aware that their freedom from this torment would not be so easy after all. Here the howling wind was strong and brutally hot, and around them chased eddies of sparks. Corpses lay scattered on the street where people had fallen at random, some barely charred or even injured but rather victims of toxic fumes or the abrupt blasts of seething hot air that had burnt out their lungs.

The three women ran on down the Grevenweg, past a couple of apartment blocks, all the time scanning their surroundings for the best way out. They watched through raised sleeves as small group of people came running towards them in the same moment as a cluster of explosive bombs screamed down, landing nearby; most of them a good few streets away but a couple quite near, rocking the ground and smacking their eardrums hard. They ducked and were momentarily deafened, but continued along in desperation, more tripping than running. Lotte was bleeding slightly from her ears. They ran past a dazed elderly couple standing still on the other side of the street, as the women headed from one conflagration to another. Behind them and out of sight, a bunch of small rod-like phosphorous bombs had dropped into an office block, flaring up bright white wherever they landed inside the now smashed inner structure, igniting the surfaces they touched. Within the building, a multitude of little fires rapidly spread through the staircase and lift area and up to all the floors, producing combustion throughout the entire inner structure with terrific speed, adding to the growing blazes around that seemed to have no limits and that were cutting off one route after the other.

Escaping from the direction of the cellars where the firemen were helping out, shambled a much slower couple in their fifties. They were heading in a southerly direction towards the same canal that the women had hoped that they too might reach. The woman in the couple was elegantly attired in a cocktail dress, her husband in a dinner jacket, as if they had just been attending a formal function. They looked pathetic in the hellish chaos and were trying to move as fast as they could, reaching a slow trot. Over them came more bursts of brightly sparkling gushes of white that fell to the ground. Some landed on the woman, and she screeched out in terror and pain. Lotte and Käthe instantly recognized the substance on her as liquid phosphorous - Lotte knew of its use in bombing from her training, Käthe from the wounds she had treated. The viscous substance would cling stubbornly to whatever surfaces it came into contact with and constantly reignite, even after being put out with water. Käthe had observed it seemingly extinguished on patients, only to start smouldering up again in wounds inside the flesh.

The clumps of this chemical had stuck to the woman's clothes and these were flaring up. As she stumbled a couple of steps further down the pavement, more was caught in her long dress. In no time, not only the woman's clothes but her flesh itself was catching fire. The fire was swift and invincible and spread all over her. She beat her hands against herself, trying to put out the persistent flames that rose up around her. Her husband attempted to intervene but was barely able to even grab his wife, as she spun round in agony as a twirling flare, falling away from her husband and onto the ground, rolling over. The flames were consuming her while the husband stumbled after her in futile assistance, screaming out loud and desperately trying to put out the flames. Meanwhile new hot gusts whistled down the street and, as he came too close to the immediate building, he too was caught up in the blaze.

Two strongly built young men in brown SA uniforms were also fleeing and ran nimbly past, dodging with a wide berth the human bonfire and the clumps of phosphorous. They hadn't got far when there came the abrupt crash as part of the upper façade of a burning building fell out and into the road, covering the latter man under a large pile of hot debris. His companion turned for an instant before continuing his sprint on into the unknown. The women considered following in the same direction but hesitated and held back, sensing that ahead the situation could be even worse. They headed back.

While the bulk of the firemen had moved on to the next block, to help another group out of their cellar, two of their colleagues had put up a ladder against the adjacent building to try to get access to a small family that was trapped on the third floor and was screaming from the balcony. The firemen had just begun transporting the first of the trapped residents out, handing her down from one to another, when there came the tell-tale whistling sound of falling bombs; two heavy dull blasts out of nowhere, followed by a third one dangerously loud and close. "They still haven't finished!" screamed Lotte, in reference to bombers above, sporadically caught in the swaying searchlights, and the still falling hail of bombs dropping out of the smoke-filled heavens.

Two houses further along they saw a building that looked unscathed, and they ducked for cover in the front gateway. They scrambled further back into the entrance to the building. Watching outwards from that position, and partly protected, they witnessed a further series of loud crashes close beside them. The firemen on the ladder screamed as a bomb exploded almost directly in front of them, smashing through the house that their ladder was leaning against. The ladder with the two firemen fell down into the burning rubble, along with those trapped inside. Another fireman, who had been moving towards his colleagues to help them, screamed as he was caught in a blast of hot metal splinters. He fell back onto the ground, clutching his groin in agony. The firemen standing by the second cellar had been dispersed by this new cluster of falling bombs, as they ran smartly for cover. Two of them could be seen fighting off flames that had begun to grow stubbornly out of their uniforms, refusing to be extinguished. The occupants of the cellar were left to their own devices now; the heavy exit hatch had slammed back down on those still waiting underneath. Meanwhile the handful of befogged escapees who had managed to get out in time, were darting off into the melee, disappearing in all directions, into the smoke and glow. The street blazed away, ever more furiously. Inge shook her head in disbelief. When Lotte said, "We can't stay here much longer," she had been about to say the same herself.

They glanced up at the building that was providing temporary shelter and saw, just as they had indeed feared, that up in the roof structures of both it and the contiguous block, the tell-tale red flames were beginning to flicker into the night. The junction behind them, particularly on the side of the Hammer Landstraße to the east, was blazing furiously. The only option left seemed to be the small Brekelbaum street just ahead of them; the same route that some of the other survivors from the nearby cellar had chosen.

They ran on down the middle of the narrow street, buildings burning on both sides. In one particularly incinerated house there was little left inside of the blackened walls, and flames were spurting right out of the cellar. The women thought of the bunker they had left behind and the people there with whom they had briefly shared this ordeal.

They ran round the corner, where a smoking burnt-out truck was parked. The bonnet was propped open, as if someone had been trying to fix the motor, and beside it lay a male corpse. Passing by quickly they glanced through the driver's window and saw a woman slumped over against the smaller figure of a child, who in turn was slumped against the incinerated passenger door. Against the frame of the vehicle were the tell-tale splattered markings of phosphorous. Ahead of them a group of about six people were running; one at the back of the group suddenly jerked and fell to the ground, lying motionless. The others didn't even notice and struggled on forward.

The howling wind had picked up again. The women ran further on too but then turned back into the Borgfelder Straße, hoping to find a safe route out of the labyrinth of fire further to the west. They saw behind them how a middle-aged woman with an older woman, possibly her mother, came into view. The ferocious wind was pulling at them, and the old woman held on to her daughter for dear life.

Around them pieces of rubble, even a wooden door, were being sucked down into a monstrous fire further away. The progress of the two was slow and eventually the younger woman, sensing she would soon not be able to hold herself upright, decided for them to duck inside the intact entrance of a building. Lotte looked upwards and saw how above the roof structure of that building was blazing too. There was nothing here but death traps. On the other side of the Borgfelder Straße, across a small grassy area with trees, was the elegant Karl-Groth-Straße, that they had just run down less than ten minutes ago, now also sinking into flames. Here the hot wind seemed to be omnipresent.

Lotte cried above the roar, "We have to try to get further down this street and then make another attempt to get south to the canals. Water is our only hope."

"But all the streets are blocked off!" shouted back Käthe. "They are all unpassable. We will never make it down that way."

The aerial bombing had ceased by now but behind them came explosions from delay-action bombs, with timing devices designed to go off long after they had fallen and so disrupt rescue services. Hazards were now omnipotent. Lotte put her hands to her mouth, almost in tears. The women knew their position was becoming increasingly hopeless. Nevertheless, they moved on, still desperately chasing survival. Following a couple of hard hit and energetically burning apartment blocks, the next few buildings they were now passing, which led up to a large junction further ahead, were still relatively untouched. However, an immense blaze was burgeoning further on beyond that, and the street was truncated by a formidable sea of flames.

They backed away a few steps, feeling that a trap was closing in on them.

As Käthe turned round to reevaluate the state of the street behind them, whence they had just come, while considering yet another strategic retreat and a re-attempt at locating a safe route, she received a sudden blast of searing air together with a rush of sparks full into the face. She screamed and covered her eyes instinctively with her hands, but when she took them away, she found herself staring into a deep dark pain.

"Help me, please help me!" she screeched. "Oh God, oh God! - I am blinded, I cannot see anything!" Lotte rushed over to her and pulled the helpless woman away from the path of the boiling hot gusts.

Inge was looking ahead at a small side road that led off diagonally from the junction, the Anckelmannstraße. She shouted "There, that is the way, that is the only possibility!" Lotte looked round in desperation while she held on to the still screaming Käthe. They moved on but a crash of rubble just in front sent them scrabbling back several metres in panic, until they fell backwards. Lotte landed awkwardly on broken glass and cut her hands and the back of her head, but Käthe hit smooth pavement and, feeling blindly around her, was able to scramble back up much quicker. Her hands guided her as she nimbly came to her feet. The hot gale had picked up strength again and she instinctively covered her burnt-out eyes with her hands. She stumbled to the side in an attempt to seek refuge away from it, heading toward a patch of relatively cool air near to her. Here was the entrance to a block in which the upper floors were blazing but the lower two not yet. Moving too fast in her disabled state, she smacked into the front door entrance and fell to the ground; stunned, but at least momentarily sheltered from the unbearable heat all around.

Inge was the furthest back of the three and directly above her a large balcony window had burst out, sending a shower of glass fragments cascading down onto the street. Two larger ones caught her in the face and left deep cuts, one slicing into her cheek. She screamed and struggled up off the ground. Another window burst and the panic sent her lurching forward and away from that spot and any further falling glass. In this rush of movement, she had now shifted her position further along the Borgfelder Straße, despite the major blaze ahead. She tripped, stumbled, and found herself slipping down the side of a large bomb crater. She slid with a shriek but to her immense relief there was a pool of water in the bottom; all that remained of the gushing contents of a mains pipe smashed up early on in the raid by the blockbuster bomb that had made the deep crater. Most of the water had long since dried up in the heat, but Inge scooped up the little pool of this wet elixir in her hand and splashed it over her face. She resisted the enormous temptation to drink some, despite her horribly parched throat and mouth, as she could see it was muddy and moreover it had a light chemical stink and an oil film on top. But it gloriously refreshed the skin on her face and neck. She bent her head down and dragged her hair through the last drops, wetting them as best she could. The wind rushing over the top of the crater increased considerably in strength.

After a moment of breathing in deeply the pocket of cooler air near the surface of the pool, Inge crawled up to the top of the crater, peering over the edge. To her left, she saw Käthe now crouched in the building entrance, holding her hands to her eyes and seeming to sob. She called out to her, although the wind was howling furiously around the street by then. Käthe seemed to react, and began to crawl away from the building in search of the voice. She turned to her left momentarily, trying to locate the person who had called her name, but started back in shock and crawled backwards to the same spot. Inge did not know it, but her companion had inhaled a gust of the searing air in that instant, and her throat and lungs were irremediably burnt out.

As Inge prepared to scramble out of the crater, she saw to her right that Lotte was with a small group of people coming toward them and away from the huge blaze ahead; it seemed, from the mixed ages and the desperate bond between them, to comprise a family. Their clothes hung as rags, their faces were dark with smoke and grime, a couple of them were limping and had clear burn wounds. The wind roaring down the Ausschläger Weg perpendicular to them had picked up to hurricane force and the group was struggling to cross it from the other side. They had tightly gripped hands but were only just holding on to one another with great effort, shuffling stubbornly towards her but barely progressing forward. Among the family was a small child and one of the women held a baby. The child was firmly held by the father, but the woman fell, still tightly grasping the baby as the two began to slide together along the pavement, drawn away by the tugging winds. Lotte had struggled forward and seized her collar, roughly pulled her up with the considerable strength that she packed in her slight frame. She helped the woman away from the traversing corner of Ausschläger Weg and Borgfelder Straße, and into the latter. The others, seeing the rescue taking place, made a consternated effort and all managed to push forward. One of them nearly lost his grip and shouted in terror as the winds pulled at him, but he was able to recover this balance. Reeling and tumbling a few metres, he was able to grasp the edge of a building on the corner, almost directly opposite over from where Käthe sat. Käthe no longer held her hands over her eyes; instead they were resting by her side while her head had lolled back and she stared diagonally upward, motionless.

A new sizzling sound caught Inge's attention and she swung her vision back to Lotte and the woman with her huddled family, now almost up beside them, though still struggling against the fierce gusts careering down the Ausschläger Weg ahead. They were pummelled by another mass of sparks and lighter flying debris. The jacket of one of the men at the back of the group had caught fire but nobody noticed. The fire began to work its way around the material and in that moment there was a sudden harsh crackle in the air. Around the junction ran a tall whirlwind of flames, feeding on the parts of that corner building that were still combustible. At the same time, some windows on the first floor exploded and flowing tongues of flame snaked out of the holes, directly above the group, belching out a demonic mess of gases from the burning objects inside. The two blazes seemed to combine, consuming everything inside and around them, alighting heaps of debris lying out on the pavement together with a bench and a shop front, as well as the whole family group. The whirlwind of fire danced around them in an incandescent twirling of flames. Lotte, in that instant having moved back and at the rear of the group, was caught up in the flames but stumbled away quickly enough to avoid the bulk of the leaping fire. But her hair was singed and smoking, her face badly burnt, and she was coughing violently. There was another crash above and more rubble came smashing down, this time with larger chunks of masonry. Lotte was caught under the salvo and lay sprawled with broken bones, her moribund body still convulsing in bursts of coughs.

During this latest series of explosions, Inge had screamed in panic and fallen back down into the crater, pushing her face hard up against the earthy wall and pressing her face deeply against the edge, still feeling pinpricks of heat inside her throat and lungs. Though in great pain, she was at least still able to take in air. She stayed in that position for around five minutes, concentrated on keeping her breathing steady, until she felt the courage to dare to climb up to the top of the crater again, and peak over the edge. To her right, she saw a group of charred corpses lying around on the ground. A metre away lay a motionless figure, half-buried under rubble and glass shards; she recognized Lotte's now frizzled mass of hair and her silver bracelet that glinted out of a blackened sleeve and hand.

The hot wind seemed to have momentarily reduced its intensity and, seeing Käthe to her left, still in the same spot, she crawled out and dragged herself over to her. She knelt beside her - "Käthe?" - but realized that the sitting body was now lifeless, the eyes looking past her. Inge gasped, closed them, and moved away, driven off by a nearby strong blaze from yet another building going up in flames just behind her, one that had seemed intact but had now also become infected by the invincible fire. She stumbled a few steps forward in the direction of the Anckelmanntrasse Straße, gripping the sides of the walls of buildings near to the corner. She felt somehow that that street might offer a way out. But at the same time, the strong current of hot air was again blowing strong, this time even more furiously along the perpendicular Ausschläger Weg. It would mean crossing this street if she were to reach the Anckelmannstraße on the other side. Now standing directly on the corner, she turned her face gingerly round the edge, looked to her left, and further on down the road she saw it: the Monster.

She had never imagined such a creature could exist, nor that it could be so immense, towering up high into the black night heaven, its dazzling glow mixing in with the enormous pillars of smoke that were billowing up around it. It must have been twice, perhaps three times as high as the burning buildings around it, a couple of which had already crumbled into nothingness. It danced and swirled and seemed to laugh with a wicked cackle. It sucked in the very air in blasts of boiling wind. And it was horribly voracious. From the surrounding area it was pulling in everything that it could feed on, all into its greedy maw, with unbelievable strength. Scattered remains in all shapes and sizes was being dragged down the street towards it; pieces of fallen masonry and tiles, burning crates, smashed plant pots, planks of wood, broken bricks, tools, a bicycle. Even larger objects were not immune. The twisted residue of a terrace along with pieces of burning furniture were pulled along. A charred pram, that had been caught up in a jumble of metal bars at the front of a building, was heftily rocked in the gale until it came free and wheeled off clumsily at first, then overturned and was crashing and sliding its way towards the inferno. Random items, that had been vomited out of surrounding buildings onto the pavement by explosions and collapses, were now pulled irresistibly into the glow. The Monster pulsated and twinkled behind clouds of smoke and sparks, fat and heaving, growing in size, looming up higher.

The very air around Inge was pure heat; every breath was painful. Behind her the situation had deteriorated yet further. The whole street was filled with flames, licking in from both directions and on all floors. Parts of the roof structure of the block standing beside the crater had crashed out into the road, and burning lumps of debris fell into and around the hole. There was just the one last chance for her, she considered; and that was a quick sprint straight ahead that would take her toward a clearing and a clump of trees. Her insides were hurting badly, her mouth and throat felt raw and swollen. She paused for a moment, as she heard the hurricane wind howl more loudly, intensifying again as the Monster roared, demanding more tributes. A building interior crashed in on itself nearby. As it fell, the heavy dull thud of the initial impact was accompanied by a succession of splintering smashes, ending in the tinkling of small shards of glass finding their resting place. Her heart raced; more than just the jumble of sharp noises near her, there was the sense of something enormous and invisible about to attack.

Inge screamed out in terror. Panic jabbed her and she threw all her energy into a last desperate dash to cross the road, but midway was caught off balance by the unexpected strength of the winds. She tripped and managed to stave the fall with her hands, struggled back up to an erect position, only to find herself inside a dense flurry of sparks. A fiery blast hit her, stronger and hotter than anything she had felt so far, and her clothing began to catch fire. She attempted one last push forward to cross the junction, but in a burning gust she was ignited in a matter of seconds. Her body fell, twitching and turning round before finishing on her back, arms instantly carbonized while still positioned as pushing up to fight off the hot gusts. The wind carried the body, jerking it a few metres further along, before it was snagged by a ruptured section of the pavement and ended up wedged in that spot. It rested there, shimmering down to charred remains, with clothing and skin having melted into one.

The fires around raged on with great intensity for several hours. The area was quite unapproachable to any rescue or fire-fighting services, who were in any case already overwhelmed to the point of inaction. When dawn arrived, the sun could not even penetrate the thick clouds of deep black smoke still surging up into the morning sky. Almost all the buildings within a large area that extended out through the best part of seven whole districts, were fully burnt out. The outer walls of the apartment blocks often withstood, damaged but erect, while the insides were gutted. Thus came the sight the next day of row upon row of empty buildings reduced to windowless, roofless husks. Whole long sections of streets offered this dismal visage and the streets themselves were littered with endless masses of charred objects, burnt out vehicles, piles of fallen bricks and sandy rubble, dead bodies lying around in random spots. Flakes of ash were carried around the streets by the ebbing wind, looking deceptively like a light fall of snow but warm to the touch.

The Flegel couple did manage to escape the fires alive, the only survivors of their shelter; though both ended up with extensive second-degree and some third-degree burns. They came through the ordeal wide-eyed, shaking, and in acute pain. They had been lucky enough to find a route out through the inferno and had eventually been picked up near the Alster inner lake by a military vehicle at around five o'clock in the morning. This took them and others it found to the Moorweide, a large and mostly untouched central park where the survivors were congregating. From there, they and a few thousand others from the area were eventually transported out of the smoking city in the early morning; by road, rail, or waterway.

Some survivors, still heavily traumatized, had even begun to flee on foot, with the simple goal of getting out of the city with just the clothes they had escaped in. Others got into transport, even though they had no idea where it was heading. Smoke billowed out of the eastern area of the city for days.

On the Wednesday morning immediately after the bombing, the streets in the east of the city were empty and silent, darkened in soot. Although the July sun shone down brightly over Hamburg, for the rescue teams gradually working their way further into the heart of the catastrophe, the smoke was still so thick it was almost as if working at night. All over the area wafted the stench of toxic fumes and burnt flesh. They found in the following days next to no survivors to rescue, neither in the cellars, nor out on the streets, nor in the surrounding canals; only corpses or ashes. Many of the remains were of huddled groups, asphyxiated and roasted in the cellars; others were charred corpses caught out by the fires and burning winds on the streets, or crushed under falling rubble; others still were found floating bloated in the canals. Some of the fires were calming by the afternoon, leaving behind the charred and silent residue of what was once bustling city life.

Trucks and military vehicles combed the streets and were loaded up with bodies; far too numerous, and often too badly disfigured, to be identified. In the end the corpses were transported to the Ohlsdorf cemetery, far up in the northern periphery of the city, and thrown there together into a mass grave. The final death toll was uncertain at first, but in the following days and weeks it climbed up above the 40,000 mark, with the knowledge that more would be found in the cellars with time and that others, now little more than burnt remains, would never be. One officer with family in Hamburg, returning in the aftermath on leave from the eastern front, commented in disbelief on the state of his home city as being "worse than Stalingrad". The radio and press duly reported the attack and Party spokesmen promised ferocious revenge on the enemy in return.

Loudspeakers around Hamburg announced the next day the evacuation out of the city of all non-essential workers. This was ordered by Hamburg *Gauleiter* Kaufmann - a ruthless, dyed-in-the-wool Nazi who had been busy trying to organize a meticulous deportation of Hamburg's Jewish residents – and put into immediate effect. Loudspeakers emitted the directive throughout the streets. A mass exodus struck up; eventually nearly a million people, around half of the inhabitants, abandoned the city in long streams. Some fled to nearby towns like Lüneburg and rural areas such as the Lüneburger

Heide with its farms and villages; others headed to family, or shelters and accommodation in more distant parts of the country.

Among the multitudes of charred bodies, picked up in the days following that fateful night, were those of Lotte, Käthe, and Inge. Käthe was still sitting back against the door, which was only slightly burnt as some softer loose rubble had later dropped from the rooftop, burying her and partly protecting the door from the outer heat. Lotte's corpse was also found immediately, out on the open street, beside the small family group alongside which she had died. Though charred, her uniform was still recognizable and she was later formally identified before being sent to the mass grave in Ohlsdorf. Her silver bracelet was passed on to the Air-Raid Protection headquarters of the Wehrmacht, and later returned to her family in Frankfurt. Käthe was also later identified, and her mother was allowed, somewhat exceptionally and through the administrative weight of a relative, to have her daughter put to rest beside Käthe's grandparents out in Rahlstedt. After the war she was therefore able, together with her son Klaus, to regularly visit them all together.

Inge was located by the rescue crews in the same round as Lotte and Käthe, burnt out of all recognition and lying on her back; set stiffly in a position of clawing up futilely at the air, as if in a last attempt to push back the advance of some terrible monster. What was left of her scorched face was distorted in agony, but the crew was used to that sight and was unmoved. She was likewise picked up with the other nearby bodies and thrown onto the back of the truck, though in her case the body could not be identified. It was the fourth round that day already and the rescue teams were exhausted and in silent shock. Once the truck was full, it drove up north to the Ohlsdorf cemetery. There, that same day, the anonymous among the burnt, crushed, and suffocated corpses were deposited together in the mass grave.

Chapter 30

That fatal night, part of a series of attacks that month by the British RAF against the Third Reich and codenamed Operation Gomorrah in reference to the apocalyptic biblical tale, gained notoriety in Lüneburg by the very next day. There were official announcements made on the national radio service as well as various hurried press releases, which all amounted to either incomplete or inaccurate information concerning a major bombing raid on the eastern side of Hamburg. It was correctly reported as the second major raid on the city, and the fifth in total, within a week; by all appearances part of a large-scale and ongoing aerial assault by the Allies.

Those living locally, in nearby towns or villages, listened anxiously to the official news as issued by the authorities. But they themselves had already perceived that very same night the enormity of the destruction. The orange glow emitted by the firestorm, with its towering flames burning up vast swathes of the city, had been visible for many kilometres around. Moreover, frightening rumours had quickly spread out to surrounding towns by word of mouth.

Many Germans had suspected for a while that something of this nature would be on the books. Obviously Germany's second city, and a port of military manufacture and industrial weight including a submarine base and extensive shipbuilding facilities, was bound to be high up on the enemy's list of targets. Like all major cities Hamburg had already been bombed on many occasions. Nevertheless, nothing had prepared the residents for the sheer scale of this barrage and in particular the disastrous effects produced by the urban firestorm that Tuesday night. It would eventually come to light that around 45,000 people, nearly 2.5% of the entire city's population, had been killed in the one night. In districts around the epicentre of the firestorm, the death toll reached as high as a third of all residents. An inordinate amount of these had died in the supposedly safe bunkers; asphyxiated as the oxygen was sucked out of the cellars, poisoned by toxic gases entering, roasted alive in the heat. In some cellars, all that was left of the inhabitants of the apartment block consisted of piles of ashes.

The first homeless refugees began to arrive in Lüneburg the very next evening: exhausted, highly distressed, often with burn wounds. They had taken the first transport out of the city made available in the morning and afternoon of the following day, including trucks enlisted with the *Marktplatz* of Lüneburg as their destination. Some had friends or relatives living there but most were simply homeless and frightened, hoping to get by as best they could by offering their professional skills or simple hard graft. In general, the town's inhabitants were charitable and found rooms for all the refugees from the bombed-out city, offering mattresses in living rooms, putting up bunk beds in offices. Gisela and Martin gave up most of their rooms in the *Gasthaus* as temporary shelter for these people.

Accompanying these people came naturally their tales of the experiences that they, and others they knew, had gone through that night. Many were still at least party traumatized, a few considerably so. There was a flurry of information exchanged between these refugees, to find out which streets had been worse hit and where one could possibly find any bulletins or communications concerning the identities of the dead or the location of the survivors. Both the *ausgebombten* ('bombed out' and homeless) refugees from Hamburg, as well as the locals in Lüneburg, were all cautious not to express any contempt or even slight criticism towards the authorities for their role in the disaster. By now, most Germans had a highly tuned ear as to which statements could and would be classified as deserving of punitive measures. Anger and the pain of mourning had to be contained so that they didn't run off into delirious rage and from there into the terrain of anti-government talk.

Furthermore, and contrary to the hopes and erroneous calculations of the RAF Bomber Command and the analysts serving the British War Cabinet, the bombing of civilian populations did not even begin to break the German morale nor the general German determination to fight on till the bitter end. Exactly in the same way that the Luftwaffe's bombing of Britain's civilian populations had not broken the British morale either. In the first week following the bombing raids, those people remaining in Hamburg were already returning to work. Public transport routes, as well as utilities pipes and connections, were swiftly repaired. For those workers hunkering down in the widely ruined but still very much operational city, daily life and the war effort went on regardless. The civilian dead were highly lauded in the press and referred to as heroes, even soldiers. Resolved to show the enemy that the survivors would not buckle under nor be intimidated, Hamburg's workers - some living in huts and garden sheds - went on to turn up at their places of work punctually each morning and with more energy, enthusiasm, and resilience than ever before. Within less than half a year, most factories were achieving production levels that were around 80% of their output before the bombings. Such displays of grit and valour from the workforce only served to confirm to the political governing forces and military commanders the necessity for the continuation of the war. It consolidated the illusion that a German victory was an actual, solid reality.

Back in Lüneburg, Gisela, like the rest of the family, was frantic for any news concerning Inge. Nothing was forthcoming thus far. In the chaos and confusion of the first few days there reigned a steady confidence at the Gasthaus that, despite the enormity of the death toll, their Inge would have been able to make her way through to safety. Now the centre of everyone's attention, they talked of her as a strong and brave woman, in possession of a high degree of common sense. If anyone was capable of finding their way out of the fires and bombs, and apparently many had if the number of refugees was anything to judge by, then she would have certainly been one of them. It was expected in that first week that she would show up in one of the trucks that often dropped off people coming out of Hamburg at the Marktplatz. Gisela held watch with unwavering loyalty and optimism for nearly two weeks, until faced with bitter frustration; in any case, the frequency of said trucks had plummeted by then. She still hoped her sister might arrive at that point, though, and make her way to the Gasthaus, hardly a two-minute walk once she had been brought to Lüneburg. Perhaps she had been injured and was in hospital, unable to get in contact, pondered Gisela.

But that day never came. The high summer passed and cooler September winds arrived, finally relieving the oppressive heat of that uniquely oppressive year. In long, silent, and daily reflections, Gisela began to come to terms with the probability that her sister had indeed been killed in the bombing that night.

Some weeks later Gisela found herself conversing with a woman from Hamburg, who happened to be staying in the house of an acquaintance of the Landeck family. She showed her the address that she had: Bethesdastraße 31. "I think she said it is near to the tram stop on the Burgstraße," Gisela added, and the woman looked at her with deep pity and simply shook her head.

Uncle Robert had already hinted on the telephone that the apartment that Inge had been staying in was situated in one of the very badly hit areas, though he had not wanted to go into any more detail. He himself was still in shock, not only due to Inge's disappearance and the general magnitude of the destruction, but also to the demise of a close friend and two well-liked colleagues in the bombing campaign. He had nevertheless sworn to do all that was humanly possible to try to find out what had happened to Inge. She could well be lying in a hospital and in a deep state of shock, he had assured them fervently; confirming a theory of Gisela's and giving her renewed hope, though not believing it himself for a minute. His subsequent silence throughout the whole of August and September had been a realistic answer in itself to the question of Inge's whereabouts. What Gisela and the others did not fully comprehend was how much he considered himself to blame by having assisted Inge in coming to Hamburg in the first place; hence his embarrassed claims to ignorance.

Eventually Gisela was able to have confirmed, through an acquaintance and sometime client who worked in an administrative position with the municipal authorities in Hamburg, that Inge's house and indeed the whole street had been completely burnt to the ground. In fact, he said candidly, almost the entire area where she lived had been decimated, indicating a high chance that she had sadly not made it out. Gisela found out how Rothenburgsort, Borgerfelde, Hamm, Hasselbrook, Eilbek, one district after another, were practically wiped from the map. No more concrete information, concerning Inge herself or her dead body, was to be received from official sources.

The death of her closest family member, and one of her very few friends in the world, shook Gisela to the bones. It had brought home to her for the first time the true meaning of the word *Heimatsfront* – the home front, now increasingly used in popular parlance. She realized that the war really was being waged here within the country; that everyone, including women and children, were now participants in the battles to be fought. She sensed the magnitude of what she now gradually regarded as the Führer's madness with the idea of going to war with the world. Furthermore, the news coming in from the fighting in the east had an underlying feel of bitter pessimism (even die-hard war-enthusiasts like Volkmar had been shocked by the defeat at Stalingrad), though few who felt that way would voice their opinion openly on the topic.

During these months Gisela often went to visit her parents, who were equally in deep shock at the likely passing of their radiant daughter. Corinna was heartbroken, and Georg was filled with rage at the world. One great war had taken his brother; the next his favourite child. In silence he stored up his anger as a bitter acid that corroded him inside.

"So much for the infinite wisdom of our *Gröfaz!*" he once exploded. The *Gröfaz* (short for '*Größter Feldherr aller Zeiten*' – 'Greatest commander of all times') was a sarcastic reference to Hitler, one of the increasingly derisive terms that were in quiet use among some of the population who, with each passing month, were seeing the folly of the war more clearly. "Greatest arsehole of all times, too. I said he would kill us all in the end! I said it!" Fortunately, Corinna had the gramophone on, playing her French chansons quite loudly at the time; but she rushed to shut the open window while Gisela tried to hush her father as best she could.

Georg now detested Hitler more than ever, looked forward to the day of his execution, which he imagined would take place in the form of a firing squad, or preferably a hanging, when the people rose up and finally deposed the tyrant. He would take his family to the cinema that day, he told himself, to see the execution personally on a newsreel. It was almost a blessing in disguise that the impotent fury he felt at the loss took a toll on his already shaky health, and thus compelled him to stay inside and away from others; out on the street his anger may well have overspilled and his words probably landed him and Corinna in prison, or worse. He suffered a minor stroke in

November and after that was more stuck to his armchair than ever, almost never leaving home and then only for very short walks to fetch bread if Corinna was up at the Gasthaus, looking after the children. Though Gisela had never been especially close to her father, she came often to visit from then on and held him tight before leaving, so that father and daughter could mourn together in silent companionship.

Corinna wept frequently but preferred to do so in private. At home, she would sneak up to her bedroom whenever she felt the tears rise up, so as to sob away her desolation in quiet. The children were of immense assistance to her in navigating her grief, and when she was looking after them at the Gasthaus, she managed to see the light again; finding an infinite number of little features in the boys – both physical and psychological – that reminded her of her lost daughter. In this way she eventually managed to overcome the pain of her loss far better than her husband did. With so much death in general around them all at this point, there was a dull brute sense of resignation that guided the thoughts and inner reflections of Corinna and many others.

It was at this point that Gisela instructed Martin to construct a proper air-raid shelter for them all. "The cellar is in no fit shape and needs a lot of work. There is no shelter door of the required strength, and the place is only provisionally equipped," she argued. His parents Volkmar and Anna would help to finance the material costs required with their savings, she went on to tell him straight up, reminding him that three of the children in the house were their own grandchildren. She herself would organize two workmen to come and help him with the digging and laying of concrete. Martin did have some basic training in construction, the only course he had successfully completed during his flunked years of education and professional training, and with the assistance of more competent workers the task was within their range.

There came to the *Gasthaus Sonnenschein* an unexpected visit toward the end of October in the form of Trudchen Lenz. She appeared on the doorstep, out of the blue without any previous announcement, one Thursday afternoon. She informed Gisela in the doorway that she worked as an assistant for the Wehrmacht, specifically in the *Luftschutzdienst* (aerial protection service), and had lived with Inge in Hamburg during the bombing raids of July. Gisela was astonished at the visit and warmly welcomed her in. Upon entering the building, Trudchen took note of the swastika flags hanging out of the windows and the portrait of the Führer in the interior hall, and these details influenced her discourse accordingly. This included a complete omission of any details pertaining to the last conversation she had had with Inge, concerning the rationale and progress of the war, on that fatal day.

Upon Trudchen presenting herself, Gisela had recognized the name and then recalled that her sister had spoken very highly of all three women she had lived with: Trudchen, Lotte and Käthe. Gisela was therefore uncharacteristically hospitable to a non-paying visitor, making a loud fuss of her and bringing in coffee and chocolate cake; even offering cognac, which was politely declined.

Trudchen could not stay long. She related how since the July air-raids she had been working nearly flat out and was due to be transferred to Kiel for further active service. Before moving on, however, she had very much wanted to come to Lüneburg and meet the family that Inge had spoken of with such affection. Gisela called down the boys who then dutifully stood in line while Gisela went through their names. Adolf brought his new Belgian leather satchel down with him and proudly showed it off to the women, proclaiming – as Gisela had already heard a hundred times but it never failed to touch her - how it was a present from his Papa who was brave and fighting out in Russia for the Fatherland. (Indeed, Adolf loved to open it just to smell the leather inside and think of his father Horst.) The women got moist eyes and lumps in the throat before the children charged off in search of a new game. Trudchen said how she wished she could have brought some possessions of Inge from the apartment with her, but sadly nothing had been left after the bombing. The apartment had been completely incinerated. Gisela nodded.

At one point, Trudchen asked how she felt and if she was coming to terms with the event; to which Gisela fell back into her old optimism and told her visitor that she was still holding out hope that her sister would reappear in the doorway at some point. At this, Trudchen took her hand and stated plainly, directly, that it was very likely, to the point of almost certain, that Inge had died in the raid on 27th July. That particular raid, she stated, had produced a firestorm in the eastern part of the city where they had all shared the apartment together. She also informed Gisela that she had seen registers confirming that Lotte and Käthe had been formally identified and buried. As their bodies had been found quite close together, she suspected that Inge must have been with them at the time and so probably belonged to one of many thousands of unidentified bodies that had been buried straightaway in the mass grave in the Ohldorf cemetry. Gisela nodded. Trudchen naturally omitted the fact that this indicated that the body had been so badly incinerated that it was unidentifiable. She restricted herself to stating that in the face of such a huge tragedy and the resulting chaotic conditions, it would have been impossible for the local authorities to have carried out a more thorough identification process. Gisela nodded and added with a cracked voice that she understood perfectly and accepted this.

It was, Gisela agreed with a few tears sliding down her cheeks, senseless to hold out hope for something that was firmly and undeniably over. Trudchen's reply was hesitant, unsure at first if there was a wider implication being made in that statement, a hint for her to express herself more freely, but she decided against deepening the conversation any further. More so with her military rank and upcoming promotion to be considered, and Gisela being an almost complete stranger who, from the appearance of her home, seemed to be of a fervently patriotic mindset. Answering a wish from Gisela to perhaps see her again some time, to talk about her sister and the last weeks she had spent with her, Trudchen said she would definitely return after the war was over and things were back to normal. She said - in all earnestness, for this was now her only access to the existence of Inge Grün, a young woman whom in a short space of time she had become very fond of - that she looked forward to seeing them all again, and how the three boys were growing up.

Gisela considered asking about any benefit payments from the state that might correspond to the guardians of Inge's children, now that both father and mother were missing, presumed dead. However, she felt it would be pushing the boundary of the framework of this first and brief meeting and may have come across as grasping and vulgar, given the nature of the visit. The women gave each other a brief but heartfelt hug and bade farewell for the time being.

Official sources may have had little hope to offer of any signs of life, but from more spiritual sources there was noteworthy activity. In the following months, Corinna became convinced she had perceived the presence of her daughter on numerous occasions; a ghostly hand that stroked her arm, a breath that she felt on the back of her neck and made her turn sharply, the sensation of someone moving around at night in the Gasthaus. She told of how whenever she went to the Gasthaus after dark, there was a shadow that seemed to briefly appear in the field of vision in the corner of her eye, but rushed away nervously whenever she tried to trap it with her gaze. Gisela had no time for such tales and showed a complete lack of interest in her mother's figments. She told her flat out and impatiently that the noises she heard at night were probably just someone going to the toilet, and to not be so foolish as to frighten the children with ridiculous ghost stories.

Georg went further and chided his wife with scorn. He laughed at her openly to her face when she related that she only saw the spirits at night: Why would a spirit prefer to operate under cover of darkness? What would a spirit have to gain or lose by being elusive? Why was she the only one receiving these so-called visitations? None of it made sense, he burst out, fully exasperated, and said she was a "silly old woman who should know better but never would." He even insinuated that she was helping herself to the alcoholic stocks at the Gasthaus on her visits there, as that seemed to be the best explanation for both her fantastical notions and the occasionally missing stock that Gisela had once mentioned. This reduced his wife to bitter tears. Generally she submitted to his mocking and verbal abuse, but that time a huge row exploded that had the neighbours on the other side of the wall worried. After that, she refrained from recounting any more of her extraordinary encounters with the afterlife.

It was the children though who were most prone to flights of imagination, which they kept to themselves and experienced them as sudden spurts of ecstasy against a poignant background of ongoing hope. Their more primitive minds, still forming amid the chaos and suffering, had not fully processed the finality of death. People, and in particular men, came and went, often for long periods of time; returned for brief periods, were off again. They heard how others around them had lost their homes and close family members, without the boys really understanding how exactly they had got to be lost. Joseph was showing a particularly fertile imagination and wondered – in his own childish grasp of concepts - if there might not be some general state of navigational confusion afoot, that kept people from returning to their place of origin. That, he assumed, was the explanation for the non-reappearance of both his parents.

It was certainly a traumatic experience for all the boys, as both parents had reassured them that they would be gone for a while but would come back eventually. How long was eventually? – they asked themselves. They had no reason to disbelieve their own mother and father. And neither Tante Gisela nor Oma Corinna, who had always been their two closest points of reference after their parents, had contradicted them either.

Aside from the issue of their parents' lengthened absence, the boys also began to develop an anxiety concerning the sense of an invisible, inexplicable something that was approaching. This was what they gathered from the snippets of conversations they picked up here and there; or the few moments of an evening radio emission that they might inadvertently catch before their aunt or grandmother would whisk them off to bath or bed. They loved to hear the music as well as the excitable voices of the presenters on the *Nordische Rundfunk* and other channels; but what exactly was going on outside of their snug Gasthaus? There seemed to be something fearful brewing in the air, but due to the adult vocabulary and concepts, they could not pin it down. Was there a monster out there, lurching across vast acres of fields and towns over weeks and months, slowly coming towards them? Was it the Devil himself?

The air raid warnings had become very regular by then. The sirens would sound up (generally at night, when the British preferred to bomb) and everyone would rush down to the newly built bunker. 'Onkel' Martin and the other workmen had by then expanded the cellar area in the basement considerably and had constructed a proper air-raid shelter, modestly small but well-designed, including air ventilation and water supply. Martin had insisted from the start on a functioning toilet for the bunker and Gisela couldn't have agreed more. It was one of the few domestic projects that Martin had been able to get enthused about and he had carried out the work with solid determination and proficiency, all to Gisela's quiet amazement. Now, with every warning, he and Gisela, the six children, and anyone who was staying, would head down and patiently wait for the all-clear signal to sound out. Almost all were false alarms, and the bombers above would continue on their way deeper into Germany. There were next to no actual attacks on the city, only three in total during the war and all of them relatively minor in nature compared to other towns and cities.

All this reinforced in the children's imagination the notion of that distant something which was creeping ever closer; now dropping death from the skies, so uncannily strong that you could not even lock the door to keep it out. Every day it approached nearer and they talked to each other, in hushed tones when Gisela was out of earshot, about how it must look in appearance; none of the boys could say for sure, apart from the fact that it walked, swam and flew.

Adolf conjectured that you could sometimes see its outer glow on the horizon, an expression he had picked up from a visitor from Winsen who happened to be discussing one day the recent firestorm in Hamburg. Adolf later explained to his younger brothers that the horizon was where the sky met the trees and rooftops, and they were both impressed and terrified by the thought. Joseph imagined that this entity might be able to smother the night itself, right down to snuffing out the very stars. They had all seen a few times by moonlight the bombers flying in formation overhead and so knew the shape of the demons that accompanied it. Little wonder that paranormal entities were frequent guests in the infantile discussions; invoked by a combination of Adolf's colourful clarifications of events in the outside world and Joseph's naturally febrile creativity, all supported by Hermann's breathless and unabating awe of this whole epic drama beyond his comprehension. Between the three of them, the most exciting of horror stories were cooked up night after night. Even before going to bed, they loved the way the whole house had to be checked to make sure the curtains were closed, the blinds were down, and no light was creeping out into the darkness. Something exciting must surely be afoot out there in the mysterious night, they concluded.

Joseph was also starting to show another talent, namely an excellent memory for reciting texts that he picked up here and there, including some that were remarkably complex for his age. His favourite, due to having heard it with such regular frequency on both their and their neighbours' radios, consisted of: "*Achtung, Achtung, wir bringen eine Luftlagemeldung: Kampfverband über Nordwestdeutschland im Anflug auf... [eg. Raum Hannover-Braunschweig].*" ("Attention, attention, here is an aerial position announcement: enemy aircraft flying over Northwest Germany and approaching the area of… [eg. Hannover-Braunschweig]"). The final part varied geographically at whim; and Joseph's perfect imitation of the martial tone almost shocked Gisela and Corinna the first time he performed his new party-piece in front of them, still only six years old.

It became one of a number of set phrases, all of a military nature, that he learnt. "Make sure Georg is careful what he says when the boy is at yours", Gisela warned her mother, after later hearing other acquired articulations. "He picks up everything and then spits it all out like a parrot."

The latest announcement of a bombing campaign was a game for Joseph, especially when the sirens went off and they all had to go down to the bunker; but they were a cause of great distress to most of the adults, who feared that it would be Lüneburg's turn for a hit sooner or later. So many familiar places had been targetted, even smaller towns, that it seemed only a matter of time. To imagine the Gasthaus reduced to a smouldering heap of rubble, with them all trapped below in the cellar, was a thought that persistently haunted Gisela. She became highly nervous whenever there was talk of urban bombing, the children noticed, which was often the case. In turn, the news of retreats by the army and the insecure nature of the fronts was a cause of great concern to their grandmother, Corinna. Adolf came to deduce this was due to her sister Hertha, who lived far away in the east where a lot of the fighting was taking place.

But these darker forces of pessimism would always be cancelled out by some of other adults. Volkmar had stopped coming round regularly as before, ever since Bernhard's Mercedes had been confiscated by the government for use by the Wehrmacht; the war effort knew no mercy. But whenever he did manage to make it, he explained tirelessly to Martin and Gisela and any other nearby ears, the tactics surrounding the *Endsieg* - this final crushing victory that was yet to come. The boys sometimes managed to eavesdrop and grasped the firmness of his optimism, while Adolf explained to his brothers the meaning of words like "defence" and "conflict". This positive turnaround was to be revealed, Volkmar would pontificate, in the form of extensive strategical angles which the Führer was certain to be exploring before arriving at a definitive and well-considered decision. War was never straightforward, he argued; that was the reason they always lasted so long. All the same, they could rest assured that the course of war being taken was the right and proper one, and the end result would bear more fruits of reward that they could imagine. (Gisela had usually found an excuse to leave by this point.) Bernhard and his wife Edeltraut likewise offered similar, though mercifully shorter, words of wisdom whenever they visited.

However, the boys' fears were confirmed after all when they struck closer to home the following year. In early 1944, Gisela and Martin's son Siggi was sent off for a continuation of his Hitler Youth training to barracks further up to the north-east, not far from Schwerin. The intention here was for him to become a *Lufwaffenhelfer* (assistant to the *Luftwaffe*). He was fifteen at the time, soon to be turning sixteen. The war was starting to pull in the youngsters too, drafting them up directly from school in its ever more desperate need to bolster up the armed forces.

Gisela was beside herself with worry but was able not to let it show. She told both the boy and everyone else that this was a moment of great pride, for the whole family of course but most of all for Siggi himself. He was becoming a man, she told him one night; a man who would serve his country with bravery. Although for many of his peers this would have been a stirring thought at such a youthful age, it excited little enthusiasm in Siggi himself who would have much preferred to stay in the comfort of the Gasthaus with his toys and his books.

He ended up training to be and becoming a search-light operator, initially assigned to a unit in Braunschweig where he experienced his first ever, and for him uniquely terrifying, major attack on that industrial city in October. The ground shook under his feet like never before, as bombs came screaming down all around. Between the fires from the burning city reflecting upwards, and those planes they hit in the sky exploding in flames, the heavens transformed into vivid shades of orange and red, an image that he never forgot. He came through this major raid with not even a slight injury and – now sixteen - learnt to operate light artillery flak. He was sent on to nearby Wolfsburg in early 1945 to help defend the *KdF* (later *Volkswagen*) motor car production works there.

To add to Gisela's woes, her husband was also conscripted, a couple of months after his son was sent to training. This had now become inevitable, as in the case of many German men under fifty, and sometimes even those in their fifties. In the wake of the resounding defeat at Stalingrad there had come the necessity for all able-bodied German men to step up and do their duty. His age (nearly forty), his familial and commercial obligations, his medical conditions – asthma and recurring stomach complaints - had been useful tools to dodge the draft thus far, but in the end nothing could save him. He was drafted, trained, and sent to the eastern front by the summer of 1944, where he was sure he would meet his death. To his commendation, he outwardly accepted this fate with great dignity, wishing for his family, and in particular his children, to at least remember him as a courageous man. Internally though, he was a panic-ridden mess and once he found himself in action he could not even shoot straight, so strong was his incessant trembling.

However, for Martin there came what a neighbour later acidly termed as "*Glück im Unglück*" – good luck in bad luck. He had only been on the front for two weeks when he was far enough away from a mortar explosion to survive it (unlike his three companions at the time who were torn apart) but close enough to have half of his left leg, along with his left hand, blown off. Though he initially lost a lot of blood, thanks to the swift and timely assistance from the field medics he survived well enough and was eventually brought back home to Lüneburg, to be placed under medical care there. Between the severe nature of the injury and above all the psychological shock endured, he was left a nervous and jittering wreck of a man. He ended up practically bed-ridden upstairs in the *Gasthaus* and only moved between the bedroom and the bathroom on that floor in order to regularly change himself; the psychological scarring had affected him deeply, from the less noticeable issues, such as memory loss, to the more awkward ones, such as incontrollable shaking and sudden inopportune bowel movements. For Gisela this was yet another added burden; but despite taking care of two of her own three children, her sister's three orphaned children, and her now invalid husband, she took it all in her stride.

Corinna tried to help relieve the burden as best she could but also had her sick husband at home who was now dependent on her. She often took Inge's three boys round to her apartment, to spend some hours there with her and Opa Georg and so keep an eye on them all together and give Gisela a well-earned break. The doting grandfather was naturally delighted to see the boys. However, as in the case of all frequent visitors, his patience eventually wore thin. After four or five hours it was usually time for them to go back home to the Gasthaus. He was also a constant liability with his '*loses Mundwerk*' (his loose tongue), as both Gisela and Inge had always called it. Not for the first time did he have to be reprimanded by Gisela, after Joseph repeated a joke of his grandfather's in front of company.

"What does the ideal German look like?" he offered up one day with theatrical flair in the back room of the Gasthaus, in front of a mixed audience that included Edeltraut and some female friends of hers from the *BDM*.

Edeltraut clapped her hands with delight, impressed to hear such a little boy commanding vocabulary like "ideal". "Go on, then, what does he look like?" she beamed at him with encouragement.

The boy stood proud and erect to deliver the punchline, exultant that his memory had served him so well. "Tall like Goebbels, slim like Göring, and blond like the Führer!"

Edeltraut blushed in shame. There came a titter of laughter from someone else at the back, that soon dried up in embarrassment upon realizing it was alone.

"Really!" Gisela chided her mother later on. "You ought to try to keep Papa more under control when the children are around. I have told you before – children repeat everything and Joseph in particular.

That kind of joke could get us into trouble! Put your foot down more." She immediately regretted her words, knowing how much her mother was psychologically worn down by the man and rarely dared to contradict him.

All the same, Gisela ensured that the boys spent less time there. "Leave them here at the Gasthaus," she told her mother one day when Corinna offered to take them off her hands. "They don't bother me in the slightest as long as they have something to keep them busy." That was not quite true, as Gisela herself well knew. Deep down she loved the boys dearly, almost as much as her own – perhaps sometimes, for sentimental reasons, a little more even. She always had their best interests at heart. But she also had a short temper at the best of times, and these they weren't.

Martin Landeck's brother Dieter, who had been awarded the Iron Cross and promoted to *Oberfeldwebel* (Staff Sergeant), fell later that year in battle in the Croatian part of Yugoslavia, killed in an attack by partisans on a German garrison there. His body was buried in situ (it had been a bloody mess and barely recognizable) and the news passed on by telegram to his family. There was a remembrance service held in Lüneburg, with all due honours. There they played what had become his favourite song through the war, of which he had fondly spoken of in one of his letters home: Lale Andersen singing *Lili Marleen*. He had heard it so many times on the *Soldatensender Belgrad* (Belgrade Soldiers Broadcaster) and hoped that he would live out the conflict to see his girlfriend again, by the barracks, in front of the street lantern.

That however was not to be the case and his parents Volkmar and Anna turned out in crisp black clothes and hardened faces that day, saying little apart from how proud they were to be mourning their son. They had the *Lüneburgschen Anzeigen* newspaper publish an announcement in the obituary section, with a smiling photograph of a handsome young man and the words underneath, "*Süß ist es, für das Vaterland zu sterben!*" (It is sweet to die for the Fatherland!) Gisela found it both tragic and tasteless. The obituary columns were filling up fast by now, taking up whole bleak pages in the newspapers when in the years before there had only been a scattering.

Volkmar, with one son dead and the other one crippled for life, was indeed as patriotic a man as any could be. His boys had fought with all their might for Führer and Fatherland, had given their all, and he could now look any man or woman in the face on the street without the slightest tinge of shame. Nothing in this world could compare to the *Heldentod* (hero's death), the greatest accolade a man could aspire to. This much he proclaimed to Gisela, with her children standing beside her, during a visit to see his sick son in bed. It was to be one of his last visits ever to the *Gasthaus Sonnenschein*. Gisela did not even deign to respond, just showed him formally to the door in glacial silence.

Though having no time or patience for her oafish father-in-law, Gisela empathized with the deep grief felt by his wife Anna. This was a profound grief that Anna ineluctably then shared with her husband, sometimes in tears, sometimes in rage. It had never been a harmonious relationship between the couple and in the end that grief fed on them both like a vampire.

For Gisela, Volkmar's near cessation of visits came as the proverbial silver lining to the cloud. It was a huge relief with one less person to have under her feet. Even so, Gisela knew that although Volkmar may be brash and resolute in public, in private he was a snivelling, hollow ruin of man. His vociferous alleged pride in the killing and maiming of his sons was but one such example. Sometimes she almost felt sorry for him.

More alone than ever, Volkmar's tendency to seek consolation in alcohol, whenever he felt under duress, blossomed into full-blown alcoholism. So, in a blurred and incapacitated manner, he spent those final war years at home with wife and mother-in-law, desperately hoping for a victory that would never come and cursing all those malignant forces – too numerous to mention here - that had thwarted the rightful destiny of the nation. When he heard on the radio in June 1944 that the Allies had landed in Normandy, he cried like a baby the whole day.

Gisela observed and noted, with her usual impassive silence in public, the movements of the SS-*Hauptscharführer* Eberhard Ritter. In the first weeks following the disappearance of her sister in the bombing, she passionately wished for his exposure and punishment, but kept that passion under check. He was a highly-positioned, well-respected military officer during a war; she was a simple wife and mother – a family woman with only a handful of friends and none with influence. Anything she pointed out, whether in public or in a court of law, would be twisted around. Moreover, at this point in time her husband had yet to be called up. Hoping that he may somehow avoid active service, she knew she needed to remain inconspicuous to the authorities. She controlled her fury and inserted it instead into the hard manual work involved in almost single-handedly running a large three-storey business. There were probably few buildings in Germany at that time that were so regularly cleaned from top to bottom as the *Gasthaus Sonnenschein* in Lüneburg. Which was a great shame considering that they had no actual formal guests. Tourism, moribund since the beginning of the war, was now totally defunct; at the train station there were signs up saying, *"Erst siegen, dann reisen"* – First victory, then travel.

Nonetheless, Gisela still kept half an eye on the movements of the man who had harassed and abused her sister. She laid the blame for Inge's death one hundred percent at the door of the *"feiges Dreckschwein"* – the 'cowardly filthy pig', as she referred to him - whose behaviour had driven her sister to Hamburg in the first place and into that terrible night that had followed.

Ritter himself was eager to move on. As Gisela herself had correctly second-guessed, he had grown bored of the provincial town. By now he sought greater challenges elsewhere, with the possibility of proving himself capable of more work responsibilities and thus receive a due promotion. He applied for, and was successful in obtaining, a position in Berlin, to where he moved in the spring of 1944. His assistant Möhring was also promoted but stayed on in Lüneburg until the end of the war, assuming Ritter's previous position in the Gestapo headquarters there.

At this time Gisela was able to access a much-needed source of income. Through a high-ranking NSADP official in the East Hannover *Gau,* also an old friend of Volkmar, she had come into contact with the organization in charge of the hiring of seamstresses, tailors and other professionals to stitch up Wehrmacht uniforms. There was an ongoing and healthy demand at the time for new uniforms, due to the sharply rising conscription rate; and corresponding to that a potentially large offer, due to the ever-growing number of fallen soldiers whose uniforms required all kinds of alterations depending on the nature of the man's death, from minor stitching to full-blown repair of badly torn and blood-stained fabric. Gisela had always enjoyed sewing and darning and knew all the tricks in the book to remove a stubborn stain, and so accepted the work straight off. In this way, she spent many days working on the materials in the back room of the Gasthaus with the dance music on. Whatever qualms she may have had considering the fate in war of so many around her, who had once worn such uniforms, it was still a very financially productive manner in which to pass the days and she had children to take care of.

Apart from the losses that every family had to bear, these were times not only of painful news but also of great material shortages and intense fear: both fear of the enemy and fear of the state itself. Defeatism was not tolerated and was a punishable criminal offense. Moreover defeatism, or any other criticism directed at the Führer or the authorities or the direction the war was taking, could be easily located; some even used the opportunity of a widespread culture of denunciation to settle old scores. A wrong word here, an ambiguous sentence there, and suddenly people found themselves in very hot water. *Denunzianten* (denunciators) were everywhere, a common feature of German life; one had to take the utmost care about what one said and where. There was no such thing as idle gossip. The fishmonger Erna Sultzbach went to prison that very year - and got off lucky with a short sentence thanks to the wife of the prosecuting judge being a regular customer of hers – merely for having been heard crying and saying to a friend, *"Mein Sohn ist sinnlos gestorben"* (My son died senselessly).

With news seeping through of the Allied forces landing in Normandy in the early June of that year, invading the mainland continent and gradually encroaching occupied territory, moving toward the German border itself, it was a clear sign of the acute danger, and inexorable decline, in which the Reich found itself. All the more reason not to lose faith in the final victory, was the official stance, and this was enforced with harsh punitive measures. The

Gestapo monitored the population more closely than ever, and dissenters and 'traitors' were swiftly taken away or eliminated.

Snitch was king, and people became self-righteous to the point of actively looking for those who they felt did not match their own moral standards; which was also an excellent way of making sure they kept the wolves away from their own door. It even came to be considered potentially offensive not only that which was said, but also that which *was not* said. If a person did not actively declare their belief in a fact, how could it be known if they truly believed it?

In this nervous silence, there now dawned through much of the Reich a stern and gloomy acceptance that the military situation was going from bad to worse and that there was no realistic way out. This conclusion had been arrived at by a whole network of high-ranking military and political figures, which led to the ultimately failed assassination attempt against Hitler in the summer of 1944, primarily conducted by the German military officer Claus von Stauffenberg. A bomb was planted in a briefcase by von Stauffenberg, during a military meeting in East Prussia. However, the briefcase was unwisely placed beside the sturdy leg of a solid oak table, and in the instant of the explosion most of those present – including the target - were shielded from the blast. Hitler emerged almost unscathed from the attempt, and true to form felt more divine than ever. That night, just after midnight, he gave a short address to the nation by radio, in which he told how a small group of unscrupulous, criminal, and ultimately stupid officers had made an unsuccessful attempt on his life, but that he was unharmed and in good health.

The revenge waged on the conspirators and their families was extensive and brutal: thousands were executed, and tens of thousands more sent to prison or concentration camps. Whole families were locked up due to the alleged involvement of one single member. There was a moment of shock and near disbelief that ran through the wider population as soon as the news became apparent; first of his death, then of his survival. For those more loyal to the regime, this shock was tinged with fear as to what would happen next, followed by relief that the old order would stay firm after all, accompanied in some layers of the population by a not inconsiderable wave of simple human solidarity with the survivor of an assassination attempt. But following this final failure to oust Hitler, for those who had been so hopeful for change there seemed to be literally no way out of avoiding a doom-laden and bloody finale to the war.

There was also, for many, still a genuine and ardent belief in a German victory; a desire for the "*totaler Krieg!*" (total war) that Goebbels had screamed to his passionate cheering audience in the infamous sports stadium episode in Berlin back in 1943. In these people there reigned an irresistible optimism, not only encouraged but demanded by the state, as well as an unwavering trust in salvation through that long-promised and miraculous turnabout that would eventually arrive to transform the gloom into glory. Like children they relied on blind faith in the invisible and the unknown, as dictated by an all-powerful commander, to see them through these uncertain and dark times; that instinctive built-in submission that can guide a person – in the face of all common sense – inexorably on toward utter disaster.

Throughout the rest of 1943 and into 1944, the aerial bombardments of towns and cities throughout Germany augmented in intensity. Whole towns, whole city areas were going down in heaps of rubble and ash. Additionally, more and more young men were being sucked into the burgeoning conflict, in particular on the hard-fought eastern front. Conscription rained down on the male population of the Reich and showed a growing disregard for age or profession. Consuming whole generations, the war was insatiable. Now men in their forties and even fifties were considered suitable for active duty. It took connections of the very best quality, which constituted top-class NSDAP *Bonzen* (high-ranking functionaries), to have any chance of not being pulled into the conflict. Even then, the universal condemnation and scorn from those around – from neighbours, colleagues, and even relatives eager to point out the shirkers and the cowards - was unbearable.

Edeltraut's husband Bernhard Bohlen had hoped for a combination of factors - age (fifty-three) and professional position (head of production at the ironworks *Lüneburger Eisenwerk*) - to escape conscription. Eventually though, he succumbed to pressure, both internal and external, to actively help out more directly. In the spring of 1943, he was able to secure a high-ranking civilian post in the armaments industry, namely in the vital sector of ball bearings production, at a factory in Schweinfurt. In this way, he felt both safe from the ravages of war, and noble in his contribution to the war effort. The former was put to the test in the August of his first year there, when a large daylight raid by American B-17 bombers hit the installations where he was employed. Bohlen was carrying out an inspection of the assembly line area at the time and due to his delayed reaction in evacuating from the area when the air-raid siren sounded, he nearly paid for his tardiness with his life. With a few bloody cuts and grazes, together with a much deeper psychological shake-up, he survived the ordeal and carried on working, now at least secure in the knowledge that his valour was no longer feigned.

Inge and Gisela's brother Ernst Hartmann had been exempted due to his hopeless medical condition: he had, amongst other things, a long history of gastrointestinal problems, including heavy bleeding and stomach ulcers, a diagnosis of severe deafness in the right ear, as well as having Pes Cavus which would have made any extended stretches of walking or marching near impossible. He went through a couple of inspections by a doctor from the Wehrmacht – who seemed almost impressed by the Ernst's physical feebleness – and was thus deemed to be more of a liability than a beneficence to the armed forces and subsequently left in peace.

Horst's brother-in-law Manfred, husband of Marianne, was also exempted due to the large wheat farm – classified as being of vital agricultural importance – that he ran on the outskirts of the village of Halmern; plus the fact of the five children (six before, one had died; but another was on the way) that he and his wife were bringing up there.

Almost no profession was now considered indispensable. Top musicians, actors and artists, teachers and professors, engineers and technicians: all were finding themselves with no other option but to submit to the will of the state and be sent to one of the fronts. A famous case involved the efforts of Sepp Harberger, the trainer of Germany's national football team, who fought long and tirelessly for the confirmation of *Unabkömmlichkeit* – being dispensed from the requirement of fighting in the armed forces – for his team members. It was hoped that at least this small but most precious group of Germans might live to fight another day. Ultimately he lost that match and the men were drafted up during 1943 and 1944. Further to that, former national team member and internationally celebrated footballer Julius Hirsch, who was Jewish, was deported to Auschwitz-Birkenau and murdered there in the gas chambers in 1943.

Schilling had gone into hiding by this point, abandoning his atelier in a moonlight flit and moving up to Harburg to stay incognito with a close friend and fellow communist there. He continued to be affiliated to the underground resistance, though it was for the most part a passive resistance and their activities and attempts at sabotage remained modest throughout the war. Schilling's main function within the group involved the copious forgery of identity card and passports, and other spurious printed material such as fake ration coupons. This finally became - more than merely a necessity for survival - his great vocation in life, and it lasted further on long after the war was over.

Not all men were trying to escape conscription, however. The most ardent national-socialist in the family, Edeltraut's son Roland, had been fighting in the armed services since the outbreak of war. The proud mother had initially been very eager to report on the latest developments in her son's career, including his rapid rise through the ranks of the SS, which he had joined in 1940. But as time moved on, she seemed to report in less detail, either through a lack of exact knowledge concerning her son's activities, or a desire to keep that information closer to her chest. He was in the east, in Poland and then Belarus, but few concrete details were offered up for the family's curiosity. Unusually for her, she then became more loquacious in this period about her daughters. Leni was serving in the Red Cross, doing her valiant duty out on the eastern front; Eva was also now in training, though had opted for a secretarial course. She already had excellent marks in shorthand and English and if the war lasted long enough, she hoped to become an assistant in the Wehrmacht.

Horst's brother Karl-Heinz had initially been sent to Paris back at the end of 1940, but with the opening out of the vast front in the Soviet Union, he had been transferred two years later to the north-east. From the scented perfumes and fine food and wines of France, he was relocated to the cold mud and brutal trenches of Russia: it was an execrable twist of fate for a man fundamentally interested in simply surviving this nonsensical conflict by whatever means. In 1944 he found himself posted in the far north of East Prussia, namely in Tilsit. There he was wounded in action that spring, treated in situ, and later assigned desk duties due to the shrapnel that he had retained in his right leg and that hindered his movement. He was transferred initially to complete administrative tasks in Königsberg, the East Prussian capital, where he survived by the skin of his teeth the heavy aerial bombings of August 1944 that turned the once magnificent city into a landscape of ruins. From there he was then relocated again, this time to Dessau, where he was employed in the area of military logistics, working in the marshalling yard at the railway station there.

Gisela then received a letter from Karl-Heinz from Dessau in December 1944. He was asking after his brothers Horst and Wilhelm, to ask if at the Gasthaus they had received any updates, as he himself had been unable to obtain any concrete information. It was a very carefully formulated epistle; Gisela sensed that between the lines he was confirming the imminent collapse of the Reich and the approaching end of the war. She was very contented to hear that news, as she imagined Karl-Heinz probably was too; a sentiment that both – and millions of others besides - were keeping quietly and cautiously to themselves. She wrote back with an equally careful pen that hinted more than it stated. She avoided all mention of the greater war itself, restricting herself to familial details: that the fate of Horst remained uncertain, but to which she was holding out a quiet optimism; the news that Wilhelm was to their knowledge alive and well and out at sea; and finally confirming the almost certain death of her sister in an air-raid in Hamburg, in the summer of the previous year.

Gisela had inquired after Wilhelm to several people on several occasions, but there was little information to be gleaned from the wider Grün family. Gisela had liked him well enough, finding him to be an aimable young man and she considered him as a solid member of her own wider family; plus there was the issue of the extensive electrical work he had carried out the Gasthaus at cut price, which had produced intense gratitude in her. But he was on active duty at sea and she had heard no word from him. Horst's other siblings lived further out in rural areas and there was a minimum of contact with them. Horst's mother had died before the war and his father was tucked away at home, passing his final years in an early stage of dementia. With Horst himself missing, probably killed, contact with that side of the family had become obscured.

Many Germans were now talking of the '*Zusammenbruch*' – the collapse. As the Reich spiralled downwards and out of control in the early days of 1945, a cynical gag began to circulate among the German troops living and fighting on those collapsing fronts: Enjoy the war, because the peace will be savage.

Chapter 31

On a bitter cold evening in late January 1945, Hertha stood by the gate of her small farm and sobbed. Behind her, endless fields of East Prussia stretched out through hushed woodland, by secluded lakes, along the iced edges of the lagoons. The air was clear and frosty and the dark sky above her weighed huge, imponderable, a multitude of star specks. As the tears dried, and with them so much of the strain and fear of the last year drained out of her, she felt strong again and acknowledged that yes, the moment to leave had come. Not an easy concept to accept – this had been her home for the last forty years of her life – but she was now relieved, unburdened. After the confusion and fear-mongering of the last few months, after having cried out her soul to the birds and trees, she could now contemplate with calm planning the cold fact that the time had come to leave her home behind, and that this would be forever. The evening had passed quickly; she heard the rooster trumpeting as she pulled herself together to make the final preparations.

Hertha had been planning to leave for months, together with her only child Bärbel and Max, Bärbel's little boy. Covertly, discreetly, but determinedly she had been planning and plotting. Many others in the town also had the intention of leaving, although no-one so far had dared. They knew deep down that it was over; they knew there would be, could be no more attempts by the Wehrmacht to advance again into the east. They had known that since last July when they heard that the Soviets had already passed Witebsk and taken over the whole area around the Beresina river, just to the east of Minsk. According to reports they had heard, the German troops there had been trapped and slaughtered in no time.

Others still hung on to their firm belief in the *Endsieg* - the final victory; the sudden last-minute course change that the Führer would engineer, either through miraculous new weapon technology or a brilliant new strategy that would turn the tables in favour of the inexhaustible troops of the Reich. The tide would turn, they were convinced: it was just a matter of waiting. At a local level throughout the *Gau* of East Prussia, this was not merely wishful thinking - those were orders that were to be strictly adhered to, by military and civilians alike. The Führer had promised that not one metre of the Reich would be lost in this conflict, East Prussia first and foremost, and there was no official reason to doubt his word.

Her husband Rudolf had fallen noticeably ill in the summer of 1944. They had both known, and internally processed, that he only had a few months left to live. All the same, he had kept himself informed as to the latest news of the progress of the war and talked about little else, as if his life depended on it. There came one *Sondermeldung* (special announcement) after another and he listened to each in silent concentration, as if it were prayer in church. He did not dwell on his own suffering, as the lung cancer inside swiftly finished him off; but rather he talked with passionate worry about where the Red Army was now, how the front was "standing up" (it was crumbling fast) and whether the Bolsheviks would be there by the New Year. They weren't, not quite, but it was clear by then that their arrival would not be far away.

A married couple in their forties from Königsberg, the then East Prussian capital, distant relatives of Rudolf and now refugees on the run, stayed with them for a few nights. They had left the city surreptitiously, taking advantage of a breakout of civilians after a series of heavy aerial bombardments, together with two adolescent daughters. This was before the city was then sealed off and designated by the Führer himself as a fortress against the invading enemy. The couple told Hertha and Rudolf in hushed tones, when the daughters were out of the room and the four were alone, of major Soviet advances taking place all along the eastern front, of atrocities committed and against civilians too, of the ever-receding line along which there would be no more counter-offensives, of the thousands of German soldiers that were either deserting and fleeing or being obliterated.

"The Russians surrounded a number of our companies last month - they only had a few hundred men in them, the others had been sent off to fight in the west - and they just wiped them out. No prisoners, just a massacre." She lowered her voice, "You must not repeat that in front of the girls, of course. We have never talked about those things to them, and I still do not."

"They will find out soon enough," sighed her husband.

Hertha said, "The last thing we heard from Bärbel's husband Richard was that he was fighting further south, near to Lemberg. They were holding off the Red Army, but in the meantime we cannot help but think...., I mean, we would not dream of saying a word to her either."

"We fear the worst, to be honest. But she is hopeful that he is still alive," added Rudolf in an energetic spurt, though visibly worn out, battered by both illness and the news of the war. "We want her to stay that way, at least for the time being. Until she has had time to adjust. Everything has changed so enormously and in such little time. For all of us."

"To think she used to be so talkative and sociable," said Hertha. "Even having little Max around her has not centred her in the way I had hoped. Children always help to bridge over tragedies, but this has not been the case. The war strikes us in different ways: some it hardens, some it rewards, but most it just crushes."

Bärbel's son was two now. He had seen his father once, the last time he was home on leave, and he was now beginning to talk little nonsense sentences that everyone adored. Bärbel had taken him and the visiting girls for a walk.

The couple continued their journey the next day, moving on westwards in horse and cart. They were taking back roads, moving in a clandestine fashion – the war was officially in full swing and people could be shot for defeatism. They were hoping to sneak through to relatives in Leipzig, perhaps even make it by Christmas.

Rudolf became weaker and weaker. He was more or less his old sharp intelligent self during September; but as the autumn progressed he fell in on himself, crumpling up. He slept more and more; in the final week most of the time. He passed away at the end of October, on the 29th, and after a quiet burial was laid to rest in the cemetery in Heiligelinde, the same town that he had been born in. Knowing what was most probably about to come round the corner, that was of great consolation to both of them.

Hertha and Bärbel returned from the church to the farm on foot, Bärbel pushing Max in a pramsot. They passed patiently through a crowd of domestic geese that had congregated at a spot on the road and didn't seem to know where best to move to. It was a resplendent day and full of those profound autumn colours that few other places could radiate so brilliantly, Hertha perceived; the light falling on the golden leaves of the birch trees - the younger ones still with white trunks - while some oaks were blazing red and behind them the deeper cooper tones of beech foliage. It was strange for her to think that this same sublime beauty was painting the same scene a relatively short distance further to the north and east of them, on the bloody battlefields of the shifting front.

The next day Hertha wrote home to Corinna to inform her of Rudolf's passing. It was the last letter that she wrote to her sister from her home in then Heiligelinde, East Prussia (now Święta Lipke, Poland). "There were not many that came to bid farewell, which was sad. His family have lived here for centuries. I saw very few people but they all offered their condolences. I feel very alone now with just Bärbel and Max. We will have to see what the next months bring." Hertha looked at what she had written and reflected, "What silly sentences! Of course they offered their condolences, what else would they do? I am starting to write without saying anything. I may just as well talk about the weather. But how much truth am I allowed to write down if this letter is sure to get through?"

Two days after the funeral she heard on the radio that the French had killed General Fritz von Brodowksi while in custody. Everyone in town was talking about it. Rudolf's brother Werner had come to pay his respects to the widow, and he related how the general was originally from Köslin, where he himself had studied, decades ago. Werner seemed very nostalgic and desirous to talk of the past. He said, "Von Brodowski was from a long line of Prussian generals. Fine soldiers, the very best in the world. They are nearly all gone now: fallen in battle, arrested, demoted, locked up. Hitler won't listen to any of them. It is going to be the end of an era when this is all over."

They both knew the Soviets would soon break through any resistance at the front, for good this time. They would surge through East Prussia, ransack the towns, mow down the *Volkssturm*, enter their land, eat their livestock, shoot at random. They knew it was over and wished to remember it how it once was.

Werner ended his visit with ominous words. He said, hushing his voice as if even the cat might snitch, that when the order was issued to evacuate, she was to waste no time and just head straight off. Werner and his family lived a good 40 kilometres further to the north-east, in Steinort, and there would be no time for visits and fond farewells once that moment had come. She knew her brother-in-law had come to say goodbye, without actually saying it. "When they break through, we have guns at home and will use them," Werner said. After he had gone, Hertha wondered whether he meant against the enemy or against themselves; realized it was both. In true Prussian manner the apocalypse was to be a simple, understated event.

Rudolf had instructed his wife and daughter - in the early summer already, months before his death - to be ready to leave on the spur of the moment. He had insisted time and time again that they prepared themselves adequately for that eventuality, more a probability, and they had done just that. At least Hertha had, with her characteristic rough pragmatism, and had spent the latter part of 1944 considering what she could take and what she must leave. She had managed to whittle down her ideas to four suitcases that she hoped to place on their cart. The sense of urgency increased through December and Hertha told her daughter that their departure was now imminent. Bärbel did finally rustle herself up and manage to take some, albeit limited, control of the situation. As Hertha had hoped, Max had eventually centred her: her father had died and her husband was missing in action, so her little boy represented all the future in the world.

Hertha chastised Bärbel until she had prepared two suitcases of personal belongings; though unbeknown to the mother these were filled mostly with books, keepsakes and clothes for the child. Everything was coming together, Hertha felt, when she realized that she had made no provisions in her calculations for food and drink during the journey. She had so far two suitcases packed with bed linen, cutlery, crockery, a single framed photograph from the 1920s of the whole family, a single change of clothes, and all the modest jewelry she had. In the third the contents had been reduced to the utter basics: two blankets, pillows, hairbrushes and toothbrushes, knives, spoons, plates, and mugs. These could be packed together neatly into a space at the back of the cart, allowing room for a fourth with potatoes, smoked meats and other victuals.

By January, they were ready to depart at a moment's notice. But they had a visit from a representative of the district committee from Rastenburg, the *Kreisstadt* (district capital) that corresponded to them. He appeared from nowhere on a freezing morning, knocked repeatedly at the door until it opened. He informed Hertha that he was issuing an official reprimand that came direct from the *Gauleitung,* no less (the administrative government of the *Gau* of East Prussia, in Königsberg). It stated that "if they continued in their efforts to make defeatist preparations to leave their district, they could reckon with severe disciplinary measures being taken against them". The two women stared at him without making a single facial expression.

The man then said to Hertha, who could hardly believe her ears, "Frau Fiebach, it has come to our notice that you have been making significant adjustments to a hay cart. This includes the construction of a protective roof structure with planks of wood, the fitting of wooden pallets to form an unnecessarily strong floor structure, and the installation of large barrels at the back of the construct, presumably for the storage of liquids during transportation." It was all true but Hertha had been carrying out the work with such secrecy, she was doubly surprised that a passer-by, and possibly even a neighbour, had apparently eyed what she was up to *and* seen fit to report it to the authorities.

After he had gone, she and Bärbel set about taking the adapted hay cart apart. It broke their hearts but they knew that an inspection would now be looming and there was nothing to be done. They removed all the adjustments and restored the cart to its original form. They returned to sitting, waiting and watching precious time flow by.

The representative had also informed the women that there was absolutely no reason for alarm concerning any possible evacuation; nor – he had added with a distinctly threatening tone – was there any reason to create the illusion thereof. But two days after this visit, Hertha heard that the town council in Rastenburg had received an order, directly from the High Command of the Wehrmacht in Berlin and announcing that all men in the surrounding area who had not yet served their country, were to report immediately for the *Volkssturm* (literally: 'people's storm' - the last-ditch army of Hitler's, ordered to be employed throughout the Reich and incorporating all civilian men between 16 and 60, grabbing whatever weapons they could find). The only ones to be excepted from this order were those over sixty or officially registered invalids.

The next day a ragged bunch shuffled up to the town hall in varying states of great distress. So-and-so was lame, so-and-so was suddenly half-blind, so-and-so was much older than stated in the registry documents and this had never been changed despite repeated requests! - all accompanied by tearful wives. None of this made the slightest bit of difference. They got cheap Italian Carcona rifles with 18 cartridges (all that was left over) and three grenades each for their pains; and were sent off that very night into the snow and the darkness. They were supposed to occupy some makeshift fortresses that Gauleiter Scherwitz had ordered constructed the summer before, from which they should be able to offer a solid defense and help keep the area free of any further Soviet advances. No-one ever found out how long they were there, nor what they achieved. Eventually the front to the east broke conclusively, the Red Army rolled on through, and none of them were ever seen again.

By now rumours were abounding, speckled with disturbingly realistic details, of just how much nearer the Red Army was getting. As early as the autumn of the previous year Hertha had noticed the first of the so-called *Trecks* – the convoys of refugees from eastern provinces of the Reich - that had started passing by their town. Back then, these came from the deepest east that had been previously occupied. Some of the refugees were already exhausted and stopped to rest and beg for food and water. Others carried steadily on, more afraid of what was coming up behind that they were hungry or tired. They came in waves. First from the most distant corners of what had until recently been the Reich: dirt-poor German peasants from Belarus with hundreds of kilometres already behind them; then more sophisticated horse-carts with wagons from the Memelland and Lithuania; finally by the winter, they were coming from the outer reaches of East Prussia itself. Hertha had been able to discern in this way how the front was definitively collapsing.

At first there had come just a few, like water trickling from a leak; then more and more, from a broken pipe that wouldn't stop. Bleak long columns of them, passing by in all manner of ways. There were no motorized vehicles such as motorcycles or cars; only the Wehrmacht had those now. But there were many carts drawn by horses or oxen, along with covered wagons and carriages. If a cart or wagon were full, family members would take turns at walking beside while the others sat inside. Sometimes there was even a cow from the farm tied to the wagon and shuffling alongside the convoy. Hertha thought that must have been wonderful in terms of having fresh milk in the morning but imagined that most would become beef at some point. There were riders on horseback with sacks of hay strapped to the side, but the horses were still usually thin and underfed. Other people were pushing bicycles piled up with luggage. A great number of the *Treckers* were simply making their way on foot, some with prams or pushcarts, others dragging handcarts or sledges behind them. They were tucked up in heavy winter coats and dressed under those in good clothes that soon became rags along the journey. Women, children, old people, all hurrying on together. A lot were families, sometimes together with neighbours. A few were carrying their possessions on their backs in self-made rucksacks, but many more were trying to carry or drag along suitcases or large bags.

Hertha watched all this with sadness, but also personal interest. She now noted how the temperature had plummeted. A cold wind drove through the area without mercy, all that day and the whole week. It was usually between -10° and -20°C, occasionally even lower. She also noticed how no-one seemed to say anything on these *Trecks*, how there reigned an atmosphere of silent gloom. The treckers, wrapped up tight in their coats and scarves and gloves, were moving along with only the will to somehow survive.

The next couple of days found Hertha looking with rising frequency out of the window, watching the drove of refugees and their rickety old vehicles roll along the road beside her house, mentally caught in anxieties that dragged her eyes and her soul away from the warm familiar interior of the house and out into the open. She considered joining the route - and had acknowledged that she eventually must do, when it would be far too late - but the visit from the district committee representative had intimidated her into obedience. She raged inside at both the blatant stupidity and the iron firmness of the control being exercised by the authorities but succumbed to it nonetheless, considering the risk too high.

Suddenly in mid-January it was announced that the *Räumungsbefehl* had been emitted - the order to evacuate the district. The news arrived in the form of an abrupt and urgent communiqué, released by the local party headquarters and disclosing what everyone had known for months: that the population was under immediate threat from the enemy and was required to abandon the area as quickly as possible, preferably within the next two days. Word was passed round by telephone or through neighbours riding around on horseback.

When she heard, Hertha was both ecstatic and outraged. She would later relate in more peaceful circumstances, "On the one hand, we had been quite unable to leave up till then, having to wait for orders to do so. And now that we had actually received these orders, we were treated as an embarrassment, as if we were simple-minded for not knowing that these were to have been our instructions all along. It was all so ironic as most of us had been itching to leave but had been held back by official threats or fear of being branded a defeatist. Now these very same officials were barking at us to make a hasty retreat!"

The gate having been formally opened for all to flee, it naturally became a chaotic free-for-all with everyone looking out for themselves. Hertha went to Rastenburg to secure some last-minute provisions and stopped off at the post office. She had to laugh once inside, seeing how in the midst of this cataclysmic chaos the post office was still functioning with fine Prussian efficiency; the clerks sitting neatly on their seats and attending the general public right up until closing time, as per their instructions. Here she posted a short note to Corinna, informing her of their upcoming flight, but it never arrived at its destination.

After her business at the post office, she passed by the town hall. It was darkened and deathly quiet. Noticing how something was amiss and nagged by an inquisitive urge, she plucked up the courage to enter into the adjacent building, which was the headquarters of the NSDAP district committee. The doors had been left open and were knocking occasionally in the wind. The building was empty with just basic furniture, piles of documents scattered around on the floor, and some wisps of burnt paper that floated in the hall further inside. Behind her a local man had followed her in. He looked around with contempt and said, "Yes, of course, they would be the first ones to clear out, the pigs." He spat on the floor and left. She briefly inspected the immediate area but found nothing of interest to her. As she was leaving, she bumped into Herr Milch, a high-ranking functionary in smart brown uniform with whom she was vaguely acquainted. She decided to ask him what exactly was going on.

"Didn't you hear?" he asked her, as if she were slow on the uptake. No, Hertha answered with feigned innocence, she had no idea; and kept her fury still. He informed her of the *Räumungsbefehl* in a matter-of-fact tone, with the air of referring to something quite mundane, and how the whole area, including her own town Heiligelinde, had to be cleared by midnight of the following day. Those were the orders that had come through from the authorities of the *Gauleitung* for East Prussia, in Könisberg. She asked him, in which manner exactly they were to depart and where they were supposed to go to. These questions clearly irritated him, Hertha saw with satisfaction, and he brusquely replied that that was of no concern to him. He added that she and everyone else should feel free to leave by whatever means they wished to: whether by land, water or air. With that, he marched off.

She was riding the way back home when she passed by a neighbour of many years, Frau Berg. The Berg family had always lived a little further down the same road, with a smallholding of similar acreage to Rudolf and Hertha's property, where they bred pigs and farmed buckwheat. They had three young sons in their twenties. Hertha had known Frau Berg for years; she had a tough presence toward strangers but was kindly to those she knew well and was a woman who had always been positive and optimistic, no matter what. Even at the beginning of the war, when she was told that their youngest son of twenty-two had fallen in action in Belgium. Now she was coming towards Hertha carrying two empty buckets and nearly went straight on past without saying a word, as if she hadn't seen her. As Hertha got up close, she realized that her neighbour's eyes were full of tears. She descended from the horse and grabbed her arm, said it was she, at which Frau Berg put down the buckets. She placed her arms round Hertha's neck and began sobbing. "Two of my boys are dead now, gone forever! The officer came round today to inform me that my eldest has been killed. In Radom, in Poland. In the next breath I was told to prepare to evacuate today, with the deadline set for tomorrow, at midnight. Tomorrow! So much hope and hardship with this war, but in the end it was all for nothing!"

Eventually she calmed herself and asked if Hertha was leaving, which Hertha quietly affirmed. Hearing this, Frau Berg beseeched her to take Fabian with her on the *Trecks*. Fabian was the middle son and had been badly injured in a battle on the eastern front, earlier in the war in 1942. He had lost his right arm - it was severed off right at the top, just under the shoulder - and had been deemed unfit for further military service and sent back home to his parents on the farm.

After the aforementioned youngest son was killed back in 1940, they had had some comfort in seeing Lothar - twenty-eight and the oldest of the three - promoted to the rank of second lieutenant and awarded various medals for brave conduct. Now he was gone too and, to cap it all, her husband had been sent away with the *Volkssturm*. Frau Berg was aware that the Russians would soon arrive, but all the same she had no intention of leaving. She knew for a start that her physical health and age counted against her having a realistic hope on such a long journey. Moreover, she wished to stay until the last minute, on the outside chance that her husband somehow made it back. In any case, she had lived there all her life and knew of nowhere else in the world. Whatever the end result was to be, she would never have entertained any thoughts of attempting to flee. More than that, she refused to leave; this was her home and she would face the enemy here and die in the same house where she had been born, half a century ago but in a different world to now. A quip, that had circulated in the area in the past few months, best summarized her attitude: "If we have to be killed by the Russians, then preferably at home."

Her only hope now was that Fabian, most probably the last survivor in the family, should make it through to the west and hopefully find safety there. She begged Hertha to convince Fabian to join them, and to take him with them. Hertha agreed immediately but when she entered the house the lad initially refused, insisting he would stay to the last and defend his mother and his parent's home. Both women pleaded with him and in the end persuaded him with numerous arguments that made them all cry. His mother handed over to him all the family photos and documents and gave Hertha two generous sacks of food to share on the journey. She told her son to start a new life in a different part of a more peaceful world, asked him not to let his brothers and father be forgotten by time. She herself had nothing else to live for and would meet the enemy's arrival with resignation, perhaps even put up a fight (Hertha could imagine Frau Berg with a pitchfork, defiant and dangerous to the last). Whenever Hertha told this tale, she always ended with: "And that was how Fabian ended up joining our little family."

That last evening at home she baked six loaves of bread and put them in a cloth, with some cheese wrapped in paper and bottles for carrying water. Another sack contained different vegetables. They packed the final items into their suitcases: fresh clothes (including pairs of extra woolen socks and gloves for everyone), all the documentation of importance, plus a few extra items that occurred to them in the last moments and that would certainly come in useful during the journey: a compass, scissors, a hammer, some rope. Hertha fetched Rudolf's rifle, an old Krupp infantry gun from the last war, from the barn. There were only a few cartridges left but she liked the thought of having it by her side, if just to intimidate where necessary.

After that Hertha went for a final walk outside around the farm, inspected sheds and stables, pulled on posts and gates to find them all still sturdy. Even in this moment of utter abandonment, she still took pride in the well-maintained state of her property. All her life she had recalled with fondness her childhood town of Lüneburg and kept in touch with her sister back there. But with the passing of decades, this East Prussia had become her *Heimat*, her home; with its well-kept little towns and cobbled roads; the tranquil village byways and lanes further out, still unblemished by the din of motorized vehicles; farms with sunflowers swaying in the front yards, cattle grazing on rich green pastures in summer; meadows of cornflowers and poppies, fields of trimmed stubble in autumn; and the vast bloated rain clouds that filled the whole arch of the sky. She remembered the long walks and horserides that she had embarked upon with Richard in spring when the cycle of life began again, circling round familiar routes in the area or heading deeper into the hinterland with its quiet sandy paths, past blue lakes rimmed with clumps of yellow reeds, hearing the cries of wild geese that headed north in spring. All this would not be lived again; all this must be left behind in the past and remain sealed off there.

And so it was on this night by this gate that she sobbed away, ten to fifteen minutes in total it must have been. This way she could make peace with the fact that she would never return.

Now resigned to her fate, she made a round of the farm, unbolted and opened wide all shed doors and gates, opened the chicken coop to let them all out, and the rabbits too. The rabbits made a dash into the darkness but the chickens and rooster were unsure of what to do. Hertha shrugged: they had their freedom now and it would now be up to them whether they were caught by foxes or hungry Bolsheviks, or managed to slip past both.

They all slept in the front room – Hertha, Bärbel with Max, Fabian. It was a short fitful slumber and they rose at three in the morning. Outside the early hours were silvery dark with a full moon, and a glacial wind was blowing. They hurriedly gulped down a small potato breakfast, made the final preparations, packed the last items into place on the cart, and embarked on their long and uncertain voyage westwards through the imploding Reich.

Chapter 32

The early winter had been relatively quiet on the eastern front, which gave the false impression – one that was quickly magnified by the government and generously spread around the news and official press releases - that the Soviet army may have finally overstretched and exhausted itself. That being the case, a sharp swift counteroffensive, one that could regain much of the lost territory of the past months, would be feasible after all. Many troops were accordingly sent to the western front to combat the increasingly bold advances being made by the enemy there.

To add to the good hope, the Reich could now finally present its famous *Wunderwaffe* (wonder weapon) – the stroke of technological genius that Hitler and his military had been promising would bring a dramatic turnabout in the development of the war, and hand Germany its final victory after all. This came in the form of the V2 flying rockets.

They were certainly innovative. (The designer of this weapon, the physicist and engineer Wernher von Braun, would so impress the Allies with his murderous invention that after the end of the war he was invited over to the US to live and work there, incorporated into their budding aerospace programme and forgoing any charges associated with his involvement in the Third Reich). And in terms of terror, the V2 rockets were extremely effective too. Sleek, swift, and unmanned, they flew at too high an altitude and too high a velocity to be intercepted by regular fighter planes or anti-aircraft guns. Timed to run out of fuel over the destination, they would simply drop at random on the designated urban area below with the goal that the explosive device would hopefully cause the maximum possible damage and death. Over three thousand were launched, mostly against Belgium and Great Britain, with Antwerp and London taking the brunt of the attacks. There was no chance, at this early stage of their development, for them to be used for precision bombing of military or industrial targets of the Allies; their sole purpose was to terrorize the civilian populations of towns and cities. In the case of one rocket that hit a cinema in Antwerp shortly before Christmas 1944, over 500 people were killed in a single strike. People would listen in fear to the whizzing sound of them flying overhead; it was in that terrible moment when the sound suddenly petered out, that danger loomed and without any time to take cover.

Meanwhile, the massive aerial bombings of cities in Germany continued. One after another, they were being reduced to ruins. Following on from the fates suffered by Cologne, the Ruhr area cities, and Hamburg, other large cities were likewise in the process of being levelled. The garrison town of Münster was so heavily bombed throughout the war that by the end barely a third of it was left standing. In others the level of destruction even rose to 80% and above. Kassel was destroyed in a firestorm similar to that produced in Hamburg. (The same fate would later await Würzburg and Pforzheim in 1945; in the latter, a quarter of the population was killed in a single night). Stuttgart was almost obliterated in four straight days of bombing in the summer of 1944. Famous and once admired cities such as Mainz, Mannheim, Bremen, Frankfurt, Hannover, Saarbrücken, Düsseldorf, Nuremberg, Dessau, Augsburg, Karlsruhe, Koblenz, and many others were also so heavily battered they were no longer recognizable. Small towns of little importance, that had been left untouched so far, were suddenly flattened in a spurt of raids in late 1944 and early 1945, leaving local populations wondering whether, or more usually when, their own hometown would be the next target. Major cities like Munich and Berlin were naturally hit by frequent bombing raids too, which were widely reported in the press. This regular carpet bombing of urban residential areas was not the only, though certainly it was the main tactic of the British RAF. The US air force, by contrast, concentrated far more on precision bombing of industrial and military targets, rather than civilians.

The clatter of bravado from the Nazi Ministry of Propaganda in defiance of these area bombings was emitted in constant government broadcasts and special announcements. They hoped to exhort the broader popular opinion into a mood of fury and indignation against the enemy, as well as simultaneously instill a high degree of optimism with a view to clinching the upcoming victory. It was a fine balancing act indeed, that could easily have sent out an equivocal message to the population given the sheer level of destruction, and it formed some of Goebbels' most challenging work.

For those who shared in the Führer's vision, Germany still found itself caught up in a monumental battle that it could not afford to lose. This was not to be like any war before it, the Nazis had already promised; this was not a war that was simply lost or won, as when the Prussians had fought the French back in the 1870s, or the disastrous Great War early that century that had ended in a German military victory but political defeat. This was to be a historical event of far far greater standing, rising to mythical proportions; for the ultimate destiny of the whole German people now depended on the victory. If Germany lost, the Führer was convinced and had convinced, then the whole German people would go under with it. Their race would be utterly annihilated, erased from the map; down to the last man, woman and child. The catastrophic city bombings aroused anger, and fear too, but they did not break the general will of the people to fight on; if anything, in many cases they only bolstered it, or at least at this point in the war. Those in power were convinced that the losses endured so far would be nothing compared to the enormity of the potential devastation if Germany lost. And through the vociferous demands and vows of the die-hards to keep fighting till the bitter end, those who saw the situation as being hopeless for Germany were in turn mostly silenced.

Such people as these, with their less fanatical attachment to the reigning ideology, saw the situation in merely pragmatic terms. In the wake of Stalingrad, many Germans knew deep down inside that the long drawn-out and endlessly brutal conflict was to be in its last throes and not far from a final resolution. Even for those optimists who held onto their faith in the *Endsieg* – the ultimate victory - it was in most cases more a self-deceiving need for hope, created for the sole purpose of assuaging their deep inner fears about the nature of life in Germany after the end of Nazism.

One of the first visible signs for the *Luftwaffe* that the defense of the Reich was already starting to rot on the inside, had come in the autumn of 1943 when a group of American fighter aircraft were shot down over the city of Aachen, a German town situated on the triangular border spot of Belgium, the Netherlands and Germany. Such had been the consternation that American planes were freely penetrating German airspace and accompanying bombers into Reich territory, that *Reichsmarschall* Göring had flat out refused to believe the report, despite the insistence of his subordinates as to its veracity.

About a year later, Aachen became the first German city to fall to the Allied ground troops. Despite heavy resistance from the Wehrmacht and numerous delays, the Allied forces had been pushing their way through western Europe ever since those first foreboding landings in June 1944 on the beaches of Normandy, that had signified the beginning of the end.

The Wehrmacht held out in Aachen tenaciously during a six-week siege, before the city could finally be taken at the end of October 1944. Between aerial bombings prior to the besiegement and the long terrestrial battle for the city itself, including its surrounding districts, it was heavily damaged: nearly two-thirds of it were destroyed. The heavily reduced but still present civilian population, living between the ruins, welcomed the invaders with open arms. A suitable figure from among them, one with a notoriously anti-Nazi past – Franz Oppenhoff – was approved by the occupying American forces to assume the role of mayor of the city. Thus began the occupation of Germany.

(Oppenhoff carried out this function from October 1944 to March 1945, when he was assassinated by the so-called '*Werwolf*' (werewolf) group. This was a short-lived guerrilla resistance movement made up of fanatical young Nazis who organized a terror campaign in the wake of occupied Germany. They carried out a series of murders and arson attacks against Germans who had surrendered, including a brutal massacre of sixteen people in Bavaria, until they were finally disbanded by the end of the war. Their reputation was far worse than their limited number of disruptions and murders, though, and nothing could stop the tide of German cities opening up to the Allies, joyful that the war was finally over.)

Nonetheless, military resistance at Aachen had been tough and the Allies were aware that a long fight stood ahead. Further points along the border began to fall. By January, the Allies had smashed through the Ardennes region in southern Belgium and Luxembourg, engaging in long and embittered battles. Hitler had taken numerous divisions from a series of precarious points on the eastern front in order to make one last attempt to defend the Reich from the enemy invading to the west. Again, the Wehrmacht put up a hard fight but were no match for the combined Allied forces. These troops were soon reported – unfathomable though it first seemed to most Germans when the news came through – to have occupied whole swathes of south-western Germany and were marching ever deeper into the Reich's territory.

In February, the war abruptly came closer to home for Gisela and her family with an (albeit relatively minor) aerial bombing raid on Lüneburg itself. A number of streets received isolated though destructive bomb clusters, including the Rotenbleicher Weg where Horst and Inge had lived for a couple of years after marrying. Various buildings, including the museum, were destroyed; but worst hit was the railway station, where a large explosive bomb fell to become a *Volltreffer* (direct hit) on the communal air-raid bunker below. Around 300 people - rail personnel, commuters arriving or waiting for trains, and residents of nearby buildings who had also taken shelter there - were all killed.

Edeltraut Bohlen was notably nervous by this point. She would comment, in her grating high-pitched voice, that it would be a matter of weeks before either the town was razed to the ground or the enemy was marching through the streets at will, firing off weapons and seeking bloodthirsty revenge; all of which frightened the children half to death. Gisela began to dread her visits, which were mercifully infrequent.

Jubilant, though very furtively jubilant, in turn were the prisoners of war and forced labourers brought over from the east to work, especially in the agricultural sector but also in factories and industrial plants, and living in miserable conditions. With the German men gone to war, they provided the workforce necessary to keep the country going; without income and receiving only the most basic sustenance, often maltreated by local farmers, stripped of all dignity and rights as they sweated for hours in torn and ragged uniforms, far from homelands and loved ones. They were naturally eager for every single piece of news concerning the advancement of the Allies and the corresponding fall of the Reich. By those early months of 1945, the situation had become catastrophic for the Wehrmacht and the end of the war was only months away. The Americans were making implacable progress throughout the west and south-west, capturing vast areas. A further important front had opened up further north in the Lower Rhine region as well, with mainly British troops pushing up towards Bremen and Hamburg.

To the east, the news coming in was even worse for the Reich. However optimistically the announcer formulated the events, the Wehrmacht was clearly falling back with terrifying speed; routed on one front after another, surrendering one town after another. By the end of that crucial year 1944, the Red Army had driven the invaders completely from the eastern lands and taken back most of the formerly occupied area of Poland, along with large parts of Hungary and Czechoslovakia. It was about to break through into Germany itself.

In East Prussia, the Red Army repeated its earlier success of using pincer movements to isolate and then encircle German divisions, cutting them off from one another before taking them out. Taking advantage of the absence of a now almost non-existent Luftwaffe, they were able to operate without worry of any aerial interference; neither bombardments nor evacuations of troops. For those Wehrmacht troops caught up in these sudden advances, there was no escape to be had. Tens of thousands were being killed on a daily basis in early 1945, but Berlin showed not the slightest sign of interest in any move toward a negotiation. Quite the contrary, the troops' instructions were very clear: to fight until the last man. That hopeless destiny was literally unfolding for the men trapped in the east, where the Russians were now keen to exact a terrible revenge for the horrors that Nazi Germany had inflicted upon their own people.

With this pincer tactic, the Red Army was able to separate East Prussia from the rest of the Reich. A major breakthrough in the eastern front came for the Soviets in mid-January, when tank divisions from the northern part of the pincer were able to advance all the way from Ostrolenka to Allenstein (today: Olsztyn) through to Frisches Haff (today: Kaliningradskiy Zaliv) on the Baltic Sea. At this point, the East Prussian province was completely cut off from the rest of the Reich. Those caught within, both military and civilians, were often slaughtered in huge numbers. Homes were burnt down, livestock was killed and eaten by the desperately hungry soldiers;

whole villages were massacred, including children and the elderly. Many inhabitants committed suicide before the arrival of the Red Army, knowing full well what awaited them. East Prussia would eventually be carved up to become part Polish, part Russian. All traces of the German culture that had existed there since the 13th Century would be extinguished forever. Meanwhile, the southern divisions of the same pincer now began to push back the Wehrmacht and move westward towards Warsaw.

Word came through in mid-February of the sudden and utter annihilation, in an Allied aerial campaign, of the famous baroque city of Dresden. Details of a series of bombing raids there, from 13th to 15th February, were carried through Germany on the air waves and in the printed press by the authorities. The destruction of the Saxon city had been devastating, as the Ministry for Propaganda announced with outrage. Indeed, the nature of the disaster was true enough: the once noble jewel of the Elbe had been reduced to smoking heaps of rubble, and tens of thousands had been killed – blasted, burnt, choked. Many of these were simple citizens or refugees stopping off to escape from the onslaught of the Red Army in the east. Nevertheless, Goebbels ministry went on to play down Dresden's true military and logistic role in the war, so as to emphasize an attack on "an innocent and beautiful city on the river"; and multiplied the true death toll to the power of ten. It was on the one side an enormous psychological blow to the Germans, but the attack was also used to boost morale in the final months and to encourage resistance among the population against the "cruel barbarians" that were invading their country.

This bombing had formed part of a strategy of increased aerial assaults in the eastern side of Germany in order to aid the advance of the Red Army, which was beginning to falter; a renewal of its previous momentum was greatly desired and required by the Allies. By late February then, whole flanks of the Soviets had moved on with ever greater agility, taking Posen, surrounding Breslau and Danzig, reaching as far up as Stettin, and penetrating deep into the Brandenburg hinterland, getting dangerously close to Berlin.

In the meantime, Gisela made sure that Inge's young boys were kept well away from sources of news as best she could, forbidding them to approach newspaper stands, censoring the radio stations they heard, hurriedly changing the subject with glowering eyes on two occasions when those around her unwittingly brought up the subject. She had a hunch that certainly Adolf or Joseph may well have picked up tidbits of information in the wake of the Dresden attack that they might connect to their mother's demise in Hamburg on that fatal night. She wished to, and was able to, smother all talk of bomb blasts and streets on fire, so as not to further traumatize them.

During February, the Allied offensive picked up a strong momentum in the Rhineland area on its march through western Germany. Cologne became a city on the front. Interior Minister and SS-chief Heinrich Himmler had decreed the order throughout the Reich that no white flags nor any other indications of surrender were to be utilized by the civilian population, with the threat of death for those that did not comply. Posters stating, "*Kampf bis zum Sieg!*" (Fight until the Victory!) or "*Mit dem Führer bis zum Sieg!*" (With the Führer until the Victory!) were stuck to the street walls. Goebbels gave a radio broadcast, full of nostalgic references to his hometown on the Rhine, imploring the people of Cologne to give their very best, their all, to defend the *Heimat* against the Anglo-American aggressors: "with bloody hands and to their last breath, then this fortress must withstand the invasion - the enemy must under no circumstances be allowed to occupy German soil."

The population had dropped during four years of heavy aerial bombing from just under 800,000 to just over 100,000. Most of the city centre lay in ruins but the resistance continued. A shoddy crowd of men was randomly cobbled together, mostly consisting of scattered soldiers, auxiliary personnel from the Wehrmacht, marines, old men, and adolescents forming the *Volksturm* (people's storm), plus some young lads from the Hitler Youth; bearing a few old weapons and *Panzerfausts*, all were furiously and pathetically thrown at the US 1st Army. The fanatical members were generally killed in action, while the more skeptical ones slunk off home and so survived the war.

Working their way rapidly from the edge of Cologne, the Americans had reached the central cathedral and western side of the city in a matter of days. Half the city was taken and there was an impromptu victory march, with waving of the US flag and the rousing sound of a brass group playing the *Star-Spangled Banner*. Once reinforcements had arrived in the following couple of weeks, the Rhine was crossed and the eastern side of the city area also taken. Some didn't even notice as the front swept through their neighbourhood, they were so occupied with basic survival. Water became a precarious resource, only available for a few hours a day as roughly hewn carts came into the city areas with large metal containers for the residents to fill up their buckets. Food supplies broke down and the locals looted warehouses and stockyards by the port; men and women were seen lugging away sacks and steering stacked up box carts. People became accustomed to bartering and black markets.

Meanwhile, far over on the eastern front most of Hungary, including Budapest, was taken during March. The German attempts to regroup and regain ground there were proving fruitless. The last, worn-out Wehrmacht battalions were thrown into battle with bitter stubbornness and the hope of one final offensive spurt that could make the difference. It was naturally all in vain. The German army was tricked into attempting to reoccupy western Hungary and, once there, was swiftly absorbed and neutralized, leaving a badly weakened eastern front. The Red Army swept on unhindered through eastern Austria and by early April had taken Vienna, together with Bratislava and most of Slovakia.

By April, the Allied troops had fully encircled and taken the Ruhr area in western Germany, the whole of the once loudly throbbing industrial heart of the Reich. The Allies were able to continue on almost uncontested, reaching the Elbe river by mid-April. British troops were poised to take Soltau and Celle, the Americans were within reach of Hannover and Hildesheim. By this point, most of the German troops defending western Germany had already been encircled in the Ruhr area, between Cologne and Essen. They were overpowered and thus the western front collapsed.

One of the US soldiers fighting in the Ruhr area was none other than Isschar Beim; the man who seven years back had married Felice on that happy spring day in the synagogue in Lüneburg, a building that now no longer existed. Isschar had joined the US army in 1943 and, in part thanks to his natural aptitude as a military thinker, in part thanks to his linguistic skills as a native German speaker, had risen to the rank of Sergeant in those many months in which he had formed part of the Allied invading force fighting Nazi Germany. By April, he was commanding a unit in the 15th Army that was involved in the taking of a wide area of the west, a two-week battle called the Ruhr Pocket. His talent in the military field, including an unflinching valour even in the face of death, had lain undetected in his youth and early adulthood, when all had liked him but few had held him in high esteem; such are the circumstances that can lead to the later flowering and discovery of hidden gifts. Upon returning back home to New York City after the war, there would be no-one, not even among his own direct relatives, who showered so much constant and vociferous praise on Isschar as his father-in-law Adam Wunderlich, who had once held a much more modest opinion concerning his daughter's marital choice.

In Lüneburg, the news was received on the radio that Hildesheim had been taken by the steady stream of Allied troops, after having been devastated by an aerial attack only a few weeks previously, its elegant inner city blasted to wreckage. Reports came through of how the population, still dazed from the level of destruction, watched apathetically as tanks and jeeps crowded with Americans swept through the dead streets and past the heaps of rubble.

By April 10th, the regional hub and major city of Hannover had also been captured. Crowds arose, mostly women in drab coats and older men, to line the Limmerstraße, still stunningly intact among the rest of the ghost-town of empty ruins and half-destroyed houses, to greet the surging line of American military. White hankerchieves wafted in the air, war-weary faces gazed happily at the entering invaders, words were exchanged; some soldiers even took photos, threw chewing gum and cigarettes into the crowd. The mood was jovial until a couple of shots rang out from somewhere. The German civilians hastily retreated into the ruins from which they had emerged, while the American military machine resumed its march and the tanks droned on through the otherwise silent city. A small pocket of resistance fought it out to the north of Hannover but, resisting dogmatic and insistent instructions from Berlin, the *Kampfkommandant* (battle chief) General Loehning recognized the futility of the situation and ordered his troops to put a stop to the defence the city and surrender. They were quickly rounded up and the tanks rolled on eastwards to Lehrte, Peine, Braunschweig, each town gobbled up.

This was the template that was repeated all through the broken nation, as the shadow of the Allied troops spread across the map; the American, British, and French troops taking the western part of the country, the Soviets the eastern side. For a very few - those who still lived, breathed, and existed for the Reich - it was like a sinister solar eclipse that gradually eats up the sun. For most of the population, it was the growing light of a new dawn.

The British army was by now reaching across through northern Germany, capturing Oldenburg and Bremen. The Americans rolled on eastwards in the direction of Berlin, although the capital looked to be soon felled by the encircling Soviet forces there. The complete dissolution of the Reich was nearly complete.

At this historic junction, Corinna's sister Hertha arrived one evening at the beginning of April out of nowhere. The day she knocked on the door at the entrance of the Gasthaus, she seemed to have dropped straight out of the sky, complete with horse and ramshackle cart and a ragged bunch of followers. It was dusk and Gisela pushed her head out of a window on the first floor in irritation, looked down and prepared to shout at the disturbance; then let her chin fall in astonishment at the sight of her bedraggled but widely grinning aunt.

The family found to their joyful amazement that she had crossed a huge expanse of the country, all with the Red Army in hot pursuit: through storms and blizzards on an old cart pulled by an older nag, now standing among a mass of battered luggage and strange faces. The sight was surreal in a way that only war can make a family reunion so special. She came across as having lost none of her old character, still standing proud and erect as Corinna had always remembered her. Apart from Hertha herself, the small silent huddled group of survivors consisted of her daughter Bärbel, four young children aged between three and twelve, and three adults - two women and a man. One of the children clung close to Bärbel's skirt and was introduced to everyone as little Max, Hertha's grandson and pride and joy.

It was near to a miracle that they had made it through, Hertha said as they were bustled inside by Gisela and Corinna, who immediately set about preparing food for them all. Corinna had quietly feared the worst, given all the horror tales that never ceased to come through from the east of the Reich. She was therefore beside herself with happiness and also eager to help accommodate the other numerous newly arrived guests. The children in particular, who all looked as if they had been dragged through hell a few times, caught her heart. They had the dulled eyes of endurance, as opposed to the sparkling ones of children who only know play and peace.

Gisela's extended family of children - with the exception of Katrina, who was out at the time - was called down from their rooms upstairs to greet the newcomers. They also noticed the run-down state of these newly arrived children and saw themselves as fortunate in comparison. Joseph asked in infantile naivety who they all were; but no-one seemed capable of giving a response to such an apparently simple but sadly complicated question. Adolf felt immediately suspicious of the crowd and hoped that none of them would be expecting to sleep in his bed.

It had been a stroke of unimaginable luck, one that defied reality, said Hertha as she was presented to the children and kissed the tops of their heads. *Großtante* (Great Aunt) Hertha became her name. She repeated again and again that evening, in a clear state of shock, that she could hardly believe that they had made it safely out of the east. Now at home with family around her, even though many of them she did not personally know, she could only talk of her amazement at their good fortune; the others who had come with her, wary among strangers, said next to nothing.

That is, with the sole exception of the youngest child, the blonde cherubic Helga. She had a besmirched face but with a determinedly merry expression, was wearing a dirty purple dress that stank notably of urine. Her right arm was badly scarred with burn marks and she had become uncontrollably incontinent. She babbled details in an incoherent narrative mess which only her companions of route could comprehend.

Hertha nodded and her eyes glazed whenever the little girl burst into one of her brief but lively staccatos of speech.

Chapter 33

Hertha and her companions arrived on the evening of 12th April without warning. All eight of them - cold, hungry, exhausted, and still frightened - were promptly fed, and beds at the Gasthaus were eventually found for all. They gulped down some soup that Gisela and Corinna had rushed up, both having to tell their unexpected new guests – even Hertha at her age - not to eat it so quickly or they would burn their mouths. Baths were poured on all floors, while Hertha assured them that none of them had nits. Later on, Hertha, Bärbel, and Max were taken upstairs to the largest bedroom on the second floor. The others were put in makeshift beds or simply mattresses on other floors of the Gasthaus: the Schwarz boys in the largest room on the first floor with Erich; Grit Vögler and Helga in the next room with Katrina; and Fabian Berg on the floor beside Adolf and his brothers. Gisela took an instant mistrust towards Grit and already looked forward to the opportunity of finding her an alternative place to stay as soon as possible.

The following day a more lucid Hertha spent some hours conversing with Gisela and Corinna, with the back door open while the children played in the yard. Occasionally Gisela would tire of the din and shout at them, sending most of the group scuttling out into the street. Adolf and Joseph stayed, fascinated by the adults' tales and careful to amuse themselves quietly so as not attract *Tante* Gisela's attention. They had a small collection of toys – little metal figures of soldiers, tanks, and planes - and discreetly occupied themselves in the corner with them.

Hertha ultimately had nerves of steel and, after one night of normal rest, was already beginning to recuperate her old self. She was back in good spirits, loquacious and nattering away with the typically East Prussian rolled 'r's that she had acquired in her many years there. She was well up-to-date with news from the family in Lüneburg, having regularly exchanged letters with her sister throughout the last years. She knew the basic details of the family events during the war (Corinna had not gone into great detail in her correspondence, rightfully fearing her letters might be censored), including the death of her niece Inge and the probable death of Inge's husband Horst. She had spent the whole morning talking with Corinna about Inge and consoling her sister, who seemed to have now arrived in her mourning at a stage of acceptance.

"It cut poor Georg to the quick," said Corinna. "It was terrible for all of us, but I think it hit him hardest of all. He did love her so. The last of his grey hairs went white overnight, and he has lost a lot of weight since then. All the spark just went out of him, and then there was the stroke too. He does try to be a bit merry when the grandchildren are around, for their sake, but then you can see that deep sadness in his eyes. Anyway, they wear him out with their noise."

Hertha nodded. "Poor Inge, going off to Hamburg like that, just to help out with the war effort."

Gisela was about to provide her aunt with more relevant information concerning Inge when she caught a meaningful look from her mother that was simultaneously grazing the two boys on the floor. They had raised their heads upon hearing their parents' names mentioned amongst the other casualties and were listening intently. Surprised at how invisible the mites could become to her, Gisela was about to shoo them off to join the other children outside. Hertha placed a hand on her niece's wrist and said, "It's so pleasant to see children like that, playing happily and carefree. Let them be for now. We can talk about their parents in peace another day." There followed some general chat about the overall state of the collapsing Reich, as gleaned from the news, and Corinna told of the increasing difficulty in finding adequate food amidst heavy rationing.

Adolf and Joseph, who had returned to the toys on the floor once the adults had begun discussing politics and food, were used to listening to these tales of death with a strange naturality. It was such a widespread phenomenon, the dead and the disappeared, that it seemed the most natural and inevitable part of life. Their crude concept of mortality was already being formed in these infant years. It seemed to them to correspond to a game in which one may be lucky and get through to the next round, or simply be unlucky and fall by the wayside. Adolf felt that death was an entity, humanoid in form like the sinister *Batzemann* that appeared out of the shadows to children who were bad. Death walked all through Germany, every night from one side of the Reich to the other; when the moment was decided, it would make off with people who were taken far away and never came back. That was what seemed to have happened to his mother - he had concluded, though there was no evidence of the fact - and he suspected that the adults were hiding from him the fact that this had been his father's fate too. He formed his three soldiers around the tank in a position that he felt would best counteract the montage that his brother was organizing. When both were finished, the soldiers could hit each other, the tanks collide, and battles would be decided. Normally they liked to shout when playing war, but this time the knocks were soft and the combat noiseless.

Hertha related – at the request of the other women - Rudolf's short but intense and painful last days in the summer and early autumn of the previous year. She stated how she was almost thankful that he hadn't lived to see the final tragedy of their expulsion from a part of the world where his family had laid roots that stretched back centuries. It was almost a blessing he never got to experience that, she affirmed with a voice that almost broke but then stayed firm, and her sister and niece nodded in silent acquiescence. It was important for her to speak, they sensed: to tell and communicate with others, as well as to solidify her experiences in words so that they ceased to be merely surreal notions or nightmarish memories, but instead acquired a factual substance.

"Rudolf was already consuming large amounts of morphine as soon as he got the diagnosis. I think, not just for the physical pain, although that came later on too, but also the mental relief. Our apothecary was very helpful and so I was able to obtain as much as he wanted. I recall how his brother Werner came to visit once, early on during the illness, and he saw all the syringes and phials lying on a tray beside him. Normally people would be shocked to find out that a relative had become a morphine addict. But naturally he just shrugged. What else was there to do? I sold a lot of things in those last months to pay for it. Nearly all the furniture upstairs, some paintings we had, most of my jewelry. I am glad I did now, of course - it made leaving the house and farm behind so much easier when the moment came. In fact, I wish I could have sold it all off."

Sitting at the table, washed and well-rested and well-fed, and still amazed at her own survival, Hertha was feeling enormously comforted by the presence of her sister and niece. Also, by the quiet droning sound outside the Gasthaus of sporadic traffic, the voices of her family speaking calmly and with an easy tone, the distant sounds of the children playing in the yard. Even the birdsong caught her ear and seemed here so serene. She had reached her goal and found an inner peace, and her perception corresponded accordingly. Her return to Lüneburg, the hometown of her childhood and the familiar family faces, had strengthened her spirit in a matter of hours. She no longer felt desperate and helpless, as she had done in the months following Rudolf's death; whether alone at home with her taciturn daughter or on the desperate *Treck* fleeing westwards away from the grinding Red Army. She had made it through to a new stage in life, though she still found it absurd to think how her home in Heilingelinde was gone and would now only exist in recollections.

Like almost everyone in the war years they normally drank *Ersatzkaffee* (coffee replacement) at the Gasthaus, in their case a local rustic brew made from chicory and with a distinctive aftertaste that Gisela found horribly bitter and had never got accustomed to. However, they had hoarded a small amount of real coffee from ground beans, and Gisela prepared it for this special occasion and poured it out for the three of them as if it were a fine vintage wine. There was naturally no cake these days but Gisela had managed to wrangle a whole extra loaf of stodgy *Graubrot* (grey bread), made from mixed wholemeal flour with bean flour plus barley and mashed sweetcorn, from the local baker that morning. It was a war-time solution to the bread shortage - heavy and dry, like eating a block of stucco plaster; but for Hertha, still famished from her journey, nothing in the world had ever been so tasty and wholesome.

It always astonished Corinna how her daughter managed to get hold off such generous amounts of food. Some mornings she would set out with her tatty little *Lebensmittelkarten* (food ration cards) in her handbag, such as the red one for bread which by this point in the war was only allowing each person 1,700 grammes per week, and yet almost always return home with much more. Today she also produced a block of fresh butter from the kitchen, modest but clearly well over the permitted amount, and was smearing it generously over the slices.

As Gisela fussed over the women with food and drink, Hertha told them her tale. "The end came quickly, so incredibly quickly. And yet most of us knew that it was going to happen. We had known for months, many months, that it would eventually have to happen.

There came the *Räumungsbefehl* (order to evacuate) - finally! Within two days we were packed and gone. It was in the very early morning. We drank our coffee and ate some *Bratkartoffeln* and just went. We left the dirty dishes on the table and did not bother to close the door. It was full moon and Fabian held a paraffin lamp with his one arm while Bärbel and I packed the last items as best they would fit. We put saddlebags on the horses with hay and oats for them, and I put the final little wooden box - with bandages, alcohol, penknife, scissors, and equipment to stitch up wounds – on top of the luggage. Plus a little bag of pears from last summer, so as to at least sweeten the beginning of the journey.

Bärbel and Max sat in the back, while I sat with Fabian – the middle son of the Bergs, he was injured in battle a few years back – in the front of the cart. We trotted off, and the road was icy and mirrored the moonlight. We joined up with the others from our part of town, with the *Treckenführer* (leader of the trek) in front. It started off quite organized but as the days went by, and more and more groups converged onto the main roads, it descended into chaos. It had already become an eternity for Bärbel and Max and we were still within East Prussia. For days and days, we were all trudging along, horses and people, only thinking to head westwards. The line that formed from this endless and shambling line of people just grew and grew. More families, all fleeing too, joined up with the convoy. We were another typical little family among many, wrapped up in rough winter clothing: an old woman with her daughter and little grandson, and a young one-armed man, taking turns to hold the reigns as the horse pulled us along the route. It was pathetic sight but that was the only way out. You know, I didn't see a single motor vehicle in the convoys - the Wehrmacht had commissioned them all.

Such a frightening experience too, devoid of any security, and horrifically unpredictable. But we knew that the Red Army was making its advance behind us, and the terror produced by that thought alone kept us moving briskly. Most of the people we talked to were from East Prussia like us; all mixed – townsfolk with trades and professions, small-holders from villages, foreign workers, foresters and farm workers, even wealthy people from the big estates out there. Some were coming from as far away as Insterburg or Gumbinnen, or from the deep interior to the east of the province. Even from right up north in the Memelland and Lithuania. I could barely imagine the journeys that they must have undertaken, and still had so far to go. Wherever the front had become thin and fragile, the Soviets were breaking through, and all the towns and estates out there were being evacuated. But what the authorities were finally doing was all too little and much, much too late. Sometimes we saw young soldiers in uniform cycling by on the same route as the *Trecks*. They were evacuating too, or simply deserting if there was no official order as such. We heard that the high-ranked officers had appropriated all the motorized vehicles for themselves and sped off as quickly as possible, leaving the lower ranks and foot soldiers to fend for themselves and grab whatever they could. It was tragic, pathetic even, but this is how a war ends. This is how a country disintegrates.

Babies and young children died frequently, as did the elderly. They were just too weak for that kind of expedition. But they were buried quickly and quietly, away from the road. If you kept yourself to yourself, you wouldn't even have known. There were never any mourning or tears, certainly no funerals, just grim silence for a moment and then the rest of the family went on their way. But in the case of the tired or injured members, the families still rallied round and kept each other going as best they could. I saw one old woman, visibly at the end, settle down in the snow to die. She insisted on staying there, telling the others she was a burden and for them to continue on without her. But after some sharp words with her family, they shuffled her back to the *Treck* and squeezed her in between some sacks onto one of the wagons. I have to say, I never saw family members left behind by the *Trekker* groups. Even in the most hopeless cases, they did their best. Later on, with those who had died, you saw more and more corpses being laid under the snow on the way.

Eventually we had the Nogat and Weichsel rivers behind us and were moving south of Danzig and on towards Pommern. I remember one point in particular; it must have been as we were passing through that Polish corridor area, where the locals did not speak any German and it was difficult to communicate with them. One afternoon we were moving along a main asphalted road. We had gone up a slight hill and there at the top, you could see down both sides, to the east and the west. It was an incredible but terrifying view. You could not see the asphalt any longer; it was just a long line of people, horses, wagons and little carriages, handcarts and pushcarts, all sorts. As far as the eye could see just this endless line of ragged people lumbering forward. They looked so miserable and said next to nothing so you could clearly hear the sound of cartwheels squeaking round.

The lines just grew and grew with ever more people the further we went. New lines of *Treckers* were incessantly coming in from sideroads, converging into the main trail, blocking up the crossroads and the highway ahead. The more rapidly the Soviets advanced, the more the towns were getting their official instructions to evacuate. The organization was such a mess, mainly because the orders to leave were coming through so late. Up to that point people could still be arrested, even shot on the spot, for defeatism; and no-one dared question the authorities. Eventually the official position was collapsing in the face of the inevitable, and people were suddenly told to get out, so more groups of *Trecks* were leaving town and joining up. Sometimes with the Soviets breathing down their necks.

At one point we were just twenty or thirty kilometres from the town of Belgard in Hinterpommern, and the whole *Treck* came to a halt. Up ahead the road was blocked with the masses evacuating and joining up. Nothing moved for hours. There was nowhere to go and nothing to do except wait for the jam to clear. During the *Trecks* you could never try to bypass a jam through the surrounding meadows, because either the snowdrifts were too high, or if it had rained, they were mud-traps. So, we all stayed on the road, moved up a short distance. Then it stopped again, then it might pick up but at barely two or three kilometres an hour, then stop again and this was how it went on continually. Sometimes these military supply columns from the Wehrmacht, motorcades of vehicles carrying machine guns and ammunition, would push through. The soldiers insisted that we made way for them, and this complicated the trail immensely. Later on, tanks would push their way through as well. They just drove the others to the side without mercy. I saw people's carts and wagons fall over or crash into the ditches and break apart.

After we passed Belgard the temperature plummeted and the trail became one big icy sheet, like crossing a mirror. The horses were slipping on the ice and the wagons kept shifting round at a sharp angle and getting stuck. My hands were sore and bleeding from so much pulling on the reins. Although little Max spent the whole time inside the shelter of the wagon, I was so worried about him getting frostbite or not being able to withstand the cold and the hunger. But he never complained. Nobody said anything really, not the other treckers either; with time we barely spoke among ourselves. Sometimes you saw dead bodies on the side of the road. People no longer had the strength nor the time, or simply couldn't bury them in the hard frozen ground.

There were terrible blizzards, even though it seemed too cold for storms. The wind would whip up all the snow so that, even though there was no snow actually falling, you could barely see ahead. Some unfortunate families had the rooftops of their wagons blown away and suddenly they and all their belongings were exposed to the wind and snow. It lashed against our coats and it made it difficult to move forward but there was obviously no choice but to persevere on, whatever the conditions. It was in these moments that we were so grateful for our warm clothes. We all had thick coats and fur caps. Plus, Bärbel had brought her sewing kit with needles and lots of thread, wool and patches, all in a little red leather bag of hers, and that became an essential part of our equipment. She was always quiet and distant, deep in her thoughts and so melancholy, but at least she could make good use of the time by darning up gloves and sewing up ripped trousers. She helped out other *Treckers* by darning gloves in exchange for food. Gloves were essential for survival out there in those temperatures. If they became worn down too thin, you soon found yourself in difficulty. It is hard to imagine what frostbite can do to a person's limbs.

Along the route there reigned a heavy silence and we became silent among ourselves, too. If anyone did speak up, it was to obtain more information about what was going on around them. They often ended up wishing they hadn't. I heard how nearly all the large estates and farms in East Prussia and Pomerania had been abandoned, with the owners fleeing as fast as they could. I spoke to someone who had come all the way down from Georgenburg and she said that at one of the houses where they stopped to look for food and water, they saw some coffee cups were still standing around on the table, half-full. The farms and houses had been evacuated that quickly! In those places where some people were still holding out, such as the more elderly who wouldn't have managed the journey outward, it was obviously plain suicide. You knew the Red Army was always behind you. You thought about that all the time, even dreamt about it in the little sleep you got. It was like a ferocious spirit, pushing you on.

Once we heard this heavy shelling. I thought it was thunder at first, and someone said that the Soviets were already in so-and-so, they shouted out the name of the place but I can't remember it now. But I do remember calculating from a signpost I had previously seen that they must have been only five to six kilometres behind us! We later heard the sound of heavy fighting from the Wehrmacht holding them back and so we were able to put more distance in between us and them. But if you were ever lacking in energy, that thought gave you all the adrenalin you needed to move on.

All this went on for weeks and weeks. It seemed to be endless. We rested wherever we could, slept a few hours, moved on. Our food supply was all gone by then and we were living on a small amount of *Grießbrei* (semolina porridge) each day, usually cold and hard. About fifty kilometres after Belgard, in Pomerania, we were hit by another strong blizzard and it was at this point that we picked up two children, the little Christian and Michael you saw when we first arrived. Their surname is Schwarz. They had become separated from their group in the storm. We asked them about the others, and it seems this group consisted of around a dozen children, all being led by a teacher and a school director and his wife. These two Schwarz children were originally from Berlin. They had lost both parents in a bombing raid and had been evacuated from the capital to a school in the Pomerania countryside along with other orphans. This group was now planning to cross the Oder further south and find shelter with other families they knew in Dresden. And these two poor children had got split up from the group, in all that flying snow and howling wind, and just couldn't find them. So, they sought protection from us. We had almost no food left but of course, who would turn away two little orphans in the snow?

We had gone about ten kilometres further when Fabian spied a farmyard in the distance, so we left the trail to see if there was any food to be begged or perhaps something left behind by others. We were so hungry - we had to find something to eat, somehow. And we were in luck! The owner and his wife came to the door when we got closer and were calling out, they even invited us in. I think they saw we had three little children and took pity on us. We entered and passed through a corridor into the main room in the house, already hearing voices ahead, and ended up in a room full of people - refugees and *Treckers* like us. The table was laden with bread and other food; they were just about to eat the evening meal. They were farmers and devout Christians and had decided to do everything possible to help those escaping and in need, if just for one night for each group of travellers. Our luck was so perfect. There were large candles all along the table; that was all they had as the electric light had been gone for over a week. The owner asked for silence while he led the prayer. There was a resounding "Amen!" from everyone at the end and then we could eat. We had soup, and bread with butter, such rich and tasty butter. There were big pieces of potato and carrot in the soup and even some little chunks of beef, too. And then cheese! Imagine that. A rich creamy cheese, it was. Then the wife opened up a big pot of jam she had stored away and all the children went mad eating that jam on their bread. The couple told us later that they were not leaving, no matter what. I think that was also a reason why they were happy to share their stock of food with *Treckers*. They knew in the end the Russians would arrive and take it all anyway. I understood their attitude. They said they just wanted to stay there to the end, where they had always lived, come what may. That made sense to us too as they must have been in their late sixties, perhaps seventies. How do you uproot yourself at that age and just head off into the night? And the chances of them surviving were far from assured. In fact, they were slim.

They told us some terrible stories. Not to frighten us, just to warn us of possible hazards. They had horses on the farm, to help out with the ploughing and other jobs. And one night they had given shelter to a woman who had originally fled all the way from a farm near Fischhausen, by Königsberg, with four other families from her town, including two of her cousins. Now she was on her own, she said, and they asked what had happened to the others, but she did not want to talk about it. The next day, she went for a walk round the farm and as soon as she set eyes on the horses, she started to sob and sob - but wild and uncontrollably, and for a long while. She came back to the farmhouse with red eyes, still snuffling, and they asked her what was wrong. So she explained what had happened to the group. Back in Fischhausen they had received the *Räumungsbefehl* - order to evacuate; suddenly, out of the blue, like everywhere. It was bitter cold, around -20°C, and the quickest route was over the Haff to the south, which was solidly frozen over. Or at least it seemed to be. So they had started to cross the ice on the lagoon with their horse-carts, when there came a low-flying plane attack, from the Russians. They were all fleeing in panic and rushing along as fast as they could. The ice began to crack and break and in no time the carts and horses and people were all slipping and sliding into the water. Plus the plane continued diving and shooting at them. Between the planes and the breaking ice, in the end only her and a boy of about sixteen survived and got to the other side. But he had got shot in the shoulder and died the next day, what with the fresh wound and the frost. She could not carry the body so she buried it there as best she could and continued on alone. She said all she could hear in her head for days was that sound of the horses screeching out from the water, when they fell in with the carts and the refugees. There was a lot of noise, with people screaming and the aircraft diving and shooting, but she had never heard such a terrible sound in all her life as the terror of those poor animals. It still haunted her, she said, as she had always loved horses so much. Everyone has their weak point and so it must have been a particularly traumatic experience for her; but then again all the stories we heard were shocking and in the end we did not talk to people much along the route. Unless it was to discuss something important or make plans according to information, but not in a companionable manner. I began to comprehend why the *Trecks* were so silent when everyone was moving along together.

That night on the farm we went to sleep with full stomachs. Mine was so full it ached and ached, but I didn't care! The farming couple had some space for us to sleep, in the cowshed among the straw. It was heavenly, the first night under a roof in so long. So warm and comfortable.

The next morning, we set off early and after about a day and a half we were not far from the Stettiner Lagoon when we heard this loud firing behind us. Heavy artillery by the sound of it. It seemed so close it was terrifying. We asked a group near us what was going on and they replied that there were not just the advancing Red Army troops and tanks to watch out for, but also the *Jabos* (Soviet fighter-bomber planes). They were launching a series of attacks on the *Trecks*, even though they knew we were just civilians escaping. I recalled the story of the woman with the horses when I heard that.

So you can see, it was important to choose the right route. Others were heading south-west, hoping to cross the Oder and then head in the direction of Stettin, ultimately going through Schwedt and then on towards Berlin, or even further west. But I personally did not consider that a sensible option, especially passing through Stettin. To move further inland might well have led us into a closing pincer trap. I was sure that the Red Army, once they had got as far as Brandenburg, would try to encircle the area around Berlin as fast as possible. So, along with some others, we opted instead to leave the main trail and move up towards the Baltic coast and head for Swinemünde. Then along the Usedom and Wollin islands. I imagined there might still be bridges intact up there, which there were, so we could cross more easily at that point, rather than try to cross the Oder which must have been near impossible by that stage.

But when we arrived in Swinemünde, it was like a nightmare. It was just a charred empty skeleton of a city that was left. It had been very heavily bombed, we found out, only one week before. By the Americans this time, the survivors seemed to think, judging from the type of planes. Those that were still there, were dazed. So many had died and many had fled after that too. Just ruins and rubble everywhere. There had been thousands killed, we heard, because it was packed full of refugees; and when the bombers suddenly came at night, many of them got lost in the streets and did not know where to run to. It was a disaster. There were still many dead that had not even been buried. We came across some Wehrmacht assistants and the odd person from the *Rotes Kreuz* (German Red Cross) who were trying to help out and take care of the injured. Of course, they were completely overwhelmed by the task. Still, we managed to get some food from them. We spent a single night in one of the burnt-out apartment blocks, the best one in a whole street of ruins. But we could hardly sleep. There were rats everywhere, squeaking all night long. And these huge cockroaches, so many, and the smell of rotting… oh, it was dreadful there. We headed off at dawn even though we were dizzy from hardly having slept in days.

We decided we would then continue on through *Vorpommern* (Hither Pomerania). That route was quiet, all things considered. And because they were so few *Trekkers* up there in the north, we could move along more quickly and make good progress. On one day we actually managed to put over sixty kilometres behind us, which lifted our spirits. It was biting cold, but we weren't attacked by the Russian *Tiefflieger* (strafers, low-flying aircraft) which had been my main worry. Luckily there was a thick grey cloud covering at that time. I learnt from another *Trekker* how the Russians do not bother flying over if it is very cloudy, which was a huge relief. But I later heard how many convoys were attacked by planes. They had to jump into muddy ditches at the side of the road and duck as quickly as they could when they heard the droning noise approaching. The pilots were very cruel by all accounts. They would chase repeatedly after targets, especially women running with children, and riddle the whole area of ground with bullets trying to hit them. But that was something our own pilots had done long before to the enemy as well, that much I knew of as well. Hatred breeds more hatred. These things always come back to haunt you.

I think it was because we managed to keep away from the main German troop and civilian movements, that it helped us avoid the

Russians too, whether on land or from the air. In war there is no safety in numbers. Worse still, you become a target that way!

We went on for a couple of days and ended up in a village by Jarmen. Poor Fabian was on the point of becoming delirious by then. He was very correct and proper and always let the children sit in the cart while he walked beside, he never took turns with them. The only times he sat in the cart for a stretch were when he was exhausted or sick, and even then I had to insist. Plus, he let the others eat first, so he ended up very undernourished. When we first entered the village, he saw a woman sitting on a wall, casually eating a pear, and he nearly had a nervous breakdown. Poor thing, all jabbering and shaking and with just his one hand left clutching his face. But we found shelter with a family and they fed us too, all six of us. The children gulped the food down like little birds. But it wasn't until we had finally reached Güstrow, five days after Usedom, that I started to think that we really could get through this whole ordeal safe and sound after all.

It was on the outskirts of Güstrow that we went round to a nearby village to see if we could find a little food and some water and somewhere to spend the night, a barn or a shed. There we came across Frau Vögler and little Helga. They had been living in Oranienburg. I think her husband was in the SS and had held a high position at the KZ there, in Sachsenhausen. She did not talk much about him, except to say that he was killed in an air-raid when he was visiting the Heinkel factory there. She had then fled to the north to stay with his family and take his last possessions to them. But they weren't getting on well and she was desperate to leave and take the girl with her. That night we all sang *Auf der Heide blüht ein kleines Blümelein*, to keep the children's spirits up. Helga already knew all the words by heart, the little angel, and we sensed they ought to come with us too."

"She has those burn marks on her arm," Corinna commented. "That must have been a terrible experience."

"She can't control herself either," Gisela added. "She wets herself all the time. And the bed, you should see how she left the bed this morning. Although she seems to have behaved herself a little better this morning - I hope it keeps up."

"I know, I know, the girl is very upset," said Hertha. "It is not surprising, she is so delicate and so much has happened to her. To think what a little girl of six must have seen already. I do not even know how she came to get those burn marks, I did not want to ask. I suppose her mother will tell me in due time. Where is she, by the way?"

"She has gone off with the girl to see if she can find some writing paper and an envelope. She wants to write a last letter to her late husband's parents, telling them that they are here in Lüneburg and plan to stay," said Gisela, shrugging her shoulders in incomprehension.

"You know, she was a great help to us in the final part of the trip. We were so exhausted, so worn out and dirty. I told her where we were heading to, and said she and the girl could come along too if they thought it a good idea. She was overjoyed and jumped at the chance. Anything to get away from the husband's parents, I thought. She said that in return she was going to sell her wedding ring to a local tradesman and she did just that, the day after we arrived. We stayed in a back room in the farmhouse and the next evening she told us it was all fixed and we could go. Good quality gold, and there was a gold bracelet that she had sold, too. So, she exchanged all that for food and soap and other basics, and she managed to get some fresh clothes. Imagine that, even fresh underwear! It was wonderful! - I began to feel like a person again. Also, she managed to get hold of some little shoes for the children, which was a blessing as the clumps they had on their feet had been worn and scuffed to scraps. Plus some cream to treat our chapped skin, which was hurting so much. She bought fresh carrots and cabbages for the horse as he had become so thin. With all that, we were able to set off again. That was six days ago now, nearly a week. Even if the younger ones had to take more turns walking by the wagon, as there were two extra members to our crew. Of course it did not bother them at all as we were all so grateful for the soap and clothes alone! And we could move so much quicker without having to beg for food. All in all, it was just the boost we needed. I have to admit I was starting to get to the end of my tether and I did not know if I had the energy for the final spurt. It had been a long and frightening journey for a woman of my age! So anyway, that was all thanks to Frau Vögler.

I told them we did not have far to go now to get to Lüneburg, and also I felt we had left the Red Army behind us for good. We were tramping along roads and down hills but joyful just to be alive and have food in our bellies. I was so thankful how everything had turned out.

And there you have it - the eight of us: myself, Bärbel and Max, plus Fabian and the two Schwarz boys, and Frau Vögler and Helga. I still cannot believe our luck at getting out."

Corinna grinned wide and said, "Well, you are all safe here now," held her sister's arm tight.

"I simply cannot believe it is all over and we got out," said Hertha, still repeating her leitmotiv. "It must have been a miracle."

"Perhaps. It certainly seems like a miracle that the war is over," said Corinna, dropping her voice low to almost a whisper for the last phrase.

"It is not over yet, Mama, but I think it soon will be," said Gisela, with an equally hushed voice. She felt that her husband, a former soldier now lying upstairs in a state of permanent nervous breakdown, was symbolic of what the Wehrmacht currently had at its disposal for the defence of the town against the approaching invader. For her, the sooner it finished and the city was taken, the better. Once the moment was ripe, the swastikas were all coming down and the Führer's portrait would be ripped to a hundred shreds. A painting of bucolic charm, with horses pulling ploughs in a field of harvested wheat, was ready and waiting in the cellar, and was already planned by Gisela to take its place in the picture frame. She was getting on well with her preparations for the aftermath; the actual end of the war was an annoying final detail waiting to be completed.

"We were just a little worried on the way here," said Hertha, "because of the danger of strafing attacks. Are the Americans are doing that too?"

"Sometimes, yes. We never let the children go out very far, and certainly not out of town or into the areas around, just in case. They say the enemy fighter planes often fly around the industrial areas, or railways or autobahns, and attack convoys. Especially military ones, but sometimes they also dive and shoot at civilians, too. So you have to be very careful. If anyone drives here from the surrounding villages to make a delivery, they try to use back roads which are more hidden by the trees and hedges, and not the main or open ones. Also, the British are still bombing all the towns they can, one after another. Pforzheim was completely destroyed a couple of months ago, we heard on the radio. There was hardly anything left and thousands were killed in the night. There was a big air-raid here too, just five days ago. Only this time it was the Americans, during the day. They bombed the railway yards and some of the town around that area, so more to the south. Some houses in Rotes Feld got badly hit but nothing fell here in the centre." She looked over her back and then dropped her voice to a low level, almost whispering. "We are just hoping it will be over before they come back for another round."

Corinna sighed and said softly, "Finally over."

There was a sudden high-pitched scream that made the women start and leap up, until they realized on hearing giggles and light-hearted shouting that it was just part of the children's game outside. They smiled at each other and sat back down, and there was a warm silence of relief for some moments.

"You know, some terrible things happened over in the east," Hertha said eventually, darkly, then looked over at the two boys, still half-playing half-listening on the floor near them; and she said nothing more. Gisela stood up and whisked a cloth in their direction as if scattering flies. "Go on! - play outside for a bit. The fresh air will do you good." They jumped up and scuttled outside and onto the street. "They need to get out in the sun more," said Gisela with a sigh.

Though unbeknown to the women, while Adolf sauntered off in search of new playmates, Joseph crept back and listened behind the door to the women's conversation. Corinna was asking her sister what she meant.

"We heard some rumours, you know, last spring, but Rudolf said at the time that it was probably just propaganda from the Bolsheviks. And if not from them, then from someone else for whatever reason, because it couldn't be true," said Hertha. Gisela frowned with concern, but Corinna sensed that it was appropriate for her sister to continue. Some thoughts needed to be expressed if they were to be overcome. "It was late last year, when the Russians took some villages. Right far over in the north-east, although they were later beaten back by our Wehrmacht. After they had been driven out, they found the bodies that were left behind. Nearly all were of women and children. It was stated in the reports, and there were even photographs as evidence. I never saw them myself, I only heard about it all through others. There were bodies lying everywhere, all around on the streets and fields, even on dung heaps, with ripped dresses. Raped first, of course, before they were shot. Even girls as young as twelve, they said. And some of the women had been nailed to gates or barn doors, with their arms stretched out, as in the form of a crucifixion." Gisela and Corinna gasped and covered their mouths. "In another village, they found the women and children lying together in a school, but without a single gunshot wound. They had all been _beaten_ to death. Over fifty of them, lying dead together in a heap." She began to tremble and Corinna held her arm.

Following a pause, she continued. "We were so lucky to get out. To make it through." Her eyes watered and she wiped them with the back of her sleeve. "So lucky to be back home with family again." She smiled tearfully at her sister and niece, looked back at the table, studying the form of the wood.

There was a silence. "We voted for him alright," said Hertha eventually. "Of course we did. In our area, we all did. Every time. Right from the moment they first started to talk more seriously about him, and his party; what they were saying, what they stood for. We were right out there on the far-flung edge of the Reich, and he was offering us all the security in the world. He was a strong man with a mission, that was clear, and we knew that in this way there would be no more threats, not from the Poles nor the Russians nor anyone. No more insecurity. We could farm our land as we had always done, feel at ease without having to worry about some foreign presence breaking in. There would be peace and prosperity for everyone. It all made perfect sense. Even when the war broke out, it still made perfect sense."

Corinna nodded. "It always does. At first."

There was a rumble of thunder. Although it was clearly just thunder, it still caused some more edgy members of the now expanded *Gasthaus Sonnenschein* community to jump. But in that way, it was a timely reminder that the enemy was not far away. It was a matter of time until Lüneburg was also to fall.

Chapter 34

The war was over long before it was over, but there was still one central mystery for each person to unwrap and discover for themselves: namely their own personal destiny in the course of the upcoming defeat. First and foremost with regards to their ultimate survival; or not.

It had been apparent to most, both within and outside of Germany, that it was all over by mid-1944 at the latest. This was not only evident to those more perspicacious minds that had smelt an irreparable burn hole in the ambitions of the Reich following the disastrous Battle of Stalingrad, but now also to the wider masses. Now nearly a year later, by the spring of 1945, there was just the widespread sense that the inevitable, gradual sinking into failure and ignominy was the certain outcome; that it should be got over with as soon as possible. The relentless advance of the Allied forces coming in from the West and the Red Army surging in from the east meant it was merely a waiting game for the population until their town had been reached and conquered by either the one or the other. There was also a small, often ferocious and not insignificant minority, that was determined to resist until the very last man and never hand over power to the enemy unless dead; as these were more often than not the men in power, this would mean a long and protracted defeat in which only a minority of the population dared to outwardly express their hopes for a swift conquest. Even though for many ordinary Germans, defeat was seen as more than just surrender to the enemy, but rather a yearned release from the tyranny of the Nazis.

There was little to do now except to prepare oneself as best one could for this end phase, and so to make it through this long conflict to a safe shore on the other side. Survival was not to be taken for granted, by anyone. The Allied aerial bombing campaigns, in particular those of the British RAF, had increased in intensity. Endless tons of bombs were still being dropped every day on urban areas filled with civilians, even though Germany was now on its last legs and about to collapse at any moment. Death came suddenly and randomly from the skies and furthermore in great dimensions, as the bombing of Dresden and the subsequent firestorm there had emphasized. The victorious seizing of towns and cities by the Allied troops on the western front was, at least, proving to be a more civilized affair. But terrible rumours were heard from the eastern side of the Reich where the Red Army was advancing: tales of rape, torture, and innumerable massacres of civilians. There had existed the expectation that the incoming Soviet forces would be especially cruel, and this was borne out by many reports coming through.

There was also now a third and inner front that had opened up for the general population, and this one was the most hazardous of them all. It was moreover omnipresent; surrounding them, subsisting among them. The loyal, fervently party-supporting authorities and armed forces which, in their majority, had not the slightest intention of giving in to the enemy, were prepared to defend their nation against the invading enemy with all the slaughter required. For some this came about because, however adverse the situation became, they still believed that they would ultimately come out victorious – it was simply a matter of tenacity and time. In other cases, it came through a sheer desperation to simply fight to the death no matter what; to go down firing off round after round of ammunition and thus find, in that last sacrifice for the Fatherland, a significance to their life, and honour in their death.

But in most cases, it was achieved through a hierarchy of pressure that pushed down from one rank to the next. This mindset had as its epicentre the distant *Wolfsschanze* (the 'Wolf's Lair'), Hitler's bunker in Berlin from which he orchestrated the final miserable section of the long lost war, through the early months of 1945. From here, pompous expressions of resolve and obduracy were pumped on a daily basis out into the population; words aimed to instill hope into an already defeated nation; words that more than ever expressed only a fanatical obsession with fighting on – without meaning nor purpose - until there was nothing and no-one left to fight for. For the people in a country at war there exist the fixed concepts of valour and heroism and those are almost always on their side, rarely on that of the enemy. And thus exhausted, depleted, battle-weary, but still burning bright with those last vestiges of courage in desperation, hundreds of thousands of German soldiers fought on.

Simultaneously, all across Germany there were political battles being fought at municipal level for control of urban areas, as mayors and local military branches decided on whether to surrender or to keep fighting. This was enabled and exacerbated by the general disintegration of all political order. Numerous Germans everywhere perished in 1945 in these internal skirmishes; many civilians were shot on the spot, or hanged and left out on display to dissuade others from taking the same route. The notion of surrender, or even the mere acceptance of ineluctable defeat, was considered '*Hochverrat*' – high treason - and punishable by immediate execution by those still in control.

At the beginning of April, on a cold Saturday 7th, Lüneburg received its largest air-raid, together with the nearby town of Uelzen. The bombers came in two waves, dropping their load in a wide area spreading from the rail marshalling yards through to the districts of Wilschenbruch and Rotes Feld to the south of the town centre. In the freight yard, panic broke out in one of the trains that was carrying 390 prisoners from the Neuengamme concentration camp, who were due to be transported further up to the Baltic Sea for forced labour assignments. The men were tightly squashed up in a group of wagons and as the American planes were heard approaching, and then started bombing, they made a desperate attempt to flee and seek shelter from the raid. Meanwhile, the soldiers in command of guarding the train – a Danish SS-officer called Jepsen together with other German troops - began to shoot or club to death those trying to escape. By the end of the raid around 150 of them had been killed, their bodies thrown into a mass grave. (Jepsen was later arrested by British officers and eventually executed in 1947. Those men that successfully managed to escape were taken into shelters by the town's inhabitants. Those that had not tried to escape were later transported to the concentration camp Bergen-Belsen, but released shortly after when the Americans captured it).

The bombing, though relatively light in comparison to that meted out to other cities, and causing very little damage to the town centre, came as a great shock to a population. They were unused to the terrifying sound of explosives screaming down around them and exploding with shattering force. Moreover, the fires set off by the bombing were voluminous, especially around the railway yards, and gave off trails of thick black smoke. The town's water and electricity supplies were initially taken out, another shock; though repaired again in the next few days. The sparsely built-up Rotes Feld district, located beside the old salt mine, was covered in bomb craters, while numerous buildings in the Wilschenbruch district, also in the south, were destroyed.

Lüneburg was a considerably larger town by now in terms of population. Between the refugees from the eastern provinces and the bombed-out refugees from Hamburg, as well as deserting and wounded soldiers fleeing into the city, the population had grown from around 40,000 before the war to nearly 65,000. This was the case with Gisela, who had found room for three people whom she squeezed into the few rooms not occupied by her now larger extended family.

Although not their first air-raid, it was still a nightmarish day for the town. With the recent news of other major bombings of seemingly insignificant towns taking place all through Germany, many thought the time for the big one had come. When the sirens went off, Gisela sent the children and the refugees rushing down into the cellar. The bunker would not have withstood a direct hit by a large explosive bomb, but for them it represented sweet salvation. Gisela had tried to persuade her husband to join them down there but – presuming that all attempts to escape an already decided destiny would be futile - he said he would stay upstairs in his room and, if need be, die a soldier's death there. Furthermore, a part of him really would rather he died, than soiled himself in front of the others in the cellar. With the sirens ringing out urgently, she left him to it and joined the others in the shelter.

As the bombs began to scream down over at the marshalling yard, and then the rumbling explosions creeping closer to the town centre, Gisela and the others feared their time had come. Of the boys, only Adolf was relatively unaffected by the drama, feeling secure inside his growing bubble of self-confidence that nothing would happen to him. Joseph and Hermann on the other hand were terrified. Everyone held each other tight as they heard the droning of aircraft approaching followed by the dull crashes nearby. They watched with hot alarm how the walls and ceiling of the shelter trembled.

Georg had refused to budge from his armchair when the sirens went off, and his wife had reluctantly though obediently stayed by his side. Like Martin, Georg had a sense of fate, of the dice having already been cast. Moreover, it was too far for him to walk, with his laborious pace marked by illness, to any of the local public shelters; and in any case, the couple were both aware from their own daughter's fate that a shelter would not necessarily be of any use if this day was meant to be their last. They waited with silent stoical patience for the end to come, listened to the whistle of falling bombs and subsequent explosions without batting an eyelid. Corinna was later amazed at how unscathed their surroundings were, once the all-clear signal was sounded and she dashed out on her way to the Gasthaus to check up on her daughter and family.

The long-awaited end of the war finally came just over a week later, in mid-April. The tenacious battle on the Lüneburg Heath had already lasted three weeks, one of the last major feats of military resistance that the Germans were to put up against the British army before it marched on over the Elbe and on to the Baltic Sea.

On 16th April came the longest day in the whole of the war for Lüneburg. Air-raid sirens sounded for eleven hours, without a single all-clear signal, from ten in the morning until nine in the evening. The population hid in the cellars, once again fearing the very worst; expecting their town to be annihilated in a hail of bombs. Their luck so far could surely not last any longer.

By this point in time, Hertha and her group had arrived and were just settling in. They now felt they had jumped from the frying pan into the fire. All those thankfully gasped acknowledgements from Hertha of how fortunate they had been to escape, only to end up cowering underground in the face of possible death. Hertha recalled the scenes she had witnessed at Swinemünde and shuddered. But the attack never came, not even a single strafing plane, and in the evening a dazed town emerged from the cellars.

The order to fight to the bitter end had already been emitted by the East Hannover *Gauleiter* and Nazi-enthusiast Telschow: "Lüneburg must be held, down to the very last man!" he had ordered. "Those who did not comply with these orders are to be executed immediately." A flyer was copiously produced and distributed around town with the grim title 'To those who hoist the white flag', reaffirming the death sentence for those who did, and confirming that two councillors from the nearby Verden area had already met their death for that very 'crime'. It further read, "Plunderers and cowards caught red-handed are to be hanged or shot, without the necessity for a trial to take place. We believe in the future of a free Germany. The enemy, who seeks to jeopardize our freedom, will not be repelled with white flags but rather with military force."

Those were the instructions issued to the Lüneburg combat headquarters, which had been set up in the manor estate Gut Schnellenberg on the western edge of the town. But as luck would have it, a new commanding officer had taken over just two days earlier: World War I veteran *Oberstleutnant* (Senior Lieutenant) Helmut von Bülow. He had immediately recognized the futility and sheer senselessness of resisting the Allied advance and was able – in the nick of time - to establish telephonic contact with the head of the Lüneburg police force. Von Bülow informed him, on Monday 16th April, that British tanks now stood only a few kilometres from the town border. They came to a mutual understanding that Lüneburg would not be defended, but rather declared an 'open city' to the enemy. This act of defiance could have easily meant the death sentence for both of them, but at that point and in this town it was too late for that.

By 18th April, those British tanks had gathered on the central Am Sande square. People who had gathered there, stared in shock, others scattered in fear. Around the tanks, the rows of previously hanging swastika flags, that had bedecked houses and businesses, were now suddenly transformed into waving white flags cut out of bedsheets. The majority of the tanks rumbled off down the Kleine- and Große Bäcker Straße, along the Bardowicker Straße and further on, heading off up north in the direction of Hamburg. But some stayed, together with jeeps and troops, to occupy the town and surrounding area.

In those final turbulent days, Telschow himself beat a quick retreat once he realized that the enemy's arrival was now imminent. He fled from his lavish villa in the Schießgrabenstraße and hid himself in a small hunting cabin out in Dahlenburg, about 25km to the east of Lüneburg. (There he was located by British soldiers and arrested; he attempted suicide but was initially unsuccessful, though eventually dying of his wounds by the end of May.)

Meanwhile, the inhabitants were listening in silent, worried expectation to the rumbling noise of the enemy's tanks passing through the streets. The occupiers sequestered and confiscated the immediate area around the town hall, giving all occupants there two hours to leave. This did not, however, extend to the stretch of the Rosenstraße where the *Gasthaus Sonnenschein* was situated; and so Gisela and the others were spared that particular order.

There were initially some minor, isolated cases reported, of plundering of food supplies as well as smaller articles of value by the invaders, but generally the operation was carried out in a humane and decent manner, it was later agreed. Families were instructed to hand in all weapons, maps, compasses, and cameras, while a curfew beginning at 19:30 was imposed for all male citizens. The first arrests of those in positions of military or political power began. It was all such a small price to pay for an end to the bombs and the air-raid sirens, the telegrams telling of distant deaths, the scarcity of food and other essentials, and the general state of fear and panic.

(After taking the town, the rest of those divisions of the British army continued sweeping up through the small villages to the north of Lüneburg and heading on upwards to the Elbe River, now closing in on Hamburg. There, in the battered port city, they would meet tough military opposition from the last pockets of actively fighting *Wehrmacht* soldiers in the north of Germany. Following three weeks of dogged battles, this resistance was finally knocked out and the British troops prevailed on 3rd May.)

For the people of Lüneburg, as for all throughout the nation, the dream of conquest that had transformed half-way through into a nightmare of slaughter, was finally over. They awoke into a new world. Bleak but anticipated news of the military situation in these conclusive weeks of the conflict, by this point rushing into German homes, informed of how the Soviet troops were fighting to take Berlin and of the fierce opposition being met from the Wehrmacht in its death throes. They then learned how it was overrun and captured, how Hitler had been shot and killed by the Russians, fighting to the last, how the thousand-year Reich had been definitively crushed out of existence. (Later on, the detail about the Führer being shot in battle would be corrected to suicide.)

At four o'clock in the afternoon on the day following that abrupt entrance of tanks into the town centre and the surrender of Lüneburg, the wary but curious townsfolk gathered in the large *Marktplatz* in front of the still intact Town Hall, in an urban centre unusually free of rubble or ruin for these times. There, they heard a general from the British Army - with a simultaneous translation into German - address them from the town hall balcony with regards to the fate awaiting them. The crowd looked up in crushed silence at the small group of British soldiers and local German officials standing on this high balcony and framed by the large clock above. They listened attentively to their words under a warm spring sun, while behind them came the background rumble of a line of British military jeeps passing through the town. They were informed that all German military units had unilaterally surrendered; that from now on their own utmost cooperation would be required; and that they would soon receive information as to how much nourishment they could expect to receive on a daily basis and how to obtain it.

Gisela Hartmann had not been present at this historic gathering. She had - erroneously - suspected the worst, and smelled a possible trap when word had gone around that there would be an important announcement to be made by the newly arrived occupiers that afternoon. With the lurid details of Hertha's flight from East Prussia still buzzing round her head, she had mentally entertained the possibility of them all being unceremoniously mowed down or, in the case of the women, taken aside to be tortured and sexually abused. Hertha had assured her this would not be the case, that the British were a very different beast to the Red Army, but she was not wholly convinced. She kept a cautious distance at first and even took refuge with the children in the cellar that day, but when it became apparent that these victorious soldiers meant no immediate harm, and that her gruesome visions had not been even remotely manifested, she was already on her way to the *Marktplatz* to find out what was going on. She intercepted Fabian there, just turning into *An den Brodbänken* on his way home. They headed back together and, in time-honoured tradition for that street, she quizzed him intensely while he faithfully reported all he had heard.

A phrase that had dominated Gisela's thoughts on this short walk, concerned food: "how much nourishment they could expect to receive on a daily basis", passed again and again through her mind, with its obvious nagging conclusion. She wondered if the rations might be assigned per family unit, in their case therefore for herself, her husband, her two children, and probably her sister's three children included too. In that way the allocated rations would have had to be spread among seven, rather than four mouths. Gisela had mentally prepared herself to sacrifice where necessary her own intake for the sake of her children, as well as her late sister's children, and considered that to be the correct thing for a mother to do. An adult would receive more than a child, she figured, and therefore half of her ration would amount to a considerable increase for her own dependants. If, however, the food rations were applied per household, and hers counted as just the one, she had no idea how she was to feed no less than fifteen hungry bellies on what would surely be sparce provisions. She felt great frustration that she was forced into such an extremely difficult position, and found the thoughts upsetting.

There was a further reason for her annoyance at this change in the process of food rationing by these new governors. Through the contact that she had maintained with a friend and political cohort of Arnold Schilling from Harburg, who had approached her following news of Inge's death as a personal favour for Schilling, she had enjoyed access to forged food ration cards. The extra little booklets had come at a reasonable price and been more than worth every Reichsmark. Many a day she had breezed home from the shops with more than double the amount of fat, bread, even eggs, to that which was officially allocated to her. She had naturally kept this irregular transaction strictly secret, not even breathing a word to her own mother. The falsification of rations was a very serious crime carrying heavy punitive measures; but by this point in the war, and with her sister dead and so many mouths to feed, Gisela had become hardened up and she took this in her stride.

And if this was not enough, the increasingly chaotic state of her home depressed her no end. Gisela and Fabian had arrived home that day to find the children already out of control, playing noisily in the back yard and kicking up a hullabaloo, and she had only been gone five minutes. She saw how Inge's boys were grimy and looked shoddy with their threadbare clothes and unkempt hair. Joseph had a hole in his shoe where the little toe poked out; Hermann had a cut on his knee that hadn't been there that morning. She sighed deeply and regarded the bunch, as they stopped their game and looked questioningly at the two adults.

"Did you see the Tommys? Is the war over?" asked Joseph with his characteristically angelic though at the same time mischievous smile that Gisela now found odious. She said nothing and another voice piped up, this time one of the Schwarz boys. "The war is over? Is it over?"

Gisela did not care to answer this enormous question which required such a simple monosyllabic response. At least not this time round. She harshly told them all to go and bath themselves and get ready for the evening meal.

For Gisela, there were still some doubts as to the finality of the war, but a week later she received at least a partial response to her inner anxiety in the form of a solid and very positive response to her most important question: the fate of her son Siggi. The boy, or rather the young man now, was able to contact them by telephone from Helmstedt to inform that he was on the way home. He had fled to Helmstedt in the chaos of early April and that decision had proved to be a lucky stroke of fortune, for the KdF plant in Braunschweig was almost flattened in a bombing raid a few days later. Helmstedt itself was taken by the Americans (as in many towns – he told his already knowledgeable mother - the inhabitants had simply surrendered and handed over control to the incoming tanks and troops). He had initially been arrested and questioned by the American forces. The seventeen-year-old, not yet an adult though with the experience of a war veteran, had been eventually let out of custody under the condition that he returned to his family in Lüneburg. He told his mother that was hoping to get a lift with a military truck the next day, that the Americans were "very nice people", and that he was already learning to speak English with them. His prompt appearance, as promised the following day, turned tough Gisela into a sentimental mess. To the lad's subsequent clear weariness, she could not contain her desire to embrace him tightly and hardly managed to let him go the whole day long.

In the same week as Siggi returned home, news came through of a less fortunate end for another family member. Cousin Carsten had fallen, killed in battle at the Seelow Heights in Brandenburg, not far to the east of Berlin. He had died on April 18th; his division – one of the fifteen comprising the 9th Army – was among those practically wiped out during the four days of ferocious battle. After delivering the crushing victory, the Soviets continued on toward their ultimate target, Berlin. The family in Lüneburg were notified by *Onkel* Robert in Hamburg and their condolences were duly passed on. It was at least a consolation for all to know that Carsten had died defending – albeit futilely – the Reich that he had once so adored, as it first began to expand and fill out the map of Europe. He then joined the ranks of the fallen heroes; at least initially. Some years later there came to light the many crimes that his particular division had committed during their conquest of the east in the early 1940s, in particular in the Ukraine and Belarus. Complete dossiers existed, including photographic evidence and witness testimonies of random executions, mass shootings, and whole villages set alight. Cousin Carsten's brief life story turned out to be an ugly book that was quietly disposed of and not opened again, even by his closest family.

Meanwhile, the Americans were rolling on inexorably eastwards, also in the direction of Berlin, although the capital looked clear to be taken by the Soviet forces well before their arrival. By the end of April, the British had taken Bremen in the north, the Americans Munich in the south. On May 2nd, after two weeks of ferocious fighting, the *Reichshauptstadt* (capital of the empire) Berlin finally surrendered and the Soviet Red Army took control of the city. Hitler and Goebbels, both together with their respective wives, committed suicide; taking with them into death and history the ignoble tale of a supposedly millennium Reich that had barely passed the age of twelve.

On May 3rd, Admiral Alfred Dönitz, the former head of the *Kriegsmarine* (German navy) and now with Hitler's death the new President of the Reich and Supreme Commander of the entire

Wehrmacht, sent a message to the British armed forces declaring Germany's intention to surrender. By 6pm on May 4th, Montgomery received from Commander-in-Chief of the *Kriegsmarine* Admiral von Friedeburg, under a vigorously waving Union Jack flag, the unconditional surrender of all German armed forces in North-West Germany, Denmark, and the Netherlands. This was signed in Montgomery's tent, pitched on a windswept hill upon the Lüneburg Heath; not far from the spot where years before Horst and Inge had strolled and talked, where she had told him of her third pregnancy with the child that had become Hermann.

Hostilities ended, the ceasefire was announced. The signing of the unconditional surrender, this time for the entirety of Germany, was repeated five days later in Soviet-controlled Berlin, with representatives from all victorious parties present. With that came the official end of the war on 9th May, now known as Victory Day. The Reich was no more.

At the beginning of May, the headline exploded out of newspapers all around the world announcing the death of Adolf Hitler in his bunker in Berlin. Among the people who had once worshipped the screaming Austrian with such devotion and passion, the reaction was surprisingly muted. There had been some scattered, hushed talk of the demise of the Führer, in the days and weeks following the event. But the past frenzy of idolatry now belonged to another era. The Devil had simply disappeared back to the hell whence he had come.

For those who had survived the ordeal, life went on with new challenges and under new commanders. In a world in which neither food nor shelter nor protection were guaranteed, there was little interest in pointless patriotism or ideological considerations. Of far more relevance - more than any sorrow over lost visions of grandeur, or any sense of the monumental historical downfall that Germany had just undergone and its significance for the future - were primordial necessities. That was all that was now of vital interest to the vast majority of Germans: pure, bare survival. In any case, most had been prepared for the eventuality of the defeat – and with it the end of the Führer - for many months. Now it was time to get on with the mundane aspects of daily life. Some were already planning how best to rebuild the cities, the nation. And so the decease of Hitler - once worshipped as almost a god - was met by the vast majority with only a passing acknowledgment, and not a drop of distress nor grief.

With one notable exception among the families of this chronicle, and that was the case of Georg Hartmann. The canny old man had hidden away a bottle of champagne that he had got Corinna, much to her discomfort, to steal from the wine stock in the *Gasthaus Sonnenschein* kitchen way back in 1939, shortly after the Polish campaign had commenced. Five and a half years had passed and now was the moment for this long-kept treasure to be opened up. There was to be no public execution of the dictator, as he had initially hoped for, but still: there was all the reason in the world to celebrate.

He got Gisela to come round, told her to bring Hertha, and all the six Hartmann children (as he often called his grandchildren) from the Gasthaus, along with some stalked glasses. Sitting in a chair by the table, he popped the cork and jubilantly toasted the death of "a wicked tyrant and an enormous arsehole". The children all giggled at the sound of '*Arschloch*' and Gisela, smiling with teary eyes, told them that today was an exceptional day for use of the word; normally that would not be the case. They sipped with pleasure the noble old juice (Corinna had inadvertently pilfered the most upmarket of all the bottles) and Georg let Inge's three little boys have some sips. Hermann, not yet six, found it dreadful and nearly had to spit it out, though quickly swallowing it instead while shuddering. He whimpered, "I have bubbles inside my nose!" and looked about to cry. Adolf and Joseph, on the other hand, adored their little tipples of this fruity sparkling drink that left their palate tingling and vibrant and their sense of perception pleasantly altered. That memory would never leave them.

Gisela mentioned that week to Hertha and Corinna in the Gasthaus kitchen, with a matter-of-fact acceptance of the fact and as if referring to the mundane termination of a business contract, "Good, so now this war is finished and done with, I can only hope there is some sort of return to normality as soon as possible. If all the corresponding documents have been signed, I see no reason why the occupying troops should not all return home as soon as possible." She looked around her, cleaning cloth in hand. "After all, there is little more to be done round here as far as I am concerned."

Catching some of the drift of conversations taking place around them, the enormous question was once again asked by Inge's boys, later that day and out in the yard. This time Gisela did see fit to answer. Their youthful simplicity caught her off guard, made her emotional when this was not her intention. Her head lowered and she muttered, "Yes, the war is over."

"Forever?" asked Hermann, ever mistrustful.

"Yes."

She looked dazed, in a state of great internal turmoil at hearing herself actually voicing those words to these children. She had ruminated on the subject for a good time now after she, like so many, had felt that first aching notion that there would be defeat ahead. And moreover, possibly a long and bloody defeat. These reflections – unusually morbid for her - had come in the wake of a growing awareness, on her part, of Horst's and Inge's absence at the end of this long and hard journey. It was to be the final stage in her processing of grief. She had shown few outer signs of her thoughts to others, not even to her husband or her own children; but she had rummaged through her perceptions, her conclusions, her hopes, until she had felt that - whether under unfavourable or even terrible circumstances - she would one day live to greet the end of this war, and would then be able to do this honour for her departed sister.

Now, asked out of the mouths of these simple babes, she voiced that peculiar phrase that months ago many others had been killed for: "*Ja, der Krieg ist vorbei*" – "Yes, the war is over".

The phrase seemed to hang in the air, lit by warm sunshine until it acquired a magical wholeness, a reality taking shape in that first spring of peace. It was a spring that had been struggling to emerge from the cocoon of winter; a winter in which all had experienced the harsh and biting cold. On this bright day, among the flitting insects in the back yard, it too had spread glorious wings. Though housing a nominal sense of faith, Gisela was not of great religious inclination, but she did feel a sense of spiritual wonderment that she was unable to define. Above all there was the shapeless and inexplicable finality of the war, which in turn left her as speechless as her little nephews.

And so she stood and regarded the sight of the three grimy angels staring dumbfounded at her. She let the seconds roll on, watched them in their silent awe, soaked up the optimism in their smiles; an optimism that they as children effortlessly plucked out of the air. It was heavenly for a moment but then that moment was pricked by practical considerations. She started, realized that the angels looked thin, gaunt-faced, ragged; they looked more like malnourished paupers than cherubs. She felt herself become wary of this illusion of serenity, recalled the horrors that had taken place, and in that instant Adolf asked, "If the war is over, is Papa coming home?"

"No," she mumbled, finding the spell broken.

"And Mama?" asked Joseph.

She shook her head. "No. No, she is not either. Neither of them are. They are both in heaven and will not be coming back here to the Gasthaus again. We must learn to live without them," she replied with a dull tone as she felt her body tighten and her mind harden up. "Listen. The soldiers are all over the town, so you are not to go near them. Keep quiet and keep as close to home as possible. If they say anything to you, you just shake your head and start to walk home. Do not run. Never run. Just walk, but walk briskly. Do you understand?"

They nodded, little heads bobbing and eyes wide open. They understood immediately because they had spent nearly two years now getting themselves accustomed to the fact. Like all finality around them, it was merely a matter of waiting for the adults to confirm it.

"But if the war is over, then there is no danger to us anymore?" pondered Adolf.

Gisela had wiped her eyes and got a grip on herself again. She grinned, her voice bordering on a rugged laugh. "Just because the war is over, it does not mean there is no danger. Wherever did you get that idea from?"

"We thought it meant there would be no more fighting," said little Hermann.

Gisela laughed out loud. "Oh, you poor innocent little mites! The war might be over, but the peace has only just begun. And that is going to be the hardest part of all."

Chapter 35

In that first summer of peace the sky was a dazzling bright blue with scattered clouds. The grating sound of air-raid sirens was gone, along with the fluttering strings of swastikas, the newspaper stands selling *Der Stürmer*, the portraits and little busts of the Führer in house and shop windows, and the pompous speeches and martial music on the radio broadcasts. Also gone was the constant tension and state of uncertainty regarding progress made or loss sustained, above all on the deadly eastern front with its fleeing civilians. The summer of 1945 shone clear and strong and in its unhindered radiance was the realization: it is all over. We have lost, and lost heavily, but it is over. No more apprehending conscription letters would be arriving in letter boxes and calling young men up to war. No-one was raising their arm to greet with 'Heil Hitler!' in shops or questioning why the other person was not. There was also no more fear that *Iwan* might be the first to arrive, bloodthirsty and vengeful, to rape the women and massacre the men. In the weeks leading up to the end, a popular phrase in the north had become "*Lieber der Tommy als der Iwan!*" – "Better the British than the Russians!" In Lüneburg the *Tommys* had already taken over and, as occupiers went, they were proving to be of a very decent nature.

But despite this underlying positive change, on a national level there still reigned confusion and uncertainty for many. Societal pillars that were once so solid, had abruptly collapsed. Millions were dead or missing, yet more millions had been displaced or made homeless, and the country was occupied by foreign troops. Nearly all major towns and cities had been reduced to streets filled with rubble. Innumerable institutions and companies had disappeared or were being radically rebuilt. The old order had crumbled and was being swept aside.

Frau Wortmann, who taught history to *Abitur* level ('A' level/High School) students at the *Johanneum Gymnasium*, told a friend how in her quarter of a century of teaching she had always known the summer as the gentle end of the old academic year; a time of holiday and rest for teaching staff. Now it was all bewilderment and whispered rumours and she had no idea what lay in store. "They will need a whole new set of text books," she quietly commented to an old colleague from the same department that she knew she could speak frankly to. "Obviously the victors will have new books printed so that we will have to tell their story. It is always that way. And this time not just in history. Also in biology and *Heimatkunde* (local studies), physical training, German language and literature, and geography. Art too, I am sure. All that degenerate rubbish will be put back at the top of the syllabus. Even in mathematics they will interfere, no doubt. The social arithmetic texts will have to be changed - they won't like the references to Versailles." Her school would not open until the following January and, as she predicted, there would be marked changes.

Frau Wortmann, together with so many others like her, had got off lucky. Despite her formerly frank sympathy toward the Nazi ideology, including a deep distrust of Jews, her natural sense of prudence had led her to avoid signing up as a party member or becoming involved in any extra-curricular activities that might now stamp her with the label 'Nazi'. This might well have ended her career as a teacher, as well as procuring legal difficulties. She escaped all that. Instead, as millions of others, she adjusted to the new times and thrived. Within a decade she would be telling new staff about how she had always disesteemed the NSDAP and known the war was a grave mistake. It seemed in the end that all that she had known of, she had disapproved of; and that which she not actively disapproved of, she had simply never known.

The situation at the *Johanneum* was complicated. Four male members of staff and around a third of the older male students were gone forever, lost in the war. Plus there were other members of staff, including the headmaster, who were being investigated for their positions as paid up members of the NSDAP. They would most likely not be returning – at least not in the near future - to the profession of education.

Likewise the running of the general town administration was plagued with staff issues. The British – like the other occupying forces - were keen to weed out those 'brown' functionaries who had worked too closely and zealously with the dictatorship, including those employed in education, healthcare, municipal administration and the police force. In Lüneburg they were able to relieve just over

80 members of staff of their positions. Those who had been more deeply involved in upholding the tyrannical regime were distinguished from the average *Mittäter* (accomplices or accessories to crime) who were too numerous to adequately deal with, and were generally interrogated only to be let free afterwards and so able to continue with their lives with no further legal repercussions. The so-called 'denazification' programme was doomed from the start to be a mostly superficial business.

The high-ranking Nazis themselves had more often than not bolted and gone into hiding as soon as it became apparent that the war was irreversibly over. Telschow was just such a case in point but a much higher beast was also captured in the area: none other than one of the highest ranking Nazis of all, Heinrich Himmler. He had been the sinister Interior Minister and *Reichsführer* (Reich leader) of the SS, and the principal driving force behind the Holocaust. Having fled from Flensburg in the very north of Germany, he had first travelled south by motorcar with a group of companions before continuing on foot, eventually being caught by British troops close to the Lüneburger Heath. From there he was taken to Lüneburg and placed under arrest in the Uelzener Straße, awaiting further interrogation. That night at just after 23:00 he committed suicide by biting into a hidden cyanide capsule. His corpse was buried the next day by British soldiers in an unmarked spot out in the woods by Lüneburg.

But among the general population there was little interest taken – beyond moments of idle gossip - in the capture or deaths of these once high-standing political figures, right up to the Führer himself. In Lüneburg as everywhere, that summer was so packed with hardship, upheaval and existential preoccupation that few had the time and the wish to stop to consider the deeper significance of the recent past or fathom its abominable form. Likewise with the concept of defeat, and all the regret and personal loss that came with it. This German nation – so young and yet at the same time so ancient - was re-born that year, albeit in a bath of blood. Life began anew. The moment of midnight 8th May 1945 became known as *Stunde Null* (Zero Hour) and the country would never be even remotely the same again.

A society's existence moves along on the undercarriage of pragmatic necessity and in the course of that very year, despite the deep gashing wounds both self-inflicted and inflicted from outside, Germany picked itself up and dusted itself down with remarkable speed and vigour. Cinemas and art galleries re-opened, people began to attend concerts and public lectures once again, while local black markets shot up all over the country to offer the general public not just bread and coal, but also perfume, cognac, chocolate. In most German towns and cities *Trümmerfrauen* (rubble women) lined the streets to clear away the immense piles of destroyed buildings and pave the way for reconstruction; in this aspect Lüneburg was one of the exceptions, having never suffered heavy carpet bombings.

With the old Nazi publications now extinct, alternative newspaper titles were appearing, this time speaking in an open and free language that had not been heard in the country since the early 1930s. In Lüneburg the British helped launch the *Lüneburger Post* which was snatched up by a town eager to find work and information, and so to begin establishing a new infrastructure. Those already employed in key areas would face the challenging task of finding their way afresh with a new outlook that would be fitting for the reborn country.

Although countless soldiers had died in those last belligerent months and many were still distant prisoners of war, some of them were starting to come home to Lüneburg that summer. The first familiar faces began to appear around town; those of men who had left to fight for the glory of the Reich and now returned home to a defeated nation. Wilhelm was expected to soon be one of them. He had written to Gisela at the Gasthaus to announce that he was alive and well and currently being held captive in Lübeck. His U-Boot crew had survived the conflict fully intact, one of a minority to do so, and he was now waiting in Lübeck for his interview with the local British occupying forces as well as his official *Entlassungpapiere* (discharge papers from the Wehrmacht) that would convert him back into a civilian again. Once this whole procedure was over, he would be coming home. Or at least that was his statement in the first letter sent in May.

Two months later came a further letter, equally effervescent as the first had been, only this time with a different purpose to that of merely reporting his survival. He told how he had met a young lady while in captivity in Lübeck (a British woman called Mandy), in whom he had fallen head over heels in love, and he had ultimately decided to stay on there with the intention of getting married to her as soon as possible. Gisela was taken aback, but it was pleasant news to pass on to everyone for a change, and she did so with a huge smile.

Not a word was said about his former sweetheart Ann-Kathrin, nor was anything heard from her, and Gisela saw fit to leave the amorous matter at that. ("Just as well," she had thought, for she never liked a woman who smoked.) Likewise, Gisela prudently informed Wilhelm that there was still no news about Horst, though there was all the hope in the world that he was still alive and well in Soviet captivity.

Wilhelm's summer of love and passion was to be the only good news in the Grün family, however. Karl-Heinz, they found out, had been killed in the final months of the war. It took Gisela some time to piece the puzzle together, but in the end she ascertained the following. He had been in Dessau in March that year when the city had suffered a heavy air-raid and was almost completely destroyed. He had fled in the aftermath and attempted to head clandestinely in a westward direction, presumably back to Lüneburg. He had been subsequently apprehended en route and following a summary court martial, shot as a deserter. His execution, along the charge he had faced, had all been communicated to his wife Ilse in the same month; but such had been the deep disgrace she had felt that she had kept the matter strictly to herself. It was only in the late summer that the truth had come out, after she had felt obliged to relate the matter to their children and from there to neighbours, friends, and his sister Marianne. Marianne in turn informed Gisela and wrote to her brother Wilhelm, too. Their father, old Konrad Grün, had already passed away the previous year after a year-long bout of ill health. Gisela thought it fortunate that he did not live to endure all the tragic news.

Bernhard was also home, back from the now defunct ball bearing factory where he had been working. Like Lüneburg, Schweinfurt had been taken by the Allied Forces in mid-April; by the end of the month, he had made it back to his home and his now thoroughly miserable wife Edeltraut. Like so many women of her attitude and convictions, she had watched the Reich crumble in disbelief and horror. Their daughter Eva, who had worked with the Red Cross in Belgium and France in the last year of war, had also got home safely. The only missing member of their household now was their son Roland, who had also survived; though it soon became apparent that he would not to be returning as quickly as first thought. Roland's fanatical adherence to the then reigning national-socialist ideology was familiar to all in the family. It transpired that he had been deeply embroiled in the *Vernichtungskrieg* (war of extermination) that the SS, along with some divisions of the regular Wehrmacht too, had waged in eastern Europe against the Slavic and Jewish populations; neither that term nor the full extent and nature of the *Vernichtungslager* (extermination camps), were known to the general population in the immediate aftermath of the war. The first open facts concerning the extensive system of concentration camps began emerging in Lüneburg that summer with the trials, concerning the nearby Bergen-Belsen complex, that were held there.

That Roland was being held prisoner in Poland, pending investigation by the occupying Soviet forces, was all that Bernhard and Edeltraut initially allowed to be made known. They hid the few more precise details that they possessed - all clearly of an ignominious nature - from family and neighbours and created a blank pretense of ignorance if anyone asked after their son. In the post-war chaos it was, after all, a perfectly believable scenario; there were still over three million men being held in Soviet captivity alone. And thus they built, with meticulous attention to detail, an inconspicuous wall of fiction around the war-time activities of Roland. They had strong suspicions as to the general nature of the accusations, though little idea of the sheer scale of the atrocities – torture, rape, forced labour, mass murder - in which he had freely participated. That would first become apparent in later years. Even then, and although Roland's father fell into an absolute silence on the subject, his mother always defended him to the hilt. There was nothing that her son – or the Führer or the SS - had done, she firmly believed, that was without some rational motive.

She had a further reason for supporting her son, aside from simple maternal instinct. Edeltraut had also been involved – albeit indirectly – in some of the range of barbarous activity that by the height of the Third Reich had been deemed quite natural and explicable during a war; but which now, in the cold light of defeat, was viewed with repulsion. The Führer had quietly decreed as early as 1st September – on the same day as his Wehrmacht invaded Poland – that the 'incurably sick', those suffering from acute mental or physical health issues, including children, should be ultimately euthanized for the greater good of the German people. Or, to use his particular words: *"den Gnadentod zu gewähren"* – to grant a mercy killing. This programme – one of many aimed at the countless 'undesirables' and enemies of the state - was immediately put into effect and most of the deaths occurring in this particular purge within German territory took place from 1940 to 1941, resulting in around 70,000 deaths. (Protests from the Catholic Church were instrumental in achieving its cessation in Germany, though in other occupied areas of Europe the 'euthanasia' continued on until the end of the war.)

Lüneburg had been one of the sights chosen for these covertly carried out mass murders, namely at the *Heil- und Pflegeanstalt* (mental health hospital) in Lüneburg-Wienebüttel. Edeltraut had been aware of the exact procedure taking place, having been contacted by a local surgeon from the hospital where she worked, with regards to this intervention. She had ultimately been of logistical and administrative though not direct medical assistance. One particular transportation in which she was involved took place on 1st October 1941; the paperwork detailed the transportation of 91 boys and 36 girls – all minors – who arrived in Lüneburg from a widespread area, allegedly being received there for 'medical treatment'. As one of the later witnesses in a legal trial centred around this event would testify, "But instead of receiving medical care, they received overdoses of luminol." As the use of this drug as a tranquilizer was common practice in any case, its presence in the children's bodies helped make the deaths medically inconspicuous. The parents were informed, through official state letters, of the tragic death of their offspring, and the killing went on.

Edeltraut had been part of this project, albeit at the periphery, and was at one point called upon to testify herself. Once her complicity had been made known to the wider Landeck family, Gisela shunned the Bohlens immediately and completely; this included her forbidding her daughter Katrina to ever have any contact with her old friend Eva again. Even the Bohlens themselves had comprehension for Gisela's rage against them. They knew how lovingly devoted she was to her youngest son Erich, and all the more so due to his physical handicap.

The town was still packed with refugees; both those who had fled or been expelled from the eastern parts of the Reich, such as Hertha, and those who had been bombed out of their hometowns, especially Hamburg. People were packed into houses, staying with close relatives or distant family, working in anything they could find in order to pay their way. Here as everywhere, the kindness of strangers had never been in such great demand.

A plus point for the local population was that the occupation by the British troops turned out to be an agreeable and even edifying experience, especially for those who had previously kept out of politics and now looked forward to this fresh beginning. They had experienced none of the horror tales that they had heard of in relation to Berlin and the eastern sector, and interaction between the German civilians and the occupying troops was very positive. Even Gisela was satisfied with the situation: "They politely keep their distance and we keep ours. That is how it should be."

After her rough war-time experiences in the east, Hertha was quite delighted with '*Tommy*' and found him very correct and well-mannered, just as she had hoped. Her naturally high-spirited and feisty approach aided her greatly in her communication with the occupier. Hertha did not speak a word of English but did not see that as a barrier at all in her – often daily - quest for information, paperwork, or supplies. Some people were more fearful of the British soldiers; Corinna, for instance, was very timid in their presence, to which Hertha told her that "she shouldn't be so soft." Even Gisela kept her distance. But Hertha would boldly walk up to them at the Marktplatz to inquire after information or demand assistance, and harangue whole groups of heavily armed squaddies if her requests were not satisfied. The soldiers in turn became fond of this audacious old lady in her floral apron - barely 160cm tall but with an unflinching stare - who was more than happy to stand up to them all in a mixture of German and sign language until she got her way. "You might have won the war but this is still our country," she would tell them straight up; fortunately few understood, and they simply helped her out as best they could, to get rid of her for another day.

With time Hertha managed to befriend – in her own peculiar concept of the word – a soldier who spoke nearly fluent German through university studies, a young Lancashire man called George Dewhurst. These two very disparate people took to each another in a feeling of mutual respect and he became her principal person of contact in the following months. Thus, through Lance Corporal Dewhurst, Hertha and both her direct and her wider adopted family were able to secure all their basic needs in terms of food, heating, fuel, and news of recent developments. By the time the military police took over in 1946, Hertha wielded considerable control over the new masters. "I do like the British," she concluded. "You can talk to them, reason with them." And all that without a word of English.

The rations were good under the British, the family concluded; notably better than in the last years of the war. They found the occupiers to be generous, which further increased their popularity: per week there were to be had (at least in theory) 3kg of potatoes, 150g of meat, 125g of fat, nearly 200g of sugar, but only 30g of coffee substitute. Hertha managed to increase the coffee allowance substantially through her new military 'friends' and Gisela likewise multiplied the meagre 15g of cheese allowed through her own private contacts. Corinna and Georg ate well during this period and Corinna commented on how lucky she was to have such shrewd and sharp-witted family. "There is nothing for those who do not take it," said Gisela.

The summer and autumn passed in this state of uncertainty and chaos on the one side, and the natural optimism that accompanied a new era on the other. But as the year progressed there came the realization that the spectre of winter lay ahead. In Lüneburg, as all across Germany, the population began to prepare themselves for the coming darkness and cold. Good quality coal was near impossible to obtain, even on the black market. At first only hospitals and essential *Handwerkbetriebe* (craft businesses and small industries) had access to it; everyone else had to make do with a mixture of low-quality charcoal and wood. As the wood was in turn also strictly rationed, it was furtively taken from the surrounding forests. Gas for cooking was only available during restricted hours, while peat made a reappearance as a popular method of heating. Volkmar's wife Anna found the scene hilarious when a sack of it came through her door the first time. "Back to the old days!" she cackled.

Those great areas of agricultural production in Prussia and other eastern areas of the Reich were now firmly in Soviet hands. With that, the traditional chains of food supply within Germany was severely interrupted. The population braced for not only a cold but also a hungry winter ahead. Those older residents who had now survived a second major war, from which they had emerged even more impoverished and utterly defeated this time, had a wisely pessimistic notion of what they would soon be facing and prepared themselves accordingly.

For all those uprooted from their homes by the war, it was a period of incertitude and the ignorance as to the fates of others. Hertha, always prolific in her correspondence, received occasional letters from those old friends and relatives who had survived the ordeal of the war and were now spread around Germany in whatever accommodation they could find. There was always news to be had and she loved relating it to her sister. As early as May she was telling Corinna and Gisela how she had found out the fate of a semi-important person whom she knew well from Heiligelinde, Frau Fratzke.

"I would often bump into her in town. She was an older and very correct woman, married to a high-ranking party member who spent long periods away on official duties in Berlin. She herself had always been a real hardcore follower and supporter of the Party. I recall her loudly celebrating every *Sondermeldung* (special announcement) of good news transmitted in the early years of the war. She became very quiet towards the end, though. She was convinced that the traitors and defeatists among us were responsible for the debacle, and for sorely letting down their own country, their own people, and after all the Führer had done for them. She said this quite openly on more than one occasion. A lot of people in our town thought that way, too. Now, I already knew that she had made her way to Danzig in December of 1944 to meet up with relatives there, and it turns out they all boarded the *Gustloff*. That was a cruise liner ship originally and then a military transporter, but at the time they were using it to ferry refugees across the Baltic Sea once the Red Army had started to close in. This was in Danzig at the end of January. There must have been thousands of refugees there at the time, hoping to make it further west across the Baltic Sea to Lübeck or Rostock. Well, it turns out that the *Gustloff* was torpedoed and sunk by a Soviet submarine. Almost all the passengers on board were drowned and she was not among the survivors. Over nine thousand dead, all drowned in the sea! And to think we got through safely on just a horse and cart. You never know in which direction fate will take you, do you?"

She related the demise of this acquaintance to her mother and sister with no emotional attachment whatsoever, even saying that in her case it was probably for the best. "Some people loved the regime so much, they would not have known what to do with themselves afterwards even if they had survived."

Those were her exact words, which her sister found unduly harsh but her niece could sympathize with. What Hertha did keep for herself, though, was the way in that she found some strange relief in the solid and irrefutable nature of this news, how it gave her a sense of finality. She felt she was quite sure of this woman's fate on the *Gustloff* and so could wrap up the issue in her mind; when she was otherwise in the midst of so much uncertainty as to the strokes of fate that had been meted out all around her. The lack of clear evidence, the lack of a body and a burial, as was the case with Inge; or worse still, the lack of any news whatsoever in the case of Horst; all this nagged at her. She knew better than anyone the grim realities of the eastern front and what the Soviets were capable of, just as she knew that their own troops had behaved in an equally brutal manner. It almost bothered her that others in the family still held out such absolute hope for Horst when she had already given up on her own son-in-law and resigned herself to his probable death. Here in Lüneburg, a town that had got through the war practically unscathed by the bombings that had decimated so many other towns and cities, and that was furthermore now living in smooth cooperation with the occupying forces, she felt there was still a naïve sense of optimism in the air.

Here they did not know of the icy hell that had raged in the east quite like she did. She knew inside that Horst had perished in Stalingrad. All that was lacking was the official confirmation per post, and she thought that it would have been in all honesty preferable to this inane wishful thinking.

Hertha did not have to wait long to have this notion put to the test. A few weeks after the news of Frau Fratzke, she received more information that was much closer to home. First of all, she and Bärbel were informed that Bärbel's husband Richard had died in a Soviet POW camp. For Hertha it came as no surprise, but her daughter was grief-stricken and became a recluse in her room, not wanting little Max to leave her proximity and worrying about his every step.

"Now they are both widows," sighed Gisela to her mother when she found out. "This has turned into a country of widows and orphans." She regretted her words immediately when she realized Adolf and Hermann had sneaked into the room and were keenly listening. She thought, this was starting to become an annoying habit of theirs.

Millions now found themselves homeless and starving in the chaotic aftermath of the war. Alone in the British zone, one of the four controlled sectors, there were an estimated 2.5 million people in dire circumstances. These included those liberated from prisoner of war camps and concentration camps, as well as German civilian refugees. Those far eastern regions of the old Reich, such as Pomerania, Silesia, or East Prussia whence Hertha and her companions had come, was now fully under Soviet control and would soon cease to be part of Germany forever. The extensive lands would pass on to form part of Poland, Czechoslovakia, and the Soviet Union, as millions of Germans, forced out of their homes and expelled out of these territories, continued to arrive in vast numbers and further aggravate the refugee crisis.

Hertha occasionally heard talk from some refugees of a future return to these old German areas which came to be known as 'verlorene Gebiete' – the lost territories. She snorted with derision at the thought. Those lands were gone forever, she would tell anyone who ventured a contrary opinion; now their lives continued elsewhere. She herself found some philosophical comfort in thoughts of nature. Of an evening she would sometimes sit alone and recollect the extensive woodland near her home and the deep dark forests beyond, of pines and spruces that were filled with fallow deer and wild boars and fleeting hares. She recalled the crystal-clear water of the lakes, the curlews and cranes which built their nests by the lakesides; the urgent call of the storks; the sweeping wings of the grey sea eagle; the swans and wild geese that would head north with the good weather and return again in autumn to nest and breed. Those birds knew of no borders and would return to the same natural sites; and it would be thoroughly irrelevant to them whether the sites were German, Polish or Russian. That natural rhythm had existed for millennia, long before the nationalities – that produced such loud and bloody and worthless battles - were even vaguely a notion, and so that existence would endure just the same. That reflection in particular gave Hertha hope for the future and much spiritual strength. She blessed the birds and their ancient wisdom.

In the winter of 1945 Hertha became friendly with two other middle-aged women living in Lüneburg, also East Prussian refugees like herself. Following a series of deep discussions they decided to set up a community café together in some premises that had become vacant near to the town centre and to move into the available two apartments on the first floor directly above. Hertha took Bärbel and Max into one with her, and there was space there for Florian too. He and Bärbel had come closer during the winter months and there was clearly the signs of a romance budding if the two parties were given the necessary encouragement, a development which delighted Hertha. Both Florian and Bärbel were quiet, introverted people, still inhabiting a traumatized post-war world, but they proved to be excellent workers once pointed in the right direction. This was a function that Hertha was more than happy to fulfill and she soon had them carrying out all manner of odd jobs. She was furthermore glad to leave the Gasthaus. She could not be more appreciative of all that Gisela had done for her, as she often told Corinna; but she also considered that Gisela was a little too peremptory for there to be any hope of long-term domestic felicity between the two women.

The café they founded was basic at first, with its primitive installations and battered old furniture, but the women were attentive to details such as order and cleanliness. With time it improved greatly and attracted a broad range of clientele from all over town. Later, in the 1950s, they would go on to open a museum beside the café, with books and maps and trinkets, to commemorate the life that they had once lived and that was now history.

Not only those from the former eastern provinces of the Reich had sought refuge in Lüneburg. A reasonably large Jewish community briefly came into existence, mostly consisting of survivors from the Bergen-Belsen concentration camp who were among the many *displaced persons*. However, none of the Jews who came to Lüneburg belonged to the community that had previously lived there: all of those had either escaped or been murdered, together with millions of others, in the extermination camps of the Nazis.

By January of 1946, there were around 600 members of a new Jewish community in Lüneburg, who regularly met up in the Café Rauno in the Große Bäckerstraße. A kitchen was set up to prepare kosher food and religious services were held together with Talmud study classes and lessons in Hebrew. Additionally, a home for children freed from other camps was set up by the Jewish Relief Unit. Through the late 1940s and into the 1950s most of these *displaced persons* dispersed out into the world; often they had families, living far away from the horrors of Europe, that they managed to contact and so had tickets and visas sent to them.

Among both the displaced persons and the Germans in their hometowns, many lived in a state of anxious ignorance with regards to the destinies of loved ones. It was estimated that nearly half of all Germans were essentially "missing someone": perhaps a male relative last heard of fighting on a front, or those who had disappeared in the aerial bombings of the past months, or refugees assumed to be fleeing from the east – all these factors helped to make the immediate period after the end of the war a muddled mess of disinformation. Orphaned or separated children were often left to their own devices. There was, for example, the phenomenon the *Wolfskinder* (wolf children), groups of abandoned orphans who formed into outlaw bands in what was formerly Eastern Prussia. These bands scavenged in search of food, hiding out in the forests like wolves in packs for mutual protection and to avoid falling into the hands of the Soviet military authorities.

Many foraged across into neighbouring Lithuania and there they were eventually taken in and adopted by local peasants. With the passing of decades they eventually became Lithuanians themselves.

A major problem throughout Germany that winter, as predicted, was malnutrition and there were concerns that small children in particular would suffer to such an extent that it would become a life-threatening issue for them. Vulnerable and abandoned children were taken into orphanages, which were soon hopelessly overfilled. New ones had to be created, set up under the auspices of overseas organizations, in particular the Red Cross as well as numerous Catholic charity groups. On the outskirts of Lüneburg an old villa was refurbished for just this purpose. There, a group of children numbering around fifty were housed. Their identities were checked and registered in case the parents should at some point be located. The children were well looked after and their health status closely monitored. Where possible – in the case of minors who definitely had no family members left to take care of them – relocation for adoption was undertaken. By the end of the 1940s many children had been sent to families in countries such as Canada, the USA, Australia or Argentina; likewise, many others ended up in other European nations, such as the Netherlands, Belgium, Britain, Ireland, or Sweden. In several cases, the children were able to be put into contact with distant relatives in the rest of Germany and sent to live with them.

It is at this point that the new life journeys of the three brothers Adolf, Joseph and Hermann Grün were to commence.

One of the women who was instrumental in the running of this orphanage near Lüneburg was an American woman of German descent called Winifred Baumgarten. Baumgarten was from Pennsylvania, the granddaughter of German emigrants. She still spoke good German, with a thick American accent that blurred the vowels and softened the consonants, and possessed a larger-than-life New World charm, all of which made her very popular among the townsfolk. She was the wife of a high-ranking US army officer stationed in Hannover and, thanks to a considerable inheritance and a strong sense of moral duty, a dedicated philanthropist. When the war in Europe had come to an end, she was determined to do her bit to help the children of the now ravaged land of her ancestors. As if feeling the need to point out the role and fate of children under fascism, her constant motto was, "The little innocent ones are always the worst-hit victims. They pay ten-fold for the sins of their fathers." This was her usual closing comment to donors on the promotional tours she held back in Allentown and Philadelphia, before she embarked on her transatlantic voyage.

Winifred Baumgarten also worked voluntarily in coordination with the distribution of the CARE food packets, which the US were sending to Europe to provide much needed supplies in the face of a growing winter food crisis. One Lüneburger resident, an ex-*Wehrmacht* soldier who had fought and survived on the eastern front for over two years, was dumbfounded the first time he set eyes on a CARE packet; with its boxes of *Minute* tapioca, *Ann Page* egg noodles, *Tootsie* fudge, *Quaker Oats* Scotch oat scone mix, and *Cream of Wheat* 5-Minute hot cereal. Moreover, they were all delicious. "And to think *they* beat *us!*" he exclaimed in awed reference to the American generosity.

By the winter Gisela decided that it was time for a purge to be put into effect at the Gasthaus, which was by now hopelessly overcrowded. Not only was the repartition of the adequate but still modest amount of food she received proving to be problematic; but she also wished to recover the rooms in the Gasthaus and have them thoroughly cleaned to be eventually put to good use. Hertha had already informed her some days before of her intention of moving out to her own new lodgings soon, and that she would take Bärbel and Max, and probably Fabian, with her. With this knowledge in hand, Gisela briskly announced to the others, one glacial December morning, that the war had been over for six months now and it was time for everyone to move on.

Part of this purge would naturally include Frau Vögler and Helga, as well as the Schwarz boys who were to be sent to the newly opened orphanage that Gisela had heard of. This posed an emotional problem as in these months after the war they had integrated well into the household. Christian and Michael Schwarz had become great friends with Adolf and Hermann, while Joseph had also found a soulmate in Helga.

Gisela explained to her mother and aunt the difficulties she was having in looking after so many. She was receiving precious little income from official sources, though already taking care of an invalid husband and six children, three of her own and three of her late sister. Now she was suddenly responsible for children and adults whom she had never seen or heard of before. To complicate matters, her father was becoming an increasingly feeble invalid, one whom her ageing mother with time would not be able to appropriately attend to. Gisela saw a sea of dependent charges stretching ahead and was starting to panic. While all the time she would have dearly appreciated more time to dedicate to her own offspring, in particular her darling Erich.

All the same, it broke Hertha's heart to think how, after all their ordeals and hazards overcome, the little group would now be separated forever. But she also recognized that the current situation was unsustainable and that it was time for everyone to move on to new pastures and begin to reconstruct their lives.

Gisela had already gone to the town hall on two occasions and explained her dire straits to the provisional municipal authorities, who were hopelessly overwhelmed. Despite Hertha's assistance in getting her appointments with the right people in the chain of command, she received little support from the British military authorities in the midst of such general and overall need. The fact that she already had a large property in which to fit all her dependants and let them sleep comfortably, meant that she was not deemed a priority. She felt out of her depth, that she was going out of her mind when the house filled every morning with the noisy and demanding din of numerous souls, most of whom had now outlived the good will of their initial welcome.

Gisela's fortune changed dramatically when she forged a contact to the Red Cross and found there a more sympathetic ear for her situation. The bleak winter which lay ahead did not look promising and Gisela correctly foresaw food and energy shortages. Through the Red Cross she got to know the American Winifred Baumgarten, and with her help she managed to obtain for the Schwarz boys two places in the nearby orphanage, and also found a home in a residence in Uelzen for Grete Vögler and her daughter Helga. With the upcoming departure of her aunt, together with Bärbel and Max and Fabian too,

Gisela's task seemed to be approaching completion. They celebrated Christmas with only modest food and decorations. There was a frosty quiet that lay over their failed attempts at festivities and overshadowed the occasion; and a chill in the air as if the ghosts of the departed were visiting. Corinna had more visions, as did Joseph, but they each kept them to themselves. Either way, there was for everyone the deep sadness that although the war was over, those absent souls would never return in corporal form. In this way, all three boys started to take an aversion to the annual yuletide celebration, the older two in particular who recalled times past with a bitter sense of loss.

To make matters worse, one morning at the beginning of January 1946 catastrophe struck. On her way out to the baker's Gisela fell badly on an icy section of the cobbled street and fractured her hip. It was a hair-line fracture but enough to immobilize her for a good while. She was examined and treated in hospital, undergoing a minor operation followed by a number of weeks at home spent lying in bed with one leg up in the air, while Martin quietly destroyed her nerves beside her as they lay together twenty-four hours a day, seven days a week. She had never spent such a prolonged period of time with her spouse and it made her wonder why she had ever married him in the first place.

Luckily for her, at least two of her children were now growing up and had become largely independent. Katrina was eighteen and wanted nothing more than to be a switchboard operator in a large telephone exchange. That was a glamorous job that appealed to her greatly. Her mother had warmly approved when she was first informed of her daughter's plan: it was a new and exciting career that seemed very promising in an otherwise desolate land. There had been little school in the last chaotic year of the war, but Katrina was determined to complete the necessary professional preparation in what was hoped to be a soon blooming nation. She looked after her mother during her convalescent period following the fall, while simultaneously busying herself with learning foreign languages: French and English primarily, though Gisela advised her to also familiarize herself with Russian. "Borders change so quickly these days, you never know where you will end up - even if you don't move house." By the autumn of the following year Katrina would leave for Hannover and commence there the *Ausbildung* (professional training course) to be an officially qualified telephone operator.

Siggi was also making plans for the future, though unlike his sister he held out less hope for any prosperous and promising future for the German nation. His short but positive experience in American captivity had made him set his sights on that country. He enrolled at the *Johanneum Gymnasium* at the end of the year with the objective of completing the final year – postponed due to his wartime combat duty – and graduating with an *Abitur*. As he waited for the school year to commence in the January of the coming year, he spent his time sedulously working on raising his English to a level of proficiency that would allow him to emigrate to the great nation in the West as soon as he was able to. He hoped to have crossed the Atlantic for good before his twentieth birthday. None of this he told his mother, of course.

Hertha was by this point in the process of moving out but naturally called in at the Gasthaus to check up on the incapacitated Gisela and Martin, to feed and keep an eye on that invalid pair lying upstairs on the third floor. Erich was sent to stay at the shabby little apartment of his grandparents Corinna and Georg, where at least he would be properly fed and looked after. Although Inge's boys continued sleeping at the Gasthaus for reasons of space, they spent much of the day, including mealtimes, with their Hartmann grandparents too. There, they spent the long weeks of Gisela's convalescence all playing merrily together in the new home and kicking up a regular hullabaloo. It was a rough time for poor old Georg who had survived two world wars only to finish up being driven mad by his own grandchildren.

As soon as was physically possible, and driven along more than anything by her exasperation with her husband, Gisela was up and moving around again; though with extremely limited mobility for at least another two to three months, so the doctors estimated. She arose to the sensation that her life and the Gasthaus were falling completely out of control.

Her mother and aunt saw the great distress Gisela was in and took her aside to discuss her predicament. Alone the fiasco of the washing was enough to drive her to desperation. Like most German women of her times, Gisela had a regular '*großer Waschtag*' (great washing day). All the clothes and bed linen were boiled in water, hung out to dry and then passed through the hulking green clothes press in the laundry room. During the years when the Gasthaus had been buoyant in its visitors, this had been once or even twice a week. By now it was only once a month, with the assistance of Katrina. Gisela prided herself on the clean clothes her family wore and the crisp sheets they slept in, and this task she viewed as a vital part of her workload and a crucial component of her domestic pride. Now left to Katrina to manage, together with some begrudging assistance from Siggi, the *Waschtag* was an abysmal mess. The two teenagers struggled with the press for hours and everything came out profusely creased.

(Years later, when Gisela had her first washing machine fitted into the *Gasthaus* in the 1950s, she stood agape in wonder and said, "If they could build so many tanks and aircraft bombers back then, why couldn't they build these?")

She confessed that she couldn't cope and admitted – although it shamed her to do so – that what was wearing her down most of all was the guardianship of her three nephews. It was an emotionally traumatic matter to discuss. She knew how much her sister had adored her children, and she in turn had adored her sister. She loved them too in her own way but they were now getting older, becoming more difficult to manage, showing a boisterous, even wild side to their characters that she found increasingly difficult to handle (this was not really the case, not more so than with any children of that age, but Gisela in her stress perceived it so). She concluded, quite simply - and Corinna and Hertha could plainly see themselves how it was the complete and unadorned truth - that she wanted only the best for the boys and knew she was not capable of giving it to them.

Corinna sympathized with her. She commented that the best place for a young German child to grow up these days was abroad. They opened a bottle of white wine and Corinna told them of the rumours she had heard while waiting in line for bread. "Apparently the Americans have come up with this plan, and the other powers are going to agree to it. They are saying they do not want Germany to have any more industry or produce any more goods or sell anything abroad. Nothing at all. They just want the whole country to be one big farm. So there will be fields of crops, especially potatoes and cereals, and orchards, and livestock grazing, but little else. They will split the country up into two parts, the north and the south. One part will be run by the Americans and the other by the Russians, but they did not say which one will correspond to us. I hope it is the Americans."

Hertha, who had devoted her life to farming, was feeling the wine's effect and had to chuckle. "What a lark! But Corinna dear, there are so many rumours going around at the moment that each new version contradicts the one from the day before."

Corinna, as usual and even more so now since her daughter's death, did not see the funny side of the prognosis. "That is all you have to say? There will be no future here in Germany. It will be a poor country forever." She morosely continued to paint a dark vision of a Germany forever under foreign control and reduced to the most primitive of economies. Considering the bombed cities and complete economic collapse in the aftermath, Gisela thought she had a point.

"If you want my opinion," said Corinna, "The best thing you could do for Inge's boys is to send them aboard. Find an adoption agency and try to secure them good homes in other countries. America, England, France, wherever. Anywhere but here. They will have a good education there and then, when they are older, all the career possibilities in the world. Imagine growing up in a country like America compared to growing up here."

Hertha nodded and agreed with her sister's remark. She knew that much of Germany was now lost forever, first and foremost her own adopted homeland of East Prussia. But inwardly she was very skeptical as to this supposed new plan that would divide the rest of the country into two. And even if it were true and they did? she mused. The Soviets were firm communists, the Americans quite the opposite. Sooner or later the fur would fly, and when that moment came it would be in nobody's best interests to have 'their' Germans spending their time harvesting corn and milking cows.

It was during this period, in early spring 1946, that Gisela was visited by Winifred Baumgarten in order to corroborate some details that were missing on the Schwarz boys' index cards; information that she hoped either Gisela or Hertha might be able to provide her with. Gisela greeted her at the door and proceeded to clumsily hobble around the kitchen to make them a pot of coffee. Baumgarten insisted she let her take over and rolled up her sleeves. Apart from making them coffee, she also helped to finish washing up a pile of plates that Gisela had not had the time nor energy to get round to. The two women developed a strong feeling of congeniality and were soon talking about all manner of topics. Gisela explained how helpless she felt with her lot and that the human responsibilities that had come her way were becoming too much for her. She complained that taking care of a disabled husband, while bringing up three adolescent children, one of whom was also disabled, as well as her three small nephews, plus the prospect of soon taking care of elderly parents, were all going to finish her off some day. She looked and sounded utterly worn out; the Pennsylvanian took pity and took up the challenge, and started to plan how she could help out.

Baumgarten probed and found out about the fates of Inge and Horst. Although there was no official indication of their actual decease, not even a body to bury nor a last memento that had been sent on, Gisela had come to terms by now with the fact that both had almost certainly died. In the case of Inge, she had no doubt. The three children were angels on the one hand, but a handful on the other, she said. They were good boys with hearts of gold, but they had developed an obstinate and difficult side to their characters since the loss of their parents. Understandable, she added, but nevertheless making the situation very demanding for her. Baumgarten asked after their religion, and the lax and agnostic Gisela assured her they were being brought up as Catholics, which was vaguely true.

Baumgarten regrettably informed her that there were no current places at the orphanage she was helping to run. Gisela responded that under no circumstances could she countenance them being taken in to an institution run by the state (she made some mental connections and shuddered); until there was a more long-term and secure private solution available, they would stay at the Gasthaus with her. She had been of the hope that some of Horst's family could perhaps help out and adopt at least one of the boys, but as yet there had been no progress made, merely a plethora of excuses. Even the newly-wed Wilhelm had not been forthcoming, which was a disappointment.

Baumgarten enjoyed the visit and upon leaving she promised to return as soon as she had any news. Gisela, well used to being fobbed off by all and sundry, expected nothing more of the conversation. She was therefore very pleasantly surprised when the assiduous American returned within two weeks to impart some unexpected and positive news. She explained to Gisela that she had located various possibilities for foreign adoption through some of the agencies that she was in contact with. The families had been thoroughly checked and approved of by the agency; once the basic forms had been filled out and the necessary health tests carried out, then she could file the applications.

"The favourable side here is that you can already provide so much information, including birth certificates. With some of the children we are working with, no-one has the slightest idea who they are. Not even whether their parents are perhaps still alive somewhere." The children would receive a routine check for diseases - tuberculosis and rickets were particularly prevalent and problematic in parts of the shattered country; also complicated long-term medical issues such epilepsy, chronic enuresis, or serious psychological trauma needed to be assessed. If all of that went well, Baumgarten felt sure she could find places in families within the next few months.

All did go well and some families matched the profile as being able to offer a good home for the young boys. It would naturally have been ideal, both Baumgarten and Gisela agreed, for the brothers to end up under the same family roof; but given the large number of orphans in similar situations and the limited number of placements available, that would sadly – in all probability - not be a viable option.

The first boys to be found a suitable home were to be the two youngest, but some initial confusion occurred due to a typing mistake in the dates of birth stated on the card indexes. This came to light while the forms were still being processed and would have meant Adolf - rather than Joseph - together with Hermann being put into adoption first. The boys had been due to be allocated to an American couple from Ohio, members of a church group participating in the adoption project. Eventually the files were corrected and reprocessed, but before all the prerequisites were completed the couple had to retract from the decision, or at least postpone it, due to an unforeseen relocation to Texas. While this error was being ironed out, a home for Joseph had already been found in England. This was with a couple in Kent who already had three young girls and wanted in addition to give a solid upbringing to an orphan of the war. This time the papers went through smoothly with no impediment whatsoever. The transportation of Joseph to London, along with four other small children from nearby orphanages, went through that very summer, in July 1946.

That same month, an alternative family position was found for Hermann, though this time it was not through connections brought about by the agency but rather through his own flesh and blood, namely a family living in Warnemünde, near Rostock. The couple, called Schukowski, were quite distant relatives; Frau Schukowski was a cousin of Horst, the daughter of his late mother's younger brother, with whom there had been some recent contact through Horst's sister Marianne. The Schukowskis had no children of their own and upon hearing by chance of the situation with the children, had offered to take in one of the boys into adoption. Preferably the youngest, they mentioned; unaware of the similar ages. The location was not ridiculously far away; somewhat over 200 kilometres further to the east along the northern coast of Germany, around two and a half to three hours by train from Lüneburg. It seemed the perfect solution and Gisela hoped that in this way there could still be at least some contact with the boy.

This left just Adolf. Between a subsequent silence with regards to offers from any of the local families they knew, and a momentary lapse in placements abroad from the side of Baumgarten's agency, it looked as if he might be destined to stay on at the Gasthaus with Gisela after all. There was a suspicion that his first name might be an obstacle for some prospective parents, and Gisela even toyed with the idea of renaming him Arnold or something else that also began with an 'A' but was more pleasing these days to foreign ears. This naturally contradicted the birth certificate that she had originally presented and that the orphanage had so meticulously copied into all its documents. But luck was on Gisela's side. Before autumn arrived, a Catholic relief agency that was active in the area had found a placement for the child with a well-positioned couple in Valencia, who seemed to have no qualms whatsoever about the boy's name.

In the early spring of 1947 Adolf embarked by motorcar, together with an administrative worker from the agency and three other children, on the long journey to the south of the continent. They reached southern Germany in the first day and spent the second night in the south of France, in Perpignan, where two of the children stayed on and were taken into homes that had been assigned to them there. Adolf and the other boy, and Señor Blanco as they learnt to address their adult companion, continued on their trek. Señor Blanco drove through the Pyrenees, across the French-Spanish border, down through the whole of Catalonia (where they spent the third night in Tarragona), on past Castellón, until half-way down the coast they finally reached their destination in the coastal city of Valencia. The two boys looked out of the window in awe at the sparkling Mediterranean and the strange palm trees. There, exhausted and confused, they spent a further night in a monastery and were each picked up respectively the following morning by the adoptive parents. In Adolf's case, the final destination was a large apartment in the historic Ciutat Vella district in the centre of Valencia.

And so with Adolf in Valencia, Joseph in Kent, and Hermann up on the north-eastern Mecklenburg coast, the three boys had the good fortune to find three caring families to give them that stabile and auspicious childhood that the forces of history had so far denied them. The geographical distance between them, though not modest, was not to be regarded as an insuperable barrier either. Gisela herself commented to Mrs. Baumgarten, after the whole project had been satisfactorily completed, that they should all still come back at some point to see her and stay at the Gasthaus. In the meantime, she was feeling more optimistic about the future and augured a renaissance of the German economy, including the tourist branch. "It is only a matter of time before things pick up. As soon as the foreign soldiers go home, the guests will come back," she told her mother Corinna, while Georg in the background rolled his eyes and sipped on his glass of schnaps.

As destiny would have it, she would never see any of her three nephews again. Nor would the brothers themselves have the opportunity of reuniting until over half a century had passed.

-END OF PART ONE-

Printed in Great Britain
by Amazon